Phillis's Big Test

Written by Catherine Clinton   Illustrated by Sean Qualls

Houghton Mifflin Company

Boston 2008

For Pat Bradford, whose talent speaks for itself.
—C.C.

For my grandmothers, Blanche E. Smith and Willie D.
Qualls. I miss you.
—S.Q.

Text copyright © 2008 by Catherine Clinton
Illustrations copyright © 2008 Sean Qualls

www.houghtonmifflinbooks.com

The text of this book is set in Regula.
The illustrations are acrylic paint and paper collage.

Library of Congress Cataloging-in-Publication Data
Clinton, Catherine, 1952–
  Phillis's big test / by Catherine Clinton; illustrated by Sean Qualls.
     p. cm.
  ISBN-13: 978-0-618-73739-0
  ISBN-10: 0-618-73739-1
  1. Wheatley, Phillis, 1753-1784–Juvenile literature. 2. African American poets–Biography–Juvenile
literature. 1. Title.
  PS866.W5Z5828 2008
  811'.1–dc22
  [B]
  2007013241

Printed in China
WKT 10 9 8 7 6 5 4 3 2 1

In 1773, Phillis Wheatley became the first African American to publish a book of poetry. When she went to London to meet with literary admirers, she became the most famous black person on both sides of the Atlantic.

But in 1772, Wheatley's book almost didn't get published, because printers in colonial Boston could not believe that an African-born enslaved girl wrote such wonderful verses all by herself.

To prove the poems were her very own, the teenage poet consented to be cross-examined by eighteen of the most learned and powerful men of Massachusetts. Phillis's big test . . .

One crisp early-autumn morning, Phillis Wheatley was crossing the Boston cobblestones with a sheaf of papers held tightly under her arm. When her master, John Wheatley, had offered her a ride to her examination, she said she would prefer to walk.

She would make her own way to the public hall where the most important men of the Massachusetts Bay Colony would examine her and settle the question once and for all: was she or was she not the author of her poems?

She had spent recent evenings copying and recopying her poetry in her own neat handwriting. She knew each poem inside out. What kind of questions would they ask? Why should she have to defend her own verse?

As she turned the corner of Mackeral Lane, reading one of her poems, the wind gusted and blew it out of her hand. As the page danced in the wind, she gave chase, catching it before it disappeared.

Even if it had disappeared, would it matter? She knew every line, every syllable, by heart. She wrapped the pages tightly in a roll, pages of poems that had come from deep inside her—and could not be taken away, no matter the outcome of today.

Still, she had something to prove.

Not just because she was young, not just because she was female, but because she was a slave and came from Africa. She paused as a billowing sail moving into the harbor caught her eye.

Was this like the boat she had arrived on one day in July more than eleven years before? A slave ship full of human cargo?

She could remember little about crossing the Atlantic, and even less about her African homeland. She was just shedding her front teeth when John Wheatley bought her on the Boston docks as a servant for his wife, Susanna. They christened their new slave Phillis, the name of the ship on which she arrived.

She remembered the strangeness of the Boston house that became her home. Her first winter was so very cold and awful. She survived only by the kindness of her masters, especially the Wheatleys' twins, Nathaniel and Mary, who eagerly shared their lessons with the young slave girl. They taught her not just English but also Latin and Greek. Soon Phillis spent more time on her studies than on serving her mistress.

It was those lessons that led her along this path, to this crossroads today. As she passed by the impressive spire of the Old North Church, it made her think of those first Bible stories Mary had read to her. They taught her not just religion, but a love of the King's English. As she began to read poetry, glorious sonnets had inspired her to try her own hand at writing. And soon she was reciting her poems to the Wheatleys' friends.

She had been staying up late, night after night, preparing for what lay ahead. Was she ready? Would she ever be ready?

Last night, her mistress, Susanna, had taken away the candle at midnight and advised: "Tomorrow you will look them straight in the eye as you answer all their questions. Your talent will speak for itself. They will discover the poet we know you to be! And when your book is published, everyone will know!"

Los Angeles Times

Los Angeles, CA, January 12, 1984

If President Reagan hoped that his Central America commission would defuse criticism of his policies in that region or even build support for them, he must be sorely disappointed this morning.

But if the President wanted the panel to point him toward effective long-range U.S. policies for that volatile region, he will not only accept its recommendations, but move to implement them. For despite reports that the panel was divided on key issues, the final document indicates that consensus was reached on a range of important and fundamental concerns. Some of the commission's recommendations will be controversial, but the supporting arguments are thoughtful and constructive.

The report of the National Bipartisan Commission on Central America was formally delivered to the White House Wednesday by its chairman, Henry A. Kissinger. As expected, the panel recommended a substantial increase in U.S. foreign aid to the governments of the region—$8 billion over the next five years, along with more financial assistance from international agencies and the private sector. This aid is to stimulate economic development in Central America, the best strategy for dealing with what the commission sees as the region's most fundamental problem—"the impoverishment of its people." We agree with this conclusion, having long held that aid is central to peace in the region.

The panel also proposed more security assistance for governments that consider themselves threatened by outside subversion, including El Salvador and Honduras. But it adds an important proviso: military aid must be legally tied to improvements in the human rights record of the region's armies and security agencies.

The Reagan Administration has belatedly begun to pressure the government of El Salvador to improve its human rights record, but progress has been limited and grudging. The Kissinger commission suggests that the best way to keep pressure on the Salvadorans is for Congress to enact legislation linking military aid to human rights improvements, legislation like that which Reagan pocket-vetoed late last year.

Citing that veto, White House Press Secretary Larry Speakes earlier this week suggested that Reagan would be "inclined" to ignore the Kissinger commission's recommendation on this point. Of all the premature reactions to the Kissinger report, Speakes's was the most unseemly and troubling. Despite the press secretary's attempt to backtrack after several commission members expressed anger at his statement, damage was done because Speakes's reaction came directly from the White House. It fed a suspicion that Reagan may try to overlook the human rights issues in the Kissinger report while stressing its emphasis on U.S. security concerns in Central America and the potential for the Soviet Union to exploit trouble.

The question of whether more military aid should go to countries like El Salvador, and under what conditions, is best dealt with on a case-by-case basis. Overly generalized policies can lead to commitments and even entanglements that this country would be better off avoiding. But we certainly agree with the commission's insistence that military aid must be tied to human rights. The sad history of Central America's military establishments provides little hope that the human rights situation will substantially improve unless this is done.

And even where the Kissinger report does focus on the danger of Soviet troublemaking in Central America—conducted through its Cuban surrogates and, to a lesser extent, Nicaragua—it is encouraging to note that the panel took a realistic view of how turmoil can best be subdued. The commission does not, as some of the more ardent anti-communists in the Administration and in Central America might have hoped, opt for military action. Instead it proposes negotiations.

To end the killing in El Salvador, the commission suggests that the Salvadoran government proceed with elections scheduled for next March, with outside observers to vouch for their openness and honesty. The newly elected government should then "pursue negotiations and reconciliation" with the political representatives of the guerrillas and other opposition groups with the aim of establishing a framework for future elections. That is a constructive and rational proposal to which we can only add a suggestion that an international peace-keeping force, not including American troops but with U.S. logistical and financial support, be considered, since it may be needed to enforce a cease fire between the warring sides.

With regard to the Sandinista government of Nicaragua, the commission concludes that military force should be used against it only as a last resort. Instead it proposes that the United States offer positive incentives to the Sandinistas, primarly the aforementioned economic aid, if they moderate their ways.

The commission also concludes that the United States can curb but not totally eliminate Soviet influence in the Caribbean Basin. This can be achieved both by social progress that forestalls violent revolutions in which the Soviets can meddle, and through cooperation with other nations of the Western Hemisphere. "Where countries of the region can agree on mutual security and the pooling of benefits, collective actions can reduce Soviet opportunities," the report states.

In the spirit of such regional cooperation, it is noteworthy that the Kissinger commission went out of its way to praise and support the "bold, new experiment" undertaken by the so-called Contadora Group—Mexico, Venezuela, Panama and Colombia. The four regional powers are engaged in a difficult but methodical diplomatic campaign to arrange a series of peace agreements among the five Central American nations. The commission report urges the United States to "genuinely" support this process, pointing out that "when countries of the region take the lead, when we (the United States) are not perceived as imposing regional goals, the prospects of a constructive evolution based on shared purposes will increase."

That phrase summarizes what may be the most important lesson to be drawn from the Kissinger commission's study of the Central American crisis. As we have noted before, the United States is not alone in seeking peace, stability and progress for Central America. And this country by itself cannot provide all the answers. Some of those answers must come from other countries in the region, working not as surrogates of the United States but as partners.

We have said before that as the dominant power in the Western Hemisphere, the United States should be confident and mature enough to accept the advice of other countries in the region in order to find ways of adapting to social and political changes that are both necessary and inevitable. If the nation absorbs nothing more than that message from the Kissinger report, then the commission's work will have been well worth the effort.

Rocky Mountain News

Denver, CO, January 13, 1984

IF the American people pay attention and Congress acts responsibly, the National Bipartisan Commission on Central America will have performed a valuable service by highlighting the complexities of the dangerous crisis smouldering in the seven nations of that region.

After studying and visiting the area since August, the 12-member commission headed by Henry Kissinger handed President Reagan a 125-page report that, in places, verges on panic.

To its credit, the panel avoided the simplistic path of blaming all Central America's miseries on the machinations of the Soviet Union, acting through its Cuban and Nicaraguan allies.

Quite correctly, the members understood that the crisis is rooted in native soil, consisting of equal parts of poverty, injustice and political systems that lock out the poor and ignore their cries for help.

Also correctly, the commission said that economic progress and social reform would not succeed while Marxist-Leninist guerrillas, supplied from Nicaragua, rampaged through fragile societies.

"The absence of reform may start a revolution," one member said, but reform alone won't end a revolution. A guerrilla war begins to take on its own momentum because it is so much easier to destroy a bridge than to build one."

To stave off collapse, especially in El Salvador, the report called for $8 billion in economic and military aid for Central America over the next five years. That is $3.5 billion more than is now projected.

We suspect that the commission really doubts that the increased aid will protect or produce democratic governments. It probably made the recommendation because it had no other answer.

The commission drew a grim sketch of the Sandinista junta. "Consolidation of a Marxist-Leninist regime would create a permanent security threat. Nicaragua's mainland location makes it a crucial stepping-stone to promote armed insurgency in Central America."

Unfortunately, the group failed to advance any promising ideas about what to do with Nicaragua. Similarly, its "solution" for El Salvador was to induce communist-led rebels, who want full power, to participate in democratic elections.

It is unfair, of course, to needle the commission for not coming up with a definitive blueprint for a good ending, when perhaps none is possible. In any case, Kissinger and fellows were dead right in saying "no quick solutions can be expected. The United States must make a long-term commitment."

ALBUQUERQUE JOURNAL

Albuquerque, NM, January 13, 1984

The long-awaited Kissinger Commission report on Central America has been completed, and for the first time in recent memory, the administration and Congress have a proposed region-wide agenda against which to measure governments, aid proposals and military situations.

By and large, the commission's view of the current situation and its proposals for the future appear to be solid framework around which to fashion a regional U.S. policy with some hope for long-term success — both for U.S. interests and for the betterment of the people of Central America.

One can argue to the point of blue faces about the greater of the evils: repressive right-wing totalitarian states, or leftist, communist guerrilla victories. But one point is unassailable: That is that a series of communist Soviet vassal states in the region would be disastrous for U.S. long-term interests, and certainly less than optimum for the people.

Providing military aid to counter communist guerrilla movements thus becomes an important and immediate central element of the commission's recommendations. But that doesn't have to require the embracing of ruthless right-wing fascists, either.

Closely allied is the specific recommendation that military aid to El Salvador — an admitted pivotal country in the region — be tied to demonstrated progress in improving human and political rights.

But in marked contrast to what seems to have been the Reagan preoccupation with the military solution alone, the Kissinger Commission recommends a series of longer range actions designed to improve the economic and social fabric of the nations of the region, thus rendering them more impervious to the blandishments of the guerrilla left.

Trade credits, reactivation of the Central American Common Market with an emergency U.S. loan to finance its activities, vastly increased economic assistance and U.S. leadership in resolving loan payment problems are among some of the longer-term, non-military recommendations.

The strength of the commission's recommendations lies in their diversity and their complexity. To follow only those that square with current administration Central American dogma would be to waste the commission effort.

The intermediate and long-term economic needs of the countries of Central America must be addressed along with the bolstering of the military efforts against the left.

The resolve of this country that death squads, political intimidation and other violations of basic human rights must be stamped out needs to be made crystal clear to the Roberto D'Aubuissons and the military juntas of Central America.

The concerns of this country must be made to reach beyond the immediate military situation to the economic situation of the common people of Central America.

The best long term defense against outside interference is internal prosperity for the majority.

The economic side of the U.S. regional policy may not sit as well with the oligarchies and the colonels as has the military aid. But the current situation in El Salvador demonstrates the moral bankruptcy of preoccupation with the military side alone.

The Kissinger Commission's recommendations constitute a solid framework for an effective U.S. Central American policy. They should be implemented without delay.

The Miami Herald

Miami, FL, January 14, 1984

LIKE a well-stocked grocery store, the Presidential commission on Central America has all kinds of products for consumers of all tastes. President Reagan got a bipartisan commission to agree with him that American national security is at stake in Central America. Democratic critics of the Administration's policy got the linkage that they wanted between military assistance to El Salvador and evidence of progress on human rights.

One problem with the just-completed study is its unrealistic price tag — $8 billion — for its proposed development aid to the region. The price is unacceptable to congressional critics of the Administration's Central American policy, and it's too steep even for the Reagan Administration.

The commission was created last year under former Secretary of State Henry Kissinger. Its mission was to evaluate the conflicts and U.S. policy there and to try to build a national consensus on what the United States should do in the region. Its report stresses the importance of American security interests in facing a Soviet-Cuban challenge in Central America. That portrayal of the region's conflicts as an East-West struggle is vintage Kissinger.

It is also somewhat oversimplified. For whether the turmoil in Central America is caused by indigenous social and economic problems or by Soviet and Cuban intervention is the essence of the long debate on Central America. If one accepts the report's rationale, it would be difficult to deny any government in the region massive U.S. military assistance to fight leftist guerrillas who endanger national security.

The fragile political consensus achieved within the commission will not diminish the vehemence of the debate in Congress and across the nation. The commission clearly was as divided as are other Americans on two key issues: U.S. covert aid to guerrillas fighting Nicaragua's Sandinistas, and on whether to link aid for El Salvador to human rights.

Still, if only because it has focused attention on the region, the Kissinger Commission report performs a valuable service. Central America — in fact all of Latin America — needs more constant and rational attention from the United States. The Kissinger Commission also put forth some intriguing proposals, such as creating a new Literacy Corps to combat illiteracy in the region and granting 10,000 scholarships so that more Central Americans can attend U.S. colleges.

For these suggestions and for focusing the national debate on Central America, the Kissinger Commission deserves credit. But — other than pouring $8 billion into the region — it failed to provide the groundwork for a national consensus, or a feasible agenda for ending the region's turmoil and violence.

DAYTON DAILY NEWS

Dayton, OH, January 15, 1984

The Kissinger Commission's recommendations on U.S. policy toward Central America are broad and enlightened in scope, offering a compromise of the more extreme liberal and conservative approaches. Although its suggestions would be difficult to carry out, they offer some promise.

Acknowledging social and economic problems, the commission calls for a broad, five-year, $8 billion economic program for the region, suggesting such new initiatives as a Literacy Corps, 10,000 scholarships for higher education and government loans to start up a private development corporation. Focusing on the East-West struggle, the commission calls for a "substantial" increase in the present level of $65 million in military aid to El Salvador.

Kissinger

Possibly additional military aid is needed. The commission says that although a case can be made for cutting off all military aid, and a case can be made for increasing it dramatically, little is achieved by continuing the present levels, which allow the Salvadoran army to achieve no more than a stalemate with leftist guerrillas.

But unless some mechanism is put in place to assure that American military assistance is not used to terrorize the populace, rather than protect it, all the economic aid and political support this country can provide will not save the region from continued turmoil.

To its credit, the commission addresses this issue, calling for a verification process to assure the advancement of human rights as a condition for receiving military aid. The United States previously set such conditions, but there never was any real commitment to advancing human rights, by El Salvador, the Reagan administration or the U.S. Congress. President Reagan even vetoed the human rights certification requirement last summer.

The report challenges Congress to form a bipartisan concensus on aid to El Salvador. At the same time, it challenges Mr. Reagan to guarantee that American assistance isn't used to bloody U.S. ideals and prospects for a civilized peace.

Many of the reforms suggested by the commission — economic, social and political assistance — already have been sponsored, to a lesser extent, by the United States in El Salvador. In many respects, they have failed, not because of a lack of American support, but because of the determination of powerful factions of the U.S.-supported Salvadoran government and ruling class to undermine the work. This is intolerable.

As the commission concedes, bold steps are needed. The United States too long has alternately ignored the problems in Central America or acted to exacerbate them, trampling the sovereignty of some nations (the proxy war now is against brash, Soviet-helped Nicaragua) to impose U.S. standards.

Balance is difficult to achieve, but the commission attempted it in a bipartisan way and has offered the president and Congress a foundation of some compromise on which to try to build an effective policy.

The Houston Post

Houston, TX, January 11, 1984

President Reagan is to receive the Kissinger Commission report on Central America today. It is expected, among other things, to recommend that future military aid to El Salvador be tied to progress on human rights. Even before the report is delivered, however, the administration has disclosed plans to request an additional $140 million in military assistance for El Salvador's armed forces in their struggle against leftist insurgents.

In the meantime, El Salvador and four other Central American nations — Nicaragua, Costa Rica, Honduras and Guatemala — have signed a preliminary agreement to a formal peace treaty for the region. The document was drafted after a year of negotiation led by the four-nation Contadora Group — Mexico, Venezuela, Panama and Colombia. It calls for withdrawal of all military advisers from Central American nations, an end to the arms buildup, free elections and protection of human rights. This is a potentially significant step in the search for regional solutions to regional problems. But it won't make the region's problems magically disappear.

The president's bipartisan Central American study commission reached a consensus that avoided a minority report. But information leaked about the panel's work indicates the 12 members were not of one mind on some of the recommendations. Even the chairman, former Secretary of State Henry Kissinger, reportedly added a warning that the human rights requirement should not be applied too strictly to El Salvador's government while it is trying to combat guerrilla successes.

Reagan recently vetoed a bill that would have made arms aid to El Salvador conditional on periodic administration certification of human rights progress there. The veto was a clear signal that he doesn't want his hands tied in implementing his Central American policy. In the short term, his insistence on a freer hand in funneling aid to El Salvador is defensible on the ground that without it, the present government could collapse. But there is also strong evidence that the El Salvador government needs more than new weapons. It needs better leadership that can win the support of more Salvadorans.

Vietnam should have taught us two fundamental lessons: We cannot fight other peoples' wars for them. Nor can we buy a victory for democracy in a country that lacks the will and the incentive to defend itself against the threat of a determined leftist insurgency. Those lessons apply to El Salvador and other Central American countries just as they did to Vietnam.

The Seattle Times

Seattle, WA, January 12, 1984

IF ANY key administration or congressional officials are of a mind to paste a part of the Kissinger Commission's Central America report on the wall, we suggest this:

"Direct U.S. military action — which would have major human and political costs — should be regarded only as a course of last resort and only where there are clear dangers to U.S. security."

True, no one in authority has called for direct U.S. military intervention into Central America's multiple conflicts. But when large U.S. fleet components are stationed off both coasts of the narrow intercontinental link and when U.S. forces hold joint maneuvers with Honduran troops, there is reason to suspect that such intervention is more than a remote option in decision-makers' minds.

President Reagan predicts that when Congress considers the report, it will not get bogged down in an argument over whether aid to Latin countries should be tied to progress in human rights. That looks like whistling in the dark. We hope and expect that progress in human rights will be among a number of strings Congress will insist be tied to heavy spending in Central America.

The Kissinger panel recommends that an extra $400 million in U.S. economic assistance be funneled to the region this year — on top of $477 million already budgeted — and a total of $5 billion over the next five years.

If sums of that magnitude are to be spent, U.S. taxpayers have a right to the strongest possible safeguards against waste. If the funds are used primarily to keep repressive oligarchies in power, they indeed will be wasted.

A U.S. failure to insist on significant political and economic reforms would play directly into the hands of the leftist insurgents who look to Fidel Castro and the Soviet Union for support.

THE ATLANTA CONSTITUTION

Atlanta, GA, February 9, 1984

Laying out an $8-billion Central American aid proposal recommended by the Kissinger panel, President Reagan declared, "If we don't help now, we'll surely pay dearly in the future." Well, yes, but there's more to it than that.

Capitol Hill debate on the aid plan will no doubt dwell on the highly publicized questions of how U.S. aid is to be tied to human-rights progress and whether the United States can afford such an expensive commitment at a time of crippling deficits. But it is likely too little attention will be focused on a pivotal point: whether the pint-sized nations of Central America can absorb massive infusions of American money.

Take Honduras: Last year Washington ticketed $101 million in non-military aid. Balance that against *$100 million in unspent funds* stuck somewhere in the U.S. aid pipeline to Honduras, some of it for projects initiated five years ago. One project was a $15.3-million program begun in 1979 to build 2,100 classrooms. Only 300 have been finished at a

cost of $2.1 million. And, to boot, there's not a single Honduran pupil in any· None of the classrooms have desks

The Honduran logjam is not an isolated phenomenon. Of the aid budgeted over the last five years for six other Central American countries, including the now-outcast Nicaraguans, fully *$379.1 million remains unspent.*

Why this snarl? U.S. law requires recipient nations to match aid money one-to-three, a threshold impoverished governments often can't reach. Local administrations are frequently inept or inefficient, or hopelessly fettered by their own — or U.S. — red tape. There are shortages of trained personnel to manage and implement the projects.

The most effective projects are often small and encourage self-help. Successes in Honduras include a $2.5 million program to help peasants rehabilitate their homes and a public health drive that has ended infant dysentery deaths.

The Kissinger commission did recommend streamlining procedures to help counter some glitches that have dogged past aid efforts, but a president who has a notable disdain for details may ignore them. Congress should make the most of its opportunity to disabuse him of the notion that Central America can be made whole with the wave of a wand or of the Yankee dollar

The Wichita Eagle-Beacon

Wichita, KS, February 12, 1984

President Reagan is right to assert a moral obligation to foster democracy, human rights and peace in Central America, but he has embraced a clumsy and unworkable vehicle for doing so: the Kissinger commission recommendations on U.S. policy for the region, which rely on lavish gifts of guns and money to achieve these goals.

One can't help feeling Mr. Reagan's $8.8 billion program, which would benefit the guerrilla-beleaguered government of El Salvador most, would do little to improve the lot of the citizens of the region. The targeted nations — with the exception of Costa Rica — lack one element crucial to the success of the big-money-and-guns strategy: a tradition of responsible, democratic leadership. Those among the region's poor who are inclined to revolution became that way because the leadership historically has shown little interest in their welfare.

Given that propensity, there's little reason to think massive economic aid to the Salvadoran, Honduran and Guatemalan governments, in the form of cash payments and loan and commercial guarantees, would reach those who need help most. Democratic attitudes and practice won't evolve naturally in those who don't somehow benefit directly, and quickly, from the U.S. bonanza.

Moreover, Mr. Reagan's exclusion of Nicaragua from that bonanza is sure to drive its leftist government deeper into the Soviet-Cuban orbit, and thus keep tensions between that nation and its neighbors high. To write Nicaragua off as hopelessly leftist, as the plan appears to do, is to assure it remains a threat to bordering nations.

This isn't to suggest the premise of the plan — that the United States has paid too little attention to the region in recent decades, and must make amends — is incorrect. As unrest in the nations targeted for U.S. aid — in El Salvador, especially — attests, the United States can afford such neglect no longer. But effective U.S. aid would address

that unrest at its source, providing the peasantry of the targeted nations a realistic alternative to communist-style revolution.

Parts of the Kissinger plan — the least costly parts — warrant enactment into policy because they could help provide such an alternative. One reason Cuba enjoys the influence it does in Nicaragua and elsewhere in Central America is its "internationalist brigades," which provide free instruction in reading and writing to the illiterate, who are legion. The Kissinger plan would create a similar program, staffed by U.S. instructors, for the targeted nations.

This is a good idea not only because literacy is one of the finest gifts one can give, but because such a program would do much to offset the United States' image problem in the region: the widely shared perception that U.S. aid cares only about the monied classes. Similarly, the plan's provision for projects that would involve citizens in public works, housing and agriculture, could do much to change the Unites States' negative image, as well as to render help where it's needed most.

Congress, as it starts work on an aid plan for Central America, should give special attention to these positive and relatively inexpensive proposals. But it seriously should consider whether the massive military and economic aid really will help foster peace and democracy.

Members of Congress last week made clear their position on Mr. Reagan's third imperative — human rights — by considering a measure to revive human rights certification as a condition of further military aid to El Salvador. If Congress is determined to force certification upon Mr. Reagan, it should be aware of the accompanying obligation: to monitor the State Department closely, lest certification again become what it was before Mr. Reagan vetoed a similar bill last year: a sham.

The Des Moines Register

Des Moines, IA, February 10, 1984

One of many fine points made by the bipartisan commission on Central America was that, without peace and stability, all the social and economic aid in the world will not solve the problems plaguing that beleaguered region.

Now comes President Reagan with his proposal to Congress to implement the recommendations of the commission. Much of the proposal, as much of the committee report, is responsible and creative.

The generous appropriation of funds, insurance and economic guarantees — $8 billion over five years — includes developmental assistance for projects such as roads, schools and agricultural services; credits for trade and agricultural-commodity assistance and guarantees for such programs as housing investments.

Then comes the difficult part. The proposal requests that $179 million be added to the $64 million already appropriated in military aid for El Salvador, with another $133 million requested for the next fiscal year.

That's $376 million in military aid for El Salvador for this year and next. Add to that a proposed $80 million in military assistance for the rest of the region this fiscal year, and $123 million next.

In the commission's scenario, and in Reagan's, this "security assistance" is essential to provide the stability necessary if the economic and social aid is to work. It is easier, however, to see how it will contribute to the instability.

•

The United States is the main source of financial and material aid for a government in El Salvador that is deeply intertwined with the grisly work of the right-wing death squads, the slowing of land reform and the suppression of the judicial system.

The president, however, rejects the commission recommendation that military aid be tied to proof that the government has improved its human-rights record. What is missing is an explanation of how stepping up the shooting will make peace more likely.

As the commission said, no peace means no effective application of aid. Congress, as it considers the pending legislation, should take note.

St. Louis Globe-Democrat

St. Louis, MO, February 6, 1984

President Reagan has wasted no time in calling for much higher military and economic aid for El Salvador and other nations in Central America, as proposed by the recently-released Kissinger Commission report.

In asking Congress for $312 million more in military assistance for El Salvador's hard-pressed army over the next two years, Reagan approximately would triple the military aid going to El Salvador. Congress approved $64.8 million in military assistance to that country this year after cutting the administration's request virtually in half.

The president also will seek $203 million in military aid for other Central American countries over the next two years, with most of that going to Honduras.

However, even this stepped-up military aid would be dwarfed by proposed increases in economic assistance to Central America. If approved by Congress, the other forms of aid would total about three times as much as the military assistance. If the full Kissinger Commission agenda is carried out, nations of Central America would receive $8.9 billion in economic and military aid over the next five years.

This means that President Reagan is seeking to provide Central American nations the kind of aid they require instead of the token help they have gotten from the U.S. so far. Reagan is determined to provide the armed forces with enough military support to defeat Communist guerrillas throughout the region. These small nations simply don't have the military or economic capacity of their own to repel the guerrilla forces supported by the combined might of the Soviet Union, Cuba, Nicaragua and other members of the Soviet bloc.

Providing a military shield is essential to making the greatly expanded economic aid program a success. Without the military support, the Communists could continue to bomb, burn and otherwise destroy key installations, businesses, crops, power stations, and all forms of transportation.

It is vital to U.S. interests, as well as to those of the people of Central America, that the increased aid program recommended by the bipartisan Kissinger Commission is carried out. The time has come for the United States to get serious about defeating the Soviet-Cuban-Nicaraguan attempt to turn all of Central America into a Communist stronghold.

To permit a Central American takeover would mean that U.S. troops probably would have to be used to prevent the Communists from driving north to the U.S. southern border and south across South America.

As President Reagan pointed out, the United States has more than enough resources to help the threatened countries preserve their freedom.

For years politicians in Washington have talked about standing up to the unparalleled Communist intervention in Central America. Now, however, President Reagan has proposed the kind of program that could allow these countries to defeat the attempt to put them in the Soviet empire.

The Houston Post

Houston, TX, February 13, 1984

Congress and the Reagan administration should take former Secretary of State Henry Kissinger's advice and compromise to avert a confrontation that could severely damage our relations with Central America. At issue is what kind of strings the legislative branch should attach to aid for El Salvador.

The House passed a bill last week requiring the administration to certify every six months that the Salvadoran government was making a "concerted and significant" effort to guarantee human rights and that it was making progress in its land redistribution program. The measure would also make military aid contingent on government efforts to negotiate with the country's leftist rebels.

If the Senate approves the bill and it becomes law, it will replace a certification law that was in effect during most of 1982 and 1983. When the law expired last September, Congress passed a measure to extend it, but the president "pocket-vetoed" the bill.

The administration opposes the new House bill on the ground that it limits the president's flexibility in conducting foreign policy. In sending his Central American aid request to Congress earlier this month, the president followed the recommendations of his bipartisan study commission on the region, which Kissinger headed. The panel proposed $8 billion in economic assistance over the next five years. It also recommended certification as a condition for military aid to El Salvador. Reagan accepted the idea of linking military aid to human rights improvements but rejected a congressional role in deciding whether the aid was merited.

Congress seems intent on having a bigger voice in El Salvador aid policy by exercising its power of the purse. But it is not equipped to cope with the day-to-day conduct of foreign relations. That is a job the Constitution assigns to the president.

The administration readily concedes that there have been horrific human rights violations in El Salvador. It has been applying diplomatic pressure to force that country's government to curb the murderous right-wing death squads. And it has offered to voluntarily report to Congress on human rights conditions in El Salvador. The White House and Capitol Hill should get together on a compromise that would allow close congressional monitoring of the situation while preserving the administration's flexibility in shaping and implementing policy.

The president's Central America commission set out sound goals — to help protect the region against Soviet-Cuban subversion and overcome its severe economic problems. Otherwise, as Kissinger warned Congress last week, we might see the day when the Western Hemisphere becomes a security problem for the United States.

Reagan, in Policy Speech, Warns of "Tide" of "Communist Subversion"

United States President Ronald Reagan May 9, 1984 appeared on national television to appeal to the public and to Congress to support his policies in Central America. The President focused on what he said was a threat to the hemisphere posed by Cuba and Nicaragua and warned that the leftist guerillas in El Salvador would win the civil war there if more U.S. aid was not forthcoming. Reagan also defended his administration's covert war against the Sandinistas, calling the U.S.-backed anti-government contras in Nicaragua "freedom fighters." Reagan blasted the Sandinista regime, stressing its Cuban and Soviet ties and what he said was its plan to spread communism throughout Central America. The president linked Nicaragua to what he called the "terror network," which he said included Libya, the Palestine Liberation Organization, the Soviet Union and other communist countries, all of which supplied Nicaragua with arms and manpower. Presenting the civil war in El Salvador as a direct threat to U.S. borders, Reagan cited threats to the U.S.'s shipping lanes in the Caribbean should communists take power in that country. Reagan maintained that El Salvador was "struggling valiantly" to establish democracy; alluding to death squads, he said there was "a small, violent right-wing" but contended that "they are not part of the government." The President urged Congress to take action on legislation proposed in February to provide funds to implement the recommendations of the National Bipartisan Commission on Central America.

The House of Representatives May 10 approved, 212-208, further military aid to El Salvador in the current fiscal year with no conditions attached relating to human rights progress. The measure was an authorization bill setting policy and not appropriating funds, but it was expected to influence an upcoming conference between the House and Senate on a $61.75 million emergency military aid bill for El Salvador.

Detroit Free Press

Detroit, MI, May 11, 1984

PRESIDENT Reagan likes to keep things simple, even when they aren't, as was evident in his speech on Central America Wednesday night. Mr. Reagan portrayed events in the region as a single, uncomplicated crusade by the United States against communism. In that cause, he explained, we support the government of El Salvador and subvert the government of Nicaragua, and Congress had better ante up the funds to keep doing so.

The trouble is that things aren't that simple. There are important differences between what the United States is doing in El Salvador, where the administration is belatedly propping up the democratic center, and in Nicaragua, where we are running a soldier-of-fortune campaign against the government, a campaign in which the CIA is deeply and recklessly involved and in which we are supporting some former Somocistas who are every bit as unlikable as the government we are encouraging them to overthrow.

In El Salvador, Congress is actually on the verge of giving Mr. Reagan most of what he wants in military and economic aid, especially since the moderate Jose Napoleon Duarte emerged as the winner of this week's election. Whether Mr. Duarte can hang onto his victory is something else. The wealthy oligarchs distrust him for his commitment to reform. The military hates him for his gestures of conciliation toward the rebels and his determination to root out the death squads. His defeated right-wing opponent, Roberto d'Aubuisson, is making dark and ominous statements about the validity of the election returns, which presage continuing political turmoil. The threat to democracy and American influ-

ence in El Salvador clearly comes as much from the violent right as from the rebels on the left, but you wouldn't know it from Mr. Reagan's analysis.

As for Nicaragua, it is legitimate to interdict the flow of weapons and guerillas to other Central American nations and to prevent the spillover of violence and revolution to democracies such as Costa Rica. It is legitimate to pressure the Sandinistas to live up to their promises of representative government and freedom, and to condemn the slaughter of the Indians there. But it is questionable how effective it is to rely on former Somoza adherents as our surrogates, or to mine the harbors used by our allies' shipping, or to thumb our nose at the World Court, which just condemned that action. Our activity in Nicaragua is not simply a mirror image of what we are doing in El Salvador (and there, often doing ineptly), and Congress is right to question it.

Mr. Reagan's advisers seem to feel his chief problem is not in his policy but in the failure to explain it adequately. Americans are indeed hard put to sort out the good guys from the bad guys in Central America. Congress, as usual, is better at rearing and kicking in opposition than in formulating an alternative. But in fact, the defects are in Mr. Reagan's policy, and not his public relations. They lie in the failure to recognize and combat the indigenous roots of discontent, in the past failure to regard repression and terror from the right with the same abhorrence as that from the left, and most of all in the compulsive oversimplification of American foreign policy and the challenges it faces right in our own backyard.

The Boston Globe

Boston, MA, May 11, 1984

President Reagan was hale, hearty and dead wrong Wednesday in his televised Central America sales pitch. The House, which yesterday approved a no-strings-attached El Salvador aid package, is just as wrong.

The President's purpose in prodding Congress into passing the massive program of military aid was to clear the way for open-ended expansion of US military operations in Central America. Reagan's speech was close in spirit to the Tonkin Gulf oration that in 1964 won Lyndon Johnson the free hand he sought to sort out Southeast Asia.

Incredibly, the House fell for it.

Most of the President's text was conventional right-wing rhetoric: A Red menace arcs from Moscow to Havana and on to Managua where the Sandinistas ("Cuba's Cubans") have established a "Communist reign of terror" for the export trade.

The Sandinistas were accused of genocide, anti-Semitism, anti-Catholicism, cynicism and bad manners. As if that were not enough, they were packaged with Cuban drug traffickers, the mad Moammar Khadafy and the Palestine Liberation Organization.

This laundry list added nothing factually new. On the key point of an alleged arms flow from Nicaragua to El Salvador, it seems the flow – if it exists – is so small that the United States cannot come up with a shred of evidence.

Although Reagan's immediate goal was to get Congress to approve a large increase in military aid for El Salvador, he did not talk much about El Salvador. Instead, his speech took a rhetorical Great Circle route across Tripoli, the Mideast, Laos, Cambodia, South Yemen, Europe "of the late '30s" and even post-war Greece.

By flitting across the globe on this magic carpet of irrelevancies, Reagan avoided the current political reality in El Salvador. Because he is ideologically committed to supporting the Salvadoran regime, he found it embarrassing to discuss the indigenous sources of revolution in El Salvador: corruption, injustice, a brutal military, and fascist terror.

It is precisely because Reagan refuses to face these realities that he has been unable to devise a policy with the remotest chance of putting out El Salvador's revolutionary fires. So instead he sends SWAT teams after Nicaragua.

Sen. Paul Tsongas made a key point in a post-speech discussion on CBS television: The battle for El Salvador is being fought *within* the Salvadoran military.

Napoleon Duarte, the moderate who apparently won Sunday's presidential election, is a decent man in a dangerous place. Many of the officers around him at the highest levels of the military have been key players in the blood-drenched past – many, but not all.

The only hope for Duarte, for Salvadoran democracy and for a peaceful settlement in Central America is to use US aid to strengthen Duarte's hand so that he can combat the terrorists of the right. That means attaching strings so that the Salvadoran military understands that it will not survive without reform.

That is not "new isolationism." It is tough-minded realism. It has been sadly absent from US policy since Reagan came to office. It is what was missing in the President's message and the House action, as time will tell.

THE DENVER POST

Denver, CO, May 11, 1984

PRESIDENT Reagan appealed to the public Wednesday to support his program of U.S. aid to Central America. We do support that aid — not because we are persuaded by the words of the "great communicator," but because we are impressed by the deeds of Jose Napoleon Duarte.

It is Duarte who emerged this week as the freely chosen leader of El Salvador, after that nation's most honest election in more than 40 years. It is Duarte who is pledged to land reform, democracy and eradication of the far-right "death squads" who have been slaughtering their own people. And it is Duarte who deserves U.S. help as he tries to steer El Salvador between the mirror evils of right-wing and left-wing totalitarianism.

If there was any doubt that intelligent Americans had cause to rejoice in Duarte's victory, it vanished when Sen. Jesse Helms denounced him as "a socialist 10 miles to the left of George McGovern." Helms, who is 20 miles to the right of the planet Pluto, probably hasn't been happy with any government since the reptile "Visitor" tyranny was overthrown in the TV space potboiler "V."

Reagan, in contrast, could hardly contain his glee over the victory of the man his administration had discreetly but effectively backed. Reagan has hardly made a habit of promoting socialists. But he recognizes that if Duarte deserves that label at all he falls firmly in the camp of moderate democratic socialists such as French President Francois Mitterand or Spanish Premier Felipe Gonzalez.

Of more importance, the president understood that the triumph of Duarte's rival, Roberto d'Aubuisson, would have meant an almost certain cutoff of U.S. aid to the struggling Latin nation, followed by victory for the communist guerillas. Congress knows D'Aubuisson has been authoritatively linked to the "death squads" who have been butchering moderate reformers like Duarte.

Heartened by Duarte's victory, moderates such as House Majority Leader Jim Wright have begun to seek a bipartisan consensus around a renewed aid package for El Salvador. The day is past when the American people are willing to pour in blood and treasure behind any tin-pot despot who calls himself anti-communist. But from FDR and Wendell Wilkie through Ronald Reagan and Walter Mondale, leaders of both parties have believed we should help those friends who deserve it.

Duarte's record shows he is such a friend. He has suffered imprisonment, even torture, for his ideals. He deserves our support to see if he can and will establish in practice the ideals he has espoused so eloquently in principle.

The Honolulu Advertiser

Honolulu, HI, May 10, 1984

The president's speech on Central America yesterday was a classic Reagan performance — smooth, eloquent and likely to at least temporarily boost congressional and popular support for his policies there.

As on past occasions, he went before the nation in what amounts to a pre-emptive strike to turn public sentiment against his critics — in this case, those who oppose his proposed military aid for the government of El Salvador and for anti-Sandinista "contras" in Nicaragua.

MANY OF US will remain unconvinced, however, of the wisdom of Reagan's approach to achieving peace in Central America, an essentially military effort based on continuing and largely uncritical U.S. patronage for those who say they're fighting a tide of Soviet- and Cuban-backed insurgency.

Reagan made passing reference to the Contadora nations' attempt to negotiate peace in Central America, but he obviously has little confidence that it will succeed. Instead, he painted a picture of Moscow-engineered "anarchy and chaos" sweeping to the banks of the Rio Grande unless it is checked now.

There is no question that the communists have fomented much bloodshed and chaos in Central America, but certainly they are not the only ones to blame. The president made no mention, for instance, of right-wing death squads that have killed thousands in El Salvador.

He failed to acknowledge any need to correct the political and economic oppression which, as Massachusetts Senator Paul Tsongas noted, makes Marxism "appealing" to those oppressed.

SO, REAGAN has painted the situation in Central America in "good guy, bad guy" terms. It is neither a fair nor accurate assessment, and it leaves the prospects for peace in that strife-torn region as elusive and remote as ever.

ALBUQUERQUE JOURNAL

Albuquerque, NM, May 14, 1984

Apparently the U.S. House of Representatives believes the United States should "draw the line" against Soviet-bloc expansionism in Central America. The House has joined President Reagan, the Kissinger Commission and the Senate in supporting a military aid policy that could backfire unless tied to demonstrated human rights progress.

Reagan went before the nation recently to argue his case that additional military aid is urgently needed by El Salvador to prevent the spread of communism being nurtured by Soviet-Cuban-Sandinista subversion. The president's analysis persuaded the House, which authorized his request for $120 million in emergency aid by a slim 212-to-208 margin.

But it is known Salvadoran rebels get about as much of their weaponry from U.S.-backed soldiers as they get from Managua and Havana. Moreover, the military assistance already provided evidently has not checked the spread of communism in Central America. If it had, Reagan would not need to request ever-larger increments. Nor has the human rights situation in El Salvador improved markedly.

Reagan's one-eyed view of foreign affairs discounts the possibility that negotiations would serve U.S. interests better than trying to impose U.S. will at the point of a gun. Reagan says negotiations will work only when all sides have an incentive to negotiate. He says the Sandinistas ruling Nicaragua have no such incentive now because they already are fulfilling their proclaimed goal of spreading revolt across sovereign borders.

True, the Sandinistas have little reason to negotiate with their neighbors. They have achieved military might unmatched in the region. They have played a big role in El Salvador's troubles, have fought with Hondurans and attacked Costa Rica, a country that doesn't even have an army.

And the Sandinistas have been partially successful in depicting the regional military escalation as the work of Reagan alone. They conveniently forget their original statements and their arms buildup that began long before U.S. military aid first went to the anti-Sandinista *contras*.

Few would say negotiations alone will end the troubles in Central America. Certainly the Sandinistas will have to be convinced their campaign to spread communism throughout the region will be forcefully resisted by the region's nations, with U.S. assistance if necessary.

That point can be driven home in the solemnity of face-to-face talks. But the talks themselves cannot be conducted in a spirit of conciliation while the involved parties continue a rapid arms buildup. If anything, the arms buildup is encouraging more fighting and less talking.

The recent House vote reflects shifts among House critics of the president's policy. It brings the lower chamber more into line with Kissinger Commission and Senate thinking about dealing with the problems of Central America. Conferees still must approve the figures and both chambers must actually appropriate the military aid money.

Before that happens, the House can draw its own line by challenging the belief that Central America's problems can be solved with U.S. guns.

The Boston Herald

Boston, MA,
May 11, 1984

PRESIDENT Reagan had the facts, and his critics in Congress had mostly their fears to rely on as they took their debate on Central America to the nation Wednesday evening.

Those facts — not disputed by the opposition — were that the Sandinista government of Nicaragua, supplied and abetted by Cuba and Russia, had created a threat to peace in the region that imperils their neighbors and us; that they are exporting violence to El Salvador, Honduras, and Costa Rica; and that the Red Tide they represent will sweep inexorably over democratic governments unless we give more and continued economic and military aid to those in danger.

Against those facts, and the president's forecast of what will grow from them unless we help our friends, Democrat opponents raised the fear that Mr. Reagan was "sabre-rattling," a claim so specious that even some of the party leadership cannot swallow it.

Sounding the alarm for a fire at our door can hardly be called warlike — and that was precisely what the president tried to alert us to when he spoke of a Cuban contingent of fewer than 200 men in Nicaragua being increased to 10,000. They are not there to till the fields, but rather to help spread the seeds of subversion to Nicaragua's neighbors.

Mr. Reagan is convinced it is both obvious and inevitable that unless we help our friends in Central America fight for freedom now we will one day be faced with a far stronger threat to ours than they face today.

"If we come to our senses too late," he said, "when our vital interests are even more directly threatened and after a lack of American support causes our friends to lose the ability to defend themselves, then the risks for our security and our way of life will be infinitely greater."

That's what this Central America debate is all about, and Mr. Reagan stated it well. He needs the support now of each of us.

FORT WORTH STAR-TELEGRAM

Fort Worth, TX, May 15, 1984

Two kinds of romanticism hobble U.S. policy toward El Salvador.

There is the romanticism that overemphasizes the importance of military assistance to that beleaguered country. And there is the romanticism that underemphasizes it.

Romanticism No. 1 afflicts the Reagan administration, which appears to labor under the illusion that bullets can bolster the Salvadoran government indefinitely. Although the administration acknowledges the need for economic and human rights improvements, it appears to be uninclined to pressure the Salvadorans to move in that direction.

That could change, however, in view of moderate Jose Napoleon Duarte's being elected president. If Duarte can avoid being eliminated himself by the right-wing death squads, he might succeed in ridding the country of menace to democracy, stability and U.S. aid.

Romanticism No. 2 afflicts a large percentage of Congress, particularly members of the House. Its central illusion is that the way to resolve the situation in El Salvador is simply to negotiate with the Marxist insurgents while addressing the economic and human rights problems that are at the root of all the trouble in Central America. There is just enough truth in that illusion to make it captivating.

While it is true that the main causes of the conflicts in Central America are poverty and political injustice, it does not necessarily follow that one can bypass the symptoms and get to the core of the problems. Indeed, it is impossible to focus any significant remedial action upon those areas without some stability. A realistic view of the situation would recognize that continuing military assistance to El Salvador is necessary to provide the stability that must prevail if the root problems are to be addressed.

A majority of Congress displayed that kind of realism in voting last Friday to authorize President Reagan's request for military aid to Central America that would provide $132 million in military aid for El Salvador next fiscal year. That same degree of realism must be exhibited when House-Senate conferees meet to consider a $61.7 million emergency appropriation for El Salvador. Without that aid, the Salvadoran government will not be able to cope with insurgents supported and supplied by the Soviet Union, Cuba and Nicaragua.

The conferees must realize that there will be no possibility of resolving the conflict through negotiations if the guerrillas believe they can win.

The administration must also be realistic. It cannot be content to provide the aid with no strings attached, when it is clear that Congress expects human rights progress in El Salvador as the price for continuing aid. The administration must work with the Salvadoran government to wipe out the death squads. Otherwise, the guerrillas will continue to attract recruits and the U.S. Congress eventually will put an end to U.S. assistance to El Salvador.

'Congratulations! Your democratic elections qualify you for certain privileges.'

THE ATLANTA CONSTITUTION
Atlanta, GA, May 11, 1984

One day after President Reagan took his case for Central American aid to the court of public opinion, the House wisely ruled in his favor. It passed a bill that (among other things) would give the president broad discretion in the expenditure of $132.5 million in military help for El Salvador.

El Salvador desperately needs the money. Unless its guerrillas are held at bay, its more civilized goals of economic and developmental resurgence will go unmet. At this point, too, military aid is necessary to protect what progress there has been in human rights and democratization. So first things first.

As the president's summation shooed straying House members into the fold, however, the World Court unanimously ruled that the United States has no business mining Nicaraguan ports. This time around, the United States responded with dignity: Very well, it said, the mining has stopped and will not be resumed.

Such restraint contrasts sharply with the stridency of President Reagan's speech last Wednesday night. While his basic stance on Central America is correct — El Salvador *does* need military help and Nicaragua, with Cuban and Soviet help, *is* exacerbating unrest throughout the region — his rhetoric and focus remain troubling.

The speech was marred by a lack of candor on a key issue: the right-wing death squads. The president is willing to attribute all manner of barbarity to El Salvador's leftist guerrillas, yet he says little about the country's murderous right-wingers. It is time for Reagan to get tough on this ugly matter.

The talk was soiled, too, by a gratuitous reliance on vintage cold-war hyperbole. The president, quoting John Kennedy, spoke of our "long, twilight struggle" to defend freedom. He suggested that America might "come to its senses too late" on Central America. It was a speech simplistically focused into terms of Ultimate Good and Ultimate Evil.

Fortunately, the president's program, crafted by the Kissinger Commission, is more to the point. Besides military aid, it contains some generous proposals for economic and developmental help. The United States would export seeds and raw materials to Central America, and would guarantee private loans and help to develop schools and health clinics.

The plan tacitly addresses a bitter truth: that poverty and deprivation, more than foreign meddling by Communist nations, is the root of current unrest in Central America. The complete plan also suggests that military aid, however necessary, should not be considered an end in itself.

Guns might preserve a democratic El Salvador for the short term. But only butter will sustain it in the long run.

Charleston, WV, May 11, 1984

PRESIDENT Reagan's simplistic belief that Central America's upheavals are caused by the Kremlin and Fidel Castro was restated Wednesday night with all the persuasiveness of The Great Communicator.

But his explanation is as unrealistic as the 1960s cry by Dixie leaders that civil rights turmoil in the South was the work of "outside agitators."

Instigators and arms-suppliers play a role, of course, just as CIA delivery of weapons to Afghan rebel tribes is a fringe factor in their revolt. But social ferment in Latin America, like the black equality crusade in America and the Islamic uprising in Afghanistan, is too profound to be blamed on a conspiracy.

Desperate Hispanic peasants, ground under the heel of landlords and generals, have been rebelling sporadically for generations and will continue to do so — with or without outside help. Revolts against the Somoza regime in Nicaragua and the ruling oligarchy in El Salvador would have occurred even if the Soviet Union and Cuba didn't exist.

Reagan's plea for America to escalate its traditional role of helping to kill leftist rebels is drawing rebuke. House Speaker Thomas O'Neill, D-Mass., said the president's "prescription is now clear: more ammunition, more U.S. involvement, more force, more deaths." Sen. Edward Kennedy, D-Mass., echoed bitterly: "President Reagan believes that more guns, more bullets, and more killing is the only answer."

Historian Arthur Schlesinger Jr. added on *Nightline*: If Reagan is correct — that communist subversion directed from abroad is gobbling up little Latin countries one after another — why doesn't the Organization of American States see it in that light? Why is the U.S. acting unilaterally, often secretly?

A world rebuke followed Thursday: The International Court of Justice at The Hague, whose judgment the Reagan administration had striven to avoid, tentatively held the U.S. guilty of breaking treaties and international law through its covert attacks on Nicaragua.

Obviously, America would be more comfortable without hostile Marxist neighbor governments such as Cuba's and Nicaragua's. But hostility from collectivists can be moderated by intelligent, realistic dealings between nations — as in Reagan's approach to Communist China.

Satisfactory solutions to Latin America's nightmare of poverty, cruelty, insurrection, oppression, will be a long time coming — and they'll never come from machine guns.

Cornell University historian Walter LaFeber, writing in *The Nation*, says President Reagan worsens the Latin problem because he tends "to see revolutions engendered by hunger and centuries of exploitation as Kremlin plots."

That simplistic view, reiterated in Reagan's Central America speech Wednesday night, is likely to draw the United States closer to direct involvement in war.

Pittsburgh Post-Gazette
Pittsburgh, PA, May 11, 1984

In his television address Wednesday night President Reagan offered the American people simple explanations and easy answers to that hard and complicated problem called Central America. That very simplicity will put some people off, but their objections will inevitably confuse style with substance.

Like the protesters in the Mon Valley, Mr. Reagan knows the value of describing a gray landscape in terms of black and white. No doubt this reflects the president's personal vision, but it also serves the ends of political necessity. After all, his target where Central America is concerned is not the liberal left — which he knows he will never impress — but middle America. With its support, he may yet get Congress to act on new aid for Central America.

Therefore, Mr. Reagan's speech contained maddeningly scant reference to the reality of poverty and oppression in the area. There was a brief mention of "historical injustices" but no hint that this legacy has often been caused, in fact, by U.S. connivance or neglect.

Instead, Mr. Reagan painted a picture of Soviet surrogates marching in lockstep to subvert the "freedom-loving people." Inevitably, there were distortions of fact along the way.

But on the major points, Mr. Reagan has the best of the argument. Central America *is* of vital strategic importance to the United States, and Mr. Reagan was right to criticize "the new isolationists" who try to pretend otherwise.

He is also right in taking a dim view of the Sandinistas and the Cubans, who both represent revolutions betrayed, and in reminding the American public that it was the Carter administration which first found Nicaragua to be unfriendly despite U.S. material aid and good will.

(However, in seeking support for the Contra "freedom fighters" Mr. Reagan highlighted something that is horribly wrong with his policy. Interdicting weapons to El Salvador may be justifiable, but trying to overthrow the Nicaraguan government, which implicitly is the Contras' real purpose, is lawless and reckless behavior unworthy of America. Yesterday the World Court agreed.)

In stating the basic truths too bluntly, Mr. Reagan did not do justice to the findings of the bipartisan Kissinger commission, which is more sophisticated and realistic on the subject. Its recommendations, which stress economic aid far more than military, and moreover are designed to keep U.S. combat troops out of the area, are now official Reagan administration policy.

The long-term cost of this remedy, originally some $8 billion over five years, still gives the Post-Gazette pause. But, especially after the seemingly hopeful outcome of the El Salvador elections, the president is entitled to a significant measure of what he asked for Wednesday.

Mexican President, Reagan Differ on Central America

President Miguel de la Madrid Hurtado visited the United States May 14-17, 1984. The issue of U.S. and Mexican differences over Central America was the main theme in meetings with President Ronald Reagan and in an address by President de la Madrid to a joint session of Congress May 16. At a welcoming ceremony at the White House May 15, Reagan spoke of the threat posed by communism in the region. The Mexican president responded by indicating his disapproval of Reagan's Central American policy, cautioning on the risk of war. Mexico's relations with Cuba and Nicaragua had reportedly been a source of irritation to the U.S. administration. Further, Reagan and officials in his administration had warned several times in recent months that instability could spread from Central America to Mexico and therefore to the U.S. border. In February, Gen. Paul F. Gorman, chief of the U.S. Southern Command based in Panama, had said Mexico was potentially the biggest security threat to the U.S.

President de la Madrid told President Reagan May 15 that the "risk of a generalized war" in Central America was growing. The Mexican president called for a rejection of "interventionist solutions of any kind" and urged the application of "principles and rules of international law established by the countries of the American continent." He listed these principles as "self-determination, nonintervention, equality of states before the law, peaceful solution of conflicts and international cooperation for development."

De la Madrid addressed a joint session of Congress May 16 and took the opportunity to warn against the use of force in Central America. The Mexican president asserted that the conflict in Central America was rooted in "economic deficiencies, political backwardness, and social injustice" and should not be allowed to become part of the East-West confrontation." He contended, "A uniform style of democratic life cannot be imposed on anyone" and that "democracy, by definition, cannot use the arms of tyranny."

THE BLADE

Toledo, OH, May 26, 1984

ALTHOUGH President Reagan had a cordial visit with Mexican President Miguel de la Madrid, it is evident that the two men are not on the same ideological wave length.

Mr. de la Madrid, in an address to a joint session of Congress, could not have been more specific. Where Mr. Reagan had said the responsible governments of the western hemisphere could not afford to close their eyes to attempts by Cuba, Nicaragua and the Soviet Union to subvert the region, the Mexican president warned against reliance on military force.

"This continent must not be a scenario for generalized violence that becomes increasingly difficult to control, as has occurred in other parts of the world," Mr. de la Madrid said. Conflict in Central America, he said, is a result of economic deficiencies, political backwardness and social injustice — a theme that has been sounded frequently by critics of the Administration's Latin American policy.

Neither leader is totally right in his assessment of the causes of ferment in the Caribbean. Nicaragua has been the channel for shipment of arms to El Salvador from the Soviet Union and its Caribbean surrogate, Cuba. But at the same time there would not be such fertile ground for revolutionary activity if it were not for the death squads, economic oppression and grinding poverty that afflict much of Central America.

In that connection it is particularly unwise for the United States to put pressure on Costa Rica, a peaceful and largely unarmed neighbor of Nicaragua, to join in what amounts to an anti-Sandinista alliance. It would be far better, in fact, if all the nations of Central America de-emphasized military tactics and minded their own business.

It is seldom that a state visit produces such a frank and public difference of viewpoints, but in this case President de la Madrid's candor is welcome. He is not a flannel mouth merely trying to placate left-wing groups with rhetorical support, although there is an element of that in his speech. His government has taken strong measures to reschedule debts, apply austerity at home and cooperate with foreign and international agencies in controlling Mexico's debt problem.

The Mexican president, in effect, has made his own people swallow bitter medicine after the excesses of his predecessor. On the basis of his track record he is entitled to a respectful ear in Washington.

The Wichita Eagle-Beacon

Wichita, KS, May 18, 1984

Mexican President Miguel de la Madrid offered some insights on Central American problems and politics that could be useful to the Reagan administration in its own pursuit of a Central American peace. Many Americans long have tended to believe, as Mr. De la Madrid told both Mr. Reagan and Congress this week in Washington, that the real causes of conflict in El Salvador, Nicaragua and other countries of the region are economic deficiencies, social injustice and political backwardness — not Soviet bloc designs on the area, as Mr. Reagan contends.

Soviet involvement in the region, both directly and through the Marxist governments of Cuba and Nicaragua, is a matter of concern to all countries in the hemisphere, certainly. This may be especially so with Mexico, whose proximity places it in even greater peril from such involvement than the United States.

Mr. De la Madrid's government has been involved in the Contadora process, with Venezuela, Colombia and Panama, in trying to resolve Central America's conflicts by negotiation, and thus achieving a regional peace. The group also has called for U.S. military disengagement from the region, along with all other outside powers. Even President-elect Jose Napoleon Duarte of El Salvador,

who is to meet with Mr. Reagan in Washington on Monday, says that while he would welcome assistance from the United States, he would oppose actual military intervention by our country or any other.

Mr. Reagan should consider the wisdom of his Mexican counterpart's insights, and re-evaluate how this country best can help Central America. Mr. De la Madrid's appeal to Congress to "ensure that the future of your country is based on tolerance, understanding of other interests, recognizing foreign identities and respecting the wishes of others" is worth such consideration. "We are confident," Mr. De la Madrid added, "that the American people will invariably prefer the limited exercise of power to the use of force, reason to domination."

Those are words well-spoken, and advice that would be well-heeded. Mr. Reagan, working with Congress, could do much to implement such "reason" in the days and months ahead, as Central America feels its way toward true self-determination for its peoples. One way to do that is through a U.S. recommitment to the Contadora principles — which the administration already tacitly supports. It's time to convert that paper support into concrete action, and begin the healing process in Central America.

The Providence Journal
Providence, RI, May 16, 1984

Receptive but wary, official Washington is unbending itself this week for the state visit of Mexico's President Miguel de la Madrid. There is to be an address today before a joint session of Congress and all the rest. It's about time that a Mexican leader received this kind of attention.

As U.S. citizens are coming to realize, few nations have Mexico's great potential to affect the United States directly, for better or worse. Gone are the days when Mexico could be dismissed as a drowsy backwater, an amiable tourist haven or a source of spicy food. Today's Mexico — dynamic, hard-charging, ambitious yet still largely poor — challenges such cliches. Part of President da la Madrid's mission is educating U.S. citizens to what today's Mexico is all about.

U.S.-Mexican friendship is genuine and important, and President Reagan did the right thing yesterday to stress the interests the two countries share. These should be nurtured. At the same time (and this will *not* appear in any communique this week), Mexico is gripped by severe problems that demand alert and imaginative responses from our own country.

Two topics — debt and Central America — are dominating this week's talks. On both, Mexico's past record gives U.S. officials reason to be cautious. Most of its $90 billion foreign debt was acquired during the heady days of high-priced Pemex oil in the 1970s. Loan deadlines are now testing Mexico's abilities to repay. As for Central America, Mexico and the Reagan administration have supported opposite sides in conflicts in El Salvador and Nicaragua.

On both these potentially explosive issues, however, Mexico has shown recent progress. Its stringent austerity plan, now in place for more than a year, has helped bring inflation down and has permitted rescheduling of $20 billion in loan principal. It is running a record trade surplus ($13.2 billion a year), chiefly on exports to the United States. And on Central America, Mexico is said to have stiffened its previously tolerant view of Nicaragua's Sandinista government, to the point of cutting back on its oil exports to Nicaragua. President Reagan has grounds to be pleased.

Even on Mexico's most critical problem — a surging population — Mr. de la Madrid is able to point to progress. A seven-year program of promoting contraception and family planning has brought Mexico's annual population growth down from 3 percent to 2.3 percent. The new goal, for 1988: 1.9 percent.

These reductions in population growth, crucial to Mexico's hopes for climbing out of its widespread poverty, carry profound and largely positive implications for Mexico's relations with the United States. If Mexico can get a handle on its population growth, it can buy time to pursue job-creating growth. More Mexican workers may choose to stay in their country instead of joining the unwieldy flow of illegal immigrants across the U.S. border.

Although he has been in office only since the first of 1983, Mr. de la Madrid deserves credit for some of Mexico's recent progress in the face of stiff odds. More than most of his predecessors, he shows an ability to approach his country's problems with constructive realism. On his success will rest much of the success of the U.S.-Mexican bond. This is why Washington this week wishes him well.

DAYTON DAILY NEWS
Dayton, OH, May 21, 1984

It amounts at least to a dent. A major dent.

The continuing determination of the Mexican government to chart a different course on Central America than the Reagan administration weakens the American case. A fundamental part of that case is that the spread of communism in Central America poses a long-term threat to the United States by posing a short-term threat to the most nearby countries in North and South America.

And here's Mexico saying "cool it." In addressing this country recently, Mexican President Miguel de la Madrid sounded like one of President Reagan's domestic critics. He referred to "the illusion of the effectiveness of force." And he insisted that poverty and "social injustice" are at the root of the current unrest, not outside interference.

If Mexico — poor, nearby and apparently a great deal more vulnerable — is not panicked by the idea of political change in Central America, why should a farther-away military and economic superpower be?

Obviously, de la Madrid is dealing with his own political situation. He is a democratic politician and must not let himself be seen as too willing to toady up to the yankees.

Nevertheless, if he really thought his republic or Mexican social peace was threatened by Central American uprisings, presumably he would find a way to make his views known.

Mexico's Central American border is with Guatemala, a tiny country which is experiencing some unrest of its own. It chooses to deal with that fact not by helping the Guatemalan government put down every perceived enemy, but by trying to keep open relations with both sides.

That kind of attitude is going to make it difficult for the United States to keep saying that our motivation in opposing revolution is to save Mexico.

Los Angeles Times
Los Angeles, CA, May 16, 1984

President Reagan and Mexico's President Miguel de la Madrid differ dramatically in their views on Central America. During their meetings this week the focus of public attention will be on what they say about the war-torn region. But they will also discuss another issue that could in the long run intensify the problems of Central America unless it is properly handled—Mexico's economy.

Mexico is barely starting to rebound from the financial shock that it suffered in mid-1981 when the price of oil, its principal export commodity, began to drop. That ended an oil-fueled economic boom and put in jeopardy more than $70 billion in loans that optimistic foreign banks and lending institutions had extended to Mexico's government and largest businesses.

The resulting economic crisis has forced the Mexican government to take drastic steps. De la Madrid's predecessor, Jose Lopez Portillo, devalued the peso and nationalized the banking system. Since taking office in 1982, De la Madrid has imposed severe austerity on the country, cutting the government's budget dramatically in an effort to cool an inflationary spiral that had reached 100% annually. Prodded by the International Monetary Fund, De la Madrid not only halted capital projects but also cut back government subsidies of food, gasoline and other key consumer products.

De la Madrid and his economic advisers have shown admirable courage in addressing their economic problems. They have been rewarded by the banks with additional loans to help pay interest on the nation's debt, which now totals more than $90 billion. But Mexico will need more help from the Reagan Administration to work its way back to full economic health.

De la Madrid wants the Administration to approve a trade agreement that will make it easier for Mexico to export manufactured goods like cement, ceramics and toys to the United States. Given Reagan's free-market philosophy, that should not pose insurmountable philosophical problems for him.

The real question is whether De la Madrid and his economic advisers can persuade Reagan that the government's annual $200-billion budget deficit is a disaster for Mexico. By refusing to scale back the deficit, Washington forces the U.S. government to borrow, increasing the demand for money and pushing interest rates up. Those higher rates could undermine everything that De la Madrid has so painfully tried to accomplish. Mexico's Finance Minister Jesus Silva-Herzog estimates, for example, that two recent increases in the U.S. prime rate added $850 million to Mexico's debts within days.

The last thing that Mexico needs now is higher interest rates. And an economically unstable Mexico is one of the last things that the United States needs. An economic downturn south of the Rio Grande not only would damage the many U.S. companies that do business with this nation's third-largest trading partner, it would also encourage more illegal immigration and add to tensions along the border. If De la Madrid can persuade Reagan how dangerous it is to gamble that the United States can stand its massive budget deficits until after the 1984 elections, the Mexican president will not be helping just his countrymen but U.S. citizens as well.

The Seattle Times
Seattle, WA, May 17, 1984

THE usual mushy platitudes that characterize the greeting ceremonies of heads of state were largely missing when President Reagan and President Miguel de la Madrid of Mexico stepped to the microphones outside the White House this week.

The two, who share a personal cordiality, used the ceremony to fire sharp shots at each other's Central America policy.

De la Madrid warned that "the risk of a generalized war, the scope and duration of which no one can foresee," is growing in Central America.

Reagan voiced an altogether different worry. He said that "responsible governments of this hemisphere cannot afford to close their eyes to what is happening or be lulled by unrealistic optimism" in regard to the same region.

In other words, De la Madrid accused Reagan of courting a wider war in Central America, and Reagan accused De la Madrid of being blind to the realities of Moscow/Havana gains there. The truly worrisome thing is that both are probably right.

Bill Plympton

Miguel de la Madrid

Many citizens of this country share De la Madrid's concerns, expressed yesterday in an address to Congress and earlier at the White House, that the Reagan administration is displaying a dangerous emphasis on military solutions to Central America's problems.

It is reasonable to ask, however, what Mexico is doing about those problems, other than to carp at the U.S. True, Mexico is a member of the Contadora group of Latin countries that seek peaceful solutions. But where is the evidence that the Contadora nations have stayed a single fire fight? Workable ideas from Latin neighbors of the combatants would surely be welcome.

Lecturing Uncle Sam is always good politics back home in those capitals. Helping shoulder the burden of hemispheric problems requires a much higher level of statesmanship.

The Houston Post
Houston, TX, May 18, 1984

Mexico's President Miguel de la Madrid reaffirmed the obvious during his visit to Washington this week. He and President Reagan don't agree on the causes of or the solutions to Central America's problems. Both in talks with Reagan and in a speech to a joint session of Congress Wednesday, de la Madrid said he doesn't believe communist subversion is a threat to the region.

The Mexican president told Congress the Central American conflict "is a result of the economic deficiencies, political backwardness and social injustice that have afflicted the countries of the area." Speaking for a country that has maintained friendly relations with both Cuba and Nicaragua, he urged dialogue and negotiation to settle the disputes that divide the region. He also advised U.S. restraint in the use of military power there.

That differs sharply from President Reagan's view that the Soviet Union, Cuba and Nicaragua are trying to sweep Latin America into the communist orbit, which he sees as a threat to U.S. security.

The truth about Central America's troubles probably lies somewhere between these divergent views. Cuba, the Kremlin's chief surrogate in the Western Hemisphere, has aided and abetted the Marxist Sandinista regime in Nicaragua, which has in turn been a conduit for arms to the leftist rebels in El Salvador. But poverty and oppression have provided fertile soil for militant leftist movements in the region. As long as those conditions exist, they will be sources of unrest with or without communist subversion.

Presidents Reagan and de la Madrid could each learn something from the other's views of Central America's problems. But both views are partly distorted by the two leaders' differing perspectives of the troubled region.

The Birmingham News
Birmingham, AL, May 31, 1984

Democratic Party politics being the harum-scarum thing they are, Jesse Jackson's trip to Mexico City to address the foreign relations committee of the Mexican Congress and to campaign against his own government should come as no surprise.

Jackson accused the United States of "arrogance" in trying to rescue Central America from the communist insurgency. Naturally, the pro-Cuban politicians in his audience cheered lustily. The problem with Jackson's demagoguery is that none in the Mexican claque can cheer him or vote for him at the Democratic National Convention in San Francisco.

The State
Columbia, SC, May 21, 1984

THE PUBLIC differences that surfaced between President Reagan and Mexican President Miguel de la Madrid after their Washington sessions were expectable and should not be over-emphasized. In at least a symbolic way, the Mexican's visit was fruitful.

Mexico, a country that prides its own "perpetual" revolution, theoretically champions other revolutions. Its leaders' public words are often aimed for home constituencies. For back home, the folks, exulting in a new national pride, are conditioned to years of anti-Yankee propaganda fed largely by memories of U.S. interventions. This fervor, which spawns a different way of looking at Nicaragua, persists despite a genuine fear in some quarters of the consequences of Sandinistan ambition in Nicaragua.

The differences with Mexico on Central American policy, of course, are substantial but they can be narrowed a bit. They are, however, not likely to be overcome soon.

Mr. de la Madrid was most critical of U.S. perception of the influence of outside powers in Marxist Nicaragua. "We are convinced," he said, "that the Central American conflict is a result of the economic deficiencies, political backwardness and injustice that have afflicted the countries of the area. We therefore cannot accept its becoming part of the East-West confrontation, nor can we accept reforms and structural changes being viewed as a threat to the security of the other countries of the hemisphere."

Mr. de la Madrid had in mind U.S. aid to El Salvador and Honduras and "covert" aid to anti-Sandinistan rebels in Nicaragua.

Indeed, President Reagan does often overplay the East-West issue, although it is manifested in communist help supplied to Nicaragua. But the issue is far bigger than Nicaraguan's socialist system or so-called liberal reforms, which the U.S. should be able to live with. The key problem is the exportation of revolution to its neighbors by a nation which has a larger army than the rest of Central America combined and by a nation whose leaders parrot "justice" but who behave more and more like the oppressors they overthrew. It is a country where Cubans and East European communists swarm like locust.

How long would the fragile hopes in El Salvador, a beleaguered country which has just conducted free elections in its search for democracy, peace and stability, survive if Nicaragua had its way? The aspirations of those people who braved guerrilla threats to trudge to the polls count for something too.

Is there a middle ground? Indeed, some hope in the region is provided by the election to the presidency of El Salvador of moderate Jose Napoleon Duarte and by the peace efforts of the Contadoran governments, of which Mexico is a member.

Mr. Duarte has already launched a common strategy for unity by his visit with heads of state of Costa Rica, Honduras and Guatemala and his subsequent weekend sessions with President Reagan.

As for the Contadoran effort, Mr. Reagan should support it more vigorously. Mr. de la Madrid implied this when, speaking to Congress, he omitted reference to the Administration's claims that it supports Contadora.

While Mr. de la Madrid was correct in saying that the United States should accept ideologies that vary with its own, he ignored the support of Nicaragua for the El Salvadorean guerrillas and the latter's refusal to cooperate in free elections.

But Mr. de la Madrid's efforts were not a bust. His visit and reception in Washington, and the sessions involving Mr. Duarte, focus much needed visibility on relations with Central America. When our President meets with such leaders, even if they disagree, it at least provides some kind of needed dialogue and sends a positive signal that the United States does consider Central America a major priority.

THE DENVER POST
Denver, CO, May 23, 1984

MEXICAN President Miguel de la Madrid argued during his Washington visit last week that Central America's problems stem far more from disease, poverty and ignorance than Soviet subversion. But while press reports played up that part of De la Madrid's message as a rebuke to Ronald Reagan, the fact is that U.S. policy recognizes those realities more than most Americans realize or the Mexican president would admit publicly. Reagan has funneled three dollars in economic aid to El Salvador for every dollar of military assistance, for example.

But De la Madrid drew less attention for underscoring a problem the administration may not realize — or more probably simply finds difficult to resolve politically in an election year. That's the degree to which internal U.S. economic policies are choking off progress in Latin America and the Third World in general. As British Foreign Secretary Geoffrey Howe noted last week, each 1 percent rise in American interest rates adds at least $3.5 billion a year to the interest the developing world owes on its debt to multi-national banks.

Thus, the chronic inability of the U.S. to its own get its own economic house in order is fostering turmoil abroad which in turn undercuts this nation's ability to defend its foreign interests. The recent rise in interest rates alone will bleed more resources from Latin America than the expansion of aid proposed by the Kissinger Commission will infuse into it.

Obviously, the problem of international interest rates is interwoven with that of U.S. government deficits, which seemingly must wait until after the election before anyone gets serious about solving it. But worried administration officials have been working on schemes to shield Third World borrowers from the worst effects of the present onerous interest rates.

President Reagan should pay more attention to at least that part of his Mexican counterpart's message. It may be politically embarassing to try to ease the interest burden on impoverished foreign debtors at a time when American voters are being asked to pay higher rates. But otherwise the president risks letting the unintended side-effects of his domestic economic policies undermine his efforts to foster stability and progress throughout this hemisphere.

DESERET NEWS
Salt Lake City, UT, May 14-15, 1984

Since President Miguel de la Madrid Hurtado took office on Dec. 1, 1982, he has been inundated with Mexico's staggering problems bequeathed by the previous administration:

— A staggering foreign debt of $84 billion, on which just the interest sops up half the value of Mexico's entire exports, including 1.5 million barrels of oil daily.

— Soaring inflation that had reached 114 percent by July of last year.

— Widespread corruption that has reached high into the political spectrum. The former director of the National Panwshop — a quasi-public agency — was accused of stealing more than $13.5 million. The former head of PEMEX, the state oil monopoly, has been charged with defrauding the government of $34 million. Under the last administration, some $10 billion worth of oil is alleged to have disappeared.

Under such circumstances, the meeting Tuesday between President Reagan and President de la Madrid in Washington takes on no little significance. The two met last August in the Mexican city of LaPaz to thresh out mutual problems.

To his credit, de la Madrid has tackled Mexico's problems head-on. He has initiated an austerity program so stringent it has brought widespread protests. He has promised to stamp out corruption, though middle-class Mexicans wonder if that can ever be accomplished in a country where it's so widespread.

De la Madrid needs U.S. financial help to avoid the prospect of a civil war. Without additional help, Mexico could easily go bankrupt. That would greatly increase pressure on Mexican nationals to flee to the United States — either legally or illegally.

One point the two presidents are sure to discuss is U.S. actions in Central America. Last August, de la Madrid told Mr. Reagan that Central American stability was endangered by "profound economic crisis and by shows of force which threaten to tough off a conflagration." Only through "dialogue and diplomatic negotiation," says de la Madrid, will Central America be able to overcome its difficulties.

Mexico was one of the architects — with Colombia, Panama, and Venezuela — of the Contadora Group's plan to negotiate a peaceful settlement in Central America. One aim of the group is to bar foreign military bases in the five Central American republics: Costa Rica, El Salvador, Guatemala, Honduras, and Nicaragua. Arms reduction is another major goal.

Mexican officials have been disturbed by Newsweek's report of April 2 that the U.S. intended to use economic pressure on Mexico to support American anti-communism policy in Central America. But any such attempt could well provoke a new wave of anti-Americanism south of the border — and increase the odds against a Central America settlement. Certainly the U.S. ought to avoid taking steps that would only aggravate an already serious problem.

FORT WORTH STAR-TELEGRAM
Fort Worth, TX, December 30, 1984

In a recent and frank interview, Mexico's President Miguel de la Madrid seemed to be saying that relations between his nation and the United States are good but could be better. He spoke highly of the opportunity for Mexico to take advantage of living next to the United States, with its wealth and developed technology.

Even as he spoke, there was a mystery developing in the abduction of four U.S. citizens in Mexico. There is a feeling among Americans that Mexican officials are not always particularly helpful in solving such disappearances.

In recent months, there have been stories of other troubles encountered by U.S. citizens in Mexico.

De la Madrid, though, spoke of the need for Mexicans to know and understand their North American neighbors better. And certainly, so interlinked are the two nations and so great are the opportunities that cooperation could bring to flower on both sides of their border, understanding their neighbors is a two-way street that would benefit both.

The danger in the recent incidents of harm befalling Americans in Mexico is that it will undo the progress already made toward understanding.

Kidnapping, robbery and even murder are not the sole province of Mexico. American tourists run a risk anywhere in the world. They, and travelers from other countries, are at risk here in the United States.

But travel from the United States to Mexico is a major industry for Mexico. It also enhances individual Americans' understanding of Mexico's potential as well as its problems. Mexico's social and economic problems are ours, too, because the United States needs a stable, strong friend to the south.

And as de la Madrid and many American leaders understand, that potential will only be realized, and those problems only eased, with American help.

Americans visiting Mexico should be good guests. They should go there as friends.

Mexico should be a good host. Mexico should show that it cares about the safety of Americans there, as well as their dollars.

It is by demonstrating mutual respect and patience that better understanding will come. To do otherwise, on either side of the border, could be tragic.

Honduran Military Chief Forced to Resign

Gen. Gustavo Alvarez Martinez, the commander of the Honduran armed forces and a staunch supporter of the United States military role in Honduras, was unexpectedly forced to resign March 31, 1984. Alvarez was immediately flown out of the country to what President Roberto Suazo Cordova said was permanent exile. Alvarez was taken first to Costa Rica, but flew to the U.S. April 5. Three other top military commanders were also ousted March 31, and a fourth two days later. Gen. Walter Lopez Reyes, the air force commander who was instrumental in forcing Alvarez's resignation, took over as armed forces commander April 4. Alvarez had been widely viewed as the most powerful man in Honduras. He had assumed the post of armed forces commander in April 1982 and quickly took a leading role in the nation's affairs. His ouster raised the question of whether his successor would be as strong a defender of U.S. Central America policy as Alvarez had been.

Honduran officials cited in press reports April 1 said that Alvarez was ousted because his autocratic leadership style, his alleged growing corruption, and his plans for restructuring the army had found disfavor with a group of young military officers. The sources said Alvarez' removal appeared to have nothing to do with his close ties to the U.S. Traditionally, military decisions were made through a consensus of the armed forces supreme council, but Alvarez had all but abolished that system. Further, he apparently aroused hostility among military officers by unilaterally imposing new regulations increasing the number of years between promotions to five from three. In effect, this blocked the rise of younger officers. Alvarez had also planned a shake-up in the officer corps in June.

Foreign Minister Edgardo Paz Barnica April 2 said that the removal of Alvarez would "allow for consolidation of democracy and provide greater impetus to a peaceful coexistence in Central America within the framework of the Contadora Group." Daniel Ortega Saavedra, the coordinator of the Nicaraguan junta, said April 1 that the developments in Honduras improved the prospects for peace in the region. He commented, "It is known that General Alvarez had an obsession of war with Nicaragua."

The San Diego Union
San Diego, CA, April 6, 1984

The recent removal of Honduran armed forces commander Gen. Gustavo Alvarez Martinez came as a complete surprise. Though it's too early to tell much about the internal state of affairs in that Central American country, this much seems certain: Saturday's bloodless coup shows that Honduras is not the U.S. puppet that many congressmen would have their constituents believe.

To the contrary, Gen. Alvarez's departure left U.S. Ambassador John D. Negroponte and his bosses at the State Department shaking their heads in disbelief. Sources close to the scene suggest the general was sent packing to Costa Rica by a corps of junior officers who were dissatisfied with his authoritarian manner. Some say he was corrupt while others claim his removal resulted from repressive policies that had led to the abduction of two prominent labor leaders and the temporary jailing of 1,000 striking electrical workers.

Whatever the reason, Alvarez and four of his key aides are currently in exile and the power has passed to Air Force chief Gen. Walter Lopez Reyes who, like Alvarez, is a staunch anti-communist, albeit less dictatorial in dealing with subordinates.

The shakeup isn't expected to interrupt joint U.S.-Honduran military exercises scheduled to span the next several months. However, there are some indications that the changing of the Honduran guard could alter the strategic equation in the region.

This new generation of military leaders is leery of increased involvement in the Salvadoran conflict. Specifically, they oppose the training of Salvadoran officers currently taking place in the Honduran coastal port of Puerto Castilla and there are rumblings in Tegucigalpa concerning the larger U.S. military presence in the country. Finally, the army-dominated Honduran National Security Council has said that nation will not become involved in a military confrontation with El Salvador unless the United States takes the lead in an overt intervention.

Better educated, more sophisticated, and concerned with modernization, these younger Honduran officers are clearly determined to pursue an independent course that emphasizes a more efficient and productive government. Thus for the foreseeable future, U.S.-Honduran relations should remain on an even keel so long as Washington treats this fledgling Central American democracy as an ally rather than an appendage.

The Miami Herald
Miami, FL, March 21, 1984

FOR YEARS critics of American foreign policy have complained that the United States lumps together all of Latin America, making too few distinctions between conditions in one country and those in a neighboring state.

Because a Marxist-Leninist regime controls Nicaragua, because of the civil war in El Salvador, because of human-rights violations in El Salvador and Guatemala, because the CIA sponsors a guerrilla force on the border between Honduras and Nicaragua, all requests for assistance in Central America are measured by the same generalizations about the region. As a result, the two countries in the region with distinctly different behavior patterns — Costa Rica and Honduras — have suffered.

The Administration had asked for $145 million in military assistance for Honduras. A House subcommittee on March 1 cut it back to $41 million and banned future American military maneuvers in Honduras. Concern was expressed that while American military assistance aids Honduras's 14,000-man army, it also presages a more-direct American involvement in the region.

Now the Administration is trying to revive its military requests for Honduras. The proposal would provide $37.5 million in additional military aid this year, $62.5 million in 1985, and $45 million over the next two years to improve a U.S.-run military base on the Honduran Caribbean coast.

In considering the request, Congress should take into account that Honduras has a difficult border conflict with Nicaragua, whose regime already has infiltrated Cuban-trained guerrillas into the country. It also should consider the civil war in El Salvador.

But in addition to external considerations, Congress should consider that internal conditions in Honduras are drastically different from those that prompted the Sandinista takeover in Nicaragua or that have nurtured the success of the guerrilla movement in El Salvador.

Honduras does not have a landed oligarchy; it never has had. More than 45,000 families own small coffee *fincas*. For more than 30 years the country has had effective unions. The Honduran army never has been a Praetorian Guard for the privileged; nor has it ever been abusive and repressive. Finally, Honduras's return to democracy is now two years old and doing nicely.

This does not mean that all is well in Honduras. Corruption in the government, although reduced, is still a problem. The country still suffers from sporadic human-rights violations.

What it does mean is that Honduras is one of the few countries in the region where American military — and economic — assistance can be productive. Congress should consider this favorably when it studies the request for military aid for the next two years as well as when it considers the current $95 million supplemental-appropriation request for economic assistance to Honduras.

The Philadelphia Inquirer
Philadelphia, PA, April 6, 1984

Full-dress U.S. military exercises — "All they are is war games," President Reagan insists — resumed in Honduras this week. The administration's comrade-in-arms, Honduran army chief Gen. Gustavo Adolfo Alvarez Martinez, wasn't around to play. To the surprise of U.S. officials who have been militarizing the country, he'd been packed off to Costa Rica in handcuffs, the victim of a barracks revolt.

That's the way power changes hands in Honduras, a two-year-old democracy where the army still calls the shots. By widening the role of such as Gen. Alvarez, the United States helped perpetuate that tradition.

There was no time for formalities. Honduras was to become safe haven to 12,000 Nicaraguan exiles, the so-called *contras*, whom the United States is paying to harass the leftist government in Managua. And it was to be the U.S. training camp for Salvadoran regulars, not to mention Honduras' armed forces.

On the strength of U.S. military aid that has grown from $8.4 million in 1981 to a proposed $62.5 million for next year, Honduras, the fortress on the isthmus, in fact, now exists. But as the Congress debates whether to support administration pleas to deepen U.S. involvement in Central America, the matter of Gen. Alvarez deserves parting comment.

Yes, the general was anti-communist. Of that there can be no doubt. But anti-communism does not a friend of democracy make. Salvadoran presidential candidate and rightist vigilante Roberto d'Aubuisson is, for that matter, anti-communist.

Gen. Alvarez had become pre-occupied — as the Reagan administration has become preoccupied — with a showdown with Sandinista Nicaragua. He meddled flagrantly in politics, undercutting President Suazo Cordova's minimal power and riding roughshod over his officer corps. While he crusaded against communism, he championed corruption.

In a nation where 70 percent of the children suffer from malnutrition, Gen. Alvarez fought communism by building two $500,000 mansions and commissioning an extravagant beach house. In a nation where the annual median income is $600, he used his office to control construction contracts, cuts of banking business, coffee exports, the shrimp catch and who knows what all. His closest compatriots were worse — smuggling shiploads of video recorders, vacationing with suitcases stuffed with cash.

This, while he donated U.S. food was diverted to the black market. While milk for children disappeared.

Mr. Reagan is wrong if he thinks such allies are bulwarks against revolution and anti-Americanism. Such as Gen. Alvarez serve only to sharpen the hunger for justice and sully the U.S. mission. Even his junior officers, in the end, could not stomach his excesses.

In June 1983, this newspaper quoted a Senate speech made by Robert F. Kennedy two decades ago. His words are even more applicable today. "If we allow ourselves to become allied with those to whom the cry of 'communism' is only an excuse for the perpetuation of privilege," he said, "if we assist with military materiel and other aid, governments which use that aid to prevent reform for their people — then we will give the communists a strength which they cannot attain for themselves."

The President's policy in Central America is doing just that — creating enemies. His support misses the point: It is the Gen. Alvarezes — the corrupt and greedy autocrats — who finally undermine regional peace and American interests as much as Soviet arms.

SYRACUSE HERALD-JOURNAL
Syracuse, NY, April 5, 1984

How is it the United States government knows so little about what's going on in Honduras?

We have thousands of troops on more-or-less permanent "maneuvers" there. We spend millions on open aid to the government and thinly disguised secret aid to anti-Nicaraguan guerillas based there. Yet, American officials were caught by surprise last weekend when Gen. Gustavo Alvarez Martinez, commander of the Honduran armed forces, was ousted.

Admittedly, the Alverez ouster didn't follow typical Central American ground rules. Usually, the military overthrows civilian governments.

That's especially true in Honduras, which was ruled by a succession of military presidents before the current president, Roberto Suazo Cordova, was elected in 1981. And although Suazo Cordova heads a civilian government, Gen. Alverez was considered the real power.

⬦   ⬦

It appears the military strongman was thrown out by other officers angry with his autocratic rule of the armed forces. The Reagan administration has tried to suggest civilian government had a role in the change but this seems unlikely. Civilians were bystanders; the revolt came about because of military dissatisfaction with a military man.

Because of its personal nature, the ouster probably does not represent a shift of policy or government in the country that is supposedly the United States' strongest ally in Central America. Nevertheless, our government's lack of advance knowledge about dissension that erupted to change the Honduran leadership picture is a bad sign. It happens too often around the world. The U.S. is constantly missing — or ignoring — changes of political currents. Ouster of the shah of Iran was the worst recent example but there are dozens of others. It's the main reason why we get stuck backing dictators who lack popular support.

⬦   ⬦

The civilian government — and the United States — may benefit from the ouster in at least once respect. The Honduran military remains stronger than the civilian government but President Suazo Cordova has a more dedicated protector — the United States. Backing a legitimately elected government is better for the U.S. image in Central America than being at the mercy of a military strongman.

But we should take little comfort. As long as U.S. intelligence gathering remains ineffective or ignored, we'll continue to be caught flat-footed in the very areas where we have the most at stake.

THE ATLANTA CONSTITUTION
Atlanta, GA, April 5, 1984

Finger-pointers who viewed with the utmost alarm the military's influence — both U.S. and Honduran — on the decidedly delicate 2-year-old civilian government of President Alberto Suazo Cordova must have had their eyes opened last weekend.

What Suazo and his allies among the subordinate ranks of Honduras' armed forces managed to pull off was a startling coup-in-reverse, cashiering Gen. Gustavo Alvarez Martinez, supposedly (but obviously not) the real power in his country, plus four other senior commanders.

The peaceable purge was carried out with behind-the-scenes finesse. Alvarez was hustled off quietly but firmly to a plane that took him to Costa Rica, and that was that. *Adios, amigo*, and don't come back.

For President Suazo, it was an expression of the primacy of civilian control and of his displeasure with Alvarez for dabbling in politics by snuggling up to Suazo's Nationalist Party rivals. For the junior officers, it was an assertion that not even their powerful commander-in-chief could highhandedly impose changes in military traditions and regulations without their having a say.

The United States shouldn't be too unhappy about the turn of events in Honduras, even though it was caught off guard by the sudden removal of one of its chummiest contacts in Central America.

Sure, Alvarez smoothed the way for the U.S. military buildup in Honduras, but the arrogant general was not an unblemished asset: He was too bellicose in his frequent denunciations of neighboring Nicaragua, and his anti-Communist zeal is thought to have been behind a disturbing upsurge in human rights violations uncharacteristic for Honduras.

With him gone, the U.S.-Honduran relationship will not likely atrophy; we have President Suazo's word on that. And the man picked to be the commander in chief, Air Force Gen. Walter Lopez Reyes, is a widely respected, apolitical professional, cordial with Americans (and a fanatic about *beisbol*).

By ridding his high command of a power-hungry element, Suazo has underscored his authority and offered credible evidence that the weight of our involvement in Honduras may not necessarily weaken the country's democratic underpinnings.

THE CHRISTIAN SCIENCE MONITOR
Boston, MA, April 3, 1984

THE situation in Central America, looming increasingly serious, needs close scrutiny by Congress.

The evidence on the ground in Honduras does not seem to jibe with explanations given by the Reagan administration about the temporary nature of US activities there. Surely the administration wants to make it clear to the American people what its interests are.

In the region, United States participation is stepped up: Another major US military exercise is under way in Honduras, and it now is confirmed that US surveillance planes based in Honduras are relaying to Salvadorean troops information about guerrilla positions.

In Washington, Congress again is debating administration requests for $62 million in emergency aid to El Salvador.

A key question Congress should address: Does administration policy toward Central America contain the proper mixture of military vs. diplomatic thrust? Many in Congress are concerned that there is an overemphasis on the military and insufficient attention to the diplomatic.

Another essential point: Just what does the US intend to do in Honduras? Both the Honduran and US governments insist military maneuvers are temporary and that no permanent US presence or bases will remain.

Skeptics in and out of Washington are not so sure. They worry that the US is deepening its involvement incrementally, without either a clear long-term plan or a reasonable likelihood that anything Washington does will result in the establishment of democratic governments.

As to Honduras itself, for some while US critics of the administration effort have been concerned that it would overly strengthen the Honduran military forces in relationship to the relatively weak civilian government. The ouster and exile of the Honduran armed forces commander, Gen. Gustavo Alvarez Martínez, in part may have resulted from concern by junior officers and the civilian government that he was becoming too strong.

In the US itself a debate now gathers force on the proper role of the US in Central America. It is somewhat parallel to the earlier debate on US participation in Lebanon, though without the immediate factor of obvious danger to US troops as existed in the Middle East.

It is Congress's responsibility to make clear to the public what the facts are. It ought to examine carefully the Reagan administration's proposals, explanations, and justifications. It should unearth the facts about current and planned US actions in Honduras and the US aims there.

Some moderate congressmen now believe that the US, despite denials, actually is constructing permanent if small military bases in Honduras. They say the US already has built or improved six rudimentary airstrips and four base camps capable of handling at least five thousand troops.

In addition, the US built two radar stations in Honduras; one was left behind after each of two previous military exercises.

It is understandable that, in part, the Reagan administration would want to keep both Nicaragua's government and the Salvadorean guerrillas guessing as to what Washington's intentions are. There is evidence that this policy is having some positive effect on Nicaragua, such as its announcement of November elections and a possible reduction in the military aid it provides to Salvadorean guerrillas.

The increasing US assistance to Central America frequently is mentioned as paralleling the step-by-step American involvement in Vietnam, with the unspoken conclusion that US action in Central America inevitably will also become bogged down.

The parallel is inexact and the conclusion unwarranted. There is no inevitability: For example, the US did not get into an endless morass in Lebanon but was able to withdraw fully from it, with US ships having just departed Lebanese waters. But the Lebanese adventure was at a heavy cost in American lives and American credibility in the region.

There is no inevitability about Central American involvement either. But there are, again, serious implications in the direction of US policy. The US does need to be clear on its commitments and its policies there — in Honduras, El Salvador, and elsewhere. And it needs to communicate them fully and clearly to its citizens.

'We have to be ready to cope with those anti-democratic forces over there.'

The Morning News

Wilmington, DE, April 3, 1984

ONE OF THE most difficult aspects of dealing with our Central American neighbors is the absence of stability in many of their governments and public institutions.

Last weekend, the commander of the Honduran armed forces and several of his top associates were removed from their jobs. The move caught the United States by surprise — a painful surprise since Gen. Gustavo Alvarez Martinez, the toppled leader, was a staunch U.S. ally who had encouraged the steady influx of American military forces in Honduras.

That our country was caught unawares in this major shift in power certainly calls into question the effectiveness of Ambassador John D. Negroponte. The ambassador, according to reports, had ignored suggestions that the Honduran military was growing increasingly dissatisfied with Gen. Alvarez.

This brings into focus another serious problem in Honduras. The two-year-old civilian government of Roberto Suazo Cordova was given little choice but to accept what was, in effect, a military coup. This is disheartening.

Apparently younger members of the Honduran officer corps were displeased with Gen. Alvarez's promotion policies and dictatorial style of leadership. So they forced him and his top assistants out.

Nonetheless, joint military maneuvers with U.S. troops proceeded on schedule Sunday with hardly a hitch.

Time after time, we are told that unless alternatives to military dominance are developed in Latin America things will not change. Honduras has just provided another example of the truth of that proposition.

The TENNESSEAN
Nashville, TN, April 8, 1984

THE forced resignation of the Honduran armed forces commander and three other top officers came as a surprise, even to U.S. observers, particularly since Gen. Gustavo Alvarez Marinez, the commander, was the one who had facilitated the growing U.S. role in that nation.

Honduran sources close to the army there say that the removal was staged by a younger generation of officers dissatisfied with General Alvarez's repressive internal policies. That came about out of their concern that the general was attempting to follow the "Argentine model" of repressive, neo-facist military rule.

The U.S. ambassador, Mr. John Negroponte said the resignations mean that "democracy is being consolidated in that country." But that seems a little optimistic. Honduran President Roberto Suazo Cordova, in comments after the departure of General Alvarez, stressed the importance of keeping the military out of politics, without any amplification about that.

General Alvarez was dismissed after a wave of repression during several weeks. There was the abduction of two prominent labor leaders, and there was the jailing of 1,000 electrical workers and other acts described as repressive.

The general was widely considered the most powerful man in the country. He commanded the armed forces and had the full support of the Reagan administration in building up the Honduran military while the U.S. had a military buildup of its own going full steam.

Some Argentine sources have said that General Alvarez was not only repressive toward civilians, but was heavy handed within the army and that alienated many of the younger officers.

According to *The New York Times*, the younger officers were dissatisfied for two reasons. General Alvarez was said to have ignored the practice of making decisions through the Supreme Council of high officers, and that he planned to restructure the army.

It is not clear whether the departure of General Alvarez will have a great deal of effect on Honduran relations with the U.S. But there could be some changes. The younger army corps may take a more pragmatic view toward El Salvador, and may oppose the military training of Salvadoran officers in Honduras. El Salvador has been the traditional enemy of Honduras.

The military changes come just at a time when U.S. forces have begun another series of joint military exercises with Honduras.

Sen. Jim Sasser, who recently visited Honduras, noted the U.S. Army engineers have constructed an 8,000 foot runway at Aguacate, one of six constructed or improved since the military maneuvers known as Big Pine I began a year ago. The Tennessee senator is concerned about what the U.S. may have in mind in that country.

It is fairly plain it could be a staging area for an attack against the Sandinista regime in Nicaragua. There are, after all, about 8,000 or 9,000 Nicaraguan insurgents in the border area, trained and financed by the U.S.

It is of more than just a little passing interest on the part of U.S. citizens just exactly what the Reagan administration has in mind for Honduras. The mystery is deepened by the unexpected resignations of top military leaders who could, at will, throw a monkey wrench into those plans, whatever they are.

Houston Chronicle
Houston, TX, April 5, 1984

In Latin America's tentative and chronically disrupted democracies, periods of instability historically have been followed by a military coup and the temporary demise of civilian government. In Honduras, however, the opposite proved to be the case.

The unexpected resignation of Gen. Gustavo Alvarez Martinez, supreme commander of the Honduran armed forces, and four other senior military officers is seen as a victory for the civilian government headed by President Roberto Suazo Cordova. While the United States maintained a close relationship with Alvarez, his resignation may prove beneficial both for Honduran democracy and the quest for peace in Central America.

Several reasons have been given for Alvarez's downfall, ranging from discontent among the Honduran officer corps to the perception that Alvarez's high-handed style made him appear to be a strongman who controlled the civilian government from behind the scene. Politics are never as transparent as some analysts make them seem, however, and the muddied political waters of Central America are particularly murky.

Regardless of its cause, the military shake-up in Honduras seems to have added to the strength of the elected, civilian government. A State Department spokesman said the Reagan administration regarded the shake-up as an internal matter, but noted that President Suazo Cordova had reaffirmed his pledge to consolidate democracy and seek a peaceful resolution of Central American conflicts. Those goals are shared by the United States, and a strong civilian government should not prove to be a barrier in the way of continued close ties.

Newsday
Long Island, NY, April 5, 1984

Most military exercises designed to train troops and enhance cooperation among allies ordinarily last only a few weeks. But in Honduras, American troops have been conducting almost nonstop exercises since August.

A new exercise started yesterday, coincidental with a Honduran military shakeup. The Pentagon says the exercise will go on through June. But announced plans calling for construction of new airstrips, radar stations and other facilities suggest that the U.S. Army plans to stay in Honduras much longer.

These virtually uninterrupted maneuvers are meant to do more than hone Honduran preparedness. They're also designed to demonstrate the Reagan administration's support both for the government of El Salvador in its civil war with leftist guerrillas and for the antigovernment guerrillas fighting the Sandinistas in Nicaragua.

It's not clear what effect — if any — the American maneuvers are having on those wars. What is clear is that they're having a dangerously adverse effect on the political life of Honduras, a country with a fragile two-year-old civilian government. Buoyed by the American military presence, the Honduran army is magnifying its own power and exercising increasing influence over the economy. While the military budget swells, education, health care and land reform suffer in a country that is among the poorest in the region.

The history of Latin American convincingly teaches that when social change languishes, the beneficiaries are left-wing revolutionaries and right-wing militarists. In the process, democratic civilian rule is undermined and the stage is set for civil war.

Honduras shouldn't be forced to run the risk of that kind of polarization. Nor should the United States, under the guise of military exercises, engage in the establishment of a permanent combat presence in Honduras without public discussion and the careful scrutiny of Congress.

Close Election Raises Tension in Panama

Panama held its first presidential elections in 16 years May 6. Both major parties out of a field of seven claimed victory as the vote count proceeded slowly and battles erupted between their supporters May 7, 1984. The commander of the National Defense Force, formerly called the National Guard, warned May 10 that further violence would not be tolerated. The actual polling May 6 was peaceful despite a bitter campaign. The major candidates were Arnulfo Arias Madrid, 83, and Nicholas Ardito Barletta Vallarina, 45. Arias was a three-time former president who had been ousted in coups during each of his former terms of office, the last in 1968. He was the leader of the Authentic Panamanian Party (Partido Panamenista) and represented a coalition of three political parties in the election. Ardito Barletta, a former vice president of the World Bank, led a six-party coalition, the National Democratic Union. He was backed by the National Defense Force. During the campaign, opposition leaders had expressed concern that the military-backed government would attempt to influence the election result in Ardito Barletta's favor.

Disturbances broke out May 7 as the vote count continued. Rival supporters of Arias and Ardito Barletta gathered in front of the legislative palace, where the count was taking place. According to news reports, members of the Democratic Revolutionary Party (PRD), the governing party, began shooting into the crowd of Arias supporters. One person was killed, and as many as 40 were wounded.

Gen. Manual Antonio Noreiga, the commander of the National Defense Force, warned May 10 that the government "will absolutely not permit partisan action to undermine the tranquility or the life and property of those involved." The day before, gunmen had fired at the offices of several government-controlled newspapers, and bomb threats were directed at the offices of the electoral tribunal. Gunmen also fired at the home of Arias.

Panama's election tribunal May 16 named Ardito Barletta the winner of the May election, ending a day of confusion surrounding the election result.

DESERET NEWS
Salt Lake City, UT, May 8-9, 1984

The election in El Salvador is getting most of the publicity, but two other Latin American nations, Panama and Ecuador, also are choosing leaders through the ballot box.

This, in itself, is notable in an area where military coups and revolutions are about as frequent as elections, if not more so.

The Panamanian election results were not yet available at this writing but both 82-year-old Arnulfo Arias and his closest rival, Nicolas Ardito-Barletta, 45, are claiming victory and their supporters are shooting each other.

The vote results might have been available sooner, but the election officials decided to knock off early without counting a ballot. Manana is soon enough.

The U.S. government apparently has no favorite in the Panamanian election. Both principal candidates are considered friendly to the U.S. Both have pledged not to change the status of U.S. armed forces installations in Panama. The U.S. military presence brings many much-needed jobs and dollars to the Panamanians.

Arias is no newcomer to Panama's political stage. He has been elected president three previous times but, as a fierce critic of the military, he has been ousted each time by the military. In 1968, the last time he held office, his tenure lasted only 11 days before the generals took over.

He still maintains his anti-military stand, but the head of the army, Gen. Manuel Antonio Noriega, has said the military will accept the choice of the people.

Ardito-Barletta, an economist, helped negotiate the economic aspects of the 1978 treaties giving Panama control of the Panama Canal. He is backed by the Revolutionary Democratic Party, founded by the late Gen. Omar Torrijos who ran the country from 1968 until 1981. Arias is supported by a political coalition.

The election is important to the U.S. not only because of our interest in the canal, which must be kept open to the shipping of all nations, but also because Panama is a part of the four-nation Contadora group that has been seeking peaceful solutions to the political turmoil in Central America. This group, consisting of Panama, Mexico, Colombia, and Venezuela, could yet play a role in settling the fierce disputes of the area.

For these reasons, the U.S. needs to act at once to establish good relations with the new Panamanian administration and give support that will enhance its stability, responsibility, and commitment to democracy and free institutions.

The Washington Times
Washington, DC, May 25, 1984

Six years ago, when President Carter was urging us to give away the Panama Canal, his arguments boiled down to three: guilt, fear, and hope.

Guilt: We should atone for our past sins against Panama, notably the 1903 Bunau-Varilla treaty. (Without that treaty, of course, the canal would have gone through Nicaragua, leaving Panama a neglected, disease-infested province of Colombia.)

Fear: If we didn't hand it over peacefully, we might have to defend it against attacks by Panamanian high-school students and/or Gen. Omar Torrijos's National Guard. (This U.S. aversion to using force to protect vital assets in Central America was heartening news to communist guerrillas.)

Hope: Our generosity to Panama would "usher in a whole new era of friendly and peaceful relations" with our neighbors to the south. (The intervening years have not dealt kindly with this prediction.)

Opponents of the giveaway said the treaty, negotiated for our side by banker-lawyer Sol Linowitz, was designed to give Panama a revenue-producing asset that would enable it to pay back billions of dollars Torrijos had borrowed from the international banks. Opponents further argued that it was folly to turn over the canal to a corrupt military dictator and to entrust the maintenance and defense of one of the world's most commercially and strategically important maritime passageways to a small, weak, chronically unstable nation.

The results of Panama's first free election in 16 years vividly recall those arguments. In that 1968 election Arnulfo Arias won with 70 percent of the vote, but was then ousted (for the third time!) by a military coup.

This time, it appears, the military used fraud rather than force to deprive Mr. Arias of the presidency. ABC-TV reported on May 16 that "a government official involved in the original counting of the votes" told them that when it became clear Arias had won "the election, officials . . . decided to fabricate 4,000 votes on blank ballot sheets and destroy 13,000" Arias votes.

Now Nicolas Ardito Barletta, the hand-picked candidate of the Panamanian military, has been declared president by the narrowest margin in the country's history — 1,713 votes. His election under such circumstances bodes ill for Panama's stability and the security of the Panama Canal.

It is interesting to note that while Mr. Arias opposed the Carter-Torrijos treaties, Mr. Barletta helped negotiate them, after which he landed a cushy job with the World Bank in Washington. He is also said to have helped draft the laws which made Panama a haven for international banks, after which Gen. Torrijos got huge loans from those same banks — with the result that today Panama has the largest per capita public debt in the world.

The Times-Picayune
The States-Item
New Orleans, LA, May 19, 1984

It may still be anybody's guess who won last weekend's presidential election in Panama, but the duly constituted authorities have declared Nicolas Ardito Barletta the victor, and unless the opposition decides to literally fight the decision, that will be that.

Mr. Barletta was the candidate of the establishment — essentially, the Defense Force, formerly the National Guard — and the opposition has made the usual charges of fraud in both voting and counting. But if the Guard were going to stuff the ballot boxes, it would surely have arranged for a more decisive "victory" than the thin margin certified for Mr. Barletta.

A Reagan administration observer called the election an "honest shambles," and the basic fact seems to be that it was so close to a tie that deciding the winner depended on deciding the validity of disputed votes. Of about 700,000 votes cast, 135,000 were challenged, and Mr. Barletta was declared winner by 1,713. That may be suspicious, but it is not necessarily false.

The interest now is in how Mr. Barletta will govern, and there is reason to hope he will govern well. He is, indubitably, the chosen president of the Guard, which has run Panama now since 1968 and whose head, Gen. Manuel Antonio Noriega, may be in effect the shadow president. But Mr. Barletta is an international economist with a wide reputation (he resigned as a vice president of the World Bank to run) and is considered intelligent, capable and honest even by many of his political opponents.

Mr. Barletta, incidentally, becomes the third Latin president elected last weekend to have been educated in U.S. universities. The others were Jose Napoleon Duarte in El Salvador and Leon Febres-Cordero in Ecuador.

The Panamanian military has been as much a populist as a conservative political force, and while it can be as corrupt and arrogant as its counterparts elsewhere in Latin America, it enjoys much genuine support. Its choice of Mr. Barletta as its civilian standard bearer suggests that it has serious, responsible government in mind and not simple power-holding.

The hope is that Mr. Barletta will be both able to and allowed to govern in that manner and that the Guard will undertake internal reforms and permit the civilian government to take a greater constitutional role. If all that happens, Panama could develop a stable, popular and demonstrably democratic government that would be a valuable anchor in a threatened region of strategic importance.

The Wichita
Eagle-Beacon
Wichita, KS, May 19, 1984

The outcome of a Latin American election held the same day as El Salvador's — one similarly crucial to U.S. and regional interests — was finally settled Wednesday, but only in the narrowest sense. The government-backed candidate for the presidency of Panama, Nicolas Ardito-Barletta, has defeated former President Arnulfo Arias Madrid. Sixteen years of military rule have ended — at least ostensibly.

But many of Mr. Arias' supporters believe the scant 1,700-vote margin between winner and loser indicates vote fraud by a military unwilling to risk true civilian rule. That belief, whether correct or incorrect, portends unstable times for a nation highly important to the United States. Mr. Arias — who won the presidency in Panama's last free election in 1968, then was overthrown by the military after 11 days in office — says he'll abide by the results of the 1984 election, but many of his supporters may not. They claim to have lost faith that fair elections ever can be held in Panama, and have left hanging the implication that loss of faith could lead to attempts to seize power forcibly.

Clearly, then, Mr. Ardito-Barletta faces some formidable challenges. Panama's per capita national debt is the highest in the hemisphere, and unemployment sometimes ranges as high as 50 percent in some areas.

These problems only will grow more serious if he can't win at least the nominal support of the opposition forces who offered Mr. Arias as their candidate. It's appropriate that news of his victory inspired Mr. Ardito-Barletta to conciliatory words toward his opponents, including hints they may have a role in his cabinet. The question now is: Will such be enough to relieve the opposition's post-election bitterness?

It's in the United States' short- and long-term interest that Mr. Ardito-Barletta succeed in unifying his country. Panama is a member of the four-nation Contadora group, which has developed a better alternative than the use of force to settle Central America's political and social conflicts: a solution negotiated within the region, in an atmosphere free of foreign — including U.S. — troops. Also, in little more than a decade, Panama will assume ownership of the Panama Canal under an agreement negotiated by the Carter administration. The success of that agreement, once executed, depends heavily on a politically stable Panama.

One hopes Mr. Ardito-Barletta, through deed as well as word, proves he isn't a military puppet installed fraudulently in office. One hopes as well that if he does such, the opposition will accept him at face value, and let him govern.

The Miami Herald
Miami, FL, May 17, 1984

JUST 15 years from now the Panama Canal will be totally under Panamanian control — and properly so. Nonetheless, the United States will retain a vital interest in the unimpeded flow of commerce through this strategic international waterway.

It is disconcerting, then, to note that the engineers and managers who will operate the canal when Panama takes over may be receiving their training right now in various Communist-bloc countries.

As Gov. Bob Graham pointed out in a speech the other day, some 600 young Panamanians already are studying in the Soviet Union. The Kremlin plans to provide up to 200 scholarships to its Patrice Lumumba University in Moscow, with 50 of them designated for the study of canal management and waterway improvements.

Governor Graham noted that Communist governments are directly providing Panamanian students 158 scholarships: 45 for study in the Soviet Union, 36 in Cuba, 17 each in Czechoslovakia and Rumania, 13 in Poland, 12 in Hungary, 11 in East Germany, and so on. Other scholarships are provided by front groups and Communist-led labor unions.

In contrast, the governor noted, the U.S. Government is providing only one direct Federal scholarship for a deserving young Panamanian to study in this country. The governor wants to change that, and he's right. The Reagan Administration, so enamored of giving military aid to prop up friendly leaders in Central America, needs to realize that some of the future leaders of that region's nations are receiving technical training and political indoctrination in Moscow and Havana today.

The United States ought to do more, and Florida should take the lead. Florida's institutions of higher education, both public and private, are natural and convenient places for deserving and able young scholars from Panama and other Central American nations to pursue their studies.

Already the University of Miami and Florida International University have taken initiatives in this area, and Florida State University has a branch campus in Panama.

To offset the concerted effort being made by the Communist bloc, however, Florida will need help from additional Federal funding and contributions from the private sector.

The urgency of the need is underscored by last week's post-election violence in Panama. Democratic institutions there are still young and in need of nurturing. The last thing they need is the subversive influence of indoctrinated students returning from Moscow and Havana to assume leadership positions in Panamanian society.

More is at stake than simply keeping the Panama Canal open, although that's certainly important. Also important is keeping Panamanian society open to the democratic currents now flowing through it.

House Bill Includes Amnesty Clause, Penalties for Hiring Illegal Aliens

The House passed the landmark Simpson-Mazzoli immigration reform legislation June 20, 1984 after seven days of emotional debate. The legislation, which would be the first substantial revision of the nation's immigration laws since 1952, would provide amnesty to millions of illegal aliens who had established residency in the United States. It would also, however, impose penalties on employers who hired illegal aliens. This measure was strongly opposed by Hispanics, who were concerned that the bill's sanctions against employers would work against the hiring of any Hispanic-Americans, whether they were legal residents or illegal aliens. The American Federation of Labor and Congress of Industrial Organizations was another opponent of the House bill as finally passed, but for a different reason. An early supporter of the legislation, the federation objected to later amendments setting up a special program for farmers who wanted to bring aliens into the U.S. as temporary workers to harvest fruit and vegetables. The provision, favored by farmers and food processors, would allow the workers to move from one employer to another to another within a specified region. The House reform bill was approved by a vote of 216 to 211. A similar bill had been passed by the Senate in 1983, and the legislation would now go into conference to iron out the differences. Both bills prohibited employment of illegal aliens, requiring employers to demand documents from job applicants verifying citizenship or authorization to work in the U.S., but only the Senate version called for a criminal penalty for a pattern of violations; both houses set civil fines of up to $2,000. The House and Senate bills also differed markedly on the amnesty issue, with the Senate's version less generous than the House's. One controversial provision in the House amnesty proposal would require aliens to show they were learning the English language and acquiring a knowledge of American history in order to become permanent residents. The proposal was presented by Majority Leader Jim Wright (D, Texas), who said the requirement was intended not to "homogenize America" but to show that the applicant could "fully participate in what our country has to offer."

The Orlando Sentinel

Orlando, FL, June 12, 1984

House Democrats began a long-delayed debate on the immigration reform bill Monday with a show of timidity. After Speaker Tip O'Neill had signaled his unenthusiasm for the bill, 100 of his Democratic colleagues voted against even considering it. Only strong support from Republicans lets the House take up this chronic, complex crisis this week.

The Democrats' gutlessness and gamesmanship can't encourage those committed to action. Clearly, control of the country's borders is still a dicey issue whose solution satisfies no one completely. Thus the reform bill is caught in a tug of war between liberals and conservatives. Each wing rejects one of the bill's two key provisions, though both are vital to its final passage and its basic fairness.

The bill would prohibit hiring illegal aliens, which liberals don't like. Hispanic politicians and civil libertarians have led a demagogic charge against penalizing employers who hire illegal aliens. Their pressure has immobilized the speaker for more than a year. But it is incredible to argue that the sanctions would force employers to reject prospective workers who look Hispanic — particularly once the influx of illegals slows.

The other hang-up is that the bill would give most workers here illegally a way to get legalized. Conservatives look at that with sand-dunked heads. They consider it an affront to law and order, when in fact with the status quo these workers can be exploited under the law. They have no legal recourse against exploitive employers or out-and-out criminals. The U.S. Congress has looked the other way while the U.S. economy has profited from their work. That's wrong.

The House's whole quaking routine on this issue is tiresome. A year ago the Senate passed overwhelmingly a similar but better bill. This week representatives will show whether they want to control borders again, whether they want to stop exploiting workers here illegally — and whether they have any courage at all. For months the speaker of the House has answered these questions negatively, so it's time for representatives not to follow their leader.

The Honolulu Advertiser

Honolulu, HI, June 21, 1984

Passage of the immigration bill in the U.S. House yesterday was both historic and remarkable. Final enactment into law later this summer could be the Congress' top achievement this election year.

The five-vote margin of House passage attests to the controversial nature of this attempt at immigration reform. This is, indeed, a measure with "something for everyone to oppose," and many are amazed it survived.

BUT THE larger fact recognized by the majority of House members is that a start has to be made at controlling illegal immigration. Not only is it a problem, it is one that has generated an anti-immigrant mood in parts of the country that would grow and possibly lead to more restrictive legislation later.

This bill, with its central tradeoff between amnesty for millions of illegal immigrants now in the U.S. and penalties for employers who hire others in the future, seems the best that can be achieved after years of effort and compromise.

Whether as now drawn it would really work in terms of stemming the tide of illegal immigrants is a question. Both employers and illegals may find it all too easy to beat a system which would rest on documents that can easily be forged; there is no consensus yet for a true national identity card.

No doubt the system the bill sets up will need adjustment later. And at best this is only part of an answer that must involve economic conditions in several countries.

STILL, it emerges as the best flawed and partial answer available to deal with an issue that can't be ignored and calls for balancing compromises.

In that regard, modest compromises will also be needed with the version passed 76-18 last year by the Senate and backed by President Reagan.

But it would seem that yesterday's House vote may have been the most difficult test for this measure which could stand as a tribute to the necessity for making tough decisions in situations where present answers, much less future results, are far from clear.

THE LOUISVILLE TIMES

Louisville, KY, June 26, 1984

Even before conferees compromise on the differences between the Senate and House versions of the immigration reform bill, critics are trying to undercut it by claiming it will be too expensive to enforce. Nobody in Congress should accept such claims at face value.

True, the budget of the Immigration and Naturalization Service — which is responsible for guarding the borders and monitoring the activities of aliens — will be insufficient to cope with all the reforms envisioned by Congress.

But the House version of the Simpson-Mazzoli bill proposed to increase the agency's budget by $80 million in the fiscal year ending Sept. 30 and would authorize spending of $700 million in 1985 and $715 million in 1986. The Senate measure authorizes $200 million for the current fiscal year for implementation and does not prescribe amounts for future years.

However, the immigration service's budget has long been considered inadequate for the job with which it is charged. Late in the Carter administration, border patrols and surveillance equipment were considered inadequate.

In the Reagan administration's early zeal for budget cutting, the agency was turned upside down. In 1981, the White House called for the elimination of 973 positions, including crucial border station slots. To its credit, in recent years the administration has supported substantial increases in funding for the agency. In fiscal 1985, for instance, Mr. Reagan has asked $574.5 million for the service, a 12.5 per cent increase.

Early this year, budget director David Stockman complained that the cost of implementing the bill, sponsored in the House by Louisville Rep. Romano Mazzoli, would be outrageous. Mr. Stockman said that amnesty provisions alone could increase the annual national welfare bill by $2 billion to $3 billion.

However, *The Washington Post* recently reported that a Rice University study estimates unemployment benefits to out-of-work U. S. citizens whose jobs were taken by illegal aliens amount to more than $18 billion each year. That is merely a fraction of the cost of continuing a system that encourages abuse of immigration laws.

Even the strongest supporters of the immigration reform measure admit it is not perfect. Nobody is quite sure how much it will cost to implement. But one thing is certain: Without it, the costs to this country will be far greater.

The Oregonian

Portland, OR,
June 17, 1984

It's a paradox: On one hand, reformers of education are talking about the need to strengthen the teaching of foreign languages in our schools. On the other, a group of U.S. senators has proposed a constitutional amendment declaring English to be the official language of the United States.

There can be no doubt that the United States, huge and diverse as it is, has benefited from having one dominant language to help hold it together. That the language is such a rich and effective one as English is an added gain. It would be a great loss if this country ever were to become seriously divided along language lines, as Canada and Belgium are.

It would not be a bad thing to require, if necessary, that all the official proceedings in the United States — its legislatures, its courts, its public records and the like — be kept in English. But having an officially designated language has other and more troubling implications.

It could, for example, endanger federal aid to bilingual education, the most common approach to teaching children who are not native English-speakers.

It could eliminate the use of bilingual ballots and other election materials.

If Congress should decide any or all of these measures are undesirable, it could eliminate them simply by changing the laws, without going to the labor of proposing a constitutional amendment.

Plainly the English-language amendment is inspired by fear of the wave of Spanish-speaking immigrants that has swept across the United States' southern border. But this country has seen surges of immigration before, and its Germantowns and Little Italys have been absorbed into the general English-speaking population without benefit of having an official language.

The amendment, which had a hearing in a Senate committee this week, threatens to focus hostile and harmful attention on America's Spanish-speaking minority. It raises some important questions, but it is not the right answer.

THE ARIZONA REPUBLIC

Phoenix, AZ, June 17, 1984

CRITICS of the notion that English should be the official language of the United States are off-base. One nation, one language is clearly an idea whose time has come.

There are compelling reasons for supporting this concept. One is the job factor. If two people, one who is fluent in English and the other who speaks, say, Spanish, but knows very little English, seek the same job, the odds are heavily in favor of the English-speaking applicant.

There is also the matter of communication. In a nation where many languages are spoken to varying degrees, English is the common tongue. With a few exceptions — such as ballots printed in both English and Spanish in a number of states — English is the means of communicating in spoken and written word. People without a working knowledge of English are lost.

There has been much ado in recent years about bilingual education. Proponents contend it is needed to help immigrant children in schools, while opponents say it promotes cultural apartheid.

Opponents are right. Bilingual education is a crutch, and as long as it is in place in the nation's schools people will be leaning on it. Moreover, since it discourages learning English, it's a disservice to the very ones it is supposed to help.

The present move away from bilingualism is toward a constitutional amendment making English the official U.S. language. It's not needed.

All that needs to be done is for the various levels of government that provide funds for bilingual education to pull the plug on the life-support system.

The Record

Hackensack, NJ, June 21, 1984

At last, the House of Representatives has passed a comprehensive immigration reform. It is much like the one proposed seven long years ago by Jimmy Carter and approved twice by the Senate. It is controversial. But its principal elements are fundamental to justice and practicality: amnesty for illegal aliens who've been here since 1982, and sanctions against employers who hire illegal aliens.

Each of these points has had vigorous and well-founded opposition. Many argue that it is unfair to law-abiding citizens to forgive (and eventually welcome into the full privileges of citizenship) those who live and work here secretly and unlawfully. Others complain that illegal aliens take jobs needed by citizens.

But the reasons for amnesty outweigh these arguments. There is no other way to persuade illegal aliens to make themselves known. Without being able even to count this underground population, the government can't begin to manage the problem. The cities that harbor most illegal aliens provide housing, schooling, medical care, and other services for which they could obtain federal reimbursement — if they could identify the illegal aliens among the recipients. But the aliens won't come forward while they know they risk arrest and deportation.

Employers and Hispanic groups oppose the idea of criminal sanctions for employers who hire — and all too often exploit — illegal aliens. Since most illegal immigrants come from Latin America, Hispanics contend that such sanctions will drive employers to shun all Spanish-speaking workers in order to avoid mistakes and criminal penalties. To answer that, the bill has been amended to outlaw discrimination against any single ethnic group.

Employers would be empowered to check Social Security numbers of applicants with a toll-free call to Washington. Civil libertarians warn of the potential invasions of privacy in such inquiries. But it wouldn't be fair to punish employers for hiring illegal aliens without giving them a means to check the status of job applicants. And without employer sanctions, there is nothing to discourage the continued flow of workers forced by fear and economics to accept miserable pay and conditions without complaint.

Amnesty is in keeping with the American tradition of generosity toward the homeless and downtrodden. Without amnesty, illegal immigration remains unmanageable. Without employer sanctions, immigration laws will continue to be unenforceable. The House has shown courage in recognizing these disagreeable truths. The bill now goes to House-Senate conference. With President Reagan's promised support, it should at last become law.

THE INDIANAPOLIS STAR

Indianapolis, IN, June 26, 1984

No crystal ball gives any hint ot the final shape of the Simpson-Mazzoli bill — actually two bills which must be transformed into one by U.S. Senate and House conferees to give the nation its first major immigration reform in more than three decades.

Differences in philosophies and attitudes and clashes of interests and perceived interests will weigh along with guesswork, widely varying estimates and controversies and uncertainties as to results in determining the final version.

The House passed its more liberal version 216-211 last week.

It would grant permanent legal status to illegal aliens who have been in the United States since before Jan. 1, 1982, after two years during which they must learn English, prove they can hold a job and stay out of trouble with the police.

It would provide for fining of employers who in the future knowingly hire "illegals."

It would widen the "guest worker" program for agricultural growers needing low-paid workers to harvest their crops. This provision aroused strong union opposition.

The tougher Senate version would give permanent legal status to those in the United States prior to Jan. 1, 1977, and temporary legal status to those here since Jan. 1, 1980. It also provides for criminal penalties and civil fines for employers who knowingly hire "illegals."

It also calls on the president to develop a nationwide verification system for employers to determine the legality of job applicants.

The House turned down a proposal for a verification system because of fears expressed by some that this could lead to a nationwide identity card system. Considering the many legislative molehills that have grown into bureaucratic mountains, anxieties over the I.D. proposal are not unreasonable.

The Census Bureau estimates that there are 3 million to 6 million illegal immigrants in the United States. Unofficial estimates say the number may be as high as 12 million. House members agreed the actual figure is unknown.

The Immigration and Naturalization Service estimates that the House bill will grant amnesty to about 2 million. But House members while debating the bill admitted it was impossible to say with any certainty how many "illegals" would seek legalization.

Rep. Daniel Lungren, R-Calif., top-ranking member of the House immigration subcommittee, said the five-year federal cost of reimbursing the states for educational and social services for legalized aliens would be $6.6 billion.

At this point no one can be certain where any of the immigration control proposals, singly or in the aggregate, will lead or that the machinery of control will not produce more ills than it can cure.

No one doubts the good intentions of the hard working sponsors, Sen. Alan K. Simpson, R-Wyo., and Rep. Romano L. Mazzoli, D-Ky.

Yet what will be the ultimate effect of granting amnesty to 2 or 3 million "illegals" now, and increasing state and local social services — and in three to six years expanding federally funded social programs -- to cover "illegals"?

Will not this add up to an invitation to millions more to try their luck?

The final version of the Simpson-Mazzoli bill should be considered an experiment subject to constant observation and subject to swift revision if the need arises.

ARKANSAS DEMOCRAT

Little Rock, AR, June 17, 1984

The Senate and House are working toward legislation that would stem the inflow of illegal aliens by making it illegal to hire them. The bills show all the earmarks of being almost lobbied to death.

Employer interests say that Americans won't do the hard work – like harvesting – that only the aliens can do. That's true. But denying them work of any kind is the only way to keep the whole Southwest from being overrun by the cross-borderers who come but never return home. However, a look at the bills shows that it wouldn't be a simple boo-we-got-you for an employer if he were caught working an illegal alien. For starters, he'd have to have three or more illegals in his employ to qualify as a lawbreaker – and even then he'd get off with a warning.

Later offenses *could* lead to fines – and the Senate version (already passed) even prescribes six months in jail. But jail would come only if a "continued pattern" of such hiring could be established.

But employers of aliens aren't the only ones fighting the bill. Congress' hispanic representatives are fighting it, too, on the proposition that the penalties would scare employers off hiring Mexican-Americans. The lobby's latest amendment to the bill is the height of stupidity – revival of the "Bracero program" of the 1940s and 1950s, under which Mexican workers are imported seasonally for crop harvests and then (laugh) go back home. That would make a joke of outlawing their employment.

President Reagan is for outlawing hiring because "We've lost control of our borders." That's obvious to all of us. Illegal residents run into the millions.

There's legislation in the offing to solve that problem by allowing any illegal to apply for citizenship if he can show he has worked here for two years. It's not a good solution but it would regularize the resident-alien situation – provided we also take action to discourage their coming, which the Bracero program certainly wouldn't.

No, the only solution is to outlaw hiring, and after years of dilly-dallying Congress appears finally on the point of doing so.

The Dallas Morning News

Dallas, TX, June 25, 1984

"Nothing," wrote C. S. Lewis, "ever does half the good — perhaps nothing ever does half the evil — which is expected of it." So it will likely prove with the Simpson-Mazzoli immigration reform bill, which the House adopted last Wednesday by a tenuous five votes.

The bill goes on to conference committee for reconciliation with the version passed months ago by the Senate. Whatever its final form, it won't provide the final answer to this country's illegal aliens' problems; still, it should help.

At the heart of the aliens problem are two phenomena: (1.) the widespread unwillingness of Westerners in general — not just Americans in particular — to take on "demeaning" jobs; and (2.) the proximity to the United States of countries with large labor forces and low-growth economies.

In other words: you have both demand and supply. These two classical conditions feed on each other. If demand remains high for farm workers, dishwashers and so on, one can bet that marginally employed, or unemployed, foreigners will try to fill those openings.

Employer sanctions, guest worker programs, amnesties — the various components of Simpson-Mazzoli — are means of rationalizing the problem: and, not incidentally, extending some protections to the workers themselves. These aren't cures. Real cures must be broader in scope.

For instance, more American jobs would be filled by American citizens if Congress lowered or abolished the minimum wage, which effectively prices teen-age labor out of the market. The Mexican economy would provide many more jobs to Mexicans but for the government's high-tax, high-spend policies, which have caused high inflation, lagging investment and the peso's feebleness.

But Simpson-Mazzoli needed enacting all the same; the House's bravery in so enacting it is commendable.

Pittsburgh Post-Gazette

Pittsburgh, PA, June 22, 1984

It is hard to overestimate the significance of the U.S. House of Representatives vote this week to overhaul immigration law. A nation that, in President Reagan's apt words, has lost control of its borders is now committed by votes of both houses of Congress to reducing future illegal immigration while dealing compassionately with "illegals" already living here.

That the House vote on immigration reform came in an election year reflects all the better on the House leadership, especially Speaker Thomas P. O'Neill, who resisted entreaties from some fellow Democrats to inter the legislation.

Mr. Reagan, too, belongs on the honor roll for his timely support last week of a bill that contains much that is not to his liking. Not covering themselves with greatness were the Democrats who aspire to Mr. Reagan's office. Rather than offend Hispanic groups that shortsightedly oppose reform, the Democrats implicitly endorsed the status quo, in which illegal aliens live in constant fear of detection or mistreatment.

As the riveting television coverage of the House debate demonstrated, immigration reform remains a political briar patch. Hispanic-Americans, increasingly active politically, opposed the legislation's sanctions for employers who hire illegals, a position that put them in the unfamiliar company of business interests. The other key element of the legislation, amnesty for aliens already living here, was resisted by conservative congressmen and those who represent areas where illegal immigrants abound — and, in popular mythology at least, take jobs from Americans.

Given the emotions on both sides of the issue, the House debate was impressive for its civility as well as its gravity. More impressive was the outcome: approval of both employer sanctions and amnesty provisions, the latter qualified by an amendment requiring that aliens seeking permanent-resident status, a step along the way to citizenship, have a "minimal understanding" of the English language or be enrolled in English classes.

Critics will charge that the amendment, introduced by Majority Leader Jim Wright of Texas, is a form of cultural imperialism. But the principle behind the Wright amendment is a sound one: Mastery of English by immigrants is not only important for social cohesion; it is an indispensable passkey for survival and advancement in the American economy.

The Wright amendment will not necessarily become law. As with other provisions of the House legislation, it will be discussed anew by a conference committee seeking to reconcile House and Senate versions of immigration reform. The Senate legislation, for example, imposes criminal penalties on employers who knowingly hire illegal aliens while the House version provides only for civil sanctions.

When the differences between the two bills are resolved, the legislation will go to President Reagan, who, in the spirit of this entire process, has agreed to subordinate his reservations about individual provisions to the pressing need for immigration reform as a whole. In demonstrating a similar sense of priorities, Congress has brought credit upon itself.

Portland Press Herald

Portland, ME, June 22, 1984

It's become almost a political axiom that Congress can be counted on to avoid passing controversial legislation during a presidential election year. The immigration bill passed by the House this week is a remarkable exception.

The legislation, which marks the first reform in the immigration laws in three decades, is plainly controversial but even more obviously necessary. President Reagan's assertion that the United States had lost "control of its borders" is all too true. Millions of "illegals" have flooded into the country.

The House-passed bill, similar to a measure already passed in the Senate, addresses two major problems: How to control the influx of illegal aliens and how to react to the plight of those already here.

As to the former, the bill would make it illegal for employers to hire illegal aliens and impose stiff civil penalties for those who do.

As to the latter, the legislation would grant amnesty to illegal aliens who could prove they had lived here for some time. In addition, those granted amnesty would be given the opportunity to eventually attain citizenship.

That the bill seems likely to become law, particularly in an election year, is remarkable. Less than a year ago, House Speaker Thomas P. "Tip" O'Neill Jr., scuttled the proposal because of the opposition of Hispanics who fear they will suffer economically under the law.

Other groups opposed the bill; businesses because they'll be fined if they knowingly hire illegal aliens, and organized labor, which fears the new legal workers will depress wages.

Nonetheless, the bill reflects reality. An estimated 6 million aliens are now here illegally. They can't be ignored. And by providing severe sanctions to those who attempt to profit by hiring illegal aliens, America may finally hope to reclaim control of its borders.

Guatemalan Moderates Win Assembly Elections

Two moderate parties, the Christian Democrats and the National Union of the Center, had come out ahead in recent Constituent Assembly elections, it was reported July 8, 1984. The Christian Democrats won 17.2% of the vote, and the National Union Union of the Center won 14.5%. Despite the better showing by the Christian Democrats, the two leading parties gained 22 seats each in the 88-member Constituent Assembly. A rightist coalition of the National Liberation Movement (MLN) and the Authentic Nationalist Center came in third with 13.2% of the vote and 21 assembly seats. The center-right Revolutionary Party took 7.7% of the vote and 10 seats. The remaining 13 seats went to five other parties. Prior to the election, the MLN, led by Mario Sandoval Alarcon, had been expected to draw the largest number of votes. An estimated 1.7 million of the nation's 2.5 million registered voters cast ballots. Voting was mandatory in Guatemala.

Guatemala's head of state, Gen. Oscar Humberto Mejia Victores, had pledged after taking power in a 1983 coup that Constituent Assembly elections would be held. However, he had stressed that the 88 deputies in the new assembly would have limited powers and that his government would continue to hold legislative authority until a new president was elected in 1985. Mejia warned that if the Constituent Assembly attempted to replace him, he would dissolve it. The Constituent assembly was to write new electoral laws and draw up a constitution in preparation for the presidential elections.

Since the election campaign began in October 1983, more than 60 political activists associated with the 17 political parties and three civic committees taking part had been murdered or kidnapped. The United States embassy in Guatemala City estimated that since Mejia Victores came to power in August 1983, 150 political murders had taken place every month, as well as 50 "disappearances." A peace commission had been formed in March to attempt to curb the violence, but its members resigned in May, complaining that the government was not supporting the commission's work.

DESERET NEWS
Salt Lake City, UT, July 3-4, 1984

Guatemala, never noted for its political stability or orderly society, took a step toward maturity last weekend when its citizens flocked to the polls to vote for representatives to a new Constituent Assembly. This is their first move toward democratic civilian rule in 30 years.

A record 1.7 million registered voters, an estimated 70 percent of the total, cast votes for some 1,179 candidates nominated by 17 parties to fill a mere 88 seats.

The assembly will be charged with the responsibility of drawing up a new constitution for the country, the eighth since Guatemala declared its independence in 1839. This will be the fourth constitution in the past 30 years.

The new document will differ from the other constitutions in that it will not be designed to legitimize a military coup and perpetuate its power. This election, although sponsored by a military government, apparently was relatively free of corruption. Hopes seem high that Guatemala might, at last, achieve a semblance of real representative government.

Certainly, people of goodwill are hoping the election will lead to the establishment of a viable constitutional government. If the Constituent Assembly operates smoothly enough to complete its task by December, elections for the new government could take place by next March.

Yet the mere adoption of a constitution, however well-framed, will not guarantee domestic tranquility. Not even the infusion of billions in U.S. aid will assure such a blessing.

Less than half of the country's 7.7 million people are literate. Education is imperative on a broad scale. People can't vote intelligently without ability to read and understand the issues. Guatemalans must develop hunger for learning.

Foreign as well as domestic investment must be fostered and protected in order that industry and jobs might be developed. This will bring on growth of a middle class — people with a real stake in maintaining an orderly society.

When Guatemalans can see they have more to gain in a government of laws than in revolutionary lawlessness, they will be able to enjoy the fruits of constitutional rule.

Until then, the best constitution in the world will be of little help to them. They still have a long way to go.

The Record
Hackensack, NJ, June 25, 1984

Guatemala has suffered under a series of ruthless military dictators for 40 years. The latest is Brig. Gen. Oscar Humberto Mejía, who led a coup last August that toppled the government of Gen. Efraín Riós Montt. General Mejía hasn't distinguished his rule from past reigns of terror, but he did promise to turn the government over to an elected civilian president.

Next week, Guatemalans will take the first step toward that goal. They'll choose 88 members to a new constituent assembly that will then draft a constitution and establish the rules for general elections in 1985. The convention may also choose a provisional president to serve until national elections are held. General Mejía at first welcomed the idea, but now he's having second thoughts. He announced last week that the assembly could only write a constitution, and that he'd remain in office until Guatemalans go to the polls.

General Mejía has backtracked on his pledge to cooperate because he's grown comfortable with his authority — and increasingly heavy-handed in his dealings with political opponents. He strengthened the military, while doing little to improve living conditions for the mostly impoverished people. He has jailed and tortured several Catholic priests and nuns who've resisted his brutality and charged that the church is riddled with "subversives."

The prospect of national elections has made many Guatemalans hopeful that a civilian government will convert the country into a showcase of democracy. There's been much talk about the need for land reform and improved education and health services — and curbing the army's excesses. If General Mejía refuses to relinquish power as he promised, he'll dash those hopes and invite rebellion. Freedom and self-determination have been a long time coming to Guatemala. It would be tragic if progress were halted now.

The Times-Picayune
The States-Item
New Orleans, LA, July 1, 1984

Today Guatemala joins the Central American march to the polls with a nationwide election for an assembly to write a new constitution that will be the basis for elections next year for a national assembly and a president. A great deal rides on the outcome, as it did previously in El Salvador and Honduras, for Guatemala is attempting to civilianize and democratize a government long dominated by a military establishment notorious for corruption and brutality.

The election is perhaps more free-wheeling than practical politicians would like — there are no fewer than 17 parties and three civic committees fielding 1,179 candidates for only 88 seats. But there are really only two major parties and one new one that is making a stir.

Typically, the two major parties are long-established rightist and center-left organizations. On the right is a coalition of the powerful National Liberation Movement and the Authentic Nationalist Center, headed by a leader of the U.S.-supported army that overthrew the communist-leaning government in 1954. Spreading over the center-right is the traditional Christian Democratic Party.

The new party, the Union of the National Center, stands midway between them and presents itself as a modern, progressive alternative untainted by the past. It is making a U.S.-type media splash, but it is anyone's guess how it will fare at the polls.

The Guatemalan military is generally credited with having smashed the Marxist-led guerrilla movement that had been growing for some years but had never achieved the strength of similar campaigners in El Salvador and pre-Sandinista Nicaragua. But it was a brutal campaign that eliminated the revolutionaries without eliminating the conditions that created their following.

The test in Guatemala is to prove that these conditions — a stagnant economy, a lack of civil and human rights, a succession of illegitimate military dictatorships can be corrected by free democratic processes instead of violent revolution. Sunday's election is the first part of the test. Others will be in the military's reaction to its results and to the constitution the assembly writes, and the later elections for a national assembly and a president.

Guatemala is the largest of the Central American nations, and has, parallel to its tradition of military coups, a tradition of progressive popular movements. It is this tradition we must all hope will be strengthened by the process that begins Sunday.

Los Angeles Times
Los Angeles, CA, July 5, 1984

There is cause for hope in the results of Sunday's elections in Guatemala—but not enough to justify the Reagan Administration's plans to renew U.S. military assistance to that country's brutal security forces.

It is encouraging that despite 30 years of repressive military rule, and periodic electoral fraud to keep the generals in power, more than 1.5 million people turned out to select 88 members of a Constituent Assembly that will rewrite the Guatemalan constitution and make other preparations for presidential elections in 1985.

It is even more encouraging that Guatemalan voters gave most of their votes to moderate political parties, including the Christian Democrats and the Union of the National Center, while the rigidly right-wing National Liberation Movement got only 12% of the vote. Almost 20% of the ballots cast Sunday were either blank or mutilated, a traditional sign of protest in Latin America and an indication to many analysts that a significant number of Guatemalan voters were upset that leftist politicians were banned from participating in the elections.

But, despite the outcome of the vote, the real power in Guatemala is still in the hands of the military. Anyone who doubts that need only read the threatening statements made before the voting by Gen. Oscar Mejia Victores, the latest in a string of military strongmen who have headed the Guatemalan government since 1954, when the Central Intelligence Agency—in one of the most shortsighted "successes" in the history of U.S.-Latin American relations—helped engineer a coup that ousted a civilian government.

Mejia warned that the military will not allow the Constituent Assembly to do anything except write a new constitution. It cannot, for example, elect a provisional president as the assembly in El Salvador did after elections there in 1982. If assembly members get out of hand, Mejia said, the army will move in. "If they want a dictator, then they shall get one," the general bluntly told one interviewer.

That attitude reflects the brutish arrogance of many Guatemalan military officers. It is the same attitude that led the Guatemalan army to reject U.S. military aid in 1977, after the Carter Administration criticized the government's abysmal record on human rights. It is an attitude that has actually worsened in recent years as Guatemalan security forces have waged a successful counterinsurgency campaign against guerrillas in the country's highlands, taking a bloody toll among the region's predominantly Indian population.

Today the Guatemalan military is convinced more than ever that it can win its dirty little war alone, without advice or interference from pushy gringos who worry about niceties such as human rights. Nevertheless, the Reagan Administration is talking about renewing military aid to Guatemala, starting with $10 million in "non-lethal" military aid in the next fiscal year. President Reagan and his aides should remember that they already have enough worries and problems in Central America in trying to control the wretched excesses of El Salvador's military. The Guatemalans should be left to their own devices, at least until civilian authority is firmly restored in that country.

The Cincinnati Post
Cincinnati, OH,
July 9, 1984

American policy makers can't claim any credit for the recent election in Guatemala. That's one of the reasons it should please them.

However fragile it proves, Guatemala's first move toward democracy in 30 years has the virtue of being indigenous.

A military head of state who enjoys next to no aid from Washington, and suffers next to no leverage from there, has announced the return to civilian rule by 1985. He set up the civilian commission that wrote the rules for the recent election, and he allowed it to do its work without interference from the military.

His officials and troops supervised the vote on July 1. High-level U.S. observers who visited polling places all over Guatemala judged the election free and fair.

This is a notable development in a country familiar with sham elections, left-wing and right-wing violence against civilians, and succession by coup. In 1977, the Carter administration cut off aid to Guatemala in protest over human rights abuses.

Only last August, Maj. Gen. Oscar Mejia Victores seized power from another general, who himself had been in power a year and a half.

Given this background of military rule and instability, the election of a new constituent assembly is only a tentative beginning. It remains to be seen whether the assembly will actually write a constitution and an electoral law that become the basis for a democratic regime.

Still, this first step should be welcomed. It should be greeted —as many Guatemalan voters greeted it, an American observer said—"with hope, if not confidence."

For the United States, it is an opportunity to encourage a process of democratization that is in this country's interests as well as Guatemala's. Through the Caribbean Basin Initiative or the resumption of direct aid, the Reagan administration should demonstrate solidarity with a neighbor and strong support for the new direction it has taken.

The Honolulu Advertiser
Honolulu, HI, May 15, 1984

Democracy still gasps for life in Guatemala, but the nation remains under control of the military, as it has been for the past 30 years.

On June 1, a record number of Guatemalans, more than 1.5 million, voted for delegates to a Constituent Assembly that will draft a new constitution and laws for a presidential election next year. Most of the votes went to candidates from moderate parties. About 20 percent of the ballots were left blank or mutilated, in apparent protest of a ban on participation by leftist candidates.

The present head of state, General Oscar Mejia Victores, announced before the election that the assembly will not be allowed to do anything beyond rewriting the constitution, and he threatened that military intervention would meet any overstepping.

Thus, the military rule that began 30 years ago when the CIA led a coup that toppled Guatemala's civilian government continues. So too does the shabby history of human rights abuses, especially against that nation's predominantly Indian population.

In 1977, Congress conditioned aid to Guatemala on human rights reforms. The Guatemalan officers rejected the conditions and the aid, and turned to other nations such as Israel and Taiwan.

Now, the Reagan administration is seeking to resume military training for Guatemala and has requested $10 million in unconditional, "non-lethal" military aid.

The right thing would be to require advances toward democracy in exchange for any aid to Guatemala. It is the least the U.S. can do to amend for abetting the demise of democracy there in the first place.

The Miami Herald
Miami, FL, March 15, 1984

WHAT can be done when an American policy of high moral standards fails to achieve its goals? What should be done when a military and economic assistance quarantine does not help curb human-rights abuses?

That issue is raised anew in Guatemala. For seven years the United States refused to grant military and economic assistance to three different Guatemalan military regimes. The lofty goals are absolute. No American assistance is acceptable for a government that has so little respect for human life. If Guatemala wanted assistance from the United States, the rampant violations of human rights would have to be curbed.

The problem was that Guatemala did not seem to care. It did not even ask for assistance. Since 1977, Guatemala has gone it alone with no American help and spurned by other countries in the region. The country was the pariah of Central America.

Because of its isolation, Guatemala never was compelled to curb its human-rights abuses. By 1982, Guatemala's record for human-rights abuses was one of the worst in the world. No reward was offered if it improved its behavior, and there was no penalty for continued abuses. In effect, the United States had lost its ability to influence events in Guatemala. In the process, the virtually isolated Guatemalan regime had beaten — or at least brought under control — the guerrilla insurgency.

Now there are indications that Guatemala is willing to mend fences with its neighbors. The government of Brig. Gen. Oscar Humberto Mejia Victores says its stay in power is temporary, that Guatemala will return to civilian rule in July 1985. The process will begin this July 1 with the election of an 88-member constituent assembly.

The question now is: How should the Reagan Administration and Congress react? Guatemala wants to buy $2 million worth of spare helicopter parts in the United States. The Reagan Administration has proposed to give $10 million in credit at current interest rates for the purchase of military equipment in fiscal year 1985.

Administration officials contend that congressional approval is not required to sell the helicopter spare parts. The proposed military credits, which do fall under Congress's jurisdiction, are conditioned on the legitimacy of the July 1984 constituent-assembly elections.

Because the policy of isolation has not helped curb human-rights abuses in Guatemala, the time may be right to lure improvements from the Guatemalan military in exchange for very limited, very tightly controlled, assistance. The spare parts for the helicopters might be a first step. Then, if meaningful elections actually are held, Congress properly could consider the $10 million credit for purchase of military equipment.

America's Guatemalan policy has not prevented continued human-rights abuses. In view of the regime's apparent new desire to rejoin its hemispheric neighbors, the carrot-and-stick approach deserves a trial.

Miami, FL, July 7, 1984

WHEN A person crippled by illness or disease begins a rehabilitative process, it is much like a child learning to walk. The first steps are tentative, falls not infrequent.

Guatemala, the largest and richest of Central American nations, embarked over the weekend on precisely such a rehabilitative process. After 28 months of military rule and a history fraught with abuses of the democratic process, more than 1.5 million Guatemalans went to the polls on Sunday. They cast their ballots to elect an 88-member constituent assembly that will write a new constitution and plan presidential elections for 1985.

This is but the start of a process that Gen. Humberto Mejia Victores, the ruling military leader, hopes will restore Guatemala's image and provide a new start for the country's always-shaky democratic system of government.

News of an election in Guatemala merits a measure of skepticism, however. For subversion, human-rights abuses, and electoral frauds are only slightly less prevalent in Guatemala than in El Salvador. Moreover, General Mejia Victores says that he will dissolve the future assembly if it attempts to elect a provisional president before it adopts a new constitution. That's worrisome, because it calls into question the Guatemalan military's commitment to returning the country to democracy.

Yet in spite of all the questions, in spite of all the doubts, the process begun in Guatemala should not be dismissed lightly. If El Salvador — with more than 40,000 dead, a raging civil war, and a history of complicity between oligarchs and the military — was able to break the mold and elect a moderate president this year, why not Guatemala?

Like a child or an infirm person, Guatemala is likely to waver and stumble. The United States, with its long tradition of democratic government, can and should help Guatemala toward this goal. Congress has approved $40 million in U.S. assistance to Guatemala for 1984 and another $187.7 million for 1985. Congress should make those funds contingent upon Guatemala's making a real effort to walk steadily on the road to democracy.

Boston Sunday Globe

Boston, MA, December 16, 1984

For years the great invisible horror story of Central America has been Guatemala. While strong-man generals have followed each other into the presidential palace, the military regime has waged war on the Indian population of the highlands with shocking depravity and chilling effectiveness. Yet the story is mostly unreported.

In mid-September the president of Guatemala's Supreme Court disclosed an incredible statistic that tells what has been happening in the remote mountains of the north and west. An official census had turned up 51,144 children who had lost one or both of their parents. The figure covered only three provinces in the highlands: Quiche, Chimaltenango and San Marcos. Other key regions, such as Huehuetenango, Quezaltenango and Solola, were still to be counted. The figure also did not include children driven into exile in Mexico or into the kills, or those who have been killed. The total figure is estimated to be 100,000.

Beatriz Manz, a professor of anthropology at Wellesley and a fellow at Radcliffe's Mary Bunting Institute, describes the killing in Guatemala in 1982-83 as "the worst violence since the Spanish conquest." Manz, a Chilean who has extensively studied Guatemalan Indians, says that in many areas the descendants of the great, agricultural Maya civilization have been reduced to a "hunter and gatherer" society, wandering in the open, subsisting on roots.

The Indians who make up about half the population of Guatemala are admired by tourists for their handiwork, but among the "Spanish" Guatemalans they have long been despised as racial inferiors and feared as potential incubators of revolution.

During the blood-soaked administration of Romeo Lucas Garcia the army began a campaign inspired by methods of insect control, on the premise that Indian areas are swamps where guerrillas can breed. In El Salvador army atrocities are often caused by retrograde officers or out-of-control troops. In Guatemala the violence is controlled and deliberate.

The military in Guatemala has been practicing these tactics for 30 years. This is where the fledgling assassins of the Salvadoran right wing were sent in 1979 to develop the concept of "death squads" under the tutelage of the National Liberation Movement, which liked to be known as the "party of organized violence."

Killing Indians out of sight stirred no protest, but Lucas Garcia brought the carnage into the cities too. He killed teachers, lawyers, journalists, labor leaders and other categories of "subversives." Eventually he overplayed his hand, and he was deposed in March 1882.

His successor, Gen. Efrain Rios Montt, improved the tourist-bureau image by cutting the urban violence and ordering his killers to stop littering the roadsides with the headless corpses for which Guatemala had become known. But he pressed the military assault in the highlands with renewed viciousness.

Rios Montt had quirks that made him in some ways unpresentable. He professed, for example, to be on speaking terms with God. In August 1983 he was replaced by Gen. Oscar Mejia Victorez, who still rules today.

Mejia Victorez resumed the urban killing and moved the campaign in the traumatized highlands into a new phase. With many of the sweeps now completed, the surviving Indians are being starved out of the hills and confined to "strategic hamlets" under military eyes and guns.

Press coverage of Guatemala has been eggregiously thin for two reasons. In general, "news" for Americans derives heavily from official voices. What the White House says is news – for example, the ephemeral Nicaraguan MIGs – is always covered. What official Washington downplays or ignores is often ignored by the media.

Second, reporting from Guatemala is chilled by military controls and a lurking security apparatus as ominous as that of any totalitarian system. No US reporters work steadily in Guatemala. Those who visit the country reach the highlands only rarely. When they do, the watchful Guatemalan security forces know they will stop, ask a few questions of Indians who are afraid to answer them – and scoot for town before sundown. This is not for want of journalistic acumen. In a country so efficiently repressive that not a single human-rights office is allowed to function, it is terrifying to do otherwise.

Even the novocained human-rights wing of the State Department stirred when Guatemalan soldiers killed some US aid employees two years ago, and Congress has been relatively steady in restricting aid shipments to Guatemala. But at high levels within the Reagan Administration the right-wing elements that have shaped general Central America policy have angled to resume the military aid that was cut off in 1977 when Lucas Garcia mocked the idea of US oversight as a quid pro quo. These elements include UN Ambassador Jeane Kirkpatrick, who has loudly accused Nicaragua's left-wing Sandinista regime of the "worst human-rights violations I know of in this hemisphere," but remains quiet about Guatemala. Nicaragua's mistreatment of the Miskito Indians is documented and grave, but mere whiffle ball compared with the mayhem in Guatemala.

□

This fall, intent on stopping funding for the illegal "covert" war in Nicaragua, Congress lost track of the Guatemalan situation, and $300,000 in military aid slipped into the pipeline. It is apparently being used to train military helicopter pilots in the United States. Aid restrictions are also circumvented through commercial sales of equipment such as "civilian" helicopters that can be retrofitted with armaments. Moreover, serving as a Pentagon proxy, the Israeli government has long been a major arms supplier to Guatemala.

Because of the terror, tens of thousands of Guatemalan Indians have fled to Mexico. Now the Guatemalan government is trying to have them repatriated so that they can be confined to strategic hamlets, evidence that the "war" is over. The Administration has been supporting a Guatemalan-Mexican effort to cauterize the border. If there are no refugees, the area will appear tidy.

Twice this year the State Department has eased its travel advisory for US tourists, suggesting that the highlands are becoming safe again. Perhaps they are, for American tourists. Confining starved-out highland Indians to fortified villages no doubt reduces the number of guerrilla skirmishes. For that matter, death camps helped control the Warsaw ghetto.

The bloodletting in the green hills of Guatemala is not over. Another major military drive is forecast against areas where the guerrillas have taken refuge. In neighboring Chiapas province, in Mexico, a Catholic bishop has developed contingency plans to receive 40,000 refugees. Guatemala, would-be paladin of the right wing of the Reagan Administration, is the heart of darkness.

Houston Chronicle

Houston, TX, July 4, 1984

Elections are being held in Latin America these days with such regularity that they almost seem to constitute a fad.

In the latest voting, Guatemalans cast ballots for a national assembly to rewrite their constitution, perhaps leading to general elections next year and an end to three decades of military rule. Guatemala has long suffered the reputation of being the home of some of the region's most repressive military regimes. The elections Sunday illustrate the pressure felt by the region's military governments and the growing momentum of democracy.

Latin America has a long way to go, of course, before it can be looked on as a bastion of smooth-running democracy: In the case of Guatemala, early returns show more ballots being ruled "illegible" and "invalid" than those actually counted for any one party. Still, democracy takes practice, and this week's election is an encouraging exercise. No doubt the election in Guatemala will increase the pressure on Nicaragua's Sandinista government to go through with scheduled presidential elections in November.

Even the region's dark cloud had a silver lining: A coup attempt to overthrow the civilian government of Bolivia was aborted by the afternoon of the same day, and President Hernan Siles Zuazo was released by the military unit that had kidnapped him. Coup attempts are hardly new in Bolivia. The novelty in this one came from its failure.

One can almost detect that such coups are becoming old-fashioned, passe, bad form. Conversely, democracy seems to be on a roll. As it gathers momentum, it will be increasingly difficult to stop.

Nicaragua Accepts Contadora Plan; Stymied Efforts Raise Tensions

In an unexpected move, Nicaragua September 21, 1984 said it would sign "immediately and without further modifications" a revised draft peace treaty for Central America proposed by the Contadora Group. In a letter sent to the president of the four Contadora countries—Mexico, Venezuela, Colombia and Panama—Nicaragua's coordinator of the junta, Daniel Ortega Saavedra, said: "Nicaragua is conscious of the need to reach as quickly as possible a peace accord for the whole region." However, the letter continued, such an accord "will only be sufficient if it can count on a formal and obligatory commitment by the United States." Ortega said that while U.S. "aggression continues the government of Nicaragua will continue defending the inalienable right to take all the necessary measures to guarantee our security." The 21-point proposal included such key provisions as: an inventory and reduction of arms, bases and soldiers in each of the five Central American nations; a timetable for the removal of foreign military advisers; respect for human rights and laws leading to free elections; and an end to the use of one country's territory as a base for aggression against another. Thus, the treaty would require Nicaragua to cease aiding rebels in El Salvador, and would require the U.S. to send home military advisers and expel anti-Sandinista contras.

In a meeting in Honduras October 19-20, 1984, Central American nations allied to the U.S. drafted modifications to the regional peace treaty. Costa Rica, Honduras and El Salvador proposed substantial changes to the second draft of the treaty, which Nicaragua had accepted without modification in September. Nicaragua boycotted the Honduras meeting, charging that it was the result of U.S. efforts to sabotage the Contadora peace process. Prior to Nicaragua's unexpected acceptance of the treaty, the U.S. had said it fully supported the Contadora peace plan. However, following the Nicaraguan move, the U.S. scrutinized the plan and urged its allies in the region to alter some provisions. Specifically, it wanted changes to limit the size of military forces in Central America and to restrict military activities there by countries outside the area. Some of the changes agreed to in Honduras were published in the U.S. press November 9 and 14, and the extent of the modifications was widely believed to threaten to set back the negotiating effort.

The *Washington Post* Nov. 6 published a leaked U.S. National Security Council document stating that the U.S. had successfully "trumped" Mexican and Nicaraguan moves to obtain a quick signing of the Contadora peace plan accepted by Nicaragua. The document, a secret briefing paper, said that following "intensive U.S. consultations with El Salvador, Honduras and Costa Rica," those nations had "submitted a counterdraft to the Contadora states...[that] shifts concern within Contadora to a document broadly consistent with U.S. interests." It said the U.S. had "effectively blocked Contadora Group efforts to impose a second draft of a revised Contadora Act." According to the document, similar "strong pressure" would be placed on Guatemala.

The Contadora Group September 12, 1985 presented a draft of a new peace plan for Central America to replace an earlier version that had been accepted only by Nicaragua. The new draft was presented at a Sept. 12-13 meeting in Panama City with the foreign ministers of five Central American nations. Nicarguan Foreign Minister Miguel d'Escoto Brockman immediately denounced the proposal, charging that it defended U.S. interests. Nicaragua June 19, 1985 had cut short a meeting of Contadora group nations and the five Central American nations, begun the previous day, when El Salvador, Costa Rica and Honduras rejected a Nicaraguan proposal to discuss renewed U.S. aid to the contras fighting the Nicaraguan government.

According to press reports, the new draft softened requirements for the removal of foreign military advisers from the region. It also called for international inspectors from four neutral nations to monitor arms levels and military activity in Central America; pledged the signatories to respect human rights and political pluralism; committed nations in the region to the peaceful solution of international disputes; and prohibited them from supporting groups seeking to overthrow the governments of neighboring states.

Houston Chronicle
Houston, TX, April 5, 1985

Another timely effort is being made to get the Contadora peace process under way again, and President Reagan's proposal for a cease-fire between Nicaragua and the contra rebels should help toward that end.

The ideal formula for peace in Central America would be one arrived at by the nations of that region. Mexico, Colombia, Panama and Venezuela met on the island of Contadora two years ago to draw up a set of principles that would lead to peace in the region.

Progress was made, with other area nations involved. Early this year, a conflict between Nicaragua and Costa Rica over an asylum matter brought the discussions to a halt. They are now scheduled to resume next week in Panama.

President Belisario Betancur of Colombia was in Washington Thursday to meet with President Reagan.

The United States has not played a direct role in the Contadora process, but has encouraged it. Reagan took the occasion of the visit to call for an end to fighting in Nicaragua and church-mediated talks between the Sandinistas and the contras.

Reagan is not backing down on his call for immediate release by Congress of $14 million in non-military aid to the contras. But he did say that the money would not be used while a cease-fire is honored. He termed this suggestion an incentive for talks that could lead to a "national reconciliation" in Nicaragua.

If the Contadora group could agree upon a set of principles calling for non-intervention, military parity and representative democracy in all of Central America, it would be a great accomplishment.

The remarkable thing is, the Contadora goal is not impossible. Difficult, yes; impossible, no.

The Honolulu Advertiser
Honolulu, HI, February 16, 1985

What little hope there was that the Contadora group might bring peace to Latin America has all but evaporated with the cancellation of meetings late this week in Panama.

Previous meetings have been scrubbed, but this was the first one that ended because of diplomatic differences.

COSTA RICA, backed by El Salvador and Honduras, refused to attend as observers because of a diplomatic incident in Nicaragua. A student in Managua last year sought political asylum in the Costa Rican Embassy. However, on Christmas Eve, the student "left" the embassy.

Costa Rica claims the student was forcibly removed. Nicaragua says he left on his own, but it would not allow independent officials to question the man. The student has since been court-martialed for avoiding the draft and is serving a five-year sentence.

The student case, however, is symbolic of the deepening rift that has been developing between Costa Rica and Nicaragua. Traditionally, the two countries have never been close.

But Costa Ricans supported the Sandinista revolution that overthrew the Somoza dictatorship, and Managua-San Jose relations were at least cordial in the early days of Sandinista rule. That has changed.

The upshot of these developments is a peace initiative that is now dead in the water. The Contadora members — Mexico, Panama, Venezuela and Colombia — have no hope of progress if Costa Rica and other Central American countries refuse to cooperate.

THE BREAKDOWN occurs a month after the United States' termination of bilateral talks with Nicaragua. Washington charges that the Sandinista government was not negotiating seriously.

Unfortunately, the Reagan administration continues to support the anti-Sandinista contras and is seeking increased aid for the guerrilla groups.

Thus at the regional and national levels, the prospects for a negotiated peace in Central America appear more remote than ever. The mix of diplomatic intransigence, traditional animosities and conflicting strategic goals by the various nations involved grows thicker.

Admist the uncertainty, one conclusion is clear: unless the situation is defused, the likelihood of military intervention will increase dramatically.

Arkansas Gazette.
Little Rock, AR, April 5, 1985

President Reagan and Congress found themselves at such odds over two issues last year that they postponed settlement until this year. One was the $1.5 billion fiscal 1985 funding for 21 additional MX missiles, which Mr. Reagan won last month after a monumental lobbying effort. The other was the question of $14 million in covert aid for the contra rebels in Nicaragua, an issue that remains unsettled, with increasing probability that Congress will prevail.

Although the Republican-controlled Senate has not been enthusiastic about resuming military aid to the guerrillas, the key obstacle to Mr. Reagan's plan may be found in the House. Four times since 1983 the House has refused to provide such aid, but last fall the $14 million was cleared only with the stipulation that the money not be spent until additional approval by each house was given this spring.

Mr. Reagan has made repeated appeals for release of the money since January. On one occasion this year he said he wanted "to remove" the "present structure" of the Nicaraguan Sandinista government, adding that it was immaterial to him how the deed was accomplished. One key member of the House Foreign Affairs Committee called the remark "a virtual declaration of war against Nicaragua." In a recent radio address, Mr. Reagan employed the language of the crusader to plead for resumption of military aid, thus giving an opportunity to Representative Bill Alexander of Arkansas to offer an alternative to addressing the problems of Nicaragua and Central America. Mr. Alexander, who is the chief deputy whip in the House, articulated the Democrats' response.

Instead of promoting the violent overthrow of the leftist Nicaraguan government, Mr. Alexander said, the President should throw more support behind the peace efforts of the Contadora nations — Mexico, Panama, Venezuela and Colombia — that would negotiate a settlement in Nicaragua, adding: "The real enemies in Central America are poverty, ignorance, hunger, social injustice and political corruption. The voices of the people are crying out for food, for shelter, for peace and for justice."

The message seems to be that the Democratic-controlled House is not about to resume military aid to rebels until the Contadora process, and perhaps other diplomatic efforts, are fully explored and ways are found to remedy the deep-seated economic and social problems correctly suggested by Mr. Alexander as being the real enemies of freedom and justice throughout Central America. The House should hold firm.

The Miami Herald
Miami, FL, August 29, 1985

SELDOM HAS democracy in this hemisphere produced quicker dividends. Four South American countries — among them three nations where democratic governments replaced military regimes in the last year — have joined the original four Contadora nations' Central American peace efforts. Not surprisingly, the first joint communiqué of the group that now includes Argentina, Brazil, Uruguay, and Peru was to urge a negotiated settlement of the conflicts in Nicaragua and El Salvador.

That message is not much different than the one that the original Contadora members — Colombia, Mexico, Panama, and Venezuela — have been unable to deliver to the warring factions in Central America. It is a difficult task in a region where the imperative to reduce poverty and social ills has become entwined in the East-West struggle.

The original Contadora group was unable to overcome these difficulties. A Contadora plan that Nicaragua could support was not acceptable to the United States, to other Central American nations, or to the rebels fighting the Sandinista government. Conversely, a plan acceptable to the United States and its Central American allies was unacceptable to Nicaragua or to the rebels fighting in El Salvador.

This was a moral crusade, an effort to move world opinion into pressuring the two sides to negotiate an end to the hostilities. Despite all their efforts, the pressure that these four countries could generate was not sufficient. The Contadora peace initiative has been stalled for months with no prospect of progress.

Now comes the communiqué of the enlarged group. Even though the message has not changed much, the presence in the group of Argentina, Brazil, Uruguay, and Peru makes the new proposal that much harder to ignore.

No longer can the United States, Cuba, Nicaragua, and other Central American countries sit back and give little more than lip service to the Contadora process. The expanded Contadora group includes the largest and most influential countries in Latin America. Their presence gives the expanded group's message much more authority.

This is a propitious time for the Reagan Administration to rejoin the peace offensive in Central America. The Administration would do well to listen to what the expanded Contadora Group is saying, lest it find itself isolated from the hemisphere's key democracies.

FORT WORTH STAR-TELEGRAM
Fort Worth, TX, August 28, 1985

Contadora lives and still offers some hope for a regional settlement of the issues that disrupt Central America, but it also is in trouble.

The Contadora group of countries — Colombia, Mexico, Panama and Venezuela — began seeking a solution in January 1983.

The thrust of the Contadora effort has been to leave Central America to the Central Americans and remove it from the larger arena of East-West and U.S.-Soviet confrontation.

It is a worthy, if naive, idea.

The United States has supported the Contadora process, but with reservations. The first Contadora draft plan, last September, foundered on U.S.-Nicaraguan disagreement because it would have removed U.S. influence from the region while leaving Nicaragua with a great military advantage over its neighbors, most of whom already feel threatened by the Sandinista regime.

The Contadora group is working still and is considering Canada or some other non-involved nation for a role as an observer to supervise a peace treaty.

The problem is that there is no peace treaty.

Nor is there likely to be any time soon. The reality is that no comprehensive plan for reduced tensions in Central America is possible without U.S. and Nicaraguan agreement and without addressing the warfare between government and rebel forces in both El Salvador and Nicaragua.

Contadora proposals have called on existing governments in those nations to stop imports of weapons and to get rid of foreign military advisers. They have failed to recognize that communist insurgency in El Salvador and U.S.-backed anti-communist insurgency in Nicaragua are fundamental. Neither El Salvador nor Nicaragua can be expected to disarm while threatened by insurgents.

Yet the involvement of other nations, particularly the Contadora group, remains one of the few hopes for eventual peace. It may be time for the Contadora planners to direct their efforts at bringing the Sandinistas together with the contras and the Salvadoran government together with Salvadoran rebels.

The plain fact, like it or not, is that the United States has a legitimate interest in Central America and legitimate fears about the spread of communism there. And if the nations of Central America and their Contadora neighbors, as well as many North Americans, would like a less active U.S. role in the affairs of Central America, they must consider ways to remove the causes of U.S. concern.

Earlier U.S. proposals for a dialogue between Nicaragua's government and exiled anti-Sandinista leaders got nowhere, but that should not preclude a Contadora effort in the same direction, and for its part the United States should back such an effort.

The Boston Globe
Boston, MA, August 30, 1985

Last weekend the Contadora mediators in Cartagena, Colombia, tried to breathe life into their plan for bringing a negotiated peace to Central America. Foreign ministers of the four original Contadora member countries — Mexico, Colombia, Venezuela and Panama — were joined by others from Argentina, Uruguay, Brazil and Peru — a "support group" of emerging Latin democracies formed this summer.

The United States is the stumbling block the Contadora group faces. The peace the Latin Americans envision is simply not what the Reagan administration wants. Contadora is suffocating, not because of intransigence in Managua or the other Central American capitals. The major problem is the spoiling game played with cynicism and lamentable success in Washington.

Contadora is not just an altruistic Latin effort to calm the Central American crisis. It is an effort at self-policing, aimed at removing the pretext for US interventionism. The Latin American leaders expect a renewal of Big Stick diplomacy, and it makes them fearful. They know that left-right violence has a way of spreading across borders, that US intervention anywhere in the region could trigger a chain reaction.

The spirit of Contadora would allow the Sandinistas to survive, albeit "on probation," with their international behavior under scrutiny. The treaty also calls for regional demilitarization, which cuts as much against a US troop presence in Honduras, El Salvador or Costa Rica as against Soviet or Cuban forces in Nicaragua.

The Reagan administration's objectives are fundamentally opposed. The hard-liners who dominate the administration want to destroy Sandinista Nicaragua, not domesticate it. Moreover, a superpower intrigued with scenarios for making its clout felt has small interest in seeing once-dependent neighbors outgrow their rancorous past and turn into statesmen.

If the Contadora mediators had been given a chance, the peace effort would probably have succeeded last fall. Last September the Sandinistas signed a treaty their neighbors had accepted. The startled administration had to twist Honduran, Salvadoran and Costa Rica arms to get them to renege.

National Security Council memorandums in October gloated over the derailment of the peace initiative. Since then the administration has broken off bilateral talks with Managua, revitalized the contras and substantially heated up the rural terrorism that is the essence of the "war." State Department officials responsible for the region, such as Langhorne Motley and his successor, Elliot Abrams, have woven a fabric of specious rationales for continuing hostilities indefinitely. Latin Americans understand the administration's cynical game. Only Congress plays dumb.

The Sandinistas show signs of having reconsidered the wisdom of subversion. The right-wing governments of Honduras and El Salvador and the more neutral government of Costa Rica understand that with the huge US commitment to the status quo in the region they have little to fear from Managua, but plenty to fear from unending instability.

If the administration had not sandbagged Contadora, for reasons that are politically shortsighted and morally repugnant, an uneasy peace would have broken out. Central America would be getting on with the urgent Third World task of economic development. Faced with sly, persistent malice in Washington, however, Latin American peacemakers are outgunned.

Detroit Free Press

Detroit, MI, December 18, 1985

IF SOME possibility for compromise between the extremes of the Sandinistas and the contras remains in Nicaragua, President Reagan's recent verbal assault will do little to strengthen it. The Reagan administration has consistently treated the country as if it were naturally polarized, as if no middle ground existed, as if no compromise were possible.

In that spirit, the president in his weekly radio address renewed his call for further aid to the contras, calling the Sandinista government "thugs" and international aggressors. The spur for this latest spate of bellicose rhetoric was the recent discovery of two Cuban military advisers on board a shot-down Sandinista helicopter of Soviet make.

The Reagan administration should remember that it was the United States that wrote the book on "military advisers." We view in that light Mr. Reagan's assertion that Nicaragua is "a breeding ground for subversion." Meanwhile, if the administration wants to see the development of a stable, democratic Nicaragua, showering the contras with money in hopes of destroying the current government is an unrealistic method of accomplishing that goal. Destabilization of Nicaragua's economy and political and social structures could well destroy any chances for the flowering of democracy in that nation for years to come.

ST. LOUIS POST-DISPATCH

St. Louis, MO, December 6, 1985

When is a war endless? When Secretary of State Shultz says it is. He asserts that the United States will go on financing the Contra rebels against Nicaragua "indefinitely." He adds, "We have staying power."

No wonder, then, that the four Contadora nations that for three years have been trying to arrange a Central American peace settlement are discouraged. Along with Mr. Shultz's promise of continued warfare, the Contadora group — Mexico, Colombia, Venezuela and Panama — confront irreconcilable positions on all sides.

Those four nations, plus four other Latin American governments, have drafted for the United Nations General Assembly a resolution calling for a resumption of direct negotiations between the U.S. and the Sandinista government of Nicaragua, and for outside powers to refrain from actions that might frustrate the Central American peace effort.

The Reagan administration does not like the resolution. Neither do three U.S. allies. El Salvador, Honduras and Costa Rica say they cannot accept a plan that conditions the Contadora peace process on talks between the U.S. and Nicaragua. And that is a strange juxtaposition of argument, because the same three nations earlier contended that Nicaragua's differences with the U.S. should be settled by direct negotiations. They made that suggestion when they accepted a new Contadora draft peace treaty for the region and responded to Nicaragua's rejection of it. The Contadora treaty is intended to reduce armed forces in the area. Nicaragua's position is that it cannot reduce its army while it is being assaulted by the U.S.-sponsored guerrillas.

While the United States remains outside the scope of the Contadora treaty, Contadora's plan for peace cannot succeed without U.S. cooperation, which does not exist. Nicaragua won't sign a peace treaty while under attack, and Mr. Shultz says the attack will continue. Both Contadora and the U.S. allies propose talks that they know are unlikely, since Mr. Shultz has said they will not be resumed. In substance, the peace project is blocked at every turn.

Mr. Shultz recently tried in a New York speech to answer charges that the U.S. has been guilty of a double standard in taking a warlike stance toward Nicaragua and a softer line against apartheid in South Africa. The secretary made the administration's standard distinction between leftist and rightist governments that abuse human rights. He called Nicaragua a "moral disaster" while referring to South Africa as a "difficult challenge." He argued that a "passionate commitment to moral principles could be no substitute for a sound foreign policy in a world of hard realities and complex choices."

So much for a double standard. The complex choices made in Washington are for prolonged intervention and indefinite war in Central America.

The Orlando Sentinel

Orlando, FL, December 14, 1985

Prospects for peace in Nicaragua grew dimmer last week when the Reagan administration charged that Cuban troops are fighting rebels alongside the Sandinistas.

But something even more important is compounding the Central American problems: Mexico has signaled that it will play a smaller role in the so-called Contadora Group, which banded together in 1983 to try to bring peace to Central America.

That's awfully discouraging. Central America would be far better off if Mexico would continue to be a full partner in these talks.

Mexico is important to the peace process because its traditional good relations with both the United States and Cuba have provided a strong moderating influence. But Mexico says it is frustrated that Contadora negotiations haven't ended Nicaragua's civil war. On top of that, Mexico is facing economic problems.

But without Mexico's leadership the Contadora Group is critically weakened and there's little hope for a peaceful settlement in Nicaragua. Nothing else had worked before Contadora efforts made it possible for direct U.S.-Nicaragua talks.

The rationale behind this group — Mexico, Venezuela, Colombia and Panama — is that regional difficulties can best be handled by regional countries with a stake in preserving peace.

Granted, the Contadora Group's enthusiasm was dampened last month when its treaty to negotiate an end to Nicaragua's civil war was rejected. But that doesn't explain Mexico's backing off.

The more likely cause for Mexico's new stance is economic.

Mexico has irritated the United States — its best source of economic aid — by defending Nicaragua vigorously in these talks. That's risky now that Mexico is seeking more trade with the United States and help in managing its $96 billion debt.

So now Mexico is cutting trade with Nicaragua and smoothing over relations with El Salvador. That's necessary. But it needn't go so far as to reduce its vital role in the Contadora process. Mexico's economic success will mean nothing if its cost is strife in Central America.

Lincoln Journal

Lincoln, NE, December 4, 1985

High scepticism is the recommended mode in judging contradictory — and inevitably self-seeking or self-justifying — statements about armed clashes inside Nicaragua. Only when the various sides agree might something be then considered within a mile of the neighborhood of the truth.

For example, there seems more-or-less agreement it was a Soviet-made SAM-7 missile which brought down a Nicaraguan helicopter last week, killing 14 men.

Whether any of the victims were Cuban military, as Washington quickly claimed, based on second-hand reports from shadowy and unidentified people but just as quickly denied by Managua, is a who-knows kind of thing. Not us, that's for sure.

Whereas U.S. weapons were being used to destroy U.S.-built weaponry elsewhere in the world not so long ago, maybe someone will regard it a "mark of progress" that Soviet arms now are being used to do the same things to Soviet-made military hardware in Central America.

Honduran-U.S. Military Games Staged as Constitutional Crisis Worsens

United States and Honduran forces February 11-May 3, 1985 participated in joint military maneuvers called Big Pine III aimed at showing U.S. readiness in Central America. A separate set of maneuvers, Universal Trek '85, opened April 23 at Puerto Castilla in northern Honduras and were to last three weeks. More than 7,000 U.S. military personnel were involved in the games, the largest yet staged by the U.S. in Honduras. The first phase of exercises in the Big Pine III maneuvers, Operation Scorpion, had been held in mid-April in Chouluteca province in southern Honduras, just three miles from the Nicaraguan border. Honduran warplanes made practice bombing runs over U.S. battle tanks and armored personnel carriers that were simulating a Nicarguan attack. It was the first time U.S. armor had been used in Honduran exercises. U.S. troops were also scheduled to build antitank fortifications and improve airfields near the Nicarguan border and at Cucuyagua near the border with El Salvador. According to one U.S. officer, the U.S. armor was using "Soviet-style" tactics in order to expose the Hondurans to "communist bloc tactics, to Russian tactics, to Sandinista tactics." Nicaragua had declined a U.S. invitation to observe the maneuvers and filed an official protest March 28.

Meanwhile, a constitutional crisis that arose in late March over control of the Supreme Court, and thus the ability to influence presidential nominations for November elections, worsened in April. The dispute had split the ruling Liberal Party. In March the National Congress had voted to remove five Supreme Court justices allied with President Roberto Suazo Cordova, charging them all with corruption. But Suazo ordered the arrest of five judges named to replace them. One of the five was now in prison and four were in hiding. The Congress also accused Suazo and the ousted judges of having cooperated to ensure that pro-Suazo candidates were nominated for the presidential elections. At the same time, labor unions had threatened a general strike if the president refused to accept the electoral reform. The military, which traditionally settled political disputes, to date had refused to intervene, but was reported to be moving behind those favoring the reforms.

The Miami Herald
Miami, FL, April 7, 1985

BEHIND its comic-opera facade, the confrontation between Honduras's president and the head of its congress has the potential to become a true tragedy. Only its own restraint has kept the Honduran military from intervening and ending the constitutional crisis the way generals in Latin America have done all too often: by toppling the government.

The crux of the crisis is that Honduran President Roberto Suazo Cordova, forbidden by law to succeed himself, is determined to choose his successor. To do that, he is trying to control not one but two of Honduras's main political parties. His appointees control both the National Electoral Tribunal and the Honduran Supreme Court, so all political disputes are resolved in his favor.

Enter the president of Honduras's congress, Efrain Bu Giron y Azcona, who himself has presidential ambitions. Furious at President Suazo's machinations, Mr. Bu Giron began his own. At his urging, the National Assembly impeached five supreme-court justices friendly to the president. Then the assembly appointed five new justices who support Mr. Bu Giron.

President Suazo struck back by moving to have the five new justices arrested. Then a criminal-court judge friendly to the president indicted 50 of the 81 assembly members who had voted to replace the president's appointees.

Not to be outmaneuvered, Mr. Bu Giron housed the new supreme-court justices at the National Assembly building, where they cannot be arrested. He further pledged to keep the National Assembly in session — even over Easter weekend if necessary — to thwart any further maneuvering by President Suazo.

The longer this absurd cycle of action-reaction continues, the greater the threat to Honduras's incipient democracy — and to a key U.S. ally in Central America. Both sides claim constitutional sanction for their actions, but both are contributing to a political deterioration that holds no good for either.

The Reagan Administration officials should tell President Suazo in unmistakable terms that it views the Honduran crisis with the greatest gravity. Washington should impress on President Suazo that successful democracy requires that the people, not he, choose his successor. For if Mr. Suazo does not abide by this principle, his successor quite possibly will bear neither his stamp nor his title of president. He'll be a general instead.

The Record
Hackensack, NJ, April 18, 1985

With the help of Patrick Buchanan, the White House's assertive new communications director, President Reagan has fired fresh salvos in his war of words with Nicaragua. But more than rhetoric is filling the skies over Central America. For two years the Pentagon has been staging continuous war games in Honduras along the Nicaraguan border.

These practice shoot-'em-ups are the longest-running military maneuvers in Pentagon history — and the most expensive. The Defense Department has spent more than $100 million, dispatched more than 10,000 troops, and built nine airstrips, a small hospital, and scores of military outposts for these "temporary" exercises.

The Reagan administration has turned Honduras into a U.S. military base for two reasons, both of them wrong. First, the Americans in Honduras are training Salvadoran soldiers, making our military commitment to El Salvador much greater than the 55 advisers Mr. Reagan has acknowledged sending. Mr. Reagan knows that Congress would probably reject an expanded role in El Salvador; since these games don't need congressional approval, they enable him to circumvent the lawmakers.

Second, the administration wants to harass the Sandinista government in neighboring Nicaragua. It's no coincidence that large numbers of anti-Sandinista "contras" are turning up in Honduras, where they have access to American medical care and supplies. Mr. Reagan's war games thus provide a cover for tactical support for the contras, which Congress has so far barred.

Honduras puts up with all this because the Reagan administration is handing over extraordinary amounts of military aid. Until 1981, military aid for Honduras hovered around $4 million a year; last year, the figure topped $62 million. Ironically, Honduras now wants a bigger army because El Salvador has increased its arsenals, mostly through U.S. assistance. The countries are traditional enemies.

President Reagan seems determined to solve our problems in Central America militarily, even if he has to use Honduras to do it. These war games are deceptive and dangerous. Mr. Reagan has managed to put troops in the region under the guise of temporary, routine exercises without letting Congress and the public debate it. He has made Honduras a partner in two civil wars, neither of them its own.

THE KANSAS CITY STAR
Kansas City, MO, March 21, 1985

The administration may be painting itself into a corner through the proposed defense declaration with Honduras. Without casting outright aspersions at the government's benevolence—that of helping Honduras if it is attacked—the pact should be recognized for just what it is: a stalling mechanism.

It is an appeasement, something to tide the Hondurans over so that the U.S. may get out of the doghouse and on with more urgent business in Central America. Honduras has hungrily watched the trail of U.S. goods strengthen Salvadoran government and Nicaraguan rebel forces, neighbors to the south and west.

The U.S. supports President Duarte of El Salvador, whose troops have trained at U.S.-sponsored bases in Honduras, and anti-Sandinista Nicaraguans, who are also in Honduras and Costa Rica.

President Roberto Suazo Cordova is feeling the squeeze from domestic dissenters who have not forgotten the 1969 border war with El Salvador and who have seen twice as many Salvadoran as Honduran soldiers trained at the military center in Trujillo on the Caribbean coast.

There also is the problem of the Nicaraguan contras, who represent a foreign guerrilla force much stronger and with newer weapons than the host country. The administration will find itself stammering, stuttering and downright choking on its declaration if the Hondurans end up tangling with either of those two.

What will become of the contras in Honduras if the 99th Congress refuses to refinance them? They certainly cannot return to Nicaragua, unless of course some miracle develops at the Contadora table. On whose side would the U.S. be if the bankrupt contras raise a ruckus in Honduras?

Honduras is the keystone to the administration's policy in Central America. President Reagan knows it. So does President Suazo, who first permitted Big Pine III, the U.S.-Honduran military exercises begun in mid-February, and then threatened to kick the Americans out if he didn't get more concessions.

Some call it political extortion, others call it effective bargaining. Honduras cut a deal and we bought it. But it's the strings that are attached which may end up costing the U.S. the most in the long run.

The Dispatch
Columbus, OH, April 4, 1985

Political events in Honduras are nearing the hysterical point as rival political factions use the country's Supreme Court as a toy in their maneuvering for power. The partisan actions are making a mockery of democracy in that country and should stop.

There are nine justices on the court. The court has been supportive of President Roberto Suazo Cordova, a member of the Liberal Party. The party holds 44 seats in the 82-member, one-house Congress. The party, however, is badly split. Congress President Efrain Bu Giron wants to be the party's presidential candidate in the November elections. Suazo Cordova is backing another candidate.

Late last week, the Congress voted 50-30 to declare five justices incompetent, fired them and named their replacements. Hours later, government prosecutors filed treason charges against the five replacements. The chief justice was jailed and the other four went into hiding.

All of this is taking place prior to the April 11-14 national convention of the Liberal Party at which the presidential nominee will be selected. Each side is trying to get the upper hand in order to secure the nomination for its candidate.

In the meantime, the politicians are severely damaging their own credibility and the trust the public must have in their leaders if democracy is to work.

The factions should put aside their differences until the national convention, and then lobby and maneuver and vote the way they wish to. Then the losing side should accept the winner as the legitimate leader of the party. If they can work with him, they should. If they cannot, they should form another party and offer their own candidate. The winner in November must then be accepted as the legitimate leader of the nation.

Until then, the destruction of the democratic apparatus that guides the country must stop. No one will gain — indeed, all will lose — if the government crumbles and anarchy is allowed to take over.

The Idaho STATESMAN
Boise, ID, April 12, 1985

By Honduran standards, the political events of the past two weeks in that impoverished Central American nation have been fairly tame.

First, the Honduran Congress ousted five Supreme Court justices for a perceived lack of cooperation in a corruption probe. The legislators then named five new justices.

President Roberto Suazo Cordova, who appointed the original justices, responded by filing treason charges against the five new justices and the 53 lawmakers who voted to oust the original justices. But Congress has refused to strike down the 53 lawmakers' immunity, so they cannot be prosecuted.

All parties involved are acting within their powers; the quick conclusion might be that Honduras' constitution could stand some fine-tuning.

But even a comedy of democracy is better than no democracy at all. Ten, 20 or 50 years ago, this sort of dispute was ended by the military, which seized power time and again, often suspending whatever constitution was in place.

Mr. Suazo has held power for $3\frac{1}{2}$ years, making his rule Honduras' most tenured civilian government in more than 20 years. That trick has not been achieved, however, because of anything having to do with Mr. Suazo's charisma or political sophistication.

The Honduran military has been dismayed by his rule, and in August forced a Cabinet reorganization. The U.S. Federal Bureau of Investigation in November thwarted a coup and assassination plot by exiles in Miami.

Mr. Suazo's survival can be attributed to U.S. policy that has placed thousands of American soldiers and tons of American hardware on Honduran soil since Mr. Suazo and President Reagan took their respective offices in 1981.

The United States uses bases in Honduras to fly reconnaissance over El Salvador and to conduct war games within a stone's throw of the Nicaraguan border.

The Hondurans like the aid and security that comes with a U.S. military presence, and Washington likes democracy among its allies. Honduras wants more aid and a stronger treaty with this country than it now has, so a coup would be an imprudent way to end the current standoff in Tegucigalpa.

Mr. Suazo has called Congress' action a "technical coup," but nobody dies in those. Elections are scheduled in November, and Mr. Suazo is barred from seeking re-election. The present tiff is viewed by some as a battle in Mr. Suazo's Liberal Party, which holds 44 of Congress' 82 seats.

The new twist this situation offers for Honduran history is that this sort of political struggle will be played out.

THE INDIANAPOLIS STAR
Indianapolis, IN, March 12, 1985

Honduras, which has 20,700 men in its armed forces, shares a long border with Marxist Nicaragua, which has military forces now estimated at 133,800, including "advisers" from Cuba, the Soviet Union and East Germany.

The people and government of Honduras have every right to be concerned about the Nicaraguan military buildup.

Nicaragua's regime says the buildup is "defensive." But the Sandinistas should not worry about being conquered by Honduras. If anyone should be concerned, it is the Hondurans. Their country has been hit by terrorism and subversion directed by the Sandinistas and Cubans.

In the current fiscal year Honduras will get an estimated $62.5 million in security aid from the United States, plus $8 million for airfield reconstruction and $13 million for a new airbase.

The Honduran government is asking for $100 million a year in military aid for the next four years. This is too much. Yet some increase in military aid to Honduras would make sense if, in return, the Hondurans would make a sincere effort to improve relations with neighboring El Salvador and work together with the Salvadoran government in counter-insurgency operations.

For a long time the Cubans and Nicaraguans have been shipping arms through Honduras to communist rebels in El Salvador.

The United States should help Honduras modernize its armed forces. It should also encourage the Hondurans to diversify their economy, liberate it from strangling governmental interference, attract foreign investment and try free-market means to improve the country's economic health.

These recommendations are made by the Heritage Foundation, whose analyst Timothy Ashby recommended a modest increase in military aid to modernize Honduras' Korean-War-era air force, urged the Reagan administration to continue joint military exercises and said there is merit in a security pact with Honduras.

Honduras is, after all, an integral part of our Caribbean Basin neighborhood, and it makes sense for the United States to be a good neighbor, doing what must be done to make sure that our friends in Central America remain good neighbors too.

THE CHRISTIAN SCIENCE MONITOR
Boston, MA, April 4, 1985

HONDURAS occupies a key position in Central America in this time of regional turmoil. It shares long borders with both Nicaragua and El Salvador. It provides sanctuary and a staging area for the *contras,* from which they attack Nicaragua.

The United States has provided Honduras with substantial funds, primarily to build up its armed forces. The US has constructed several military facilities within it, and American troops conduct frequent maneuvers in the Honduran countryside.

It is in the interests of Central America and of the United States that Honduras have governmental stability, and that it experience an orderly transition from the current regime of President Roberto Suazo Córdova to that of the next president, to be elected in November. In a week the ruling Liberal Party will open the convention at which it is to select its nominee. Preconvention political action is fierce.

Political jockeying is old hat to Honduran politics. But the current degree of internecine political warfare, centering on who should be the Liberal Party's next presidential candidate, is more serious than politics as usual. Factions in the two main parties are involved; members are making cross-party alliances; and the legislature is wrestling for power with President Suazo Córdova.

The depth of the struggle threatens the stability of the current government and holds the possibility of producing governmental stalemate. That, in turn, might entice the military into the fray, at least to the point of dictating a settlement among the warring factions.

The last time Honduras's armed forces were deeply involved in politics, it took the nation 20 years to move from military to civilian rule; military control ended only three years ago. For the sake of the Honduran people and the stability of an already fragile Central America, the military should not reenter the political arena. But it may find the temptation irresistible unless the political situation soon stabilizes.

During this decade the US has spent a great deal of time and money in building up the Honduran military. Less attention has been paid to the nation's political structure or to its societal needs.

The United States now should make maximum effort to persuade all political elements in the dispute to back away from confrontation. President Suazo Córdova in particular should drop the charges of treason leveled against some 50 congressmen who defied him and tried to fire five Supreme Court justices. Politicians on all sides should sheathe their swords and let the new bipartisan commission study the dispute over the treason charges. It is a time for cool heads and sound judgment.

Long Island, NY, February 17, 1985

It would be a huge blunder if the Reagan administration's efforts to destabilize Nicaragua wound up destabilizing neighboring Honduras instead. Yet administration policies entail just such a risk.

Washington is pressuring Honduras to continue providing a safe haven for thousands of Nicaraguan rebels even though Congress seems likely to refuse further covert aid to these contras. But the Honduran government is afraid that if the contras operating from bases inside Honduras ignore an amnesty offer and go on fighting, they may provoke a full-scale

Nicaraguan military strike. And even if the contras now inside Nicaragua are only driven across the border by the Sandinista regime, Honduras may have a serious problem coping with renegade bands of armed men roaming its countryside.

Hondurans are also sour about El Salvador's military buildup, which they see as a greater long-term threat than any posed by Nicaragua. In the background is a lingering border dispute that the Salvadorans tried to settle in 1969 by invading Honduras. No wonder Honduras takes a dim view of Washington's plans to reopen

training facilities in Honduras to Salvadoran soldiers.

Given these anxieties, it's hardly surprising that Hondurans are seeking some accommodation with Nicaragua even as they're asking the United States for security guarantees firmer than the oral commitments they've received so far. Washington shouldn't try to bludgeon Honduras into abjectly ignoring its own security concerns; the Honduran military might not stand for it. Too heavy a hand in Washington and it could be the civilian government of Honduras that needs a safe haven.

MARGULIES
©1985 HOUSTON POST

THE KANSAS CITY STAR
Kansas City, MO, November 27, 1985

Latin American politics, known for their dubious integrity, sunk to an even lower depth in Honduras recently. What President Roberto Suazo Cordova did was despicable in itself, but his latest attempt at undermining last Sunday's presidential elections unfortunately dragged the United States into the mire.

President Suazo, who is constitutionally forbidden to seek another term, borrowed a U.S. Army helicopter to drop leaflets over Marcala, a small town in north central La Paz province, according to press accounts. The leaflets accused opposition presidential candidate Rafael Leonardo Callejas of being a "sodomite," stricken with Acquired Immune Deficiency Syndrome, better known as AIDS.

Mr. Suazo and three aides boarded a UH-1H helicopter from Palmerola Air Force Base near Tegucigalpa, sources said. A U.S. Army pilot flew the vehicle. U.S. embassy spokesman Arthur Skop told one reporter that "U.S. aviation assets may be provided to a foreign government or official in support of official business requests only."

If these sources are correct, Mr. Suazo misled officers at the base. He allegedly telephoned the headquarters for 1,000 American troops, and asked that the helicopter be available for "an official mission." A second U.S. chopper followed. Since when is mudslinging, even by air, part of official business? Mr. Suazo was backing his hand-picked successor, Oscar Mejia Arellano.

Honduras is a valuable American ally in Central American, where Washington insists the Sandinista-led Nicaraguan government must be stopped. Honduras receives millions of dollars in economic and military aid, such as the helicopter used for the president's joy ride.

But the administration, by way of the State Department, must alert the outgoing president that such abuses will not be tolerated. If Mr. Suazo wants to stoop in the gutter, let him do it alone. But he and the incoming president must know in no uncertain terms that they cannot drag this republic down there, too.

DAYTON DAILY NEWS
Dayton, OH, December 13, 1985

Honduras, until recently considered by political circles in the Western Hemisphere to be laughably obedient to Washington, D.C., seems to be trying to live down its reputation. The government there is blocking delivery of U.S. supplies to the anti-Sandinista Nicaraguan contras.

Honduras seems to be proceeding on the assumption that the Sandinistas are going to be around for a while. It does not relish the prospect of long-term animosity with a neighbor. It can foresee the day when the Sandinistas get serious about aiding anti-government forces in Honduras.

Even as it is, the Sandinistas are making forays into Honduras. Their rationale is exactly the same as the American rationale in the 1970s for moving into Cambodia: That's where the rebels are staging their attacks from.

The Reagan administration thinks Honduras ought to be willing to make this little sacrifice for the United States, given how much money Honduras has received from us (a lot!) and how much is still in the pipeline.

But the Hondurans are wondering how much help Washington will be if the Nicaraguan civil war spreads. How much patience would the American people have for full-fledged regional conflict?

Good questions.

PRI Claims Victory in Mexican Midterm Elections

Amid allegations of widespread fruad, the ruling International Revolutionary Party (PRI) July 8, 1985 claimed an overwhelming victory in midterm municipal, gubenatorial and congressional elections held July 7. The PRI said it had won all seven contested governorships and most of the 300 directly elected seats in the Chamber of Deputies, the lower house of the National Congress. However, that National Action Party (PAN) charged widespread fraud and demanded new gubenatorial elections in the states of Sonora and Nuevo Leon. In the run-up to the elections, the conservative PAN had been given a good chance of winning the governorships of Sonora and Nuevo Leon, and these races were closely watched because of the unprecedented challenge the PRI faced. PAN claimed it could only lose these races through fraud by the PRI. On the day of the election, foreign observers and press and members of PAN reported several instances of anomalies and irregularities, but the PRI claimed that these were "minor and typical" and would not affect the outcome of the races. PRI accused PAN of charging fraud to impress foreign reporters. PRI had won every race for president, senator and state governor in Mexico since the party was founded in 1929. However, in the wake of the economic crisis that gripped Mexico in 1982, PAN had been widening its base of support and winning some local offices.

Some violence was reported in the north on election day. In the PAN stronghold of San Luis Rio Colorado in Sonora, PAN supporters set fire to a police station after several arrests were made when demonstrators opened 10 ballot boxes before the election and found them already stuffed with ballots marked for the PRI. Five gunmen July 1 in Mexico City abducted Arnaldo Martinez Verduga, who had been the candidate of the leftist United Socialist Party in presidential elections in 1982. His abductors said they belonged to the Party of the Poor, a Marxist group. Martinez had been running for an at-large congressional seat in the July 7 elections.

The official results of the July 7 midterm elections, announced July 16, showed the PRI as having won 291 of the 300 congressional seats contested. PAN was 6 given seats in the Chamber of Deputies, the lower house of the National Congress, and the Authentic Party of Mexico three. PAN claimed it won 37 seats.

THE BLADE
Toledo, OH,
July 15, 1985

DESPITE reports that the opposition National Action party in Mexico might win one or two governorships in states bordering the United States, the durable Institutional Revolutionary party apparently has accomplished another electoral sweep.

Charges of vote fraud were inevitable, and it is difficult to know just how much credence to give to those accusations. Still, the PRI has not lost at the polls in more than a half century, and it was under a good deal of pressure to make a good showing even in the border areas where disillusionment with the corruption-ridden federal government runs high.

As early election returns indicated, there were some curious anomalies. For example, in the home town of the PAN opposition candidate for governor of Sonora, which borders Arizona, the results in several districts were: PRI, 400, PAN 0; PRI 320, PAN, 0, and so on. There were numerous charges of ballot-box stuffing as well.

Although the results are not yet official, the PRI claimed overwhelming victories in both Nuevo Leon and Sonora, where the PAN had been given a good chance to win. Mexico would not have fallen apart if PAN had won the governorships of either or both states. In fact, it would have been a healthy development.

Mexico has had a remarkably stable government under the PRI, which continues to assert that it carries on the heritage of the Mexican Revolution early in this century. But the country is wracked by economic problems and political agitation by both left-wing and right-wing factions.

This would be an excellent time for the PRI to take some of the heat off itself by giving more breathing room to opposition political parties. The PRI cannot forever be all things to all people. The only hope for long-range stability in Mexico is a political system that offers some choice to the Mexican people.

That cannot happen as long as the PRI, in one way or another, keeps on flattening opposition parties every time they begin to show promise of maturing into reasonable alternatives to the ruling party.

Los Angeles Times
Los Angeles, CA, July 7, 1985

Other countries seldom notice non-presidential elections in Mexico. But today's voting in several Mexican states, especially the border state of Sonora, is of special interest because some key races are in doubt. That is rare in the tightly controlled Mexican political system.

Opinion polls indicate that the gubernatorial candidate of the opposition National Action Party, known by its Spanish acronym, PAN, has a chance to defeat a rival nominated by the powerful Institutional Revolutionary Party, or PRI. PAN might well win an honest election in Sonora, whose citizens are angry about the economy—an anger intensified by still another recent plunge in the value of the peso. PAN candidate Adalberto Rosas is an articulate and popular former mayor of the state's largest city. Rosas' PRI opponent, Rodolfo Felix Valdez, by all accounts an honest civil servant, is a colorless campaigner. Should Rosas win, it would be the first major loss for PRI since it was founded 56 years ago.

But even before the polls opened there were troubling signs that PRI leaders have no intention of losing in Sonora, even if they must resort to questionable tactics to win. State election officials, all appointees of the current PRI government, disqualified some PAN candidates and poll-watchers on last-minute technicalities. The number of polling places in cities and districts where PAN candidates have run strongly in the past were unexpectedly reduced. State voter lists suddenly bulged with electors newly registered by the PRI while PAN sympathizers were being dropped.

Such heavy-handed maneuvering will surprise no one who has watched the PRI political machine in operation. But it is regrettable to see all this pre-election activity in Sonora running so entirely contrary to a pledge by Mexican President Miguel de la Madrid that the 1985 elections would be the most open and, by implication, the most honest in the nation's history. It also slows, if not reverses, a recent trend by Mexican political leaders, to open the system to opposition parties.

Many thoughtful observers argue that, for all its faults, the PRI has given Mexico political stability during a transition from a poor, rural country to a modern nation that is increasingly urbanized and industrial. But if Mexico is to become the great nation that its leaders want it to be, it must open its political system to many more voices. The hope in today's voting in Sonora, and elsewhere in Mexico, is that the nation is closer than ever to having a truly open political system. But if those elections are less honest than they should be, and especially if voter frustration over that fact results in the protests and even the violence that some observers fear, it will be a severe setback not just for well-intentioned leaders like De la Madrid but also for the nation as a whole.

The London Free Press

London, Ont., July 11, 1985

Regrettably for democracy in Mexico, the long-governing Institutional Revolutionary Party (PRI) has again claimed overwhelming victory in mid-term elections, particularly in two prosperous northern border states where it appeared the opposition National Action Party (PAN) had a chance to win.

The PRI, which has never lost a presidential or gubernatorial race, has claimed victory in 300 Chamber of Deputies seats, with the remaining 100 to be divided among other parties based on the proportion of votes they received. The PRI national committee also claimed the party had won the seven gubernatorial races and most of the local contests.

While the claims are predictable, they could spell trouble for the nation and the PRI, which has maintained its hold on power through a combination of corruption and intimidation since 1929. Official results will not be available until Sunday, but PAN is already charging widespread vote-tampering.

If corruption does indeed prove to have a been a factor in the northern states, increasing tensions are quite possible. Last year, for instance, supporters of a defeated mayoral candidate in Piedras Negras burned down the city hall in protest over disputed election results. Such violence shows signs of spreading. Tensions ran high during the vote and the army deployed all of its 90,000 troops to support police at polling stations.

Since ballot box corruption has been a tradition with the PRI for more than half a century, there's reason to believe reports by PAN of scattered violence, ballot box stuffing and "threats" and "beatings" of PAN supporters.

President Miguel de la Madrid has provided a sterling example for the rest of the world in his handling of the economic crisis facing the nation. It is unfortunate he appears unwilling to exert his influence to set an example in democracy.

Since there is little danger of the ruling party actually losing its grip on power, de la Madrid would have been wise to have throttled the PRI corrupt practices and allowed PAN a token victory, if for no other reason than to ease tensions. That does not appear to be the case and Mexico will likely pay a heavy price in festering frustration.

The Dallas Morning News

Dallas, TX,
July 22, 1985

Of Mexican President Miguel de la Madrid, Alan Riding writes in *Distant Neighbors*: "De la Madrid's principal objective was to preside over an honest administration, to clean up the corruption of the future."

He isn't there yet. Outside de la Madrid's Institutional Revolutionary Party (PRI), which has had a chokehold on Mexican politics since 1929, the consensus is that PRI last week conducted aggressively corrupt national elections.

Pointlessly corrupt, one might add. PRI candidates would in any case probably have won the great majority of state and local offices up for election; yet the party furiously stole votes.

Ballot boxes were stuffed in broad daylight, while others with uncounted votes were hauled off to unknown destinations. "In Nuevo Leon," reports the *New York Times*, "the local congress did not even bother to wait for the official results before declaring the governing party candidate the winner."

Either de la Madrid is insincere about cleaning up corruption (unlikely) or lower-level party and government officials are so strong they ignore him (highly likely).

The defeated National Action Party (PAN) has so far eschewed violent response: mute acknowledgement, perhaps, of PRI's still-awesome power. But the matter does not really end here. The PRI has egg all over its face. The election has been praised only in model democracies like the Soviet Union and Southern Yemen.

Mexico, to avoid internal strife, with accompanying gains for communism, needs one of two things — a rejuvenated, sanitized PRI or fair elections that result in the PAN's taking charge. Just now — *iay bene!* — it seems unlikely to get either.

The Boston Globe

Boston, MA, July 13, 1985

The vote fraud in last weekend's Mexican congressional and state elections suggested an air of political crisis. In fact, the elections, fraud included, reflect the survival strategy of that country's troubled political system.

President Miguel de la Madrid is beefing up the party machinery in preparation for a smooth presidential transition when he leaves office in 1988. There is no institutionalized nominating process in Mexico.

A Mexican president consults widely and then picks his successor, but to have his personal choice accepted, he needs supporters in key offices. That is why midterm elections are important to the "ruling" party.

Charges of vote fraud by the conservative opposition offer a glimpse of the methods long used in Mexico to maintain stability despite potentially volatile social problems.

Mexico has been wracked with misery, corruption and injustice since the Spanish conquest, and now faces a deepening economic crisis due to falling prices for its oil and a huge foreign debt.

The political system resembles Chicago machine politics under Mayor Richard Daley. Mexico is less a democracy than a one-party state in which the Institutional Revolutionary Party (PRI) has held on for 56 years, by fair means and foul.

The PRI ceased being "revolutionary" decades ago. It keeps the social lid on through multitudinous political deals, rewarding loyalties and diffusing pressure from the left. There is inefficiency, endemic corruption and repression, but somehow the system has survived.

Seen from Washington, the Mexican tendency to rebuff US pressures on international issues, especially on East-West issues like Nicaragua, is vexing. Some in the Reagan administration think that if the PRI machine were weakened, Mexico would be less frisky in putting forth independent policy initiatives.

Mexico is a cosponsor of the Contadora peace plan, whose live-and-let-live approach to Nicaraguan Marxism is at odds with Reagan's approach. For that reason the administration has encouraged a conservative, pro-business, pro-American opposition called the National Action Party (PAN).

The PAN has been a negligible factor in Mexican politics, and although recent discontent has swelled its ranks, its showing in the elections appeared weak, even adjusting for the "big shutdown" of vote fraud.

In a curious way, Mexican tolerance of fraud may be partly explained by the national sense of insecurity. Hanging on to sovereignty is a more deeply ingrained priority than clean government or social justice. Because of Mexico's susceptibility to US influence, a smooth presidential succession has been a high concern.

The most enlightened course for the PRI, like any political machine facing serious troubles, would probably be to open up the system and share the burden of governing with the opposition. One danger, however, is that a weakened "ruling party" and an emboldened opposition would provide openings for US efforts aimed at neutralizing Mexico's calming influence in Central America.

Many Mexicans are certain that the one crisis their society could definitely not withstand would be active US military involvement in Central America. They believe that Mexico's wobbly social balance would collapse and that the country would be polarized and inflamed along with the rest of the region.

This insecurity does not pardon vote fraud, but it helps explain why it seems so much a part of the system. Mexico's need for political evolution runs counter not only to the PRI's narrow self-interest, but also to the suspicion that weakening the machine will lead to an erosion of national sovereignty – and to chaos.

ALBUQUERQUE JOURNAL

Albuquerque, NM, July 18, 1985

Is a nation a democracy when:

■ The same political party has controlled virtually all elected offices for 56 years?

■ A clique chooses the nation's chief executive?

■ Elections are routinely rigged and vote counts inflated?

▫ Official corruption is a way of life?

■ A candidate for the strongest rival political party loses 50-to-one in his hometown?

■ Foreign television newscasts about the nation are censored in that nation?

Each of those questions describes a troubling aspect about Mexico, a nation of political and economic contrasts. It allows its people to speak, publish and move freely but its elections are shams. Political stability has been maintained by the systematic undercutting of opposition political parties.

The country's ruling Institutional Revolutionary Party (PRI) has had little serious opposition since 1929. It has used political chicanery to crush political opposition. It has compiled an unenviable record for corruption and economic mismanagement.

Promises by President Miguel de la Madrid Hurtado, whose term ends in three years, to root out official corruption and to conduct honest elections have been empty. In the recent midterm election, PRI won all seven governorships that were at stake, all but five of the 300 elected seats in the Chamber of Deputies and all but a few of many state and local offices.

During the elections, particularly in the northern states, observers saw ballot box fraud conducted openly against PRI's only serious political opposition, the National Action Party (PAN). Boxes of uncounted ballots were taken from the polls. People were seen stuffing handfuls of ballots into other boxes. Hundreds of fictitious names were on the voting rolls while names of eligible voters had been purged. Less than half the voters did not cast ballots. A poll taken in Mexico City before the election found only 13 percent of those polled expected honest results. A PAN candidate for governor was outvoted 1,000 to 20 in his hometown.

News about Mexico, particularly if it might seem adverse, is frequently censored from cable news broadcasts in Mexico. But a growing, educated middle class is spawning political opposition and dissatisfaction with the ruling party. PRI has not helped its cause with dishonest elections.

Rigged elections, government corruption and news censorship diminish Mexico's status among democratic nations. If Mexico is to occupy an increasingly important place in the family of nations — as it should — its politics cannot escape scrutiny and its people must not be denied news — as seen by others — of their nation's strengths and weaknesses.

The Honolulu Advertiser

Honolulu, HI, July 25, 1985

It was no surprise that Mexico's ruling Institutional Revolutionary Party (PRI) swept the country's recent federal elections. PRI has maintained strong control for 56 years, usually giving only a handful of legislative seats to the token opposition.

But this year the opposition National Action Party (PAN), with growing backing from Mexico's disgruntled middle class, mounted one of the strongest challenges to PRI in years. And in response to a growing dissatisfaction with its rule, PRI went to extraordinary lengths to ensure "victory" for its candidates.

Fraud was rampant and brazen. One reporter wrote: "PRI used every trick in the book — and wrote a few new chapters."

The heavy-handed methods used to win the election have damaged the reputation of President Miguel de la Madrid, PRI and the country. De la Madrid had promised honest elections. When the crunch came, the president retreated from his lofty promises. "Those who think the moment has arrived to bury the revolution . . . to turn back Mexican history . . . are mistaken," he told a campaign crowd.

Had a truly free election been held, PRI would probably have maintained a strong majority. But by openly tampering with the results, the ruling party has further weakened its credibility at home and abroad.

The State

Columbia, SC, July 20, 1985

THE ELECTION returns are in. Mexico remains a one-party state. The ruling Institutional Revolutionary Party (PRI) maintained a tight political grip by winning a strong congressional majority in midterm elections. In a nation with more than its share of problems, that party will continue to have its hands full.

The cries of fraud, protests and demonstrations by the most disappointed loser, the conservative National Action Party (PAN), will be the least of the victors' problems. The election winner, the PRI, will process those complaints, and the world will never know how pure the election really was.

Nevertheless, the world must hope that the balloting brings to President Miguel de la Madrid, who has completed half of his six-year term, a mandate to face squarely up to two of his nation's most devastating problems: the economy and corruption.

It is difficult to measure how effective his gradualistic and stylistic "moral renovation" has been in coping with corruption. Favorable reports tend to be offset by spectacular revelations of rampant bribery and drug smuggling.

But Mr. de la Madrid certainly must redouble his efforts to cope with his nation's debt problem, which has deepened despite sporadic and often ineffective efforts.

A good argument could be made that the socialism that permeates much of Mexico's economy invites inefficiency and throttles initiative, but there is little hope that Mr. de la Madrid and his followers will convert it into more of a free-market economy in the near future.

Meanwhile, low demand and prices for oil are making it tougher to earn foreign exchange to service Mexico's bank debts.

Mr. de la Madrid must recognize that it is imperative to push exports. As the British publication, *The Economist,* puts it, "That means realistic exchange rates, liberalized trade and curtailed bureaucracy. It also means putting out the welcome mat for foreign investors, not merely foreign credits, as Southeast Asia has done and revisionist China and India are starting to do."

Many imports into Mexico are subject to licenses that promote efficiency, as well as corruption, petty and bigtime.

The Economist noted that "Mexico let its peso appreciate to the point where it was nearly as overvalued in real terms as it was at its peak in January, 1982. The recent effective 33 percent devaluation was conceded by the government only after capital flight had carried away a big chunk of the central bank's rebuilt foreign reserves."

Unfortunately, realistic exchange rates will mean more sacrifices on the part of the Mexican people. Mr. de la Madrid is fortunate that his party has retained its overpowering strength in Congress. He will need all the support he can muster to do what must be done.

THE LOUISVILLE TIMES
Louisville, KY, July 15, 1985

The roots of Mexico's present government can be traced to a document, the Plan de San Luis Potosí, which contained a plea for honest elections. Ironically, 75 years later, the conduct of Mexican elections is again an issue.

Amid charges of widespread vote fraud, the ruling Institutional Revolutionary Party (PRI) won majorities in last week's contests for seven state governorships, 300 seats in the national Chamber of Deputies and hundreds of municipal and state legislative offices on such a scale that any member of New York City's old Tammany Hall machine would have been delighted.

According to most observers, however-er, the party had faced its strongest challenges ever in the northern states of Sonora and Nuevo León from gubernatorial candidates of the National Action Party, known as PAN. Inflation, austerity programs designed to reduce the country's foreign debt problems and middle-class unrest had emerged as major voter concerns.

When the ballots were counted, PRI's margins were astounding, as were the detailed reports of ballot-box stuffing and other irregularities. Of the vote totals in his home district, one candidate observed, "This would mean even my relatives did not vote for me."

PRI has dominated Mexican political life for more than half a century. And it

has been relatively easy for the United States, during that time, to abandon its abhorrence for one-party government because of the stability PRI has brought to Mexico. But the U.S. shouldn't be lulled into believing that when elections are no more than a charade, citizen frustration won't rise there, as it has elsewhere in the world.

The frightening and, some say, growing possibility of unrest is a major concern, and all the more so because Mexico is deeply indebted to American banks. The President wouldn't be inappropriately meddling by voicing our displeasure with the Mexican government. It's time they allow what their founders longed for, an honest election.

Newsday
Long Island, NY, July 18, 1985

There's a saying that democracy exists in Mexico every day of the year but one — Election Day. And it's a fact that important Mexican elections aren't normally fraught with suspense. For over half a century, the candidates of Mexico's Institutional Revolutionary Party (PRI) have won every contest for president, senator and governor.

Still, several dozen foreign reporters seemed unprepared for the blatancy of what they saw during the PRI's anything-but-clean sweep of this month's midterm gubernatorial, congressional and local elections. They witnessed ballot boxes being filled with PRI votes before the voting officially

began, people leaping from cars to stuff multiple ballots into the boxes, uncounted ballots being whisked away by armed men in cars without license plates. They found voting rolls filled with fictitious names. They saw polling places opening late and closing early in opposition neighborhoods.

Even without this evidence of fraud, the results themselves were wildly improbable. The PRI might have won handily despite credible challenges in Sonora and Nuevo Leon states. But in a clean election, a party that is widely blamed for three years of high inflation and sharply lowered living standards can hardly be expected to increase

its popular showing — as official results purport to show that the PRI did.

These were obviously not the honest elections promised for months in line with President Miguel de la Madrid's recurrent campaign for "moral renovation." And they belie Mexico's self-portrait as democracy's leading champion in Latin America. Mexicans are relatively free even under their one-party system. They speak, write, publish and move about as they like. But full democracy means that power derives from the consent of the governed — and that this consent is tested periodically — and honestly — at the polls.

Military Ousts President in Panama

President Nicolas Ardito Barletta Vallarina resigned from office September 28, 1985, citing pressures from the National Defense Force and members of the governing National Democratic Union coalition. As provided for in the constitution, he was replaced by the First Vice President Eric Arturo Delvalle. Ardito Barletta, the first democratically elected president in Panama in 16 years, had been in office since October 1984. He was selected as a presidential candidate by the National Defense Force chief, Gen. Manuel Antonio Noriega, and his election victory was said to have been engineered by the military. Despite his experience as vice president of the World Bank, which many believed well qualified him to deal with Panama's economic problems, Ardito Barletta had proved inept at gaining political support for harsh austerity measures that were backed by the International Monetary Fund. There had been a series of strikes and protests against the measures. For some time, speculation had been rife that Ardito Barletta would be replaced because of his poor performance. Noriega recently had publicly criticized the handling of the economy.

Press reports Sept. 30-October 2 also cited as a factor in his ouster divisions in the military that had threatened to topple Noriega, in the wake of the brutal murder of a critic of Noriega, Hugo Spadafora. Ardito Barletta had reportedly been considering bowing to demands to appoint a commission to investigate the murder, for which the National Defense Force had been blamed. According to political observers, Noriega Sept. 26 had summoned Ardito Barletta from New York City, where he was attending the 40th session of the United Nations General Assembly, and demanded the president's resignation. The president apparently agreed to resign only after being held for several hours and threatened, according to sources cited by the *New York Times* Sept. 30. Delvalle, who replaced Ardito Barletta, belonged to the rightist Republican Party, which was a member of the governing coalition. Reportedly to make clear its displeasure at Ardito Barletta's ouster, the United States administration Oct. 1 announced it was suspending $5 million in aid to Panama.

The Dispatch
Columbus, OH, October 3, 1985

The agreement among the United States, Japan and Panama to study shipping alternatives to the Panama Canal is a positive step that engenders the kind of international cooperation that is beneficial to the world. The study will be good for the region, in particular, and for world trading stability, in general.

The 5-year study is expected to cost $20 million and the tab will be shared by the three nations. The United States agreed to participate in the study back in 1977 when it ratified the treaty turning total control of the canal over to Panama at the end of the century. Panama is, of course, interested in remaining a vital shipping locale. Japan's interest in the study stems from the difficulty some of its large ships have in using the 40-mile, 73-year-old canal. Many of them — especially car-carriers — are too large for the canal and must go around the tip of South America, thereby increasing shipping costs.

Several options will be examined. One is to enlarge the size of the present canal. Another is to build a larger canal parallel to the existing one. Another is to build pipelines to move oil and rail lines to ship freight that cannot be transported through the canal easily.

If the new canal option is selected, it will have to be determined whether it will employ a lock system similar to the present canal or whether it will be a sea-level canal, using no locks. The locks are cumbersome and slow. However, planners of a sea-level canal would have to contend with tidal differences between the Caribbean Sea and the Pacific Ocean and the possible environmental damage that could result from a sea-level passage.

U.S. Secretary of State George Shultz, speaking at a ceremony here at which the agreement was signed, said there are "major implications for maritime commerce and international trade" and added that the agreement "underscores a basic U.S. foreign policy objective in Central America — the promotion of regional economic growth and stability as a means of strengthening the development of political democracy."

This study will, indeed, be a step toward economic stability for the region. It is a good indication of what nations which share common goals can do when they wish to work together.

The Wichita Eagle-Beacon
Wichita, KS, October 1, 1985

"FRAUDITO Barletta," they called him, after his election 11½ months ago was stripped of much of its significance by widespread charges of fraud. The voters had thought they were choosing Panama's first democratically elected president in 16 years. Any pretense at "democracy" was dropped, however, when the opposition candidate, former president Arnulfo Arias, pulled ahead in the balloting, and the count was stopped. When the count resumed, Nicolas Ardito Barletta inexplicably zoomed into the lead, and went on to win by a narrow margin. "Fraudito Barletta," indeed.

Now that Mr. Ardito Barletta has been overthrown by the country's Defense Forces — and that's what his replacement by Vice President Eric Arturo Delvalle over the weekend amounts to — Panama is further removed than ever from the democratic ideal many had hoped yet would emerge. There can be no question now the military is

running the country, and Panama — for all the government's window dressing — has drifted back toward dictatorship.

The free nations of the hemisphere — particularly the United States, which had been closely aligned with Panama — should let their displeasure be known. They should inform Gen. Manuel Antonio Noriega — as head of the Defense Forces, the real leader of the country — that Panama cannot expect to share in the good will and material benefits that have flowed to other, newly democratic countries of the region.

Disappointment is the main emotion felt by those who had thought Panama truly might be on its way to becoming a free nation of free people. Not yet, the events of the weekend demonstrate. Not until the military realizes its stranglehold on the democratic process must be released if Panama is to have the credibility and the influence in world councils that its people deserve.

BUFFALO EVENING NEWS
Buffalo, NY, October 8, 1985

ANYTHING THAT might affect the Panama Canal rightly raises concern in the United States. That is why the debate over the Panama Canal Treaty dragged on so long in the 1970s and why recent signs of instability in Panama have raised alarm signals.

The first president to be democratically elected in 16 years, Nicholas Barletta, has been ousted by the army after only 11 months in office. The real power remains the army leader, Gen. Manuel Noriega, who hand-picked Barletta last year. Now he has replaced him — apparently because of unpopular austerity measures and also because Barletta was hinting at an investigation of a recent political murder.

There has been a heartening trend toward democracy throughout Latin America recently, but unfortunately it has not reached Panama. The death of Panamanian strongman Gen. Omar Torrijos in a plane crash in 1981 threw the political situation into confusion.

Torrijos had planned democratic elections in 1984 and was expected to run for president. The elections were held on schedule, but political life has been turbulent without Torrijos' steadying influence. In the past three years, the army has installed or deposed five presidents.

A grisly side of the army's dominant influence showed up recently when the murdered, decapitated body of a prominent critic of the army was found in a mail bag on the Costa Rican border. The deposed president was considering an investigation when he was bullied into resigning. The American ambassador advised him not to return to Panama from the United Nations sessions he had been attending in New York.

This political instability is worrisome, but it does not justify any I-told-you-so reaction from the foes of the Panama Canal Treaty. One of the arguments made against the treaty was that there was no way of knowing what the political situation might be when Panama takes control of the canal.

The treaty has, however, served American interests well, and it will doubtless stand in history as one of the great achievements of the Carter administration. For generations, the American-occupied Canal Zone stood as a symbol to all Latin Americans of an earlier colonialist era, marring U.S. relations throughout the region. Since the treaty was ratified in 1978, the canal has dropped from sight as an international issue.

The United States still controls the canal and will do so for the next 15 years. Thus, the current political instability in Panama poses no direct threat to the canal. When the canal is turned over to Panama in the year 2000, the United States will still retain the right to take any military action to protect the canal or to keep it open.

New exploitation of the canal issue by quarreling politicians in Panama is always a possibility, but it would be hard to create much political heat over the canal when it is already scheduled to be handed over to Panama in a few years.

The Miami Herald
Miami, FL, October 4, 1985

PRESCRIPTION for a Latin military government: First you oust the civilian president. Then you intimidate the press. If that doesn't work, then you permit street thugs to attack any newspaper that dares to be independent.

Gen. Manuel Antonio Noriega, head of Panama's National Defense Forces (NDF), knows the formula well. He and his henchmen have imposed or deposed five Panamian presidents in the last three years. The last coup came on Friday, when General Noriega demanded the resignation of President Nicolas Ardito-Barletta and appointed former Vice President Eric Arturo del Valle to replace him.

That done, General Noriega turned to La Prensa, Panama's fiercely independent opposition newspaper. (La Prensa, coincidentally, prints part of The Miami Herald's international edition in Panama.) La Prensa knows what happens when the NDF objects to its independence. The NDF has closed the five-year-old newspaper twice.

The American ambassador is reported to have warned La Prensa's editors that the NDF wants it closed. And columnist Guillermo Sanchez Borbon, Panama's most respected political commentator, bade farewell to his readers the other day. His photograph has been distributed among NDF members, he explained. Fearing for his life, he said that he is going into hiding.

Mr. Sanchez Borbon merely was being prudent. The last time La Prensa was closed, thugs broke in and poured acid on its presses and in the computers.

This time, matters could be worse. For La Prensa, and particularly Mr. Sanchez Borbon, have insisted adamantly on an independent investigation into the murder and decapitation of Dr. Hugo Spadafora, one of General Noriega's enemies. Dr. Spadafora's mutilated body — his head is still missing — was found two weeks ago in Costa Rica, near the border with Panama. Witnesses say that cars similar to NDF vehicles, and men dressed in military uniforms, were seen in the vicinity shortly before.

General Noriega should consider carefully the consequences of muzzling La Prensa or harming columnist Sanchez Borbon. That would bring upon him the condemnation of democratic governments and human-rights advocates throughout the hemisphere. Moreover, it would elongate the shadow already cast upon the NDF by the death of Dr. Spadafora. If General Noriega and the NDF have nothing to hide, they have nothing to fear from a free press demanding an independent investigation.

The Kansas City Times
Kansas City, MO, October 5, 1985

Confidence in the democratic and fiscal futures of Panama must not be especially high right now. President Nicolas Ardito Barletta, the nation's first elected leader in 16 years, resigned Sept. 28 after serving for less than a year. Mr. Ardito Barletta was succeeded by his vice president, Eric Arturo Delvalle.

Mr. Ardito Barletta announced his resignation in a letter which explained that he lacked the military and political support to help pull the country out of the red, namely its $3.7 billion foreign debt. His explanation comes as a surprise to those who remember that it was Mr. Ardito Barletta who was accused of being a puppet of the military in the days preceeding last year's election May 6. Such allegations led U.S. lawmakers like Sens. Lawton Chiles of Florida, J. Bennett Johnston of Louisiana, and Daniel K. Inouye of Hawaii, to suggest that the administration send an official delegation to monitor the Panamanian election.

Money problems are not new to Mr. Ardito Barletta, an American-educated economist and former World Bank vice president for Latin America. As a member of that international lending institution, the Panamanian leader knows that austerity, not popularity, is the key to economic recovery. But his choice of austerity was met with protests and strikes. He is not the first Latin leader to have difficulty getting his citizens to accept tightfisted, but requisite, realities.

Mr. Ardito Barletta is also a leader in the Democratic Revolutionary Party, the military-backed party which propelled him to victory. Politics and the need for tactical suasion of the populace are not alien to him, either. But he must have faced a rude awakening in his role as president, a job which requires a delicate balance of doing what's good for the career or ego and what's good for the country. Stepping down last weekend was probably the one time he was able to accomplish both.

"I want to make a contribution to the maintenance of the peace of our country and I resign the office to which I was elected," he said in a broadcast message. Panama lost nothing when it lost a leader who realized he could not be its best representative. The question now is whether Mr. Delvalle, a critic of his predecessor, is the one.

Guatemalan Election to End 31 Years of Military Rule

Guatemala held general elections November 3, 1985 to end 31 years of military domination. Christian Democrat Marco Vinico Cerezo, 42, easily beat his rivals but did not gain the clear majority required to be named president. A runoff would be held December 8 between Cerezo and National Center Union leader Jorge Caripo Nicolle, 54, who finished a distant second. Of Guatemala's 2.7 million registered voters, about 71% went to the polls. Voting was compulsory; many voters cast blank ballots. Guatemala's military had ruled the country either directly or indirectly since a United States-supported coup in 1954. The current chief of state, Gen. Oscar Humberto Meija Victores, had pledged to permit whoever won the election to take power in January 1986 and vowed that the military would stay out of the government. There was apparently no army intervention in the current balloting. U.S. observers said the bipartisan delegation had concluded unanimously that "these contests were fairly and efficiently conducted."

The election took place against a background of economic crisis and a longstanding war with leftist guerillas, neither of which the military government had been able to bring to an end. On the economic front, inflation was running at about 30%, and unemployment and underemployment together were about 40%. On the military front, leftists had stepped up their activities in recent months. The army's ruthlessness in its fight against the guerillas had resulted in Guatemala being generally considered the worst human rights violator in Central America. Since 1980, an estimated 50,000 Guatemalans had been killed and more than one million moved out of their homes in the military's offensive against the left. Cerezo, an opponent of the military, had pledged to improve the army's human rights record but said he would not prosecute the army for past abuses.

The Miami Herald

Miami, FL, November 7, 1985

DEMOCRACY in Central America is definitely rising. The latest example is Sunday's election in Guatemala. Who wins the second round — or even if there is a need for a runoff election in December — is less important than the manner in which the elections were conducted and what the trend toward truly democratic elections portends for the region.

Scholars need not dig too far in history to see the positive change in Central America. Six years ago when the Sandinista revolution triumphed in Nicaragua, only tiny Costa Rica and Belize could be called legitimate democracies in the region. El Salvador, Honduras, and Guatemala were ruled directly by the military or by civilians who were allowed to govern by the grace of the armed forces. Today El Salvador and Honduras are governed by civilian presidents. And now Guatemala is about to join them.

In the climate of six years ago, neither Jose Napoleon Duarte, president of El Salvador, nor Vinicio Cerezo, the leader in Sunday's election in Guatemala, would have been permitted to run for office, much less dream of getting elected and governing. Less than a decade ago the military in Central America considered membership in a moderate Christian Democratic party only a shade better than being a Communist.

A year ago it was Mr. Duarte's turn to prove that a man of progressive views could co-exist with the military. In effect, his election persuaded El Salva-

Guatemala Votes

dor's conservative military establishment that things could be better under the presidency of a man such as Mr. Duarte. Now that lesson is bearing fruit in Guatemala.

Mr. Cerezo, who has survived several assassination attempts during his political career, won nearly 40 percent of the popular vote in Guatemala's election, almost double that of his nearest rival.

Much of the progress in the region derives from the emphasis on human rights first underscored by President Jimmy Carter. But credit for gently nudging the regimes to accept democracy as the best antidote for Communist insurrection belongs to the Reagan Administration and to Congress. Together — though often for different reasons — they have forged a consistent pro-democracy U.S. policy in Central America. That policy is working. The changes came first in Honduras and El Salvador. Now it is Guatemala.

After decades of military control, one election does not constitute a triumph for democracy. It remains for Guatemala's military officers to oversee a second election. And they must prove that whoever wins the December runoff will be allowed to govern.

Nevertheless, with continued internal cooperation and gentle prodding from Washington, democracy can take hold as it has in other countries in Central America. That is a welcome prospect.

The Boston Globe

Boston, MA, November 7, 1985

The US Embassy's haste in declaring last Sunday's election in Guatemala "the final step" in the return of democracy to that traumatized nation suggested no goal beyond an electoral whitewash of a savage, military-dominated government.

The motive of the assessment is to get Congress to renew aid immediately to Guatemala's armed forces. Washington expects that a dependency on aid will provide the leverage to bind Guatemala into an active role in the regional strategy against Nicaragua.

It would be nice to believe that the election will bring real change, but Guatemala's history provides such a grim context that space for optimism is narrow. The repression of highland Indians and of urban moderates trying to open Guatemalan politics has been the most ghastly in the hemisphere. In cynicism, method and style, Guatemalan repression has been in a different league from El Salvador's, suggesting a weird hybrid of modern Argentina and the Spanish Conquest.

That background must be acknowledged in any assessment of the encouraging first-place showing by Christian Democrat Vinicio Cerezo in Sunday's election. Although Cerezo's party stands far to the right of other Christian Democratic parties, in Guatemala he is considered a leftist. Perhaps his victory can bring a measure of change.

The administration's overriding desire is to gain leverage over Guatemala's maverick foreign policy. Despite its conservatism, the Guatemalan military has pursued a neutral role between Washington and Managua, refusing to endorse the contra war against Nicaragua and displaying scorn for nations in the region, such as Honduras, that have compromised their independence in return for US aid.

Guatemala's army took power in a US-engineered coup in 1954, overthrowing a left-leaning democratic regime that threatened the interests of the United Fruit Company.

That coup is regarded as the tragic watershed of modern Central American politics. It emboldened dictators in El Salvador and Nicaragua and alienated the democratic left, making the polarization of the region all but inevitable.

There will be a runoff election in a month between Cerezo and his closest contender, center-right candidate Jorque Carpio Nicolle, who would be more pliable from Washington's viewpoint.

Whoever is installed as president, it is hard to be sanguine about the possibility that the civilian government will evolve into more than a facade. Unless the tightest of strings are attached, US aid is bound to fortify the military and weaken the civilian government, as has happened in neighboring Honduras.

The people of Guatemala have suffered grievously. Congress must make certain not to undercut the possible beginning that Sunday's election represents.

The Houston Post
Houston, TX, November 11, 1985

Guatemala is trying to restore civilian rule. It has the acquiescence of its military leaders, who can't cope with the country's basket-case economy. And it has the encouragement of the United States, which wants to strengthen democracy in Central America.

The first round of national elections last week ended in a runoff for the presidency between Vinicio Cerezo, who led the eight-candidate field with 38.6 percent of the vote, and Jorge Carpio, who won 20.2 percent. Cerezo, a moderate, and Carpio, a conservative, will face each other again Dec. 8. The winner will be Guatemala's first civilian president in 16 years — unless the military prevents him from taking office. It wouldn't be the first time in Latin American politics that the army brass nullified the election of a candidate they didn't like.

The odds are against that happening, however, because the military wants nothing more to do with Guatemala's economic problems. Besides, the runoff winner will have to listen to the generals since they command the guns. After three decades of being governed directly or indirectly by the military, Guatemalans wonder if their votes will help improve conditions in a country wracked by poverty, inflation and high unemployment.

The United States, to its credit, used economic aid to pressure Guatemala's military regime into calling the elections. No matter who wins the presidential runoff, we must continue to manipulate the aid lever to promote democracy and economic stability in the country. It is the only way we can get our money's worth and the Guatemalans can be persuaded that their votes count.

The Dispatch
Columbus, OH, November 9, 1985

Guatemala took a major step toward democracy this week when the nation went to the polls to vote for its first civilian president in 16 years. We can only hope that all involved with this important transition from military domination of the country exercise restraint in the months ahead.

Christian Democrat Vinicio Cerezo Arevalo received 39 percent of the votes cast in a campaign that had no fewer than eight candidates. By law, the winning candidate must receive a majority of the vote and a runoff election has been scheduled for Dec. 8 with Jorge Carpio Nicolle of the National Union of the Center, who received 20 percent of the vote. While Carpio has vowed to go through with the runoff, it is possible that a national unity government could be formed with Cerezo as president.

It is remarkable that Guatemala has moved this close to a democracy. There are some crucial steps to be taken between now and Jan. 14, the day the new president is scheduled to take office. The biggest step is for the military to reaffirm a promise by the current president, Gen. Oscar Mejia Victores, to abide by the results of the election. Many are hopeful, but some are fearful.

An estimated 50,000 civilians have died or disappeared since 1978 in the military's campaign against leftist guerrillas, but neither of the two top presidential candidates plan to prosecute military personnel if they get into office. "It would be difficult to prosecute," Cerezo said in a pre-election interview. "I would have to put the whole army in jail."

Civil rights proponents could certainly hope for more, but will probably be happy to settle for an end to the abuses and power in civilian hands. Each nation has to settle its disputes and solve its problems as its people wish. The process may be a slow one in Guatemala, but at least it has begun.

THE CHRISTIAN SCIENCE MONITOR
Boston, MA, November 5, 1985

WITH its presidential election Guatemala has stepped out onto the bumpy road several other Latin American nations are traveling, from military to civilian rule. It is encouraging for the forces of democracy that the preliminary weekend vote was held at all, that it was without violence, and that, from first reports, it appeared to be reasonably honest.

Yet the fundamental issue remains to be adjudicated: the relationship between the civilian government that is to assume office Jan. 14 and the military, which has ruled this northernmost Central American nation for 31 years.

Guatemala deserves a strong civilian government that will actually run the country, along the lines of the Argentine government of President Alfonsín, which in legislative elections over the weekend received strong public backing for its policies. Guatemala should avoid falling into a situation akin to Panama's, where the head of the National Guard, not the civilian President, wields the effective power from behind the scenes.

The several Guatemalan presidential candidates may have made preliminary contacts with the military. But the task of establishing a power relationship between the two forces will begin in earnest when the victor emerges from the presidential runoff expected Dec. 8. To one degree or another the civilian-military jockeying is likely to be protracted.

The incoming civilian leadership will have a difficult task in putting down a leftist uprising while taking charge of the military.

The new government should be forceful in its efforts to end the widespread human rights abuses that have plagued Guatemala in recent years. To do so, it will have to control those in the military believed to have committed or indirectly controlled the abuses, which include killings, torture, and "disappearances" of persons suspected of being antigovernment.

The Reagan administration has an important role in establishing civilian supremacy over the military: It should not propose any military aid for Guatemala until the new president asks for it.

US military aid was cut off in 1977, in reponse to concern over the severity of Guatemala's human rights abuses; despite some sales of military equipment and grants for economic assistance, the United States has not resumed financial grants for weaponry.

The US should force Guatemala's military to strike a deal with the new president, by making it known that military assistance will be provided only when the Guatemalan president seeks it. Such a stance would give him needed leverage in dealing with the military.

By contrast, a US offer of military aid, without waiting for a request, would signal to the military that it need not cooperate with Guatemala's civilian leadership to gain the supplies, and increased strength, it seeks. That would jeopardize democracy.

The Washington Post
Washington, DC, November 15, 1985

IN GUATEMALA, there is a keen appreciation of the power the military retains behind the civilians it has allowed to run for office. In the ranks of the Reagan administration, however, there is a marked tendency to see the elections not only as fair in procedure but also as important ("the final step") in restoring civilian rule after three decades of dictatorship and repression. The elections are also being portrayed in Washington as proof of a swing to democracy that the United States has been effectively encouraging almost everywhere in Latin America and the Caribbean except in Nicaragua and, of course, Cuba.

Something can be said for positive reinforcement of any turn for the better in a country that has seen the grief of Guatemala. The valor of politicians such as Vinicio Cerezo and Jorge Carpio, who ran first and second in the elections' first round (the second round is Dec. 3) and who are not the military's pets, is exemplary.

But Guatemala remains not just the largest, richest and most strategically important Central American country. It is also the most feudal. The generals did make a certain "democratic opening"—at least in part to attract more international aid and respectability. Still, the permitted parties cover only the center and right in a popular spectrum with a powerful left. Great issues—land reform in a landlords' country, income distribution in a land of impoverished peasants, the accountability and the methods of a military with a record of savagery—were ruled out of bounds.

"For over a hundred years we have suffered from regimes that have been at the service of feudal oligarchies but have utilized the language of freedom," Octavio Paz wrote in "The Labyrinth of Solitude." "The situation has continued to our own day."

It's a fair question as to how the United States ought to engage with a rough place like Guatemala. Staying at arm's length, as Washington has for most of the last 10 years, spared American taint from Guatemalan abuses but left the generals free to conduct a brutal internal policy. It also stoked Guatemalan pride and produced a disinclination—distressing to the Reagan administration—to cooperate with the United States on isolating Nicaragua.

Moving closer risks some of that taint, even in what everyone hopes are improved circumstances. But moving closer also offers a chance for the administration, Congress, the human rights people and others to advise, press and nag in their respective fashions. The administration is readier than most to give it a try, but it needs to show it's not just winking at a farce in order to enlist Guatemala on the anti-Sandinista team.

The Wichita
Eagle-Beacon

Wichita, KS, December 10, 1985

SATURDAY night in Guatemala was election eve, as the Guatemalan people prepared to end 19 years of cruel military rule, and elect a civilian president. It also was the night the people celebrated the "Burning of the Devil," a traditional event that has its roots in the country's Mayan heritage.

The coinciding of the two events could not have been more appropriate, for the next day's election of Vinicio Cerezo Arevalo as the country's new president did indeed represent the burning of the devils of Guatemala's recent past. The Christian Democratic candidate attained a 2-1 margin over Jorge Carpio Nicolle of the relatively young National Centrist Union.

Sunday's run-off election between the top two candidates in last month's presidential balloting sets the stage for Guatemala's long-awaited return to democracy on Jan. 14. Skeptics say the transition never will occur, that even if Mr. Cerezo takes office, the military will retain its stranglehold on government. Mr. Cerezo recognizes the danger more than anyone, having survived three assassination attempts himself, and seen 300 of his Christian Democratic colleagues murdered by right-wing death squads in recent years.

He says flatly, however, that his administration will reduce the role of the military, or there will be civil war. "We want to put to rest those old ghosts," he says of the horrifying human rights image that is the legacy of five successive military regimes. "We are going to work for democracy."

Vinicio Cerezo probably has the best chance anyone ever has had to make democracy a reality in Guatemala. His stunning election margin can be a springboard to ending the repression of the past, keeping the military in its place, and addressing the causes of the country's worst depression in 50 years. The devils still will be there. But with iron determination and an unwavering faith, he can and will exorcise them from this beautiful, though tortured, land.

The State

Columbia, SC, December 17, 1985

COULD Guatemala, a nation disgraced by massive human rights violations over the years, emerge as another Argentina? Hardly, but the election to the presidency of Vinicio Cerezo holds the potential to end 31 cruel years of military-dominated rule in the turbulent Central American country.

And if Mr. Cerezo's victory holds, it would be one more solid forward step in Latin America in recent times.

But one must wonder whether the notorious Guatemalan military will balk at the new leader's promises to reform security forces and restore human rights.

Mr. Cerezo has stared Guatemalan violence in the face. The moderate Christian Democrat has survived at least three assassination attempts. Now, he vows, "We must end the process of disappearing," a problem that also plagued Argentina until it swept out the military lords and took human rights violators to court.

Mr. Cerezo, who overwhelmingly won an election that U.S. observers called free, honest and orderly, faces other enormous problems. His nation is staggered by a paralyzing foreign debt and an annual inflation rate of more than 30 percent. One party official lamented, "We are inheriting a destroyed country."

Mr. Cerezo also must confront an insurgency, one that has shrunk in intensity, and still must control a menace from the far right embodied in the military.

Mr. Cerezo, who promises no magic solutions, is looking to the North for help. He will journey to Washington next week to ask for more economic aid, which he wants with no strings attached.

The U.S. State Department has already hailed the elections as a "demonstration of faith in the democratic process that will mark the beginning of a new phase in Guatemalan history."

While Yankee fingers remain crossed for Guatemala, it stands as one of several nations in the region that have lurched toward democracy, sometimes staggering two steps forward and one backward.

Meanwhile, Sandinista Nicaragua's Marxist-tinged revolutionary menace to its neighbors has been at least stalemated, allowing Honduras, El Salvador and Costa Rica to breathe a bit easier. Costa Rica and Honduras have been able to maintain their somewhat democratic processes. Even El Salvador, although still beleaguered by leftist guerrillas, has held fairly free elections.

Despite a history of human rights abuse, a strong undercurrent of democratic sentiment runs through Central America. The U.S. should nurture this sentiment.

Mr. Cerezo deserves a fair hearing in Washington. But in the real world, aid without strings is scarcely heard of for nations with records like Guatemala's.

The British news magazine, *The Economist*, suggests, "the Americans can offer to re-equip Guatemala's army in exchange for its promise to help the new government curb the country's endemic death squads." That might be a string Mr. Cerezo could accept.

Certainly, the U.S. should actively foster the humanizing trend in Guatemala. A free, strong and even quasi-democratic Guatemala may be only a dream but even less probable dreams have bloomed into reality.

Pittsburgh Post-Gazette

Pittsburgh, PA, December 13, 1985

Hail one piece of good news from Central America, amidst the continuing bad news from El Salvador and Nicaragua.

That is the return to democracy of Guatemala with the overwhelming vote for a civilian politician, Marco Vinicio Cerezo Arevalo, 43. With 68 percent of the vote, the 42-year-old Christian Democrat polled more votes than any other candidate in Guatemalan history.

The new president is an independent-minded liberal in a nation long dominated by rightist military officers and noted for an environment of ruthless terror. Mr. Cerezo himself has survived at least three assassination attempts, all during the regime of Gen. Fernando Romeo Lucas Garcia (1978-82) when death squads claimed thousands of lives, giving Guatemala one of the worst human rights records in the hemisphere.

Significantly, the military stood aside during this presidential election, leading to hopes that they have learned the same lesson as other Latin American juntas in recent years. That lesson is that in a time of economic uncertainty and recession, the gun and the whip will not spur their own people, let alone international interests, to take the steps necessary to improve the situation.

The Salt Lake Tribune

Salt Lake City, UT, December 20, 1985

In one of his first acts as Guatemala's new president, Vinicio Cerezo has formally said he would improve relations with the United States. Doing so could materially help Guatemala, but the prospects aren't particularly bright.

There's little immediate cause for excessive elation over Guatemala's recent elections, ostensibly returning government to civilian control. Nonsoldier though he may be, the country's president faces a daunting task in trying to induce economic recovery and political respectability for his long-suffering country.

Christian Democrat Cerezo inherits conditions which threaten whatever reforms he might attempt. Factions responsible for driving this Central American nation into military dictatorship will be monitoring his every move.

Similar to most Central American countries, local control in Guatemala has shifted between the military and certain wealthy families. When one or the other wasn't dominant, the two together prevented any emergence of a truly popular, participatory form of politics. Consequently, a familiar Central American development persistently lacerates Guatemala: a virulent anti-establishment guerrilla movement.

At one point, the military-dominated government became so repressive in combatting rebel elements that Guatemala gained the distinction of being declared the world's worst human rights violator. It led to the United States refusing further arms sales to Guatemala, a situation Senor Cerezo says he intends to reverse.

Unfortunately, Senor Cerezo won only 68 percent of the vote which was, was, itself, about 65 percent of the eligible electorate. It was believed any new civilian president would need between 70 and 75 percent of a 70 percent turnout to succeed with meaningful reforms.

But some attempts at change are essential. In one of the country's deepest recessions, Guatemala suffers 50 percent inflation and 45 percent unemployment and underemployment. The Christian Democrats have said they would end private coffee growers' tendency to invest profits abroad by making the government the wholesaler of Guatemalan coffee exports. Bank nationalization and higher taxes on individual wealth have also been mentioned, not inappropriate for Third World countries having economic difficulties as severe as Guatemala's.

And while Senor Cerezo has said he would not strip the Guatemalan military of its prerogatives, his plans, if appearing too socialist, could mobilize entrenched wealth against him. He could use more U.S. aid, but without some signs of human rights improvement — which the army and its business allies could prevent — that remains questionable.

Nonetheless, Guatemala held elections largely because the country generally grew tired of instability and insecurity. Realistically, the former power structure must grant concessions to gain restored normalcy. If that proves impossible, Guatemala's slide into desperate turmoil will surely continue.

BUFFALO EVENING NEWS

Buffalo, NY, December 21, 1985

THE HEARTENING trend toward democracy throughout Latin America continues in Guatemala, where a newly elected civilian president is due to take over after 30 years of repressive military rule.

The incoming president, Vinicio Cerezo, has been the target of death squads, believed backed by the army, three times since 1980, but the Christian Democratic, reform-minded leader is expected to have a good chance of building a new democratic tradition in Guatemala. The army did not interfere in the free, orderly election.

The army does, however, remain in the background as a force to be reckoned with. The outgoing president, Gen. Oscar Mejia, who has ruled since 1983, said, somewhat ominously: "Let us hope the army never again has to participate in rescue actions because of problems in the government."

One reason the generals have stood aside is that they are conscious of the strong anti-military feeling in the country and the anti-military trend throughout Latin America. Over the past decade, right-wing generals have virtually disappeared from presidential palaces in the region. Only two remain — in Paraguay and Chile.

In view of their lack of popularity, the Guatemalan military leaders had doubts about their ability to deal with the guerrilla forces in the country and felt a popular civilian government could avert the development of another Nicaragua.

The president-elect also has a strong hand in dealing with the generals through his overwhelming 68 percent election victory and the exhilaration felt by the people in their newly found freedom. Cerezo does not, however, plan to tempt fate by bringing any military leaders to trial, as the civilian Argentine government has done.

The Reagan administration has properly requested economic and military aid for Guatemala. But the incoming president wants no assistance until after he is inaugurated in January, shrewdly preferring that such aid be handled by his government rather than the current military leadership.

The Washington Post

Washington, DC, December 19, 1985

GUATEMALA DEFIES the common image of Central America as a place where nothing important happens without an American hand. On its own—true, with a viciousness that repelled the United States—Guatemala beat down a guerrilla challenge in the 1970s. Again on its own —and with a promise that is attracting the United States now—Guatemala is putting an elected civilian government atop the country's military-run power structure. The question is how the United States ought to reengage in this dominant Central American land.

The prime requirement is to keep full solidarity with the democratic cause. President-elect Vinicio Cerezo, 42, a man of courage and vision, won a huge popular mandate, and his Christian Democratic party controls the legislature. This gives him a foundation on which, necessarily by degrees, to assert the claims of democracy and law against a military unaccustomed to acknowledging either.

Some suggest the armed forces are ready to yield their traditional privileged but demeaning role as the far right's gendarme and to become a self-respecting professional army. But it's a long way from happening. The United States can help a bit by taking its cues in these matters directly from Mr. Cerezo—in particular, by deferring all talk of military and police aid until he indicates interest. In Washington this week, he put this matter off. The United States also needs to be responsive to Guatemala's economic needs. Brazil's drought, pushing up Guatemalan coffee prices, won't be enough.

The second requirement for Washington is to subordinate its concern about Nicaragua to the American interest in a democratic Guatemala. A country whose whole modern history was bent by the American-directed coup of 1954, Guatemala has pursued neutrality in Central America's raging conflicts. Mr. Cerezo visited Managua before coming to Washington. He looks to a policy of "active neutrality," a vague concept but one that the apparent eclipse of the Contadora process may leave a little room for. Guatemala shares no border with Nicaragua, feels beyond the reach of its guerrillas, and hopes to gain both in trade and in regional standing by keeping lines open to Managua. In any event, no direct support that Guatemala might conceivably lend to U.S. policy in Nicaragua could serve Americans more than stability within Guatemala itself.

Guatemala has been a metaphor for state violence. Four hundred members of Mr. Cerezo's party have been assassinated, and yet men and women like him are still willing to put their lives on the line. His election is a moment of rare potential to a country that desperately needs democracy and peace. The United States must help him, carefully, to use it well.

Arias Elected President of Costa Rica

Oscar Arias Sanchez, leader of the ruling National Liberation Party, emerged as the winner of presidential elections held February 2, 1986 in Costa Rica. Arias, 44, who had said that he modeled himself after the late United States President John F. Kennedy, became Costa Rica's youngest president ever. With 94% of the ballots counted Feb. 3, he had won 52.4% of the vote. His nearest rival, former foreign minister and 1982 presidential candidate Rafael Angel Calderon Fournier, 36, of the Social Christian Unity Party, had won 45.7%. The winning margin was wider than expected; the day before the election the outcome had been considered too close to call.

Arias, a lawyer and economist who was educated in the U.S. and England, had been national planning minister in the 1970s. Calderon had lost to the outgoing president, Luis Alberto Monge, in the 1982 election. Calderon and Arias had campaigned on similar platforms. Each had emphasized economic recovery and the continuation of Costa Rica's traditional neutrality while at the same time supporting U.S. aid to the Nicaraguan contras fighting to overthrow the Sandinista government. Each candidate had criticized the government of the neighboring Marxist-Leninist dictatorship as threatening the peace in Central America. Costa Rica is the only country in Central America with no army, operating only with a militia. The main difference between Arias and Calderon was the latter's stronger anticommunist stance. Arias had accused Calderon of being a hawk who would drag Costa Rica into war with Nicaragua.

In his victory speech February 2, Arias said "the people have chosen bread" over rifles. He warned the estimated 3,000 Nicaraguan contras based in Costa Rica that he would not permit them to abuse the nation's hospitality, "much less put at risk our sovereignty." In addition to selecting a new president, the electorate of 1.2 million people also voted for legislative and municipal officials. Arias would begin his four-year term May 8.

ST. LOUIS POST-DISPATCH

St. Louis, MO, February 5, 1986

Central America has produced relatively recent elections in El Salvador, Honduras and Guatemala, and now in Costa Rica — but with a vast difference. Costa Ricans have chosen Oscar Arias Sanchez as their president without electoral fraud, political killings or military meddling.

Unlike all its neighbors, Costa Rica has a democratic tradition going back to 1824. Its 2.5 million inhabitants, living in an area slightly smaller than West Virginia, have in the past come closer to middle-income status than other Central Americans, basing much of their livelihood on small farms and coffee exports. Costa Rica abolished its army in 1949; once it had to borrow a cannon to give a new president a 21-gun salute.

But for two reasons Mr. Arias will step into something less than an ideal situation when he takes office May 8. He will have to deal with some public corruption that produced a scandal. Moreover, Costa Rica's economy is sluggish and the country is more than $4.4 billion in debt. Perhaps, as a trained economist, the 44-year-old Mr. Arias is equipped to deal with that.

The other problem facing Costa Rica involves its long policy of neutrality. The United States has been training the Costa Rican police in military tactics and both Mr. Arias and his election opponent harshly criticized the Sandinista government in neighboring Nicaragua. Both, however, opposed using their country as a base for the U.S.-supported Contras attacking Nicaragua, or for outright U.S. military bases. The test for Mr. Arias will be to resist pressures to involve his country in the ideological warfare in Central America.

Los Angeles Times

Los Angeles, CA, February 9, 1986

In keeping with a proud tradition that is unique in Central America, the citizens of Costa Rica peacefully elected a new president last weekend. In choosing between two candidates who both distrust the Sandinistas in neighboring Nicaragua, Costa Ricans thoughtfully opted for a man who offered a peaceful approach rather than hawkish rhetoric.

Oscar Arias Sanchez will succeed his fellow National Liberation Party member Luis Alberto Monge into San Jose's presidential palace. Arias, like Monge, has no illusions about the problems posed by Nicaragua's revolutionary government for the rest of Central America. But unlike his election opponent Rafael Angel Calderon, Arias did not promise to send Costa Rica's poorly-armed border guards in pursuit of Sandinista troops if there were more border incidents like those that have strained relations between the two nations in recent years.

More than anything else in the Costa Rican campaign, it was Calderon's hot-headed posturing against Nicaragua that convinced the electorate to support Arias in an otherwise close race between middle-of-the-road candidates. That is a hopeful indicator not just for Costa Rica, but for all of Central America. If Arias now joins Guatemala's newly-elected President Vinicio Cerezo in an effort to begin a dialogue among the new leaders of Central America's five governments—and especially if he helps Cerezo revive the stalled Contadora Group peace negotiations—the Central American crisis may yet be settled without further bloodshed or a heavy-handed and disastrous U.S. intervention.

Of course, Arias must be concerned with issues other than his country's relations with Nicaragua. Costa Rica is beset with the same domestic financial difficulties—foreign debt, rising inflation, poverty and rising unemployment—that plague other Latin American nations. But if he helps reduce the danger of a regional war in Central America, the other problems will be easier for Arias to tackle.

Houston Chronicle

Houston, TX, February 4, 1986

Several messages came out of this week's presidential election in Costa Rica, the principal one underscoring the importance of free and fair elections.

Since 1949 Costa Rica's democracy has been moving along smoothly, with free presidential elections every four years and no coups in between, giving the country one of the most stable governments in Latin America. Costa Ricans obviously value their ability to have a voice in government. Voter turnout is always good, and this time about 80 percent of the country's 1.5 million qualified voters went to the polls to elect Oscar Arias, a pro-American moderate.

The voters' overwhelming election of Arias sent a message to the Sandinistas: Arias has emphasized the threat the Sandinistas pose to Costa Rica and has vowed normal relations will not resume under the present circumstances. He also has said he will retain the 700-member Costa Rican counterterrorism force trained by the United States.

Another message is directed to those who might want to use Costa Rica as a base for operating against Nicaragua. Arias is adamant about maintaining neutrality, including restricting anti-Sandinista rebels from operating out of Costa Rica.

Such a functioning democracy must be galling to the Cubans, who find fertile ground for their borrowed ideology in troubled countries and among disillusioned people, and to the neighboring Sandinistas, whose lies and distortions are obvious when comparisons can so easily be made.

The Orlando Sentinel

Orlando, FL, February 7, 1986

Haiti's troubles drew attention from peaceful Costa Rica, where on Sunday citizens reaffirmed their commitment to democracy by electing a new president, attorney Oscar Arias.

Though he is the youngest man to be the country's chief executive, the 44-year-old Mr. Arias is highly qualified and has been prominent in national politics for 14 years.

Democracy and strong leadership in Costa Rica are particularly important now because two neighbors, Nicaragua and El Salvador, are fighting civil wars and a tradition of repression. The benefit of keeping Costa Rica stable in such a tumultuous region is clear: It exerts a moderating influence.

Mr. Arias should be accepted quickly as a man of peace. Already, Nicaraguan President Daniel Ortega has said that his country and Costa Rica have a good chance to work out their differences. Costa Rica has not dealt directly with Nicaragua since last year when two Costa Rican civil guardsmen died in a border clash.

A challenge for Mr. Arias is his country's weak economy. Costa Rica buys far more than it sells and owes foreign creditors $4.5 billion — the largest debt per capita in Latin America.

Some of these problems are being addressed in an austerity program directed by the International Monetary Fund. But the new president could do more to revive the economy by lessening dependence on agriculture.

Even in hard times, Costa Rica is the longest standing democracy in Latin America, and that's worth protecting.

Los Angeles, CA, February 4, 1986

Costa Rica, that democratic exemplar in Central America, lived up to its reputation last weekend by holding another in a string of free, peaceful presidential elections — a string that dates back to 1948. The winner this time, Oscar Arias Sanchez, and his main challenger, Rafael Angel Calderon Fournier, ran on virtually identical platforms, including pro-U.S. and anti-Sandinista planks. What set the candidates apart was history. Calderon's father was president in 1948 when civil war forced him to flee; Arias heads the party that led the revolt.

It is a testament to Costa Rican democracy that none of this provoked the kind of violence that is all too common elsewhere in a region noted for its bloody coups and ruthless dictatorships. Costa Rica is not only the U.S.' most reliable Central American ally; it is also a beacon for other emerging democracies. In Honduras, for example, voters last week chose a new president — the first time in 50 years that the country has seen a peaceful transition from one elected president to the next. And, in Guatemala, with a 40-year legacy of armed revolt and military reaction, civilians last month took back some control over their government by electing a new leader.

Meanwhile, Costa Rica is not without major problems, of course, including a growing foreign debt, a lagging domestic economy and the need to coexist, if possible, with Nicaragua's more powerful Sandinistas. The point is that, thanks to its free political system, Costa Rica has a shot at solving these problems, a point its neighbors will ignore at their peril.

Recent developments suggest that the future in Central America belongs to democracy. If so, Costa Rica and the Reagan administration deserve much of the credit. But this is no time for resting on laurels. Continued U.S. support for democratic instincts in Costa Rica and anywhere else they may appear, is crucial.

THE PLAIN DEALER

Cleveland, OH, February 10, 1986

Many Costa Ricans think they are taken for granted and even ignored by the United States. That's because Central America's longest and strongest democracy has been, since 1948, notable for its tranquility in the otherwise stormy region. Though Americans have come to expect nothing else of Costa Ricans, the nation's residents do not take their democracy for granted.

Last week, after a sometimes heated but scandal-free campaign, Costa Rica elected a new president, Oscar Arias. The 44-year-old leader will serve one four-year term. When inaugurated in May, he will face two major problems. His nation, dependent mostly on banana and coffee exports, is crippled by a $4 billion debt (minuscule when compared to Mexico's $96 billion debt, but no less troublesome to Costa Rica). He also must deal with tensions along the border with Nicaragua.

Arias will not have to worry about a coup. Unlike the leaders of the region's other nations, Arias will feel little, if any, pressure from the military in determining domestic and international policies because his country has no military, only a relatively small national guard.

Most of the Reagan administration's attention and most of U.S. Central American aid have flowed to El Salvador, to fight a leftist insurgency, and to Honduras, for assistance in upstaging the leftist government of Nicaragua. Unfortunately, Washington's policies in Central America, particularly the campaign against Nicaragua, also threaten the stability of Costa Rica.

Evidence in the last two years suggests that other Central American nations are beginning to follow Costa Rica's example. While not ignoring the legitimate problems of those nations, Washington should be working even more closely with Costa Rica to ensure that it remains a bright and stable beacon for democracy.

FORT WORTH STAR-TELEGRAM

Fort Worth, TX, February 6, 1986

The recent rise of free elections and civilian rule in Latin America — Argentina, Brazil, Uruguay and El Salvador are examples — should be recognized and applauded, but it should not obscure the achievement of Costa Rica.

Costa Rica, since 1949, has maintained a functioning multi-party democracy. Sunday's elections were the first in many years in which the party in power stayed in power, but the election of Oscar Arias of the National Liberation Party was not tinged with any hint of repression.

Costa Rica stands out for its lack of a standing army and for its democratic traditions.

Costa Rica has problems. Its foreign debt is huge. It relies heavily on U.S. economic aid.

But it has prospered nevertheless from a stable civilian government. It has the highest per capita income in Central America and the inflation rate has been reduced in four years from 100 percent to 12 percent.

If political upheaval has not been a problem, participation in the political process is one reason. Eighty percent of Costa Rica's eligible voters went to the polls Sunday. The result was a close election but one whose result was not disputed.

Costa Ricans do not go to vote amid armed guards. They go joyfully, celebrating their freedom. And they go in great numbers. They care about democracy.

That is as it should be, everywhere.

Viva, Costa Rica.

THE CHRISTIAN SCIENCE MONITOR
Boston, MA, February 4, 1986

OSCAR Arias has been declared the winner, according to preliminary figures, in Costa Rica's presidential elections.

But whichever of the two front-runners — Mr. Arias or former Foreign Minister Rafael Calderon Jr. — had won, the most important thing is that this small country continues to demonstrate that democracy can flourish in Central America. A record turnout was reported, and the margin of victory decisive, 53.3 percent to 44.8 percent. Another sign of the sturdiness of democracy there is that Costa Rica has had no compunction about voting out the ruling party over the years. Although Mr. Arias, like current President Luis Alberto Monge, is a member of the National Liberation Party, he is the youngest chief executive ever in Costa Rica and represents a break with his party's old guard.

Costa Rica has its troubles, notably getting along with its Sandinista neighbors in Nicaragua and paying off its foreign debt. Mr. Arias has some way to go toward articulating solutions to these problems.

But at a time when democracy can seem so fragile in Latin America, it is heartening to see signs of a healthy political process.

The Houston Post
Houston, TX, February 7, 1986

That nation is a shining contrast in a sea of revolution, violence and tyranny. Costa Rica has proven it once more, with its recent presidential election which saw Oscar Arias Sanchez win with about 53 percent of the vote. A campaign vow was to keep his country out of Central American conflicts.

Arias was a candidate of the governing National Liberation Party; President Luis Alberto Monge could not succeed himself. Ruling party success is common in Central America, but in Costa Rica it was only the second time in half a century this had occurred.

Arias, a London-educated economist, defeated Rafael A. Calderon Fournier, a lawyer and the more conservative of the two. "The people gave their verdict, and I respect it as a citizen who loves his country," Calderon said in a concession statement. Such talk isn't uncommon in Central America after elections are held, but there is every indication Calderon really meant it.

Costa Rica has some problems — economic difficulties and a $4.5 billion foreign debt, and there is a growing distrust of officials because of recent corruption scandals. But it is the only established democracy in Central America, and its people are the region's best educated and most affluent. This is, all in all, a success story, an example we can wish others in Central America might emulate.

The State
Columbia, SC, February 9, 1986

COSTA Rica, the small Central American nation which, contrary to its raucous neighbors, has built a tradition of democracy and relative stability, has pulled off another peaceful election.

The winner for president is British-educated economist Oscar Arias Sanchez, whose National Liberation Party has long dominated the nation's politics.

Mr. Arias was less hawkish toward his threatening neighbor, Marxist Nicaragua, than his main opponent, Rafael Calderon of the centrist Social Christian Unity Party. He approves of the Reagan administration funding of Contra rebels fighting the Sandinista Nicaraguan government "only if it is used as an instrument of pressure to make the Sandinistas sit down and negotiate."

But Costa Rica remains a reassuring ally of the United States. It also remains a comforting reminder that democracy can work in Central America. It certainly deserves Uncle Sam's continued support.

The Seattle Times
Seattle, WA, February 4, 1986

WHILE pro- and anti-government violence rages around the Third World from Uganda to Haiti to the Philippines, the tiny Central American state of Costa Rica has yet again staged a model presidential election.

Peace and order prevailed as usual when Costa Ricans elected one moderate over another, displaying no interest in the extremes of right or left. Democracy is taking shaky hold throughout much of Latin America. It long has been rooted in Central America's smallest country.

As a matter of deeply ingrained heritage, most Latin Americans prefer not to look to the United States as a model. They need not. Tiny Costa Rica, in their very midst, provides example enough in the processes of peaceable self-government.

Times-Colonist
Victoria, B.C., February 10, 1986

In 1948, Jose (Pepe) Figueres, a Costa Rican farmer-philosopher, stunned Latin America.

The story started the year before, when the government of the day annulled an election it had just lost. Figueres raised an army and defeated the government forces.

He governed provisionally for a time. Then, after disbanding the army he'd led and the army he'd defeated, Figueres turned power over to the winner of the annulled election.

In the years since, Costa Rica has thrived as a genuine democracy.

At age 79, Don Pepe's insights are still illuminating. Consider his comments on the U.S. role in Nicaragua.

"I've always been pro-U.S.," he said. "But at the moment, the Americans are doing one wrong thing and one right thing in Latin America.

"The wrong thing is intervening in Nicaragua. The right thing is backing elected regimes in Latin America.

"The worst danger to peace in Central America is a lack of respect for those who want to be Marxists. I don't think the Nicaraguans should be Marxists at all, but they're not a threat to anyone. I have tremendous faith in democracy — I think it's strong enough to compete."

If only President Reagan had the same faith.

The Birmingham News
Birmingham, AL, February 8, 1986

The oldest democracy in Central America went peacefully through the process of choosing a president again last Sunday. Once more, Costa Rica demonstrated the strength of its form of government, which is enduring without an army in that volatile region.

Attorney Oscar Arias, who won the presidential election convincingly over five opponents, has plenty of problems, including strained relations with the Marxist government of neighboring Nicaragua and a massive foreign debt.

Arias, a pro-American moderate, has pledged to continue his nation's policy of unarmed neutrality. "We already chose bread over rifles in 1948 when we abolished the army," he told *The New York Times* shortly before his victory.

He also has said he will not deal directly with the government of Nicaragua until it apologizes for a border incident last year in which two members of the Costa Rican civil guard, the nation's security force, were killed. That policy was set by President Luis Alberto Monge, Aria's predecessor and a member of the same National Liberation Party.

At the same time, Arias has said that although there is "some justification" for U.S. aid to anti-Sandinista guerrillas, they should not be allowed to operate on Costa Rican soil.

It is a difficult path that Costa Rica has chosen, existing without an army next to a well-armed dictatorship, insisting upon neutrality in an extremely polarized region and clinging to democractic institutions all the while. We should, as a nation, respect and support this peaceful partner in democracy.

Los Angeles Times

Los Angeles, CA, November 19, 1986

One of the things that frustrates Latin Americans when they deal with the United States is the unfortunate habit that many North Americans have of defining regional issues as they want to see them, rather than trying to comprehend them from the Latin perspective.

A classic case in point was a speech made before the U.N. General Assembly by Oscar Arias Sanchez, the president of Costa Rica, which has been seized on by the Reagan Administration to justify its obsessive crusade against Nicaragua's Sandinista government. In his speech Arias accused the Sandinistas of betraying the popular revolution that overthrew the U.S.-backed Somoza dictatorship in 1979. He argued that the Sandinistas bear part of the blame for the crisis in Central America, because by aligning their new government with the Soviet Bloc they created an East-West confrontation where none had existed before.

To hear U.S. officials like Secretary of State George P. Shultz talk about Arias' speech, one would think that the Costa Rican president had volunteered to lead the U.S. Marines into Managua. In fact, he showed no enthusiasm at all for efforts to overthrow the Sandinistas. Arias said flatly that he would not allow his nation's territory to be used by any armed group fighting a neighboring state—a clear reference to the *contra* rebels funded by President Reagan to overthrow the Sandinistas. Arias also said that the Contadora peace process is not dead, and that he would support a peaceful resolution to the Central American crisis "so long as there is one thread of hope."

That sounds a great deal like what most other thoughtful Latin Americans are saying these days about Nicaragua and Central America. They have no illusions about the Sandinistas, but they also have no illusions about the overbearing Colossus of the North. While they want Nicaragua to have true freedom and democracy, they know that the contras can't deliver those things any more than the Marines did during all the U.S. military interventions in Nicaragua during the 1920s and '30s. That is why every major democracy in Latin America supports the Contadora Group and has repeatedly urged Reagan to give up his war against tiny Nicaragua.

A more recent example of this was last week's debate on the crisis in Central America at the meeting of the Organization of American States in Guatemala City. Some very harsh, and valid, criticisms were leveled there against the Sandinistas. But no one was willing to align himself with Reagan's bloody strategy. The OAS resolutions on Central America called for democracy in the region—a slap at the the totalitarian Marxist state that the Sandinistas are trying to build. But they also called on the Contadora countries (Mexico, Venezuela, Colombia and Panama) to continue their patient effort to negotiate peace in the region—a slap at the United States.

Unfortunately, it is likely that the Reagan Administration will again focus single-mindedly on the implied criticism of Nicaragua and ignore the implied criticism of the United States. But that is par for the course in Washington. Whenever Reagan, Shultz or any other representative of the Administration hears criticism of the misguided policy in Central America, such as that offered in official state visits by Argentine President Raul Alfonsin and Mexican President Miguel de la Madrid, it is blithely ignored. But let any Latin American even whisper something negative about Nicaragua, and it is almost gleefully seized on as evidence that, deep in their hearts, our little Latin brothers want us to squash those bullies in Managua. What arrogance! What ignorance!

The Boston Globe

Boston, MA, November 10, 1986

Anyone concerned about US policy in Central America – especially members of Congress – ought to be on the alert between now and mid-February when the new Congress will swing into gear. Their attention should now focus on Costa Rica.

The Reagan administration's aim is to broaden the war against Nicaragua and deflect the possibility of a peaceful Contadora settlement. The long recess while members of Congress are out of town provides an opening to further tangle the region and perhaps put Contadora lastingly out of reach.

Costa Rica is under intensifying pressure from the administration to abandon its long-standing neutrality. This small, democratic but economically weak nation disbanded its armed forces three decades ago and is proud of it. Many Costa Ricans were dumbfounded several years ago when Jeane Kirkpatrick visited San Jose and urged them to remilitarize.

That turned out to be only the warning shot in the administration's effort to make Costa Rica become more "Central American": more pliant, more military and more under the thumb of the State Department and the Pentagon. The problem is now acute because the administration is trying to expand the attack on Nicaragua to include a "southern front" before Congress returns and is asked to vote more contra aid.

To do that requires building bases, airstrips and staging areas for the contras on Honduran soil, but most of all it means leaning hard on President Oscar Arias.

Last spring in Central America a US diplomat said: "There is a great irony in this administration's newfound love for democracy. Sometimes it turns out to be center-left democracy, and then the hidden bill is that all of these guys are jumping ship on Nicaragua."

Arias has made a consistent effort for even relations with Nicaragua by closing contra camps, jailing contra leaders and exploring the establishment of a Contadora-backed border commission. That kind of statesmanship is what the administration would like to torpedo, along with Contadora.

Pressured by a right-wing domestic press, as well as by administration emissaries who swoop through San Jose, Arias is vulnerable because his country depends on US aid.

The covert project to "Central Americanize" Costa Rica is particularly grotesque. Over the next three months, Americans who disagree with the administration's plan for a larger war in Central America must help Arias resist this role.

DESERET NEWS

Salt Lake City, UT, March 24-25, 1986

Though the U.S. is used to teaching other nations about democracy, there are times when the tutor can learn from the pupil.

As a case in point, take Costa Rica, which almost invariably manages to get high percentages of its voters to the polls in sharp and embarrassing contrast to the chronically low election turnouts in the U.S.

The reason for the difference? Possibly the fact that while young Americans often learn from their elders to treat politics cynically, young Costa Ricans are taught to take voting seriously.

Here's how. It's the custom in Costa Rica for parents to take their children with them to vote. While the parents cast the real ballots, the children also vote as a learning exercise.

But that's not all, as Executive Editor Max Jennings of The Mesa, Ariz. Tribune discovered during a trip to Costa Rica a couple of weeks ago right on the heels of elections there. Even though it has no official status, the vote of the children is tallied and reported.

The practice is bound to have some effect on elected officials in Costa Rica. More important, making voting a family experience can't help but teach these youngsters the importance of going to the polls when they grow up.

In the U.S., many schools encourage their students to participate in mock elections on election day. But the practice isn't universal and doesn't involve family participation the way it does in Costa Rica.

Americans need not wait for Congress to act before starting something similar here. Individual states could act on their own. Utah, with its customarily high turnouts in presidential elections but unenviable record in other vote contests, could appropriately lead the way. The costs involved shouldn't be excessive, particularly where voting is done with electronic machinery. But imagine the long-range benefits of teaching young Americans the importance of exercising their rights at the polls.

U.S. Drug Criticism Opens Riff; Charges Against Mexico Disputed

United States federal officials May 13, 1986 offered harsh public criticism of Mexico and its handling of drug trafficking, illegal immigration, government corruption and the ailing economy. The comments, made in hearings before a Senate subcommittee, angered Mexican officials, and the government issued a formal note of protest May 14. U.S. Attorney General Edwin Meese 3rd apologized May 22, but tensions between the two countries remained high as the officials who testified at the hearings stood by their remarks. Mexico was currently reported to be the major conduit for marijuana and heroin in the U.S., having taken over in 1985 from Colombia and Asia, respectively, as the leading suppliers of those drugs. Mexico was also said to supply some 30% of all the cocaine entering the U.S. The hearings began with with a closed session May 12, followed by the unusual public session the following day. The hearings before the Senate Foreign Relations Committee's subcommittee on Western Hemisphere affairs were called by the panel's chairman, Sen. Jesse Helms (R, N.C.), to discuss U.S.-Mexico relations. Mexico had apparently pressured Helms to cancel the hearings on the grounds that they would interfere with its sovereignty.

In the May 13 session, U.S. Customs Service Commissioner William von Raab, speaking of the drug trade in Mexico, contended that there was "massive" corruption by Mexican officials and "ingrained corruption in the Mexican law enforcement establishment up and down the ladder." He further charged that the governor of Sonora state, whom he did not mention by name, owned four ranches that produced marijuana and opium. He said the ranches were protected by the Mexican Judicial Police. The commissioner's charges against the Sonora governor, who von Raab aides later identified as Rodolfo Felix Valdes, were immediately challenged. Valdes denied the charges against him and threatened a lawsuit against von Raab.

In a related development, the *New York Times* May 25 quoted one senior U.S. administration official as saying that assessments of Mexico's situation by the Central Intelligence Agency showed that if present trends were not reversed, political instability and widespread violence could result.

FORT WORTH STAR-TELEGRAM

Fort Worth, TX, May 19, 1986

Mexico's angry reaction to accusations by American officials of widespread corruption in high places within the Mexican government is not really surprising. It's a shame, though, that the anger is being vented in the wrong direction.

A Mexican government statement had this to say in response to charges before a U.S. congressional committee that drug smuggling along the Texas-Mexico border is aided by massive corruption in Mexico:

"Mexico categorically rejects the accusations and slander that were issued against our country. The government of Mexico expresses its repudiation for the series of declarations of an interventionist nature that were produced in those audiences and that attack the sovereignty and interests of Mexico."

Rubbish.

Nobody testifying before a Senate foreign relations subcommittee was attacking Mexico's sovereignty. And the only interests being assailed by the witnesses were those of the misery merchants whose drug-smuggling activities along the U.S.-Mexican border have reached epidemic proportions.

Mexico has every right to be angry — but not at the Americans who told the subcommittee horror stories about high-ranking Mexican officials and military officers being paid for their help by drug dealers. The anger should be directed at those who commit the crimes, not those who report them.

The Mexican statement labeled those who testified as "minor U.S. officials" and said their statements "do not conform to reality."

More rubbish.

Among those testifying were Elliott Abrams, assistant secretary of state for inter-American affairs, and U.S. Customs Commissioner William Von Raab. They are hardly "minor" officials. And, unfortunately, what they told the committee conforms only too closely to reality.

Abrams told the senators that "fully a third" of the cocaine consumed in the United States in 1985 may have entered this country through Mexico. An official of the Drug Enforcement Administration said Mexico supplied about 32 percent of the heroin available in this country in 1984 and 38 percent in the first nine months of 1985.

Seizures of marijuana along the border have increased from 27 metric tons in 1983 to 78 metric tons in 1985.

Those alarming figures aren't something those reliable government spokesmen plucked from thin air in some kind of conspiracy to damage Mexico's reputation. They represent the cold, hard statistics of a drug war this country is losing. We need much more help from Mexico in fighting that war, and some Mexican officials apparently are not only not doing anything to help but are instead doing things that actively hurt.

That's what should anger the Mexican government, not the fact that Americans are telling the rest of the world about it.

BUFFALO EVENING NEWS

Buffalo, NY, May 25, 1986

FRUSTRATED BY the increasing flow of narcotics into this country from Latin America, American officials have lashed out at Mexico with strong public criticism at a hearing before a Senate subcommittee.

While the frank criticism drew a sharp protest from Mexican officials, it seems justified and may prompt the Mexican government to redouble its efforts to stamp out the traffic in heroin, cocaine and marijuana.

Much of the problem lies with corruption among both Mexican officials and the workers who spray herbicides over the narcotics crops. Americans were afforded a glimpse into the sordid world of drugs a year ago with the brutal kidnapping and murder of a U.S. drug-enforcement agent and a Mexican pilot in Guadalajara, Mexico.

A key suspect in the case escaped — apparently with the help of some Mexican police — just as other Mexican police were closing in on him.

In the most dramatic revelations at the recent Senate hearing, the head of the U.S. Customs Service accused the governor of one Mexican state of growing marijuana and opium on his own farm, guarded by the Mexican army.

Angered by this unusual frankness of U.S. officials, Mexico cited its considerable efforts to cooperate with the U.S. program against narcotics. It pointed out that a major part of the problem is the high demand for the narcotics in the American market. This is unfortunately true.

The huge amounts of money involved in the drug trade create serious temptations for all connected with narcotics. A Mexican pilot, hired to spray herbicides over marijuana or poppy fields, can make a year's pay simply by missing a field here and there. Law-enforcement officials may be similarly tempted to look the other way. But this only underlines the need for Mexico to crack down on corruption.

There is no simple solution to this many-faceted evil. Besides assisting foreign nations in eradicating narcotics crops, the United States is seeking to penetrate the infrastructure of the international drug network. It is also trying to improve law enforcement in this country to stem the deadly drug flow.

While there remains a lucrative market for the drugs, the flow will continue to some extent, and some foreign nations see the problem as an American one, caused by the big demand for drugs in the United States. But to be effective, the drug war must be fought, not only in the United States, but on many fronts abroad.

The harsh criticism of Mexico, while it may cause some resentment, indicates to Mexican officials how seriously the rise in drug smuggling from that country is viewed by the United States. It should spur new joint efforts to curtail it.

THE SACRAMENTO BEE

Sacramento, CA, May 24, 1986

For all the increased awareness in this country of Mexico and how its problems affect the United States, the Reagan administration's handling of bilateral relations often suggests both a lack of understanding of our southern neighbor and a lack of coherence in developing U.S. policy. A vivid illustration is the recent public criticism by U.S. officials of their Mexican counterparts for failing to get control of the massive flow of illicit drugs across our southern border.

It's hard to fault the criticism itself. U.S. agencies have abundant evidence of official corruption in Mexico. But the manner and the tone of the most recent verbal barrage, at open hearings before a Senate subcommittee, is scarcely likely to help matters. Customs Commissioner William von Raab's charge of Mexican official corruption at all levels was so harsh and unqualified that Alan Nelson, commissioner of the Immigration and Naturalization Service, publicly rebuked von Raab for "excess rhetoric."

Von Raab's broadside was also puzzling, because it seemed at odds with accounts of recent meetings between Attorney General Edwin Meese and his Mexican counterpart, at which Mexico agreed to greater cooperation in sharing intelligence information and in jointly verifying the destruction of marijuana and poppy crops. One explanation of this apparent contradiction is that Mexican officials continue to make promises but are either unwilling, because they themselves are being bribed, or unable, because they have no control over corruption at lower levels, to deliver on those promises.

Even if that's true, however, the bitter U.S. attack seems to have been launched with little consideration of how its impact will affect overall bilateral relations. Mexico's economic condition is so perilous — drastically reduced revenues due to lower oil prices, a foreign debt approaching $100 billion and massive unemployment that increases the flow of jobless Mexicans to this country — that the potential for worsening relations is considerable. Perhaps worst in the long run, it may contribute to weakening a political system that, for all its corruption, has been stable for more than half a century.

By all means, the administration should keep up the pressure on Mexico to clean up its drug-enforcement act. But to do so in such intemperate terms, and to fail to develop any clear U.S. strategy for helping Mexico deal with the economic crisis that hurts both countries, is irresponsible and self-defeating.

The Times-Picayune
The States-Item

New Orleans, LA, May 20, 1986

Demand and supply, those two ancient cornerstones of economics, are at the heart of the debate over the illegal drug trade these days. Without a doubt, both those who generate the demand for illegal drugs and those who supply them are equally to blame for international crime, immense social problems and even political tensions between nations.

When U.S. officials, testifying before a U.S. congressional committee, recently accused Mexican officials of being corrupted by the illegal drug traffic, the Mexican government reacted angrily. The Mexican drug problem would not be so great, they retorted, if demand for what the drug runners supply was not so high in the United States.

They had a point. It is one that the White House has come to accept, and it is one that the American people must acknowledge if the long and costly campaign against illegal drugs is ever to succeed.

Figuring that the best hope of cooling the demand for drugs is to start at the bottom, White House officials are planning a new drug-education program for 57 million school-age youngsters.

They do not have to look far to see the roots of the problem. Less than two miles from the White House drug pushers sell cocaine, heroin and other drugs to teenagers from the suburbs.

"It goes on 24 hours a day," Jack Kleppinger, an agent of the Drug Enforcement Administration, says. "On weekend evenings, there'll be hundreds of teen-agers here on dope-buying sprees."

Similar tragedies are to be found all over the nation.

Despite decades of anti-drug efforts by police agencies, the use of illegal drugs in American society has risen and drug trafficking has increased.

Realizing that law enforcement cannot begin to do the job alone, the Reagan administration has taken aim at the demand side of the problem. It hopes to enlist school administrators and educators in a nationwide effort to educate youngsters to the perils of illegal drugs.

"We've got to create a society where drugs are not acceptable," says Attorney General Edwin Meese. "Enforcement is important, but the demand side is equally important. To the extent that you can take away the customer, you're diminishing the profit."

The "demand side" anti-drug campaign is scheduled to get under way in full force when schools reopen this fall. It will utilize the resources of the U.S. Departments of Education and Health and Human Services, the Drug Enforcement Administration and U.S. attorneys' offices.

It also should have the support of all school officials, parents, civic and religious leaders, athletes, entertainers and all others who have important influences on the nation's youth.

Take away the market for illegal drugs and the supply will soon wither.

The Dallas Morning News

Dallas, TX, May 21, 1986

Along the Texas border, in more than 250 "twin" plants (*maquiladoras*), 120,000 Mexican citizens produce goods for American companies. More than 10,000 U.S. citizens commute to Mexico to work in the plants.

The beauty of the twin-plant approach is that it encourages investment along the border by giving employers access to less expensive labor in Mexico, discourages illegal immigration to Texas by creating jobs within Mexico and creates jobs for Texans living in border areas as well.

But, as Lt. Gov. Hobby points out, the use of twin plants in Texas is insufficient compared to areas such as Miami where more than 35,000 workers are employed in Florida and an additional 500,000 in the Caribbean.

Hobby says Texas needs aggressive marketing, not only to encourage more *maquiladora* operations on the border, but to push the use of industrial parks and trade zones farther into the interior of Mexico.

Rather than seek less expensive labor in Asian countries, it makes more sense for American companies to produce their goods closer to home in Mexico. That would help stabilize the Mexican economy and reduce the immigration pressures on Texas — which is certainly making a day's work pay off in more ways than one.

The Washington Times

Washington, DC, May 19, 1986

The way the Mexican government is howling you know a sensitive nerve has been hit. Last week the Senate Foreign Relations subcommittee on Western Hemisphere affairs did just that. It dropped the diplomatic niceties and let Mexico have it right in the chops about its role in the drug trade and the corruption that affects nearly every level of government south of the border.

We're talking world-class corruption here, not the usual payoffs to cops and political grafters. U.S. Commissioner of Customs William von Raab told the panel that one of the chief obstacles to drug enforcement is the "ingrained corruption in the Mexican law enforcement establishment" — a diplomatic way of saying everyone from the local *perro* catcher to state governors is on the pad.

Speaking of governors, what was Miguel Felix Gallardo, a fugitive drug trafficker wanted in connection with the murder of a U.S. drug agent, doing as a house guest of Antonio Toledo Corro, governor of Sinaloa state? More to the point, what does Mr. Corro do with the four posh ranches he owns? According to Mr. von Raab, the governor's ranches "are believed to grow opium and marijuana" — all under the protection of the Mexican Federal Judicial Police, of course.

The plaintive cries of Mexican officials in Washington — that the subcommittee's probe is "interventionist," "libelous," and designed "to fracture relations" — are so much *frijoles*. Talk about interventionism. What about the attempt by Mexico City to pressure Sen. Jesse Helms, the subcommittee chairman, into canceling the hearings? If anything threatens relations between the United States and Mexico, it is the raging drug trade, now out of control, and Mexico's porous borders. As Mr. von Raab put it, "There's no way to secure an 1,800-mile border. You have to be able to rely on the integrity of your neighbors."

Exactly. Without that integrity there might as well be no war on drugs. A lot of Mexican police officers have paid with their lives, some in unspeakable ways, to enforce Mexico's anti-drug laws, and it dishonors their memory, among other things, for high Mexican officials to collaborate with the criminals who murdered them.

DESERET NEWS

*Salt Lake City, UT,
May 19-20, 1986*

Venality plays a major role in drug trafficking — a fact that becomes devastatingly more clear with evidence of huge sums of money paid to get drugs into the lucrative U.S. market.

Latest evidence came last week from Customs Commissioner William von Rabb in testimony before Congress. Corruption among Mexican law officials, he said, is so massive that Mexico has become "the major source" for heroin and marijuana reaching the U.S.

In addition, said Von Rabb, there's increasing evidence that drug dealers from Colombia are extending their operations into Mexico. The U.S.-Mexican border has become a sieve for drugs.

What to do? One recent proposal is to use Army National Guard and Air National Guard troops from several states to augment the present border patrol. The troops would use their own planes, helicopters, and radar as part of the effort.

Such use of military forces in civilian missions is unprecedented, and raises some thorny questions. One is the prohibition against the use of military troops in making civilian arrests. Those backing the proposal say National Guard troops would be used only for "detection and mobility" while leaving the actual arrests to others.

Another difficulty concerns training. Guardsmen are on active duty for only 15 days a year, and when they're federalized. If they're on narcotics patrol, when will they train for their regular military mission? And won't such short terms of duty mean excessive expenses and troop movements, as well as compromising the quality of U.S. drug enforcement?

Granted, the drug problem is becoming so serious that extraordinary measures are needed. But the U.S. needs to take a long, hard look at all the problems before using National Guard units in such an effort.

Los Angeles Times

Los Angeles, CA, May 20, 1986

There he goes again. Harold Ezell, Western regional commissioner of the Immigration and Naturalization Service, was on location this time, helping Los Angeles Supervisor Mike Antonovich to film a television commercial for his U.S. Senate Republican primary campaign against the background of the Mexican-U.S. border that is policed by Ezell's forces.

Ezell perceived no wrong in his personal role facilitating the filming. He praised the candidate for sharing his view that the nation is menaced by the flow of undocumented aliens from Mexico, and said that he would welcome any candidate to a first-hand view of the problem. As usual, the commissioner betrayed problems in distinguishing right from wrong behavior for a government employee like himself. Of course the immigration service should cooperate with anyone wanting a better understanding of the illegal-immigration problem. But, clearly, immigration should have no role in a partisan political campaign. The event brought to mind another of his unprofessional actions—his recent intervention in inspiring and helping to organize a citizen group, the Americans for Border Control, to support his service.

The Most Rev. Roger Mahony, Roman Catholic archbishop of Los Angeles, went to the heart of the matter in a letter to The Times questioning the exploitation of the border situation for a partisan political piece of propaganda. He called on Antonovich to apologize to the Mexican-American community and to cancel the airing of the commercial. The archbishop was right.

There are serious border problems that, as the archbishop emphasized, need to be addressed. But they will only be complicated by those seeking to convert the complexities into simplistic campaign posturings. The border problems will be controlled only by an immigration service that is professional and that is led by professionals, faithful to the highest standards of law enforcement and to the ethics of public service.

The Kansas City Times

Kansas City, MO, May 29, 1986

One of the most amazing things about the latest tensions between the United States and Mexico is that the White House and the offices of State, Customs and Immigration have all managed to do to the Mexicans what outgoing Ambassador John Gavin could do alone. They infuriated them.

Truths about increased drug trafficking and how corruption in Mexico's government contributes to the problem are irrelevant. Shrewd diplomacy is, and always must be, the key to this border ally. Most ambassadors, including brash Mr. Gavin on rare occasions in his five years of service, know this.

How ironic, then, that the soothing should come from U.S. Attorney General Ed Meese, head of the department which oversees Mexico-bashers like the Immigration and Naturalization Service and Drug Enforcement Administration. Mexico certainly deserves to be blasted about lax enforcement of drug trafficking and illegal immigration. They are serious problems and legitimate concerns of the United States.

But the U.S. must not stare down at Mexico with the public righteous indignation which has arisen of late. Poor Mexico is a supplier nation. We in the U.S., with an abundance of disposable income and demands, are the users, both of narcotics and cheap Latin American labor. Each is a crime in its own right. Both nations have crooked law enforcers.

The U.S. and Mexico must quickly work together to solve these and other problems. They certainly are not new. But they will never be solved so long as President Reagan does not name a replacement to Mr. Gavin, who has left Mexico, and this nation continues to send mixed signals to the Mexicans. This irrational screaming across the border must stop. Even Ed Meese, of all people, agrees.

San Francisco Chronicle

San Francisco, CA, May 19, 1986

RELATIONS BETWEEN the United States and Mexico, sinking to a level of acerbity, can best be bettered when the Mexican government improves its handling of illegal immigration, drug trafficking and the country's sorry economy.

These sore points were made by U. S. officials before a Senate subcommittee. Customs Service Commissioner William von Raab charged that the governor of one Mexican state grew marijuana and opium poppies with the Mexican army as guard. Roger P. Brandemuehl, head of the U. S. Border Patrol, estimated 1.8 million illegal aliens from Mexico will enter the United States this year, a 50 percent increase over last year. Elliot Abrams, assistant secretary of state for Latin American affairs, expressed concern over Mexico's economic problems, including a $99 billion foreign debt.

Mexico responded with a categorical denial and lodged a rare and formal protest with the State Department, a departure from Mexico's normal manner of handling disputes unobtrusively through diplomatic channels.

IT IS TO THE BEST interests of the United States to share its southern border with a robust, productive and thriving neighbor that is free of widespread corruption and is embarked on major economic reform. The ultimate stability of Mexico is dependent upon the earnest efforts of Mexico itself.

The Birmingham News

Birmingham, AL, May 16, 1986

Mexico's angry reaction to testimony before the Senate Foreign Relations Committee was predictable. In that testimony, William von Raab, U.S. Customs Service Commissioner, laid the blame for increased importation of illegal drugs squarely on corruption throughout the Mexican law enforcement system.

The Mexican government denounced the testimony as slanderous and an attack on Mexico's sovereignty.

Not only is corruption present, von Raab said, "in one word, corruption is massive." Those who testified were careful to suggest that the corruption was mainly among the lower echelons of law enforcement in a vain attempt to avoid exciting high government officials. Mexico's reaction leads one to conclude that its top officials are either powerless to stop the corruption, are indifferent to it or even sympathetic toward it.

To be candid, corruption is endemic to the Mexican socialist system and has been for much of this century. Taxes are only a down payment for government services: For a specific service, a bribe or a tribute must be paid and, in many instances, to officials up the chain of command.

The United States has labored long and hard with only partial success to persuade Mexican officials to go after the illegal drug cartel. It has been a losing game. Now increasing evidence indicates Colombian drug dealers have extended their activity into Mexico. U.S. officials also complain of increasing production of marijuana and heroin in Mexico itself.

Only through official corruption on a wide scale could the flow of drugs increase in the proportions now evident. For the United States to tell the truth is no libel or slander. Neither is it interference with Mexico's sovereignty.

Since efforts for joint action against the drug cartel are no longer effective, the only responsible course Washington can take is to open the books for the world to see in the hope that national pride will induce the Mexican government to shut down its own drug industry, as well as close the valves on the drug pipeline from Colombia.

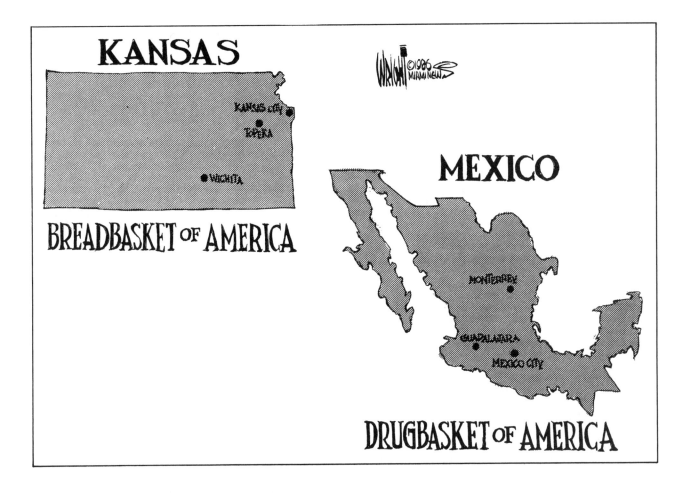

Contadora Talks Collapse; Latins Oppose Contra Aid

Efforts to revive the peace negotiations sponsored by the Contadora Group foundered April 5-7, 1986 over Nicaragua's insistence that the United States cease supporting anti-Sandinista contras before it would sign a Central American peace plan accord. After three days of talks in Panama between foreign ministers of the Contadora Group, its support group and five Central American nations, the meeting broke up in disfavor.

Three U.S. allies in Central America—Costa Rica, Honduras, and El Salvador—maintained that a Nicaraguan demand for a halt to U.S. support for the contras fell outside the Contadora framework. At the end of the current meeting, Costa Rica, El Salvador and Honduras signed a communique, the "Panama Commitment," vowing negotiations leading to the signing of the Contadora draft treaty by June 6, 1986. Nicaragua refused to sign the communique. In an apparent appeal to Nicaragua, the Contadora nations—Mexico, Venezuela, Panama and Colombia—and their support group—Argentina, Peru, Uruguay and Brazil—issued a separate draft communique. It called on the five attending Latin American nations to say within eight days whether they were willing to immediately resume negotiations on treaty issues that remained unresolved.

Three U.S. congressmen who met with diplomats involved in the Contadora talks said in Panama April 6 that the Contadora foreign ministers all said they opposed U.S. aid to the contras. The congressmen were Reps. Michael Barnes (D, Md.), James Slattery (D, Kan.) and William Richardson (D, N.M.). Barnes said the foreign ministers were "unanimous" and "strong" in their opposition to U.S. aid for the contras.

THE ATLANTA CONSTITUTION
Atlanta, GA, April 11, 1986

Quick, somebody check the pulse of the Contadora peace process. Its breathing is labored; its pallor is alarming; its best friends are dusting off their mourning clothes. If not yet a candidate for the morgue, it desperately needs to be rolled into intensive-care.

A fragile creature from its inception three years ago, Contadora has been gasping ever since — only partly attributable to the minor failings of its Latin parents. What it required to thrive was sincere cooperation and nurturing from the major players in the Central American conflict, the United States and Nicaragua. What it received instead was lip-service, neglect and, earlier this week, a jolting stiff-arm from the Sandinistas.

Nicaragua's Foreign Minister Miguel d'Escoto stuck by his country's seven-month-long insistence it would not sign any peace accord so long as it was under attack by U.S.-backed rebels. That's an odd tack for Managua to take now, considering (a) that it has strengthened its bargaining hand by all but stifling the contras' guerrilla operations and (b) that by thwarting the peace process it makes it easier for the Reagan administration to whip up support for providing the contras with military supplies and training.

Well, just because Sandinista strategists stubbornly insist on not making sense is no excuse for Washington to do likewise — but, alas, it is poised to do just that. Pointing an accusing finger at Managua for sabotage of Contadora and for a murky incursion into Honduras, the White House has put increasing pressure on the U.S. House to reverse its month-old rejection of guns for the contras.

The point to bear in mind is this: The only way the United States, on its own, can achieve President Reagan's goal — the removal of the Sandinista government — is through force of American arms; his surrogates, the contras, can't do it for him. However, neither recourse to the military option is the slightest bit acceptable to America's Latin allies, even though the great majority of them are no admirers of the Sandinistas.

Without resort to drastic action, the rest of the hemisphere may have to put up with *Sandinismo* in Nicaragua for the duration, but it doesn't have to tolerate its spread elsewhere. The way to proof Nicaragua's neighbors against subversion and bullying is through full U.S. support for the objectives of Contadora and careful attention to those nations' needs, economic *and* military.

That's why it's essential that U.S. House members hold the line against new arms assistance to the contras or, failing that, that they so condition the aid that the president is required to try his hand at negotiation before manipulating puppet soldiers.

THE RICHMOND NEWS LEADER
Richmond, VA,
April 15, 1986

Sometimes you almost want to pity the congressional opponents of U.S. aid to the Contras. Sometimes you do. Just think of how embarrassed those poor dears must feel. The real world just refuses to co-operate with them. Their buddy Danny Ortega always lets them down.

Last year they disputed the administration's contention that Nicaragua looks to the Kremlin for guidance. The House voted against Contra aid. Danny immediately boarded a jet and flew to Moscow.

Late last month, the House again voted against Contra aid, this time saying that the Sandinistas deserved time to demonstrate a commitment to "pluralism." Danny immediately invaded Honduras.

Throughout the protracted Contra debate, the administration's critics have said the U.S. should rely on the so-called Contadora talks as a means to bring "peace" to Central America. The Contadora group includes several Latin American countries. It tried to negotiate a settlement to Nicaragua's problems.

It failed. The other day the talks collapsed. The participants blamed Nicaragua. "Nicaragua rejected everything, everything that was presented to it," explained a Contadora spokesman. "There is nothing left to talk about."

The Contadora collapse came as no surprise. Communist countries — and Nicaragua is as Communist as Vietnam — never negotiate in good faith. Such talks appeal primarily to TV commentators, the children of ex-Presidents, and people who plaster "arms are for hugging" stickers on their BMWs.

First came Danny's Moscow junket. Then came his invasion of Honduras. Now comes the Contadora collapse. The anti-Contra Congressmen are running out of excuses. But don't worry, they'll come up with another spurious reason to vote against aiding Nicaragua's anti-Communists.

The TENNESSEAN
Nashville, TN, April 29, 1986

THE Contadora group's initiative for ending the conflict in Nicaragua is showing new signs of life, partly because of presidential envoy, Mr. Philip Habib, who suggested a possible compromise between the Reagan administration and the Sandinista leadership.

In a letter to congressmen, Mr. Habib said the administration interprets existing peace proposals by the Contadora nations "as requiring a cessation of support to irregular forces and/or insurrectional movements from the date of signature."

The objectives of the Contadora countries — Panama, Mexico, Venezuela and Colombia — would include promoting democracy and national reconciliation, an end to military intervention and support for guerrilla wars, restraint on the size of the military, a reduction of the number of foreign military advisers and a ban on foreign bases in the area.

At a Panama meeting earlier this month, Nicaragua refused to sign any agreement until the administration first halted aid to the contra guerrillas fighting the Sandinista government.

It is not clear what the administration really thinks of the Contadora process. It has given lip service to the effort, but almost nothing more. In his nationwide address on March 16 in which he urged more aid to the contras, Mr. Reagan didn't even mention it.

Although Mr. Reagan's request for $100 million in aid for the contras is languishing in the House, he has given no indication of modifying his request. If the aid continues, there is no possibility of an agreement.

There are several obstacles in the way of any agreement. The U.S. has demanded that the Sandinistas must negotiate with the contras, which they have refused to do. Another is the U.S. position on enforcement and verification of a peace agreement, and whether it would be content with a Contadora proposal for a four-nation enforcement commission or would insist in making its own judgments on whether the Sandinistas live up to any agreement.

The Contadora nations hope to arrange a signing of a Central American peace agreement on June 6, with Nicaragua joining El Salvador, Costa Rica, Honduras and Guatemala in endorsing the pact.

Whether the signing will take place on that date is uncertain. But it seems quite likely that there will be no vote in the House on contra aid until after that date, however much pressure the administration brings to bear on the lawmakers.

The Habib letter has encouraged several lawmakers, who said they are pleased that a compromise is even being discussed. "I think it creates a historic opportunity for us to end the contra war," said Rep. Jim Slattery, D-Kan.

Many in Congress and this country are convinced that a military solution to the Nicaraguan problem is not in the cards — at least not without direct U.S. military intervention — and that the best hope for the situation would be some kind of diplomatic solution. Mr. Habib has pointed in that direction and that offers some encouragement. ∎

THE PLAIN DEALER
Cleveland, OH, April 19, 1986

For the moment, the issue of providing U.S. military aid to Nicaragua's contra rebels has been put to rest. House Republicans, unhappy that the $100 million aid request was attached to a spending bill President Reagan is certain to veto, sank the measure by voting for an amendment barring any military aid to the rebels. Unless the Republican leadership succeeds with a long-shot ploy to force a floor vote as early as May 12, the aid request will not move.

That would be a serious defeat for the administration, which maintains that the contra campaign is necessary to moderate Nicaragua's behavior and force the Sandinistas to negotiate peace. But the aid defeat also presents an opportunity for critics to press more forcefully for alternatives, of which there are plenty. Among them:

• Honest support for the Contadora peace process. Few people seriously think the administration has given genuine support to Contadora. Yet, in order for a policy toward Nicaragua to be effective, the U.S. administration must build a Latin concensus. Contadora is just that—a Latin American approach to a largely Latin American problem. It provides the best chance for a peaceful resolution of regional conflicts and, if properly implemented, also could safeguard the security interests of the United States.

• Define the threat. Questions have been raised about the administration's contention that the Sandinistas threaten U.S. security. If Nicaragua really is the threat the White House claims it to be, direct troop involvement would seem to be called for

rather than the small aid package the president seeks. If the administration is prepared to send in troops, why isn't it saying so?

• Negotiate with the Sandinistas. Because the hostility and distrust are so high, bilateral talks between Washington and Managua are a necessity. Such talks, however, should complement rather than replace the Contadora process.

• Provide more aid to the region. Washington should provide greater assistance to its struggling democratic allies in the region, including greater military aid for defense against insurrection. A greater emphasis also must be given to the economic and political grievances of the populations within Central America. The major causes for instability are internal, though such struggles frequently are aided by external forces.

• Consult with the Cubans and Soviets. Though there is no direct role for the United States, Cuba or the Soviet Union in Contadora, each of the parties could sabotage it. All are involved in Central America, which itself is reason for talks over the region's political and economic future.

Unfortunately, the administration is ideologically opposed to a leftist regime in Managua and refuses to give the regime the legitimacy required for negotiations. Yet if peace is the goal, ideology must be set aside. Congress, most Latin leaders and the majority of Americans are asking the administration to support a negotiated settlement. If Congress holds the line against contra aid, perhaps the White House eventually will do as it should and move seriously explore the diplomatic alternatives.

The Des Moines Register
*Des Moines, IA,
April 10, 1986*

Nicaragua has done it again. The Sandinista government rejected a reasonable regional-security pact drawn up by the so-called Contadora nations, and rejected it only a week before the U.S. House of Representatives is to cast the deciding vote on aid to the contra insurgents.

A year ago, Nicaraguan President Daniel Ortega paid a call on his allies in Moscow soon after the House had turned down contra aid, which so embarrassed and angered many members that they reversed the vote.

Last month's Nicaraguan incursion into Honduras just before a Senate vote on new aid to the contras was one of many and was blown out of proportion by the Reagan administration. Nonetheless, it was dumb timing.

And now this. Nicaragua refused to sign the guarantee of regional security unless the United States made a commitment to stop supporting the contras. This is a reasonable condition, given the U.S. military buildup in Honduras and the clear U.S. intent to overthrow the Sandinistas, but it simply is not going to happen.

What the Sandinistas don't seem to understand is that the victory they won last month in the House and the strong support they drew in the Senate came not from any love for their Marxist government, but because 222 House members and 47 senators think there is a better way to bring peace and security than by financing a rebellion: That better way is negotiation.

In both chambers, contra aid came with a built-in 90-day delay to give talk a chance. The April 15 second vote in the House has been expected all along to reverse the first and authorize delayed aid. But one of the strongest arguments opponents of arming the contras could muster, the only possible chance to defeat the aid, was the case for negotiation.

Now the Sandinistas reject the fruits of negotiation, raising doubts as to whether talking will do any good. But the Latin American nations should keep trying, though without U.S. cooperation the outlook is bleak.

This latest experience suggests that the Contadora process may be as frail a hope for those Americans who oppose a military solution to the contras are for those who want a new government in Managua.

THE DAILY OKLAHOMAN

Oklahoma City, OK,
April 28, 1986

CONGRESSMEN who see a potential compromise that would end U.S. aid for the Contras of Nicaragua if the Sandinista regime straightens up and flies right may be looking through rose-colored glasses.

The basis for their optimism is a reported April 11 letter from presidential envoy Philip Habib stating the Reagan administration's interpretation of peace proposals by the so-called Contadora group of Latin American nations.

The congressmen quote it as saying this requires a cessation of support to irregular forces and insurrectionists. The United States would support and abide by an agreement fulfilling the Contadora peace objectives —as long as Nicaragua supports and abides by such an agreement.

Ah, there's the rub. Those objectives include free elections in Nicaragua, and Marxist ideology, which guides the Sandinista leadership, simply does not contemplate a true democratic process. The Soviet Union, East Germany, Poland, Angola, Cuba all provide instructive models.

The Sandinistas reportedly would sign an agreement June 6 if the United States ends aid to the Contras. But then the United States would no longer have leverage to see that the agreement is carried out, except for the Sandinistas' signature, whatever that is worth.

Interestingly, among the congressmen pushing this "compromise" is Rep. Michael Barnes, D-Md., a liberal who has opposed President Reagan's Central America policy all along.

The Philadelphia Inquirer

Philadelphia, PA, April 8, 1986

The rhetoric, the cost, the stakes escalate over Nicaragua. Sen. Bill Bradley (D., N.J.) throws his lot, grudgingly, with the contras, but wonders aloud if overthrowing the Sandinistas has become "the holy grail of a new American crusade." Another vote is scheduled in the House, which last month rejected the President's appeal to fund the rebels. The House is wavering.

As the escalation creeps upward — there is talk now of sending Stinger missiles and U.S. combat advisers — a sub-plot emerges in Panama City where anxious Latin American leaders have not given up on a regional peace plan. It has been three years since these so-called Contadora nations have been holding what some call "ritual talks."

But something curious is going on. As both Washington and Managua unsuccessfully try to browbeat Contadora leaders into joining their propaganda wars, the negotiators refuse either to back the contras or to blame the shooting match on the United States. "We are not here to hand down verdicts," said a Costa Rican emissary. "We are here to negotiate."

Longtime observers say a new urgency cloaks the talks, with a sense, as New Mexican Democrat Rep. Bill Richardson reported, that "it may be the last opportunity for peace."

Even reluctant Honduras, caught between U.S. pressure and Sandinista incursions, says it considers the contras not liberators, but bargaining chips toward a regional agreement to demilitarize Nicaragua. The contras — commanded by the rear guard of the ousted Somoza dictatorship — have grander goals in mind.

And there's the rub. While the Reagan administration argues that the contras are leverage against the spread of leftist ideology and ambitions, that they are "tools in the toolbox" of such as special ambassador Philip Habib, not the contras, the Sandinistas, or much of Latin America believes those limitations.

Yet the contras are not considered close to victory, nor are they a bunch of liberal democrats. They are a CIA-managed coalition of former Sandinistas, former Guardia, former international bankers and young recruits in uncomfortable alliance. They bicker internally, shifting U.S. tax dollars in a shell game that moved Sen. Tom Harkin (D., Iowa) recently to call contra leader Adolfo Calero "a Ferdinand Marcos before his time."

So the concern grows, not that the contras will liberalize Nicaragua, but that they will radicalize it; not that they will contain the conflict, but be party to spreading it.

That is why Contadora deserves more time: The alternative is an escalating conflict; a war without clear objective, without boundary, without domestic or regional support and, perhaps worst of all, without productive or foreseeable end.

DAILY⚓NEWS

New York, NY, April 9, 1986

CONGRESS IS SQUARING up for yet another battle over aid for the Nicaraguan contras, and talks on a regional peace treaty have collapsed. That's the "Contadora process," the attempt by eight Latin American nations to mediate between Nicaragua and its neighbors.

The latest meeting broke up Monday, and the hopes of bringing off a negotiated settlement look exceedingly dim.

Nicaragua insists that before signing, the U.S. must abandon support for the contras. Its neighbors say Nicaragua must agree in advance to cut its 100,000-man army and militia down to reasonable, defensive levels. The proposed treaty would send most of the Sandinistas' Cuban and Soviet-bloc advisers home, cut back American military maneuvers in Honduras, and would stop Nicaragua exporting revolution.

If a real treaty along these lines could be reached, backed by international guarantees, the worst problems in Central America would be resolved. Terrorists in El Salvador would be cut off; the contras could disband with honor; there would be no more Cuban bridgehead on the American mainland, and the Sandinistas would have to face up to the economic disaster they have brought upon Nicaragua.

That's one reason they won't sign. They aren't afraid of the contras, and hope the Cubans and Soviets will keep the economy afloat. That's a miserable future for the Nicaraguan people, but Commandante Ortega, he of the elegant sunglasses, believes they should be ready to suffer for the cause.

The Contadora countries blame Nicaragua for the failure of their peace treaty, but it doesn't mean they should give up. The best hope for the future of Central America remains the Contadora formula. The U.S. and the contras are using military pressure to push the Sandinistas that way. The Contadora allies must continue the diplomatic pressure.

Wisconsin 🏛 State Journal

Madison, WI, April 29, 1986

It's probably been nothing short of baffling for the average American, but the weeks of indecision that have characterized congressional debate over President Reagan's Contra aid proposal may prove to be a blessing.

Early this year, it seemed the Reagan administration would consider only one route of dealing with the ruling Marxist regime in Nicaragua — that being $100-million worth of military aid to the anti-Sandinista rebels.

Now, thanks to the game of legislative pingpong Congress has played with the administration package, the diplomatic option is getting fresh (and welcome) attention.

Signs of life

The Contadora initiative, which was once held in such low esteem by President Reagan that he refused to mention it during his March 16 nationwide address urging more aid for the Contras, is showing signs of life.

Presidential envoy Philip Habib helped revive Contadora (a peace effort involving four of Nicaragua's neighbors and four South American nations) in a recent letter to several congressmen. Habib suggested the administration would halt military aid to the Contras when the Sandinista government signed a peace accord true to the original objectives of the Contadora nations.

Those objectives were spelled out in September 1983. They included promoting democracy and national reconciliation in Nicaragua; an end to military intervention and support for guerrilla wars; restraint on the size of the Sandinista army; a reduction in the number of foreign (mostly Cuban and Soviet) military advisers; curbs on foreign military maneuvers; and a ban against foreign bases.

The path to an agreement that could involve the Contadora group as well as the United States and Nicaragua is heavily mined. It is unclear whether the repressive Sandinista regime would be forced to hold another national election; also unaddressed is the specific U.S. demand that Managua negotiate directly with the Contras, which the Sandinistas have thus far refused to do.

But as perilous as the road to a regional peace solution may appear, it must be fully explored. Habib is on a 12-nation tour of Latin America to discuss the Contadora process, and there is no reason to believe he is not seeking a diplomatic solution.

June target date

The Contadora nations hope to arrange a signing of a Central America peace agreement in June, with Nicaragua joining its closest neighbors — El Salvador, Costa Rica, Honduras and Guatemala — in endorsing the pact.

Congress has refused to embrace Reagan's $100-million military aid proposal for several reasons, not the least of which being a feeling that diplomatic means have not been exhausted. Lawmakers also detect the lack of a national consensus for military involvement.

Legislative delay on some issues can be maddening (the federal deficit and tax reform quickly come to mind) but in the case of U.S. policy toward Central America, congressional hesitation has promoted the possibility of compromise.

San Francisco Chronicle

San Francisco, CA, April 9, 1986

THE CONTADORA TALKS aimed at achieving peace in Central America under Latin American auspices have broken down — due primarily to what the participants refer to as Nicaraguan "intransigence." Nicaragua has previously accused the Reagan administration of trying to sabotage the Contadora peace process, begun three years ago by Colombia, Mexico, Panama and Venezuela to negotiate a regional non-aggression treaty. But this time it is clear that only Nicaragua was bent on torpedoing the talks.

Such calculated and peevish obduracy only does the Nicaraguan cause a disservice. It is widely believed now that the breakdown in the peace talks has dealt a substantial blow to those in Congress who hope to defeat President Reagan's plan to send $100 million in aid to the Contra rebels. Indeed, it seems every time it is argued that reasonable discourse may be held with Nicaragua, that country's leaders quickly disabuse us of such hopes through unreasonable and truculent action.

It does not help the Nicaraguan cause, either, to hear 10 Roman Catholic bishops accuse the government, as they did recently, of trying to undermine and silence the church.

NICARAGUA CLAIMS it cannot go along with Contadora unless the U.S. specifically agrees not to support the Contras. But the truth of the matter is that Nicaragua is playing the spiteful prima donna in kicking back against the peace efforts of its neighbors.

Edmonton Journal

Edmonton, Alta., April 26, 1986

Despite Ronald Reagan's attempts to link Libya and Nicaragua, the U.S. appears to be seriously considering a diplomatic settlement to its war against Nicaragua.

With legislators unwilling to give America's surrogate army the funding the U.S. president demands, diplomacy is in the forefront. U.S. special envoy Philip Habib believes the broad terms of the Contadora peace plan — worked out by several Latin American countries — can be met.

This is welcome news. The civil war has created a siege mentality in the Sandinista government and ruined the economy. A diplomatic solution may mean life without war for Nicaraguans. But they must also have freedom.

Those who believe a Leninist state is firmly entrenched in Nicaragua point to the suspension of civil rights. They are not confident that rights will be restored if the civil war ends.

Censorship, restricted mobility rights and other deprivations are common to many countries fighting a war.

Canada, Britain and other nations restored the civil liberties suspended during the Second World War; full rights were returned to Quebecois after the October, 1970 crisis.

Those cases were different because democracies were involved, argue the Sandinistas' critics. They say there's no case of a junta or a dictatorship restoring freedoms.

The critics may have a point. The only modern dictator who reverted to free elections was India's Indira Gandhi, who was voted out of office for suspending the constitution and abrogating rights. Yet she won re-election.

Why can't the restoration of civil rights be a condition of any Nicaraguan peace? If the Contras are disbanded, the U.S. ends its economic blockade and the Sandinistas agree not to export revolution, could normal political conditions be re-established? Sounder economic conditions could certainly prevail, replacing four decades of oligarchy under the Somoza family and the austere Sandinista war economy.

Would the Sandinistas call fresh elections to seek a new mandate? America's covert war sapped the Nicaraguan economy of what little strength it had — if the Sandinistas know that renewed American military action is the alternative, would they feel pressed to move toward an opn society?

Contadora offers Nicaraguans freedom from economic terrorism; it must also offer them full political rights.

The Idaho STATESMAN

Boise, ID, April 11, 1986

The collapse of the Contadora peace conference signals dangerous times ahead for Central America and an escalation of hostilities between the United States and Nicaragua.

The conference was perhaps the last chance for Central American nations to agree on a regional peace plan. Ministers from 13 Latin American countries – including the so-called Contadora nations of Mexico, Panama, Colombia and Venezuela – broke off talks in Panama City Monday, leaving a future that appears to hold more United States aid for the Nicaraguan contra rebels followed by an escalation of tension between the Reagan administration and the Sandinista regime.

The failure of Nicaragua to work out a compromise with its neighbors represents another Sandinista political blunder that will help President Reagan's $100 million contra aid request.

The Nicaraguans insist that we stop supporting the contras before they will sign a regional peace pact. While that carries some logic, they're letting pride and machismo betray their better judgment. The United States remains confused and divided over its proper policy toward Central America. With the House set to vote again next week on the funding package, many Americans favor negotiations over bullets. The Sandinistas threw away a golden opportunity to leverage that good will into a political settlement. Instead, they gave moderate congressmen one less reason to vote against the contras.

The Reagan administration, more unabashed then ever about its goal of overthrowing the Sandinistas, should rethink this destructive course and refrain from exploiting the peace talks' collapse. The covert aid turned overt, the inflated stories of Nicaraguan "invasions," the talk of sending in military advisers recall unpleasant memories of other escalations in other jungles.

If the Sandinista regime truly represents a threat to our national security, as the president submits, let him build a factual case to the American people. Without their support, foreign military intervention, as we saw in Vietnam, is doomed from the start.

A better path, for both Nicaragua and the United States, lies in shelving the rhetoric, addressing the real differences between the two countries and finding a peaceful way to settle them. A stable, democratic Central America with growing, egalitarian economies would provide the best guarantee for our national security.

THE DAILY OKLAHOMAN

Okalahoma City, OK, April 11, 1986

AMONG other things, the leftist Sandinista rulers of Nicaragua suffer from a bad sense of timing.

A year ago, Nicaraguan President Daniel Ortega flew off to Moscow a few days after the U.S. House rejected President Reagan's request for resumed aid to the Contras. The Democratic majority took that as a slap in the face and some members began to have less sympathy for the Sandinistas.

Now, just a week before the House's scheduled second vote on Reagan's request for a $100 million aid package for the "freedom fighters," the Sandinistas dug in their heels against a peace treaty signing deadline. Nicaragua's four Central American neighbors said the Sandinistas refused to accept a June 6 date and, thus, caused the breakup of peace talks in Panama City by 13 Latin American foreign ministers.

A Nicaraguan official claimed the document varied from the Carabelleda declaration signed in January by the Contadora nations. But the refusal follows a long Nicaraguan pattern of resisting peace negotiations.

It also cuts the rug from under U.S. congressmen who keep urging Reagan to "to give diplomacy a chance" in Central America.

One key to understanding the situation is a report two Cubans were advising the Nicaraguan delegation to adopt an unbending attitude. That, too, fits a Marxist pattern.

The Providence Journal

Providence, RI, April 9, 1986

The Contadora process has broken down. Again. After negotiations between 13 foreign ministers seeking a nonaggression pact for Central America dissolved Monday, the vice president of El Salvador said, "Nicaragua rejected everything, everything that was presented to it. There is nothing left to talk about."

That may be premature. Contadora has been declared dead before only to crank into operation again. But the latest breakdown makes it ever more clear that the Nicaraguan negotiating strategy accommodates its military strategy — rather than the other way around. In light of the recent Sandinista incursion into Honduras, that strategy seems to be to defeat their rebel opposition before it can win aid from the United States. By rejecting the pact, Daniel Ortega has proved he is no blunderer, as some in Congress prefer to view him. Rather, he is an expert at keeping the United States off balance while he keeps Central America aboil. Would the Soviets lavish aid on him for anything less?

His efforts rely upon the canard that the Reagan administration is the chief obstacle to a treaty. In late 1984 the Nicaraguans said they were ready to sign the latest draft. When Honduras, Costa Rica and El Salvador refused to sign, the administration was accused of pressuring them to refuse. Critics ignored the concern of Nicaragua's neighbors that a treaty without verification would leave them vulnerable. Meanwhile, the Sandinistas announced that if such provisions were added they would not sign.

This concern, treated with such disdain by opponents of *contra* aid, was manifest in the official Honduran reaction to the Nicaraguan incursion. Officials in Tegucigalpa were so fearful of even tacitly admitting that *contra* bases were on their soil that they claimed instead that Nicaragua had attacked Honduran troops. Their dicey situation was exploited back in Washington by critics fearful that the incursion would translate into support for *contra* aid.

A Contadora treaty acceptable to the United States, Honduras, Costa Rica and El Salvador is in the final stages of drafting. According to Alfred Lun of the Permanent Mission of the United States to the Organization of American States, the draft contains "enough bows" to the security needs of Nicaragua's three neighbors that "they'd sign now." So now it's the Sandinistas who refuse to sign. They contend now that they will not sign anything until the United States abandons the *contras*. This punctilio was of no concern to them in 1984. Obviously they are not interested in regional security, only their own.

Last Dec. 9, Nicaragua cast the only no vote on a resolution before the OAS to the effect, merely, that the Contadora process is helpful and should be continued. Senate majority leader Bob Dole, referring to President Reagan's proposed $100 million package of aid to Nicaraguan rebels, said that Nicaragua's intransigence in the Contadora talks would make passage of the aid more likely when the House votes on it again next week, after having rejected a similar package last month by a 222-to-210 vote.

"Some of the Democrats," said Mr. Dole, "will no longer be able to hide behind the Contadora process" as the Nicaraguans (have) torpedoed that."

The Courier-Journal
Louisville, KY, April 9, 1986

THE COLLAPSE of the Contadora talks Monday in Panama could very soon have tragic consequences in Central America.

Next week, the U.S. House of Representatives is due to vote again on President Reagan's plan to send $100 million worth of weapons and "humanitarian" assistance, and up to 55 American military advisers, to guerrillas battling Nicaragua's Sandinista government. If enough lawmakers see regional peace negotiations as fruitless, the House could reverse its earlier opposition to this aid. Such a reversal would guarantee more bloodshed in Nicaragua and would increase the risk of a broader war in Central America — a war in which the United States could become directly involved.

D'Escoto balks at signing

Nicaragua is being blamed by its Central American neighbors — and by diplomats from several of the eight other Latin American countries involved in the so-called "Contadora process" — for the failure of the 13-nation parley in Panama.

The Nicaraguan foreign minister, Miguel D'Escoto, reportedly refused to sign any document that didn't specifically condemn U.S. support for the anti-Sandinista guerrillas — or contras. The Nicaraguan delegation, accompanied by Cuban advisers, is also said to have balked at several provisions of a draft treaty that Latin American sponsors hoped would be signed June 6.

If, in fact, the Nicaraguans were the heavies in this diplomatic drama, it wouldn't be the first time the Sandinistas have blundered into a political trap laid by Ronald Reagan. A visit to Moscow last year by Nicaraguan President Daniel Ortega prompted Congress to approve $27 million in "non-lethal" aid for the contras. And last month's attack by Nicaraguan forces on a contra camp in Honduras, though initially downplayed by Honduran officials, allowed the White House to ring alarm bells about an "invasion."

The Sandinistas can sometimes be every bit as inflexible as President Reagan, which is why some Latin American diplomats despair of finding a peace formula acceptable to both Managua and Washington. But exasperation with the Nicaraguans evidently hasn't been transformed into support for Mr. Reagan's war-by-proxy approach. Diplomats in Panama repeatedly warned that U.S. support for the contras was counterproductive.

If the Contadora talks have reached a dead-end — or are at least momentarily stalled — how should Congress react? The Reagan administration's answer is more of the aid-to-the-contras policy that has pushed Nicaragua into greater and greater dependence on the Soviet bloc. But even within the administration, some officials concede that the contras can't win. The real goal of Mr. Reagan's policy — if, in fact, he has a clear goal — is to bleed Nicaragua to the point where it can't subvert its neighbors.

Protection of all Central American nations from subversion — and from open aggression — is a major goal of the Contadora process, too. But it aims to achieve that goal through verifiable agreements, border patrols, removal of foreign troops and reduction of Central American armies. Despite the collapse of the talks in Panama, Contadora remains preferable to contras as the road — the very bumpy road — to peace in Central America.

The Miami Herald
Miami, FL, April 10, 1986

ONCE again the efforts of eight Latin American nations to bring peace to Central America have broken down. This time they collapsed over Nicaragua's rejection of a purely procedural point — an agreement to continue negotiations and sign a peace accord by June 6.

Nicaragua insists that it will sign nothing until the United States halts its aid to the anti-Sandinista rebels. Managua's stubbornness shook the Latin American peace brokers as well as those members of Congress trying to prevent approval of President Reagan's $100 million in aid to the contras.

"If the talks break down, the vote to stop aid to the contras is lost," said Rep. Bill Richardson, a New Mexico Democrat.

Even though the collapse of the current round of peace talks falls squarely on the shoulders of the Sandinista regime, the Reagan Administration is hardly blameless. The eight Latin American nations that are seeking an end to the Central American turmoil — the four Contadora nations and the recently formed support group — strongly urged that the Administration's requested aid to the contras be rejected.

In the collective mind of the eight foreign ministers gathered in Panama, the United States as an observer is just as guilty of torpedoing the talks as was Nicaragua as a participant.

The final conference communique says: "To gain peace in the region it is imperative that all sides and the countries with ties and interests in the region abstain from giving support to irregular forces or insurrectional movements that operate in any of the countries of the region."

Two presidents — Daniel Ortega in Managua and Ronald Reagan in Washington — should weigh carefully the consequences of their mutual intransigence.

They are like two trains headed toward each other on the same track, each engineer insisting he has the right-of-way. Each now appears to think that if the trains are allowed to continue on a collision course, his side will survive the crash and remain on the track.

Both Washington and Managua should think instead of the thousands or tens of thousands who will die needlessly unless both sides tone down the rhetoric and pursue peace talks in earnest. Let them do so now. Time is running out.

THE ARIZONA REPUBLIC
Phoenix, AZ, April 9, 1986

THE Sandinistas walked out of the Contadora peace talks after rejecting all offers — and it is Ronald Reagan's fault. At least that is the position of Rep. Michael Barnes, D-Md., and two other Democrats down in Panama City, Panama, who have been trying to conduct their own American foreign policy.

Barnes and his entourage argue that continued U.S. support for the contras is blocking the negotiations. The Sandinistas refuse to negotiate with the Contadora nations until the Reagan administration renounces its support for the Nicaraguan democratic opposition. The commandantes also refuse to accept a deadline, preferring, instead, open-ended talks.

Some people can't seem to learn how Marxists view and use negotiations. The Sandinistas want to stall the Contadora talks long enough for the contras to wither away. That is why they reject the Contadora nations' deadline for arriving at a settlement.

Not one bullet of American military aid has gone to the contras for nearly two years, so Sandinista assertions that continued U.S. support is the chief obstacle are plain nonsense.

What the Sandinistas want out of Contadora is to crush their domestic democratic opposition. Nicaragua's neighbors apparently are willing to abandon democracy in that country for a treaty protecting their own borders. The United States, however, is not prepared to abandon the forces of democracy in Nicaragua.

Barnes and his crowd of Sandinista sycophants are willing to surrender Nicaragua to a Marxist dictatorship, cynically bartering away democracy for "a regional settlement to the Central American conflict." In other words, the Marxist commandantes can have Nicaragua if they just lay off their neighbors.

There is no precedent for Marxists abiding by treaty agreements unless they are maintained by military force. Those who constantly bleat about the "Vietnam syndrome" and espouse unreserved faith in negotiations apparently learned nothing from North Vietnam's calculated abandonment of a solemn peace treaty and invasion of the south. No piece of paper will keep the Sandinistas behind their borders.

As Jean-Francois Revel observes, Marxism necessarily looks outward because it is a failed system incapable of engendering a viable, productive, free human society. It is left with no choice but to direct its revolution toward expansion abroad to hide its failures at home.

The United States must stand firm in its commitment not only to containing Sandinista expansion in Central America, but also to the restoration of democracy inside Nicaragua. The United States must insist the Sandinistas negotiate with their Nicaragua opposition.

The House of Representatives should vote for contra aid to pressure Managua into good-faith negotiations, now that the perfidy of the Sandinistas has been displayed.

Sanctuary Defendants Convicted; Liberation Theology Debated

A federal jury in Tucson, Arizona May 1, 1986 convicted eight Christian activists of smuggling or harboring illegal immigrants from El Salvador and Guatemala into the United States. Among those convicted was Rev. John Fife 3rd, a Presbyterian minister who helped found the movement to give church sanctuary to illegal aliens from Central America. He was convicted of conspiracy to violate U.S. immigration laws, the most serious charge against the defendants. It carried a maximum penalty of five years in prison and a $10,000 fine. Fife was also found guilty of two misdemeanor counts of aiding and abetting, and a felony charge of transporting an alien. Another founder of the sanctuary movement, James Corbett, a Quaker rancher, was found not guilty on all counts.

The prosecution, focusing on the immigration laws, called 17 witnesses, 15 of them Central Americans, the others a government informant and an undercover agent. The defense called no witnesses and said the government had failed to make its point. Defense attorneys stressed the moral and religious aspect of the case and said the U.S. immigration law failed to provide a safe haven for those with a "well founded fear of prosecution."

U.S. District Court Judge Earl H. Carrol ruled out testimony on the religious or political issues. The argument that an alien was a "refugee" and entitled to enter the country without proper immigration papers was "a mistake of law," he told the jurors in his instructions. "Good motive is not a defense to intentional acts of crime," he told them.

Afterwards, the defendants pledged to persist in the sanctuary effort. "We will continue to provide sanctuary services openly and go to trial as often as is necessary to establish the legality, or more directly, to actualize the Nuremburg mandates that the protection of human rights is never illegal," Corbett said.

THE SACRAMENTO BEE
Sacramento, CA, May 3, 1986

Five Sanctuary activists have been convicted by a federal jury in Tucson of conspiracy to violate federal immigration law. They and three others were convicted also of assorted lesser charges of concealing, harboring or transporting illegal aliens. "I think this jury's verdict," the prosecuting U.S. attorney said, "is going to have a significant impact" on the Sanctuary movement throughout the country, changing the thinking of "those persons who were well-intentioned but misguided." One can only hope not.

"Those persons" in Tucson knew they were breaking the law — or at least the law as interpreted by the Immigration and Naturalization Service. Under the Reagan administration, the INS, far from welcoming those fleeing political persecution, as the law requires, has refused even to consider the possibility of political persecution in the cases of most Central American, and particularly Salvadoran, refugees.

The Sanctuary activists did what they did, not in ignorance of INS policies, but with the conviction that those policies have failed to protect refugees whom the law was meant to protect, whom the nation ought to "harbor." In flouting those policies they did not expect to escape the consequences to themselves; their intention was, rather, to spark public outrage and get the policies changed.

And in that, the conduct of the Tucson case has, if anything, abetted them. The government went after the Sanctuary leaders — priests, nuns, ministers and church laypeople — with an alacrity rarely if ever applied to the widespread importing and "harboring" of illegal workers for profit by employers throughout the Southwest. The government turned refugees into informers and sent spies and provocateurs into church meetings to record and catch these "criminals." The judge in this case refused to allow the jury to hear any argument about the government's maladministration of the refugee law. And all that evoked precisely the injustice that the Sanctuary defendants meant the public to see in the immigration system.

"What was the U.S. government to do?" the prosecutor asked reporters after the verdicts came in. "Was it supposed to look the other way?" No; disobedience of the law is supposed to set in motion a chain of prosecution. But neither should the country look the other way when its commitment to provide refuge to those who flee persecution is being broken in the administration of its refugee programs. Those whose purpose was to force the nation to face that issue have not failed. And those who still support them are no more misguided than they ever were. The verdicts in the Tucson case may not be unwarranted, but they are irrelevant to the issue at the heart of the Sanctuary effort.

The Des Moines Register
Des Moines, IA, May 5, 1986

The U.S. government has won its case against eight men and women who now face jail for 18 counts of conspiracy, illegal smuggling and harboring. Those convicted include a Presbyterian minister, two Roman Catholic priests and a nun.

Their crime: Providing aid and comfort for refugees from war-torn Central America.

An injustice? Yes and no.

First, these religious workers knowingly committed acts of civil disobedience. They were aware that giving sanctuary to aliens who might be in this country in violation of immigration laws is itself a violation of federal law. But, in the ancient tradition of churches giving refuge to victims of oppressors, they believed they answered to a higher authority in violating a law they do not believe in.

Civil disobedience is an honored tradition in this nation, from Henry David Thoreau to Martin Luther King. We believe in the principle for which these religious workers have fought. But before the civil disobedients can be rewarded for their good deeds, they must answer to the authorities at home. Therefore, the government had every right to investigate, bring charges and prosecute the offenders.

To conclude otherwise is to suggest that the federal government ignore a city that refuses to enforce civil-rights laws because racist city-council members believe the Constitution is wrongly interpreted by the Supreme Court.

Does this mean that the Arizona sanctuary workers' efforts have been for naught?

Not necessarily.

Surely before these good people rot in jail for the crime of helping a few hundred people escape persecution or perhaps death in their homelands the Reagan administration will come to its senses and change its inconsistent immigration policy.

THE ARIZONA REPUBLIC
Phoenix, AZ, May 2, 1986

FROM the beginning, the Sanctuary trial in Tucson has been used as a pulpit by disciples of the movement to preach their gospel of selective morality, or breaking the law with impunity. It was the Reagan administration that should be on trial, they claimed, for its immoral policies in Central America.

Their overblown rhetoric was deflated Thursday when a federal jury, after nearly nine days of deliberation, convicted eight of 11 defendants accused of running an underground railroad for Central American refugees.

The jury convicted six people on charges of felony conspiracy to bring aliens into the United States. Two others were convicted of harboring an alien and transporting an alien.

Acquitted were three defendants accused of conspiracy, harboring an alien and aiding and abetting unlawful entry.

The numbers are not important. The significant fact is that the jurors recognized that the United States is a nation of laws — laws that must be upheld to protect the public interest.

It is not that the jurors, or the public for that matter, were unsympathetic toward those on trial.

One juror, David McCrea of Tucson, said the jury was far from agreeing on a decision, even hours before the final verdicts were announced.

"Even earlier this (Thursday) morning, it looked like it might end up (with a hung jury)," McCrea said shortly after the verdicts were revealed.

"It wasn't easy to come to a decision, but we thought about it a long time," he said. "I don't think necessarily that the law is right, but that's the law. I sympathize with them, but we had to go by the law. We couldn't go by our sympathies."

The Sanctuary trial verdict is a victory for the principle which holds that no one is above the law — including members of the clergy who claimed they were acting out of what they believed to be a higher morality.

The dictates of conscience do not justify civil disobedience. The clergy's concept of churches as sanctuary has no standing in American legal tradition.

The United States has the most liberal and generous immigration policy in the world, legally admitting half a million people every year, more than all other Western nations combined.

If the Sanctuary movement is so concerned with bringing in refugees from Central America, let it build its railroad aboveground, subject to the same laws as everyone else.

The message from Tucson is clear: Those who break the law must be prepared for the consequences.

The Cincinnati Post
Cincinnati, OH, May 5, 1986

"I had sympathy for the defendants but we had to follow the law," said a member of the jury that convicted eight Sanctuary Movement members of smuggling or harboring illegal aliens. That sentiment is exactly right.

The movement, founded by Presbyterian minister John Fife of Tucson, believes the U.S. government is too harsh toward Central Americans who claim to be fleeing political persecution. Its members have taken the law into their own hands, running an underground railroad for Salvadorans and Guatemalans who fear U.S. authorities will turn them down if they apply for asylum.

Sanctuary activists are not the only Americans with strong opinions about immigration. Many think it's too easy for foreigners to move here; others want to restore the open borders of the 19th century. All are free to seek change through the democratic process: to publicize their views, lobby public officials and campaign to elect new officials. But they also must respect the results of that process. Just as nativist groups have no right to harass legal immigrants, Fife and his followers have no right to harbor illegal ones.

Sometimes, of course, men of conscience decide a law is so immoral that they must break it in obedience to what they see as a higher law. If so they should be willing to accept the consequences. But modern protesters sometimes seek the best of both worlds: They want the public to see them as martyrs, but they want the courts to let them off.

The truly heroic course for Fife and his fellow defendants would have been to decline to contest the government's charges—or to plead guilty, as Cincinnati Sanctuary activist Lorry Thomas did. Now serving a two-year prison sentence in West Virginia, Ms. Thomas refused to plea bargain or to sign a statement promising not to break the law again in return for a reduced sentence.

Just as citizens cannot choose which laws to obey, officials cannot choose which to enforce. Answering his critics after the recent Sanctuary trial, Assistant U.S. Attorney Donald Reno said, "What was the U.S. government supposed to do? Was it supposed to look the other way while illegal acts were being committed?"

Though painful for some, the Tucson trial's outcome was a victory for the rule of law. To let people decide which immigration regulations to obey—or which taxes to pay—is to court anarchy.

Chicago Tribune
Chicago, IL, May 8, 1986

Four years ago, the Southside United Presbyterian Church in Tucson informed then-Atty. Gen. William French Smith that it planned to "publicly violate" the nation's immigration laws. The stage was set for the inevitable confrontation that resulted in convictions last week of some members of the sanctuary movement.

This was no *denouement*, merely a scene perhaps midway through the first act of a debate involving the church, the state, foreign policy, humanitarian action and civil disobedience.

A federal jury in Arizona convicted 6 of 11 defendants of conspiracy to violate U.S. immigration laws by smuggling Central American refugees into this country. Two others were convicted of various felonies involving the transport and harboring on illegal aliens. Three were acquitted of all charges.

It was not a clear victory or defeat for either side in the controversial sanctuary movement, but it will be viewed that way by those on both sides who want to use the verdicts for their own ends.

The sanctuary movement, now claiming some 300 American houses of worship, 18 cities and one state (New Mexico), contends the federal government is violating U.S. immigration laws by failing to admit large numbers of refugees fleeing troubled El Salvador and Guatemala. Advocates of the sanctuary movement say many of these are political refugees who face death if they are sent back; the government says they are economic refugees fleeing poverty and random violence.

And at the same time, the sanctuary people contend, the government is letting in as political refugees a disproportionate number of Nicaraguan citizens.

At the heart of this debate is the fact that the U.S. opposes the Marxist Sandinista government in Nicaragua and supports the governments in El Salvador and Guatemala. Immigration policy reflects this foreign policy judgment, perhaps more than it needs to.

But rather than simply politicking to get a change in the law, the members of the sanctuary movement have declared themselves to be adherents to a higher law than federal statutes and have openly engaged in smuggling refugees into the country.

The government could no more ignore this conduct than it could look the other way when taxpayers declare themselves conscientiously opposed to tax laws. Those who oppose the law through civil disobedience must face the consequences and hope that their dramatic defiance moves the country to change its policies. By becoming martyrs, perhaps they will turn a light on some of the darker aspects of U.S. immigration policies that attempt to give rational reasons for saying "yes" to the handful and "no" to the multitudes who want to come to this country.

But that does not mean they stand above the law. All sides in this case—prosecutors, judge, jury, defense attorneys, defendants—did what they must.

DENVER POST

Denver, CO, May 7, 1986

SUPPORTERS OF the eight church workers found guilty of breaking U.S. immigration laws in Arizona last week weren't allowed to argue theology. But they may find an ultimate haven in Gandhiism, the principle of non-violent protest of government laws one disagrees with.

The theology argument was put off limits in the courtroom in Tucson. "Good motive is not a defense to intentional acts of crime," said the judge in instructing the jury. Federal lawyers contended that the defendants' actions in smuggling illegal aliens into the United States had no defense in law — and the jury agreed. Appeals are pending.

The debate is far from over, however. It doubtless will continue long after the Rev. John Fife III and his seven co-conspirators are sentenced on July 1, assuming an appeal doesn't intervene.

The legal flaw in the defendants' case is that they haven't proved that "their" Central American refugees were really fleeing oppression created by U.S. support of evil regimes, particularly in El Salvador. Federal officials said the refugees were fleeing poverty — not repression. And if flight from oppression was their chief goal, why didn't they stop in Mexico, rather than flee all the way to Tucson?

The legal point is clear: The law has been broken. But the moral argument remains: not only the doctrinal dispute on whether the U.S. fosters repression, but also whether a distinction between "political" and "economic" refugees is valid or fair.

That debate can be cast in terms of Gandhian activism. Mohandas K. Gandhi stirred millions and won freedom for India by preaching non-violent opposition to the oppressive laws imposed by colonialist Britain.

We might disagree that U.S. laws are oppressive. But there is something noble about non-violence and the principle — which Gandhi insisted on — that his followers bravely endure the penalties provided by the offending laws. But the Tucson Eight may never make it that far. Their leader, Reverend Fife, went off to appear on the Phil Donahue TV show. Possibly he will find real truth in something more modern than Gandhiism: a media blitz.

The Hartford Courant

Hartford, CT, May 8, 1986

The claims of conscience and the requirements of law often conflict: Under a government of law, conscience sometimes loses, even if it is right. That may seem to mock justice. In fact, it doesn't.

The conviction by a federal jury in Tucson, Ariz., of eight sanctuary workers on charges of smuggling and harboring illegal aliens demonstrates the tension between the law and conscience. The government prosecuted 11 activists, who are either Christian clerics or lay workers, accusing them of violating immigration laws. The activists claimed that it was the government that broke the law.

Two founders of the sanctuary movement, which has been endorsed by about 300 churches, 20 U.S. cities and the state of New Mexico, were among those charged. The movement is committed to providing sanctuary to Central Americans who say they are fleeing government persecution, especially those from Guatemala or El Salvador.

Federal law requires that refugees apply for asylum and it specifies that only those determined to be fleeing persecution are entitled to remain here. Those seeking a better quality of life, so-called economic refugees, are not eligible for asylum.

The sanctuary activists claim, with some justification, that the Reagan administration misapplies that law; that it puts certain refugees in the economic category to avoid offering asylum to those fleeing the persecution of right-wing governments friendly to the United States. So disaffected are the activists by the administration's policy that they have taken the law into their own hands, harboring refugees who haven't even applied for asylum.

But disregard for the law invites anarchy. In his instructions to the jury, U.S. District Judge Earl H. Carroll said: "Good motive is not a defense to intentional acts of crime." He did not allow the defense attorneys to address the defendants' religious motivations, the political and economic situation in Central America or U.S. policy on refugees. The issue was simply "whether defendants conspired to smuggle immigrants across the border and harbor them." The jury thought they did.

U.S. law requires that an applicant for asylum present a claim to the Immigration and Naturalization Service that he faces persecution in his country of origin. The service then submits the claim to the State Department for review. If a request is denied, an applicant can then pursue his claim in the courts. Each case is reviewed on its merits. For a refugee to be entitled to asylum, he or she must be granted that status by the federal government. No private group can declare who is and is not entitled to asylum.

It may be that the law needs changing or that the admininistration needs to be shamed into upholding it. Civil disobedience can point the way — but not with impunity. Until Congress is convinced of the need to change the law or the courts rule against the administration, the burden of proof falls on those who claim that justice requires that the law be broken.

The Kansas City Times

Kansas City, MO, May 6, 1986

Americans actively involved in the so-called Sanctuary Movement, which smuggles selected Central Americans into this country, knowingly break immigration law and openly defy the federal government. Some who smuggled Guatemalans, Salvadorans and Nicaraguans into this country held news conferences where journalists interviewed their Latin charges, whose kerchiefed faces kept them anonymous.

These media shows challenged federal authorities. Yet even the INS knows that it is not good PR to be seen carting away nuns and other Sanctuary activists in handcuffs. Unfortunately, it stooped to wiretapping and other methods to find what was already out in the open.

Nonetheless, the INS did have the good sense to know that legally something had to be done. It scored a victory in federal court last week when a jury in Tucson convicted eight Sanctuary activists of smuggling or harboring illegal immigrants. Sanctuary activists tend to forget the rest of the taxpayers after they've made their political point.

Clearly, the federal government and Sanctuary activists are each political animals.

Sanctuary has support across the nation, but the INS went straight to Tucson, home of the Rev. John M. Fife, co-founder of the movement. The federal plan must have been to nip the thing in the bud. In addition, however morally correct Sanctuary may seem, it is clearly a protest against the Reagan administration's foreign policies in Central America and immigration laws, many of which, admittedly, need overhaul.

If Sanctuary were purely moral, then why didn't anyone help the Haitians when their fractured bodies and boats washed ashore? There were certainly tortures, killings and poverty there, just as in Guatemala and El Salvador. And is it mere coincidence that many of the Latin Americans smuggled here denounce this country, their new home? We think not.

The Sanctuary people knew that convictions were possible and should not be shocked when the prison doors slam behind them. Perhaps the good to come from this will be a careful review by Congress of laws concerning refugee and asylum status, what the Sanctuary people said they wanted all along.

Detroit Free Press
Detroit, MI, May 5, 1986

COMPARISONS between the sanctuary movement and the civil rights movement come easily. Both movements — involving individuals willing to risk jail — have called the nation's attention to injustice. Both have touched our consciences, forcing us to think about our society, its laws and their application.

That people who aided refugees from violence in Central America may be jailed for their actions is, of course, shocking. The eight sanctuary movement workers found guilty of felonies last week by a U.S. District Court jury in Tucson face the possibility of lengthy prison sentences and hefty fines for their acts of conscience. But as tempting as it is to second-guess the jury, to do so might be to miss other implications of the case.

Even more troubling than the prospect of the sanctuary workers being jailed are the methods used by the Immigration and Naturalization Service and the U.S. Department of Justice to build the case against the 11 sanctuary activists — three of whom were acquitted of all charges. The questionable methods included infiltration, electronic surveillance of church activities and the use of paid informants.

Like the tactics used by Southern lawmen two decades ago against civil rights workers who were challenging Jim Crow laws, the U.S. government's overzealous pursuit of sanctuary activists raises serious questions about our most basic freedoms. A civil suit that accuses the government of violating religious freedom in gathering evidence against the sanctuary movement has won the support of a broad cross section of religious groups.

Appeals in Tucson can also be expected because of restrictions placed by a federal judge on the kind of evidence that could be introduced by the defense. The sanctuary workers' ethical and religious motivations were said to be immaterial. Neither would the judge allow the defense to explore the issue of whether the Reagan administration's policy of rejecting nearly all Salvadoran and Guatemalan applicants for political asylum is a violation of international agreements.

Sanctuary workers insist that because of United States support for the governments now in power in those countries, it has turned its back on refugees who have a "well-founded fear of persecution" if they go home. They cite impressive evidence of a double standard at work that endangers thousands of men, women and children who, under great hardship, have made their way to the United States only to be told there is no place for them here because we don't acknowledge the terror that forced them to flee their countries.

Outside the courtroom, attempts to keep attention narrowly focused were less successful. Publicity surrounding the trial in Tucson has stimulated healthy debate about U.S. government policies. That was one of the results sanctuary movement workers hoped for when they decided to challenge civil authorities out of a sense of moral duty.

BUFFALO EVENING NEWS
Buffalo, NY, May 9, 1986

A FEDERAL JURY in Tucson, Ariz., has dealt a blow to the sanctuary movement for Central American refugees by convicting six church workers of conspiring to smuggle Salvadorans and Guatemalans into the United States. Two others were convicted on lesser charges. The verdict, which acquitted three remaining defendants, seems a fair one.

It is unfortunate but true that the United States cannot throw open its doors to all foreigners who would like to live here, even those fleeing from poverty and strife.

American law does provide for the admission of refugees who can show that they would face political persecution if returned to their homelands. And it is important that these cases be handled humanely and impartially by immigration authorities.

As federal prosecutors argued in the Tucson case, however, the granting of asylum is a matter for the courts and should not be decided by private citizens and groups — even those motivated by the highest moral and religious concerns.

The Buffalo area director of the U.S. Immigration and Naturalization Service, Benedict J. Ferro, recently reminded the public of the distinction between legal acts of providing compassionate assistance to illegal aliens in distress and unlawful acts of harboring them and helping them to evade deportation.

America is a free country, and those opposed to the government's policies on Central America or its handling of refugee cases have every right to speak, lobby and demonstrate for their views. What cannot be condoned is breaking the law, and those who engage in civil disobedience must accept the consequences.

The Tucson case did have one troubling aspect — the extent to which the government used secret informants and covert taping of church activities to obtain evidence of illegal harboring of aliens.

While churches have no right to violate the law, decisions on infiltration of church activities must be carefully balanced against the First Amendment guarantee of freedom of religion. The role of federal agents in this case is now the subject of a lawsuit filed by the American Lutheran Church, the Presbyterian Church (U.S.A.) and four of their congregations.

Still, there can be no quarrel with the basic verdict of the Tucson jury. As INS chief Alan C. Nelson said, "this case has demonstrated that no group, no matter how well meaning or highly motivated, can arbitrarily violate the laws of the United States."

The Chattanooga Times
Chattanooga, TN, May 10, 1986

Eight of 11 church workers, defendants in the Tucson sanctuary movement, have been convicted of smuggling Salvadoran and Guatemalan aliens into the United States, thus violating U.S. immigration law. Three of the defendants were acquitted, even though the trial judge, whom the defense accused of partiality toward the prosecution, excluded much of the defense's evidence. Those convicted plan an appeal, and it can't come too soon. There are grave issues of constitutional rights and religious freedom at stake in this case.

Chief among these was the government's infiltration of the churches involved. It used a paid informer who secretly recorded meetings where activities of the sanctuary movement were planned. The judge admitted the informer's recordings and testimony into evidence, ruling that such conduct was "unacceptable but not outrageous."

Of course it is outrageous. Are we now to conclude that the government has the right to infiltrate any church where it suspects illegal activity is going on, is being planned or, to stretch the point, is being condoned?

The issue this time was the government's charge that the churches were violating U.S. immigration laws. But if the judge's ruling on the admissibility of the informer's testimony is not overturned on appeal, what's to stop other officials from using paid spies to infiltrate other churches in the future? It is ironic in the extreme that the federal prosecutor in the sanctuary case argued that defendants in the movement were politically motivated. What could be more politically motivated than the administration's selective enforcement of the immigration and refugee laws as a means of promoting its policies in Central America?

As evidence, consider the hypocritical inconsistency of the administration's approach to such issues in Central America. In Tucson it prosecuted the church sanctuary movement because of its efforts to help men, women and children escape violence in countries that the administration supports — El Salvador, Guatemala and others. At the same time, the administration makes much of its efforts, admittedly laudable, to aid refugees from communist countries, and not just those in Central America. Of course, there would be no need for a sanctuary movement if the administration would use the 1980 Refugee Act to help those trying to escape repression, whether by the right or the left.

All of this is bad enough. Far worse is the dangerous precedent set by the judge's ruling in the sanctuary case that permits government infiltration of churches. If this ruling stands, no church is safe from the prying eyes of government agents. Repressive measures have a way of being used against those who initiate, or support, them.

U.S. Ties Army Chief to Drugs, Murder

Panama's army commander, who was effectively the leader of the country, was deeply involved in a number of illegal activities, including drug trafficking and the supply of arms to the Colombian rebels, according to information gathered by U.S. intelligence sources. The officer, Gen. Manuel Antonio Noriega, was also involved in the 1985 murder of a political opponent, Dr. Hugo Spadafora, said senior State Department, Pentagon and intelligence officials. The charges were published in the June 12, 1986 edition of *The New York Times*. The *Times* said senior White House officials were aware of the charges against Noriega but initially refused to discuss them for fear of damaging relations with Panama. Panama was vital to U.S. interests in Latin America. The U.S. had a vast intelligence-gathering network there to monitor all of Central America and most of South America. It was through this network that the extensive file on Noriega's illegal activities was said to have caused a dilemma for successive U.S. Administrations, which had to weigh Panama's strategic value to the U.S. against denouncing illegal activities by its top officers. The *Times* said officials in the Reagan and past administrations had decided to overlook Noriega's various illegal operations because he had cooperated with U.S. intelligence agencies and permitted the U.S. military to cooperate in Panama.

The *Times* cited a recent classified report by the Defense Intelligence Agency that said Noriega tightly controlled drug trafficking and money laundering by associates in the Panama Defense Force. According to a White House official, Noriega directed the most significant drug trade in Panama, which had been described in a 1985 assessment by the U.S. House Foreign Affairs Committee as a "drug and chemical transshipment point and money-laundering center for drug money." U.S. intelligence sources were quoted as saying Noriega played the role of a "facilitator." As such, he was paid a percentage of drug profits through his secret investments in Panamanian companies and his involvement in a number of trading concerns. Noriega and President Eric Arturo Delvalle denied the charges June 12 after an emergency meeting of top Panamanian government officials.

THE SACRAMENTO BEE

Sacramento, CA, June 26, 1986

Officially, the Reagan administration is treating accusations of political murder, election fraud, drug smuggling and gunrunning by the military strongman of Panama as "basically a Panamanian affair." That's as it should be. At the same time, key administration officials are letting it be known that they consider the allegations to be true. That, too, is as it should be.

If even half the charges in the intelligence dossier on Gen. Manuel Antonio Noriega — officially the armed forces chief but in fact Panama's dictator — are true, the calculated risk Washington is taking in confirming press reports of his misdeeds is one worth taking. There's strong popular opposition to Noriega, so that making known U.S. displeasure with his behavior is less likely to be seen, as it would elsewhere, as unwelcome Yanqui meddling. It's important, though, for the U.S. response to remain a low-key one. This country has 10,000 troops and a strategic interest in Panama, which by treaty will take full sovereignty over the Panama Canal in just 14 years.

For years U.S. officials found it expedient to deal with Noriega, who supplied intelligence information about Cuban activities in Panama (all the while keeping Havana posted about U.S. operations there). But since becoming Panama's kingmaker, Noriega apparently has committed the sin of excess. He is charged with subverting Panama's return to democratic rule, first by rigging the 1984 presidential election for his handpicked candidate, Nicolas Ardito Barletta, then, in 1985, by forcing Barletta to quit after he dared to call for an investigation of a political murder that opponents say Noriega ordered. At the same time, the general is accused of supplying leftist Colombian guerrillas with weapons in return for narcotics whose final destination is this country.

Narcotics production for export, mostly to the United States, has become a major industry in a number of Latin American countries. Poverty, corruption and intimidation of officials make eradication of large-scale drug trafficking all but impossible. Given the unsavory history of its ruling military clique, that may be the case in Panama. It's just possible, though, that the spotlight now focused on Noriega will persuade his colleagues that such egregious behavior mandates a change. Whether that happens or not, it's important that this country dissociate itself from a dictator's ugly abuse.

Detroit Free Press

Detroit, MI, June 22, 1986

U.S. RELATIONS with the military strongmen of Latin America have long been problematic. Often, our policy has been to close our eyes to their human rights abuses because they have brought stability to a part of the world where it is often lacking. Yet sometimes their excesses become too great to ignore.

The activities of Gen. Manuel Noriega, head of Panama's armed forces and the power behind the Panamanian president, appear to be just such a case. And, according to recent news reports, U.S. self-interest and Gen. Noriega were on a collision course in 1972 when his alleged involvement in drug trafficking prompted the suggestion that he be assassinated. Cooler heads in the Nixon administration wisely rejected that notion.

Recent news reports have alleged the general's continuing involvement in the drug trade, as well as in gun-running and money-laundering activities. They also claimed that he has close links to Libya, Cuba, the Palestine Liberation Organization, and leftist insurgents in Colombia and El Salvador, and, citing U.S. intelligence officials' secret testimony before Congress, that he planned and supervised the murder last year of a political opponent.

Understandably, as Secretary of State George Shultz said last week, the reports about Gen. Noriega are "of importance and concern" to those responsible for formulating U.S. foreign policy, particularly as they look ahead to the year 2000, when Panama is to take over defense of the Panama Canal.

In anticipation of the transfer of responsibility for that strategic waterway, the Panama Defense Force has already swelled to 15,000 members and is expected to reach 20,000. Its budget is approximately $90 million. Panama is nominally a civilian-run country, but few deny that Gen. Noriega is the boss.

Though the allegations against him should not be used as an excuse for heavy-handed U.S. meddling, they must be taken seriously, and the situation closely monitored.

THE PLAIN DEALER
Cleveland, OH, June 28, 1986

The disclosure that Panama's military leader stole his country's 1984 presidential election for a comrade was leaked to the press by the Reagan administration for a reason. The public should keep that in mind the next time the president or CIA Director William Casey denounces government leaks.

In this case, the leak was orchestrated by the administration to counter Sen. Jesse Helms' efforts to undercut the treaty that returned the Panama Canal to Panama. To save the pact and neutralize Helms, who has been hammering away at Gen. Manuel Antonio Noriega, the administration has been forced to acknowledge the sordid details of the stolen election.

Noriega is said by administration officials to be involved in drug dealing and in feeding sensitive information to Cuba. They say he is responsible for stealing the 1984 Panamian presidential election from Arnulfo Arias Madrid, a popular nationalist the United States considered anti-American and a threat to U.S. interests in Panama.

The White House instead supported Nicolas Ardito Barletta, whose candidacy also was supported by Noriega. When it became apparent that Barletta was losing the election—Panama's first for a president since 1968—Noriega halted the vote count. National guard troops seized ballot boxes and the count was rigged in Barletta's favor.

In blowing the whistle on Noriega, who among his other misdeeds forced Barletta from office in 1985 when the president insisted on probing the murder of a Noriega critic, the administration now admits:

• That it knew before the election that Noriega was prepared to steal it for Barletta.

• That Noriega did steal it and the United States had massive evidence of the fraud at the time it was being committed.

• That the administration adopted a policy to ignore the vote theft and to support Barletta because it was in the United States' interests to do so. Thus, in response to widespread charges of fraud after Barletta was declared the winner, the United States claimed it had received no evidence of fraud. Yet, before the election, the administration had warned that any attempt to steal votes could result in a cut off of U.S. aid to Panama.

Only the naive would consider that threat genuine, given the strategic value of Panama and its canal to the United States. That warning, however, in light of what the administration now admits happened, places the United States in an awkward situation. Does the United States stand four-square behind the democratic process or doesn't it?

Noriega undoubtably is a bad egg. He has only been exposed now by the administration, in a rare airing of dirty linen, because of Helms' use of previously classified information to undermine the canal treaties.

The affair reveals much about the struggle for influence over foreign policy in Washington. It also points to the historical weak link in America's policy toward Latin America.

Gratitude is only temporary for foreign political or military leaders whom Washington buys politically. The administration's policy in Panama was to look the other way while the Panamanian people were being deprived of the right to elect the person a majority wanted to be their president. Neither they nor the interests of the United States have been served well by that bit of double-dealing.

THE KANSAS CITY STAR
Kansas City, MO, June 17, 1986

Panama's armed forces chief, Gen. Manuel Noriega, received a most unpleasant welcome while in the U.S. last week. The general, who has made certain his path is unobstructed in pseudo-democratic Panama, walked right smack into a real democracy and its free press. While in the U.S., Gen. Noriega was treated to a front-page story in *The New York Times* in which intelligence sources accused him of drug trafficking and other corruption, running guns to terrorists, murder, and supplying information to the Cubans and the U.S. simultaneously. What was not in the newspaper was broadcast on NBC television.

As the general is the true head of state in Panama, not President Eric Arturo Delvalle, it is safe to assume that Panamanian newspapers would not have carried such stories. The general runs the country and things have a way of happening to uncooperative media people and dissidents. The decapitated body of one outspoken critic, Hugo Spadefora, was found last year at the Panama-Costa Rica border.

The charges against the general, if true, could have adverse affects on U.S.-Panamanian relations. Regional peace plans would also be imperiled. Gen. Noriega has been accused of supplying Colombia's leftist M-19 guerrillas with guns to overthrow the Colombian government. Panama and Colombia are half the Contadora Group.

Gen. Noriega seems to be loyal only to himself. He has supplied the U.S. with intelligence information about Cuba and the Nicaraguan Sandinistas and offered the same to Cuba on American activities in Panama, the media reported. Panama is a training ground for numerous military exercises and other national security activities. For this reason, the administration must step lightly in solving what is not only a domestic problem for Panamanians, but a bilateral one, requiring U.S. action.

St. Petersburg Times
St. Petersburg, FL, June 26

It's common knowledge that Gen. Manuel Antonio Noriega is the true power behind the presidency in Panamanian politics. Authoritative U.S. intelligence reports show that Noriega, commander of the Panamanian army, worked to rig Panama's 1984 presidential election in favor of Nicolas Ardito Barletta — and then forced Barletta out of office last year because of a fear that the new president would pursue charges that Noriega was involved in the torture and murder of a political opponent.

And unless the Reagan administration and Congress act quickly to determine the facts surrounding the 1984 Panamanian election — including the American role in its staging and outcome — it will appear that Noriega also is capable of wielding inordinate power behind the closed doors of our own government.

Administration officials acknowledge that Barletta was chosen as a figurehead presidential candidate equally acceptable to Washington and Noriega. Among other assets on Barletta's resume was a stint as an economics student under George Shultz at the University of Chicago. Still unexplained, however, is the logic behind the Reagan administration's apparent decision to do business with Noriega, who was already known to be a corrupt and unreliable ally.

Panama had had no presidential election since 1968; in the meantime, the country was led by a government controlled by a succession of military strongmen. Noriega's predecessor, Brig. Gen. Omar Torrijos Herrera, was generally considered a dependable friend of the United States. But questions of Noriega's character and ultimate loyalties have been unresolved for more than a decade.

Documents show that officials of the Nixon administration were so concerned with Noriega's involvement in illegal drug trafficking that they considered several proposals, including assassination, to remove the general from power. Beyond that, U.S. officials accuse Noriega of having provided vital intelligence information to Cuba and other governments (as well as our own) for at least 15 years.

The United States' connection, however tenuous, to Noriega's strongman rule makes a mockery of the Reagan administration's general policy of promoting democratic reform in Latin America. Of more immediate importance to our own security, Noriega's erratic leadership threatens the future of the agreement under which the United States gradually turns control of the Panama Canal over to Panama.

The United States obviously has a vital long-term interest in the maintenance of a friendly, reliable government in Panama. But that interest will not be served by a marriage of convenience with a tyrant whose loyalty is constantly on sale to the highest bidder.

Noriega was warned prior to the 1984 elections that any attempt to subvert the political process would result in a cutoff of U.S. aid. Despite evidence of fraud at the time, aid continued unabated. A similar threat, with real meaning behind it, is needed to convince Noriega and his associates that Panama must join the democratic movement that has swept most of its Latin American neighbors.

The Washington Post

Washington, DC, June 24, 1986

Suddenly in parts of the press and television there is a retelling of the more or less familiar story of Panama's strongman, Gen. Manuel Noriega, accused drug trafficker, weapons peddler, murderer, double agent (spying for both the United States and Cuba), election fixer and coup maker. Interesting details have come to light, but what is even more intriguing are the possible explanations of why the rerun is occurring and of whose interest it serves.

The more innocent explanation is that the information on Gen. Noriega took on a shape so ominous and undeniable that the American intelligence agencies collecting it and the political bureaus receiving it simply could not keep it to themselves. The administration was caught between an American habit of winking at local foibles in order to enjoy the strategic comforts of close association with Panama, and its growing apprehension that Gen. Noriega's misrule was threatening to undermine the American interest in the stability of the country and its great canal.

A darker explanation is that elements on the American right who have never reconciled themselves to the Panama Canal treaties are pumping out damaging information about Gen. Noriega in order to make a case for going back on the American treaty commitment to turn over the canal to Panama in the year 2000. Sen. Jesse Helms (R-N.C.), who has used his Senate Foreign Relations subcommittee to air some of the charges, allows that "it may be entirely necessary down the road" for the United States to try to assume power over the Panama Canal again. An odd political matchup is taking place in Washington: conservatives whose interest is to demonstrate Panamanian frailty, liberals appalled by Gen. Noriega's human rights record.

In this murky scene, two things are clear. Gen. Noriega, who presides over a system that does not permit a fair judgment of the shocking charges against him, does not have a mandate from the Panamanian people and must allow the country's admittedly frail and uncertain democratic process to get back on its feet. Meanwhile, the United States—and this means Congress, too—cannot afford to give the slightest sustenance to the notion of revising the canal treaties. That way lies a cynical cultivation of instability in Panama and a threat to the strategic assets that the United States removed from risk precisely by the treaties some would now casually reopen.

Birmingham Post-Herald

Birmingham, AL, June 16, 1986

As if the United States did not have enough headaches in Central America, it now must decide what to do, if anything, about a Panamanian businessman whose business is, well, Panama.

The amigo in question is Gen. Manuel Antonio Noriega, head of the Panama Defense Force, who rules the strategically placed nation through a dummy civilian president, Eric Arturo Delvalle.

According to U.S. intelligence sources, quoted by The New York Times and NBC News, Noreiga is a busy beaver who intends to get as rich as such world-class crooks as Baby Doc Duvalier and Fredinand Marcos.

Noriega and his cronies in the Panamanian military run money-laundering activities for drug dealers. They protect drug shipments in and out of the country for a price. And they provide weapons to M-19, pro-Cuban guerrillas who are fighting to overthrow the democratically elected government of neighboring Colombia.

In addition, the good general is a secret investor in a Panamanian company that sells embargoed American technology to Cuba and the communist bloc in Europe. And for 15 years he has provided valuable information to the CIA, while evenhandedly furnishing Havana with intelligence on the United States.

Noriega presents a dilemma to Washington policymakers. He clearly is an asset to international drug traffickers who are ravaging this nation's youth. He also permits American actions that a successor might not: He allows the National Security Agency to eavesdrop on much of Latin America and the U.S. Army to conduct clandestine missions from Panama.

For this newspaper, the choice is easier than for the CIA and NSA. When you stay too close to a corrupt dictator for too long, as with Cuba's Batista, Nicaragua's Somoza and Iran's shah, you end up with virulently anti-American successor regimes.

Thus, if the Reagan administration can figure out how, it ought to facilitate Noriega's departure and his replacement by an honest democrat. He already has a vast fortune hidden in European banks and a house in southern France, not far from Baby Doc's, and the French economy needs all the help it can get.

Lexington Herald-Leader

Lexington, KY, June 24, 1986

Don't look now, but there's a crisis to the south. A Central American nation located near a vital U.S. strategic interest has been selling secrets to the Cubans. Its leaders are involved in smuggling drugs into this country. The military helped rig the country's last elections.

Clearly, it's time to send the Marines in to clean up this mess in Nicaragua, right?

Wrong.

The country in question is Panama, not Nicaragua. And the Reagan administration seems perfectly tolerant of this state of affairs.

This is a peculiar state of affairs. The Reagan administration has repeatedly denounced Nicaragua's government for its ties to Cuba and the Soviet Union, alleged that the Nicaraguans are involved in drug smuggling, and dismissed Nicaragua's 1984 elections as a sham.

The administration has known about the situation in Panama for some time, and has begun to tell reporters about it. But officials remain curiously silent about it in public. Although the government had extensive knowledge of the election irregularities, Secretary of State George Shultz congratulated the Panamanians on their 1984 elections, which he described as offering "Panamanians of all political persuasions a new opportunity for progress and national development." Our government recently sent the Panamanian government a note assuring them that we would keep quiet on the topic.

From one perspective, our desire not to stir up trouble with Panama is understandable. The Panama Canal remains a key strategic concern. The United States military's southern command center is in Panama, and overall the government remains friendly to us.

This policy is nothing new, of course. It is precisely the same kind of tack we took with the Somoza regime in Nicaragua and with scores of preceding military dictatorships in other countries in the region. So long as a government remains ostensibly friendly toward us, we will ignore its shortcomings.

This short-sighted attitude has gotten us into trouble before, and it will get us into trouble again. In fact, it is likely to cause trouble for the Reagan administration in short order.

The administration is trying again to push through Congress $100 million in aid to Nicaraguan rebels. Revelations about the rebel leaders' misuse of funds have made the administration's job harder. The news concerning Panama is apt to make it even more difficult.

This sort of double standard is at the heart of the administration's problems with its Central American policies. If Panama and the Nicaraguan contras are the best we can do for friends in that part of the world, maybe it's time to try embracing our enemies.

The Houston Post
Houston, TX, June 24, 1986

Panama's Gen. Manuel Antonio Noriega has been the target of allegations that he was involved in illicit activities ranging from narcotics-smuggling and money-laundering to assassination and election-rigging. U.S. officials have privately corroborated many of these disclosures, and Sen. Jesse Helms, R-N.C., has charged the Panamanian military chief with running "the biggest drug-trafficking operation in the Western Hemisphere."

Now a State Department spokesman says the reports that Noriega is connected with drug-smuggling are hearsay, circumstantial or speculative. That raises questions about other claims. Did the general, for instance, order the military to intervene in Panama's 1984 presidential election?

Political opponents of the Panamanian government have also attempted to tie Noriega to the death of a political dissident. Is this, too, hearsay? If we have hard evidence that Noriega is involved in corruption, that he has acted against U.S. interests, we shouldn't leak it and then issue a qualified repudiation of it. Such contradictory behavior damages our position in a strategically crucial region and our relations with the country that will control the Panama Canal in another 15 years.

The Providence Journal
Providence, RI, June 25, 1986

General Manuel Antonio Noriega, the strongman of Panama for the past five years, poses an interesting problem for the United States.

On the one hand, he is a strategic player in the broad scheme of Central American events: He is now, and has been for some time, a useful source of intelligence information for the region. He has granted the United States considerable latitude for military operations within Panama. And of course, he is the most important Panamanian with whom this country deals in the proposed transfer of authority over the Panama Canal. The canal treaties, ratified in 1977, take effect at the end of the century.

But General Noriega is also "head of the biggest drug trafficking operation in the Western Hemisphere," according to Sen. Jesse Helms (R-N.C.), and "a business partner with (Fidel) Castro."

Senator Helms is the first public official to confirm details of two-week-old news reports that accuse General Noriega of drug trafficking, money laundering and the murder of a political opponent. It also claims that he has been systematically providing intelligence data to Havana, as well as Washington, and sold restricted American technology to Cuba and various Eastern bloc governments. He is also alleged to be supplying arms to pro-Cuban rebels in democratic Colombia.

Such revelations put the United States in a quandary. Of course, in his day, Senator Helms was the most vocal opponent of the Canal treaties, and is no friend of the regime in Panama City. But as a senior member of the Foreign Relations Committee, he speaks with considerable authority, and his assertions have been met with a disconcerting silence in the two capitals.

After all, as armed forces chief, General Noriega is the real power in a country where his hand-picked prime minister is the nominal administrator. And for many strategic, military and diplomatic reasons, the United States must reckon with whomever or whatever governs Panama.

General Noriega has many friends in Washington. His predecessor, General Omar Torrijos, had many friends, too — and even some exotic admirers, such as the British novelist Graham Greene. But General Torrijos died in a mysterious helicopter crash in 1981, and his successor seems to have wormed his way into the confidence of military, intelligence and political circles in a variety of hemispheric capitals.

Senator Helms was asked over the weekend whether the United States should intervene in Panama, to oppose the government, as we have sought to exercise influence in Nicaragua, for the same reason. He declined to answer, partly because he does not wish to speculate about hypothetical matters, but largely because President Reagan is the Commander-in-Chief "and I am not."

Accordingly, President Reagan should take a hard look at the Panamanian in charge, and ask some pointed questions of his own: Are these allegations true, or can General Noriega prove that they are false? And if they are true, is this the sort of person with whom the United States can do business as we divest ourselves of the strategic waterway between the Atlantic and Pacific oceans?

These questions should be asked in Panama, by General Noriega's military associates and fellow countrymen. Perhaps they can furnish some answers about which Washington can only speculate.

Chicago Tribune
Chicago, IL, June 27, 1986

Even hardshell cynics might concede that Gen. Manuel Antonio Noriega of Panama has compiled for himself a fairly impressive resume as all-around villain and menace.

The military strongman, ostensibly an American ally who currently runs a country in which vital U.S. interests are at stake, is accused, on what appears to be substantial evidence, of: ordering up the assassination of at least one political opponent, who was, in especially grisly style, decapitated and deposited in a U.S. mailbag; possibly arranging the helicopter crash which killed his predecessor; providing intelligence information and American technology to Cuba; running guns to a pro-Cuban guerrilla organization in Colombia; and stealing the 1984 Panamanian presidential election for his candidate (whom he subsequently and unceremoniously dumped).

When not occupied with such delicate affairs of state the general, whose official title is commander of the army, also is accused of dabbling in a major-league money laundering operation and presiding over what Sen. Jesse Helms (R., N.C.) calls the "biggest drug trafficking operation in the Western hemisphere."

Sen. Helms, ardent conservative and achingly disappointed leader of the fight against the Panama Canal Treaty, which provides for the U.S. to turn the canal over to Panama in the year 2000, is floating another option.

Asked on a TV interview program if he thought the U.S. should move to reassert authority over the canal, Sen. Helms responded, "Well, I think it may be entirely necessary down the road. That depends on how the present situation involving Mr. Noriega is handled."

No, it doesn't. Even to suggest reopening the canal treaty question, to threaten now to take back and reclaim sovereignty over part of of another people's country, is as dumb and as extreme an idea as was the suggestion by law enforcement officials in the 1970s that the general be assassinated.

What the U.S. might do, for a start, is quit turning a blind eye to Gen. Noriega in return for his willingness to permit extensive American military and intelligence operations in Panama. For the State Department spokesman to declare only that "we find these allegations to be disturbing," which is approximately all the administration has done so far, is hardly an adequately robust response.

IMF Accord Signed After Finance Minister Resigns in Mexico

Fianace Minister Jesus Silva Herzog resigned unexpectedly June 17, 1986 at a critical point in months-long negotiations with Mexico's international creditors on its $98 billion foreign debt. Some political observers and international bankers were reported to believe that Silva Herzog had been fired. A cabinet dispute over the terms of an economic program being negotiated with the International Monetary Fund (IMF) in return for a fresh loan was cited as the possible cause. Silva Herzog's departure indicated to a number of observers a toughening in Mexico's stand on repayment of its $98 billion debt, but a senior Mexican official, who asked not to be identified, said June 18 that the government intended to continue seeking a negotiated solution to the debt crisis.

Mexico had been negotiating with the IMF since the fall of 1985. A major stumbling block in the talks was a budget deficit, which currently equaled 13% of the nation's output. As the talks entered 1986, Mexico's stance hardened with the precipitous decline in the price of oil. Mexican officials threatened a unilateral moratorium on debt payments, claiming that the nation had reached the limit of its ability to pay. An agreement with the IMF would clear the way for a new financial package from commercial banks, and Reagan Administration and international banking officials said June 10 that such a package was near. The banks had refused to consider new loans to Mexico unless an IMF agreement was reached.

But, after months of negotiations, Mexico July 22 signed an agreement with the IMF for a $1.6 billion loan. The pact was expected to pave the way for more than $10 billion in additional new loans for Mexico by the end of 1987. In signing the pact, IMF Managing Director Jacques de Larosiere urged a "major cooperative effort" by the world financial community to provide Mexico with the funds it needed. The objective of the new agreement, he said, was to "help Mexico deal with its economic imbalance, which had been intensified as a result of the oil price drop."

St. Petersburg Times

St. Petersburg, FL, June 16, 1986

Mexico is like a sick, possibly dying, next-door neighbor. All of our immediate instincts tell us to do whatever we can to ease the neighbor's obvious suffering. But the suffering doesn't end in a day or a month: Our compassion for our neighbor begins to compete with our own problems and concerns, and the efforts that we do manage to make may seem futile and painful.

Eventually, we may come to resent the neighbor, to consider his very presence a reminder of our own fragile well-being, a reminder of our failure to do as much for him and others as we might — a reminder that we, too, are more dependent on our neighbors than we might like to believe.

Each season seems to bring a terrible new dimension to Mexico's ever-worsening economic and social crises. Mexico's $100-billion foreign debt would require serious economic austerity, with all of the political instability that it implies, even in the best of circumstances. The ironically named Institutional Revolutionary Party, despite some sincere recent efforts to extricate Mexico from its hole, has survived decades of poor industrial planning, inequitable distribution of wealth and corrupt control of power. No true democratic opposition now exists to challenge that tradition.

Add a catastrophic earthquake and a catastrophic (for Mexico) drop in world oil prices, and Mexico's situation seems almost terminal.

And without the long-term help of the rest of the world, especially the United States, Mexico, at least as it now exists, will not be able to survive. On at least one level, the world, led by the United States, is responding once again. The Reagan administration, in concert with the international banking community, has developed a plan for as much as $6-billion in new loans to help Mexico through its immediate economic crisis.

That intervention brought at least a temporary halt to the sharp decline in the value of the peso. Perhaps even more important was the psychological lift it gave to a government and people badly in need of good news and good luck.

The mood of the Mexican government and people also would be greatly improved if a handful of Washington demagogues would quit trying to score petty political points at Mexico's expense. North Carolina Sen. Jesse Helms presided over a recent subcommittee session in which all sorts of loose charges of criminal conduct were casually tossed in the lap of the Mexican government. When Mexican officials protested, Helms responded with his inimitable brand of offhand racism: "All Latin people are volatile people," he said. "Hence, I was not surprised by the volatile reaction."

No one in the Reagan administration has stooped that low in slandering Mexico, but administration officials did participate in Helms' media event, and they should have known to expect Helms' ugly buffoonery. Other White House officials have been publicly critical of Mexico's economic efforts, when private guidance would have been more appropriate.

The new loan package seems to signal a change in administration policy toward Mexico. The White House also is pressuring the International Monetary Fund and other creditors to ease their demands for new Mexican austerity measures as a condition for new loans. Even the administration's language was more conciliatory, praising the Mexican people for the "sacrifices" they have already made.

Mexico's economic and political problems have reached the point of becoming serious economic and political problems for the United States. For many reasons, we owe Mexico our help — even our occasional helpful criticism — rather than our scorn and inattention.

DESERET NEWS

Salt Lake City, UT, June 24-25, 1986

If you borrow enough money, once commented Texas phosphate dealer Billy Sol Estes, you don't have a creditor — you have a partner.

Mexico may have achieved that delicate distinction. Mired in $98 billion worth of foreign debt, Mexico is acting more and more like a partner rather than a debtor nation. With the sudden resignation last week of Finance Minister Jesus Silva Herzog, a well-known and moderate figure in finance, there's talk that Mexico may toughen its stand on international debt.

The International Monetary Fund, which must approve debt measures taken by Mexico before it can hope to get any more bank loans, is haggling with Mexico over how much the country should cut spending in order to pay its debt commitments. Herzog, of course, was at the center of those talks. Whether he fell from power or was pushed out is still uncertain.

Sen. Jesse Helms stirred up further trouble this week by accusing President Miguel de la Madrid of stealing the 1982 elections. He claimed Mexican sources gave him documents showing de la Madrid actually won only 39.8 percent of the vote, but had proclaimed himself president with 71.2 percent of election ballots cast.

Such charges, even if they can be substantiated, can only harm U.S.-Mexican relations and contribute to the instability of the Mexican government. Pushed too far, Mexico may just renounce its $98 billion in foreign debt — $70 billion of which is owed to commercial banks, including those in the U.S. In that case it would have to take its chances on the world markets.

If Mexico defaults, it can shake the U.S. economy, greatly increase the flood of illegal immigrants now entering this country, and add to drug trafficking problems between the two nations. Most of the $98 billion debt was contracted in the palmy days of rising oil prices and vast new petroleum discoveries. Since then, the fall in oil prices has wiped out 30 percent of Mexico's foreign-exchange earnings and 12 percent of its total government income.

The primary difficulty now is that Mexico cannot meet the austerity measures laid down by the IMF without plundering its already-shaky economy. It already has tightened up considerably since 1982 when it was forced to adopt tough IMF economic measures to qualify for a $9 billion rescue plan. Further belt-tightening may be counterproductive.

The Times-Picayune
The States-Item
New Orleans, LA, June 24, 1986

Mexico's chronic international debt problem appears to be reaching another juncture of special significance. The beleaguered government of President Miguel de la Madrid is said to be on the verge of offering a new plan for repaying Mexico's $97 billion foreign debt.

Only last week Finance Minister Jesus Silva Herzog suddenly resigned amid reports of sharp disagreements within Mr. de la Madrid's Cabinet over the debt issue. The resignation sparked speculation that Mexico was about to take a tougher line toward repayment of its huge debt.

It now appears that Mexico will ask for, and have trouble getting, major new concessions as part of any new debt-restructuring accord.

Mexico is believed to need an additional $5 billion to $6 billion in financial help this year. Before Mr. Silva Herzog resigned, there had been reports that Mexico had been close to an agreement with the International Monetary Fund and its foreign creditors on a new $8 billion financial aid package. Apparently those reports were premature.

The collapse of world oil prices has already eliminated some $6 billion in oil revenues the Mexican government had expected to receive this year. The nation's international reserves are believed to have dwindled to about $5 billion, increasing the pressure on the Mexican government to find some relief from its debt payments.

Two key issues could snag efforts by Mexico to renegotiate a new debt plan on its own terms. The International Monetary Fund has insisted that Mexico cut its budget deficit from about 13 percent to 6 percent. Heretofore, the de la Madrid government has resisted, fearing the additional political pressure that would result from the severe cutbacks in social programs required to meet the IMF's demand. A new debt accord depends on a compromise.

Mexico also might insist that its foreign creditor banks, including a number of major U.S. banks, agree to lower their interest rates on Mexico's existing debt. The banks, which are reluctant to make further loans to Mexico for obvious reasons, have already signaled their unwillingness to trim interest rates on existing loans. Many have substantial outstanding loans to other countries and do not wish to provoke other demands for cuts in interest rates.

So the Mexican debt problem grows trickier. Before he resigned or was fired, Mr. Silva Herzog had hinted that Mexico might decide to default on its debt payments.

President de la Madrid apparently has discarded so drastic a step, but there is an implicit threat of possible default in his apparent willingness to take a tougher line with Mexico's creditors.

Mexico's debt problem is the United States' problem as well, and it is not getting any easier.

The Washington Post
Times Herald
Washington, DC, June 19, 1986

THE SENSE of strain is rising in Mexico, and the crisis that began with its foreign debts four years ago is becoming sharper. The dismissal of the Mexican government's chief debt strategist, Finance Minister Jesus Silva Herzog, seems clearly to be related to the divisions within the government over its next move. The drop in the price of oil since January represents a loss to Mexico of one-fourth of its federal revenue and one-third of its export earnings. The enormous budget deficit is pushing up the inflation rate, and capital flight has begun again. In the midst of these tensions, the Mexican government is being subjected to Sen. Jesse Helms's abusive and inflammatory hearings here in Washington.

It's easy for Americans, who know Sen. Helms well, to brush off his attacks on Mexico. But it's harder for Mexicans. There are fears in Mexico that the United States is trying to do to President Miguel de la Madrid what it did last year to President Ferdinand Marcos of the Philippines—to undercut his reputation and authority in preparation for a change of government. That suggestion is considered ludicrous here. But to many Mexicans, accustomed to their own tightly centralized politics, it is inconceivable that a senator of President Reagan's party could launch hearings of this nature except at the administration's direction.

Last month Sen. Helms took testimony—much of it evidently inaccurate—on corruption and drugs. This week he charged massive fraud in Mexico's last president election, a direct assault on President de la Madrid's legitimacy. If the administration does not intend to let Sen. Helms take over its Latin American policy, President Reagan is going to have to step forward, personally and publicly, to reassure Mexico that the senator speaks for no one but himself.

Why is Sen. Helms doing it? To punish Mexico for its refusal to support the United States in Nicaragua is some part of it. Perhaps he also hopes that a change of government in Mexico would bring the far right to power. That is a grievous misconception of Mexican politics, for nationalism there pulls to the left.

But it would be an equally serious mistake on the part of the administration to underestimate the degree to which the Helms hearings can poison the atmosphere in which the debt negotiations go forward. For Mexico and its friends, dealing with the debts this year is both easier and harder than in 1982, when it suddenly declared its inability to repay. It is easier because Mexico is now an isolated case. The falling oil prices that have caused Mexico's distress promise to benefit most of the other Latin economies. But dealing with the debts is harder because Mexico is wearying of the long years of negotiations and the feeling that it's at the mercy of the foreign bankers. There's a rising temptation to indulge in a sweeping gesture such as a unilateral moratorium on payments, despite the knowledge of the great economic damage that would follow.

To keep the talks on a rational and productive level will require great strength on the part of President de la Madrid and his government. It may also require a more visible demonstration of American support than the administration has yet provided.

Detroit Free Press
Detroit, MI, June 30, 1986

PRESIDENT REAGAN'S invitation to the president of Mexico, Miguel de la Madrid, to come to the United States for a visit in August is a welcome development in the effort to maintain good relations with our southern neighbor. The relationship has become at least temporarily "very touchy," as described by an unnamed U.S. official.

The touchiness proceeds both from real problems — Mexico's debt problems, the traffic in drugs and people across the border, and alleged corruption in Mexico — and from insults traded back and forth across the border, sometimes for no good reason. One of the more egregious blunders was the statement, by the customs commissioner of the United States, William von Raab, who testified before a Senate Foreign Relations subcommittee that the governor of the Mexican state of Sonora was growing marijuana or opium poppies on his ranch. The Reagan administration has been embarrassed by that and other inaccurate assertions made in testimony before the subcommittee, which is chaired by Sen. Jesse Helms, R-N.C.

The United States is going to be walking a tight and thin line between the need to address Mexican policies and problems that affect this country and the need to try to maintain civil relations with a close neighbor. The border problems seem to get progressively worse; descriptions of what Border Patrol officers encounter virtually every night are incredible. It is not racism or chauvinism for this country to refuse to be what the Mexican foreign minister calls "a safety valve" for Mexico. Neither is that the kind of discussion that is likely to improve relations with Mexico.

The president will need to use all his considerable diplomatic skills to try to get U.S.-Mexican relations onto a sounder footing. We have our agenda, and where it concerns debt, drugs and illegal immigration, our government should not simply accede to whatever abuses occur. Sen. Helms, though, cannot be allowed to set the tone for those relations. And the United States cannot afford to try simply to bully its neighbor. Balance is harder to produce than bombast.

Newsday

Long Island, NY, June 16, 1986

After months of dickering and uncertainty, Mexico and its American bankers appear to be near agreement on new lending to that debt-ridden nation. And the Reagan administration, after publicly accusing Mexico of corruption and indifference to drug trafficking, is now pressing the International Monetary Fund to approve a Mexican austerity program that would be the final piece of a wider lending plan.

That's good. Mexico has been flirting with the idea of reneging on its outstanding loans — a tactic espoused, though not practiced, by other Latin American leaders. Default could have disastrous consequences for Mexico, which needs foreign trade and capital to pull out of its slump.

Mexico owes about $25 billion to U.S. banks and has found it more and more difficult to keep up payments. Last year's deadly earthquake took an economic toll as well, and the plunge in the price of oil has knocked the bottom out of Mexico's major source of revenue from abroad.

Fortunately, Mexico now appears to have rejected any unilateral renunciation of its debt — perhaps because the American banks have rearranged their balance sheets to reduce the impact of a default. That makes the threat of one less effective as a bargaining tool.

But the new financing agreement, which would provide Mexico about $6 billion in additional loans, won't be final until the IMF approves a Mexican austerity plan.

No matter how hard Mexico has worked to put its house in order, it still hasn't moved to quit money-losing government enterprises or open its doors wide to foreign investment — both necessary steps to put its resources to more productive use.

Some analysts in this country argue that Mexico can never meet IMF austerity demands and pay its debts. Trying to do that, they say, keeps the country from making the kind of investments that could help its economy grow.

But it's foreign pressure — such as Treasury Secretary James Baker's campaign last year to get debtor nations to open their economies to investment from abroad — that has spurred Mexico to look seriously at real reform. Now it's the IMF's turn to press for cuts in inefficient government spending.

Mexico probably can't pay back as much or change as fast as foreign lenders would like without creating severe political problems at home. But Mexico is too deep in debt to turn away foreign capital or to continue wasting its own. Change is hard, but for Mexico to make any real economic progress, there's really no other choice.

THE TENNESSEAN

Nashville, TN, June 17, 1986

THE debt crisis in Mexico is an issue of growing concern in the U.S. and elsewhere with fears that faced with growing poverty and political alienation, that country could begin to come apart.

Conjectures about Mexico's intentions regarding its $98 billion foreign debt has been intense, dominating financial, government and political circles. With that country's foreign reserves shrinking and its loss of crude oil revenues this year expected to top $6 billion, its situation is certainly grave.

There appears to be an aid package taking shape, but a source of frustation is Mexico's unwillingness to get its economic house in order through policy reforms. The one-year rescue plan under consideration would provide the country with $1 billion from the International Monetary Fund; $1 billion from the World Bank; $2.5 billion from commercial banks and about $900 million from other countries.

But until the IMF approves a debt plan, private bankers are not willing to provide new funds. The IMF wants Mexico to cut its budget deficit to 6% of national output instead of the current 12%.

A budget cut of that size would impose intolerable pain on Mexico's citizens, already pinched by the flagging economy. Unemployment and underemployment and inflation are constant threats to the people.

Needed development capital is being sent out of the country in a flow that would probably match half its debt.

Mexico was bankrupt when President Miguel de la Madrid Hurtado took over in 1982, but people were willing to undergo some tough times in order to see their economy grow again. But the problem was the drop in oil prices. Last year Mexico counted on oil for about half its domestic debt collections and three quarters of its foreign sales revenues.

President de la Madrid said recently that the drop in oil prices from more than $25 a barrel to as low as $12 has slashed Mexico's foreign-exchange earnings by 30% and cut government income by more than 12%.

Part of the problem is political. The ruling party has been in power since the revolution and its dominance has led Mexico into a statist system of top-heavy and inefficient industries. There is widespread corruption.

It needs to denationalize some of its state-owned businesses, to crack down hard on corruption and to make other policy changes that are going to be difficult. Its range of choice is quite narrow, however, but the reality is that it must choose.

A stable Mexico is crucial to the Americas and to the United States. It does need all the help that this country can muster. ∎

Los Angeles, CA, June 17, 1986

The $6 billion rescue package being hammered out between international financial agencies and Mexico may alleviate the symptoms of that nation's sickly economy, but it won't cure the illness.

Mexico may never be able to repay its $100 billion foreign debt, even if the deflated oil prices that have triggered the latest crisis begin turning upward. Sooner or later, the U.S. banks that loaned most of  **De la Madrid** the money will have to come to terms with that possibility.

If Mexico were to default on its loans, several U.S. banks would be devastated financially. In turn, many Americans would be affected. So it's no surprise that bankers are postponing that day of reckoning by preparing to bail Mexico out again. The International Monetary Fund also has tried to stave off that catastrophe by making new loans contingent upon Mexico's adopting a strict austerity program.

Mexico has imposed discipline in some areas, but it has failed to do much to cut either its massive corruption or the bloated state-run enterprises that are sucking the economy dry. The economy is shrinking, and poverty is exploding. And Mexico has been unable to generate enough export earnings to pay the interest on its debt, let alone the principal.

A solution to Mexico's predicament will come about only with changes instituted by both Mexico and its creditors. In the short term, lenders will have to put some cap on Mexico's interest payments, protecting the nation from sky-high interest rates so the economy can start to dig itself out of its hole. Some of the debt probably will have to be written off.

For Mexico's part, the government must be far more aggressive in its attempt to unshackle its economy: President Miguel de la Madrid should not only earnestly crack down on corruption and privatize many state-run industries, but he should also promote new investment both within the country and from the U.S.

It's possible that the Institutional Revolutionary Party (PRI), which has dominated Mexico for 57 years, is incapable of making these hard choices. Perhaps new, bolder leadership will emerge from the alternative National Action Party (PAN), which is challenging PRI in the country's state elections next month. Whatever the outcome, it's clear that the time for change has come.

HELMS' HAT DANCE

Mexico

6/20/86, THE PHILADELPHIA INQUIRER
UNIVERSAL PRESS SYND.

WINSTON-SALEM JOURNAL

Winston-Salem, NC, June 20, 1986

Mexico, our neighbor to the south, is in trouble. She has come once again to the brink of financial chaos. And once again, found a temporary rescue. The chairman of the Federal Reserve Board, Paul Volcker, made an unpublicized trip to Mexico City. He subsequently put together a bail-out package sponsored by private banks, the IMF, the World Bank, the Japanese and the Paris club of banks.

To make matters worse, Sen. Jesse Helms has discovered Mexico and its problems: A debt so great that it threatens the international banking community, (albeit with cash-flow difficulties, not collapse) and a swell of illegal emigres fleeing worsening poverty and corruption. The loan figure is $6 billion.

That will pay the bulk of interest on the debt. Twelve percent of Mexico's GNP goes toward it. The peso has fallen to, conservatively, 627 to the dollar. From 1935 to 1982, the Mexican economy grew by some 6 percent a year. Since 1982, Mexico has experienced zero economic growth. The experts say the standard of living in Mexico is now comparable to what it was in 1966.

The Volcker fix done, the American banks will get their cut. Mexico itself will need more than a debt repayment plan or "conciliatory default," though this may help in the short run.

In addition to economic growth and stability, Mexico has traditionally been politically stable. One reason has been the way that national wealth has been distributed. To put it kindly, the citizenry, or enough of the right target groups in it, were co-opted. Now Mexico must either face reducing the welfare and graft it doles out to keep the citizens of a sham democracy quiet, or continue the payoff at current rates, hence continuing to be unable to pay off the debt.

The deeper problem is political. The Mexican governors find themselves in a conundrum. It is that while more democracy and economic freedom might, in past times, have been an apt trade off for a stagnated standard of living, to liberalize in a period of depression is almost certainly to lose power.

Today the Mexican ruling party (the PRI) is hoarding power illegitimately. They are losing their base with the middle class, and the opposition party (the PAN) is increasingly strong. President de la Madrid was initially inclined to open up and let the PAN have their day. But they got too many votes, especially in the North, where the Californian way of life is visible. No wonder 80 percent of the Mexican people say they do not believe their government.

More, relations between the United States and Mexico are perhaps at an all-time low. The United States has bullied Mexico about the debt, and about drugs and immigration. The administration had just begun to soften its voice when Helms began ranting. The Mexicans feel humiliated. And relations have not been helped by the ambassadorship of John Gavin, a former actor and friend of the president's. He is a fellow who fits Winston Churchill's characterization of an American diplomat: a bull who carries a china shop with him. Now Gavin has resigned and is being replaced by a retired rubber executive.

Which shows the lack of understanding for the problem in Washington, D.C. Mexico is not of minor concern to us. We are in danger of losing that buffer between ourselves and the more unstable areas of the hemisphere. Mexico could fail to become completely democratic — could, in fact, slip backward — and that would be a far greater problem than the Sandinistas in Nicaragua.

The essence of the new isolationism is to insist upon displays of American power where they are of marginal or no importance or to insist upon an illusion of American omnipotence, which can only be sustained for the length of a Las Vegas lounge act.

We should make a special commitment to Mexican oil, encourage investment in Mexico and defer to Mexico in Central American affairs instead of shunting her aside. When we do the latter, we decrease the ability of Mexican leaders to appeal to pride, which gives Mexicans, as every people, hope and a sense of efficacy. We should create a new Marshall Plan to help the Americas, as we did when we rebuilt Europe.

At this point, militarism will win some grudging respect but books and bread, not bombs, are the ways to counter the Marxian promise of social and economic equality. It's fine to tell the Mexicans to open their markets, but they need consumers to inhabit them.

Part II: Nicaragua

The United States has been involved in Central American affairs for more than 100 years. U.S.-orchestrated invasions and occupations throughout this century placed dictators acceptable to the U.S. in power and succeeded in establishing temporary stability but left behind a legacy of ruthlessness that has been challenged and in some cases erased. The legacy of U.S. involvement in Nicaragua, for instance, has given the revolutionary Sandinista government ample reason not to trust the "Colossus of the North." U.S. Marines invaded Nicaragua twice in the 20th Century, occupying the country from 1912-1925 and from 1926-1933. During the latter intervention, American troops helped usher into power the Somoza family, which ruled Nicaragua for two generations until overthrown by the Sandinistas in 1979, by handpicking Anastasio Somoza to head the despised National Guard.

Guerilla bands named for the martyred patriot Augusto Sandino began challenging the U.S.-sponsored Somoza regime in the 1960s. But it wasn't until Anastasio "Tachito" Somoza, son of the first dictator, scandalized even his supporters by misappropriating disaster-relief funds for the devastating 1972 earthquake that virtually destroyed the capital of Managua that the opposition movement began to garner popular support. By 1978 the revolution was successful and Somoza fled the country. But as the Carter Administration's early support was frustrated, the Reagan Administration's immediate impatience with the Sandinistas was blamed on reasons that included the postponement of elections, a growing Cuban and Eastern-bloc presence, the militarization of Nicaragua and the suspension of certain media freedoms. President Jimmy Carter, in the last days of his tenure, charging the Sandinista's with arming the guerillas in El Salvador, suspended a pending aid package and blocked international financial loans. In April 1981, the new Reagan Administration canceled the assistance in spite of evidence that aid to the Salvadoran guerillas had decreased in response to the suspension under the Carter Administration.

The Central Intelligence Agency (CIA) received congressional authorization in November 1981 to assist covert counterrevolutionary groups (contras) already operating against the Sandinistas. Although the congressional authorization was ostensibly to assist the contras to deter Sandinista support for the Salvadoran guerillas, the contras themselves stated from the outset that their goal was to overthrow the Sandinistas. Congress cut funding for the covert activity in June 1983 after authorizing some $80 million in aid to the contras over a period of two years. Nevertheless, the contras, some 500 strong in 1981, had reportedly grown to 15,000 by 1985 and had broadened their political and military base. However, they were unable to occupy any Nicaraguan territory and continued to operate out of bases in Honduras and Costa Rica. From the outset, the contras have been charged with killing innocent civilians and have caused great loss of life, disrupted important economic activities such as the coffee harvest and forced the Sandinistas to institute an unpopular draft and increase military spending.

U.S.-Nicaraguan tensions increased in 1985. Congress at first rejected continued aid to the the contras, despite massive lobbying by the Reagan Administration. Some members, however, were able to encourage the president to use his emergency powers to declare an economic embargo against Nicaragua. But when the Sandinistas continued to persue closer relations with the Soviet Union, one of their last remaining allies, many in Congress who had opposed direct military aid to the contras voted for $27 million in aid for "humanitarian" purposes. The U.S. aid for food, clothing and medical supplies kept the rebels in business by allowing them to channel funds raised privately to the purchase of weapons without direct U.S. involvement. This proved to be a key factor as the Iran-contra arms scandal unfolded in late 1986.

Disclosure of CIA-Directed Mining of Nicaraguan Ports Creates Furor

Following revelations April 6-7, 1984 that the United States Central Intelligence Agency (CIA) had directed the mining of Nicaraguan ports, the U.S. Congress voted to condemn U.S. participation in the operation. Press reports cited unidentified U.S. Administration and congressional official sources who revealed that Salvadoran and other Latin America nationals operating from a CIA-controlled ship off Nicaragua's Pacific coast had planted mines in the ports of Corinto and Puerto Sandino under the direction of the Americans. Previously, U.S. personnel were believed to have played no direct role in covert action against the Sandinista government. The disclosure sparked an outcry in Congress and prompted sense-of-the-Congress votes in both houses April 11-12 condemning the mining. Federal law required that the CIA inform Congress about intelligence operations. The Administration said April 11 that the mining had been halted.

The mining operations began in February 1984, and until the April disclosures, at least eight ships from six nations had been damaged. Kenneth Dam, Deputy Secretary of State, told the House Foreign Affairs Committee April 11 that the mining had ended in late March, whereas other officials had reportedly said it was ended only in recent days. Dam declined to acknowledge that the U.S. was directly involved, but said that if that were the case, the U.S. role was justified as an act of collective self-defense. The Senate nonbinding resolution, approved by a vote of 84-12, opposed the use of U.S. funds to plan, direct, execute or support the mining of Nicaragua's territorial waters. It marked the first time that the Republican-controlled Senate had blatantly opposed the administration's Central American policy. Nicaragua April 9 asked the International Court of Justice in The Hague to order the U.S. to halt the mining and cease aiding attacks on its territory. In anticipation of the Nicaraguan move, however, the Reagan Administration April 8 announced that, for a two-year period, it would not accept the court's jurisdiction in U.S. disputes involving Central America.

The Des Moines Register

Des Moines, IA,
April 12, 1984

That was strong stuff coming out of the Senate about U.S. involvement in Nicaragua.

Assailing the administration both for the U.S. role in the mining of Nicaragua's harbors and for its renunciation of World Court jurisdiction, senators of both parties registered their unhappiness on two counts: the extremism of the tactics, and the lack of consultation

Heightening the anger was the recollection of President Reagan's recent chastisements of Congress for meddling in foreign policy once it is formulated. That's all the harder to swallow for a Senate that learns how little involved — or even informed — it has been in the formulation, as Barry Goldwater's sizzling letter (printed on this page) shows.

Of course, the Senate only last week approved money for the covert operations in Nicaragua and rejected attempts to put constraints on it. One amendment would have left the money intact, but stipulated that it could not be used to support acts of terrorism. The Senate voted 47-43 to table that measure, with Iowa's two senators splitting on the issue — Roger Jepsen voting to table, Charles Grassley voting against tabling.

But on Tuesday, when U.S. involvement in the mining became clear and public, the sentiment changed. The Senate voted 84-12 against what many called this "act of war"; both Iowa senators, along with the Republican Senate leadership, supported the resolution.

•

It was the first time the Republican-controlled Senate had rejected an element of Reagan's Central American policy. Combined with the anticipated House rejection of the $21-million appropriation for the operation in Nicaragua, it made a strong statement indeed.

It was an outcry of the American people against the extraordinary tactics of an arrogant administration, it was representative government at its best ... and thank goodness for it.

Charleston, WV, April 11, 1984

TUESDAY'S outcry by hawkish Sen. Barry Goldwater, R-Ariz., that President Reagan committed an act of war by ordering mines planted in Nicaraguan harbors — plus rising protests by other Congress members — indicates the tide of national opinion is turning against Reagan's warmongering.

Until now, Congress has acquiesced to Reagan's trillion-dollar arms buildup, his Grenada invasion, his 10-warhead MX missiles, his secret Nicaraguan war — but events of the past week are horrifying:

▲ It was learned that CIA agents put mines in Nicaraguan harbors, damaging ships of Holland, Britain, Japan, the Soviet Union, Liberia and other nations..

▲ France offered to help Nicaragua remove the mines, and Britain protested that the U.S. act violated laws of the seas.

▲ The U.N. Security Council voted 13-1 to condemn outside military intervention in Nicaragua. The lone opposing vote was a U.S. veto.

▲ The State Department notified the World Court in The Hague that America won't accept its judgment on U.S. actions. But Nicaragua filed a World Court protest anyway.

Harvard law professor Abram Chayes, top State Department lawyer under President Kennedy, drafted the Nicaraguan complaint to the World Court. He said the Reagan administration is violating the U.N. Charter and solemn treaties in which America pledged not to molest neighbor nations.

Roberts Owen, top State Department lawyer under President Carter, said Reagan's renouncement of the World Court proves his guilt. If Nicaragua were keeping a ship off the U.S. coast and sending speedboats at night to plant mines in New York harbor, America certainly would regard it as a violation, he said.

Now Goldwater says Reagan personally gave written approval for the mining. "It is an act of war. For the life of me, I don't see how we are going to explain it."

Superpower America obviously can smash the weak new government of Nicaragua, an impoverished little nation of only 2.6 million people.

But, in the process, President Reagan is dishonoring the United States, violating the American conscience, breaking treaties to which the United States has put its name, alienating U.S. allies, defying the world's highest law tribunal — and turning Congress against his militarism.

The Evening Gazette

Worcester, MA, March 13, 1984

The Reagan administration is playing a dangerous game in Nicaragua. Its policy may be justified, it may even be successful, but it is dangerous all the same.

The policy is to encourage and support insurgents to blow up bridges, power stations and fuel tanks in Nicaragua to put pressure on the Marxist regime in Managua. The insurgents are based mainly in Honduras, where the United States has been building up military strength. Some rebel units are reported to have penetrated more than 70 miles into Nicaragua.

But have the Sandinistas sued for peace? Not so far as is known. Instead, last month a Soviet delegation flew into Managua to discuss increased Soviet assistance to the beleaguered Marxist regime. If the aim is to loosen the tie with Moscow, it doesn't seem to be working.

The Reagan people say that they are not aiming to topple the Sandinistas, but only trying to get Nicaragua to stop supplying and helping the guerrillas who are trying to overthrow the government of El Salvador. Few Latin Americans believe that Washington's goals are limited to that.

It may be that the Sandinistas will finally bow to the growing military pressure. But they may not. They may militarize the country even further. They may get even greater support from Cuba and Moscow. And the war in El Salvador may continue to go badly for our side.

In that case, what will we do? Will we move steadily toward direct U.S. military intervention or will we decide to negotiate? And, if so, is it better to negotiate now or later?

Arkansas Gazette.

Little Rock, AR, April 13, 1984

It really is 1984, the year when doublespeak has come to full flower as George Orwell foresaw in his prescient novel. A State Department spokesman has described the CIA's mining of Nicaraguan waters as an act of "collective self-defense." Fact and reality have flown the coop in this fourth year of the rule of Ronald Reagan.

Even Orwell would have been impressed at the claim that putting mines in the waters of Nicaragua, a sovereign country no matter how scruffy its government, is somehow an act of defense on the part of the United States, acting through its Central Intelligence Agency. The American policy toward Nicaragua is evocative of Vietnam, where we were engaged for so many years in defending the shores of California from the perfidious communists — or so the Vietnam War's loudest advocates would have had us all believe.

In Nicaragua we do not even have a government in residence to support. In any event, President Reagan and his warhawks have over-reached themselves this time, for the Congress is having no part of the astonishing argument advanced by the administration. The Senate rushed through a bipartisan resolution, 84 to 12, calling for a halt to the mining of Nicaraguan waters. The House prepared to follow suit. The most influential members of the Senate's Republican leadership were aghast. Barry Goldwater was furious at his not having been consulted even though his committee has the CIA in its purview. The Foreign Relations Committee was not consulted either in this outrageous enterprise undertaken by the CIA under authority of the President.

How much of the Reagan foreign policy, in its deliberate provocation of every adversary, real or fancied, large or small, is the American public prepared to accept and endure? It is unlikely that anything except a sustained wave of popular indignation will bring this administration to its senses.

EVENING EXPRESS

Portland, ME, April 13, 1984

The near unanimity of congressional condemnation of the mining of Nicaraguan harbors should put the Reagan administration on notice: Covert activities in Central America—or anywhere—must stop short of anything resembling overt actions of war.

The direct involvement of the CIA in the mining operation constitutes such an action. Sen. Barry Goldwater put it plainly in an anguished letter to CIA Director William J. Casey: "This is an act violating international law. It is an act of war. For the life of me, I don't see how we are going to explain it."

And Goldwater is a friend of the administration, a leading supporter of the president's confused Central American policies. If he can't explain it, who can?

Acts of war cannot be tolerated by a nation in which only Congress has the power to declare war. International lawlessness cannot be accepted by a nation whose whole history and tradition rests on a devotion to the principles of law.

The administration only compounds the offense by airily withdrawing from the jurisdiction of the World Court when it is called to account for actions we would not condone by any other country.

The secret warfare in Central America holds the same insidious danger which carried us by barely perceptible degrees into the Vietnam disaster.

There is the same taking of sides in a civil war, justified in the name of democracy and resistance to communism, the same CIA machinations, the same gradual burning of bridges to the rear.

In Vietnam this nation first became quietly entrapped, then obsessed, drained, divided and ultimately defeated.

The parallel to Central America may not be exact, but we dismiss the similarities only at our peril.

THE SACRAMENTO BEE

Sacramento, CA, May 31, 1984

All along we thought it was CIA Director Bill Casey who was handing out the disinformation about the mining of the Nicaraguan harbors. But now here's the president telling a European television crew that the mining was "much ado about nothing" fueled by the Communists' "worldwide disinformation machine." Those were just little itty-bitty "homemade mines," the president said, "that couldn't sink a ship," probably something put together in some contra's garage out of a few pieces of wire and some of those exploding cigars the CIA once hoped to use on Castro.

You have to wonder. The president says all those people who worried about the mining probably had good intentions; it's just that they've been propagandized by that Communist disinformation. But he doesn't say how they're confused. The president says the mines were planted in Nicaraguan harbors by Nicaraguan rebels; does that mean the president doesn't know that people in his own administration have already acknowledged that the CIA directed the mining operation?

The president says the mines "couldn't sink a ship" (although they've damaged some ships and injured members of their crews); does that mean we were running an operation — which we have since said we have discontinued — that, while it violated all international law and was thus sure to get the United States another black eye, was bound to be ineffective? If it was all so harmless, why did Casey fail to tell the Senate Intelligence Committee, as the law requires? Whose disinformation was that?

The president says he doesn't want to be presumptuous, "but is there any one of (the critics) who has access to all the information that the president of the United States has?" Now that's begging a real question.

The Chattanooga Times

Chattanooga, TN, April 11, 1984

Things are not going well for President Reagan and his "secret war" against the government of Nicaragua. For one thing, the word is out that the CIA has crossed the line to active involvement in the military operations of the anti-Sandinista rebels. For another, Nicaragua has asked the International Court of Justice to rule on the legality of U.S. actions in suppport of the insurgency. Anticipating Nicaragua's initiative, the Reagan administration advised the World Court Friday it would not accept its jurisdiction in the matter, but sufficient notice may not have been given to avoid exploration of the question in that international forum.

Mr. Reagan was asking for trouble when the CIA-sponsored insurgency escalated efforts at economic sabotage by mining Nicaragua's harbors. Exploding mines have damaged several ships, including Japanese and Soviet vessels. This highly provocative act has aroused opposition even among U.S. allies, notably, Britain and France. And reports that the CIA supervised the mining and that CIA operatives actually laid the mines has fueled the fire of congressional opposition to Mr. Reagan's secret war.

The House of Representatives twice in the past year attempted to halt funding for the "contras," as the CIA-backed guerrillas are called; but the Senate has not shown such wisdom. Last week the upper chamber approved another $21 million for the "contras," but we are encouraged by comments from Democratic leaders in the House that revelation of the CIA's direct role in military operations in Nicaragua has doomed the financing measure.

"Up to this point," House Speaker Thomas "Tip" O'Neill said Monday, "I have contended that the . . . secret war against Nicaragua was morally indefensible. Today is it clear that it is legally indefensible as well." The Reagan administration's attempt to avoid scrutiny before the World Court can be easily interpreted as an admission that current policy contravenes international law. That impression will not be erased by the administration's self-righteous explanation that it is merely trying to keep Nicaragua from diverting attention from its export of revolution in Central America by staging a "propaganda spectacular" before the World Court.

The administration cannot so easily wash its hands of the dishonesty in its conduct of foreign policy toward Nicaragua. Mr. Reagan has denied intentions of toppling the established government of Nicaragua while financing and directing rebels intent upon that very goal. The administration still will not officially admit direct CIA involvement in the "secret war," and the "covert" nature of the Nicaraguan operation precludes the full congressional debate which it warrants. Before the Senate vote last week, Sen. Joseph Biden Jr., D-Del., a member of the Senate Intelligence Committee, told his colleagues they would vote against the bill "if you knew what I know. ..."

Covert intelligence activities have a place in international affairs, but it should be strictly limited. Using the "covert" label to shield a broadening military operation from congressional and public scrutiny is an abuse of the freedom allowed such activities. And basing a foreign policy on this abuse of official secrecy is a dangerous proposition. It's time for Congress to stop this dirty little war in Nicaragua — before Mr. Reagan's adventuristic policies precipitate a bigger war.

WORCESTER TELEGRAM.

Worcester, MA, April 24, 1984

Brent Scowcroft, retired general and presidential adviser on national security matters, says that the CIA's involvement in the mining of Nicaraguan harbors "is hurting the CIA." That is a point that has not been given enough attention.

After the failure at the Bay of Pigs, President John F. Kennedy tried to limit the CIA to intelligence responsibilities. Kennedy and his advisers had learned that when an intelligence agency starts to run operations, the quality of intelligence may be compromised. Allen Dulles, head of the CIA, told Kennedy that the Bay of Pigs invasion would succeed. It would have been surprising if he had said anything else; he set up the project.

If some other agency had been responsible for the Bay of Pigs operation, Dulles might have given a more objective and negative assessment of the chances of success.

In Central America, the CIA once again is mingling intelligence with covert operations. That makes its intelligence reports suspect. It cannot be objective.

As Scowcroft pointed out, the revelations of the mining has diminished public and congressional confidence in the CIA. It is seen as irresponsible and out of control.

Maybe the country needs another agency strictly concerned with operations, covert and otherwise. The prime function of the CIA is to provide the government with accurate intelligence. All else is secondary.

The Philadelphia Inquirer

Philadelphia, PA, April 11, 1984

Gradually the United States has come to this point. It has plowed Honduras with airfields and training camps. It has funded rebels bent on breaking Nicaragua's government. It has labored to prop up a Salvadoran regime that has been impotent against its leftist enemy and rightist death squads.

The United States is, in April 1984, at a threshold: President Reagan stands ready to rout revolutionaries from Central America by any means — by secret war, by open war, with proxies or with American troops.

The veil has dropped, but the deception remains. It is disclosed that Americans have supervised the mining of Nicaraguan ports, damaging the ships of at least five nations. Secretary of Defense Caspar W. Weinberger denies the United States is behind it, but says he's not talking about "anything the Central Intelligence Agency is doing or not doing."

Mr. Reagan proclaims "Law Day USA." "Without law," his tribute declares, "there can be no freedom, only chaos and disorder." The same day, Nicaragua calls on the World Court to act against U.S.-sponsored terrorists. The administration rejects the court, contends there is no jurisdiction — declares it is above the law.

Britain and France recoil. Had not the U.S. secretary of state days before called state terrorism "really a form of warfare" and hinted that it should be dealt with pre-emptively?

Reports circulate that the Pentagon is preparing contingency plans for U.S. combat forces on the isthmus. Officially, the administration denies them. Anonymously, it encourages the speculation. If Congress refuses to fund proxies, the President's men threaten, U.S. troops must be dispatched, "regardless of public opinion here and abroad."

Such is the talk from an administration that crusades in the name of "democracy." Such are the actions from an administration that castigates the Soviet Union for its "totalitarianism" in Afghanistan, that berates Syria for supporting terrorism in Beirut, that deplores violent outlawry in Ireland and in Israel.

A nation's ideal, its most fundamental principle, the rule of law, is being tested.

In that test, the machinery of government that is built on that principle — that of checks and balances — is directly challenged.

Mr. Reagan has created a dilemma of illogic. There is more than simply a hemispheric foreign policy on the table as the House reviews military aid to El Salvador and covert funding to Nicaragua's rebels.

The President demands millions for rebels, covertly to stop Nicaraguan arms flowing to Salvadoran leftists, but — because of the hypocrisy of his position — he can offer no proof, no evidence. On the record, the United States is not involved.

"Exercises" in Honduras draw U.S. engineers and troops ever closer to harm's way, toward border incidents. U.S. reconnaissance planes overfly El Salvador. The United States is not "directly" involved.

The margin of error narrows. The Gulf of Tonkin whispers off stage. Will the United States be maneuvered into war? Or shall its people, their representatives and constitutional process control its destiny as befits a free and democratic — and legally accountable — nation?

It is time, on this threshold, to say "no" to an administration that would deny the supremacy of the law over its own acts, to a president who would wage war in the peoples' name, without their consent. To remain silent is to nourish the seeds of tyranny.

THE PLAIN DEALER
Cleveland, OH, April 15, 1984

Perhaps the present furor on Capitol Hill regarding the Central Intelligence Agency's role in the mining of Nicaraguan harbors will bring about something that is long overdue—the cessation of covert American operations against the Sandinistas.

Those operations have created nearly as much friction between Washington and its allies as between the administration and Congress. Ships from Japan and the Netherlands are included among the dozen that have been damaged by the mines. And both Britain and France are among the growing number of nations that have been critical of the minings in specific and U.S. covert operations in general.

In the past, President Reagan has said it is "common sense" for the United States to offer aid and support to rebels opposing the Sandinista regime. The administration has accused Managua of providing arms to insurgents seeking to topple the government of El Salvador—which the Sandinistas deny—and claims its support of the contras is not intended to topple the Nicaraguan government but to keep it from exporting its revolution abroad. The White House also claims the activities are designed to persuade Managua to honor the promises of the Sandinista revolution, which include holding elections.

The Sandinista regime has joined the Contadora peace process begun by Mexico, Venezuela, Colombia and Panama. It has offered to negotiate proposals for a regional peace, a partial amnesty to anti-Sandinista guerrillas, increased dialog with the Roman Catholic hierarchy. It has, further, expressed a willingness to reduce its number of foreign military advisers and curb support for revolutionary movements elsewhere in Central America. The Sandinistas also have scheduled November elections for a president and constituent assembly.

Despite what the administration claims, covert operations against Nicaragua have not denied war materiel to rebels in El Salvador. Indeed, much of the guns and ammunition Salvadoran rebels use are American, confiscated or purchased by the rebels from the Salvadoran military. Why then do the covert operations continue?

The administration has cast a skeptical eye at Managua's proposals, citing instead the size of the Sandinista military and the presence of Cuban, Soviet and East European military advisers. The administration is right to be concerned about the size of Nicaragua's military, estimated at 50,000 regulars. It is right to be concerned about the thousands of foreign military advisers in the nation.

Yet how can the White House expect Nicaragua to curb its military buildup when there are 13,000 guerrillas along its borders, united by a desire to bring about the Sandinistas' destruction? Can the administration simply "turn off" the contra campaigns at some future date?

The administration has shown little willingness to test the sincerity of Managua's proposals or to cease covert activities. But diplomatic efforts should be preferable to covert military operations. Do not covert operations endanger what few chances may exist in Nicaragua for democracy, while increasing the prospects for an expanded regional conflict?

Successfully bringing change in Nicaragua only can heighten the chances for greater regional peace and stability. Those chances diminish, however, with each new attack against Managua by the CIA surrogates. That is all the more reason for Congress to deny further funds for such counterproductive efforts as mining Nicaraguan ports, and insist the administration spend more time exploring viable but little-used diplomatic channels.

THE COMMERCIAL APPEAL
Memphis, TN,
April 12, 1984

THE Reagan administration has blundered badly by permitting the CIA to mine Nicaragua's ports and by rejecting the jurisdiction of the World Court over its activities in Central America for the next two years.

By ducking a World Court hearing on Nicaragua's complaint, the United States in effect pleads guilty in the eyes of the world and seems to admit that it has a weak case.

In fact this country would have a good case if the administration had the wit and courage to make it.

The United States could have and should have argued that until Nicaragua leaves its neighbors alone, it enters the court at The Hague with bloody hands and is not entitled to a ruling that its neighbors leave it alone.

However, trust the CIA to screw up. Its mines are dumb, indiscriminate, capable of damaging friendly as well as unfriendly vessels and an affront to international law and world opinion.

In addition, they cannot do the job of stopping the flow of arms from Cuba to Nicaragua for the El Salvador guerrillas. Even if the mines closed Nicaraguan ports, Havana could use its fleet of Soviet-supplied transport planes to move weapons to its proteges.

The mining has been effective, though, in inflaming Congress against administration policy for Central America. An angry House is likely to cut off funds for covert activities against Nicaragua and to slash aid to embattled El Salvador. With Republican leaders joining in, the Senate passed a nonbinding resolution Tuesday calling for an end to the use of CIA funds for the mining of Nicaraguan ports.

THE CIA'S announcement that the mining has been stopped still leaves a burden on the administration. Having set up the illegal blockade, what moral and legal grounds will the United States have to protest if Iran, as it has threatened, cuts the oil-shipping lanes in the Persian Gulf?

There are enough forces in the country, in Congress and abroad that want to see the administration fail in Central America. Why does it help them with self-inflicted wounds?

CIA Manual Advocates Terror Tactics for Nicaraguan Rebels

United States President Ronald Reagan October 18, 1984 asked Central Intelligence Agency (CIA) Director William Casey to investigate a manual issued by the agency that instructed Nicaraguan contras in techniques of political assassination and guerilla warfare. The focus of the manual, whose existence was disclosed by the Associated Press, was on political propaganda. It described how to build a guerilla force and train guerillas "in psychological operations and their application in the concrete case of the Christian and democratic crusade in which the freedom commandos [contras] are engaged in Nicaragua." However, the manual also endorsed the "selective use of violence" and gave instructions on how to blow up public buildings and blackmail ordinary citizens. The manual did not use the words "assassinate" or "kill" but it did refer to "neutralizing" specific targets. An executive order signed by President Reagan in 1981 prohibited United States employees from engaging or conspiring to engage in assassination.

Disclosures from the CIA manual brought an angry response from Democrats in Congress, and it was announced Oct. 17 that the House Select Intelligence Committee was undertaking an investigation. The committee's chairman, Rep. Edward Boland (D, Mass.), proclaimed that he was "appalled by the image of the U.S. that the primer portrays" and charged that the manual "embraces the communist revolutionary tactics the U.S. is pledged to defeat." Boland contended that the manual, like the mining of Nicaraguan harbors by CIA-trained rebels revealed earlier in the year, was "a disaster for American foreign policy." White House spokesman Larry Speakes stated that "the tactics contained in the manual would never have been condoned by the president or the national security community," and administration officials were reported to assert that the manual had been written by an "overzealous" independent low-level employee under contract to the CIA. Nicaragua's Sandinista government objected to the CIA manual in a note sent to the U.S. State Department Oct. 24, characterizing the booklet as "new material proof of the official policy of state terrorism being waged by the United States Administration against the people of Nicaragua."

THE BLADE
Toledo, OH, November 15, 1984

FOR what is supposed to be an agency that shrouds its activities in secrecy, the Central Intelligence Agency again has had its cover blown. Even though "corrective action" of a sort has been taken, the CIA still looks inept.

Several weeks ago a CIA warfare manual to aid Nicaraguan rebels surfaced. It described how to win popular support and influence the populace through acts of assassination, blackmail and mob violence.

The booklet was another example of the agency's poor judgment, a continuation of a U.S. policy that allows the CIA to pour millions of dollars into support for guerrilla groups fighting to overthrow the established leftist government in Nicaragua.

That has been a dubious activity. U.S. involvement through the CIA has amounted to an act of undeclared war against a Central American neighbor, a reflection of the fact that the United States has little use for the Communist leanings of the Nicaraguan leaders.

The manual produced a public uproar, and last week President Reagan approved disciplinary action against junior CIA operatives involved in preparing it. The nature of the punishment was not spelled out, but it could include letters of reprimand and suspensions.

The agency's first mistake was not to run the offending booklet past the appropriate congressional committees, which probably would have rejected it immediately. Secondly, the fact that no higher-ups were punished is a reflection of the Pentagon's wrist-slap approach for a matter that deserved penalties for those individuals who approved the manual.

Ironically, the document reads like a Marxist tract for revolution. Its existence made it appear, in some persons' eyes, as a reflection of an unsavory drift in U.S. foreign policy. The CIA should have halted the document long before it was circulated in Nicaragua.

THE MILWAUKEE JOURNAL
Milwaukee, WI, October 19, 1984

Halloween is the time, just a few weeks away, when children dress up like goblins, witches and other scary creatures and go from door to door, playing trick-or-treat. The Central Intelligence Agency has been teaching some scary tricks of its own. But it hasn't been teaching them to children, and the tricks aren't harmless, seasonal pranks.

The CIA has produced and given to Nicaraguan rebels a 44-page book of instructions on terrorist tactics, including murder and kidnaping, blowing up buildings, blackmail, inciting mob violence, even killing supporters so they can become martyrs "to the cause."

The world does not always play according to Marquess of Queensberry rules, so there may be situations that require violent solutions. But the CIA book was not given to rebels fighting a country with which the United States is at war — or even a country that directly threatens US security. The CIA publication was given to rebels trying to overthrow the government of Nicaragua — a country that's irksome, and sometimes worse, but with which the US is carrying on negotiations and diplomatic relations.

The instructions to the rebels were provided without the knowledge of Rep. Edward Boland (D-Mass.) and Sen. Barry Goldwater (R-Ariz.), chairmen of congressional committees that are supposed to oversee CIA activities, and apparently even without President Reagan's knowledge. One of the terrorist tactics covered in the booklet — assassination — is explicitly prohibited by presidential and CIA directives issued subsequent to Watergate-era disclosures of CIA misconduct.

It is hard to resist the conclusion that the CIA is not operating as part of a coherent strategy, but is making up its own rules and running its own operations, free of outside supervision, as though the Watergate reforms had never been made. Thus, Reagan's order that the CIA investigate its own conduct in the production of the booklet is not sufficiently credible.

This CIA terror booklet not only smacks of the excesses of the past; the state-sponsored terrorism taught by the CIA is exactly the kind of thing this country and others rightly condemn when practiced by Iran and Libya. State-sponsored terrorism is defensible only in time of war, and war under the US system of government is an act that Congress must formally approve.

Did the CIA conceal its activities from Congress, or has Congress been too tame to demand the truth? Either way, it's time for the lawmakers to demand accountability and compliance from CIA Director William Casey. If he can't or won't rein in the agency, then he ought to be replaced.

THE PLAIN DEALER
Cleveland, OH, October 21, 1984

Americans have solid reason to be angered by reports that the CIA had prepared a primer for contras in Nicaragua, instructing them—among other things—on how to kidnap and kill government officials.

The message that conveys about this country contrasts remarkably with the image of a nation that claims to prize state morality and condemns the Soviet Union's use of surrogates to do its dirty work. The hypocrisy is near absolute. If the United States is a true opponent of state-supported terrorism, then how can it justify supporting it—and inviting the retaliatory use of it in this country? Perhaps the president will provide a strong answer during tonight's debate in Kansas City.

At least four investigations have been ordered to determine the facts surrounding the document. Two are to be conducted by the CIA at the direction of President Reagan.

The administration says that it "has not advocated or condoned political assassination." Is the CIA out of control then? The president says, "Not at all." Consider, however, the damage-control remarks of a "senior administration official" who spoke anonymously to the media. His explanation is that the manual was written by a "free-wheeling, free-lancing" low-level CIA contract employee who produced it without the knowledge of his superiors.

Is that possible? Yes. Is it probable? No. On July 27, in an interview with Bryan Barger of Pacific News Service, Edgar Chamorro, a Honduras-based contra propaganda officer, said that the CIA provided the "freedom fighters" with the manual and a comic book advising Nicaraguans on how to overthrow their government, along with technical assistance and funding.

The choice is to believe President Reagan. The CIA is in control. The question then is, who controls the CIA? Director William Casey? The president? Congressional oversight is blunted for the simple reason that the CIA distrusts Congress and tends to ignore the intelligence committees. The mining of Nicaragua's harbors proved that. Casey chose not to inform the committees, in violation of the statute requiring advance notice of any significant covert intelligence action. The mining was a probable breach of international law.

That failure to notify was deliberate and is profoundly disturbing. The outrage expressed by individuals such as Sen. Daniel P. Moynihan, D-N.Y., does not stem from innocence on the part of well-intentioned, but naive people.

The intelligence committees have funded CIA paramilitary activities in Central America for years. Members have not suddenly become fainthearted. They are well aware of the rough nature of clandestine intelligence work.

The CIA, however, once again has assumed an extra-legal mindset and is improperly operating as a fourth branch of government. To what end? If it justifies the illegal war against Nicaragua not because a leftist government has seized power, but so that other countries in the region may not follow suit, the agency is killing itself not so softly with its own song. The record needs to be broken.

The Philadelphia Inquirer
Philadelphia, PA, October 21, 1984

After the last Beirut embassy bombing, President Reagan suggested that U.S. intelligence capabilities had been hobbled by his predecessor. Turned out that was not quite the case, though Mr. Reagan did manage to drag the Central Intelligence Agency into the election spotlight.

Now there are reports that it was the security, not the spying, that may well have been at fault in Lebanon. But there is news from another front — from Central America — that may, in the end, inject the CIA into the presidential campaign more deeply than Mr. Reagan could ever have imagined.

He is faced now with disclosures that the CIA wrote a primer for U.S.-backed counterrevolutionaries in Nicaragua that, among other things, gave practical advice in the black arts of political assassination, mob violence and extortion.

The mere publicizing of the manual — the President says he knew nothing of its existence — probably has done more to subvert U.S. objectives in the region than anything the Sandinistas could have hoped to do militarily.

The administration is trying to fob the manual off as the work of a low-level spook. But that won't do. The agency is replete with contract employees and, disturbingly, there are signs that they are being given free rein — or reined in for the wrong reasons.

Thus, the spectacularly embarrassing CIA harbor-minings in Nicaragua, reports of CIA comic books advising tire-flattening and toilet-clogging and, on the other extreme, public charges by a senior CIA analyst that agency Director William Casey was distorting data on Mexico to support administration policy.

The revelations put the United States in a bind. Secretary of State George P. Shultz has made it a major point that "our" *contras* in Nicaragua are not like those other terrorists — the state-sponsored murderers from Libya and Iran and Syria.

Yet, here is the CIA advising the *contras*, in writing, to "neutralize" troublesome officials; to set up kangaroo courts; to seduce gullible civilians into violent mob action.

Not only that, the document contradicts express presidential directives against assassination and such.

The President promptly has ordered the agency to investigate itself. But that only pushes the matter aside. He must address it squarely, denounce such operations unequivocally, and search his soul to determine whether Mr. Casey's effectiveness at the agency has come to an end.

When covert action gets out of control it ceases to be, as Vice President Bush likes to call it warmly, "quiet help for a friend." It too often corrupts American ideals and distorts U.S. foreign policy. And too often, as in the case of the secret war in Laos, the Bay of Pigs, the overthrow of Chile's Allende, it has offered little in return.

The case of the CIA primer for the *contras* has done both — it has dragged the flag in the mud and caused harm this nation will not soon, nor easily, see repaired.

Minneapolis Star and Tribune
Minneapolis, MN, November 13, 1984

President Reagan says he has "cleared the air" on the manual prepared for rebels fighting the Nicaraguan government. The opposite is true. The manual appears to encourage the assassination of Sandinista leaders. The Reagan administration's efforts to hide that appearance shows a cynical disregard for the truth and for U.S. law.

The CIA-prepared manual's central topic is not violence, but psychological warfare to win popular support for the rebel cause. It stresses that unfocused violence undermines that support. It says, for example, that rebels should "kidnap all officials or agents of the Sandinista government ... " but warns that these " 'enemies of the people' ... must not be mistreated in spite of their criminal acts."

However, buried within this cautionary emphasis on the limits of force is a section titled, "Selective use of violence for propagandistic effects." The section opens with the statement, "It is possible to neutralize carefully selected and planned targets such as court judges ...." Thus, while winning over the people requires strict limits on force, carefully selected Sandinista officials may be "neutralized" by violence. The wording is vague, but the message seems clear: Selective assassination of government officials is justified.

When the manual's content was made known during the presidential campaign, two investigations were ordered — by the CIA and by the Reagan-appointed Intelligence Oversight Board. The administration promised that the reports would be released before the Nov. 6 election. Later, their release was postponed until after the election. Now the air-clearing administration refuses to release them at all.

A week ago, Reagan offered the gentlest possible interpretation of "neutralize." It means, he said, that, "You just say to the fellow who's sitting there in the office, 'You're not in the office anymore.' " The president's interpretation is implausible. The manual advocates wholesale kidnapping of Sandinista officials. Reagan would have people believe that a special section on "selective use of violence" merely involves how to tell Sandinistas that they've been removed from office.

Reagan also applauded CIA Director William Casey's "very forthcoming" statement to Congress that the manual's purpose was to make the rebels better at "face-to-face communication." That's not forthcoming; it's disingenuous. Casey was right about the manual's general purpose, but he sidestepped the questions raised by the "selective use of violence" section.

According to the administration, the two studies concluded that "there had been no violations by CIA personnel or contract employees of the Constitution or laws of the United States, executive orders or presidential directives." U.S. law and a Reagan executive order prohibit intelligence agents from taking part in or urging the assassination of foreign officials. Yet the studies also concluded, in White House words, that the CIA committed "poor judgment and lapses in oversight at lower levels." The president cannot have it both ways: Either the manual is defensible or it is not.

Far from clearing the air, the Reagan administration has sought to evade questions surrounding the manual's production. The American people deserve straight answers to those questions. Congress should ensure that it gets them.

The State

Columbia, SC,
November 21, 1984

SIX middle-level Central Intelligence Agency officials have been reprimanded for authorizing a controversial, clandestine warfare manual to be given to Nicaraguan rebels. The booklet included a section on "neutralizing" government officials.

The manual became a late issue in the recent Presidential race, Democrat Walter Mondale saying it showed lack of control by President Reagan of his Administration. A long-standing Presidential executive order has barred U.S. involvement in assassinations.

Six CIA employees were held responsible for the publication by the agency's inspector general after an investigation. President Reagan approved disciplining them. But the CIA officials are reported to be objecting because no higher-level authorities were also punished. Morale is said to be sagging at the CIA.

Although the disciplining has taken place, and the President's Intelligence Oversight Board found the CIA had not violated the "Constitution or laws of the United States, executive orders or Presidential directives," the controversy will be prolonged.

A senior member of the House Intelligence Committee — a Democrat — has called the CIA report a whitewash. And a ranking Senate Intelligence Committee member, Sen. Patrick Leahy, D-Vt., declared "you don't have to be very cynical to realize that somebody is being protected."

Ultimately, within the agency, the director, William Casey, is responsible for actions of all his subordinates. In this case, Mr. Casey is said to have personally supervised the covert operations in Nicaragua since the President approved them in 1981.

It is easy to see where the congressional probers are headed. The second Reagan administration is in for a rough start.

THE INDIANAPOLIS NEWS

Indianapolis, IN, December 5, 1984

From the beginning, CIA Director William Casey has been an embarrassment to the Reagan administration. Now, Casey is more than an embarrassment and he should be asked to resign.

Controversy has dogged Casey since he was appointed in 1981. Late in the summer of that year, questions about Casey's business dealings surfaced during a Senate Intelligence panel investigation of Casey's decision to appoint the clearly unqualified Max Hugel as his No. 2 man.

Hugel's hasty and forced departure and some charity toward the Reagan administration from Sen. Barry Goldwater kept Casey's financial dealings from becoming a scandal at that time, but questions about them were to arise again and again.

Not three months later, Casey was accused of conflict of interest when he refused to put his multimillion-dollar stockholdings in a blind trust. After a good deal of political pressure, Casey first agreed to make his financial holdings public and, after nearly two years and a series of accusations that he was using CIA information to pump up his bank account, he finally put his holdings in a blind trust. Even then, there were accusations — and denials — that Casey still was manipulating the trust. But no proof.

These unsavory incidents cast a shadow over Casey's personal integrity and should have been reason enough for his resignation. Yet he wasn't forced to resign.

Now, on the basis of two Casey decisions within the past year, he should be.

In January, Casey authorized the mining of Nicaragua's harbors — a questionable policy decision in itself. The decision provoked world criticism and landed the United States in front of the World Court. Last week, the court ruled the actions were illegal.

What made Casey's authorization worse still was that he did so without notifying members of the Senate Intelligence panel, including senators who were firm supporters of the Reagan administration's policies in Central America. It was a major political gaffe and it revealed that Casey had little regard for the proper channels of government.

Now comes news that Casey authorized the CIA-prepared "terrorist" manual to help the Nicaraguan rebels foment unrest and unseat the Sandinistas. Casey probably was not aware that the manual would evolve into a primer on murder and other violent terrorist measures, but he should have been. He authorized its preparation and publication and he should have known what was going into the manual. If he had seen the final copy, he should have stopped publication immediately. He did not and he must assume responsibility for it.

The President has already mentioned a fair penalty for Casey's mistake. In the second presidential debate, President Reagan promised to fire whoever was responsible for the preparation and distribution of the manual.

The President should hold himself to his promise. In his time as director of the CIA, William Casey has damaged his own credibility, that of the CIA and that of the United States. It is time for him to go.

St. Petersburg Times

St. Petersburg, FL, November 14, 1984

Imagine this, if you can. The mayor of some small Nicaraguan town, a loyal Sandinista, looks up from his desk as a delegation of U.S-backed *contras* walks in the door. "*Compañero,*" they say, "we want you to resign."

"*Sí,*" he says. "I'll go."

This scene, more suggestive of a Woody Allen comedy than of real life, is how President Reagan chooses to wash his hands of the murder manual that was issued by the CIA to the guerrillas waging his undeclared war in Nicaragua. The manual explicitly advised the guerrillas to "neutralize" government officials who stand in their way. In the spy trade, "neutralize" is a euphemism for assassination. But in Mr. Reagan's inventive mind, it assumes a wholly benign meaning. "You just say to the fellow who's sitting there in the office, 'You're not in the office anymore,' " he explained last week. Having led himself to this reassuring conclusion, Mr. Reagan now advises the American public that the issue is "much ado about nothing."

AND WHAT about his campaign promise to dismiss any official involved in the production of the manual? With the same facility that makes murder look something like a recall petition, the administration now intends dismissal to mean nothing more than a few wrist taps (and sly winks) for a handful of low-level CIA functionaries. What a difference one election makes!

If one accepts the intended meaning of "neutralize," the manual represents a violation both of federal law and Mr. Reagan's own 1981 directive against the assassination of foreign officials. His failure to take it seriously can only invite similar disregard for U.S. law whenever anyone surmises that his ends justify their means. It may be too late for the voters to act on that problem, but not for the Congress, which must necessarily be that much more reluctant to give the President blank checks in Central America or anywhere else.

Assassination was only the most vivid of the indiscretions that were committed to print in this case. The manual also suggested kidnapping "all" Nicaraguan government officials, hiring criminals to murder fellow rebels in order to create martyrs for the cause and the use of blackmail to force citizens to join the rebel movement. Such repugnant measures put to shame any nation that would employ them. Indeed, there was some speculation at first that the manual might have been a forgery planted by the Soviet KGB, which has been the undisputed master up to now in the theory and practice of such dirty tricks.

IT TURNS out that the Soviets had more to do with the manual than even they knew. Edgar Chamorro, the Nicaraguan rebel leader who was responsible for publishing the manual, has revealed in an interview that the CIA employee who wrote it admired Communist successes in guerrilla warfare, "and he was going to teach us how they do it."

When the colors of their flags are all that distinguish one side from the other, who will be left to care which one wins?

Richmond Times-Dispatch

Richmond, VA, October 20, 1984

Congressmen and commentators across the country are all aquiver over the discovery of a CIA psychological warfare manual in the hands of Nicaraguan rebels. President Reagan has responded by ordering an immediate investigation to determine if the agency has acted improperly in producing it. Until more information becomes available, however, we would recommend a tempering of criticism lest it lead to the same type of witch hunt that has weakened the agency in the past.

Not long ago President Reagan was criticized for suggesting that the CIA had been undermined in the years preceding his administration by agency critics who thought that "spying was dishonest." Subsequently the president made clear that he was not specifically referring to the Carter-Mondale years; the problem was long term.

Indeed, the agency's decline, and Walter Mondale's part in it, probably started in the early 1970s. Those were the days when a Senate committee headed by the late Sen. Frank Church and dominated by Democrats, including then Sen. Mondale, went on a 15-month rampage against U.S. intelligence agencies for a variety of "abuses" — using covert action excessively and tailoring intelligence data for political purposes, for example — many of which had been ordered by president after president. It was great politics and good publicity for committee members, who got the chance to bash agency staffers and heads at public hearings. But it didn't do much for the morale and efficiency of the intelligence agencies, the agents themselves or the people who worked with them.

In its ensuing report, the Church committee detailed its criticisms again and publicized once-secret information, to the dismay of the Ford administration. It also recommended that the 535 members of Congress have greater power regarding intelligence operations, and the agencies less. Sen. Barry Goldwater, a committee member, refused to sign the report, saying that it would "cause severe embarrassment, if not grave harm, to the nation's foreign policy." Sen. Mondale did sign the report, complaining only that the committee was unable to release still more information that would have been "embarrassing or inconvenient" to the CIA. No doubt the more than 1,000 Soviet officials and agents whom the committee knew to be operating in this country at the time would have loved that.

Under the Reagan administration, there has been an attempt to revitalize the agencies, and they are growing stronger. We now know that U.S. intelligence had warned of the most recent Beirut bombing, a warning that sadly did not get the attention from government officials it deserved. Nonetheless, that failure only serves to remind us of the vital role that the agency can play in national security.

Is Mr. Mondale, however, still stuck in his anti-intelligence rut? His current foreign policy adviser is the same man who counseled him during the Church committee hearings. Now his running mate, Geraldine Ferraro, and other Democrats upset over the manual are shooting at CIA Director William Casey first and asking questions later. Its origin and circulation do bear investigation, but not more political posturing. Sunday's debate would be a good time to see which course Mr. Mondale prefers.

THE LINCOLN STAR

Lincoln, NE, November 16, 1984

It's news that at least two CIA employees among five ordered disciplined by President Reagan in connection with that guerrilla warfare primer prepared for Nicaraguan rebels are balking at accepting punishment. That takes some spine.

The middle-level agency workers apparently think they are being picked on as the fall guys. Meanwhile, equally culpable superiors are escaping any formal blame.

The story leaked to the *New York Times* by "a senior intelligence official" — not otherwise identified — made the case that language in the manual which could be read as suggesting political assassinations was missed because CIA reviewers were so terribly busy. They did not pay sufficiently close attention.

Thus we can expect that's the company line which will be followed when the House Intelligence Committee begins interviewing the workers singled out for reprimands.

The disciplinary action followed President Reagan's acceptance of a CIA inspector general's report targeting only middle-level CIA operatives, including at least one man in the field. Reagan is satisfied — even if Democratic congressmen aren't — that the manual didn't violate an executive order forbidding U.S. participation in or planning assassinations.

That's what happens when euphemistic words capable of several meanings are used. The Spanish-language primer looks favorably on "selective use of violence" to "neutralize" local government leaders who tilt toward Nicaragua's Sandinista regime. Neutralize could mean forcing booze down their throats to get them drunk or maybe kidnapping them and putting them on a slow boat to Sri Lanka. Agreed, it could mean something other than assassination.

We trust the congressional committee will provide a full list of non-lethal activity possibilities. And a full review of the chain of responsible command.

Sandinistas Claim Election Victory; United States Calls Vote a Farce

Daniel Ortega Saavedra, the coordinator of the Nicaraguan government junta, November 5, 1984 claimed victory for the ruling Sandinista National Liberation Front (FSLN) in elections held Nov. 4. The election was the first in Nicaragua since 1974. Of the 1.55 million registered voters, about 80% were not reported to have turned out to elect a president, vice president and 90-member National Assembly. Voting was not compulsory. Five parties challenged the FSLN, but they did not include the opposition Democratic Coordinator (CD). The CD candidate, Arturo Cruz, had refused to register for the election on the grounds that the election laws unfairly favored the ruling FSLN. (The CD had unsuccessfully negotiated for a postponement to give the party a longer campaign period.) With 69% of the returns counted by Nov. 6, the FSLN had won 67% of the vote, according to the Voice of Nicaragua state-run radio. In second place was the Democratic Conservative party with 13.5% of the vote. United States Administration officials proclaimed the vote a sham. A State Department spokesman declared: "The Sandinista electoral farce, without any meaningful political opposition, leaves the situation essentially unchanged."

Five parties challenged the FSLN: the Popular Social Christian Party, the Marxist-Lenninist Popular Action Movement, the Democratic Conservative Party of Nicaragua, the Communist Party of Nicaragua and the Nicaraguan Socialist Party. Many voters were reported to have praised the election as the first free ballot in the nation's history. However, a large minority reportedly said they feared difficulties with the authorities if they did not vote and expressed the wish that CD candidate Cruz had joined the election. Opposition poll-watchers and foreign observers reported no irregularities, although some observers from abroad noted a shortage of poll-watchers from opposition parties. Some unofficial U.S. observers were said to have commented that the ballot was fairer than the U.S.-backed election held in El Salvador earlier in the year. A team of observers from the Washington Office on Latin America, a lobbying group, described the electoral process "well-conceived" and giving "easy access to vote with guarantees of secrecy." However, the team said in a statement that the "skewed political climate" had marred the election, referring to the lack of separation between the state and the FSLN.

The Dallas Morning News
Dallas, TX, November 4, 1984

The landslide the pollsters and pundits say Reagan could win Tuesday will be nothing next to the landslide Sandinista leader Daniel Ortega is sure to win today in Nicaragua. The Sandinistas have ensured that they have no serious opposition.

"Serious" opposition means opponents who enjoy the right to free speech and free assembly, access to a free press and freedom from police harassment and dizzying technical obstacles to participation. None of this was accorded Arturo Cruz, the only potential challenger who had enough organizational and popular strength to worry the Sandinistas.

Nicaragua surely is, as Walter Mondale says, "an increasingly totalitarian state," and today's sham election should shove it farther in that direction. Indeed, it's doubtful that the Sandinistas would feel obliged even to stage the sham were it not for the heat they've felt from the U.S.-backed rebels fighting to oust them.

But the recent congressional vote to cut off aid to the rebels undercut what leverage Cruz had in trying to persuade the Sandinistas to allow him to campaign freely and fairly. Why should the Sandinistas make any concessions to pluralism when Congress will reward them for totalitarianism?

"Democracy," Ortega intoned in a recent speech, "is literacy, democracy is land reform, democracy is education and public health." Voters here may notice that something is missing: In the Sandinistas' Orwellian design, "democracy" has nothing to do with such bourgeois formalities as free elections.

THE SUN
Baltimore, MD, November 6, 1984

Nicaragua's so-called election changes nothing about the reality of power in that Central American nation. The Sandinista junta still rules, as it was destined to keep ruling, or the balloting would never have been allowed in the first place. Carefully timed to precede the U.S. election by only two days, the Nicaraguan referendum neither increases nor decreases the legitimacy of the Marxist-leaning regime. Which is to say its legitimacy remains in question.

The junta had calculated that by holding an election in which opposition parties would be allowed to participate, it would increase its standing by making good on its long overdue pledge to establish a pluralist system. But after censorship and harassment early in the campaign made it impossible for a genuine opposition to operate, the Sandinistas wound up with more of a charade than an election. The huge turnout and the overwhelming majority for Commandante Daniel Ortega Saavedra as president were more in the Soviet than the free world tradition.

Mr. Ortega would be wise to acknowledge his ballyhooed election did not achieve its purposes. He should direct the newly elected General Assembly to draft a new constitution quickly so a more creditable election can be held next year. Not only would this be gratifying to opposition elements whose appetites for freedom have been whetted; it would enhance prospects for some kind of regional peace agreement under the aegis of the Contadora nations — Mexico, Venezuela, Panama and Colombia. The Contadora approach can never really work unless Nicaragua adopts a political system compatible with its neighbors and stops menacing them with a Soviet-Cuba backed army that is huge by regional standards.

But this is only half of the equation. The Contadora approach can never really work unless the Sandinista regime feels secure enough to reduce its forces, curtail its Soviet-Cuban ties and move toward democracy, as Washington demands. And so far, it has little reason to feel secure. The United States has spent $80 million since 1981 to finance an insurgency that has turned into a mirror image of the leftist civil war aimed at overthrowing the U.S.-backed government in El Salvador. While President Reagan insists he has no "plans" for an invasion of Nicaragua, his pressure against the Sandinista revolution has given Mr. Ortega a pretext for maintaining an authoritarian regime with a strong military component.

This week's elections give Nicaragua and the United States an opportunity to stop antagonizing each other. Both sides in El Salvador have started to talk. Perhaps a similar process could take shape in Nicaragua. Peace in Central America is a long way off, but it deserves a chance.

Richmond Times-Dispatch
Richmond, VA, November 8, 1984

If elections are about choices, Nicaragua has yet to have one. Before the first vote was counted after Sunday's balloting, the Sandinista press had declared the Sandinistas the overwhelming winners.

Before the first vote was cast, they had ensured they would be. The Sandinist solution to electoral competition was not to limit the number of voters — an 80 percent turnout of even unenthusiastic or intimidated voters looks good — but to circumscribe their choices. The directorate has been setting up the machinery to do so for the past five years. The few media the Sandinistas don't control they censor severely. They command and employ the means to disrupt opposition meetings and rallies.

When their major competition, refusing to be set up for a loss, dropped out, the Sandinistas made a show of regret. When even minor parties tried to bow out, the Sandinistas either bought them back into the race with additional campaign funds or simply refused to let them quit.

Tammany couldn't have done it better.

Yet some of the same people who would be excoriating New York, or Chicago, or Biloxi, or San Salvador are excusing Managua — and blaming Washington for contributing to the "skewed political climate" in a nation the Sandinist regime intended all along be a one-party state. Only under international and domestic pressure, fueled though far from fabricated by Washington, did the Sandinistas agree even to go through the motions. Without continued pressure, will they allow even the small gains made by the more moderate, minor parties in a Sandinista-dominated national assembly to develop into a democratic alternative?

Not likely, by their record. But the argument over which pressures — economic? diplomatic? military? — should be applied on a little-changed Managua by a little-changed Washington will continue. Neither the U.S. nor the Nicaraguan election settled the future of the *contras*, who struggle on in spite of Congress, or of the Contadora process, which bumps along despite Nicaragua. Sunday's demonstration of the Sandinistas' contempt for democracy in Nicaragua could spur the *contras*, enfeeble Contadora and still leave the administration's congressional critics unconvinced of the Sandinist threat to democracy throughout the region.

Yet even they should be interested to know what Soviet freight is being offloaded in Nicaragua these days and to obtain corroboration for Managua's explanations. Managua, meanwhile, ought to know that the likeliest way to settle the argument — and to galvanize this Congress and the next behind this and the next president — is to unload MiGs in Corinto.

The Times-Picayune
The States-Item
New Orleans, LA, November 6, 1984

Nicaragua's ruling Sandinista party got one thing it wanted in Sunday's elections — it got elected. But it did not get the other thing it wanted — legitimacy.

Running against five minor opposition parties after the major opposition group boycotted the election, the Sandinistas were voted into the presidency and into control of a new national assembly that will write a new constitution.

But they may have a difficult time persuading the world that the election was in fact a referendum on their record and that they now have a genuine and credible national mandate. The Democratic Coordinating Committee, a grouping of three opposition parties, dropped out of the election campaign when it became clear that the Sandinistas were stacking the deck in their own favor. Arturo Cruz, who was the group's presidential candidate, called the election "ridiculous and illegitimate."

Like most machine-run elections and all communist-run elections, the election went smoothly. More than 80 percent of registered voters went to the polls, and early returns gave Daniel Ortega, head of the ruling junta and Sandinista candidate for president, about 70 percent of the vote. The final returns may not be known until Thursday, but there is hardly any suspense.

This was the first election since the Sandinistas took over the broad-based revolution that threw out President Anastasio Somoza in 1979. It is a tragedy that post-Somoza Nicaragua's first election should have been robbed of true democratic meaning by a new political machine. Observers of the Nicaraguan scene say that there is significant opposition to the Sandinistas, and a properly run election would have given it voice.

Now the future looks dim for those in Nicaragua who intended the ouster of the Somoza family machine to lead to a pluralistic democracy. Instead, one machine has been replaced with another even worse. The Marxist Sandinistas, now able to claim electoral victory and with the continued help of their allies, Cuba and the Soviet bloc, will doubtless move more confidently toward the communization of Nicaragua.

This refusal of the Sandinistas to allow the Nicaraguan people political expression puts new importance on the anti-Sandinista armed forces called the contras. They see themselves as continuing the 1979 revolution for democracy, a revolution that was stopped half-way when the Sandinistas used it to put themselves exclusively in power.

And this in turn faces the United States with serious decisions. President Reagan supports the contras as "freedom fighters," but Congress has cut off aid to them. One of the first tasks facing the United States after its election today will be to decide what policy steps must be taken to help the Nicaraguans and protect their neighbors against Sandinista subversion.

AKRON BEACON JOURNAL
Akron, OH,
November 6, 1984

AS AMERICAN voters visited the polls today, results were being celebrated in another election of interest to the United States: Nicaragua's first nationwide vote since the Sandinistas came to power five years ago.

The results are not surprising — the coordinator of the leftist regime, Daniel Ortega, will become president and the Sandinistas will control the National Assembly.

Despite holding the election up as a symbol of democracy, the Sandinistas probably gained little from it. Legitimate opposition was missing from the campaign. The claims of the Reagan administration — that it was the kind of one-sided election that might be expected in a marxist state — have merit. No doubt the United States will continue its opposition to the Sandinista rule and Nicaragua will see little if any support from other Western nations.

The Sandinistas had hoped for more. A few weeks ago, they signed an agreement with other political parties, pledging scheduled elections, freedom of the press and freedom of political action. Of course it is not only altruism that makes the rulers act this way.

Nicaraguans are showing signs of fatigue at living in a military state and being at war with the U.S.-supported contras. The Nicaraguan economy continues to disintegrate and there is growing tension between the Sandinistas and the Catholic Church.

None of this means the people are ready for another revolution, but the Sandinistas know they must head off major dissent if they are to build a nation. This means establishing themselves as legitimate in the eyes of Western democracies and attracting aid that could help improve the standard of living for their grumbling citizens.

U.S. support is, of course, a key. The Reagan administration is not only financing a war against the Sandinistas, it has worked against international loans for economic development to Nicaragua.

One election is not likely to end this tension. Potential supporters of the Sandinistas have been waiting for a meaningful gesture, a move toward true democracy, that even the United States would have to recognize as a definite step in the right direction.

After this Nicaraguan election, however, in which credibility was as absent as the opposition, the wait goes on.

The Boston Herald
*Boston, MA,
November 9, 1984*

DANIEL Ortega Saavedra, leader of the Marxist junta which rules Nicaragua, has proclaimed his nation's recent election a famous victory. Ortega's enthusiasm is understandable. His Sandinista party won a landslide victory, in both the presidential balloting and voting for the nation's Constituent Assembly.

In reality, however, the election was a farce

The principal opposition parties boycotted the balloting. These groups recognized the futility of running in an election in which they were denied fair access to the government-controlled media, where their rallies were attacked by Sandinista street gangs.

The Sandinistas will doubtless point to the high voter turnout (over 80 percent) as evidence of the election's validity. But many who cast ballots did so out of fear of reprisals if they abstained. Throughout the campaign, the government insisted that those who did not vote were "traitors."

That the Marxists in Managua would even permit an election, albeit one carefully orchestrated, is an indication of their concern over growing opposition to their rule — from the Catholic Church, anti-communist guerrillas and the population at large. They hope that this bogus electoral process, and the results will legitimize their reign.

Alas, they have deceived only themselves. Until the Sandinistas hold real elections, end censorship and stop suppressing internal dissent, they will be marked by world opinion as just another totalitarian regime — ruling in the name of the people without the latter's support. And no Soviet-built jet fighter is going to help cure that image.

THE ATLANTA CONSTITUTION
Atlanta, GA, November 7, 1984

As Americans were waiting out the results of their own elections last night, Nicaraguans finally were getting the picture from their own Sunday balloting. There were no surprises, and couldn't have been any. The Nicaraguan vote won't be complete until Thursday, but it is clear that voters have shown support for the ruling Sandinista National Liberation Front.

The procedures observed in the Sunday election were, by all accounts, fair. No one was marched off to the polling place at gunpoint. Ballots were secret. There hasn't been the slightest suggestion of tampering.

No matter. The results were tainted from the moment that three important opposition parties, and later a fourth, decided — with good reason — that the Sandinista-sanctioned conditions for campaigning for office were basically unfair and opted to sit out the election. There was no contest from that point.

On that basis, the U.S. government and the Nicaraguan opposition, both peaceable and guerrilla, have labeled the entire exercise a farce. Their characterization is probably as wide of the mark as the calculations of Sandinista stalwarts, who consider the results a mandate.

The Sandinista government's projections — and there is little reason to doubt them — indicate that two-thirds of the 80 percent of the electorate who voted cast their lots with the FSLN. That's an absolute majority of voting-age Nicaraguans, but not by much — certainly far too slim to suggest universal, lockstep adherence to the FSLN's credo, but significant backing just the same.

The Reagan administration has to recognize that the Sandinistas, for all their numerous failings, have gathered around themselves a sizable and committed popular following. For many impoverished Nicaraguans, the government of President Daniel Ortega is a big improvement over what they remember of the sleazy Somoza dictatorship that preceeded it. For the nation's indoctrinated youth, to whom the Sandinistas' revolution is ostensibly dedicated, it is an institution in which they feel a personal stake.

Most Nicaraguans are poor and young; weaning away that bloc of enthusiasts from Ortega's brand of revolution-without-borders won't be easy.

The United States has strong and legitimate interests in its case against the Sandinistas — their massive military buildup, suppression of basic liberties, willing service to Soviet and Cuban interests, ambiguity about their designs on neighbor states.

But as long as the Reagan administration sponsors an undeclared war against Managua and as long as it erects impassable barriers to peace (as it has in ongoing bilateral negotiations with Nicaragua), it plays into the Sandinistas' hand: Uncle Sam is a bogeyman, a tool with which to whip up internal support and, at the same time, enforce compliance.

Sunday's election endorsement of the Sandinistas ought to be a lesson to the White House: Playing tough hasn't neutralized them; playing smart might.

FORT WORTH STAR-TELEGRAM
Fort Worth, TX, November 12, 1984

Could it be that Professor Michael Dodson of Texas Christian University wore his rose-colored glasses when he went to Nicaragua last week to observe the national election there?

Or, could it be that he saw only what the Sandinista dictators wanted him and 15 other Americans invited there as observers to see?

We beg to differ with the esteemed TCU professor when he said that the election in Nicaragua was "very much like those in the United States," other than the presence of gun-toting guards at the Nicaraguan polls.

Without question, the Sandinistas put on a good show at their Nov. 4 national elections. Other than having armed guards at every polling place, it probably appeared that they were actually conducting a free and open election.

But in order to make an educated appraisal of the election in Nicaragua, one needs to be fully informed about what went on leading up to election day. Beyond that, one should probe deeply into the background of that election.

Basically, it was a mock election which was designed, staged, produced and executed by the Marxist faction that controls the Sandinista political apparatus — the National Liberation Front which rules by the guns of its 50,000-man military force.

And just to be sure that the election results came out right, the Sandinistas set up their own Supreme Electoral Council with bottom-line control of the entire election process.

The council members also are Sandinistas and are members of the National Liberation Front. It puts on elections and is totally involved in the process from printing the ballots, to staffing the polling places, to counting the ballots to approving who is eligible to run for public office.

When the balloting is over, the council then receives, counts and "confirms" the results. And there is no appeal from its decisions. There is no court in Nicaragua with jurisdiction over the council's decisions.

The Sandinistas have tried to convince the outside world that its Supreme Electoral Council is comparable to the Federal Elections Commission in the United States. That is like comparing the U.S. Congress to the Supreme Soviet, which meets only to rubber stamp rules and regulations already approved by the Soviet Union's Communist Party.

Nicaraguan voters were only given a choice to vote between the Sandinistas and smaller Marxist parties that support the Sandinistas. The two non-Marxist parties involved in the Nov. 4 vote there were so small as to be insignificant. One of them tried to withdraw before the election, but a mob of youths, orchestrated by the government, broke up their national party meeting before a vote could be taken.

Yes, professor, there was an election in Nicaragua. No, it was not "very much like those in the United States."

© 11/18/84 THE PHILADELPHIA INQUIRER
1/6 WASHINGTON POST WRITERS GROUP
AUTH

BOOM

THE GOVERNMENT OF NICARAGUA HAS MINED NEW YORK HARBOR, BUZZED AMERICAN CITIES WITH SUPERSONIC FIGHTERS, AND IS FUNDING AN ARMED INSURGENCY BY LIBERAL DEMOCRATS IN AN EFFORT TO FORCE THE REAGAN ADMINISTRATION TO HOLD LESS ONE-SIDED ELECTIONS.

— IMAGINARY NEWS ITEM

THE LOUISVILLE TIMES
Louisville, KY, November 6, 1984

The results of Nicaragua's first election in 10 years won't be official for some time. However, the ascendancy of leftist leader and strongman Daniel Ortega Saavedra to the presidency is a foregone conclusion. The question now is what he and his Sandinista colleagues, who will dominate the 90-member constituent assembly, will do with the voters' mandate.

Since this event coincides with the U. S. presidential election, however, Mr. Ortega has an opportunity to turn his own victory into something more than the "sham" that President Reagan said it would be.

Doubtless there will be hard-liners who will encourage Mr. Ortega to come down firmly in traditional Marxist style. With an electoral mandate, it might indeed be possible to clamp down on press criticism and on dissident priests and bishops. The introduction of Soviet fighter planes may give the Sandinistas a sense of military security they've lacked as well, but would inevitably destabilize the region even more.

But recent events indicate that Mr. Ortega and some of his supporters don't want to go down that path unless they are forced to.

Just two weeks ago, concessions were made to political dissidents assuring them periodic elections, the freedom to organize, to speak and to conduct a free press. Also, the Sandinistas surprised many by expressing a willingness to go along with the terms of the accord proposed by the Contadora group of regional peace negotiators. As far as the United States is concerned, the most important promise is that Nicaragua would stop trying to export revolution to its neighbors, provided the "contras" and other rebels hostile to the Sandinistas end their challenge.

These are more than election year goodies for war-weary Nicaraguans.

They are clear signs that Nicaragua's economy is in trouble and the Marxist government is increasingly nervous after five years in power. No electoral mandate changes those grim facts.

Until recently, the Sandinistas were bolstered by support from the middle class and the Roman Catholic church. That is changing. Farmers and businessmen, distressed by long years of strife, balk at demands that they meet the government's production quotas.

Though Moscow and Havana can offer moral, political and even military support to their friends in Managua, hard currency is increasingly something that they can't provide. But Washington can, and there is reason for the Sandinistas to hope that it might provide aid if certain conditions are met.

They do this advisedly. Neither Ronald Reagan nor Walter Mondale has been charitable toward Nicaragua in this campaign. If the country fails to follow the Contadora approach, Mr. Mondale has said, he would impose a quarantine. Mr. Reagan, continuing to speak of the contras as freedom-fighters, evades the possibility of an invasion, but in Nicaragua the fears of a grander Grenada-type operation are widespread.

What happens in Nicaragua next, of course, depends a lot on how leaders of the United States respond to their own and to their neighbor's election returns. Attempts to show the flag, especially through more substantial "war games" in Central America, will be a setback for closer ties.

Neither Nicaragua nor the United States can in the end escape credit or blame for what happens next. If both think first of their national security and the prospects of regional peace, decisions shouldn't be difficult.

THE PLAIN DEALER
Cleveland, OH, November 4, 1984

Today's election in Nicaragua is not the kind that the Reagan administration had hoped for. The election process has not been as open as most Americans would have liked. Arturo Cruz, the main opposition candidate, has decided not to take part in the election because of restrictions on his candidacy.

But that is not the reason for the administration's frustration. The president and his advisers have been calling the campaign a sham ever since Managua announced the date of the elections earlier this year, well before Cruz pulled out. The real source of the administration's opposition is the firm belief that today's results will add legitimacy to Nicaragua's leftist Sandinista government, something Washington is unwilling to accept.

There even have been reports that the administration, though publicly supporting Cruz, privately dissuaded Cruz from participating in the elections in the hope that a Cruz withdrawal would reinforce Washington's position that the elections are flawed. That's the same kind of doubletalk that had the administration supporting the Contadora peace process until surprised by Nicaragua's acceptance of the Contadora terms.

Still, Nicaragua's election will include seven political parties, including the Traditional Liberal and Conservative parties. And though you may question their sincerity, the Sandinistas did make efforts to accommodate Cruz' demands. The election, despite serious flaws in the process, does represent a willingness to allow more opposition sentiments to be represented in the government.

The best interest of the United States will be served if Washington abandons its hostilities against Managua, particularly support for the contras, and attempts to work with Nicaragua's elected leaders in developing a politically and economically healthy democracy—even one that is not in Washington's image.

Shipment of Soviet MiGs Denied, U.S. Invasion Plan Charged

Following United States charges November 6, 1984 that a Soviet freighter was approaching Nicaragua with a cargo of MiG-21 combat jets, Nicaragua Nov. 6-8 issued firm denials, maintaining that the U.S. government was attempting to establish a pretext for an invasion. The U.S. Nov. 6 and 7 warned the Soviet Union that it would not tolerate the delivery of MiG fighter aircraft to Nicaragua. The administration admitted, however, that intelligence reports were insufficient to confirm conclusively that the Soviet freighter's cargo included MiGs. The Soviet ship *Bakuriani*, was docked at the Nicaraguan Pacific port of Corinto Nov. 7. Reporters, who were permitted to watch the unloading of the freighter, saw no indication that there were MiGs on board. The U.S. also charged Nov. 6 that Nicaragua had recently received a number of Soviet-built attack helicopters. A senior administration official said the White House viewed the delivery as a "very serious development."

Nicaragua had recently unveiled a new military airport still under construction and said it was seeking to buy Soviet MiGs or other advanced combat aircraft. In a news conference Nov. 7, U.S. President Ronald Reagan said that the delivery of such aircraft to Nicaragua would "indicate that they are contemplating being a threat to their neighbors here in the Americas." The President declined to comment on "any plans on what we might do" if Nicaragua obtained MiGs. In the following days, sonic booms caused by U.S. reconaissance aircraft were heard across Nicaragua, contributing to what was widely viewed as a U.S. campaign of psychological pressure. Nicaragua's defense ministry Nov. 12 ordered the armed forces on full combat alert and deployed tanks in defensive positions around the capital. The U.S. continued to deny that an invasion was imminent, as charged by the Sandinista government, but vowed Nov. 13 that it would come to the aid of Honduras and El Salvador if Nicaragua attacked either of those countries.

The Times-Picayune
The States-Item
New Orleans, LA, November 14, 1984

The U.S. public can only be bemused and perhaps amused by the Nicaraguan Sandinistas' squawking like so many Chicken Littles about an impending U.S. invasion. Their expressed fears, said Secretary of State George Shultz, are "a self-inflicted wound ... based on nothing, and I don't know why they are doing this."

What they are doing is putting the whole nation on alert — issuing rifles right and left, reopening trenches dug two years ago during another panic, rolling their Soviet tanks and East German trucks through Managua and in general acting like Keystone Kops.

The general public is apparently taking it all in its stride, though there are worries about what effect all this may have on the real world they are having increasing difficulties living in. "It's been five or more times they've alerted us about an invasion, and it's going to tire people," remarked one man on the street. A Managuan offered, "The bad thing about all this is that factories and crops are neglected because of the military alerts, and we don't know what we're going to have to eat come July."

One suspects that the Sandinistas are protesting too much for a purpose. President Reagan, identified with a firm position against the Sandinista's power grab in Nicaragua and efforts to export Marxist revolution throughout Central America, has just been re-elected by a landslide. The Sandinistas, two days before, won a carefully controlled election not by the 90 percent they had predicted but by a touch over 66 percent. The anti-Sandinista rebels, supported by the United States, are gaining recruits and treatening expanded operations.

An easy way to create national unity and support is to focus attention on a foreign threat. The Sandinistas have pointed at the United States and cried wolf ever since they took control. The U.S. invasion of Grenada clearly scared them, but Nicaragua is not a tiny island. An open U.S. invasion of Nicaragua would require preparation of the U.S. public for such a step, and much of the U.S. public, according to opinion polls, doesn't really know much about the Central American situation.

The only U.S. military threat made against Nicaragua that we know of has been the U.S. refusal to rule out a possible surgical pre-emptive strike to take out MiG-21s fighter planes should the Soviets send the Sandinistas any. Whether this possibility extends to the combat and transport helicopters the Sandinistas admit the Soviets have just sent is , we think, best left unspecified.

THE SAGINAW NEWS
Saginaw, MI,
November 14, 1984

What if they gave an invasion, and nobody came?

It almost seems as though the Sandinista commandantes of Nicaragua are sending out engraved invitations.

They say they fully expect an invasion. They have raised their people's emotions and fears to a war pitch.

And they are goading the Yankees on with steady dockings of Soviet freighters carrying — what? Helicopters, apparently, not MIG jets. But if the U.S. thought those crates contained MIGs, then Nicaragua was not going to any great pains to contradict the impression — even knowing the risks. The past week's blunt warnings against MIG shipments only reiterated long-standing U.S. policy that the introduction of aggressive weapons would not be tolerated.

Both sides, actually, are playing a dangerous game. The U.S., with its maneuvering around the MIGs, may be preparing the public for a strike. We hope not — because it's just as likely that the Sandinistas are setting a trap.

Consider that the invasion has been "imminent" for years now. How long can Nicaragua cry wolf to its people without some evidence that the beast is real?

The regime has other troubles as well. This month's elections fell far short of a mandate for Marxism. The contras, led by former Sandinista heroes, are plugging away despite a U.S. aid cut-off.

The situation almost demands something dramatic, and what would serve better than provoking an attack?

The U.S. should resist the bait. It ought to know, as the Sandinistas surely do, that this isn't Grenada, that in the Central American swamp, if the quicksand doesn't get you, the 'gators will.

Should the Sandinistas really bring in MIGs, all parties have been given due warning. Otherwise, the U.S. should stand by Secretary of State George Shultz's assurances that the invasion alerts are "based on nothing."

The question remains of what the Sandinistas intend to do with their 50,000-man army, backed up by an equal militia, that is by far the most powerful military force in the region.

If it's invasion in the other direction, that's one, extremely dangerous, thing. But if Nicaragua keeps its peace, just let the troops, tanks and misled citizens dig in. The way to win this crisis is to let the Sandinistas lose it. They'll find a way to save face, but the U.S. shouldn't save it for them.

THE ATLANTA CONSTITUTION
Atlanta, GA, November 15, 1984

U.S. blood is being spilled over Nicaragua, but, thank goodness, so far only figuratively, in policy feuds within the Reagan administration. The debate, intensified by last week's MiG false alarm, must be resolved — wisely, decisively and rapidly — before the United States commits preventable blunders.

Simply put, the State Department favors a measured response to the militarization of Nicaragua while drastic action is being championed by influential spheres within the Defense Department, the Central Intelligence Agency and the National Security Council.

The policy struggle is complicated by the fact that the administration continues to project conflicting objectives: To contain the Sandinistas or to crush them?

State's point is well taken: The hawks have to realize they cannot achieve the latter without spending American lives and squandering good will throughout Latin America. Isolating Nicaragua and its Marxist-Leninist virus is a sound policy goal; eradication without a justification acceptable at home and abroad is too costly a remedy.

Let us then clearly set forth a threshold of tolerance. Let us say we will commit ourselves militarily before Nicaragua becomes a mirror-image of Cuba, a heavily armed Soviet proxy subverting weaker neighbors and providing bases for Moscow's submarines, missiles or high-performance warplanes.

But let us also recognize that, short of that threshold, the Sandinistas cannot be overthrown. A U.S. live-and-let-live policy would be best, with non-belligerent efforts both to press and to entice the Sandinistas into acceptable neighborliness.

Nicaragua, for all its sins, is not yet the rightly feared second Cuba. Nor is it clear that the Kremlin would commit its prestige and resources to that end. Its Nicaraguan venture seems more opportunistic than calculated.

Granted, the recent weapons shipments — patrol boats, helicopters, anti-aircraft guns — are a legitimate worry. But the weapons seem essentially defensive, justifiable by the argument that a sovereign government has the right to defend itself against rebels ("our" rebels, in this case) bent upon its destruction.

The Managua monster may be partly of our own making. Nicaragua's militarization began before the *contra* threat was credible, but economic realities might have restrained the Sandinistas from further weapons shopping if Washington hadn't upped the armaments ante by all but openly creating an army of exiles.

The searing glare of attention the administration has focused on Nicaragua has set it aboil. Reducing the heat and pressure might help make the problem there more manageable. That means leaving the *contras* to their own devices but at the same time removing one of the Sandinistas' best propaganda props.

Washington should underscore its expressed willingness to make peace with the idea of a revolutionary government in Managua so long as — but only so long as — it doesn't violate clearly understood codes of conduct regarding its neighbors. Meanwhile, let's strip Managua of its excuses for its own national mismanagement. Instead of nourishing the *contras* with our "covert" assistance, let them feed on the Sandinistas' own blunders and excesses.

THE ⛰ SUN
Baltimore, MD, November 14, 1984

A key to resolving tensions between the United States and Nicaragua lies not in Managua but in Moscow. If the Russians continue shipping weapons to Nicaragua at what the State Department calls "an unprecedented rate," we could have the kind of crisis the Sandinistas constantly invoke. Invasion, air strikes, naval quarantines — all these are "contingencies" that cannot be ruled out. An administration official said yesterday that the situation "bears some similarities to the Soviet behavior in the weeks and months preceding the 1962 Cuban incident in which the Soviet Union built up a considerable amount of armaments in Cuba and then used that to create a leverage to have a permanent presence in that country."

Does that mean the United States is confronted with "another Cuba"? Secretary of State George P. Shultz has charged that the Sandinistas "seem to be in the process of militarizing their society on the Cuba model." Defense Secretary Caspar Weinberger says "Cuba is a big problem and a second Cuba would be twice that kind of problem."

If we read these comments right, it means that the absence of Mig-21 aircraft on the Soviet freighter that unloaded in Corinto last week does not alleviate the administration's main concern, which would be Nicaragua's conversion into another Cuba — another Soviet base in the hemisphere. According to Western intelligence sources,

there are some 10,000 Cubans in Nicaragua plus more than 2,500 Soviet bloc advisers. The Sandinista armed forces, with 61,800 troops in uniform, are equipped with more than 60 T-55 main battle tanks and with armored personnel carriers that would overwhelm the land forces of neighboring El Salvador and Honduras. Now that the Sandinistas are getting Mi-24 assault helicopters, Nicaragua may be in the process of trying to match the superior air power of its neighbors.

If Moscow wanted to create a crisis atmosphere in the aftermath of the U.S. and Nicaraguan elections, it has succeeded in doing so. Armored units prowl the streets of Managua as the regime issues new wolf-warnings about a U.S. invasion; the capital resounds each morning to the sonic boom of reconnaissance U.S. aircraft.

The question still facing President Reagan and his Soviet counterpart, Konstantin Chernenko, is how large the Nicaraguan arms buildup can go before the United States is provoked. Obviously part of the answer lies in Washington. But the other part lies in Moscow, not in Managua. The Kremlin may be interested in nuclear arms negotiations and a larger diplomatic role in the Middle East, but these objectives would go smash if there is a clash in Central America. There are still opportunities for peaceful rather than military solutions, but they are diminishing.

The Salt Lake Tribune
Salt Lake City, UT, November 12, 1984

It's MiGs and it rhymes with eggs and, at the moment, that looks like what the Reagan administration has on its collective face.

After indulging in considerable provocative saber rattling by threatening all manner of reprisals, albeit unspecified, if that Soviet freighter were carrying advanced MiG jet fighters to Nicaragua the administration was forced to admit it was virtually certain there were no jets on board

The whole affair was far more bellicose than need be and it was another demonstration of the senseless paranoia, relative to the Soviet Union, that permeates the Reagan White House.

Also it suggests that Reagan aides have a very limited insight, or appreciation of, where the Soviet Union's priorities lie.

The Soviets have far too many urgent considerations on their agenda with the United States to risk jeopardizing them for the sake of tweaking Uncle Sam's nose by shipping some jets to Nicaragua, a cash-short country, incidentally, that is probably unable to pay for them.

Among the high priority items on the Soviet agenda are things like arms control, Asian security and the conflict between NATO and the Warsaw Pact; all issues that Moscow is unlikely to complicate in order to get some planes to the Sandinistas.

Evidence that these items are far higher on the Soviet agenda than shipping U.S.-provoking jets to Nicaragua comes from an unidentified U.S. official who told the Associated Press that the Soviets have recently shown interest in reopening talks to curb nuclear missiles under the "umberella" framework Mr. Reagan advanced at the United Nations in September.

Also, the Soviets did, it is useful to remember, tell the administration early last week that there were no jets aboard that freighter. Certainly such assertions have to be consumed well-salted, nevertheless the denial was made and should have been assessed a little more critically instead of being rejected out of hand.

Likewise, while that freighter justifiably needed to be monitored closely, the job should have been done in a less flamboyant fashion. And certainly, without the accompanying publicity. On that count the administration could have been far more discrete.

The affair of the mistaken MiGs leaves the United States looking bad; like an overbearing bully that is trying to throw its weight around in Central America. That is an image the United States has never really been able to rid itself of and the last week's provocation only perpetuated it.

The Burlington Free Press

Burlington, VT, November 9, 1984

U.S. intervention in Central America has reached a critical juncture.

While questions have been raised about the wisdom of providing military aid to El Salvador to fend off a purported left-wing overthrow of the government, an even greater furor has erupted over U.S. support of guerrillas who are trying to unseat the Sandinistas in Nicaragua. The extent of that effort is not yet clear. Available information, however, has led Congress to take steps to control funds that are being allocated for covert action against the Sandinistas.

But if the Reagan administration carries out its threats to destroy Soviet MIG-21 fighters which are reportedly being delivered to Nicaragua, the region could become a battleground in a Vietnam-type war.

Because U.S. meddling in the internal affairs of Central American nations already has gone some distance beyond the limits which have been set by the treaties that define relationships among the countries of the hemisphere, doubts have been expressed about U.S. respect for the sovereignty of its neighbors. Apparently blind to the inequities that have sowed the seeds of dissent in several Central American countries, the Reagan administration has chosen military action over economic and humanitarian aid as a means of dealing with the region's problems. Thus it is likely that a precipitous response to the delivery of Soviet warplanes to Nicaragua could widen the gulf between the United States and people in the region who are working for social change.

Mistake after mistake has been made by U.S. diplomats in their efforts to avert what they perceive as a leftist takeover of Central America. The principal error, however, has been the blind pursuit of policies that ignore the need for developing programs which will release millions of people from the clutches of abject poverty. Indiscriminate use of military power cannot assuage hunger pangs. Misery cannot be swept away through the use of force.

But the jingoistic rhetoric which is emanating from the Reagan administration indicates that the message of the region's people is not being heard. In a post-election news conference, President Reagan warned that he would regard the arrival of the Soviet planes as a serious matter and a "threat" to Central America. He said the Sandinista regime has been informed that it is "absolutely unnecessary" for them to bring in the Soviet fighters. Such a move, he said, constitutes a "threat to their neighbors here in the Americas."

There is an ironic twist to the situation. While Washington is alarmed by the possibility that the Sandinistas may be planning to build an air force in the hemisphere, U.S. missiles in Europe are but a breath away from targets in the Soviet Union. Several European and Mideastern nations have been supplied with U.S. planes which could be used against the Russians. And American arms are being shipped to many countries on the periphery of the Soviet Union.

What is even worse is that the United States has neglected several opportunities to reach some type of agreement with the Sandinistas which would preclude intervention by outsiders in Central American affairs. Policy-makers have instead concentrated their attention on activities which are designed to overthrow the Managua government.

Should the United States attack Nicaraguan airfields with the intention of destroying the Soviet planes, it may well find alienate leaders of several Latin American nations who up to now have been silent witnesses to intervention in El Salvador and Nicaragua. They will not sympathize with this country if a full-scale war develops in Central America.

The administration's wisest course now would be to concede that the Sandinistas have a right to govern Nicaragua as they see fit even to the point of using Soviet planes to guard its borders.

At the same time, Nicaraguan leaders should be invited to sit down at the bargaining table to discuss with U.S. diplomats acceptable arrangements which would guarantee peaceful relations in the region for years to come.

The Honolulu Advertiser
Honolulu, HI, November 13, 1985

The tenuousness of U.S.-Soviet relations has been particularly evident over the past few days. President Reagan held out an olive branch after his re-election, saying improvement of superpower ties would be a major priority during his second administration.

At the same time, the Soviets issued what might be construed as a "peace feeler." In a congratulatory message to Reagan, the Soviet government expressed its hope that "the coming years will be marked by a turn for the better in relations."

Then the possibility of Soviet MiG fighters being sent to Nicaragua brought any tentative steps toward improved relations to a halt. Fortunately, the crisis seems to have passed, even if Sandinista leaders are still using the possibility of an American invasion to keep Nicaraguans on edge.

OF COURSE, just because Washington and Moscow appear willing to talk of better relations does not guarantee the outcome. There are considerable obstacles.

For instance, how deep is the Reagan administration's desire for a U.S.-Soviet rapproche-ment? This president and many of his principal advisers have been among the most hard-line in recent memory. Has there been a dramatic shift in attitude?

The Soviet Union, for its part, has not encouraged a more trusting Western attitude. It continues a brutal occupation of Afghanistan; it maintains support for rebel causes in Central America; Vietnamese imperialism in Southeast Asia is possible because of considerable Soviet aid; despite detente, the Kremlin pushed ahead with a dramatic build-up of nuclear forces; and it has made clumsy attempts to influence Western European democracies with anti-American propaganda.

Add to that the continuing uncertainties about the Soviet leadership, and a cautious American attitude toward Moscow's "peace offerings" is understandable.

SO WHAT we seem to have is a situation in transition.

Certainly the hopes for peace are greater than they have been in four years. But the obstacles that have prevented movement toward better superpower relations remain formidable, and they cannot be discounted.

Los Angeles, CA, November 9, 1984

For a year now, the Reagan administration has made it clear what would happen if the Marxist regime in Nicaragua acquired advanced Soviet jet fighters: The U.S. is ready to use force, if necessary, to eliminate the threat such aircraft would pose to the rest of Central America. The warning has been so explicit that it is hard to believe the Kremlin and the Sandinistas would go out of their way to pick a fight they can't possibly win (barring the possibility, perhaps fanciful, that they thought they might slip something past Washington when the nation was occupied with the presidential election).

On the other hand, it was also hard to believe back in 1962 that the Soviets would dare provoke the U.S. by sending nuclear missiles to Cuba. Yet they did so. MiGs in Nicaragua would endanger U.S. interests less directly than ICBMs in Cuba, but they would upset the regional balance of power, which is why the White House has drawn the line.

At this point, it is far from clear that the Soviets and their clients have crossed that line, or even intend to do so. There may be some reason to suspect that the Soviet freighter that has docked at a Nicaraguan port might be carrying Soviet jets, but if so, that has not been established, and the Sandinistas have denied the allegation. Still, there is no reason they should necessarily be taken at their word, particularly since the regime in Managua has insisted all along that it has the right to obtain MiGs if it wants them.

Regardless of whether this particular alarm proves false, if advanced Soviet fighter aircraft turn up in Nicaragua, some sort of U.S. action would be justified. The Sandinistas already have armed forces far larger than they need for self-defense. They lack only a modern air force to obtain unquestioned military superiority in Central America. Although it is silly and dangerous to be "licking our chops," as one gung-ho administration official put it, at the prospect of denying them that superiority, we have the right to do so to protect our allies.

It would be most unfortunate if the Sandinistas and Soviets chose to challenge that right. ■

The Star-Ledger
Newark, NJ, November 14, 1984

Have the Soviets been conducting a military buildup in Nicaragua by supplying their allies there with offensive weapons? The recent controversy about the suspected presence of MiG fighters has added grave new concern to this question of several years duration. The question is a serious one that deserves a prompt and serious answer.

Unfortunately, the United States hasn't been able to get convincing assurances from either the Soviets or the Nicaraguans. What it has gotten from the Soviet and Sandinista regimes is the usual Communist blather—wild, unsubstantiated statements about how the United States is preparing to invade Nicaragua.

This is not reassuring. Indeed, it sounds very much like a rationale for justifying the importation of MiGs into Nicaragua and the buildup of other offensive weapons. The Nicaraguans have denied that a Soviet vessel brought a shipment of fighter planes and the Soviets, while refusing a formal comment, are said to have sent informal assurance to Washington that there was no MiG shipment. But this in itself is not enough.

Doubts remain. The State Department has sounded a warning expressing its concern. Intelligence reports tell our diplomats that the most recent shipment received from a Soviet vessel at a Nicaraguan port contained cartons of a type usually used for the transportation of fighter planes.

* * *

If that is indeed the contents of the shipment, the State Department is quite right to view it "with profound concern." It seems quite possible that the accumulation of such war materiel is for use against Nicaragua's neighbors—and is even a potential menace to the United States. Under these circumstances, it seems quite reasonable that the State Department is refusing to rule out the use of retaliatory force to destroy any fighters.

The Sandinista regime replaced the Somoza dictatorship in Nicaragua but has not proved a friend of democracy. What it has chiefly proved to be is a Soviet client fomenting revolution in bordering nations, such as El Salvador.

The concern by the United States over its intentions is quite legitimate and genuine. The question of whether there has been a shipment of planes from the Soviet Union may not be answered, but the controversy it caused reflects the concern our nation has with a militarily expanding Nicaragua.

Notice has been served on both the Nicaraguans and the Soviets that we will not sit idly by and permit an unrestricted military buildup of sophisticated offensive weapons. This is a warning that our adversaries had best heed. The hemisphere doesn't need another Cuba crisis.

Reagan Seeks to 'Remove' Nicaraguan Government

United States President Ronald Reagan February 21, 1985 asserted that his administration's goal in Nicaragua was to remove the Sandinista government "in its present form." In the past, the administration had said that its covert aid program in Nicaragua aimed to stem the flow of arms from Nicaragua to leftist rebels in El Salvador. In appealing for a resumption of aid to the contras, Reagan used his harshest language yet to denounce the Nicaraguan government. His appeal was part of a stepped up effort by the administration to persuade Congress to release funds for the contras. It drew strong criticism from some Democratic Party leaders and from the Nicaraguan government, which accused the U.S. of distorting the truth. However, Nicaraguan President Daniel Ortega Saavedra Feb. 27 announced that his government would halt the acquisition of new weapons and would send home 100 Cuban military advisers in an effort to reduce tensions in Central America. In 1984, Congress had allocated $14 million for the contras for the current fiscal year but had suspended release of the funds until it took another vote sometime after the end of February 1985. Democrats and Republicans alike had expressed the view that the funds almost certainly would not be released.

Reagan made his Feb. 21 comments in his first televised news conference of his second term. Asked whether the goal of his administration was to remove the Sandinista government, he replied: "Remove it in the sense of its present structure, in which it is a communist, totalitarian state and it is not a government chosen by the people." Reagan charged that the present government in Managua had betrayed the revolution that brought it to power and violated a pledge to the Organization of American States to bring about democracy. He maintained that the contras wanted to restore the original goals of the revolution. The president maintained that if the Sandinistas would "say uncle" and invite the contras to "come back into the revolutionary government and let's straighten this out and institute the goals," then their removal would not be necessary.

The Times-Picayune
The States-Item
New Orleans, LA, February 25, 1985

It sounded like a shocker. At his news conference Thursday night, President Reagan seemed to be calling for the overthrow of Nicaragua's Sandinista government. Does that mean he is ready to send in the Marines to oust a "brutal, cruel, communist totalitarian state"? The answer clearly is no. The president was using an excess of rhetoric to put pressure on two groups: the Sandinistas and the U.S. Congress.

To be sure, Mr. Reagan would like very much to see the Soviet- and Cuban-backed Sandinistas replaced by a democratic government or, at a minimum, have the Sandinistas share the government with the U.S.-supported rebels, or contras. His remark that the U.S. goal is "removing . . . the present structure" of government in Nicaragua is a blunt statement of the administration's purposes, but the goal has been obvious all along. Otherwise, why bother to support the rebels?

Still, Mr. Reagan's blunt call for political change in Nicaragua marks a significant, if subtle shift in the administration's policy. Until recently, the administration had argued mainly that the U.S. was backing the contras to block arms shipments from Nicaragua to El Salvador. But at his news conference, the president charged that the Sandinistas had betrayed the democratic promises of the 1979 Nicaraguan revolution and, therefore, do not have "a decent leg to stand on."

Mr. Reagan apparently wants to give the Sandinistas something to think about by,

in essence, saying their regime is illegitimate and unacceptable to the United States. At the same time, he held out the possibility of a negotiated settlement, provided the Sandinistas are willing to open the government to the contras.

As for Congress, Mr. Reagan was trying to put pressure on it by going over its head to the American people. The president wants the public to accept his harsh description of the Sandinistas and the very real subversive threat they pose to other Central American governments. Then he wants the public to pressure Congress to resume funding for the contras.

Last year Congress voted to halt funding for the contras' covert war against the Sandinistas after the administration had spent more than $80 million on a covert aid program directed by the CIA.

In saying that the Sandinistas had shut out other factions that had helped to overthrow the dictatorship of Anastasio Somoza, Mr. Reagan is simply restating historical fact. The Sandinistas have aborted the purpose of the revolution against the Somoza regime by replacing a rightist dictatorship with an oppressive leftist regime supported by Moscow and Havana.

Mr. Reagan is putting pressure on the Sandinistas to negotiate while also pressuring Congress to give him the leverage, in the form of renewed aid to the contras, to make his tough new rhetoric carry weight.

The Miami Herald
Miami, FL, March 4, 1985

PRESIDENT Reagan's Nicaragua policy is in trouble. Since its beginning, the Administration's "covert" aid to guerrillas seeking to overthrow Nicaragua's Sandinista regime has incurred the displeasure of U.S. allies abroad and congressional critics at home. Now, as he turns up his anti-Sandinista rhetoric, the President may be alienating yet another group: the voters who re-elected him.

According to a nationwide *Washington Post*-ABC News poll conducted last weekend, Americans now oppose by almost a 4-1 margin any U.S. involvement in trying to overthrow Nicaragua's leftist government. Distaste for American intervention transcends party affiliation, moreover. Among Republicans, 60 percent oppose it and only 26 percent favor it, with the rest undecided. Among Democrats, 76 percent are opposed, only 12 percent in favor.

Almost no one suggests that American foreign policy ought to be governed by plebiscite. Voters, in the absence of a perceived military threat to the nation or its allies, are a remarkably complacent lot. In murkier contingencies, it is frequently a President's burden to act now and seek voters' approval later.

And yet, as Defense Secretary Caspar Weinberger has pointed out, no foreign policy can succeed in the long run without public support. When decisive Executive action nets immediate results, as in the invasion of Grenada, voters are quick to give the President the benefit of the doubt. But initiatives that resist quick fixes — witness the recent U.S. military role in Beirut — soon are undermined by the public's impatience.

That's why popular opposition to Mr. Reagan's Nicaragua policy is likely to build, rather than diminish, unless he can persuade the public that it's in America's best interest. By the Administration's own reckoning, it will be years before the guerrilla's war of attrition compels the Sandinistas to moderate their policies. Prospects for overthrowing the regime are even more slight. What is envisioned, then, is precisely the kind of holding action for which Americans historically have demonstrated no tolerance.

There's little doubt that the voters who overwhelmingly re-elected Mr. Reagan share his antipathy for the Sandinistas. But the public's distinct lack of enthusiasm for U.S. aid to the *contras* indicates that the Administration has failed to translate that general distaste for Marxist regimes into support for Mr. Reagan's specific remedy.

Opinion surveys alone shouldn't determine American foreign policy, of course, especially in so critical a region as Latin America. Even so, any policy that fails to command the electorate's acquiescence is doomed in the long run. As things stand now, public disapproval is a formidable obstacle to the Administration's aspirations in Nicaragua.

Houston Chronicle
Houston, TX, February 28, 1985

President Reagan is not finding it difficult to express his mind on the subject of Nicaragua. He wants that government to shift away from communism and toward democracy.

However, the president is careful how he phrases the means by which he would like to achieve his goal. As illustrated in his recent press conference, he carefully avoids using the word "overthrow." That word is not permitted. It is not acceptable to Congress. It speaks of armed intervention by a superpower in the affairs of a small neighbor.

So, the U.S. policy must be one of exerting pressure for change.

One means of pressure is to provide "covert" assistance to the contras fighting the Sandinista government. President Reagan refers to the contras as "freedom fighters." If the Soviet Union is supplying attack helicopters and if the Cubans are supplying other military equipment to help the Sandinistas defeat the rebels, it is appropriate, the reasoning goes, for the United States to help those fighting the communists. That's why the administration is appealing to Congress to approve $14 million in military aid.

There is little expectation that the contras will be able to achieve a military victory in Nicaragua under existing circumstances. Once the Sandinistas won their revolution,

they set about building the largest military force in the region. The contras are exerting pressure on the Sandinistas, but they alone cannot force change.

Beyond the military, there are diplomatic and economic levers available.

Regional governments, through the Contadora negotiations, may extract democratic concessions from the Sandinistas. Some church groups which once backed the Sandinistas are now discovering the true impact of communism and pushing for greater liberty. Direct U.S.-Nicaraguan talks were not productive, but could be tried again.

Economically, the United States is not powerless. The United States remains one of the principal customers of Nicaragua. The Sandinistas are having problems meeting the basic needs of Nicaraguans and productivity is down. They could use financial aid.

Interestingly, congressional leaders came out of a meeting with President Reagan this week speaking of a carrot and stick approach to Nicaragua, of using all three means of pressure — military, diplomatic and economic. With the added element of time, such an multifaceted approach would produce effective pressures toward the kind of necessary change in Nicaragua the president seeks.

ST. LOUIS POST-DISPATCH
St. Louis, MO, February 24, 1985

In his latest press conference, President Reagan at last was a little more specific about just what he intends the administration's war against Nicaragua to accomplish. He wants the Nicaraguan leaders to say "uncle."

Until recently the administration has had varying explanations of why it is using the CIA to promote a guerrilla war against Nicaragua: to interdict supplies to El Salvador, to jostle the leftist government to turn to the right, etc. But this time, when asked if he wanted to overthrow the Nicaraguan government, Mr. Reagan said, "Not if the present government would turn around and say 'uncle' to the Nicaraguan rebels."

Saying "uncle" to the CIA's surrogates would be tantamount to surrendering to the supporters of the former Somoza dictatorship who provide much of the rebel leadership. Hardly anyone inside Nicaragua wants a return of that kind of oppressive regime. Mr. Reagan may talk of those rebels as "freedom fighters" but their record also includes civilian murders and torture. Certainly it takes a flight from reality to view the Nicaraguan situation as either black or white, with the U.S. totally on the side of what is totally right.

Yet that rigidly ideological view is one that the administration seems to have adopted. Supporting demands for more U.S. military aid for the CIA's rebels, Secretary of State George Shultz recently told the House Foreign Affairs Committee that the

U.S. has a moral duty to keep Nicaragua from falling behind the Iron Curtain. And he later hinted that the U.S. might eventually have to take direct action against Nicaragua.

What Mr. Shultz said was mild compared to the explicit advice that Curtin Winsor, the U.S. ambassador to Costa Rica, gave visiting congressmen. Astonished legislators say he suggested that the U.S. consider invading Nicaragua with 120,000 Marines who could get the job done "in three days." The State Department had to reject this nonsensical remark. After all, a major administration charge is that the Sandinistas are building up the largest military machine in Central America. Outright invasion would not be another Grenada; it would be a senseless and bloody affair.

Still, the administration is exploring the idea of getting Nicaraguan rebel groups to form a united organization so that they could receive U.S. aid openly, not covertly. An advocate of that idea, Sen. Durenberger of Minnesota, says "the only difference is that when we do it covertly, we lie a lot." But another Republican, Sen. Lugar of Indiana, warns that public aid to the rebels would be close to declaring war, "and there's no consensus in the public for that."

Indeed there is not, nor is there justification for it in Mr. Reagan's conclusion that his government has the absolute right to force another government to say "uncle." The best thing to do with this war, covert or open, is to call it off.

The Chattanooga Times
Chattanooga, TN, February 25, 1985

"I don't think the Sandinistas have a decent leg to stand on. What they have done is totalitarian; it is brutal, cruel. And they have no argument against what the rest of the people in Nicaragua want." In delivering himself of that assessment of the current regime in Nicaragua, President Reagan was on reasonably firm ground. The Sandinistas did in effect betray the revolution that six years ago overthrew the Somoza government there.

But however reprehensible that is, does that give the United States the right to do whatever it can to encourage the overthrow of that government? Mr. Reagan seems to think so. He doesn't like the Sandinista government, and thinks it ought to be removed "in the sense of its present structure": a Communist, totalitarian state, not chosen by the people. The present government could avoid being removed, so to speak, if it "would turn around and say [to the contra rebels] — all right — if they'd say uncle, or all right, and come back into the revolutionary government and let's straighten this out and institute the goals."

But as Mr. Reagan surely knows, the Sandinistas are unlikely to say "uncle," and invite the contras back into the government to institute goals for which conservatives like the president were criticizing them back in 1978. That raises the obvious question: If the Sandinistas spurn Mr. Reagan's gracious request that they surrender in a war that they aren't now losing, what happens next? That is precisely the question that worries Congress. It led to adoption last year of the Boland amendment.

Under that amendment, about which Mr. Reagan professed ignorance during his press conference Thursday evening, the administration's request for $28 million in new aid to the contras was cut to $14 million, none of which could be spent before Feb. 28, 1985 (next Thursday). If Mr. Reagan decides he wants to spend the money, he must certify to Congress that the funds are needed to combat the Sandinistas. The report has to be approved by both Houses, which means either has the power to veto any spending.

Any way you look at it, the Boland amendment is — and should be — a strong deterrent to the adventurism implicit in Mr. Reagan's Nicaragua policy. Moreover, the president's bellicosity suggests that Congress would be well advised to renew the Boland amendment, if for no reason than to ensure that the United States doesn't get more deeply involved in Nicaragua. If Congress allows the administration to resume funding the contras, it will put this country once more on the slippery slope of increased, direct involvement.

It is proper to sympathize with those who feel they were betrayed by the Sandinistas' totalitarian tendencies, but does that mean the United States should be intervening to ensure more democratic government? No. If that were the chief criterion, the administration would be underwriting rebels in Chile, South Korea and other countries headed by right-wing totalitarian leaders.

Mr. Reagan denigrated the Boland amendment by saying that "some of the proposals ... in Congress have lacked a complete understanding of what is at stake out there and what we're trying to do." On the contrary, Congress knew exactly what it was doing: acting as a check on the administration. It should continue to do so as long as Mr. Reagan continues to encourage U.S. interference in other countries.

Arkansas Gazette.

Little Rock, AR, February 25, 1985

That the Reagan administration is determined not to take "no" for an answer from Congress on covert aid to the pro-United States rebels — the contras — in Nicaragua seems more apparent daily, in remarks not only by the President but also by Secretary of State George Shultz. Some of it is pretty scary stuff, too, and it surely will not go unanswered in either house.

President Reagan remarked at his news conference last week that he wanted "to remove" the "present structure" of the Nicaraguan government, adding that it was immaterial to him how the deed was accomplished. Mr. Reagan remarked that the change could come about through action of authorities in Managua acting on their own or through agreement with other nations or "through the collapse of the Sandinista regime."

A clear message came across to a good many in Congress and elsewhere, and it may be best summarized by the remark of a senior member of the House Foreign Affairs Committee, Representative Stephen J. Solarz of New York: "I think it was a virtual declaration of war against Nicaragua. I think that his statements last night totally ignored the Contadora process and the very real possibility that the problems we confront in Central America can be resolved at the negotiating table rather than on the battlefield."

Secretary Shultz, the next day in San Francisco, hit another disturbing note in the anti-Sandinista campaign. If more aid was denied to the rebels, he said, Nicaragua would fall into "the endless darkness of Communist tyranny," possibly requiring direct and costly American action later. Americans, the secretary said, have "a moral duty" to help "the freedom fighters" battle the Nicaraguan government. Meanwhile, back at the White House, Mr. Reagan remarked to some editorial writers that he did not see an American invasion of Nicaragua as a possibility.

The implication in all this is that "you can pay now" with the $14 million more in aid to the contras or "you can pay later" to eradicate "the endless darkness of Communist tyranny" in Nicaragua.

But that is not the choice before Congress, and there are many indications that Congress knows it in spite of the administration attempt to appeal directly to the American people, who have learned the hard way how to read between the lines when the subject is possible intervention in foreign lands.

The Knickerbocker News
Albany, NY, March 4, 1985

As the war of words between the Reagan administration and Managua escalates, so do the chances for misinterpretation, or worse — stumbling into a war neither nation wants. That's why it's important for the White House to speak both cautiously and clearly.

President Reagan says he wants the Sandinistas to say "uncle" and all will be well. But what if they do not? What is the administration prepared to do to remove the Sandinistas from power? There's no clear answer, just ambiguity.

If the contra rebels can't defeat the Sandinistas — and most military experts agree they cannot, at least at their present strength — who will? America's allies in Central America show no willingness to commit troops. If not, what options remain — American Marines?

Mr. Reagan isn't saying anything to indicate he's planning an invasion, but he's hinting broadly that his patience with Nicaragua's Marxists is running out. Having scared the Soviets back to arms negotiations by raising the possibility of a Stars Wars nuclear defense, Mr. Reagan appears to be using charged rhetoric on the Sandinistas as well.

So far, he's had limited success. Nicaragua's President Ortega says he's willing to send home 100 Cuban advisers — out of 3,500 in his country — and talk peace with American officials.

The White House, correctly, detects a public relations ploy. Spokesman Larry Speakes characterizes Mr. Ortega's proposal as a somewhat sophisticated attempt to sway Congress away from continued American aid to the contras. In fact, both sides have become disturbingly sophisticated at shaping the truth to suit their purposes.

Last week, Secretary of State George Shultz labeled Managua a major drug trafficker — until critics pointed out that the label fits other Central and Latin American nations that also happen to be our allies.

Weeks before the drug claim, the administration was raising alarms that Nicaragua might be importing Soviet missiles. Closer scrutiny showed the shipments were in facts helicopters and other defense weapons — not nuclear rockets.

But the White House isn't alone in revving up the truth. Sandinista sympathizers are doing it as well. New York Congressman Ted Weiss, for example, charged Secretary Shultz with red-baiting on Nicaragua in a McCarthy-like fashion — a charge even the congressman has now recanted.

Other sympathizers, and the Sandinistas themselves, are portraying the Oretga regime as beleaguered innocents who, while Marxist in outlook, are free of Soviet domination. But if that is so, why are so many Soviet arms streaming into Nicaraguan ports? Why are North Korean and Vietnamese military advisers training pilots to use Soviet missile-firing helicopters? All because of the motley contras?

Or could it be that Nicaragua, like Cuba before it, intends to export revolution once the contras are crushed. Could it be that the Sandinistas, like the Cubans, will one day install Soviet missiles aimed at American cities? Given the Soviet edginess over Star Wars, Moscow might feel safer with another arms base close to the American mainland.

These questions, along with the Sandinistas' previous deceptions about harboring democratic ideals, give the Reagan administration good cause for opposing the Ortega regime. But that cause will be weakened if the administration continues to use overstatement and intimidation to drive the message home.

The majority of the American people will support a firm hand toward Nicaragua, provided they know the facts. That means telling them the truth and the truth alone — in all its complexity.

'UNCLE' RON

THE LOUISVILLE TIMES

Louisville, KY, February 26, 1985

Sometimes President Reagan makes sense, and occasionally when he does, it's downright scary.

Such was the case Thursday night in his press conference, with his irresponsibly provocative threats to "remove" the "present structure" of Nicaragua's government unless the Sandinistas there "say uncle."

In a startling change of rhetoric, the President explained the need for removal. It's not to stop the flow of arms into neighboring El Salvador, a claim that had been used to justify opposition to the leftist Nicaraguan regime in the past. Rather, it is the very nature of the Sandinista government: "What they have done is totalitarian, it is brutal, cruel. And they have no argument against what the rest of the people in Nicaragua want."

There's a big difference between disliking the kind of government that Nicaragua has — as many Americans do — and talking about removing it. But the fear across Central America over the last four years has been that Mr. Reagan isn't hung up by such niceties, a fear substantiated by the invasion of Grenada in the fall of 1983.

It's fair to say that no matter how oppressed many Nicaraguans may feel under the Sandinista regime, few of them are anxious to return to power some leaders of the so-called contra movement, which has received $80 million in U. S. aid for its "covert" rebellion since late 1981. Many of the contras were once linked to the U. S.-backed Somoza regime, which was toppled by the Sandinistas and others in 1978.

What Mr. Reagan has consistently failed to understand is that communism and democracy are relative terms in underdeveloped countries — even ones that are as near the United States as Nicaragua, El Salvador and others in Central America. When Secretary of State George Shultz talks about "freedom fighters" the expression may warm the hearts of patriotic Americans but rings hollow for those who have had firsthand experience with the contras.

Until last week, at least, Mr. Reagan adhered to some niceties in his public pronouncements about U. S. goals in Nicaragua. Usually he justified opposition on the claim that the Nicaraguans were determined to export revolution. In the last year, particularly, he seemed willing through Mr. Shultz to discuss some kind of negotiated settlement.

The Sandinistas are not the only group Mr. Reagan wants to cry "uncle," however. He's also talking to Congress, which has resolutely knotted the purse strings to prevent further aid to the contras. Ever since the CIA was linked to the mining of Nicaraguan harbors last spring, neither party on Capitol Hill has been willing to finance further international embarrassment.

And reports over the weekend that the intelligence agency put together plans to overthrow the Sandinistas is unlikely to win many more votes. Even conservative Republican leaders in the Senate express doubt whether Mr. Reagan can get enough support this spring to renew covert aid.

Not only must Congress refuse that aid, but it must send word to the White House that negotiations must become a true priority. Dangerous words about removing any foreign government — whether we like its policies or not — can lead to devastating consequences.

Mr. Reagan's brazen talk deserves a not so gracious rebuff. Otherwise, there's a danger that when the President carelessly talks about making a nation "say uncle," it will be interpreted to mean "Uncle Sam."

Come to think of it, we like it better when Mr. Reagan *doesn't* make sense.

Richmond Times-Dispatch

Richmond, VA, February 23, 1985

President Reagan apparently intends to turn his fight to obtain congressional approval of American aid for Nicaragua's contras, seeking to wrest that country's revolution from communist Sandinistas, into a crusade. And his principal weapon, he told a group of editors at a White House briefing yesterday, will be the truth.

The president believes that the American people, indeed the world, have been misled about the situation in Nicaragua by a vast disinformation campaign. It seems to be generally believed that the Sandinist regime is a thoroughly legitimate government that enjoys wide popular support. Not so, says Mr. Reagan. The Sandinistas seized control of the revolution and have replaced the dictatorship of Somoza with a dictatorship of Marxism, betraying Nicaraguans who had hoped to establish a true democracy in their unfortunate country. Many of the *contras* are these betrayed revolutionaries, he says, who are engaged in a legitimate struggle for freedom. And they deserve the United States' support.

Reagan

Exactly how does he intend to try to convince Congress of this? By telling it "the truth," he replied. But in conveying the truth to Congress, he will not communicate exclusively with that body. The Great Communicator plans also to try to persuade the legislators' constituents to join his crusade for the *contras*. If he is successful, Congress, of course, will get the word.

That Mr. Reagan will go to the people was revealed by White House Chief of Staff Donald Regan, who preceded the president at the White House briefing. Mr. Regan seems certain that most Americans will agree that the United States cannot "tolerate a Marxist state just north of the Panama Canal," a state that would constitute a festering point from which communism would spread throughout the region.

All this prompted the editors to ask whether direct American military intervention could be justified and whether it is contemplated. The president replied that because the gunboat diplomacy the United States has practiced at times in the past in Latin America has created a lingering image of this country as the "colossus of the North," countries in that region would not "tolerate" the use of United States troops in the Nicaraguan conflict. While it is conceivable that conditions could change to justify such intervention, he foresees no such development.

And so President Reagan will concentrate on efforts to extend American moral and material support to the *contras*. For this he will need the support of Congress; and the chances are good that, with the help of the American people, he ultimately will get it.

Compromise on U.S. Aid Fails; House Bars All Aid to Contras

The United States House of Representatives dealt President Ronald Reagan a crushing blow April 24, 1985 by rejecting all forms of aid to the Nicaraguan contras. The rejection came after efforts to work out a compromise on humanitarian aid failed. Efforts by the White House and Congress to work out a specific compromise plan failed largely because of disputes over the U.S. role in peace negotiations. The Democrats insisted that release of funds be linked to the resumption of direct talks between the Sandinista government and the U.S. Administration. The White House, on the other hand, emphasized the importance of talks between the Sandinista government and the contras, a step that had been rejected in Managua. There was also disagreement about how the funds would be disbursed; Democrats opposed the channeling of aid via the Central Intelligence Agency, favoring disbursement through the State Department.

The wording of a resolution that was endorsed by the Senate April 23, by a vote of 53-46, called for funds for "military or paramilitary purposes," but was accompanied by a letter from Reagan pledging to restrict the aid to food, clothing and other nonlethal uses. In his letter, Reagan vowed to resume talks with Managua and to push for a cease-fire and church-mediated talks between the Sandinista government and the rebels. He said he would also "favorably consider" economic sanctions against the Sandinistas to encourage them to negotiate in good faith with the contras. After the Senate vote, Reagan praised the action as "a historic vote for freedom and democracy in Central America." The House later that evening rejected the same resolution in a 248-180 vote. In debate before the vote, Rep. Joseph Addabbo (D, N.Y.) charged that "a letter from the President, a press release from the President, is not law" and noted that the language before the House would legally permit the use of funds for military purposes. In a series of votes April 24, the House then wiped clean the legislative slate on U.S. aid to Nicaragua, defeating all amendments including the original Democratic plan for aid to the region.

THE ATLANTA CONSTITUTION
Atlanta, GA, April 26, 1985

Ronald Reagan can keep butting his head against the walls of the U.S. Capitol or he can reshape his administration's Nicaragua policy in ways that can and should command wide support.

This clear choice should be evident to all but the most intransigent of the advocates of a Nicaraguan military strategy after the U.S. House, for the fourth time in little over a year, rejected aid to the contras, even a trifling $14 million worth of arguably humanitarian assistance.

Regrettably, the president seems not to have taken Wednesday's blow to his prestige to heart. Before the fiscal year runs out, the White House will submit a request for $28 million in military supplies for the Nicaraguan guerrillas, and supporters in Congress may try to wear down the opposition by attaching contra aid requests to a host of unrelated bills. It is a formula for futility.

A commanding body of House members and a near-majority in the Senate simply will not buy the Nicaraguan "realities" as depicted by the president. His rhetorical excesses (equating the contras to our Founding Fathers), his false claims of support for his most recent Nicaraguan initiative (repudiated by no less than Pope John Paul II), his subordinates' blunders (the CIA's harbor mining and assassination comic book) — all have undermined the administration's Nicaraguan policy more effectively than any resistance that Managua has raised.

When the president made his latest Nicaraguan gambit — a six-month period in which to test the preposterous notion that Managua might negotiate with the contras — he spoke unconvincingly of a time "to give peace a chance." But the president has never seriously given peace, or peaceful if punitive means, a chance to reduce the turmoil in Central America or to teach the undeniably distasteful Sandinistas to mind their manners.

Wednesday's House action probably won't seriously impact on the contras or Managua. The rebels are sure to continue their low-intensity incursions, funded from private right-wing sources and sympathetic Central American governments. The Sandinistas will clear their northern border areas for free-fire zones and hone their combat skills against the contras. Sadly, the death toll, now pegged at 10,000 after more than three years of fighting, will mount.

The president should be resolutely testing and implementing all diplomatic and economic means to minimize the arms buildup and subversion in the region. After all, the flip side of congressional disapproval for his contra strategy is strong, bipartisan support for a no-nonsense, sustained U.S. hand on all other levers.

If Reagan ever does need resort to any military option — and it is not impossible that he will — it will be most readily available to him if an honest effort to secure legitimate U.S. interests by other means has proven unequal to the task.

The Register
Santa Ana, CA, April 25, 1985

The House vote Tuesday against sending $14 million in aid to Nicaraguan rebels is being called a severe defeat for President Reagan's policy to force democracy on that country. It should not be seen as a defeat, but rather a bittersweet victory for those who believe that freedom from repressive governments sometimes means freedom from the U.S. government as well.

The Reagan administration wants to focus on the Senate, which did approve the aid, but the split between the two houses makes it unlikely that aid will be approved soon. Presumably, now that the military — or discretionary — aid apparently will not be sent, the opponents of the pro-Marxist Nicaraguan government will have to turn to other sources for their funds — to individuals and groups that understand and sympathize with their cause.

Anti-government groups in Nicaragua began just such fund-raising efforts last summer, when Congress stopped their access to U.S. taxpayer dollars through the CIA. Funds have since flowed from appeals to private individuals in this country, as well as from individuals and governments in Central America.

Importantly, because those funds did not come from the U.S. government, the contra cause is not as easily identified as a Yanqui cause. That's important to a revolution that wants the support of the Nicaraguan people.

If the revolution is not seen as backed by a foreign government — the Soviet Union, say, or the United States — then it is ever so much more a revolt of the people whose future it determines. And it well could be ever so much easier to win support for the cause.

That was one of the lessons of Vietnam, as it has been in almost every war where the United States has tried to interfere. When foreign governments get involved, the focus changes, from the people and the government of the country involved to the superpowers engaged in their symbolic battle for "image." And the people? They begin to see little difference between one foreign power running their lives and another.

The House vote temporarily will save Nicaragua from that fate. It is a bittersweet vote because it may well mean the contras face a much more difficult — and longer — fight against the Sandinista government. It is a bittersweet vote because surely anyone who believes in freedom believes in aiding the cause of a people trying to overthrow a repressive government as quickly as possible.

The $14 million in aid President Reagan wanted to send to the contras might well have speeded their revolution in the short run. But in the long run, it would have hurt, for it would have been a victory not of the Nicaraguan people, but of one superpower over another

The Houston Post

Houston, TX, April 25, 1985

What has happened in the House of Representatives the past two days can only encourage Nicaragua's Sandinista regime to go its Marxist way with less concern about U.S. reaction.

Partisan politics and the "Vietnam syndrome" were key factors in the House defeat of President Reagan's request for $14 million in aid to anti-Sandinista rebels in Nicaragua. The amount of money was small by federal spending standards, but the vote was a potentially heavy blow to the administration's Central American policy. It could reverberate throughout the region, including El Salvador, where the government is battling leftist rebels backed by the Soviet Union, Cuba and the Sandinistas.

The president didn't help his case by first conjuring up an imminent Communist military threat to U.S. security and then offering eleventh-hour compromises that came close to embracing the Democratic position, including no arms for the rebels. Though the tactic worked in the Republican-controlled Senate Tuesday, it didn't in the Democratic-led House.

On Wednesday, after approving a Democratic alternative to the Reagan plan and defeating a GOP compromise, both by narrow margins, the House voted down the final bill. The Democratic plan would have substituted Nicaraguan refugee aid for Contra funds.

If Congress doesn't eventually agree to resume aid to the Contras, effective insurgency will become increasingly difficult. Most of the rebels are peasants who oppose Sandinista policies that include Soviet-style collective farming and population relocation to quell unrest. By aiding the Contras, President Reagan hoped to pressure the Sandinistas into keeping their promises to build an open, democratic society. But weakened Contra resistance will allow them to pursue their radical-leftist agenda that much faster.

The Dallas Morning News

Dallas, TX, April 25, 1985

THE vote Tuesday on aid to the *contras*, Nicaragua's anti-communist rebels, proves that what the majority of Congress learned from Vietnam is worse than nothing.

We're pleased that most of the Texas delegation, including Sen. Bentsen, supported the president's watered-down proposal. We greatly regret that Reps. Wright, Frost and Bryant didn't.

The first thing to notice is what had already happened to the president's original proposal for $14 million in military aid.

By the time the vote was taken Tuesday the president had pledged that under *no* circumstances would the aid be used for military purposes, and that he was willing to resume negotiations for a cease-fire with the Soviet-backed Sandinistas.

Even that wasn't enough to satisfy his opponents, who had the numbers in the House, though not the Senate, to doom the aid measure.

Now attention turns to ways of compromising previous compromises.

House Democrats want to give $10 million to Nicaraguan "refugees," and $4 million to enforce a regional peace plan. Which is rather like making grand plans of what you'd do if you were rich, but darn the luck you're not.

There is little likelihood that the Sandinistas, in the absence of pressure from the *contras*, will seriously consider bargaining away any of their totalitarian power just because some regional group says it would be nice if they would.

What this means is that the *contras* will be crippled at least for the next several months.

Time is crucial, for even if Congress wakes up eventually, by then the Sandinistas could be too solidly entrenched behind their military machine and state police to be budged.

If the United States is quiescent when its security interests and values are threatened on its southern doorstep — what? A refugee flood? Intensifying instability in Mexico? We probably ain't seen nothin' yet.

Worse, as Undersecretary of State Fred Ikle says, "Morale is just now turning in favor of a diminution of insurgency in El Salvador," but with waning support of the *contras*, "insurgents in El Salvador will take heart. They would know that they just have to wait a few years until the Sandinistas are done with Nicaragua, and then they can get all the help they need."

No doubt the Central American mess will get plenty messier with the Sandinistas free to join the Cubans as a growing regional menace.

Lovely, Congress, just lovely.

Wisconsin State Journal

Madison, WI, April 26, 1985

If House Democrats and President Reagan had bargained a few weeks ago as they started bargaining Wednesday, the United States might today have a coherent and constructive policy on Nicaragua.

But that didn't happen. Instead, Democrats voted down in succession several variations on Reagan's proposal to send $14 million in U.S. aid to Contra rebels fighting Nicaragua's Sandinista government.

For the moment, U.S. policy toward Nicaragua is rubble. Yet there are timbers in the rubble that should be salvaged and used to construct a sound bipartisan strategy.

That strategy must start with the principle that the United States should *not* seek to overthrow — even indirectly — a sovereign government recognized by the United States and against which we are not at war.

Nor should the United States condone or be party to the terrorism committed on either side of the conflict between the Sandinistas and Contras.

Next, congressional leaders and the president should agree that events in Nicaragua remain a legitimate U.S. concern.

The Sandinistas are being armed and advised by the Soviet Union, via Cuba and other routes; the military strength of Nicaragua and its intentions in Central America are a genuine worry for neighboring countries; and the United States has a proper interest in these developments within its "sphere of influence."

Those who contend another Soviet satellite in Central America should be of no concern to the United States should recall the Cuban missile crisis of 1962, the closest the world has yet come to nuclear war.

What, then, should U.S. policy be?

Its outlines emerged in the proposals and counterproposals between the White House and Congress this week.

First, the United States should work toward a cease-fire in Nicaragua and provide financial support, if necessary, for a neutral peacekeeping force. These ideas were contained in one Democrat-sponsored alternative presented Wednesday in the House.

Second, the administration should resume bilateral talks with the Sandinistas. Reagan told Senate Republicans Tuesday he would support such talks.

Third, the administration and the Congress should unite in a firm bargaining position, insisting that the Sandinistas restore fundamental freedoms in Nicaragua and satisfy the legitimate security concerns of the United States and other Central American countries.

With their votes against both military and non-military aid for the Contras, Democratic leaders in the House have dealt Reagan a foreign-policy defeat.

But with that victory comes a heavy burden of responsibility. Democrats must help fashion a policy that respects not only the security of the Sandinistas, but the security of the United States and the region.

TULSA WORLD

Tulsa, OK, April 26, 1985

THE U.S. House of Representatives has rarely looked worse than it did Wednesday in killing the last hope for uninterrupted U.S. aid to anti-communist rebel forces in Nicaragua.

The only thing to say in defense of those who handed this good news to the Soviet-backed Sandinista regime is that they reflected the will of many of their constituents.

That's the real problem in dealing with Soviet meddling and aggression in Latin America. Every poll shows that many Americans, frightened by the memory of Vietnam, are in no mood for the use of American power or influence to promote our own interests or to support democracy abroad.

Victims of the Vietnam Syndrome see hobgoblins in every proposal to resist aggression. Some are afflicted with a kind of political nihilism that is scary. This is a belief that all systems of government are more or less equal (i.e. bad) and any dispute between democracy and communism is a moral standoff. Both sides are to blame. And, finally, what happens in the rest of the world is none of America's business.

These attitudes make people want to believe the Marxists in Managua when they say, with perfectly straight faces, that they aren't Marxists and that they would be good boys if the Americans would get off their backs.

It is disappointing that Oklahoma's Reps. Jim Jones, Dave McCurdy, Mike Synar and Wes Watkins voted no on the key roll call on the aid issue. Their best argument is that, regardless of their own views, they do not want to make a serious commitment abroad that does not have broad support from the American people.

Reps. Mickey Edwards and Glenn English voted yes. Sens. David Boren and Don Nickles both supported a Senate version of the aid bill.

Wednesday, April 25, 1985: A bad day in the U.S. House of Representatives.

The Chattanooga Times

Chattanooga, TN, April 26, 1985

In pushing his policy of financing a war to overthrow the Sandinista government of Nicaragua, President Reagan has employed vastly overblown rhetoric and outright distortion. But the country was unpersuaded by Mr. Reagan's depiction of Nicaragua as a major security threat to the United States or his view of the contras as the moral equivalent of our Founding Fathers. And the lack of public support for Mr. Reagan's policy translated this week into the president's first major congressional defeat of his second term.

The House of Representatives voted Wednesday to kill all active legislation to renew aid to the anti-Sandinista contras during this fiscal year. But that action has not put the matter to rest. Congress is certain to be faced, in a matter of weeks or months, with another request for military aid to the Nicarguan rebels. The administration has a pending proposal for $28 million in such assistance for the fiscal year beginning Oct. 1 and may well attempt to resurrect the issue of immediate aid to the contras by attaching it by amendment to some other legislation.

But surely the United States can do better in terms of conducting foreign policy within this hemisphere than to continue this tug-of-war between the White House and Capitol Hill over an ill-conceived and demonstrably unpopular war in Nicaragua. After this prolonged and often vitriolic battle, it is time for a true bipartisan effort to forge a policy toward Nicaragua which can command both popular and congressional support — and which can succeed.

Despite bitter divisions over tactics, there is a consensus on what our goals should be. Nicaragua must not be allowed to export communist revolution in Central America. The Sandinistas must be pushed toward accommodation with the legitimate democratic opposition within Nicaragua and toward fulfilling their pledges to ensure human rights and social and political freedom for that nation's people. And the Contadora countries which have long been seeking a regional peace agreement in Central America must be strongly supported.

President Reagan has proclaimed these goals but has limited his policy toward Nicaragua to one of military pressure through a covert war organized and financed by the United States. Diplomatic efforts have been undertaken half-heartedly and only to maintain support for a militaristic policy. This was demonstrated most recently by the fact that Mr. Reagan agreed to reopen direct talks between the United States and the Sandinistas only as a last-ditch effort to garner congressional support for aid to the contras. Moreover, the president has not matched his words of support for the Contadora process with actions. He has, in fact, thwarted the process when it appeared that the Sandinistas would agree to a proposed settlement, and he has cynically attempted to pressure the Contadora nations into supporting his policy of making war in Nicaragua.

President Reagan should accept the actions of Congress this week as a repudiation of his militaristic approach to Nicaragua. He was saved from defeat even in the Republican-controlled Senate only by retreating from his request for military aid and promising that the funds would be used only for non-lethal purposes. Rather than regroup for another battle for military funding for the contras, the administration should work with congressional leaders of both parties to devise a policy which can united this country behind agreed-upon goals and promote the cause of peace in Central America.

The Philadelphia Inquirer

Philadelphia, PA, April 26, 1985

So has dawned the morning-after: President Reagan insists he will not take "no" for an answer on his aid package to Nicaragua's rebels, Congress fumbles for new directions, and Nicaraguan President Daniel Ortega announces he's off to Moscow to plead for economic aid. The feeling is more bad hangover than fresh start.

House Majority leader Jim Wright (D., Texas) had glimpsed "a breathing spell ... a cooling-off period" in the policy vacuum following the defeat of military aid bills for the *contras*. It was wishful thinking.

Within hours Vice President Bush was pledging the administration would be back "and back and back" asking for funds to fight "a Marxist-Leninist dictatorship" in Central America. Secretary of State George P. Shultz said the mistake in Vietnam was pulling out — and the United States shouldn't make it twice.

In a monumentally stupid move, Mr. Ortega — all sweetness and light before the vote — rushed to confirm his critics' deepest fears. Instead of reaching out to the Contadora peace process, as his government has done before, he began packing his bags for Moscow.

If ever there was a time to demonstrate Nicaragua's professed policy on nonalignment, this was it. Mr. Ortega has played into the hands of those who view Nicaragua merely a pawn in the East-West geopolitical struggle.

This is no time to dig in, to pledge fealty to failed policies. This is a time to listen — to leaders of virtually every Latin American nation who frown on continued military buildups on *both* sides of the Nicaraguan border; to the mood of an American people who long ago rejected the piecemeal, incoherent military involvement of Vietnam; to such as Pennsylvania's Sen. Arlen Specter who see no future in "supporting one set of bad guys against another set of bad guys."

Throughout Latin America — from Argentina to Brazil to Peru to Mexico — the United States faces grave policy challenges. White House rhetoric about the surge of democracy in the hemisphere ignores the fragility of that trend and the ever-burning fuse of Latin American debt. Against that backdrop, the problem of Nicaragua palls.

It need not remain insoluble. Nicaragua need not become a threat, either to its neighbors or the United States. There is a structure and a process in place for negotiations that could satisfy a whole host of regional agendas. That is the Contadora forum.

It is time the White House embraced that forum publicly and unambiguously. It is time to reject not only the tactic of armed intervention, but its logic as well.

It is time Mr. Reagan dialed down the hysteria. Time Mr. Ortega displayed a smidgen of political judgment. Time for Congress, having broken the momentum toward military solution, to point the way to peace.

To do less is to dig blindly in the ruins, awaiting impotently an incident that will trip the wires of war.

ARGUS-LEADER

Sioux Falls, SD, April 29, 1985

Congress has a fight on its hands — a fight almost as tough as the one faced by the Nicaraguan Contras President Reagan so much admires.

In an appropriate move, Congress last week rejected Reagan's proposal for $14 million in aid for the rightist Contras trying to overthrow Nicaragua's leftist government.

Editorial

Like the fight in Nicaragua, the fight in Washington, D.C., is not over. Reagan's political forces are lining up for another charge at the money. Congressional opponents should dig in and again say "no."

In Reagan's thinking, a vote to keep the rebels fighting the Sandinista government armed and in fighting shape is a vote for peace — not war. Vice President George Bush has drawn a suitably ridiculous skirmish line: "We will be back and back and back until America does the right thing."

The right thing? As in George Orwell's *1984*, war is peace.

Bush and other supporters should stick to the argument that the United States should not turn its back to people fighting for democracy against a Marxist-Leninist dictatorship. They should knock off the self-righteous claims about fighting for the "right thing." Phantom justification like that led to protracted U.S. failure 10 years ago in Vietnam. The lessons of that failure are reason enough to say "no" to financing another war on foreign soil.

Where will U.S. involvement stop? Clearly not with $14 million.

Contra leader Adolfo Calero has said his 15,000-man rebel army needs at least twice the $14 million in Reagan's current proposal if it is to pose a serious threat to the leftist Sandinista government in Nicaragua. Calero says his army could increase by 20,000 troops and force a turning point in military balance in Nicaragua if the United States provides $30 million to $50 million.

Indeed, Reagan wants to spend an additional $28 million in military support for the rebels in fiscal 1986, which starts Oct. 1.

Congress should draw the line now by rejecting Reagan's plea for aid. We don't need another Vietnam.

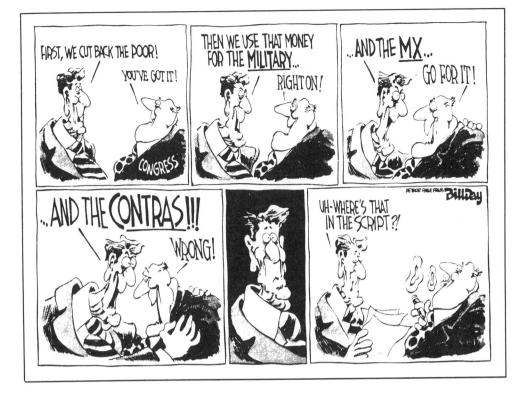

The Boston Globe

Boston, MA, April 28, 1985

Congress said no last week to military coercion of Nicaragua. The legislators who stood up to weeks of shrill attacks can take pride in having stopped a policy that would have led eventually to ruin. Now comes the hard part. US policy toward Nicaragua, in shambles at this moment, must somehow be rebuilt.

There are formidable obstacles to sensible policy, some in Washington, others in Managua. In Washington the executive branch, which controls the instruments of foreign policy, is still adamantly resisting a peaceful settlement that would leave the Nicaraguan government in power. If policy is to be redirected, that may have to happen in spite of the executive branch.

In Managua the Sandinistas are equally stubborn. It is an article of their revolutionary faith that they will not bow to Uncle Sam, whatever the costs. Their country needs reconciliation, but Nicaraguans who have become tainted by their association with the Reagan Administration's belligerent policy have put themselves beyond redemption in Sandinista eyes.

There is talk now in Congress of turning to economic and political pressure on the Sandinistas to replace support for the contra war. This sounds like an improvement, but it will not be unless there is a clear idea of what the pressure is supposed to produce and how.

A continuing effort by the United States to grind Managua into the dust, albeit now by non-military means, will deepen misery in Nicaragua. It will make the Sandinistas more dependent on the Soviet bloc, sending Daniel Ortega off on more trips to Moscow such as the one announced last week (with exquisite ill timing) in search of oil, feed and fertilizer, as well as arms, to replace what the Sandinistas cannot acquire in the West.

Carried far enough, a policy of non-military pressure would produce much the same fortress Nicaragua that the contra war has produced. Where is the statecraft in that?

It might be time for Americans to begin considering incentives as well as punishment in formulating policy toward Nicaragua. It might not hurt to try a peace gesture like the gestures Ortega made in February – and reaffirmed this week – to send some Cuban advisers home and pardon some political prisoners. The United States is powerful enough to risk a small reciprocal concession.

If it is too much to expect so sharp a shift in US policy, from belligerence to token generosity, at least Americans could begin developing new habits of thought about Nicaragua, look more coolly at the facts of Sandinista behavior before leaping to conclusions about it.

The Sandinistas have a number of ugly traits, and their behavior has done much to place their people in an unhappy situation. Still, the track record suggests that the Nicaraguan leaders are pragmatic, learning as they go, moderating directions both in foreign and domestic policy.

The apparent breakthrough last week in negotiations with a leader of the Miskito Indians is an example of that moderating trend. The Sandinistas make a distinction between Indians seeking to guarantee their traditional way of life and contras trying to topple the government in cahoots with the CIA.

Managua's willingness to negotiate with the Miskito leader, Brooklyn Rivera, does not mean the Sandinistas are ready for peace with the leaders of the National Democratic Front, who include the cronies of the former dictator Anastasio Somoza. But it is a sign they understand the need for reconciliation.

The Sandinistas have taken a step in the right direction, and it is only fair to give them a measure of credit. One thing can lead to another. The move should be encouraged by a reciprocal move from Washington.

The Oregonian

*Portland, OR,
April 27, 1985*

The rejection by U.S. House Republicans of a Democratic plan to send humanitarian aid to Nicaraguan refugees was a mistake and will prove a tactical blunder. The defeated compromise proposal would have provided $10 million to help people displaced by the Nicaraguan fighting and added $4 million to encourage and enforce a peace settlement between the contras and the Sandinista government.

The American people want the killing stopped, and like the Congress, they have rejected President Reagan's efforts to overthrow the Sandinistas with a dirty little war in Central America.

In a series of votes that resulted in killing military aid and the so-called White House non-lethal aid that would have been doled out to the contras by the CIA, the Congress has put the issue down, but it will not rest. The administration, led by a president bruised by a major foreign policy defeat, has vowed not to give up the fight to send more weapons to the rag-tag forces opposing the Sandinistas. American foreign policy in Latin America is now in a mess, lost in the contradictions of a wrongheaded presidential determination to use guns instead of diplomacy to further democratic institutions.

Administration efforts will be made to tack contra aid dollars onto other bills. Momentum will be sought in a new struggle not only to give the contras their lost $14 million for arms, but to add the $28 million in contra weapons aid Reagan has proposed for fiscal 1986 that starts Oct. 1. The CIA has funneled $80 million in covert aid to the contras since 1981.

Had the House Republicans gone along with the Democrats, there not only would have been a carrot encouraging negotiations between the opposing groups, but a legislative vehicle to carry compromise legislation to the Senate.

It is not inconsistent to oppose military aid for the killing fields of Nicaragua and also to recognize the need for national unity and compromise on the issue that has made American foreign policy appear impotent, like a tiger with hen's teeth.

Ortega's Visit to U.S.S.R. Prompts U.S. Criticism

Nicaraguan President Daniel Ortega Saavedra arrived in Moscow April 28, 1985 to discuss economic aid. Ortega was believed to be seeking some $200 million in emergency aid for food and consumer goods. Ortega met with Soviet leader Mikhail Gorbachev April 29. The Soviet news agency, Tass, quoted Gorbachev as having pledged to "continue to give friendly Nicaragua assistance in resolving urgent problems of economic development, and also political and diplomatic support in its efforts to uphold its sovereignty." No specific amounts of aid were reported. Earlier April 29, the two nations signed an accord to set up a joint commission on economic, trade, and scientific and technical cooperation. Ortega was also to visit other Eastern European nations after leaving Moscow. In a voice vote, the United States Senate April 29 approved a resolution contending that the visit was "clear evidence of a continuing Sandinista effort to strengthen ties with the Soviet Union, in support of Sandinista policies of militarization, repression and interference in the affairs of its neighbors.

Ortega followed his controversial visit to Moscow with a tour of several Eastern and Western European nations April 30-May 20 to gain political and economic support for the Sandinista government. Ortega's first stop after leaving Moscow April 30 was Belgrade, Yugoslavia, where he said he was counting on cooperation and "paternal solidarity." The nations signed a cultural, scientific-technical and educational pact, which was the first agreement between Managua and Belgrade. After visiting Bulgaria and East Germany, Ortega unexpectedly added several Western European stops to his schedule. He arrived in Spain May 11 where he held a joint news conference with Premier Felipe Gonzalez and then traveled to France May 13, where he met with French President Francois Mitterrand. Ortega ended his tour with visits to Italy, Sweden and Finland.

On his return to Nicaragua May 20, Ortega said Moscow had pledged to provide the nation with as much as 90% of its oil needs in 1985. Ortega denied that the agreement with Moscow meant that Nicaragua was aligned with the Soviet Union.

THE SACRAMENTO BEE

Sacramento, CA, June 14, 1985

Now that both the House and Senate have caved in to presidential pressure and voted to give official U.S. aid to the Nicaraguan rebels, the way is open for the Reagan administration to pursue its efforts to unseat the Marxist regime in Managua by almost any means. For in addition to providing money to the contras, Congress also scuttled the Boland amendment, an action that lifts all restraints on CIA activities in support of the rebels. By October, the agency will be able to run its own kind of war with discretionary funds that could well exceed any official aid.

The two houses must reconcile remaining differences over the amount to be delivered to the contras — $27 million or $38 million or some compromise figure — and the means of delivering it. But those are mere details. The administration is now free to act, and it would be fatuous to assume that it will stop at this level, especially when it turns out — as it will — that stepped-up pressure will not achieve the White House's avowed aim of making the Sandinistas "say uncle."

To the extent that President Reagan's obsessive policy makes any sense, its logic will sooner or later "compel" the United States to take sterner measures. Any number of options exist: a travel ban to keep curious Americans away from Nicaragua; a break in diplomatic relations, which would at least be consistent with the policy course already being taken; a naval blockade, which is an act of war by any standard, and, ultimately, direct involvement of American troops, first as "advisers" and then as overt participants.

If that is the administration's policy — and the White House insists it is not — then the steps now being taken are understandable, even if madly wrong. If it is not, then what is now being undertaken makes no sense at all, for it leads nowhere while squandering American money and much of this country's international standing.

The probable scenario is obvious, and depressing. When the contras fail to bring down the Sandinistas, as they will, it will be argued by the administration that this country has tried every reasonable, non-violent means of persuading the junta to make the democratic reforms Washington has demanded. Then, some convenient pretext will be found to justify the next turn of the screw, and the next. It is the worst kind of cynicism, and a majority in Congress is now a party to it.

House Speaker O'Neill bitterly characterized President Reagan's motives as growing out of romantic notions of "leading a contingent down Broadway ... kind of like a Grade B motion picture actor coming home the conquering hero." At one time, that might have seemed to be a fanciful explanation for what possesses the president, and perhaps it still is. But it makes as much sense as anything else in this senseless march toward a needless war.

WORCESTER TELEGRAM.

Worcester, MA, June 11, 1985

The renewed debate in Congress over sending more aid to the rebels in Nicaragua reveals much about the liberal Democratic mind set.

Politicians like Sen. John F. Kerry and Rep. Gerry E. Studds are furious at Nicaraguan President Daniel Ortega. Ortega had the effrontery to visit Moscow a few weeks ago, right after Kerry had visited him and got assurances that the Sandinistas would act nicely. After Kerry announced his deal with Ortega, Congress killed President Reagan's request for $14 million in non-military aid to the Contras. The Ortega trip, says an indignant Kerry, was "an act of political stupidity: an act of clear insensitivity to the dynamics of American politics."

Ortega's trip "presents a real political problem," says Kirk O'Donnell, chief political adviser to House Speaker Tip O'Neill.

Well, we suppose it does. As long as Ortega could be passed off as just a patriotic Nicaraguan who was trying to bring freedom and democracy to his country, the liberals in Congress could attack the Reagan plan with impunity. But when Ortega showed his true colors and hugged Gorbachev, it got a lot harder to pretend that the Sandinistas are just an amiable bunch of democratic types.

If we follow Kerry's logic, it would have been much better if Ortega had gone along with the charade, concealing the real nature of his junta. By being so open about his preferences, Ortega has made the liberal deception in this country that much more difficult.

We Americans owe Ortega thanks. Unlike his supporters in the U.S. Congress, he is honest about where his loyalties lie. But why is anyone surprised? As Sen. Christopher Dodd put it, "Where did my colleagues think he was going to go? Disney World? The man is a Marxist."

Tut, tut, Dodd. You're not supposed to say things like that.

The Record

Hackensack, NJ, June 14, 1985

Just when it appeared that Congress had put the brakes on President Reagan's mischief in Nicaragua, lawmakers have foolishly done a turnabout. The Senate recently approved a $38-million aid package for the Central Intelligence Agency's war against the Sandinista government. The House followed this week with $27 million, at the same time lifting a ban on use of those funds for direct military actions.

The vote comes just seven weeks after the House firmly rejected Mr. Reagan's request to arm the contras. Guns and ammunition, as well as essentials such as food and clothing, have been in short supply since Congress first cut off aid 13 months ago. Opponents of the president's plan said then that military aid to the contras would violate international law and widen the war in Central America. It would also frustrate efforts of the Contadora group, the U.S. allies who are trying to negotiate a truce between the Nicaraguan government and the rebels.

The situation — and the stakes — haven't changed much in the last two months. So why has Congress reversed itself? One reason seems to be the Sandinistas themselves. On the heels of the first vote, Nicaraguan President Daniel Ortega flew off to Moscow to ask for a line of credit to purchase farm equipment and supplies. The visit had been arranged weeks before, but some members of Congress considered the trip a flagrant display of anti-Americanism. They switched votes to send Mr. Ortega a message that cozying up to the Kremlin would result in a tougher stance by the United States.

But the main reason for the congressional shift has been a disingenuous publicity campaign by the White House to discredit the Sandinistas. Whenever he takes to the stump these days, Mr. Reagan hyperbolically portrays this poor, tiny country of 4 million people as a threat to our borders, a communist launching pad, a menace to all our allies in the region. Declaring a "national emergency," he recently cut off trade relations with Managua to further cripple Nicaragua's faltering economy.

Members of Congress gave in to the rhetoric, worried that they would appear unpatriotic if they didn't. But Mr. Reagan's efforts to overthrow another government run counter to our best interests. More aid to the contras makes a mockery of our pledge to promote democracy. It will create havoc in the region and force Costa Rica, Guatemala, and Honduras to spend scarce resources on beefing up their armies. It dismays U.S. allies, who warn against heightening tensions between East and West. And it could lead the president to send in U.S. troops. Mr. Reagan is risking American prestige on an untrained, ill-equipped band of mercenaries who have no chance of winning. When they lose, the president may decide that he can make good on his investment only by sending American fighting forces.

As House Democratic Leader Jim Wright of Texas warned his colleagues, "You are absolutely, clearly voting to do away with the restraint that exists in the law today against the United States financing an invasion of the country and the overthrow of that country's government." Said another opponent of the plan, Rep. Bill Alexander of Arkansas, the vote is "a declaration of war against Nicaragua." It is something else: a shameful and dangerous abandoning of a sensible and sane policy to keep the peace in Central America. Congress, like the president, will live to rue this decision.

THE SUN

Baltimore, MD, June 14, 1985

President Reagan would be in error if he interprets the House reversal on aid to Nicaragua rebels as a mandate to "go for it" in Central America. Public opinion remains strongly against either U.S. military involvement or U.S. military aid. A Louis Harris poll on May 23 reported that Americans oppose a U.S. invasion of Nicaragua by a margin of 75 to 20. On the aid issue, the poll was 73 to 23 against military aid for "contra" forces battling the Sandinista regime and 58 to 37 against even the non-military aid that has now been approved by the Senate and the House.

By zigging in late April and zagging in mid-June, the House has demonstrated once again that it is a weathervane institution. Much attention is currently focused on the defection of 27 Democrats, mostly Southerners, to the administration side. These switchers are said to have been incensed over Nicaraguan President Daniel Ortega's handout-grubbing trip to Moscow the day after the April vote in the House and concerned that they might be labeled "soft on Communism" by hardline Republicans in Dixie.

But that is only part of the story. Democratic disarray in the House is due in large measure to strident and inept leadership on the part of Speaker Thomas P. O'Neill and his chief lieutenants. So intent were they in opposing the president at every turn during the April rollcalls that they wound up with no House policy at all, a situation that left party moderates exposed and embarrassed.

Just before the administration turned the screw this past Wednesday, the speaker said Mr. Reagan "is not going to be happy until he has our marines and rangers down there for a complete victory." House Majority Leader Jim Wright said "we are now accessories to an attempt to overthrow the government of Nicaragua by force." Deputy Leader Bill Alexander said what the House had approved was "tantamount to a declaration of war." No wonder White House spokesman Larry Speakes said it was all so sad. Such rhetoric overshot.

What Congress now should do is craft careful guidelines that will keep U.S. forces out of Central America while putting pressure on Nicaragua to reach a settlement with contra forces seeking the kind of centrist democracy taking shape in El Salvador. The House is now ready to go along with the Senate in providing non-military aid to the contras. For the first time in three years, it is also willing to have the CIA share intelligence information with rebel forces. But these pressure moves need to be constrained by provisions that will keep U.S. forces or agents out of direct involvement in overt or covert military operations.

Mr. Reagan has no need to fulfill Mr. O'Neill's prophecies. Public opinion polls give fair warning that if he sends U.S. forces into Nicaragua he could undercut all his hopes and plans for the remainder of his presidency.

The Honolulu Advertiser

Honolulu, HI, June 11, 1985

U.S. Senate approval last week of spending $38 million in non-military aid over two years for anti-Sandinista guerrillas is a blow to the weak and scattered forces of moderation in Central America.

At this point, the vote is a symbolic victory. The less-favorable House of Representatives must still act this week on the measure, an amendment to the State Department's funding bill.

BUT THE impact of the Senate's action only reinforces the image of a United States loaded for bear in a region where the main target is rat-sized.

Not all the blame must be shouldered by Congress and the administration. Earlier this year, lawmakers snubbed the president by denying him aid for the contras.

Then Nicaraguan President Daniel Ortega made a highly-publicized trip to Moscow, where he was feted by Soviet leaders. The effect of Ortega's trip, planned or not, was to infuriate those congressional leaders who want a non-military solution to the Nicaraguan conflict.

Worry about the administration's intentions would be less if there were some sign of a serious U.S. attempt to tie a diplomatic initiative to the pro-contra policy. This president, however, has not applied his often vaunted "quiet diplomacy" approach in the case of Nicaragua.

THE NICARAGUAN government gives cause for concern: The Sandinista leadership has abandoned the democratic goals it originally stated and has been replacing a dictatorship of the right with one of the left.

Still, Washington errs in using a bludgeon to deal with this odious regime. Diplomatic pressure, applied with patience and with regional support, would have far better effect.

And the best vehicle for that approach remains the Contadora peace process. The Reagan administration and Congress should pay as much attention to the Contadora group as they do to the anti-Sandinista guerrillas.

Houston Chronicle
Houston, TX, June 3, 1985

Assessing political and social developments in Nicaragua is a difficult task, even for experts on the scene. However, a consensus seems to be growing that the Sandinista regime represents an increasing threat both to its own people and to its neighbors.

That consensus has developed extremely rapidly. Until recently, much of the world seemed to be willing to give the Sandinistas the benefit of a doubt. Even in Congress, most members were more worried by the possibility of further U.S. entanglement in Central American affairs than about the Sandinista threat. That is no longer the case.

The recent trip to Moscow by Nicaraguan leader Daniel Ortega served to confirm the suspicions of those who see Nicaragua becoming "another Cuba." A CIA report says the Sandinistas are well along toward completing the well-established Marxist pattern of consolidation of power, including state control of the media, the economy and education.

Individual peace activists still return from visits to Nicaragua defending the Sandinista regime, pointing to its advances in education and health care and to what remains of private enterprise. However, groups that have conducted sustained investigations are increasingly inclined to criticism. Even such organizations as Amnesty International and the Lawyers Committee for Human Rights have reported a growing number of political prisoners and instances of physical torture, detention without trial and failure by the Sandinista rulers to recognize decisions of the independent judiciary.

For the Sandinistas, all this adds up to an image problem. For the Nicaraguan people and their Central American neighbors, it adds up to a regime bent on repression and subservience to Soviet-Cuban aims in the region.

SYRACUSE HERALD-JOURNAL
Syracuse, NY, June 10, 1985

Is this trip necessary?

That's the question Nicaraguan President Daniel Ortega should have asked himself before he trundled off to Moscow last month. That journey gave U.S. senators just the excuse they needed to reverse their votes on aid to the Contras, the rebel Nicaraguan group that's fighting Ortega's leftist Sandinista regime.

As a result, the Senate last week approved a package of "humanitarian" aid to the Contras totaling $38 million over the next 18 months. If the House goes along this week, the aid will be dispensed under the auspices of the CIA, that renowned champion of humanitarian concerns.

President Reagan praised the Senate action as "a display of bipartisan concern for the people of Central America and our own national security."

Wrong on both counts, Mr. President.

For the people of Central America, *any* aid to the Contras means pumping new life into a bloody conflict that has killed their sons and devastated their economy. And as far as our national security is concerned, we're still unable to make the connection between that and the fortunes of a tiny nation that is struggling just to feed, house and educate itself.

The only "bipartisan concern" the senators were demonstrating was for their own political hides. The Great Communicator had spent the weeks since the aid package originally was voted down trying to convince the American public that any-

one who opposed the plan was likely the illegitimate son of Joe Stalin and the Wicked Witch of the East. He struck a chord when he cited Ortega's visit to Moscow, and 55 senators harmonized.

The concept of humanitarian aid is a noble one, and the poor people of Nicaragua, by all accounts, need it badly. But their lot has been made more wretched, not less, by recent actions by the Reagan administration. The trade embargo slapped on by the U.S. in April has hurt them badly, according to reports from within the country. That won't win the U.S. any friends among the Nicaraguan people; it can only give the Sandinistas more ammunition for their anti-U.S. propaganda.

Assuming the House approves the Contra aid package this week — and House Minority Leader Robert Michel has said its chances are good — Congress will have lent its support to a policy pointed squarely at eventual U.S. military involvement. It is saying, in effect, the U.S. is within its rights to promote the overthrow of another government. Once that precedent has been established, use of troops is a logical extension, especially as it's likely nothing less will bring down the Sandinistas.

If and when the U.S. goes to war against Nicaragua, where does Ortega turn? Why back to his buddies in Moscow, of course. When that happens, we'll have a real problem. The Reagan predictions will have fulfilled themselves.

The Times-Picayune
The States-Item
New Orleans, LA, June 14, 1985

The House of Representatives came to its senses Wednesday with its vote to approve $27 million in nonmilitary "humanitarian" aid to the Nicaraguan contras opposing the communist Sandinista government. Even though it was not the whole loaf — military aid is needed to keep real pressure on the Sandinistas — it was still a significant victory for President Reagan's attempt to prevent irreversible installation of a Soviet satellite on the hemisphere mainland in the United States' neighborhood.

The House narrowly defeated the whole-loaf bill in April. In Wednesday's vote, 23 Democrats and seven Republicans switched their votes. Some of the voters' switches may be attributed to the difference between the bills, but many were doubtless the result of embarrassment at their revealed naivete following the April vote.

Sandinista leader Daniel Ortega, after weeks of wooing public and congressional opinion, left for Moscow the day after Congress voted his way, was feted and photographed with Soviet leader Mikhail Gorbachev and came back with pledges of aid.

"He embarrassed us, to be perfectly truthful," commented House Speaker Thomas P. "Tip" O'Neill, D-Mass. For a national leader who accuses President Reagan of not understanding the situation in Nicaragua, it was an extraordinary admission of his own misunderstanding.

An even more significant feature of Wednesday's vote was the trouncing, by a strong bipartisan effort, of the Boland Amendment, attached to the last congressional action on contra aid and due to expire in September. The amendment prohibits military or paramilitary aid to forces fighting the Sandinista government.

In leaving that door open, the measure keeps sharp pressure on the Sandinistas and encourages those working against them. Three of the major opposition leaders have joined into a Nicaraguan Opposition Union to give clear shape to their program. Their goal is political pluralism, free elections and civilian control of the military — the first two promised but never provided by the Sandinistas, the third to prevent the rise of another Somoza type.

The issue is not one of an American attempt to thwart a popular revolution and install a new client ruler. It is one of a classic communist attempt to commandeer a popular revolution to put itself in total power.

Those who profess to see all the telltale elements of "another Vietnam" should pay more attention to the telltale elements of the assemblage of communist power under the guise of popular support, glaringly obvious in Nicaragua and with far more numerous precedents — the first, the 1917 Bolshevik coup in Russia — than wars like the Vietnam war.

In Nicaragua we have a proto-communist regime that has not yet been able to fully clamp down and a broad, active opposition that has a chance, given adequate, appropriate support, to take the country back for its citizens.

Los Angeles, CA, June 14, 1985

Two things were accomplished by the House of Representatives' decision to approve $27 million in "humanitarian" aid to the Nicaraguan *contras* (a.k.a. "freedom fighters") who are trying to overthrow the Sandinista government: Representatives got a chance to vent their anger at Sandinista President Daniel Ortega's latest visit to Moscow, which came on the heels of a House vote in April to *deny* the *contras* aid; and it provided an opportunity to prove to the voters that they aren't soft on

communism. (It's possible, of course, that Congress acted out of a sense of moral obligation to the rebel forces it helped create — possible, but not probable.) Still, the decision fails to confront the question of what U.S. policy regarding Nicaragua really is.

If the goal is to overthrow the Sandinistas and their Marxist proclivities — and that is probably what the White House, at least, would like to do — then $27 million, or even the $38 million that the Senate voted last week, won't do the job. The rag-tag *contras* would probably be no match for the government's troops in any case. Indeed, little short of a U.S. invasion or a massive popular uprising seems likely to rid the hemisphere of Ortega & Co.

If, however, the point of *contra* aid is to discourage Nicaraguan support for guerrillas in El Salvador (as President Reagan originally said), then the House could at least lay claim to a certain degree of logic. The fact is, however, that the White House has all but dropped that rationale itself, presumably for lack of hard evidence that the Salvadoran guerrilla war is any longer — if it ever was — a made-in-Managua affair.

All of which leaves us as confused as Congress itself seems to be. Nothing in Central America has changed fundamentally since aid for the *contras* was rejected two months ago, except that our fickle lawmakers have handed Reagan a considerable political victory. What happens next? We're not sure we want to find out.

THE MILWAUKEE JOURNAL
Milwaukee, WI, June 15, 1985

The credulity and shortsightedness of Congress, combined with the international clumsiness of President Daniel Ortega of Nicaragua, can be blamed for the House's decision to aid rebels seeking the overthrow of the Nicaraguan government.

By a vote of 248 to 184, the House decided to provide $27 million in aid to the anti-government contras. The bill required that the aid be nonmilitary — it couldn't include vehicles, weapons and ammunition — and that the Central Intelligence Agency and the Defense Department have no role in delivering it. Earlier, the Senate passed a similar bill that provided a looser definition of nonmilitary aid and gave the CIA a role in providing it.

The restrictions in the two aid bills are merely a smoke screen. So is President Reagan's recent claim that he does not seek to overthrow the Sandinista government in Nicaragua or replace it with followers of the ousted (and hated) dictator, Anastasio Somoza. The fact is, Reagan previously stated his desire to replace the structure of the Nicaraguan government. That is the whole point of the aid program: to topple the Marxist-oriented regime.

The $27 million in aid would go to rebels who repeatedly and proudly espouse that goal. The leadership of the principal rebel group, moreover, is made up of old Somoza followers. Whatever these rebels don't spend on nonmilitary items can be spent on weapons that will be provided by private sources, with the blessing of the administration.

Thus, the money (however it is packaged and tied with strings) will aid a right-wing rebel effort to overthrow by violent and almost certainly illegal means a duly-constituted government with which the US has formal diplomatic relations. That is what the House authorized.

And for what? Because the Sandinistas are a threat to the US national security, as the administration has claimed? Is Reagan so unsure of this nation's strength that he feels it vulnerable to a challenge mounted by a country whose population is two-thirds that of Wisconsin? Such a claim is preposterous. Yet the House bought it.

Reagan also claims the US wants to promote pluralism in Nicaragua, that it wants to fight communism there and elsewhere in the region. Congress bought this bill of goods, also. By voting to aid the contras, the House played into the hands of the Marxists in Nicaragua; it provided an excuse for the regime there to become even more repressive, intransigent and totalitarian, not less; it will make the Sandinistas more dependent on Soviet aid, not less. And it will perpetuate the war and worsen the suffering.

To be sure, Ortega contributed to this dismal circumstance. Shortly after the Congress rejected a similar aid proposal in April, Ortega flew to Moscow for a well-photographed meeting with Soviet leader Mikhail Gorbachev. The visit was a red flag in Reagan's face and an embarrassment to those in Congress who opposed the contra aid. The visit made more difficult the urgent and neglected task of producing change in Nicaragua through cooperative measures with Nicaragua's influential neighbors in the region and in the Contadora Group of countries.

Yet the inept, infuriating behavior of Ortega was not sufficient reason for Congress to support a misguided effort to overthrow him.

Reagan, Cutting Air, Sea Links, Bars Trade With Nicaragua

United States President Ronald Reagan May 1, 1985 ordered an embargo on trade with Nicaragua and banned Nicaraguan aircraft and ships from the U.S. In an executive order and an accompanying letter to Congress, Reagan justified the moves by charging that Nicaraguan policies and actions constituted a threat to U.S. security. The embargo was made public hours after Reagan had arrived in West Germany for an economic summit with the leaders of major industrial nations. The measures followed a resounding defeat the previous week for Reagan's request for $14 million in aid to the Nicaraguan contras. Some administration officials were reported to hope that the embargo would show Reagan's assertiveness in the wake of that defeat.

The president's executive order stated that he found that the "policies and actions of the government of Nicaragua constitute an unusual and extraordinary threat to the national security and foreign policy of the United States" and that he was therefore declaring "a national emergency to deal with the threat." The order barred U.S. imports of goods and services from Nicaragua and all U.S. exports to that nation, "except those destined for the organized democratic resistance, and transactions relating thereto."

In the letter to Congress, Reagan cited Nicaragua's "continuing efforts to subvert its neighbors, its rapid and destabilizing military buildup, its close military and security ties to Cuba and the Soviet Union and its imposition of communist totalitarian internal rule."

The U.S. trade embargo against Nicaragua, which went into effect May 7, ran into criticism from Western European and Latin American leaders May 3-8. The four Contadora Group nations—Colombia, Mexico, Venezuela and Panama—opposed the embargo.

Buffalo Evening News
Buffalo, NY, May 8, 1985

THE U.S. trade embargo against Nicaragua is unlikely to produce any dramatic shifts in the policies of the Marxist Sandinista regime.

For one thing, trade between the United States and Nicaragua has already declined markedly in recent years. And economic sanctions have proved of limited value in the past, especially when not supported by other countries.

Indeed, there is concern that the trade embargo could backfire on the United States by causing the Sandinistas to deepen their economic ties with the Soviet bloc and by weakening the private business sector that still operates in the Nicaraguan economy.

All this raises questions about the wisdom of the embargo decision. But now that the action has been taken, it must not be a substitute for efforts to settle the region's problems through the diplomatic process initiated by the nations of the Contadora group — Mexico, Panama, Venezuela and Colombia.

The United States does need to apply pressure on the Sandinistas to moderate their policies, but the best hope of achieving this still lies in joint action through a Contadora-sponsored treaty aimed at halting the export of subversion in Central America.

Congress was justifiably angered by Nicaraguan President Daniel Ortega's visit to Moscow last week in search of economic aid. That trip took place before the trade embargo was imposed and almost immediately after Congress had voted to end U.S. military aid for the contra rebels seeking to overthrow the Sandinistas. There had been suggestions earlier that if Congress cut off contra aid, Nicaragua would respond with significant concessions. Instead, the Sandinista leader cynically took off for Moscow.

In spite of this, the logic of supporting the Contadora regional peace initiative remains. President Reagan has applied the stick of economic sanctions. He should now attach to this the carrot of renewed negotiations on a comprehensive political resolution of the region's ills.

The Boston Globe
Boston, MA, May 5, 1985

The trade embargo that President Reagan has ordered against Nicaragua is consistent with the policies his Administration has pursued since coming to office.

Whatever its real effects, the embargo gives the appearance of being "tough." Those who have weighed the embargo on its merits, however, have long since concluded that it is a poor idea. Sen. David Durenberger (R-Minn), chairman of the Senate Intelligence Committee, said that when the CIA was asked a few weeks ago what an embargo would accomplish, "their response was that sanctions wouldn't do much good or we would have done it already."

Each legislator who opposed the contra war should think twice before embracing economic warfare as an alternative. Yes, it is legal, at least under US law. But the embargo is a blunt instrument that will most injure the people the Administration says it cares about, the private-sector farmers and businessmen who have struggled along in a war economy under a stumbling, state-oriented government.

So where is Nicaragua to turn? To the World Bank and the International Monetary Fund, where the United States is blocking loans? To Western European allies? Nicaragua will turn to Moscow. The embargo narrows the chances that this unorthodox leftist regime will muddle through to nonalignment.

It is disheartening that Daniel Ortega asked for Soviet-bloc help so ostentatiously and so soon after the vote in Congress. Page-one photographs of handshakes with a Soviet leader were bound to embarrass those trying to keep Congress on an even keel: tough on valid US security issues such as East bloc bases or military conquest, but flexible on how Nicarguans organize their society.

Ortega's quest for credit, seed and fertilizer is a poor pretext for declaring a US "national emergency," all the more so when measured against Sandinista acceptance of the Contadora peace process and the series of Sandinista concessions and peace gestures to the United States in recent months.

Seen symbolically, the President's trade embargo is a rejection of the spirit of the American people reflected in last week's votes in Congress. That vote was not an absent-minded lapse. Rarely if ever has a decision about peace and war been aired so carefully and at such length.

A savvy US Administration would have accepted the need for a time-out following last week's vote in Congress. It would have called a recess to bellicosity and coupled a few months of watchful waiting with renewed diplomacy aimed at supporting the multilateral peace efforts of Nicaragua's Contadora neighbors.

Instead, President Reagan imposed a unilateral Yanqui embargo. However gloomy the situation, thanks in part to the heavy-footed globe-trotting of Daniel Ortega, fair-minded Americans should consider where this embargo came from and where it leads – to unilateral, reckless intervention in Central America.

The San Diego Union
San Diego, CA, May 2, 1985

When Democrats in the House blocked President Reagan's request for aid to anti-communist guerrillas in Nicaragua last week, the White House was left with little choice but to take some action on its own to pressure the Marxist regime in Managua. Otherwise, Mr. Reagan's critics could continue wondering aloud why he wanted military aid for groups trying to overthrow the Sandinistas while declining to impose lesser political and economic sanctions.

The President's response was to impose the trade embargo he announced yesterday against Nicaragua. He also banned Nicaraguan ships from U.S. ports, revoked landing rights for Nicaraguan airliners, and abrogated a 27-year-old U.S.-Nicaraguan treaty of friendship. The last three actions are largely symbolic. Only the economic embargo will worry the nine-member Sandinista directorate that, despite last November's "elections," remains the *de facto* government of Nicaragua.

The embargo could hardly come at a worse time for the crumbling Nicaraguan economy. Living standards and real per-capita income for most Nicaraguans have already shrunk to early 1960s levels. Inflation is running at a rate of about 200 percent per year. And the Sandinistas have run up a foreign debt of more than $4 billion. For a country with a population of barely 3 million, that represents the highest per-capita debt in Latin America.

Now a Nicaraguan economy already half ruined by the mismanagement and socialism of the Sandinistas will be further hurt by the U.S. embargo. Despite the war of words between Washington and Managua, the United States had remained Nicaragua's largest trading partner, although that trade had declined over the last several years. Still, as recently as 1983, the United States had accounted for about one-fifth of Nicaragua's exports and imports.

New economic hardships for a population already prone to blame the Sandinistas for hard times will not be good news in Managua. But more than mere popularity is at stake. The Sandinistas know that each drop in the economy generates more resentment among ordinary Nicaraguans and more recruits for the so-called *contras* who have taken up arms against the regime.

Officially, the Reagan administration hopes that economic sanctions will persuade the Sandinistas to moderate their policies inside Nicaragua, curtail support for Marxist revolutionaries elsewhere in Central America, and open negotiations or at least a dialogue with the armed, democratic resistance movement opposing them.

Privately, the administration probably recognizes that an embargo by itself will not induce the Sandinistas to give up their radical politics or sever Nicaragua's ties with Cuba and the Soviet Union. Indeed, there is a chance that those ties may be strengthened in the short term as the Sandinistas look for ways around the embargo and for aid to offset it.

But it made no sense at all for the United States to remain the single most important market, source of hard currency, and supplier of imports for a regime nonetheless bent on subverting U.S. interests and allies in Central America. How well the trade embargo serves U.S. interests will depend on what else the Reagan administration and the Congress are prepared to do about the second Cuba developing in Nicaragua.

Birmingham Post-Herald
Birmingham, AL, May 4, 1985

As expected and as urged by Congress, President Reagan has ordered a halt to trade, shipping and airline service between the United States and Nicaragua, and two points ought to be made right away.

One, the embargo is unlikely to change the behavior of the Marxist-Leninist regime in Managua that the president finds unacceptable. And, two, Reagan really had no choice but to impose economic sanctions.

Last week when Congress rejected $14 million in aid to rebels fighting the Sandinistas, conservatives who opposed military action called for a trade boycott. And so did many liberals who feared accusations that they had voted to lock into place a communist government.

In addition, President Daniel Ortega embarrassed Congress and virtually invited sanctions when after the vote he flew to Moscow for a begging-bowl tour of the communist bloc seeking $200 million in aid.

Since Reagan could not and would not appear softer on the Sandinistas than the doves he had criticized, cutting trade became inevitable — regardless of whether the step will do any good.

After the Sandinistas seized power in 1979 and embraced the Soviet Union and Cuba, Nicaragua's trade with the United States plummeted. It sent only $58 million, or 10 percent, of its exports here, a loss that will pinch but not cripple its economy.

In fact, the embargo could inadvertantly help the Sandinistas. Their efforts to impose Marxism and militarize the country have weakened the economy and led to widespread shortages — and grumbling. Now they will try to make Reagan's "trade war" the scapegoat for the people's hardships.

Nevertheless, Reagan's moves are not necessarily fated to fail. If he can get much of Latin America and Western Europe to reduce trade with Nicaragua, pressure will build on the Sandinistas to move toward his goals: democratic reforms, a smaller army and an end to exporting revolution.

In any event, bananas and coffee are in plentiful supply and there is no reason the United States must do business as usual with a distasteful regime that threatens its neighbors.

Winnipeg Free Press
Winnipeg, Man., May 11, 1985

Instead of waiting timorously to see what other countries are going to do about the U.S. trade embargo on Nicaragua, External Affairs Minister Joe Clark should be saying that this country will do nothing.

No action is required from Canada, which trades with Nicaragua and will continue to do so, as it did with Cuba after the United States government imposed a trade embargo that is still in force.

U.S. President Ronald Reagan is free to impose his embargo. Canada is free to ignore it. There are no Canadian reasons to do otherwise.

Some Canadians, notably Liberal MP Charles Caccia, want Canada to get very excited about Mr. Reagan's embargo. In a hearing of the House of Commons standing committee on external affairs and national defence, Mr. Caccia suggested that Canada express disapproval by raising the embargo issue at the United Nations in New York. He also urged that the government of Canada put pressure on Canadian businessmen to expand their trade with Nicaragua immediately.

Fortunately, Mr. Clark did not pay much attention to these ill-considered proposals. Nicaragua itself raised the embargo in the UN Security Council, an obvious step to everyone but Mr. Caccia. Were Canada to have made the kind of sanctimonious intervention suggested, the result would not have helped Nicaragua, which was doing fine on its own, but it would have enraged the Reagan administration and hurt Canada's national interests pointlessly.

Similarly, Mr. Caccia's talk of pushing Canadian businessmen to expand their trade with Nicaragua displays a lamentable incomprehension of how such trade works in a state like Canada that does not have a centrally-planned economy. Canadian businessmen decide to buy or sell abroad on the basis of whether they can make a profit and whether they will be paid. Their doubts about both questions explain the current modest level of Canada-Nicaragua trade, not the politics of the Sandinista regime.

Any expansion or contraction of Canadian trade with Nicaragua can be safely left to individual business decisions by those who stand to gain or lose by the transaction.

Mr. Clark raised some doubts about where the government may be going when he said that a review of Canada's policies towards Nicaragua is under way, in consultation with other countries in Central America and Western Europe. He said: "I think it important that Canada try to take action in concert with others and that's why we are consulting with other countries as to their assessment."

Beyond carrying on trading normally, it is hard to see what "action" he thinks may be necessary. Canada's biggest trading partner is the United States. He should bear that in mind if any other country, whose trade with the United States is less important, tries to involve this country in some quixotic crusade to counter the Reagan administration action in a significant way.

THE ATLANTA CONSTITUTION
Atlanta, GA, May 6, 1985

In declaring a total trade embargo against Nicaragua and denying its ships and planes access to the United States, President Reagan moved in the right direction — toward nonbelligerent pressures on the Marxists in Managua.

The trouble is he swerved off abruptly several exits too soon, without using his turn signal and with no indication he has a road map tucked away in his glove compartment to guide him the rest of the way.

How much wiser might it have been if he had waited to announce the sanctions, so they would seem the product of thoughtful deliberations rather than personal pique at his *contra* aid defeat in the U.S. House?

How much more effective might they have been if he had taken the time to consult with hemispheric and Western European allies and to solicit their support?

How much more prudent might it have been to apply the trade cutoffs step by step — bananas, say, then beef and so on — rather than firing off a full clip at one burst?

And how much more appropriate might it have been if he had given our economic weapon a double edge, enumerating steps the Sandinistas could take to restore terminated trading privileges?

Setting aside the misgivings (including those of his own advisers) about the potential effectiveness of the punitive steps he took, the United States *has* been provoked sufficiently by the Sandinistas for Reagan to make it clear that we will not do business as usual with Nicaragua.

But from here on out, he would be wise to parcel out punishment — such as declaring the Sandinistas in default on their debts or freezing their assets in the United States — as it befits their offenses. He should accentuate *specific* Nicaraguan skulduggery — like the squad of subversives caught in Honduras or the impending arms shipment from Iran — rather than generalizing, too broadly to be believed, about the wicked Communist *commandantes.*

Reagan should be aware that many who share his low opinion of the Sandinistas but doubt the wisdom of ousting them at the point of a gun will be watching for signs of less bellicose but no less firm anti-Sandinista policies.

If he follows that path and if he sticks to the facts in reciting the case against Managua, he can count on the requisite support in Congress and among interested third countries to do whatever is necessary to minimize the turmoil in Central America.

Houston Chronicle
Houston, TX, May 3, 1985

In rejecting military aid to the contra rebels, Congress delivered a clear message that it favored a nonmilitary approach toward conflict in Central America. President Reagan's trade sanctions against Nicaragua are the logical next step in that approach.

Critics have argued that the sanctions would further drive the Sandinista regime into the arms of the Soviet Union. But as Sen. Lloyd Bentsen points out, "They are already there." After Congress rejected military aid for the contras, Nicaraguan President Daniel Ortega promptly journeyed to Moscow to seek closer Soviet ties and increased aid.

Since 1980, Nicaragua's trade with the United States has declined from 30 percent of its total to 17 percent. Its trade with the Soviet bloc has increased from 1 percent to 20 percent. In addition, the Soviet bloc and Cuba have injected thousands of military personnel and tons of weaponry into Nicaragua.

A pattern has already been clearly established here. The new U.S. sanctions can hardly be blamed.

Another argument that has been made against the trade embargo is that it would hurt the small private sector that remains in Nicaragua. However, private businessmen and farmers have already been crippled by state harassment, collectivized farming, price controls and the unjustified military buildup that uses up much of Nicaragua's funds.

The United States is more than justified in using every peaceful means to encourage democratic reform and to halt Nicaragua's export of armed revolution to its neighbors. The U.S. trade embargo will put pressure on the Sandinistas to reconsider the repressive and militant course upon which they have embarked.

"BOMBS AWAAAAY!!!"

Detroit Free Press
Detroit, MI, May 5, 1985

PRESIDENT Reagan's trade embargo is not so much a policy as an act of frustration. As such, it may be a momentarily useful and emotionally satisfying response to Daniel Ortega's trip to the Soviet Union, but it is not likely to yield the long-term results our government wants in Central America. The search for a policy that blocks out Soviet meddling but doesn't have the liabilities of the contra policy or the weaknesses of an embargo must go on.

The Ortega trip and the Moscow promise of additional aid demand a response.

The United States does have a legitimate interest in blocking the projection of Soviet power in this hemisphere. That can be done in a number of ways. One way is to invoke a range of punitive measures to signal that the United States will not tolerate certain kinds of military action by the Soviet Union in this hemisphere. The other is a diplomacy that offers some hope for a more promising course of action for the Sandinista government and some reinforcement for those elements of Nicaraguan society who want a truly democratic, truly independent government.

The chief virtues of the trade embargo are that it is apparently legal and that it has some appearance of being a decisive, if limited, action in the face of the Moscow trip by Mr. Ortega. The liabilities, though, are that it may serve to weaken the private sector in Nicaragua, that it could tend in the long run to increase the dependence of Nicaragua on the Soviet Union and Cuba, and that, while it may put added stresses on the fragile Nicaraguan economy, the markets and supplies Nicaragua gains in trade with the United States can eventually be found elsewhere. There is considerable evidence that the U.S. embargo on trade with Cuba has in fact been more inimical to U.S. interests than to Cuba's.

One problem is that the U.S. government has been so shrill and so lacking in credibility in its assessment of the Soviet or Cuban threat in Nicaragua that it now seems to believe its own stereotypes. There is a Cuban presence in Nicaragua, a profoundly important presence though partially a defensible one, and there is certainly evidence of Soviet military aid. But the threat posed by Nicaragua to its neighbors has been consistently overstated and poorly documented.

If there is to be a change for the better in Nicaragua, if the anti-civil libertarian and pro-Soviet tendencies of some of the Sandinistas are to be reversed, if there is to be a chance for a non-communist, democratic model in Central America, it is important that the Foreign Service and the president and secretary of state get beyond the stereotypes and the oversimplifications. It is not enough that a policy look superficially tough and aggressive; it is important that it have some probable value and some realizable goals. The offhanded embargo is likely to have a short shelf life as a policy of any real meaning.

We are not opposed to the application of certain kinds of pressures to the Sandinista regime, and we are not so sure the Soviets can effectively preserve, protect and nurture the Sandinistas even if they want to and even with the restrictions on aid to contras. We don't like patently illegal interventions in another country's affairs, especially with an instrument of such uncertain intent and direction as the contras. But what the policy desperately needs, in addition to some selectivity in the choice of weapons invoked, is a clearer definition of what it is our policy is seeking in Nicaragua. If our policy is merely to force the Nicaraguans to "say uncle," as the president once quaintly put it, it is likely to help, rather than retard, the creation of "another Cuba." U.S. pressures in various other parts of Latin America have often helped to foster the evolution of democratic institutions. There is even evidence that this administration's policies in El Salvador are yielding such fruit, on what certainly appeared to be unpromising ground.

The cliche-ridden and often patently silly U.S. pronouncements on Nicaragua, though, have made it harder and harder to devise an American policy that is either strong or sensible. If the administration really wants to devise a post-contra-vote policy to bring about peaceful and constructive change in Nicaragua, it needs to get beyond the embargo and devise a more clearly defined policy capable of attracting a consensus here at home.

Herald News
Fall River, MA, May 7, 1985

The visit of Nicaragua's president, Daniel Ortega, to Moscow seeking aid was certainly a mistake if he had any hope of convincing the American public that he was not seriously committed to paralleling Castro's course.

He got what he was looking for, an agreement from Gorbachev to provide more help for Nicaragua.

But he also got what he was presumably not looking for: a trade embargo from the Reagan administration.

After all the argument over U.S. aid to the rebels fighting Ortega's regime, the House killed the measure the administration had submitted.

But had the House members known that Ortega was about to take off for Moscow, they might have been less willing to refuse the administration $14 million to continue the fight against him.

Now Ortega has gone a long way toward justifying the administration's attitude toward him.

Furthermore, Gorbachev's assurance to him makes perfectly apparent that the Soviet Union does not intend to stop its meddling in the Caribbean area.

None of this will come as a surprise to the Reagan administration, but it may come as a surprise to those who deluded themselves into thinking the administration was misrepresenting the Ortega regime.

Now the Nicaraguan minister of trade says this country's embargo will "boomerang." He does not say how.

What the administration has done is apply the policy to Nicaragua that this country has long since used in relation to Castro's Cuba.

It amounts to a policy of peaceful hostility.

The Nicaraguan minister of trade says that only 17 percent of his country's foreign business is conducted with the United States. The vast bulk of it, he insists, is with various Latin American countries.

Fair enough, if so. But there is no reason why the United States should continue to trade with a nation whose government has such close connections both with Cuba and the Soviet Union.

If Nicaragua can manage without U.S. trade, then it will have an opportunity to do so.

But it is nonsense to make believe that Ortega's mission to Moscow is irrelevant to Nicaragua's relations with the United States.

On the contrary, it is an overt statement of where the Ortega regime stands.

It is committed to the Soviet Union.

This is what the administration has been saying, and why it has been trying to support the Nicaraguan rebels.

Perhaps its tactics in those terms were not as effective as had been hoped, but that does not mean it was wrong to try to keep the Soviet Union from gaining a foothold on the Central American mainland. It still is trying. That is what the trade embargo is all about.

And that is why, now that Ortega has made his own position clear, the administration will have less trouble in getting help from Congress to limit his influence in and out of Nicaragua.

After all the controversy and criticism, the administration turned out to be on the right track.

U.S. Panel Seeks Contra Aid Records

A United States House foreign affairs subcommittee investigating possible misuse of $27 million in U.S. humanitarian aid to the Nicaraguan contras voted unanimously May 8, 1985 to subpoena U.S. bank records of contra suppliers and brokers. The Western Hemisphere subcommittee voted 9-0, to subpoena records from 13 banks, 11 of them from Miami, Florida. The records pertained to 16 brokers and suppliers who had received funds from the contras and who also did business with the Nicaraguan Humanitarian Assisstance Office (NHAO), a U.S. State Department agency set up to disburse the funds. The 16 had refused to turn over their records to the NHAO. In addition, the General Accounting Office (GAO), the investigative arm of Congress, had been denied access to intelligence reports said by the State Department to show that the funds were not being misused.

The subcommittee took its action at the end of a hearing on a new report by the GAO, which had audited the contra aid program. The GAO said it could not account for how $13.3 million of the $27 million approved by Congress had been spent. Of the $27 million, $21.1 million had been disbursed by April 25. The $13.3 million that could not be accounted for was spent in Central America. The remaining aid was spent in the U.S. Allegations had surfaced charging that some of the money might have been spent on items not considered humanitarian in nature, such as aircraft spare parts and on military equipment. Further U.S. news stories May 9 said that Honduran military officers had received part of the U.S. aid. They were said to have received profits from a Honduran supermarket that supplied the contras with some $1 million of goods a month, in return for allowing U.S. supplies to reach contra bases in Honduras.

In a related development, the *Miami Herald* reported April 20, 1985 that of the $132 million in U.S. aid provided to the contras since 1981, $116 million had never been independently audited and it was likely that some of it had been misappropriated. Of particular concern, the *Herald* said, was the period between 1981 and 1984 when the contras were provided with $100.5 million in covert aid. Receipts were said to cover only a small portion of expenditures, and the Central Intelligence Agency had refused the GAO permission to audit the program.

LOS ANGELES HERALD EXAMINER

Los Angeles, CA, June 20, 1985

Congressional auditors reported last week that a good portion of U.S. aid earmarked for the Nicaraguan *contras* has instead been diverted to private bank accounts and officials in the Honduran military. Secretary of State George Shultz and his chief lieutenant, Elliott Abrams, dealt with this bad news in timeless governmental fashion: by discrediting the messenger. But their public harrumphing is no substitute for answering questions every taxpayer should ask.

The investigation, conducted by the respected General Accounting Office, was begun two months ago after government officials couldn't account for more than half the $27 million in non-lethal aid Congress appropriated for the *contras* last year.

In tracking this money from the Treasury, the GAO found that at least $3.6 million of it ended up in private bank accounts in the U.S., the Bahamas and the Cayman Islands. Another $1.2 million was paid to a Honduran supermarket, which quickly wrote checks to the armed forces of Honduras and that nation's commander in chief, since retired.

The auditors also discovered that only a small fraction of the money went to businesses that supplied food, medicine and clothing to the *contras*. In most cases, it's not clear yet who did get the money or what they spent it on. The GAO is still digging.

As might be expected, congressional foes of *contra* aid have greeted the report gleefully. They will no doubt get political mileage from its shocking findings next week when the administration tries to persuade Congress that the *contras* need another $100 million to continue their war against the Sandinista government. The State Department's disdainful response to the GAO report hasn't bolstered the administration's case.

Shultz and Abrams complain that the whole investigation was a put-up job, a politically motivated effort designed to embarrass the White House at a crucial time. They claim there has been no wrongdoing, no corruption, and that the *contras* received the money they were supposed to get. If that is so, the administration should back it up with facts instead of smears.

THE PLAIN DEALER

Cleveland, OH, May 7, 1985

When Congress cut off direct military aid and CIA support two years ago for the contra rebels trying to overthrow the Nicaraguan government, the focus shifted to the private sector to keep the war going.

One of the largest outfits funneling money to the contras is the U.S. Council for World Freedom. Founded and headed by retired Maj. Gen. John K. Singlaub, it enjoys questionable federal tax-exempt status. Questionable because, in reply to IRS questions regarding its application for tax exemption, the council's treasurer stated that "at no time will the USCWF ever contemplate providing materiel or funds to any revolutionary, counterrevolutionary or liberation movement."

The group, with State Department approval, recently sent a refurbished Vietnam-era UH-1B Huey helicopter to the contras for use as a medical transport, to be based in Honduras. Because the UH-1B is a military ship, a license was required from the State Department, and was granted four days after Singlaub's group requested it.

In approving the license for use in Honduras only, the State Department said the helicopter is to be used for transport of the sick and wounded only, and cannot be armed. A Washington contra spokesman interviewed by the New York Times said he hoped the copter would be used in Nicaraguan territory occupied by the contras because that it is where it most obviously is needed.

There is more than a simple failure to communicate here. Singlaub's group previously has told government officials one thing to comply with the letter of the law, and then gone ahead and acted otherwise. In its charter, USCWF says it will provide "materiel support to [anti-Communist] liberation movements." When pressed for an explanation by the IRS, the organization's treasurer said that USCWF considered "materiel support" to be sponsorship of seminars for people of countries under communist rule, to present their views to the American public.

Despite what the treasurer told the IRS, he later confided that "we had always intended to give support of other types to those [anti-Communist rebels] in Angola and elsewhere." The administration knew that. President Reagan has endorsed the assistance USCWF provides the contras and counts on it because of his inability to persuade Congress to approve funding for his rebel aid plan, which includes helicopters and other military gear.

The Huey clearly is not a seminar. The contras clearly are a counterrevolutionary group. The question is why USCWF continues to enjoy tax-exempt status obtained through deceit. Has the IRS been politically influenced to go along with the charade? If not, why has it failed to revoke the organization's tax-exempt status and to seek recovery of tax money from USCWF?

It is folly that some Americans are funding an illegal war in Central America and getting a tax write-off for their contributions. Congress should act to stop the practice.

SYRACUSE HERALD·JOURNAL

Syracuse, NY, May 12, 1985

Even those folks who like the idea of sending big bucks to what some of us perceive to be a rag-tag gang of cutthroats in Nicaragua, the so-called "freedom-fighting" Contras, have to be concerned at recent reports from that part of the world.

For instance, nobody in the Reagan administration seems to be able to account for $13 million worth of "non-lethal" aid sent to the Contras. They don't know whether the money has gone for food, or guns, or swimming pools in Miami.

So, quite naturally, there are some members of the Congress who have gotten uptight about sending another $100 million that has been requested by President Reagan.

▽   ▽

Then there is the little matter of allegations of cocaine trafficking and gun-running by the Contras and their American supporters. That's being looked into, as well.

And last week, the National Catholic Reporter quoted a report from Honduras that 145 U.S. Army Green Berets were headed there to take part in a secret training exercise with the Contras. A U.S. military information officer in Honduras was quoted as telling a Knight-Ridder correspondent the exercise would involve "wiring things and blowing them up."

The correspondent, Sam Dillon, said the Americans will be based near the Nicaraguan border in an area used by anti-Sandinista Indian rebels as a rear-guard base.

None of these news tidbits is necessarily related to the others, other than the fact they all concern developments in an area of the hemisphere where we seem to be losing our grip on sanity.

Is it not, indeed, at least bordering on insanity that we have sent $12.9 million to the Contras and lost track of it immediately upon funneling the money into a dozen Miami banks?

We understand that to the administration and some congressmen this is not considered a great amount of money. We would dare say, on the other hand, that to the Contras it's a considerable sum, more, we would suspect, than we could expect them to handle with any degree of honesty.

As a matter of fact, we understand there is more than circumstantial evidence that certain Contra leaders have been skimming big bucks off the top while their troops die for lack of medicine and food.

▽   ▽

And is it not insanity that between raids the Contras could be (probably are) moonlighting in a trade that's almost as lucrative a profession as stealing from Uncle Sam, hauling cocaine and other substances northward as a token of thanks for what we've done for them?

And how many more Green Berets will be sent to Honduras to "blow things up" before we recognize the insanity of sending *any Americans at all* to take part, either actively or otherwise, in that horrid little war?

In addition to the sense of deja vu about this entire situation, we also get a feeling that we are in a strangely hazy dream world where some things are not as they appear. Which side of Alice's looking glass are we really on?

The Pittsburgh PRESS

Pittsburgh, PA, May 12, 1985

Anti-government rebels in Nicaragua have been described many times as a ragtag band of ill-equipped guerrillas maintaining their fight through sheer determination and patriotism.

Hold that description. How about a well-heeled army with ready access to whatever today's well-dressed young fighting man should be wearing, including baseball caps, ponchos and four pairs of boots each?

And that's not even to mention a new fatigue pants pocket possibly stuffed with cordobas, the Nicaraguan currency, or maybe a rifle or spotter telescope, all bought with American financial aid.

The new picture of a spiffier Contra fighter began to emerge in Washington last week with disclosure of an internal financial summary of goods bought with U.S. "humanitarian" aid.

The classified summary, prepared by the State Department's Nicaraguan Humanitarian Assistance Office, details Contra purchases only from last October through Feb. 21 of this year. Listed among the purchases were 57,000 pairs of boots, nearly four pairs each for the 15,000 rebels, and 90 rifle or spotter scopes, which would be in violation of previous congressional restrictions against providing arms to the Contras.

More than $356,000 of American money was used to purchase cordobas. If exchanged on the bloated Nicaraguan black market, $356,000 would buy as many cordobas as $10 million would at the official rate.

The money spent during the period covered by the summary was part of $27 million in American aid given the Contras thus far. The Regan administration wants Congress to approve $100 million more.

Fortunately, some members of Congress want to do first things first, such as finding out just what was done with the $27 million already sent.

Twenty-four members of the House Foreign Affairs Committee voted unanimously last week to subpoena records of about 15 American banks which were used to funnel the aid to the rebels. The subpoenas were necessary because the General Accounting Office, the investigating arm of Congress, has no access to confidential bank records and can't trace about $15 million of the aid without those records.

The Foreign Affairs Committee's vote to subpoena the records was a prudent move in an attempt to find out if some of the aid was misused once it got out of the country.

To match that move, President Reagan ought to back off on his push for the additional $100 million until we find out just what the Contras did with the money and goods they were given thus far.

The Miami Herald

Miami, FL, June 7, 1985

ALLEGATIONS daily grow wider that the *contra* rebels seeking to oust Nicaragua's Sandinista regime have misappropriated or misused U.S. assistance funds. The first allegations of impropriety came from Honduras and involved the Nicaraguan Democratic Force, the largest *contra* group. Now, from Costa Rica, come reports that the smaller Nicaraguan Revolutionary Armed Forces has billed the United States for thousands of dollars in food, clothing, and other supplies that merchants say were never sold or delivered to the insurgents.

The two most logical explanations for these irregularities are that *contra* leaders are diverting these "humanitarian" funds to purchase much-needed arms, or that they're stealing the money to enrich themselves. Either explanation leads to the same conclusion: The United States Congress, and America's taxpayers, are being defrauded.

If proof turns up that rebel leaders are stealing American aid money, that would be — and absolutely should be — the absolute end of this country's involvement with them. Even if the lesser offense is proven — diversion of nonlethal aid to buy arms — that would constitute a clear violation of Congress's will. When Congress voted in 1985 to give the *contras* $27 million in humanitarian aid, it specifically excluded arms purchases. U.S. aid was to be for nonlethal supplies exclusively.

This newspaper and others have turned up evidence of misuse of U.S. aid, evidence too strong to be explained away. The *contras'* leaders must be made to understand that every dollar of American aid must be accounted for fully. To drive that point compellingly home, it's imperative that Congress continue its investigation into what became of these funds. Not until it knows how that humanitarian aid was spent should Congress even begin to consider giving the *contras* another cent.

THE TENNESSEAN

Nashville, TN, June 3, 1985

WITH the Congress scheduled to vote again this month on President Reagan's request for $100 million in military and non-military aid for the Nicaraguan rebels, investigations have been under way to find out what happened to previous aid.

The House Foreign Affairs Committee has subpoenaed bank records to try to determine what happened to $13 million to $15 million in aid money. The Reagan administration itself raised questions about the contras by its inability to give a full accounting of how the most recent aid has been spent.

The result has been a number of reports on two kinds of allegations. One is that the money was diverted into private hands, or spent on supplies that never reached the contras. Another is that contra leaders and Honduran officials have made enormous profits by exchanging U.S. aid dollars for local currencies on the black market.

Some $13.3 million was deposited in bank accounts of brokers, most located in Miami, who were to buy uniforms, food and other items from suppliers in Central America. According to the General Accounting Office, the State Department's Nicaraguan Humanitarian Assistance Office made the bank deposits on the basis of invoices from suppliers, but couldn't prove the purchased items were delivered.

A major reason for lack of verification, according to both the GAO and the State Department, is that the Honduran government would not allow the U.S. to monitor shipments made to the contras, most of which were made through supply routes in Honduras. That county has declined to acknowledge that contras operate from its terroritory.

According to a report by *The Miami Herald* contra rebels in Costa Rica were paid thousands of dollars for food, clothing and medical supplies which merchants say were never purchased. The rebels based in Costa Rica allegedly charged the U.S. for enough supplies to outfit at least 1,000 insurgents, though their numbers total less than 400.

Although only $1.89 million in humanitarian aid was given the rebels in Costa Rica, records examined by *The Herald* reportedly reveal a trail of financial irregularities and missing funds. Records show that on Nov. 6, the U.S. paid $16,764 for purchases from the Farmacia Upala, a small drug store in Upala, Costa Rica. But the owner denied such large purchases were made, said the newspaper.

Another store owner in the town said she sold $370 worth of jeans, dress shirts and underwear to the contra group in January, but nothing sizable since. U.S. records show she sold $26,766 in food to the rebels Nov. 6.

The obvious question is that if the U.S. can't account for $13 million or so, how can it expect to account for $100 million? Congress ought to know the answers to that before it votes to spend any more money. ■

The Burlington Free Press

Burlington, VT, June 10, 1985

Substantial amounts of U.S. foreign aid dollars have a remarkable capacity for disappearing after they are poured into the pipeline in Washington and channelled toward their recipients.

The latest fiasco involves padded and phony invoices submitted by two Nicaraguan rebel groups who are part of the network that makes up the contras. The contras ostensibly are fighting against the Sandinista government in Managua. Some contend the aim of the contras is to force the Sandinistas to liberalize their human rights policies. Others claim that the contras are dedicated to the overthrow of the Ortega regime. Whatever the case may be, the Reagan administration has thrown its support behind the contras as "freedom fighters" who are seeking to save Central America from the Communists.

To help the rebels in achieving their goals, the administration has appropriated millions of dollars for military and non-military aid and next week will ask Congress to approve President Reagan's request for another $100 million for the same purpose. Charges that between $13 million and $15 million in taxpayers' money have been misappropriated certainly are not calculated to persuade lawmakers to send more money to the contras. Reagan's case has been seriously, perhaps fatally, damaged by accusations from former contras and Americans who worked with them that the rebel organization has been involved in corruption, drug-smuggling, gun-running and assassination plots.

That the administration advocated intervention in Nicaraguan affairs through the contras was wrong to begin with. Instead of dealing with the regime that was established after the overthrow of Anastasio Somoza, the White House chose to deal with the issue on an ideological basis, claiming that the Sandinistas were the Kremlin's surrogates in spreading Communism through Central America. And there should be little doubt in anyone's mind that contra champions in the administration would cheer lustily if the government in Managua were overthrown.

Interfering in the internal affairs of Nicaragua or any other country in the world, however, is a violation of the right of self-determination. That principle should be a fundamental element in American foreign policy to which presidents must subscribe.

To insure that it is observed, Congress should reject Reagan's request for more aid to the contras and should demand that he seek a diplomatic solution to the differences between Washington and Managua.

The State

Columbia, SC, June 21, 1985

THE REAGAN Administration's failure to assure critics that aid to the Contras will not be misused may have hurt its cause in Congress.

Instead of providing adequate answers, the State Department has challenged congressional findings that millions of dollars in non-lethal aid to Nicaraguan rebels were diverted to offshore banks and to the Honduran military.

The Administration may have been on target when it accused Michael Barnes, the Democratic chairman of the House Foreign Affairs Subcommittee on Western Hemisphere Affairs, of misusing the General Accounting Office to investigate the Contras. But it has taken a defensive, blustering stance that invites animosity.

The Administration claims it hasn't had equal access to the GAO's information. The other side claims the State Department is stalling until after the Contra vote, scheduled for next week, is taken.

At this late stage, it is difficult to pierce beneath the fuzz. Apparently, Democratic foes of the Contras are quite willing to use Congress' investigating clout to cloud a bigger issue. If the Administration has not monitored aid closely enough, it should pledge to do so in the future.

In the mire of Central America, accounting for use of every penny in aid will always be difficult. But the Administration must give it its best shot.

In the meantime, Congress should not use this diversion as an excuse to deny aid to those who seek relief from an oppressive, Marxist regime.

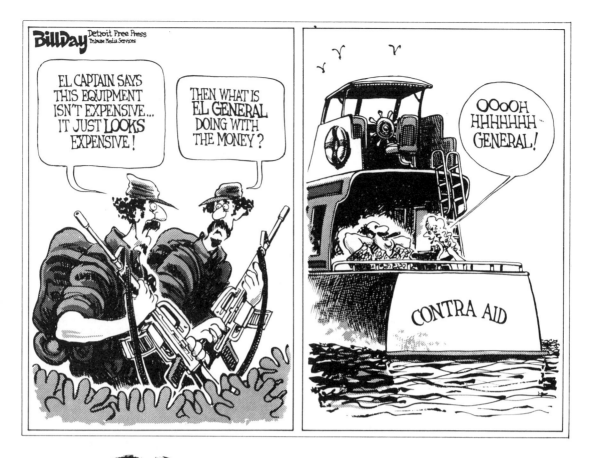

The Sun Reporter

San Francisco, CA, June 12, 1985

The House Foreign Affairs Committee, concerned about possible misuse of U.S. aid to rebels in Nicaragua, has approved subpoenas for the bank records of 16 people and the companies receiving the funds.

Some members of Congress are worried that much of the $27 million in U.S. humanitarian aid to the contras has not been accounted for properly.

The Foreign Affairs Committee is taking the proper steps to investigate how American taxpayer's money that was allocated to provide humanitarian aid to the real poor people in Nicaragua is being spent. We don't think such an investigation would be conducted by the congressional committee if the money was being used in the manner in which the supplicants, whom President Reagan defined as "Freedom Fighters," were truly interested in any significant social changes in their country.

From all accounts that have been publicized, the leaders of the rebel cause in Nicaragua are just the leftover lieutenants of the discredited Somoza regime, whose primary aim is to bring about a restoration of a Somoza-type administration, whose primary goal was a systematic looting of the public treasury for their own personal enrichment.

It could be possible that the remnants of the Somoza regime, who are called freedom fighters today, were unable to get any of their ill-gotten gains out of the country to banks in Switzerland and Rio de Janeiro like Somoza did.

Much of the loot that Somoza stowed away in foreign banks came from aid money from the U.S. and from private American businesses.

The rebels are well aware that as long as they declare themselves leaders of a movement to eradicate so-called communist encroachment of their tiny nation that they could talk to some high officials in Washington and convince them that they were engaged in a holy crusade against the forces of evil.

We have long felt that the so-called freedom fighters, whether in Angola, Nicaragua or any other place on the planet, are simply persons who are engaged in campaigns to enrich their personal bank accounts at the expense of the American taxpayer.

There are many programs in the United States designed to provide some amenities to poor Americans which are scheduled to get less money than in the past because the Reagan administration seems more interested in creating more millionaires in Africa and Latin America just because of the ability of such leaders to convince the Reagan administration that they are freedom fighters.

We have never seen or heard of any of these freedom fighters' activities as being anything other than terroristic campaigns against neutral people in their countries who do not take sides in the issues.

We hope that the house committee will push their investigation in a diligent manner, with the added hopes that, if it is possible, the U.S. can regain the aid money from what seems to be nothing but confidence men.

At least the new Philippines government is taking action to recoup money from the Ferdinand Marcos ill-gotten bank accounts.

San Francisco Chronicle

San Francisco, CA, June 13, 1985

CHARGES BY AUDITORS for Congress that a sizable portion of American aid supposedly going to Nicaraguan rebels never got there must be fully investigated, particularly if the administration expects approval of its request to ship another $100 million to the Contras.

Asked to follow the paper trail of some of the $27 million in non-military Contra aid approved by Congress last year, auditors from the General Accounting Office found that nearly $1.2 million was paid to the Honduran armed forces (including $450,000 to its commander in chief) and another $3.6 million ended up in bank accounts in places such as the Bahamas, the Cayman Islands and Florida.

One particular oddity was the discovery that $6.6 million found its way to a small food market in Tegucigalpa, Honduras, which then turned around and made the payments to the Honduran military. If the whole matter weren't so deadly serious, it would seem like a scenario for a Woody Allen movie.

REAGAN ADMINISTRATION officials are probably correct when they charge that the GAO report is being used for political purposes by opponents of aid to the Contras. But that response doesn't answer the very real questions raised by the auditors or justify possible misuse of federal funds.

The serious questions that have been asked about the actual use of the first millions sent to the Contras must be answered before more American taxpayer dollars are shipped south. Congress meant the money to aid the anti-Sandanista movement, not to line the pockets of generals and sharpies on either side of the border.

U.S. Gave Contras Military Advice

The Reagan Administration August 8, 1985 acknowledged that National Security Council (NSC) officials had given advice on military operations to Nicaraguan contras fighting the Sandinista government. The White House role had been disclosed in a *New York Times* article published that day. The *Times* story said that since Congress cut off military funds to the contras in 1984, NSC officials had given advice on military operations and had had "tactical influence" on the contras. In addition, they had helped the contras raise money from private sources, the story said. According to the article, the operation was being run by a military officer who was a NSC member. The officer had frequent meetings with the contras, was in contact with the Central Intelligence Agency (CIA) and briefed President Reagan, the *Times* reported. The *Times* cited a Nicaraguan exile who said the officer had aided efforts to coordinate the two main contra groups: the Nicaraguan Democratic Force (FDN) based in Honduras and the Costa Rican-based Democratic Revolutionary Alliance (Arde).

News organizations subsequently identified the officer as Marine Corps. Lt. Col. Oliver North. *The Washington Post*, in an article Aug. 11, gave details of North's role in Central America. The officer was an aide to national security adviser Robert McFarlane and held the position of deputy director for political-military affairs, focusing on Central America. He was said to have drafted a controversial terror manual for use by the contras that suggested "neutralizing"—assassinating—Sandinista officials. The manual had caused a furor in the U.S. Congress. Adolfo Calero, president of the FDN, acknowledged Aug. 13 that he had met several times with North but said reports that North was a key adviser to the group were "silly." He maintained that neither North nor any other NSC officials had given military advice to the FDN.

The New York Times Aug. 10 cited a senior administration official who said CIA officials had been concerned at the activities of the NSC. Referring to the legislation originally sponsored in 1982 by Rep. Edward Boland (D, Mass.) that restricted or prohibited direct or indirect U.S. aid to the contras, the unidentified official said CIA Director William Casey "hasn't wanted to know some of the things the NSC was doing because of the Boland Amendment."

Chicago Tribune
Chicago, IL, August 14, 1985

When a President becomes so frustrated that he begins running national security operations directly out of the White House, it is time to beware. Whatever the motives, the shift is a sign of trouble. And the results can be disastrous.

Some time back, the White House replaced the Central Intelligence Agency with the President's National Security Council staff in handling relations with the anti-Sandinista guerrillas who have been harassing the Nicaraguan government. The reason seems to be to circumvent congressional restrictions on the CIA.

It is no wonder the White House is frustrated. Congress has behaved abysmally on the question of aid to the Contra rebels. It has not been able to decide which is worse, American support for the Contras or getting blamed for the collapse of the rebellion against the Sandinistas. It has twisted and turned, first cutting off all aid, then discovering, to its horror, that the Sandinistas were allying themselves with the Soviet Union, then valiantly voting to provide "humanitarian aid" to the armed rebels, whatever that is supposed to mean.

The administration is quite right to want to keep the pressure on the Sandinistas, though it has added to the policy confusion by its lack of clarity about what it hopes to achieve that is within the realm of possibility. A military alliance between Nicaragua and the Soviet Union would be dangerous in a region which, after all, sits on the United States' southern flank. But at times the administration seems to be seeking the overthrow of the Sandinistas rather than some kind of accommodation by which Nicaragua would steer clear of Soviet influence in return for U.S. cooperation. And the hapless, factionalized Contras are not in a position to overthrow anybody.

Congress has compounded the difficulty by its timorousness and vacillation. But little as the administration likes it, the way to straighten things out is to work on Congress, not to try to work around it by setting up a special team in the White House.

The danger of usurping the role of the CIA or other government institutions is twofold. First, it stinks of trickery and discredits the orderly processes of government as well as the specific program, which needs to be sold to the public and Congress if it is to have any chance of success. Second, the Executive Office of the President is not equipped to handle such sensitive operations. It has no institutional memory. And it is prone to going overboard in its zeal.

Unlike the agencies, the White House is filled with people with a single-minded view of how to get things done. There is no bureaucracy, no institutional restraint. This can seem like a blessing to a President who is having trouble getting the government to respond the way he wants it to. But as the experience of the Nixon administration in creating an investigative unit within the Executive Office of the President demonstrated, responsiveness can easily run out of control.

Now that the story of the White House role in handling the Contras has begun to come out, the administration reportedly plans to shift responsibility to the State Department. That is a good idea. But already a certain amount of damage has been done to the credibility of the program. Not only will the administration have to try to coax a balking Congress into supporting its Central American policy, it will have to defend itself against charges of arrogance and subterfuge.

ST. LOUIS POST-DISPATCH
St. Louis, MO, August 29, 1985

Though not much in the news lately, President Reagan's war against the Nicaraguan government proceeds with both U.S. government and private help. Indeed, the two forms of aid supplement each other.

Congress finally assented to $24 million in "humanitarian" aid for the contra guerrillas backed by the CIA. That represents food, clothing and medical supplies essential to continuing the war. But what about weapons? *The New York Times* quotes officials and retired Maj. Gen. John K. Singlaub as saying the contras have received as much as $25 million in donations from private individuals in the United States. That allows for the weaponry.

Certainly the administration is not discouraging this private funding, and President Reagan says official involvement in advice and aid to the contras is "not violating any laws." But is it? The neutrality laws prohibit American citizens from helping to fund or plan warfare against nations with which the United States is at peace. In diplomatic terms, if no other, the U.S. is at peace with Nicaragua.

There is a further question about private assistance. Gen. Singlaub, as chairman of the U.S. Council for World Freedom, takes credit for funneling more than $100,000 in aid to the contras. His council obtained federal tax-exempt status from the Internal Revenue Service three years ago after pledging never to provide "materiel or funds" to insurgents.

The general says White House national security officials advised him on private fund-raising when Congress voted against direct CIA funding. He insists that his money was used to buy only non-lethal supplies, while arms funds were raised elsewhere. The IRS ought at least to be investigating whether the pledge not to provide materiel or funds has been violated.

While there is nothing particularly covert about Mr. Reagan's war, the mixture of public and private funds to keep the war going has been clandestine enough — and so is the express purpose of the war. Robert McFarlane, Mr. Reagan's national security adviser, recently repeated that "it is not now, has not been and shall not be our position to overthrow the Nicaraguan government." But that is not what spokesmen for the contras say, that is not what other administration officials have privately told reporters, and that is not how the administration has acted in closing off talks with Nicaraguan leaders and in ignoring appeals of the Contadora nations trying to negotiate a solution to the war.

So the war continues, and it leaves the U.S. without reasonable options. Negotiations have been shut off, yet the contras' terrorism shows no promise of a military defeat of the Nicaraguan government. Before the administration is tempted to resort to further U.S. involvement, it ought to call off its intervention and substitute peaceful diplomacy.

Roanoke Times & World-News

Roanoke, VA, August 12, 1985

EVEN BEFORE the infusion of $27 million in "non-military" aid from the United States, the Contras of Nicaragua have been showing new military zing.

After a six-month hiatus on major military operations, the Honduras-based Contras have struck deep into Nicaraguan territory. They now have new air transports, which can fly needed supplies into Nicaragua and eliminate the need for the guerrillas to return to their Honduran bases. This cuts down on the danger of ambush from Sandinista forces. The rebels expect soon to acquire a short landing and takeoff aircraft, which can fly supplies into small jungle air strips.

The source of financing for this new equipment is unspecified. But there can be little doubt that congressional approval of non-lethal supplies to the Contras has given them new leverage in the arms market. It also, undoubtedly, figures in the ability of Adolfo Calero, who heads the Contras' political appendage, to offer a $1 million reward to any Nicaraguan who will turn over to the Contras one of Nicaragua's Soviet-built MI-24 attack helicopters.

While the Contras are a long way from overthrowing the Nicaraguan government, they can certainly cause the Sandinistas a lot of grief. Calero has threatened to destroy the country's only oil refinery if the government uses its MI-24s against the rebels.

What if the Contras do succeed?

Democracy is unlikely to follow their trail into Managua. The Contras' military command consists largely of former officers in dictator Anastasio Somoza's notorious National Guard. If the Sandinistas use Castroite Cubans as their role models, the Contras use the disreputable Argentine military as theirs.

Calero's political organization is a CIA creation designed to take some of the Somoza taint off the Contra operation. It has no proposed constitution and no clear political program for a post-Sandinista Nicaragua. Neither can it give any assurance that it can control the men who are directing the military action. These men are cutthroats who cling to the Argentine military mentality. Edgar Chamorro, a former member of the Contras' political wing, wrote in The New Republic:

The political dimension of the struggle meant nothing to the commanders. They all had the simplistic belief that Somoza lost because he had his hands tied by Jimmy Carter and that if he hadn't he could have killed a lot of people and won. The Argentine officers who trained them had told them, "We're the only people in Latin America who've beaten the communists in a war. The way to win is to fight a 'dirty war' like we did in the '70s." I became convinced that the combination of Argentine training and National Guard mentality was one of the major obstacles to putting the Contra movement on a truly democratic path.

In view of this mentality, it is reasonable to expect that a bloodbath would accompany a Contra march to power. Nor can we expect a pacification of Nicaragua after a Contra triumph. The Sandinistas fought long and hard to overthrow Somoza. The diehards among them probably would continue to organize resistance to a regime that included former Somoza supporters.

It is misleading and naive to regard the Contras as freedom fighters. They are an unpredictable lot with questionable motives. They play ball with the CIA at this point, because they need American support to continue their battle.

But we should not kid ourselves that we are promoting democracy in Central America when we back the Contras. We will no more be promoting democracy there than we were in 1934, when American Marines left Nicaragua in the care and keeping of the corrupt Somoza family; than we were in 1953, when we overthrew a leftist government in Iran and restored the shah to his throne; than we were in 1954, when we toppled the regime of reformist President Jacobo Arbenz in Guatemala and doomed that country to another generation of right-wing military rule; than we were in 1973 when we watched the downfall and death of Salvador Allende in Chile and the ascension of Augusto Pinochet to the dictatorship.

We can join other countries in the hemisphere in seeking a peaceful solution to the turmoil that wracks the isthmus. Or we can continue our historic policy of supporting any despot who will cooperate with Washington. If we do that, we may cure the immediate headache, but the underlying cancer will surface again and another generation will pay the price.

Houston Chronicle

Houston, TX, October 14, 1985

The various contra groups opposed to the Marxist Nicaraguan government are in dispute about how U.S. aid funds will be distributed.

The United States has $27 million in non-lethal assistance to give to the rebel forces. U.S. officials say the aid will all be channeled through the United Nicaraguan Opposition, which was formed just last June.

Some rebel leaders say this is an attempt by the United States to force them into a subsidiary role and they don't like it. The leaders of an Indian group are particularly incensed. There's not complete unity in the UNO.

Wouldn't it be a mess if the rebel groups start shooting at each other over their share of U.S. funds?

The Philadelphia Inquirer

Philadelphia, PA, August 27, 1985

In the beginning, there were the "routine maneuvers" in Honduras. They are still going on. Then there were the Nicaraguan harbor minings, attributed to "freedom fighters," but orchestrated by the CIA. Now there is $27 million of "humanitarian aid" flowing to rebels trying to oust Managua's Sandinistas.

Those rebels, called contras, know a wink when they see it. They've put in their bids for chunks of the "nonlethal" aid, asking for helicopters, planes, jeeps, boats and communications equipment.

And why not? Words have ceased to have real meaning in the Reagan administration's Central American policy. "Routine maneuvers" mean semipermanent presence. "Support for peace talks" means sabotage of peace talks. "Humanitarian aid," of course, means logistical backing for armies in the field.

Last week brought news that a group called the U.S. Council for World Freedom, which won tax-exempt status from the Internal Revenue Service after pledging it would never provide "materiel or funds" to insurgents, in fact has been claiming credit for slipping tens of thousands of dollars to the contras.

Can you blame the council? When it comes to Nicaragua, it is official policy of the United States government to say one thing and do another. And heaven forfend that the IRS read the council the riot act while it is following the doubletalk game plan so scrupulously.

THE PLAIN DEALER

Cleveland, OH, August 25, 1985

When Congress cut off direct military assistance funds and CIA support for the Nicaraguan insurgency last year, private fund-raising for the rebel contras increased to aid the war effort. The effort has been backed by both President Reagan and the Treasury Department, which granted a tax break to the leading donor group.

The organization, the U.S. Council for World Freedom, was founded and is directed by retired Army Gen. John K. Singlaub. Because of funding from the council and other supporters, the assistance "has made the difference . . . and the freedom fighters have not just continued—they are expanding," Singlaub boasted to Newsweek magazine.

While the general is keeping the faith, American taxpayers are getting stuck with the tab as those donating money to the USCWF can deduct such contributions from their taxable income. In 1982, only a few months before the CIA set up the contra directorate known as the Nicaraguan Democratic Force (FDN) in Florida, Singlaub's group obtained questionable federal tax-exempt status.

The freedom council's treasurer, in responding to questions from the Internal Revenue Service regarding the organization's application for the exempt status, filed documents stating that "at no time will the USCWF ever contemplate providing materiel or funds to any revolutionary, counter-revolutionary or liberation movement." To explain the organization's charter reference to providing "material support to (anti-Communist) liberation movements," the treasurer told IRS officials that the USCWF considered "material support" to be sponsorship of seminars for people of countries under communist rule, to present their views to the American people.

Despite what the treasurer told the IRS, he now says "we had always intended to give support of other types to those (anti-Communist rebels) in Angola and elsewhere." And Singlaub knew it.

So did the administration, which gave its blessing to the contra aid project. Because the president backed the effort, Singlaub argues that the assistance provided the anti-Sandinista forces to help them overthrow the Nicaraguan government is proper under the exemption granted.

It is not. At best the exemption was obtained through deceit; at worst, because of administration support of the "freedom fighters," the IRS was influenced to go along with the charade.

If political influence does not affect the tax code, as claimed by the tax agency, it should immediately revoke the USCWF exempt status, seek recovery of tax dollars from the organization and pursue legal penalties against the council's leaders for violation of tax laws.

The Providence Journal

Providence, RI, August 16, 1985

Only a few weeks ago, debate over proposed U.S. military aid for the *contra* rebels in Nicaragua was running clippety-clop. Opponents variously argued (1) that such aid is illegal, (2) that it is immoral and (3) that it is futile: the rag-tag rebels could never do much more than annoy the Sandinista army.

So the Congress approved $27 million in "non-lethal" (and lawful) aid — food, medicine, etc. — for the rebels. Then came the "revelation" — which had for months been common knowledge among reporters inside the Beltway — that the National Security Council was giving advice to the *contras.* Pro-Sandinista editorial writers sniffed that this was only "technically" legal. Thus the argument from illegality wears through at the elbows.

The argument from immorality will never end, because there will always be apologists for Marxist regimes such as the Sandinistas; their blinkered eyes will always see Daniel Ortega as a liberator, and his enemies as reactionary puppets of American imperialism. So let that argument continue; time will out.

As for the futility of the *contras'* military campaign, reports recently dispatched from Nicaragua tell a different story. Nicaraguan citizens have been increasingly fleeing the Sandinistas and joining the rebel forces. In March 1984, the *contras* numbered fewer than 8,000. Today, their strength is estimated to be 16,000 and growing at a rate that could nearly double that figure during the next year.

For a while, after U.S. military aid ceased last October, the *contras* could not train and equip all the volunteers who were joining their fight. But advisers such as Maj. Gen. John K. Singlaub, a retired U.S. Army officer, have been teaching the rebel leaders not only how to train soldiers and wage war, but how to raise money and buy weapons on legal markets. General Singlaub estimates that they have raised some $25 million from private U.S. donors and foreign nations.

And the *contras* apparently have learned to organize. Rebel groups operating out of Honduras have united under the United Nicaraguan Opposition; aid from the $27 million provided by the United States will go only to groups who have joined UNO. The primary holdout is Eden Pastora, who commands a large rebel force based in Costa Rica; it is reported that many of Pastora's commanders have left to join UNO in the north.

These northern forces, once capable of only brief skirmishes across the border, have recently penetrated deep into Nicaragua, as far south as the town of La Trinidad. Tens of thousands of Sandinista troops failed in an attempt to seal the northern border. It is reported that peasants have led *contras* through Sandinista lines. The size and organization of rebel forces, together with popular support from such peasants, are making them a formidable adversary.

We do not delight in telling war stories. The point is that these recent successes show promise of continuing in a scenario that is not unrealistic: the UNO is expected to demand observer status at the United Nations, such as is enjoyed by the Palestine Liberation Organization. If UNO armies can occupy some portion of Nicaraguan territory — which seems ever more likely as their strength increases — they could establish a provisional government that would certainly be recognized by the United States.

On that scenario, peaceful negotiations worthy of the name could begin. The promise of democracy, once extended and as quickly retracted by the Sandinistas, could be restored. Such a scenario is not so far away as it might have seemed only a few months ago. As one U.S. official put it: "The end is not in sight, but it is much, much closer. This is not going to take 10 years."

Let us hope not.

St. Petersburg Times

St. Petersburg, FL, September 7, 1985

The Reagan administration is waging two private wars: one with the government of Nicaragua and one with our own Constitution. The administration is fighting both battles privately, because it wants to avoid the glare of public scrutiny of these costly and dangerous adventures. That leaves it to Congress to do the job of bringing them to light, and thus bringing them to an end.

The President has all but said that he supports the overthrow of the government of Nicaragua, and his administration has worked toward that goal in a variety of direct and indirect ways. But the President and his advisers apparently do not trust Congress and the American people to support that policy. Instead, they have used public resources to arrange a privately supported war against Nicaragua, with the White House acting as behind-the-scenes organizer, fund-raiser and strategic planner.

BY USING AGENTS and employees of the U.S. government to wage a "private" war against Nicaragua, the administration undermines our Constitution, ignores the will of Congress and violates international law — all in the name of a cause that it has failed to explain to its own citizens.

The Constitution gives Congress the sole power to declare war, and the administration hasn't even attempted to win such a formal declaration. Instead it has sought military and "humanitarian" aid for our anti-government surrogates in Nicaragua. But even in the case of such an undeclared war, Congress still controls the power to authorize public funds. It cut off all military aid to anti-government rebels in Nicaragua during the fiscal year ending Sept. 30, and the so-called Boland amendment prohibited the administration from, among other things, soliciting private funds for that cause.

Even that explicit prohibition failed to affect the administration's plans. Officials have acknowledged that a member of the National Security Council, Lt. Col. Oliver L. North, has been deeply involved in organizing the activities of the Nicaraguan rebels, including coordinating some of their military activities and helping to solicit private money for their cause. All such activity clearly violates the law.

Top administration officials, including National Security Adviser Robert McFarlane, have engaged in some tortured reasoning in attempting to make the case that White House actions have violated only the spirit, rather than the letter, of the law. Col. North has not actively solicited money for the rebels, they say. Instead he has merely organized meetings of wealthy sympathizers; if they happened to ask how they might go about contributing to the rebel cause, the ubiquitous Col. North was prepared to answer in detail. But isn't solicitation, either active or passive, still solicitation?

THE COLONEL also violated the Boland amendment if, as seems almost certain, he spent any public funds during his blitz of passive activity. No intelligence agency is permitted to support "directly or indirectly, military or paramilitary operations" of the Nicaraguan rebels. As with so much of the rest of its little war in Nicaragua, the administration has not bothered to explain just how, except through executive-branch expenditure, Col. North could have managed to find the time and money to support his travels on behalf of the rebels. Nor do we know how many other executive-branch employees may have contributed to the cause.

If the administration wants to subsidize a war against Nicaragua, let it go to Congress and say so. Otherwise, its actions are as cowardly as they are unconstitutional. By encouraging a surrogate war fueled by private funds, we create a dangerous new form of warfare. And by going to so much trouble to prevent Congress from exercising its constitutional control, the White House may soon find itself in a deadly situation over which it loses its control of its own surrogates.

Faced with those public consequences of private irresponsibility, Congress must reassert itself while it still has the opportunity.

The Chattanooga Times

Chattanooga, TN, August 13, 1985

When President Reagan signed a bill last week which included $27 million in non-lethal aid to the rebels fighting the Sandinista government of Nicaragua, he again referred to the so-called contras as "freedom fighters." He made no mention of the abduction, by a band of contra rebels, of 29 U.S. civilians and more than two dozen journalists.

The abduction took place after Eden Pastora Gomez, leader of the Revolutionary Democratic Alliance (ARDE), threatened the American peace activists. The group's abductors at one point identified themselves as belonging to Pastora's Costa Rica-based rebel army, but ARDE denied any connection to the abduction. The kidnappers then changed their story, saying they were members of an independent anti-communist group fighting the Sandinistas from Costa Rica.

Thankfully, the kidnapping was short-lived and without violence. It was, nevertheless, an outrage, hinting that these rebels took the administration's bellicosity toward the Sandinistas to mean the United States wouldn't care if U.S. citizens who opposed Reagan policy were taken captive. Surely we have not sunk to that. The kidnap victims do strongly oppose U.S. support of the contras, as is their right. They are church activists in the Witness for Peace program which seeks to deter rebel attacks in the Nicaraguan countryside by maintaining a consistent presence of U.S. citizens there. In this case at least the deterrent didn't work. The Americans themselves became the target of rebels supported by their own government and financed at least in part by private donations from their fellow U.S. citizens.

But the kidnapping was not the only incident last week which should cause members of Congress to have second thoughts about going along with the administration on Nicaragua. There was also the revelation, later confirmed by President Reagan, that while there was supposed to have been a congressionally-imposed suspension of direct U.S. aid to the contras, the White House was directly overseeing the guerrilla war through the staff of the president's National Security Council.

So the bill-signing last week did not signal the resumption of direct U.S. aid to the contras so much as it signaled Mr. Reagan's victory in bringing Congress back in line with his Nicaraguan policy. When the National Security Council connection was revealed by *The New York Times* the administration stoutly maintained no laws had been broken. If that is true, it is only in a strict legalistic sense. The White House circumvented the will of Congress. But it's really no surprise. The Reagan administration's conduct of its once-secret war against Nicaragua has been marked from the beginning by subterfuge and obfuscation. When will Congress ever learn?

The Des Moines Register

Des Moines, IA, August 26, 1985

Meet the war in Nicaragua.

A retired U.S. Army general is advising it on site. He wants to bring on more old Somoza guardsmen, but runs up against some nervousness on the part of rebel leaders, who know that too many guardsmen mean a low opinion of the rebels both at home and abroad.

The general not only advises, but helps raise money, a role he took on when Congress cut off funds for the "covert war."

The money comes from all over: from Nicaraguans in exile who lost property when the Sandinistas took over; from a 90-ish woman in Texas who wants to save the free world. In the past year, they've raised from $15 million to $25 million.

The military advice comes from all over, too: Germans, French, retired military officers, people on "leaves of absence" from their governments.

Directing it all is an administration official working out of the White House. He says he is proud of how well the troops are functioning on their own, without the Central Intelligence Agency, which used to run the show.

"When the agency was pulled out of the program, these guys didn't know how to buy a Band-Aid," he says. "They knew nothing of logistics; the CIA had been doing all of that. Since then, they have learned to raise money, recruit and defend their cause in a coherent way. They know how to go on on the legal international arms market and buy boots, guns, everything."

Now that the rebels are so self-sufficient, the new influx of "non-military" aid from Congress will be a nice supplement. The rebels can go on buying their $2,000 M-72 antitank weapons and their $2,800 machine guns with private money, and buy other supplies on Congress.

●

This is not the war that Ronald Reagan describes — not the picture he paints — when he speaks of our brothers, the freedom fighters. This is not the U.S. policy that Congress intended when it cut off aid, and it is not going to become the policy Congress intended when it resumed "humanitarian" assistance.

This private, surreptitious, undercover war, smelling less of liberation than of old accounts being settled, is not a war that a respectable country would want to claim.

But this is the war that Nicaraguans are getting.

Nicaragua Declares State of Emergency

Nicaragua, citing "brutal aggression by North America and its internal allies," imposed October 15, 1985 a yearlong state of emergency under which civil rights were suspended. The measures were contained in a decree read over national radio and television by Nicaraguan President Daniel Ortega Saavedra. The decree suspended the right of free expression and public assembly, allowed the interception of mail and telecommunications, and permitted searches of homes and offices without prior authorization by civil authorities. The decree also withdrew the right to strike and gave the government sweeping powers of arrest and detention. Under the decree, censorship was strengthened with the requirement that material to be broadcast or published first be submitted to the interior ministry. Previously, material for publication by the main opposition newspaper, *La Prensa*, had to be submitted to censors only if it dealt with military affairs or Nicaragua's economic problems.

The Washington Times
Washington, DC, October 17, 1985

The Sandinistas suspending civil rights is a bit like Ethiopia cutting back on food production. You're talking about a place where the one remaining independent newspaper is under steady censorship; where block committees of the revolutionary faithful report to the comandantes on the manners and mores of those under their eye; where priests who don't go along with the state-sponsored "popular church" are humiliated in public. This list does not begin to tap the stories coming from Nicaraguan refugees.

Now, things are going to be different: no more of what was left of press independence, free expression, free association, or mail privacy. There was a similar "state of emergency" from March of 1982, lasting until shortly before last year's national elections. Now that that little ritual is out of the way, the comandantes can carry on.

Once again the pretext is the resistance movement; yet Daniel Ortega, interrupting television transmissions to announce the new order, specifically lashed out at "certain political parties, the press, and religious institutions." He did not announce the next certain date of the American invasion, but, if he's true to form, he will soon.

It is a fair guess that this state of emergency will be lifted the next time the Sandinistas can be pressured into holding an election, or when the resistance marches into Managua. Hope, but don't hold dinner for either eventuality.

The Wichita
Eagle-Beacon
Wichita, KS, October 20, 1985

SANDINISTA rhetoric is getting stale. "To support the terrorist policy of the American leaders," said President Daniel Ortega, "allies and agents of imperialism who act from some political parties, press outlets or religious insitutions are stepping up their actions to sabotage national defense efforts, hinder our economic policies and provoke discontent and confusion in the popular bases."

The speech was occasioned by the Sandinistas' suspension of civil liberties in Nicaragua. "They made us do it," is the Sandinistas' now-familiar refrain. The tune is becoming tiresome.

The Sandinistas' paranoia about outside agitators now is being extended to their own people. To save the revolution, they have suspended fundamental democratic rights of free speech, assembly, strike, religous freedom, and habeas corpus. How can ordinary Nicaraguans come out of this as winners?

Sandinista rulers have constructed a fantasy world where their actions have no consequences. Mr. Ortega blames the state of emergency on (among other things) Congress' vote to send renewed aid to the contras. Mr. Ortega won't admit that Congress had voted against contra aid until his disastrous mission to Moscow, during which he genuflected, sloganeered, and generally gave the impression of being the Soviet puppet he claimed not to be.

Commander Lenin Cerna (let us guess — a Bolshevik?), the director of state security, reports that the Sandinistas foiled a plot by a "terrorist cell" just two days after the emergency crackdown. Without a free press, though, who can say whether the Sandinistas are battling real enemies or their own paranoia? The Sandinistas like to play revolutionaries, to dress up in uniforms and spout Marxist jargon. They should decide whether such play-acting is in the best interests of Nicaraguans.

Mr. Ortega has been issued an unrestricted visa to travel in the United States and take his case directly to the "enemy." But he has forbidden honest debate within his own country. The Nicaraguan opposition has been critical lately of the harsh military draft, poor economic performance and other legitimate problems. Instead of stopping up his ears, maybe Mr. Ortega should start listening to his critics. They may have something to say.

THE DENVER POST
Denver, CO, October 21, 1985

NICARAGUA'S ruling Sandinista junta has finished plunging its country into a Soviet-style dictatorship worse than any imposed by the late Anastasio Somoza. The new Somoza, Daniel Ortega, has revoked the rights of free expression, public assembly, strikes and the privacy of postal communications.

The junta also tightened its grip on Nicaragua's news media, requiring journalists to submit all material to government censors prior to publication or broadcast. Previously, La Prensa, the main opposition newspaper, had been required to submit to censors only material dealing with military and economic affairs.

Predictably, Ortega lashed out at Nicaragua's journalists, trade unionists and other victims of his decree as "pawns of imperialism" and attempted to blame the United States for his latest outrage. But in fact, the latest wave of repression seems aimed primarily at the Catholic Church, which Ortega rightly believes is the chief remaining independent force in Nicaragua. Ortega may also have been spurred by his eroding international relations. Ecuador last week became the first Latin American government to formally break diplomatic ties with the communist regime.

In the U.S., the Catholic Bishops Conference, which has opposed President Reagan's support for the Nicaraguan contra rebels, wired Ortega protesting "the excessively broad restrictions."

That's pretty mild criticism, especially since Catholics seem to be the special target of Ortega's repression. But at least it's a sign that the repression has not gone unnoticed in this country.

Many other groups in the U.S., such as Witness for Peace, have been offering apologies for Nicaragua. We challenge them to speak out against the renewed police state policy. If the Sandinistas realize their repression is repelling their friends, they may restore some rudimentary freedoms.

On the other hand, if those who have criticized U.S. policy toward Nicaragua don't speak out against the Sandinistas now, Americans can justifiably conclude that Ortega's apologists actually share the new dictator's ruthless goals.

THE ARIZONA REPUBLIC
Phoenix, AZ, October 17, 1985

THE allegedly benign agrarian reformers of the Sandinista junta have at last shown their true colors to the world and Nicaraguans are now seeing red.

The government Tuesday announced what amounts to, virtually, a total suspension of civil rights in Nicaragua.

Using the growing strength of the U.S.-backed *contra* forces as a pretense, the Sandinista politburo suspended the right of public assembly, freedom of expression, freedom to move about the country, freedom to organize labor unions, all guarantees of "individual freedom and personal liberty" and legal protections against police-state tactics.

La Prensa, the courageous independent newspaper that opposed both the old dictatorship of Anastasio Somoza and the leftward drift of the Sandinista revolutionary regime, will now be required to submit to even greater censorship than has been the rule over the past five years. Any pretense to freedom of the press in Nicaragua is now dead.

President Daniel Ortega is, of course, blaming the actions on the United States, claiming they are necessary to combat the *contras*. Ortega apparently has not asked himself why thousands of his fellow countrymen have joined the democratic opposition forces.

Marxist regimes always have used the presence of democratic opposition and the hobgoblin of foreign imperialism as an excuse for imposing totalitarian rule, an argument the Soviet Union employs daily to justify its genocide in Afghanistan.

Tuesday's actions only complete the drift that has been evident in the Sandinista regime since a popular uprising threw dictator Somoza out in 1979. The Marxist faction of the old anti-Somoza coalition has now completed its capture of the broad-based revolution. Lest there be any doubt, consider the character of the top Sandinista leadership:

■ President Ortega, most popular among the left wing jet-set in the United States and Europe, is a dedicated Marxist-Leninist committed to a "revolution without borders."

■ Ernesto Cardenal, a suspended Roman Catholic priest and minister of culture, lauds Cuba as an example of a Christianized, classless society. He said in his four-volume work, *The Gospel in Solentiname*, that "not only can a Christian be a Marxist, but that in order for him to be authentically Christian, he must be a Marxist."

■ Tomas Borge, minister of interior and powerful head of S-7, the state security force, is responsible for enforcing the suspension of civil rights. Borge is a hardcore communist who, like Cardenal, received his revolutionary training in Cuba.

At Borge's insistence, Nicaragua has become a haven for terrorist groups, including the Palestine Liberation Organization, Italy's Red Brigades, Germany's notorious Baader-Meinhoff gang and Colombia's April 19 Movement. He has repeatedly and publicly called for a regional Marxist revolution in Central America.

■ Humberto Ortega, the president's older brother, is minister of defense. He has called the Soviet Union's Red Army "a vital pillar in the fight for world peace." Controlling the largest and best-equipped army in Central America, he is perhaps the most powerful man in the Sandinista junta. According to a former associate, he is a Marxist of the Stalinist variety.

■ Miguel d'Escoto is Nicaragua's foreign minister. As a Maryknoll priest and the son of a wealthy friend of Somoza he was an opponent of Salvador Allende, the Marxist president of Chile. In 1975 he was conveniently converted to Marxism and joined the Sandinista revolution. Today he lives like a millionaire on a palatial estate in Managua.

With credentials like these, it should not be surprising that the Sandinistas have tightened their totalitarian grip on Nicaragua.

Minneapolis Star and Tribune
Minneapolis, MN, October 18, 1985

Minnesotans concerned about Central America felt a diplomatic tremor this week when a shock wave named Alvaro Baldizon came to the Twin Cities. A former chief investigator in Nicaragua, Baldizon accuses the Sandinista government of oppression on many counts. Some are familiar. We have alluded in these columns to such abuses as intimidation, harassment and needless censorship. This week's abrogation of civil rights carried such oppression further. But from the start, a redeeming quality of the Sandinista revolution was the evidence that it refrained from the most brutal abuses: the political murders that have long been a prominent, ugly part of the Central American scene. The Baldizon shock comes in his claim that such evidence is wrong; that Sandinista-sanctioned assassination is commonplace.

If Baldizon's assertions are true, they demand that U.S. defenders of the Sandinistas rethink their positions. As Ned Crosby and Julie Heegaard point out in an article on the next page, credible charges of human-rights abuse need to be taken seriously even if they run counter to cherished assumptions; to do otherwise would be to apply a double standard.

We recognize the possibility that someone may make a compelling case that Baldizon is a liar. It often happens that what appears to be fact in Central America proves to be myth. But Baldizon's charges cannot be readily dismissed; nothing in his manner or experience discounts his credibility. He is intense, and he is explicit. The people killed, he says, were "soldiers, peasants, anyone who opposed" the regime. His job, until he slipped out of Nicaragua last summer, was to investigate allegations of abuse. He says he found plenty. He recounts them in detail. He says the government buried the findings and deluded friendly foreign observers. He tells of assassination orders by Interior Minister Tomas Borge.

But this picture of bloody abuse does not justify a U.S. policy of support for the anti-Sandinista contras, whose record of terrorism is clear. One of their leaders spoke recently of the need to clean up the contras' act: specifically, to stop killing prisoners. The United States has no business championing "freedom fighters" whose actions belie that title. And Americans who praise the Sandinista revolution should mute their applause while pondering the new evidence offered by Baldizon.

WORCESTER TELEGRAM.
Worcester, MA, October 19, 1985

No doubt the communist regime of Nicaraguan President Daniel Ortega is feeling pressure from the U.S.-backed Contras, but they are not the only reason he decided to suspend civil rights in the Central American nation.

Communist nations and emerging totalitarian states are perfectly willing to put on a show of individual freedoms until the peasants are "educated" enough to realize the state knows better. That showcase of token freedoms is fine, until honest dissent comes along. Then, rights must be sacrificed for the good of the state, and not incidentally for the continued political careers of the rulers.

Ortega's pressures are not all external. They continue, incredibly even under his harsh regime, to be internal. One person he hopes to silence is the popular archbishop of Managua, Cardinal Miguel Obando y Bravo. There is a charismatic leader to strike fear into the heart of any Marxist. The Sandinistas hope the ban on public assembly will cut the archbishop off from his audience. Free expression is dangerous.

La Prensa, the only opposition newspaper, continues to publish despite the crippling censorship and economic sanctions under which it operates. The new measures will be even stricter. Divergence of opinion from the state's cannot be tolerated under totalitarian governments of any persuasion. Communism hands even raw information over to the state to be managed. Individual thought is unhealthy.

As much as any success the Contras have had against economic targets, Ortega cannot abide the persistence of the Nicaraguan middle class. It only makes it worse that these independent entrepreneurs are the only ones who can deliver the goods to the people. Central economic planning, communist style, is a failure in Nicaragua as elsewhere.

The only thing that keeps Daniel Ortega and his pals in power is the war hysteria they continue to orchestrate against the Contras and the United States. Removal of civil rights satisfies two goals: It fans that hysteria, and it pushes Nicaragua one step further down the road to Marxist totalitarianism.

The Philadelphia Inquirer

Philadelphia, PA, October 30, 1985

Nicaragua's Sandinista regime "suspended" civil liberties Oct. 15. President Daniel Ortega decreed that henceforth Nicaraguans no longer possess a right to speak freely, to travel freely, to assemble peaceably, to strike. The regime now asserts the official right to detain people indefinitely without cause, to disband labor unions, to inspect mail. State censorship of news was tightened, state control over the Roman Catholic Church and other once-independent institutions was increased.

Since a state of emergency was imposed in March 1982, Nicaraguan civil liberties have been progressively restrained. The latest decree only intensifies and formalizes the regime's assertion of right to control every aspect of Nicaraguan life. To be sure, the Sandinistas offer reasons. They are, after all, under attack by thousands of U.S.-backed guerrillas. Ending civil liberties is necessary, President Ortega says, to prevent internal enemies from assisting the guerrillas.

Presumably that's why Sandinista security forces seized nearly all copies of the first edition of a new Catholic newspaper, Iglesia, on Oct. 12. They seized the press and printing equipment too. Necessity must be the reason security agents have arrested more than 100 people since the Oct. 15 decree and charged them with plotting against the regime. Surely that's why Interior Minister Tomas Borge summoned Cardinal Miguel Obando y Bravo, the archbishop of Managua, to warn him that henceforth he had better obtain official permission before speaking to crowds. How else to defend the regime, which of course is always every citizen's paramount goal?

Regimes always have reasons for oppression, after all. Gen. Wojciech Jaruzelski surely had his reasons for imposing martial law in Poland, Ferdinand Marcos must have had his for destroying democracy in the Philippines, Stalin and Hitler and Anastasio Somoza — all doubtless had their reasons for crushing law and liberty and human lives in order to extend the raw power of their states. Tyrants always can justify tyranny.

Tyranny it is that the Sandinistas impose upon the long-suffering people of Nicaragua — make no mistake about it. Even so, the U.S.-backed guerrilla war against that tiny impoverished nation remains unjustifiable. If the presence of tyranny justified such aggression, then America long ago should have invaded Nicaragua's neighbors, such as El Salvador and Guatemala, where civil liberties are enjoyed exclusively by those in power, and those who dare dissent risk death.

Freedom of the press? Since 1979, according to the Washington-based Council on Hemispheric Affairs and the Newspaper Guild, 31 Salvadoran journalists have been killed primarily by right-wing death squads — a censorship method considerably harsher than the Sandinistas'. Tyranny? For years the generals of Guatemala have slaughtered whole villages of peasants on suspicion of leftist sympathies.

America's rightists are blind to oppression by Latin fascists. America's leftists will not see that the Sandinistas employ different methods no less oppressive to ensure, above all, that they alone will control power. Whether the boot on one's neck holds the right foot or left makes little difference to the victim. Pity the Nicaraguans, the Salvadorans, the Guatemalans — victims all.

The Knickerbocker News

Albany, NY, October 22, 1985

By government decree, Nicaragua's Sandinista army can detain people on the spot, open private mail, ban political rallies, smash labor unions and shut down the press. That's the army of the leftist Sandinistas, mind you, not some right-wing banana dictator.

Nicaragua's President Ortega seeks to blame the United States for his nation's state of siege. The "brutal aggression by North America and its allies" left him no choice but to suspend basic liberties, he claimed last week.

That claim rings hollow. By "brutal aggression," Mr. Ortega no doubt means American aid to Nicaragua's contra rebels and neighboring Honduras. But that aid has held steady for some time. Why the sudden crackdown on human rights, if not to solidify a Sandinista dictatorship?

Moreover, American aid to the Contras might have been shut off by now if Mr. Ortega hadn't shown the same ill sense of timing earlier this year, when Congress at first denied Mr. Reagan's request for additional assistance. But no sooner had the vote been recorded than Mr. Ortega was off to Moscow to discuss military matters. That left an embarrassed Congress in no mood for indulgence; it reversed itself and voted for continued assistance to the contras.

Now Mr. Ortega is once again slapping at those who are trying their best to accommodate him. The latest decree renders empty the peace initiatives by the Contradora nations of Panama, Colombia, Mexico and Venezuela. Before the crackdown, some Contradora leaders had openly disputed the Reagan administration policies toward Managua. Now they must be having second thoughts.

More and more, it appears the Sandinistas coveted power all along, but tolerated a token amount of opposition at home so as to divide American opinion and cool any urge by Mr. Reagan to launch a Grenada-style invasion.

In an awkward attempt to repair his image, Mr. Ortega is now suggesting the crackdown is more precautionary than real. During a visit to New York City this weekend, he told reporters that Nicaraguans are still free to move about as they wish, at all hours. For now, perhaps. But so long as the decree remains in effect, the Sandinistas can trample dissent at a moment's notice.

New York's Senator Moynihan was right all along in labeling the Sandinistas as Leninists from start to finish. The proof is in the repression.

DESERET NEWS

Salt Lake City, UT, October 21-22, 1985

The Sandinista government of Nicaragua showed its Marxist face last week when it abolished most remaining civil liberties, tightened censorship, put more restrictions on labor unions, and seized printing presses of the Roman Catholic Church.

Apologists for Nicaragua have criticized the U.S. for its hostility to the regime, arguing that the Sandinistas are essentially peaceful, that peoples' rights are protected, and that dissent is tolerated, that private property and religion are protected, and that the lives of people are greatly improved.

Anti-Sandinista guerrillas backed by the U.S. are painted as armed remnants of the Somoza dictatorship overthrown by the Sandinistas in 1979, or at best, not much more than mercenaries.

But the Sandinistas are Marxists and have admitted it publicly. The fact that they did not immediately impose a totalitarian state on Nicaragua may have had more to do with gaining support and consolidating power after the revolution than any respect for freedom.

In their action this week, the Sandinistas suspended freedom of expression and guarantees of individual freedom and personal liberty. Searches, arrests and detentions without warrants are allowed. The right to a speedy trial and the right of appeal were cancelled. The right to meet publicly and to travel were revoked. Last week, an opposition politician protesting government policy was arrested.

Nicaragan president Daniel Ortega said the suspension of civil rights was necessary because of U.S. hostility and "agents of imperialism" operating within certain political parties, the press, and religious institutions. That's a handy excuse to seize control of those groups that are normally the bastions of democracy.

It's an old, sad story in Latin America. A country that overthrows one dictatorship soon finds itself in the grip of another — the newest one run by the former liberators.

THE SAGINAW NEWS
Saginaw, MI, October 31, 1985

By now the roster of repressions is familiar. No right to assemble. No right to strike. No freedom of expression. No right to move freely about the country, or even to send mail with privacy.

Should there be violations, there is no right to a speedy trial, or to an appeal, or protection against indefinite detention without charges.

Surely such a regime deserves worldwide condemnation.

Yet, what a deafening silence from the activist corners.

For, as of this month, all of the above describes Nicaragua after the total suspension of civil liberties.

How do the Sandinistas explain it? In the drearily usual Marxist cliche, President Daniel Ortega described these as "correct" steps. His decree cited "an extraordinary situation" created by North America and, pointedly, "its internal allies."

Who might those be? Not the Contras, who would hardly worry about a right to strike in Managua. And the Sandinistas claimed a broad popular mandate after elections less than a year ago.

But the targets indeed are key elements of society: Labor unions, the Catholic Church, private business, what's left of the opposition press. As of the moment, Nicaragua, election or not, is a totalitarian nation, like its buddy, the Soviet Union, which has been playing paranoid for decades.

Once again, Ortega's timing is odd. Just after Congress accepted his arguments against aid to the Contras, he took off for an intimate meeting in Moscow. This crackdown came just before Ortega headed for the United Nations to denounce the United States as the cause of all his troubles.

His mirror knows better, even if some of his American friends do not. As Ortega does the talk-show tour, no doubt a certain number will support his contention that a new U.S. policy is all that's needed to restore liberties. But the message to Nicaraguans is clear enough: Their "rights" are held hostage to the whims of the regime, and this regime will not tolerate dissent.

Nicaragua can behave internally as it chooses. Others, though, risk all credibility if they continue to picture this regime as some sort of a model for "justice." Should the Sandinistas manage to export their idea of democratic rule, there will not be enough churches or campuses in all the U.S. to provide sanctuary to the victims.

No doubt most Nicaraguans remain loyal to the original revolution that promised progress and liberty. The various Contra forces are something of a mixed bag. But there is also no doubt what the Sandinistas' bag is. Their version of revolution equates with repression. And where have we seen that before?

Houston Chronicle
Houston, TX, October 22, 1985

While the focus has been elsewhere, has something important and relatively unremarked been going on in Central America?

Specifically, are the Marxists in trouble? Both the Marxist government in Nicaragua and the Marxist rebels in El Salvador?

There is reason to suspect that this may be the case. It is almost surely so in El Salvador. Despite continuing upheaval, it seems a nearly universal opinion that President Jose Napoleon Duarte's government has for some time now been gradually winning its struggle.

And Nicaragua? The tone of the reports out of Nicaragua began to change a few months ago. From the entrenched, unshakable Sandinistas they were, they began to be an increasingly embattled bunch with large internal unrest on their hands — serious unrest. On top of that came the resumption of U.S. aid to the contras and the disenchantment of Western governments which had been friendly.

Now comes the Sandinista suspension of what little civil liberties are supposed to have remained. President Daniel Ortega is at the United Nations in New York telling anyone who will listen that the crackdown is because the Sandinistas are winning their fight against the contras. It takes a large leap of faith to believe that when his own officials in Managua are saying it is because of the problems they are having with the opposition, both contra and noncontra.

The signs are that something may be going on in Central America that is all to the good. If that is the case, this is the time to keep the pressure on. Both in Nicaragua and in El Salvador.

U.S. Congress Approves Aid for Nicaraguan Contras

In a major foreign policy victory for President Ronald Reagan, the United States House of Representatives June 25, 1986 voted 221-209 to approve his request for $100 million in aid for the contras fighting to overthrow the Nicaraguan government. Passage of the measure marked the first time that the House had granted overt military aid to the contras. In the last vote on the issue, in March, it rejected Reagan's request. Considerable maneuvering had gone on since then to bring the issue back to the House floor, but in a modified form. Success of the measure was attributed in large part to President Reagan's personal lobbying, which garnered as many as 10 converts in the days preceding the vote.

The U.S. Senate August 13, 1986 voted 52-47 to approve his request for $100 million in aid to Nicaraguan contras. A further $300 million in economic aid would be given to four of Nicaragua's neighbors: Costa Rica, El Salvador, Guatemala and Honduras. Republicans blocked day-long efforts by Democrats to amend the contra aid package. After debate ended 11 Democrats joined 42 Republicans in voting in favor of the aid. After the vote, the military construction bill to which the contra aid amendment was attached was passed 59-41. The entire bill still had to go to a House-Senate conference.

Senators had agreed to link the contra aid with another contentious issue, proposed sanctions on South Africa, in an effort to break a deadlock on the handling of the two issues. A delay on the final action on one would delay final action on the other. The Senate took separate votes Aug. 13 to end debate on contra aid and South Africa sanctions. In an initial vote on ending the debate on contra aid—which would have averted a filibuster threatened by a group of Democrats—supporters gained only 59 of the 60 votes required for cloture.

Detroit Free Press

Detroit, MI, June 27, 1986

THE VOTE IN the U.S. House of Representatives on Wednesday to give $100 million to the contra rebels trying to overthrow the Nicaraguan government sets a dangerous precedent. Assuming Senate concurrence, Congress will have approved overt military aid to forces trying to overthrow a sovereign government with which the United States has diplomatic relations.

Last year, the United States sent $27 million in so-called humanitarian aid to the contras. In March of this year, the House defeated President Reagan's request to give the contras $100 million in aid. Earlier this month, the federal General Accounting Office reported that much of the $27 million in U.S. aid to the contras last year cannot be accounted for — and that much of what can be accounted for has been traced to mysterious bank accounts in Miami and the Bahamas.

Mr. Reagan's backers dismiss the report of the GAO — a non-partisan government accounting agency — as "biased." And the House approves a $100-million package for the contras, $70 million of which is for military use. With its 221-209 vote, the House finally gave in to Mr. Reagan's obsessive campaign to fund a band of mercenaries, which this country cannot control, which includes many anti-democratic and corrupt elements, and which has been generally ineffective.

Supporters of the contra aid package argued that it will force the Sandinistas to the bargaining table. But what the aid will do, in fact, is exactly the opposite: It will continue to give the Sandinistas a pretext — and not an unjustified one — to stay away from negotiations. There already exists a sound and reasonable peace plan for the region, which is endorsed by a majority of the countries in Latin America. That plan is the Contadora treaty, and it would ban all foreign intervention there — the Sandinistas' Cuban advisers as well as the Americans' contras. A huge increase in U.S. aid to the contras simply gives the lie to the Reagan administration's sanction of the Contadora process.

The contras badly need an infusion of money because they have been unable to garner enough support from the Nicaraguan people. Their numbers have dropped significantly from the peak of 15,000 two years ago; their leadership has been shuffled repeatedly in an attempt to lend the appearance of legitimacy to a reactionary core still dominated by former officers of the deposed dictator Anastasio Somoza; Eden Pastora, who commanded respect as one who had fought with the Sandinistas against Somoza, has left the contras' ranks because of their bad company.

When will Congress confront the inherent weaknesses of our present contra policy? Probably not soon. Members of Congress are easily intimidated by the fear that they may be called soft on communism. Thus, they continue to support a policy that does not promise success or bring credit to the United States.

THE SUN

Baltimore, MD, June 27, 1986

President Reagan now has the Nicaragua policy of his choice, having orchestrated a turnabout in the House to provide direct military aid to "contra" forces battling the Sandinista regime. His victory denies the administration the option to blame future problems on its political critics. While Rep. Michael Barnes (D, Md.) overstates when he says "Now, it is [Mr. Reagan's] war," there is no question that it is Mr. Reagan's operation.

To secure House approval of overt assistance to the contras, the president accepted proposals put forward by swing-vote legislators seeking an end to the congressional stalemate that has compromised the United States position in Central America. The $100 million in contra aid will be treble-matched with a $300 million support program for the region's fragile democracies — El Salvador, Costa Rica, Honduras and Guatemala. And a bipartisan commission which is to monitor the whole situation will have to validate later installments of weaponry.

In a national address the day before the showdown House vote, President Reagan made a pledge that should not be overlooked:

"As a condition of our aid, I will insist on civilian control over all military forces; that no human rights abuses be tolerated; that any financial corruption be rooted out; that American aid go only to those committed to democratic principles. The United States will not permit this democratic revolution to be betrayed nor allow a return to the hated repression of the Somoza dictatorship."

Even as he spoke, civilian control of the military remained shaky, Amnesty International had published evidence of human rights abuses by contra forces and Mr. Barnes was complaining about the diversion of covert U.S. aid to private bank accounts by contra officials. Obviously, a lot of cleaning up is in order now that the United States is poised to give overt backing to the anti-Sandinista rebels. It is, indeed, Mr. Reagan's operation.

While we would have preferred the tighter congressional reins on contra aid implicit in a compromise proposal that never came to a vote, we find the president's pledge reassuring. If it holds up, the nation will be much better served than if liberal Democrats had prevailed by denying any aid whatsoever to the forces opposing the Soviet-backed, Cuba-cloned junta in Managua.

Communism cannot be checkmated in Central America by pretending Nicaragua's leaders would liberalize if only U.S. pressure were turned off. On the contrary, their oversized army could be counted upon to harass and intimidate weaker neighbors. Nor is the solution a U.S. armed intervention that could bring a Johnsonian denouement to the Reagan presidency. The Sandinistas must be contained in part by contra forces and in part by U.S.-backed democracies until a peaceful, pluralistic government emerges in Nicaragua.

LEXINGTON HERALD-LEADER

Lexington, KY, June 27, 1986

The Great Communicator has done it again. His latest achievement is persuading the House of Representatives to approve $100 million in aid to the contra guerrillas fighting to overthrow the government of Nicaragua.

It is Ronald Reagan's greatest strength that he can make people overlook niggling details. In this case, that strength may be the nation's weakness.

In voting to send the money to the contras, a majority of House members chose to overlook a number of inconvenient details. Among them: After five years of fighting, the contras have yet to make any major inroads in terms of popular support. On the other hand, they have established a solid record of atrocities against civilians. Their leaders appear to have siphoned off a considerable amount of American aid for their own purposes.

Against this demonstrated record of ineptitude, brutality and theft, members chose to accept the president's word that such things would not happen again. But what reason is there to believe this? Can anyone really believe

that the United States can control the actions of its surrogates in their remote bases in Honduras and Costa Rica or on the mountainous battlefields of Nicaragua?

No matter, apparently. The president's persuasiveness carried the day in the House. Now the Senate, which has previously approved a similar aid request, is the only thing that stands between the United States and a misguided policy of escalating militarism in Central America.

Where that policy may ultimately lead no one can say. It is intended, its proponents say, to counter Soviet influence in Nicaragua. Now Nicaragua faces the prospect of facing a much better-financed foe in a bloody civil war. If past form holds, Daniel Ortega and other Nicaraguan leaders are now on the phone to Moscow, begging for more and better arms.

Instead of lessened Soviet influence in Nicaragua, sending aid to the contras seems likely to achieve the opposite. But what's a minor detail such as that compared to the reassuring salesmanship of the Great Communicator?

The Sunday Record

Hackensack, NJ, June 27, 1986

Tegulcigalpa, Honduras, Oct. 14, 1988 — A mixed force of U.S. and Honduran troops swept across the Nicaraguan border today to deliver what American military authorities hope will be a quick death blow to the Sandinista regime in Managua.

The invading force encountered only light resistance in Nicaragua's thinly populated, heavily forested north, although Sandinista troop were reported to massing in the provincial city of Esteli to the south.

In Washington, meanwhile, Republicans were jubilant over the long-awaited invasion. Democrats were upset that President Reagan had scheduled the attack just three weeks before the presidential election. "Frankly, we don't know how to respond," moaned a high-ranking strategist for Democratic presidential candidate Mario Cuomo. "We favor negotiations, but no one feels comfortable criticizing the president now that the country is at war. The smartest thing, we figure, is to concentrate on other issues."

A few years ago, such a scenario would have seemed well-nigh impossible, but after Wednesday's 221-209 vote in the House of Representatives in support of $100 million in aid for the Nicaraguan contras, it seems more and more likely. The reason: the House vote will escalate the level of fighting and widen the circle of suffering and corruption throughout Central America, but it will not topple the Sandinistas from office. The Nicaraguan army is a far more formidable force than it was two or three years ago when U.S.-armed guerrillas ranged nearly at will across large portions of the countryside, and it is not easily dislodged.

These days, in fact, the army is well-armed,

well-trained, and — most important — well-motivated. Despite initial resistance, the draft is now accepted throughout the population. Mothers visit their sons at forward bases, and once their two-year tour is completed, the conscripts are welcomed home as heroes. The government crack anti-guerrilla battalions, which are lightly armed and highly mobile have proved particularly successful.

As the Sandinistas' fortunes have risen, so have the contras' fortunes fallen. In their Honduran border bases, the contra top brass seems to have nothing better to do than smuggle drugs and siphon U.S. aid into offshore bank accounts. Morale has dropped as more and more rank-and-file contras wake up to the scam that their officers are pulling. In Washington, meanwhile, contra representatives have appealed repeatedly for anti-tank and anti-aircraft weapons and even heavy artillery, even though the last thing a fast-moving guerrilla needs is a big bulky piece of equipment to weigh him down. Yet the Reagan administration has endorsed the request, and now Congress has shown its willingness to satisfy it.

The likelihood is that the Sandinistas will keep on getting stronger, while the contras grow weaker and more corrupt. It's hard to imagine, however, that President Reagan will face up to that hard reality.

Sometime in 1987 or 1988, therefore, we could all wake up to screaming headlines about U.S. troop movements, bombing runs, and cross-border raids as President Reagan sets out to do directly what he could not do with ill-trained contras. If so, Wednesday's House vote will have turned out to have been a kind of Eighties replay of the 1964 Gulf of Tonkin Resolution, in which Congress gave Lyndon Johnson the green light for the Vietnam War. But instead of a war in Southeast Asia, it will mean a land war much closer to home — in Central America.

The Washington Post

Washington, DC, June 27, 1986

BY TRAVELING a very small political distance on Nicaragua, President Reagan has traveled a very long policy distance. He needed only a few additional votes in the House for military aid to the Nicaraguan resistance. Unfortunately, he got them. With this result he moves from a condition of sinking stalemate to a situation with a whole new and riskier range of possible gains and losses: from a wasting or at best a holding operation to an attack.

Politically, Mr. Reagan had drawn a line in the dust and had been moving a reluctant Democratic-controlled House toward it. Now he has pulled the House across the line: 51 Democrats supported his position against the passionate counsel of their leadership. For the president the arms vote is a political feat, which he celebrates as a triumph of bipartisanship. For the Democrats the vote is a party-fracturing event whose implications will hover over its search for a post-Vietnam identity and its quest for a 1988 presidential nominee.

In foreign policy terms, the United States is now in a strange position. It is newly committed to a war against a government with which it is not formally at war and with which it observes diplomatic relations. It is doing so, moreover, not only with congressional consent but in the noonday sun. No longer is there the slightest bow, as there was when the United States funded the contras early in the first Reagan term, to the discretion once associated with CIA operations.

It may be argued that American support of the contras will be the more potent and constant for having been suspended and then renewed in an intense multiyear debate. But there is a problem here: the president and Congress, the Republicans and the 51 Democrats, are agreed on arms aid but not on its purpose. For Mr. Reagan the purpose presumably follows from his pledge to enable the contras "not just to fight and die for freedom but to fight and win freedom." Others who support contra aid, however, do so without expectation of victory but simply to raise the Kremlin's costs of empire, and still others do so to build a position of strength from which to negotiate more effectively.

The excitement of the turnabout may conceal these fissures for a time. But they are likely to emerge later, especially if things do not go well in the field. Mr. Reagan may then have to face the familiar and fateful dilemma of whether to raise the ante, this time perhaps with a direct commitment of American forces, or to cut his losses. Optimists see the Sandinistas buckling. Realists should start thinking about the choices that the president, plainly, has not been thinking about.

AKRON BEACON JOURNAL

Akron, OH, June 27, 1986

THE U.S. HOUSE is now on record as supporting the overthrow of a government with which we are not at war. The House voted Wednesday to provide $100 million in military and other aid to guerrillas fighting against the Sandinista government in Nicaragua.

Little sympathy is due the Sandinistas. They are just one more corrupt and oppressive regime in one more impoverished Latin American nation. They are also communist-led and that's what makes them a different case, at least as far as American foreign policy is concerned.

President Reagan has an irrational fear and hatred of the Sandinistas, even though it is a petty, bumbling regime that can barely keep its buses running, much less launch an assault on the United States. But Mr. Reagan is a powerful persuader so the United States has drifted into a policy that can only make matters worse in Central America.

The anti-Sandinista rebels, the Contras, cannot win against the Sandinistas. That is the estimate of U.S. intelligence. What the Contras can do, and are doing, is make raids into Nicaragua and create mischief. And with every international news report that the Contras have ambushed another wedding party or destroyed another school or clinic, the prestige of the United States sinks lower; and the justification grows for the Sandinistas to apply more oppression to their own people and to seek more arms from the Soviet bloc.

Maybe nothing will turn the situation around now, but the best hope remains the Contadora peace plan that involves other Latin American nations, and would require the removal of foreign troops from the area, an end to fighting, a respect for human rights, and limits on military power. The Reagan administration has never been enthusiastic about that effort, sending mixed diplomatic signals while escalating the CIA-backed war against the Sandinistas.

A case can be made that the Contadora plan cannot — at this late date — remedy the situation in Central America. But no matter what the options, the Contras are a thin support on which to pile so much American honor and influence. Contra atrocities against Nicaragua have been documented. The Contras and their supporters are also being investigated by Congress for drug-running, gun-running, and violations of the Neutrality Act; the General Accounting Office cannot account for half of the last $27 million in aid Congress sent to the Contras, although much of it went to individuals and corporations in the United States and was never converted into rebel supplies.

It is amazing that Congress could vote more aid without having those charges resolved.

The aid package voted by the House Wednesday was not even the best proposal before the House. The plan approved 221-209 will provide $70 million in military aid and $30 million in non-military aid beginning Sept. 1. No questions asked. A Democrat plan that was voted down would have provided the non-military aid immediately, but would have held up the military aid until after a second vote in October. That would have given the United States some leverage. It would have said to the Sandinistas, negotiate now or face a rearmed rebel force.

The Senate still must vote on the package, in the form of an amendment attached to the military construction appropriations bill. But the Democrat-controlled House was clearly the biggest hurdle to Mr. Reagan's policy. It was also perhaps a death blow for a diplomatic settlement in Nicaragua, and a signal that the war will escalate.

The Pittsburgh PRESS

Pittsburgh, PA, August 15, 1986

President Reagan has hailed the Senate approval of $100 million in new aid to the Nicaraguan Contras as "a truly bipartisan policy on Central America" and "a historic vote in favor of democracy." But neither description appears accurate.

The Senate action, as earlier in the House, demonstrated deep disagreement and uncertainties among the lawmakers over just what the $100 million package is going to accomplish for this country or for Nicaragua.

And the public may be even more divided on Contra aid and skeptical of the outcome than Congress, if the polls are any indication.

If the vote showed anything, it was that most lawmakers don't want to run the risk of being tagged as "soft on communism" in an election year or opposed to a popular president.

Mr. Reagan has painted the Sandinista government in Nicaragua in the most fearsome terms, a Soviet puppet and the spreader of revolution and communism through Central America, while labeling the Contras as "freedom fighters" who need and deserve this country's support. The "democratic" credentials of these guerrillas are fuzzy, however.

The president's extreme rhetoric and continuing pressure on Congress has paid off twice in recent years, with congressional appropriations to keep the Contra movement alive if not noticeably kicking.

The latest package contains $70 million for military hardware and $30 million for non-military items.

Clearly, it is in this country's strategic interest to ensure Nicaragua does not become another Soviet camp on our flank. But, just as clearly, Contra aid will not provide a resolution to the problem, as Mr. Reagan sees it.

But it assuredly will keep the guerrilla war going — and perhaps can exert some pressure on the Sandinistas to move for a diplomatic solution.

The next-step question continues to haunt Mr. Reagan's Nicaraguan policy. Congressional critics believe the latest gesture of support for the Contras inevitably means a greater entanglement, and finally a direct commitment of U.S. troops on their side.

The similarity to Vietnam is repeatedly invoked, although that is highly unlikely given the mood of this country.

But the deeper and longer the involvement, the more difficult it will become for the United States to extract itself from the Nicaragua quagmire.

□ □ □

While the Senate handed Mr. Reagan a victory on Contra aid, the House was dealing him a setback on Star Wars, another of the president's pet projects.

The House, working on a massive Pentagon authorization bill, chose to freeze spending for the space-based, anti-missile defense system at this year's level of $3.1 billion. The administration had sought $5.3 billion.

While the White House expressed anger at the cutback, and raised the old argument about how it would hurt arms negotiations with the Soviets, there still remains a lot of money for developing the Star Wars space-based missile defense system.

If there's any message to be read in the House action, it might be that the Pentagon's money and Star Wars program need to be better managed when the country faces a projected deficit of $230 billion-plus this year.

THE SACRAMENTO BEE

Sacramento, CA, August 15, 1986

Nothing's changed in Nicaragua since 1984, when Congress refused to supply any more military aid to the Contra forces fighting the government there. The ruling Sandinista regime hasn't gotten any more attractive, but neither have the Contras. The impropriety of the United States abetting their civil war, the illegality of American interventionary tactics before Congress pulled the plug, and the risk that a military association with the Contras will draw U.S. troops into a widening war, are of no less concern now than they were then.

The need remains as critical as ever for the United States to participate in the peacemaking negotiations that Nicaragua's Contadora Group neighbors have been trying to foster. But where before the U.S. Congress was attentive to all that, now it's caved in.

Wednesday night, the Senate voted, as the House did in June, to approve $70 million in military aid and $30 million in other aid to the Contras, with no strings attached. Even an amendment that would have required regular reports to Congress on how the money is being spent (an amendment prompted by reams of recent reports on the corruption and misuse of earlier "humanitarian" aid to the Contras) was defeated.

Indeed, the Senate went beyond overt military support; it voted as well to lift its previous ban on CIA involvement in the Nicaraguan war. And it imposed no limit on the

amount of additional, covert money the CIA could spend on the Contras out of its own contingency funds, without any specific congressional authorization. Various sources report that the CIA plan is to use those opportunities to "seize operational control of the war." But if that poses a risk of an escalating U.S. involvement, the Senate ignored it. No one is saying this is a U.S. proxy war, but neither would the Senate pass an amendment prohibiting the dispatch of regular U.S troops to Nicaragua.

As to the regional peace process: A motion to limit U.S. use of Honduras and Costa Rica to further the war effort was defeated. A proposal to force the Reagan administration to talk to the Sandinista government (with which, through all this, it still supposedly maintains diplomatic relations) was defeated, too. Even a last-ditch attempt to at least terminate military aid to the Contras in the event a regional peace settlement is somehow reached without us was defeated. There is thus nothing to require an unwilling administration to engage in diplomacy or negotiation.

The votes were close, but the results are radical. Congress has caved in to an administration policy that is no less a mistake now than it was when Congress had the courage to oppose it.

The Providence Journal

August 15, 1986
Providence, RI

The U.S. Senate last March passed a $100-million aid bill for the Nicaraguan *contras*. After a bruising battle in July, the U.S. House followed suit — but with changes requiring another vote by the Senate, which Wednesday reaffirmed its earlier stand. However, the form of the aid measure now sends it to a House-Senate conference committee, following which it must face final votes in both chambers. At this pace, will the needed aid ever get to the *contras* in time to do any good?

Such delay may suit the purpose of congressional opponents on this very divisive issue, but for them to obstruct further what now is, by majority vote, national policy serves only to subvert the effectiveness of that policy. While Congress has dithered on letting an eager President Reagan carry out a decision both chambers in actuality approved awhile back, the repressive Sandinista government of Nicaragua has encountered no hesitation at all from its aid partners — the Soviet Union and Cuba.

These two communist nations continue to pour military equipment into a country already boasting by far the largest armed force in Central America. Their intent is to solidify a satellite state within the Red orbit, one in strategic position to later force its neighbors into the same sphere. U.S. support for the Nicaraguan *contras* aims to block this Soviet incursion into America's own backyard.

That effort was showing good success — the *contras* at one point controlled up to a third of the countryside — until Congress in 1984 put a halt to U.S. military assistance to them. Now that the Sandinista threat has become clearer, the repressive nature of that government more obvious, the aid program that should have been pressed uninterruptedly is to be reinstituted. But it will be tougher going, what with USSR helicopter gunships among other embellishments to the Sandinista arsenal.

If the *contras*, notwithstanding the nay-saying of Senators Chafee and Pell and other lawmakers from this area, are to have a chance, they've got to be helped promptly. So let's move the aid bill, and the aid, along quickly. Success for the *contras* is a top-priority, U.S.-security interest.

Nicaragua Downs U.S. Plane; Charges CIA Supply Operation

The Nicaraguan government October 7, 1986 charged that the United States Central Intelligence Agency (CIA) was responsible for a contra supply plane shot down over southern Nicaragua Oct. 5. Eugene Hasenfus, a U.S. ex-Marine, survived after parachuting from the plane and was captured Oct. 6. Two other Americans died when the plane was downed. The Reagan Administration and the CIA denied any link to the plane, despite a claim by Hasenfus that the CIA supervised the flight and previous supply operations. CIA aid to the contras was currently restricted to the sharing of intelligence. The restrictions would be removed once the Congress gave the final approval for $100 million in military and economic aid to the contras. Despite repeated denials of any official U.S. involvement with the downed plane or knowledge of who operated it, questions were raised as to whether the administration was revealing all it knew. Coming at a time when the administration was under attack for allegedly misleading the press in a disinformation campaign directed at Libya, the incident prompted new warnings that the administration's credibility was on the line. The downed aircraft was a C-123K cargo plane reportedly carrying Soviet-made ammunition, grenades and rifles intended for anti-Sandinista contras seeking to establish a front in southern Nicaragua. It was shot down some 18 miles north of San Carlos near the Costa Rican border. The two Americans who died were identified as William Cooper of Reno, Nevada and Wallace Blaine Sawyer, Jr. of Magnolia, Arkansas. Both were said to have worked for the CIA many years before.

At a brief news conference at which the surviving American was presented, the Nicaraguan government Oct. 7 gave details of alleged contra air supply operations using U.S., Filipino and other pilots based in El Salvador. On being captured, Hasenfus, 45, of Marinette, Wisconsin, identified himself as a U.S. military adviser serving in El Salvador. Salvadoran air force identity cards describing the three Americans as military advisers for the U.S. were found in the wreckage. Hasenfus told local journalists that the downed plane began its journey in Miami, picked him up in El Salvador and then stopped in Honduras, where a Nicaraguan boarded. It then flew into Nicaragua airspace from Costa Rica. Hasenfus, who served in the U.S. Marines from 1960 to 1965, elaborated on the supply operation at a second news conference Oct. 9. He maintained that the flights were directly supervised by CIA agents in El Salvador and were coordinated by two Cuban-Americans who worked for the CIA. He identified the two as Max Gomez and Ramon Medina. Hasenfus said that, along with Cooper and Sawyer, he worked for Corporate Air Services, which operated out of Ilopango air force base base in El Salvador. He said Corporate Air was part of Southern Air Transport Co., an air cargo company based in Miami owned by the CIA from 1960 to 1975.

A volley of denials of responsibility was issued by U.S. and Salvadoran officials Oct. 7-8. U.S. Secretary of State George Shultz asserted Oct. 7 that the flights were organized by private citizens. The CIA the same day denied that the downed plane had any direct link to the U.S. government.

U.S. Vice President George Bush and a Bush aide, Donald Gregg, Oct. 10 were linked to the supply operation to provide arms to anti-Sandinista contras in Nicaragua. The *San Francisco Examiner* had reported Oct. 10 that Vice President Bush, and not the CIA, was the Washington connection to the contra supply operation. Citing unidentified intelligence sources, the *Examiner* stated that the National Security Council, in particular, was involved. The *Examiner* stated that Max Gomez had been assigned in 1984 to the Ilopango air force base in El Salvador by Gregg, national security adviser to Bush, on the vice president's instructions. Through a spokesman, Bush Oct. 12 acknowledged that Gregg had recommended Gomez for a job as counterinsurgency specialist for the Salvadoran air force. The *Examiner* said Gomez was introduced to Bush by Robert Owen, identified in news reports as a former employee at the State Department's Nicaraguan Humanitarian Assistance Office (NHAO). The office oversaw the supply of nonlethal aid to the contras. Bush, director of the CIA from 1976 to 1977, Oct. 11 denied "unequivocally" that he had played a role in directing the supply flights. He acknowledged that he had met Gomez on three occasions but said they had not talked about Nicaragua. He described Gomez as a "patriot."

Detroit Free Press

Detroit, MI, October 9, 1986

THERE IS NO absolute proof of CIA involvement in an aborted attempt by some Americans to deliver arms to rebel forces in Nicaragua. But the incident is suspicious enough that it ought to strengthen the hands of opponents of this country's wrongheaded policy of escalating aid to the contras.

The American-built cargo plane that was shot down over Nicaragua on Sunday was operated by a private group led by a retired United States Army major general, according to the administration. It reportedly had flown down to deliver ammunition and supplies to the Nicaraguan rebels.

Spokesmen for the administration, the State Department, the Central Intelligence Agency and the Department of Defense all denied any government connection to the flight. Somehow their denials were not enough to silence the troubling questions spawned by the incident.

One official said that the company set up by Gen. John K. Singlaub in El Salvador had been used by the CIA in the past, but claimed that this particular flight was not a CIA operation. That is a very fine distinction to try to make. Moreover, the plane was a C123, a turbo-prop formerly used by the Air Force to carry cargo and paratroopers. Only a few remain in service, and one would not expect them to be readily available to private groups.

Congressional prohibitions against military aid to the contras remain in effect, with $100 million in new aid awaiting final approval in Congress before new supplies and training can be offered legally to the insurgents. What this incident suggests is that the Reagan administration remains committed to finding ways to funnel covert military aid to the contras at all costs.

If it can be shown that the administration has been working through private groups to circumvent the prohibitions on contra aid — along with disregarding the War Powers Act and the Constitution — that ought to galvanize Congress into voting down any new aid for the rebels.

Already, there is disturbing evidence of misuse of the $27 million in so-called humanitarian aid that the United States has sent to the contras, with nearly two-thirds of the money going to Central American suppliers whom the U.S. government cannot control. There is still no answer, either, for this question: What will we have won if we succeed in toppling the Sandinista government and installing the contras — either for the long-suffering Nicaragua people or for U.S. interests in the region? The cargo plane incident makes it all the more compelling that we find the answer.

The Hartford Courant

Hartford, CT, October 8, 1986

Who is responsible for the military cargo plane shot down in Nicaragua Sunday, with four crewmen aboard who apparently were Americans?

Nicaraguan officials were quick to point fingers at the CIA and at the U.S. military advisers' mission in El Salvador. The CIA denied involvement, and Secretary of State George P. Shultz said the plane had been hired by private American citizens who have no connection to the U.S. government.

The accusations from Managua and the denials from Washington were all predictable, but they mean little and there's a need to clear the air.

What seems to be beyond dispute is this: A large cargo plane was brought down southeast of Managua by a surface-to-air missile fired by Nicaraguan troops. The plane contained ammunition, rifles and other supplies presumably meant for the contra rebels who are fighting the Sandinista government. Three crewmen, thought to be Americans, were killed and a fourth American was captured.

There's a good chance the Americans were breaking U.S. law, whether they were acting as private citizens or working for the CIA. For the past two years, during which Congress denied President Reagan's requests for military aid to the contras, some American citizens — in defiance of congressional intent — have been working behind the scenes to help the contras overthrow the Nicaraguan government.

The efforts apparently have had the tacit approval of the White House and have been under the unofficial direction of the CIA. Both the House and the Senate have passed bills providing the contras with $100 million in military and non-lethal aid for this fiscal year, but there has been no final action. The supplies in the downed plane were not part of the new aid program.

Moreover, the aid to the contras bill does not permit the involvement of U.S. personnel in the war through fighting on Nicaraguan soil or flying over Nicaragua.

Congress should look into the sub rosa efforts by Americans to aid the contras. It has an obligation to investigate the evidence of secret and illegal war-making. If it's found that U.S. officials have been involved, they should be held accountable.

Los Angeles Times

Los Angeles, CA, October 9, 1986

It looks bad enough for the United States to have an airplane packed with arms for Nicaragua's rebels and flown by an American crew crash inside that country's borders. It makes it look unacceptably worse to have one of President Reagan's chief advisers on Latin America use the incident to encourage free-lance attacks a sovereign government with which we are officially at peace.

There will be more details in the days to come on the activities of Marine Corps veteran Eugene Hasenfus, the Wisconsin man who is the sole survivor of the four-man crew aboard the C-123 transport that Nicaraguan troops shot down Sunday near the Costa Rican border. Two other U.S. citizens, and a Nicaraguan, were killed when it crashed. Hasenfus has reportedly admitted his mission was to resupply anti-Sandinista *contra* rebels.

The U.S. government has disavowed any official connection with the airplane or its crew, but there can be little doubt the flight was part of a pattern of covert operations, either overseen directly or encouraged indirectly by the Central Intelligence Agency, in support of the contras, who Reagan considers freedom fighters. That an Administration irrationally obsessed with Nicaragua is linked to such activities is no surprise. What is amazing is how consistently U.S. officials, and their contra allies, botch up these operations and embarrass themselves before the world.

Take the way Assistant Secretary of State Elliot Abrams, the chief coordinator of Reagan Administration policy in Central America, praised the work of private U.S. groups that aid the contras, going so far as to call the downed plane's crew "heroes." They probably were brave men. But there are serious questions as to whether such activities are even legal under the Neutrality Act of 1972.

Quite apart from their legality, there are millions of Americans who consider such activities improper and unwise. Even the Republican chairman of the Senate Intelligence Committee, Minnesota's David Durenberger, is asking whether the CIA could bring free-lance contra aid operations under control if Congress were ever to allow it to go after Nicaragua unhindered. For Abrams to go out of his way to praise that kind of activity reflects profound arrogance.

But then, ignorance and a belief that we know better than the rest of the world what to do in Central America runs through all of the Administration's tactics and pronouncements with respect to Nicaragua. Reagan, Abrams and the rest are apparently determined to wage their war there regardless of what it costs in human lives or damaged U.S. prestige. The only way their campaign to overthrow the Sandinistas will be forced into a more constructive channel—like the Contadora negotiations suggested by our Latin American allies—will be if Congress flatly refuses to go along with it.

Congress should now delay final approval of the $100 million in contra aid it voted recently, until the Administration answers the many questions raised by the aircraft's downing. Congress must find out if the Administration is already using the contra aid money despite the fact it has not been finally approved, or whether the CIA is using its operating funds against Nicaragua, a strategy Congress specifically banned two years ago when it was revealed that CIA operatives had mined Nicaragua's harbors.

Congress must have a clear answer to those questions before allowing Reagan and his fellow adventurers to plunge deeper into the jungles of Central America.

The Des Moines Register

Des Moines, IA
October 10, 1986

Private adventurers may have financed and flown the American-built cargo plane shot down over Nicaragua last Sunday, but Congress and the president are responsible for the undeclared, but no longer secret, United States war against Nicaragua.

The Constitution gives the president the authority to make foreign policy and Congress the right to declare war. But in Central America, the president seems to prefer CIA covert operations and private vigilantes rather than risk public debate by asking Congress to declare war.

Congress, for its part, has ducked its responsibility to debate whether this country should be at war by not declaring the war a war.

The Senate Foreign Relations Committee is now conducting an inquiry to determine if the U.S. government was directly or only indirectly behind the plane that was shot down. But it doesn't take much investigation to note that Congress itself endorsed the spirit and the financing of the secret war last August when it approved another $100 million in aid to U.S.-trained contras fighting to overthrow the Sandinista government.

Congress even failed to pass an amendment offered by Senator Tom Harkin of Iowa to limit the number of American advisers in Central America, so that now the administration can send 20 or 2,000 or 20,000 "advisers" and still not call it a war.

Last year, Congress contributed further to the secret war by refusing to approve a bill drafted by congressmen James Leach of Iowa and Mel Levine of California that would update the neutrality act to forbid private intervention in countries with which the United States is at peace. If the Leach-Levine bill had passed, two Americans might not have died last Sunday in Nicaragua.

●

But people die in wars. That is why the founding fathers gave Congress, and therefore the people, the responsibility to declare war. And in instances when Congress has tried to stifle public debate by fighting war without declaring war, such as in Vietnam, public outrage exploded when it became clear that Americans were killing and dying without having the chance to vote on whether they wanted to go to war.

If Congress and the administration approve of sending American money, equipment and citizens to support killing in Central America, they should at least have the courage to call it war and to stop pretending that such a policy can bring peace to Central America.

The News and Courier

Charleston, SC, October 12, 1986

The brother of Eugene Hasenfus, the American veteran who is a "prisoner of war" in Nicaragua, has been complaining about the U.S. government. He says that his brother is a "political orphan" who has been deserted by his own country.

Since that complaint, however, Mr. Hasenfus has been claimed. The Nicaraguan Democratic Force (FDN), one of the groups of anti-Sandinista guerrillas known as the Contras, has announced that all four men aboard the plane shot down over southern Nicaragua have worked for the FDN since 1984.

It is in the interests of the Sandinistas to establish a CIA link with Mr. Hasenfus, the only man aboard the plane with a parachute and the only survivor. While there can be no doubt about CIA involvement with the Contras, there is also no reason to jump to the conclusion that the four men were hired by the agency. The FDN has private funding and can operate independently of the CIA.

If Mr. Hasenfus was working for the FDN, he cannot claim, nor should his relatives expect, the United States government to do any more for him than they would for any other U.S. citizen. Were he to be a CIA agent, he would know that he could not expect any special help in his present predicament. Whoever was his employer, Mr. Hasenfus must have read the job description and, given his background, would have known the terms of employment.

Mr. Hasenfus has not been deserted by his country or his government. A prominent member of the adminstration, Assistant Secretary of State Eliott Abrams, has described Americans who work for the Contras as heroes. It takes more to be a hero than parachute out of a crippled plane, but Mr. Hasenfus' courage will certainly be tested by the Sandinistas.

Not surprisingly, the Sandinistas are exploiting the downing of the plane, the deaths of three of its crew and the capture of Mr. Hasenfus, in their propaganda, which is stridently anti-American at the best of times. The delivery to the U.S. Embassy in Managua of the remains of two of the crewmen, and the unexplained retention of a third body, seem to be part of a campaign to keep this matter before the public eye. Although the description of the delivery of the coffins containing the remains of the two Americans as "ghoulish" may seem somewhat exaggerated, there can be no doubt that the Sandinistas are determined to picture the United States in the worst possible light. Because they are so insensitive themselves, the Sandinistas invariably end up by shooting themselves in the foot. That is precisely what they did when, instead of taking the bodies of the pilot William J. Cooper and co-pilot Wallace Blaine Sawyer Jr. to the embassy in the least conspicious way possible, they dumped two coffins containing their remains on a stretch of grass outside the embassy. The objective was to emphasize the symbolism of the delivery of two coffins to the embassy gates. It may not have been "ghoulish" exactly but it showed scant respect for the dead men, their families or their fellow citizens.

Regardless of Sandinista provocation, the U.S. response must be measured and decorous. President Reagan has never made any secret about his support for the Contras. He has called them "freedom fighters" from the start. The administration has no reason to be ashamed of CIA involvement with the Contras, or of private American citizens who work for them, as long as such activities are legal. The administration will, however, have to take some political heat because of the incident. President Reagan is likely to find himself in crossfire between the right and left extremes. He will be called upon by the former to adopt Mr. Hasenfus and by the latter to disown him. The right policy is to steer a centrist course, ignoring those who would like to see an invasion while turning a deaf ear to those who would like to see the United States abandon its support for democracy in Nicaragua.

Wisconsin ▲ State Journal
Madison, WI, October 10, 1986

The seeds of doubt planted by the government's alleged use of disinformation against Libyan leader Moammar Gadhafi are bearing bitter fruit thousands of miles away in Nicaragua.

A cargo plane loaded with arms for anti-Marxist rebels has been shot down along Nicaragua's southern border, leaving two Americans dead and a third, Eugene Hasenfus of Marinette, Wis., in the hands of gleeful Sandinista captors.

President Reagan says Hasenfus has no official connection with the U.S. government. Secretary of State George Shultz says the same. Yet there are signs the ill-fated mission was connected with an organization headed by retired Major Gen. John Singlaub, who has enthusiastically supported the cause of the "Contras" through private means.

Also, there are reports the two dead Americans had links to Southern Air Transport, a Miami firm once owned by the CIA and reputedly still used by the intelligence agency.

Coming when it did, at the height of an uproar over government disinformation in the case of Libya, the mysterious circumstances surrounding the downing of the C-123 cargo plane have raised a host of questions.

Opponents of Reagan's pro-Contra policy are asking — not without good reason — whether the administration is encouraging private parties to carry out those portions of the president's plan which Congress has yet to approve. "It will bother me," said Sen. Patrick Leahy, D-Vt., "if this turns out to be connected with adjunct soldiers of fortune sent out there with a wink and nod or a shrug as a way of getting around our foreign policy or the law."

Reagan insists that is not the case, but adds: "We're in a free country where private citizens have a great many freedoms." History suggests those freedoms do include the right to get involved in other people's wars, but only so long as those individuals don't drag the rest of us along.

The Senate Foreign Relations committee, chaired by Sen. Richard Lugar, R-Ind., will conduct an inquiry into whether or not the cargo plane had ties with the Reagan administration.

Given Lugar's record for parting company with the White House when he believes necessary (the Philippines and South Africa come to mind) such a probe begins with a strong measure of credibility.

Reagan is right — it's a free country. But those freedoms do not extend to private formulation of foreign policy without the advice and consent of the president and Congress.

THE ASHEVILLE CITIZEN
Asheville, NC, October 9, 1986

The U.S. government should render what aid it can in securing the release of Eugene Hasenfus from Nicaragua — and the return of the bodies of two Americans who were killed when his cargo plane was shot down.

It isn't enough for U.S. officials simply to shrug and do the "Who, me?" routine. Our government has an obligation to help Hasenfus whether it was involved in the operation or not.

The official position is that government agencies were not involved. Yes, private mercenary groups are active in supporting the Nicaraguan rebels, but they are working entirely on their own. What they do is their business. If "patriotic Americans" want to aid the cause of freedom in Nicaragua, that's admirable — but they have no connection to the government.

President Reagan upheld the official line Wednesday when he spoke to reporters. "We're in a free country where private citizens have a great many freedoms," said Reagan innocently.

The CIA is denying everything it can: that the plane was a government plane, that the Americans involved worked either directly or indirectly for the government, that the CIA had any role in what they were doing.

All of that may be true. The CIA tries to maintain what it calls "deniability" in operations of the sort that American civilians are carrying out in Central America.

Nonetheless, the private groups active in the region work with the encouragement, if not the advice and support, of the government. It was Miami-based Southern Air Transport that serviced the plane and issued identity cards to the crew. Southern Air was owned by the CIA until 1973 and still does contract work for the agency.

As far as the fate of Hasenfus goes, CIA involvement in the operation is irrelevant anyway — or should be. The U.S. government tries to render assistance to any American citizen who gets into trouble abroad, whatever the circumstances. Whether the trouble is his own doing or not, our government is there, ready to offer whatever aid is possible.

We should do no less with Hasenfus. It would be unfortunate if U.S. officials abandoned him simply to prove they have clean hands.

They should try to get him back — which may not be too difficult. After the Sandinistas parade Hasenfus around and milk all the public relations they can from his capture, they probably would be willing to release him to show their "humanitarian" concern.

THE SACRAMENTO BEE
Sacramento, CA, October 9, 1986

Eugene Hasenfus and his fellow soldiers of fortune are being portrayed by the Reagan administration as private mercenaries. It contends that their free-lance gun-running mission into Nicaragua, in which an American plane was shot down and all but Hasenfus were killed, had no official connection with the U.S. government. So far there's no reason to dispute that, but to argue that the mission was not inspired and encouraged by the administration's Central American policy would be absurd.

Hasenfus (whose name, ironically, means "rabbit's foot") and his companions were not just solitary adventurers. Their mission, and doubtless many others that don't end up on the front pages, are part and parcel of the Reagan administration's crusade to oust the leftist regime in Managua by force.

For the most part, that crusade has had to be waged surreptitiously and obliquely in recent years, through private organizations like the one that sponsored Hasenfus' adventure, because Congress forbade direct U.S. government involvement. That hasn't deterred the administration from cheering on the mercenaries, however, a fact that was demonstrated again when a State Department official praised men like Hasenfus as "very, very brave people."

But Congress reversed course this year and legitimized the war by approving $100 million in direct aid to the Contras, who will now resume the offensive against the Sandinista government. Presumably private mercenaries will continue their work, too. But to what end? The war against the Sandinistas is either doomed to abject failure, because the effort is too small, or destined to expand into a regional conflict on a far larger scale, with uncertain but certainly horrendous consequences.

How a tiny, impoverished nation of 2.5 million people threatens the United States is hard to see. It ought not to be beyond the capacity of our policy-makers to devise a strategy of containment against this "threat" without getting into a shooting war with it. As long as the administration continues on its present course, there will be more mercenaries like Eugene Hasenfus, more American deaths, and a growing risk of wider war.

Nicaragua, Honduras Clash; U.S. 'Copters Ferry Troops

Honduran aircraft struck against Nicaraguan troops on the border between the two countries December 6-7, 1986 after Sandinista soldiers penetrated Honduran territory in an operation against contras based in that country. The Sandinista government charged that the aircraft also bombed two Nicaraguan villages. On Dec. 7-8, for the second time in 1986, United States helicopters ferried Honduran troops to a staging point near the battle area. The U.S. military played no role in the fighting to push back the Nicaraguan troops. The clashes between Nicaraguan and Honduran troops took place in the Las Vegas salient of Honduras' El Paraiso province, which juts into Nicaragua's Jinotega and Nuevo Segovia provinces. The largest contra camps were located in the area, and the contras main infiltration routes into northern Nicaragua passed through it. A basic aim of the contras operating in Las Vegas was to capture territory in Nicaragua that would be exclusively under contra control, and to establish a provisional government that would receive the official recognition of the U.S. The Nicaraguan government sought to prevent a large-scale contra penetration at a time when the rebels were beginning to receive funds from the $100 million aid package recently approved by the U.S. Congress.

The incident prompted the involvement of the Honduran military and the request for the use of U.S. helicopters Dec. 4. That day, Nicaraguan troops overran a Honduran border post at Las Mieles, wounding three Honduran soldiers and capturing two. The next day, Sandinista troops were reported to have advanced to within a half mile of the main camp of the Nicaraguan Democratic Force (FDN). Nicaragua denied that its troops were inside Honduras and rejected a Honduran note protesting the attack. The Honduran air force joined the fray Dec. 6-7, using U.S.-made A-37 Dragonfly planes to bomb Sandinista targets. Honduras claimed that the attacks had taken place over Honduras territory, but the Sandinistas said the planes had hit targets inside Nicaragua. The air attacks on Nicaraguan targets were reported to be the first by fixed-wing aircraft. As the fighting raged, nine unarmed U.S. helicopters Dec. 7 ferried some 1,000 Honduran soldiers to a staging point at Jamastran airfield, joining hundreds of other troops in the battle area. The U.S. role, involving some 60 American soldiers, had been requested by Honduran President Jose Azcona Hoyo Dec. 6 and was approved by U.S. President Ronald Reagan later that day. Jamastran was 25 miles from the fighting and 15 miles from the nearest Nicaraguan border point. The U.S. State Department said the ban on U.S. soldiers aiding the contras within 20 miles of the Nicaraguan border did not apply because the action was in support of the Hondurans, not the contras. The contras reportedly did not play a role in the clashes.

THE SPOKESMAN-REVIEW

Spokane, WA, December 4, 1986

When President Reagan fought successfully for a congressional appropriation to aid the Nicaraguan Contras, he and his supporters repeatedly assured the American people that they had no intention of sending in U.S. troops if U.S. dollars proved insufficient to topple Nicaragua's Sandinista government.

Now, the Sandinistas are stronger than ever. And the Contras are in deep trouble, militarily and politically. The presidents of Guatemala and Costa Rica both have declared that the Contras don't have a chance of military victory and the Contras are becoming increasingly unpopular in Honduras, as well. The chance of more congressional appropriations to the Contras looks slim, thanks to disclosure of the National Security Council's unorthodox and probably illegal methods of funding the Contras and the Republican Party's loss of its Senate majority.

Against this backdrop, what did President Reagan do? As if to distract attention from his current domestic political crisis, he sent U.S. personnel up to the threshhold of the combat he said he didn't want.

With Reagan's authorization, 14 American Chinook helicopters, each manned by a five-member crew from the 1,100 personnel based at Palmerola Air Field in Honduras, ferried 700 Honduran soldiers to a U.S.-built dirt airstrip 18 miles from the Nicaraguan border. From there, Honduran choppers flew the reinforcements into combat in a triangle of Honduran territory where the Contras maintain their supply and training bases. Sandinista forces, who maintain positions there as well, had raided a Honduran army outpost. That led to the call for reinforcements, and after a skirmish the Sandinistas faded into the jungle.

When U.S. aircraft carry reinforcements to battle, they become active participants and give the Sandinistas both a reason and an opportunity to shoot them down. This goes a step beyond building airfields or supplying weapons or furnishing military advice — all of which the United States has done for the Contras.

By taking this step at a time when his beloved "freedom fighters" are in deep jeopardy, President Reagan flung down a gauntlet at the feet of Congress. Congress should waste no time in accepting the challenge.

Central American leaders such as Jaime Rosenthal, a vice president of Honduras, say that while Contra leaders have been "living a very good life" off U.S. aid, they haven't even been able to dislodge Sandinista positions within Honduras, let alone make military progress within Nicaragua itself. Rosenthal says Honduran public opinion runs against the Contras, who are viewed as a source of trouble.

No justification exists for a fullblown U.S. invasion of Nicaragua, and further support for the Contras would be difficult to justify. It's up to Congress to break off this entanglement.

THE PLAIN DEALER

Cleveland, OH, December 12, 1986

The contras battling Nicaragua's government are in bad shape. The Iran scam threatens to rob them of further support in the U.S. Congress. And now, things are getting even worse. Honduras, which has been the home of several contra camps, reportedly has told the Reagan administration that it wants the contras out of its territory by next April. Huge amounts of U.S. aid for the Honduran military and economy apparently aren't enough to sway Honduras to risk its future for the American-backed war.

And that's just as well. Central American countries, while anything but happy with the Sandinistas who are ruling Nicaragua, long have been nervous about the Reagan administration's policies toward the region. The latest Honduran request underscores the destabilizing nature of those policies. It should give Congress, already dubious over the administration's sleight of hand funding of the war, further reason to question contra aid.

Some analysts contend that Honduran officials don't want their country to become the Lebanon of the Western Hemisphere, torn apart by its role as host to a foreign rebel force. The comparison is overdrawn. Honduras doesn't have near the level of class, ethnic and religious strife that is present in Lebanon. Nonetheless, the presence of the contras does threaten Honduras' already fragile political stability, as well as its economy.

That is all the more reason to pursue other alternatives to ensure that the Nicaraguan revolution is contained in Nicaragua. This week, Central American sponsors of the Contadora peace process have been meeting, again, to assess how best to keep their proposal alive. The Reagan administration has undercut them at just about every turn and has declared the effort all but dead.

Fortunately, that's not the view shared by others. A high-level European diplomat in Cleveland the other day said the European community regards Contadora as very much alive. He counseled more hard work, and patience.

Desperately, some movement is needed by one side of the dispute, or both. The Sandinistas could make a gesture such as sending home some of the Soviet bloc personnel advising its military forces. But because of the contras—recently more active thanks to the infusion of money from Iran—Nicaragua isn't likely to act so responsibly.

The Reagan administration, which could make a major gesture by offering to sit down with the Sandinistas, isn't likely to make any positive moves either. Which means the responsibility continues to lie with Congress to say "no" to the contras.

The Washington Times
Washington, DC, December 10, 1986

While Washington examines its navel, the world keeps spinning round — or, more accurately, marching on. Self-possessed by the Iran affair, and especially the "contra" connection, many U.S. congressmen continue to ignore the steady consolidation of a pro-Soviet regime in this hemisphere. Several work overtime to make Nicaragua safe for Communism.

Sandinista troops, 1,000 of them at least, entered Honduras last Thursday in an apparent attempt to wipe out the resistance forces. Managua, as is usual, denies breaching the border, which is news to the Honduran government, air force, and army. But U.S. Democrats, traditionally against incursions (i.e., the U.S. move into Cambodia) have yet to take much umbrage, preferring to label Oliver North as the chief threat to Central America.

Like the Sandinistas, U.S. anti-resistance forces want to make progress under cover of the Iran-"contra" arms struggle. Cries have arisen to revive the lifeless "Contadora process," though nary a word is said about the bipartisan Kissinger Commission report. Congressmen quote the Boland amendment, which states that U.S. money is not to be spent to overthrow the Sandinistas, forgetting that they voted money for that purpose earlier in the year.

These are not the boldest efforts. Sen. Christopher Dodd, for example, has bragged that he's going to pull the plug on the resistance once and for all. A trip to Managua this week could result in the release of Eugene Hasenfus, allowing Mr. Dodd, like the Rev. Jesse Jackson in Syria a few years back, to fly home with a goodwill token, supposedly proving Managua's peaceful intentions. But the Sandinistas, like their Soviet masters, do not free prisoners out of the goodness of their hearts. By releasing one captive, they hope to further insure the enslavement of a nation.

Much of the press is in full bay as well. Look for more references to "President Reagan's war on Nicaragua," as a *Wall Street Journal* headline termed it last Friday. Such a formulation suggests that Nicaraguans would not be fighting to overthrow a tyranny on their own account. It says that the same people who fought against the oppression of a Somoza would accept the oppression of an Ortega if it weren't for Ronald Reagan. This is liberalism's version of "The devil made them do it."

As is the case with apartheid, it has become necessary to preface every statement on Nicaragua with a disclaimer: "Illegal activities are not to be condoned, but . . ." If laws were broken, justice must be served. But as is the case with South Africa, a sizable number of congressmen are suggesting remedies for Nicaragua that could kill the patient — or at least all hopes for democracy there. The president is in a weakened position, which means his friends — or those of them who ha✴ ✴t cut and run — have a heavier burden ✴✴y. Now is the time for them to stand up.

THE ATLANTA CONSTITUTION
Atlanta, GA, December 12, 1986

The latest and mercifully short-lived "skirmishlet" between Honduras and Nicaragua mustn't be shrugged off.

It wasn't just more of the same sporadic and mostly harmless exchanges of fire along their remote and rugged border regions. The stakes keep getting higher.

For the first time, Sandinista forces burned Honduran villages. For the first time, President Daniel Ortega publicly spelled out Nicaragua's conviction its forces can and will engage in hot-pursuit attacks against contra guerrillas based in Honduras. For the first time, Honduran warplanes attacked Sandinista military positions inside Nicaragua, an ominous escalation.

The U.S. military role in all this was limited, the State Department said — simply ferrying Honduran forces by helicopter to drop zones out of range of unfriendly fire. The administration's version might be more reassuring if its reputation for leveling with the public, especially with regard to Central America, was unspotted, but it's not.

Ortega has his own sagging credibility problem, having cried wolf so often about imminent U.S. invasions. You have to discount again his assertion that President Reagan is itching for a justification to order U.S. troops to fight Sandinista forces.

Still, as long as Nicaragua and Honduras are at each other's throats, that, alas, is a distinct possibility.

That painful realization is sinking in among Honduras' civilian and military leadership. Publicly, President Jose Azcona is saying the contras' battlefield is inside Nicaragua, not Honduras. Privately, he is reported to have told the U.S. ambassador the contras must leave Honduran soil by next April.

From 1982 till now, Honduras has been a sometimes willing, sometimes grudging host to "secret" contra military facilities, partly because of Washington's aid and encouragement, partly out its own deeply felt conservative animus toward the Sandinistas. But its patience is thin and its apprehension runs high. It's fair for Azcona to ask: If the contras have a legitimate claim on Nicaraguans' loyalty, why haven't the rebels in all this time established a single beachhead for themselves on their own soil?

They have not and they surely won't if April is to be Honduras' deadline — and not because of President Reagan's Iran-contra troubles, either, but because of the contras' own glaring organizational weaknesses.

With Honduras backing off, the White House must survey its options, the diplomatic ones especially. The hard truth is that its "freedom fighters" have just about worn out their welcome in Central America. And the American public is not about to offer its Caribbean fleet, stationed off Nicaragua, as the contras' next base of operations.

The Miami Herald
Miami, FL, December 10, 1986

HISTORY is replete with examples of confrontations escalating out of control in unstable times when neither side is able to judge the other's intent. That is why the weekend skirmishes between Nicaraguan and Honduran troops, the latter with U.S. support, are so worrisome.

Border clashes between Honduran and Nicaraguan forces have occurred before, of course — most notably last March. But last March, officials in Washington, Managua, and Tegucigalpa knew with relative clarity what each of the three sides would tolerate. Iranscam and its effect on the Reagan Administration's internal functioning, as well as on how other countries view U.S. foreign-policy moves, has clouded that foreknowledge. This opens the way for disastrous misinterpretation.

Is this latest Nicaraguan incursion into Honduras an attempt to test the will of a Reagan Administration in crisis? Did the Administration encourage Honduras's retaliatory air raids on Nicaraguan border villages in an attempt to regain its foreign-policy initiative in the region? Or did Honduran officials respond with such force to test the United States's support for its ally's national sovereignty in turbulent times?

Nobody can say with certainty, although it should not make a difference. What is of paramount importance is that these events do not mushroom by accident because of a real or perceived absence of U.S. policy.

It is therefore imperative that the Administration and Congress take great pain to reiterate the objectives of American policy in the region. That needs to occur apart from the continuing debate on aid to the *contras*.

The Administration should make extraordinary efforts to keep key congressional leaders advised of its intended actions in the region. Congressional leaders in turn should join the Administration in stressing that this country's commitment to safeguarding the national sovereignty of Honduras and other Central American nations from an assault from Nicaragua is unchanged.

American interests in Central America are clear. Those interests need to be made unmistakably evident to friends and foes alike in the region. If the United States is to become directly involved in hostilities with Nicaragua, let it be after deliberation, not by accident.

THE SACRAMENTO BEE

Sacrmento, CA, December 9, 1986

Once again, the Reagan administration's proxy war in Central America has shown that it's no respecter of borders. The map says it is Honduras on the northern side of the line running through the Central American mountains, but for months it has been Nicaraguans, Sandinista and Contra, who've fought there. Honduras has been forced to accept the Contras' use of its territory to launch their attacks against the Sandinistas; in return, it has had to tolerate near-continuous patrols by Sandinista troops chasing their Contra enemies.

So why this weekend's fighting by Honduran troops against the uninvited Sandinistas? Had Tegucigalpa decided the Nicaraguans have become too brazen? Did Washington fear the Contras would suffer major losses without a screen of Honduran and American power?

Don't expect good answers to those questions. Two weeks of Washington revelations about the Contra war — about illegal arms purchases from slush funds in Swiss bank accounts, about "humanitarian" flights to Nicaragua ferrying guns and ammunition for the Contras, about American officials shaking a tin cup for the Contras around the sultanates of the world — have taught that truth is hard to come by in this unsecret secret conflict.

But this much is still plain: The fighting in Honduras is an inevitable consequence of the administration's Contra policy. As long as Contra troops use Honduras as a sanctuary, Sandinista forces will cross the border in pursuit. And as long as hot pursuit and pre-emption are a militarily useful option for the Sandinistas, the danger of a wider war, involving Honduras, and ultimately the United States, will grow.

That danger has always existed, but with the Iran-Contra scandal in Washington, perhaps there will be a new willingness to face it. The last two weeks have exposed the Contras to be less than they seemed. Cut off from official American aid for two years, the Contras did not, as advertised, survive on their own wit and resources, but on money collected by the White House and on logistics and direction provided by Lt. Col. Oliver North and his network of arms-dealing confederates.

In both Congress and some parts of the administration, the revelation of the White House role is forcing a more realistic evaluation of Contra prospects. Events in Honduras and Washington must also lead, at long last, to a clearer-eyed assessment of Contra risks — to America's reputation, to the processes of government, and, above all, to Honduras and the peace of Central America.

THE CHRISTIAN SCIENCE MONITOR
Boston, MA, December 9, 1986

One can understand the widespread unease about President Reagan's weekend decision to allow United States helicopters to carry Honduran troops into the border region to battle Nicaraguan forces. The problem in such a US action, as clearly stated by Indiana Democratic Congressman Lee Hamilton, is that it "raises the risk of American involvement in that area."

That the US decision was ostensibly based on a request for help from the President of Honduras may be beside the point. So too is the Hondurans' claim that their military action occurred in response to an incursion into Honduras by up to 1,000 Nicaraguan soldiers. That is not to say that legitimate requests for help from Honduras should go unheeded. Rather, it is to recognize that at this moment, the US public must be wary about becoming drawn into a conflict. That is especially the case regarding Central America.

Why "at this moment"? Because of the turmoil now surrounding American foreign policy. Granted, the Honduran request apparently came directly from that nation's President, and was endorsed by the US State and Defense Departments. Still, the danger of miscalculation cannot be ignored. A US chopper could, for example, inadvertently make contact with Nicaraguan forces. At the same time, as it hardly seems necessary to mention, there is a wariness over the prospect of a military diversion from all the bad news about the Iran-contra affair. Secretary of State George Shultz was asked about this prospect during his testimony before the House yesterday. The secretary correctly replied that each foreign policy activity had to be considered on its own merits.

The Honduran operation is said to be winding down. The Hondurans do have legitimate concerns about the border region, called the Las Vegas salient.

Jurisdiction over the area, an inhospitable mountainous terrain, has long been disputed between the two nations, although a World Court decision a few years back recognized Honduran claims to the region. Most of the small, rural towns have been evacuated. Contras maintain bases there.

Pressure has been building within Honduras for some government action to "reclaim" the salient, both from the Nicaraguans, who make frequent sallies into the area, as well as the contras, who are detested by many, if not most, Hondurans. Opposition members of the National Assembly are expected to put pressure on the government about that territory when the Asssembly meets early next year. So this weekend's Honduran action may as much reflect internal Honduran politics as it does larger regional considerations. Indeed, in Honduran military thinking, the traditional adversary continues to be neighboring El Salvador, rather than Nicaragua.

Congress should require a careful accounting regarding direct US operations in Central America, lest all parties be inadvertently drawn into a larger – and unwelcome – conflict.

The Charlotte Observer

Charlotte, NC, December 11, 1986

The fallout from revelations about illegal funding for the contras, along with Democratic control of the next Congress, ought to prompt a sober reassessment within the Reagan administration of its Nicaraguan policy. Even before reports about Iranian arms money surfaced, and before the Democratic victories of November, there was growing pessimism about the ability of the contras to sustain their war against the Sandinista government.

Now the government of Honduras is asking the United States to get the Nicaraguan rebels out of Honduras, which will be no easy task. And the administration is unlikely to persuade the next Congress to provide enough aid to keep the contras in business.

The American people are deeply divided on the issue, which makes it even more difficult for the administration to win continuing congressional support for its policies. Most Americans surely have no illusions about the repressive and expansive nature of communist governments, and they overwhelmingly oppose the spread of communism in this hemisphere. But Americans haven't united behind Mr. Reagan's policy of opposing a Marxist regime in Nicaragua.

One reason is that so many Americans who visit Nicaragua on trips sponsored by religious and other organizations return with reports that the U.S.-backed rebels are fighting a guerrilla war primarily against innocent civilians — blowing up roads and medical clinics and schools. That is hardly the way to win the support of the people in the Nicaraguan countryside — or in the United States.

There also are reports that the Sandinistas, for all their repressive Marxist inclinations, are taking steps to make life better in fundamental ways for the people of Nicaragua, specifically in such areas as education and health care.

If the contras collapse, the United States will be left with two options: to do nothing or to send in American troops. Before matters reach that unhappy point, the administration ought to use whatever leverage it has left to try harder to get negotiations underway between the Sandinistas, responsible opposition elements in Nicaragua and Nicaragua's neighbors. The goal of such negotiations should be assurances from the Sandinistas about human rights and free elections in Nicaragua, and peaceful relations with neighboring countries — in return for an end to U.S. support for rebel forces and the possibility of U.S. humanitarian aid to the Nicaraguan government.

THE ARIZONA REPUBLIC
Phoenix, AZ, December 11, 1986

FOR nearly four decades after the Civil War the Republican Party did its best to keep the Democrats out of the White House by waving the "bloody shirt" at every opportunity, branding the opposition as the party of slavery and secession. Today, the Democrats have their own bloody shirt. It is called Vietnam.

These neo-isolationists trot out the Vietnam War and wave it over their heads every time the United States does something that in the slightest way hints of a foreign military action.

The latest hysteria to seize these myopic isolationists — for whom everything beyond the Washington Beltway is a big blur — is the new Vietnam being cooked up in Honduras. Here the appalling prospects are of the Reagan administration approving the use of 14 U.S. helicopters to ferry Honduran soldiers to their southern border to confront a force of 700 Sandinistan troops that have again invaded the country. What cheek of those Hondurans to object to the invasion of their country.

Rep. Michael Barnes, D-Md., the isolationists' head pooh-bah and chairman of the House Foreign Affairs Committee's Western Hemisphere subcommittee, fairly hyperventilated over the incident. "I hope that they don't make the mistake of getting the United States further involved in the regional war that's going on in Central America," Barnes warned in duly apocalyptic tones.

What "regional war"? It's Barnes and his congressional allies who hold the view that the Sandinistas do not constitute a regional threat so long as they keep their Stalinist revolution inside Nicaragua's borders. Now all of a sudden there's a "regional war" in Central America, but it's one that doesn't concern the United States, and in which we shouldn't get involved.

Barnes called the use of the American helicopters "enormously dangerous," saying that such recklessness "can only lead to disaster." Hyperbole and phony hysteria are the big guns in Barnes' neo-isolationist arsenal, but they are aimed exclusively at American targets. The unprecedented and massive buildup of the Soviet-equipped Sandinistan military apparently isn't a danger of comparable enormity.

What Barnes and some others seem unable to grasp is that the United States is a part of the region in which this regional war they are talking about is being fought. Central America might seem like a faraway place from Maryland or the posh bars and restaurants of Georgetown, but four states border the region. The fortress of Barnes' isolationist ideology is unassailable by grade-school geography.

Barnes and his buddies in Congress are quick to declare, lest they be thought wimps, that they agree to the use of military force where American security is directly threatened. The only problem is, they are unable to name such a place or situation outside the borders of the United States. Paralysis is their policy.

The United States has vital security interests in Central America which must be defended against the gang of would-be Castros and their enormous military establishment in Nicaragua. The United States offered reasonable and minimal assistance to a friendly government facing a foreign invasion. Barnes had best look for ghosts of Vietnam elsewhere.

The Oregonian
Portland, OR, December 12, 1986

U.S. efforts to help Honduran-based Contra rebels overthrow the Nicaraguan Sandinistas are raising the dangers to Honduras as well as to the United States. The Hondurans now doubt that the rewards are worth the price. The United States should have similar self-doubts.

Honduras, whose conservative administration deplores the leftist tilt of its southern neighbor, has offered haven to 12,000 insurgents — so long as there have been military aid benefits but no costs to Honduras.

The Hondurans even winked at most incursions into their country because the Sandinista forces only attacked Contras, not Hondurans. But in last week's cross-border foray, Sandinista soldiers attacked a Honduran army border position and inflicted casualties. That prompted a Honduran military response, assisted by U.S. helicopter pilots serving as chauffeurs.

Correspondents in the region increasingly interpret the Honduran assessment as follows:

— U.S. support of the Contras since 1982 has not yet enabled them to carry their rebellion effectively into Nicaragua.

— By contrast, the Popular Sandinista Army has become increasingly bold in preventing insurgent infiltration across the border and in projecting the fighting north.

— Continuing U.S. military aid to Honduras and backing in the event of a major escalation of fighting are in doubt. Congress increasingly doubts that the Contras can win and is angry at the Iran arms sale link to Contra funding as a deliberate effort to evade congressional intent.

— Domestic discontent is growing over the displacement of border-area villagers by Contras and the impact the fighting has on growing the coffee crop.

In essence, the Hondurans now want the Contras out of their country. The United States is downplaying the request, for it runs counter to its military strategy vis-a-vis the Sandinistas. The irony of this affair is that the policy intended to destabilize the Sandinistas increasingly has become a candidate to destabilize Honduras.

The Washington Post
Washington, DC, December 10, 1986

AMERICANS have only begun to tote up the costs of the Iran arms deal as they apply to Central America. There the costs go beyond the political embarrassment arising from disclosure of the fund diversion. They reach into the whole structure of confidence on which the American-led program of support for the Nicaraguan rebels is based. An operation that just a few months ago appeared to be moving into a high forward gear on the strength of a $100 million congressional authorization is now threatened with being thrown into neutral, if not reverse.

The difficulties only begin with the addition of the fund-diversion to the still-creeping disclosure of the American role in routing arms and money to the contras while Congress had outlawed military aid. Defenders of government policy insist that on the merits of contra aid, nothing has changed. But in any issue so long and hotly disputed, the merits always include one side's trust in the other's part in any of the temporary policy bargains struck along the road. The administration will have a hard time recovering here.

Meanwhile, events are weakening the fragile support available to the Nicaraguan resistance in the three countries closest by. Accidental revelation of the gun-running out of El Salvador's Ilopango military airfield seems to have closed off that crucial supply route. The new president of Costa Rica declines to keep winking at contra use of his country's territory as even a modest military sanctuary. Honduras, where most contra fighters remain based, is eager to see to their early removal to Nicaraguan soil so that it can shed the double burden of the contras' presence and the Sandinistas' attacks. The three neighbors, fearing the Sandinistas, would like to wake up some morning and see them gone. But they will have to live with the Sandinistas—and live next door—if the resistance fades, and this inclines them to take out a certain insurance by keeping the door open to the best accommodation with Managua that might yet be gained by diplomatic means.

President Reagan has embraced no policy goal more ardently than victory for the democratic resistance in Nicaragua. But recent frustrations only sharpen the question of whether the United States can accomplish that goal by relying on the contra military forces alone. The administration plainly hopes the resistance will be on the move before the funding issue is joined again in Washington next year. But it is not too early to review the policy bidding to determine whether the old $100 million strategy still makes sense.

Contra Drug Smuggling Charged

Two alleged drug traffickers claimed that the Nicaraguan contras had smuggled drugs into the United States from Colombia via remote air strips in Costa Rica, according to *Newsweek* magazine in its January 26, 1987 issue. *Newsweek* had interviewed the two men, who were being held in federal prison in Miami. They were Gary Betzner, 45, who said he had flown planes used in the operation, and George Morales, a former speedboat champion, who said he had provided the aircraft. Betzner and Morales claimed that U.S. Central Intelligence Agency operatives and other U.S. officials had helped in an operation in which drugs were shipped out of Costa Rica and guns were shipped in. Betzner claimed that the U.S. Drug Enforcement Administration (DEA) also knew of and assisted in the drug flights. Both men charged that contra leaders pocketed the money, which did not reach the contras in the field. *Newsweek* said a third alleged smuggler claimed to have seen planes belonging to Southern Air Transport Co. loaded with cocaine in Colombia in 1985. Southern Air had been linked to the El Salvador-based contra supply network set up by former National Security Council aide Lt. Col. Oliver North.

The Washington Post reported Jan. 20 that Jorge Ochoa Vasquez, reputedly a leader of Colombia's Medelin Cartel, said to be the world's largest drug ring, was in charge of the contra drug operation using Southern Air.

Separately, U.S. officials said Jan. 19 that DEA agents in 1986 had discovered evidence that the crews of the private contra supply network based in El Salvador were ferrying arms to El Salvador and then stopping in Panama on the return trip to pick up cocaine and marijuana. Officials were said to believe the Americans were motivated purely by personal profit and that a claim that they were protected by Lt. Col. Oliver North was a bluff.

St. Petersburg Times

St. Petersburg, FL, August 28, 1986

The Reagan administration's get-tough policy on drugs is by no means universal or consistent. While some officials go forward with plans to force millions of presumably innocent Americans to submit to the indignity of individual drug testing, another side of the administration is proving itself remarkably tolerant of well-documented drug smuggling activity on the part of its favorite "freedom fighters."

The White House's attitude seems to be that a little cocaine trafficking is okay, as long as the profits go to a good cause — such as an undeclared war on the government of Nicaragua.

It was reported last December that Nicaraguan rebels operating out of Costa Rica had become involved in a scheme to smuggle drugs into the United States. The profits of that operation helped to pay for their guerrilla war against the Sandinista government of Nicaragua.

White House officials didn't want to hear the story. Not long before the Costa Rican operation was exposed, the administration had made similar — but unsubstantiated — charges of drug smuggling on the part of the Sandinistas. When U.S. intelligence confirmed the *contras'* involvement in cocaine trafficking, the State Department publicly repudiated the charges.

In the meantime, Nicaraguans who said they were acting on behalf of the *contras* have been convicted in connection with two cocaine smuggling operations broken up by San Francisco authorities. Investigations showed that the profits from those operations also helped to finance the *contra* war.

At long last, a new report compiled by the State Department admits that "the available evidence points to involvement with drug traffickers by a limited number of persons having various kinds of affiliations with or political sympathies for resistance groups." The report says, however, that it is "inevitable that there will be some who have had drug connections" among the 20,000 or so active *contras.*

Incredibly, even the evidence included in this report — lamely worded and at least eight months late — is more than some administration officials want to admit to. A cover letter accompanying the report says "the administration believes these allegations are false."

A *contra* leader reading the language of the administration report must feel that he has been given official approval to continue to raise money by fair means or foul. After all, the number of rebels involved in trafficking, whether 10 or 1,000, will always be "limited." If such connections are considered "inevitable," there isn't much reason to bother trying to eliminate them. And some members of the administration will continue to question the validity of the accusations even after *contras* are convicted of criminal charges.

The administration's single-minded crusade against the Sandinistas has blinded many people to the troubling moral problems raised by our proxy army in Central America. The obvious unwillingness to crack down on the *contras'* drug trafficking is just another obvious example of that moral blind spot.

The Register

Santa Ana, CA, April 14, 1986

As debate in the House of Representatives over supplying $100 million from U.S. taxpayers to anti-government forces in Nicaragua heats up, the charge has predictably been renewed that the so-called *contras* have been dealing in drugs to finance their insurrection. Rep. Michael Barnes, D-Md., says he thinks Americans will be outraged by this perfidy, while Rep. Bob Dornan, R-Garden Grove, suggests that it's understandable that the *contras* have turned to drug dealing since the United States cut off funds some time ago.

These allegations of drug-dealing by governments and political movements surface constantly, and it's likely that there is some plausibility to most of them. As long as the United States continues to try to outlaw certain substances for which there is a strong demand, thus driving up prices and potential profits, drug-dealing will be attractive to those who think they need lots of money (preferably not too traceable) quickly. Governments and political movements certainly fit this category.

Governments and insurrectionists are also well situated to deal drugs. Governments may be able to use diplomatic pouches and other prerogatives to move contraband. Insofar as governments and rebel movements effectively control territory and have weapons, trucks, airplanes and helicopters, they can be useful to drug dealers. And the government or political movement doesn't exist that doesn't think it can use more money.

Drug trafficking is no respecter of ideology. In recent years Bulgarian customs guards have resold seized heroin and both Colombian colonels and left-wing insurrectionists in Colombia have protected or dabbled in cocaine and marijuana. There is good evidence that some Nicaraguan government officials have trafficked in drugs. It is almost certain that the North Korean diplomatic service has smuggled heroin in diplomatic pouches and that the anti-communist, CIA-backed Hmong irregulars financed operations during the Vietnam war with opium and heroin.

Those facts are not pleasant, but they are facts. Drug dealing by political movements and governments is likely to continue unless the United States decides to decriminalize the possession and use of certain drugs. Having junkies indirectly finance political movements of varying degrees of unsavoriness is simply one more predictable result of U.S. laws against drugs.

The Courier-Journal & TIMES

Louisville, KY, February 15, 1987

IN MIAMI, prosecutors are having trouble getting drug convictions because alleged smugglers have begun resorting to what might be called the coke-and-*contra* defense. Instead of denying that they were dealing, the accused claim they worked secretly for the U. S. government, raising money for Nicaraguan "freedom fighters."

These claims may often be lies, but it's tough for law enforcement officials to disprove them. Prosecutors also worry that such stories may have emotional appeal to Miami juries that include Cuban Americans, many of whom favor U. S. support for the *contras*.

This is a sorry state of affairs. It's no worse, however, than the fog of lies and half-truths generated by the Reagan administration to obscure its arms trafficking with Iran and its efforts to skirt congressional restrictions on funding for the anti-Sandinista guerrillas.

According to *The Washington Post*, this willingness to resort to lies led some administration officials to work out a plan for misleading Congress — a plan that countenanced perjury.

William Casey, who has since resigned as head of the Central Intelligence Agency, was scheduled to submit testimony to a Senate committee last November on arms sales to Iran. In a story concocted by the CIA and the National Security Council, Mr. Casey was to allege that U. S. officials believed a shipment a year earlier from Israel to Iran had contained oil drilling equipment. In fact, as Mr. Casey, President Reagan and Secretary of State George Shultz evidently knew at the time, U. S.-made Hawk missiles were being shipped to Iran.

Mr. Shultz, according to *The Post*, got wind of the lie Mr. Casey planned to tell. The secretary of state then had what *Post* reporter Don Oberdorfer called "a tense showdown" with the President.

As a result of the Shultz protest, Mr. Casey's testimony was revised — though he still claimed that, "to the CIA's knowledge," the November 1985 shipment had contained drilling equipment, not missiles.

Four days after Mr. Casey told this tale to the committee, Attorney General Edwin Meese announced he had found evidence that proceeds from the Iran arms sales had been diverted to the *contras*.

Since then, congressional investigators have been trying to untangle a much larger skein of lies, and a special prosecutor is also looking into the Iran-*contra* connections.

Getting to the truth promises to be a daunting task. Compared to some high-level officials and former officials in Washington, those alleged drug smugglers in Miami sound like small-time fibbers.

The Philadelphia Inquirer

Philadelphia, PA, February 24, 1987

President Reagan wasn't content in his anti-Sandinista speeches last winter to paint Nicaragua as "a second Cuba, a second Libya," "a mortal threat to the entire New World." He liked to save up a kidney punch for the peroration. The punch was something called "narco-terrorism" and it focused on a Sandinista drug connection.

There was one photograph that would show up in State Department booklets and one — the same one — that the President would use on nationally televised appeals for contra funding. It purported to show a Sandinista official loading cocaine at a government-owned airfield. "I know every American parent concerned about the drug problem will be outraged to learn that top Nicaraguan government officials are deeply involved in drug trafficking," the President would say.

Exactly *how* deeply has remained something of a question, although the larger question in recent months has been not the Sandinista drug connection, but allegations that the contras' hands are pretty dirty themselves. The House subcommittee on crime, chaired by Rep. William J. Hughes (D., N.J.), has been investigating and now the Senate Foreign Relations Committee is about to take a look at both sides of the question, especially the contra side.

Given the state of affairs in Washington and the disarray over Central America policy in particular, the Nicaraguan drug connection (Colombia, let's face it, is the *real* connection) might seem like a sidelight. But it's time the administration's assertions were put to the test on issue after issue where official disinformation has obscured reality.

If the contentions of contra drug-running are substantiated, Mr. Reagan should explain why parents shouldn't be equally outraged at the administration's mercenaries. If there's a serious Sandinista connection, the White House can have satisfaction that it beat Senate investigators to the punch.

ST. LOUIS POST-DISPATCH

St. Louis, MO, February 28, 1987

For years, rumors have linked the Miami-based Contras with another group that has its unofficial headquarters in that city: cocaine smugglers. Now there's growing evidence that those sordid rumors may be based in sordid fact.

The FBI, which is investigating drug-running out of Miami, has a witness who swears he saw Southern Air Transport planes being loaded with cocaine in Barranquilla, Colombia. Southern Air Transport, you will recall, was the carrier of choice in the Contra arms supply scheme orchestrated by Lt. Col. Oliver North. Investigators suspect the planes would drop off a load of weapons to the Contras and fly on to Colombia before returning to Miami, where the drugs would be exchanged for more weapons and the trade triangle begun again.

Supporting testimony comes from two admitted drug smugglers, Gary Betzner and George Morales, in federal prison in Miami. The Contras weren't interested solely in buying weapons, Mr. Morales told *Newsweek*. The ringleaders pocketed the proceeds, he said, leaving the Contras in the field without even enough beans to eat.

More disturbing yet are these witnesses' accounts of complicity by CIA agents and officials of the U.S. Drug Enforcement Agency, who, the witnesses say, not only knew what was going on, but participated in the drugs-for-weapons exchange.

It's an unholy, implausible alliance, if it exists at all. At one point it would have been unthinkable — a radical, mind-bending suggestion entertained only by political enemies of the Reagan administration. In the wake of the Iran-Contra scandal, though, barriers to the unthinkable have come tumbling down. And that, more than evidence that may have been around for years, has made the start of congressional investigations of these rumors not simply justified but urgent as well.

U.S. Profits From Iran Arms Deal Found Sent to Nicaraguan Contras

United States President Ronald Reagan November 25, 1986 said he had not been informed about an aspect of his Iranian policy and as a consequence had accepted the resignation of national security adviser Vice Adm. John Poindexter and fired a key aide, Lt. Col. Oliver North. This was followed by the disclosure that $10 million to $30 million in profits from the Israeli-brokered sale of American arms to Iran had been secretly diverted to help the contra rebels fighting the Nicaraguan government. The revelation of the Nicaraguan connection, following a week of unprecedented public bickering among top administration officials over who to blame, left Reagan facing the most serious crisis of his presidency.

Both Republican and Democratic leaders on Capitol Hill expressed shock at the news and promised full-scale and wide-ranging congressional investigations. They noted that a number of laws might have been broken by the diversion of funds at a time when United States aid to the contras had been banned by Congress. Some lawmakers described Reagan's foreign policy as being in "total disarray." They viewed the claim that a major covert operation had been run out of the White House without the president's knowledge as having raised damaging questions about his competence and credibility.

Reagan made a brief statement to reporters. He said that previous week he had directed Attorney General Edwin Meese 3rd to review the Iranian arms-supply policy, which had been aimed chiefly at establishing links with Teheran and winning the freedom of U.S. hostages in Lebanon. He said a preliminary report of Meese's findings had "led me to conclude that I was not fully informed on the nature of one of the activities undertaken in connection with this initiative." He added, "This action raises some serious questions of propriety." Reagan said he would appoint a special review board to conduct a comprehensive review of the National Security Council (NSC) staff in the conduct of foreign and national security policy. The NSC, which was created as a policy coordinating and advisory body, had run the Iran arms operation—skirting Congress and the State and Defense Departments in the process. Reagan said further actions would wait until after he received the reports from the Justice Department and the special review board. "I am deeply troubled that the implementation of a policy aimed at resolving a truly tragic situation in the Middle East has resulted in such a controversy," Reagan continued. "As I've stated previously, I believe our policy goals toward Iran were well founded." But in one respect, the policy's implementation "was seriously flawed," he said.

According to Meese, a preliminary investigation by the Justice Department had established the following outline of what happened: Between January and September of 1986 the Central Intelligence Agency (CIA), under NSC direction, sent $12 million in Defense Department weapons stocks to Israel, which had agreed to broker the covert U.S.-Iranian operation. "Representatives of Israel," not necessarily in the Israeli government, sold the arms to Iran with a premium of $10 million to $30 million added on to their cost. The Israelis gave $12 million, plus transport costs, of the Iranian payment to the CIA, which in turn reiumbursed the Pentagon. Either the Israelis or the Iranian representatives, acting with the knowledge of North, then transferred the extra funds to Swiss bank accounts controlled by "the forces in Central America which are opposing the Sandinista government there." Meese said that none of the other members of the NSC—including CIA Director William Casey, Secretary of State George Shultz and Defense Secretary Caspar Weinberger—had known about the Nicaraguan aspect. Meese said President Reagan knew nothing until the day before.

Some U.S. officials Nov. 25 noted that the disclosure of the skimming off of Iranian arms profits for the contras could partly explain how the rebels had been able to finance their resupply operation over the previous two years, when U.S. aid had been cut off. It was suggested that, at least since early 1986, the Iranian funds had paid for a large part of the resupply effort, which involved hundreds of covert drops over Nicaragua. The rebels, along with Lt. Col. Oliver North and other administration officials, had maintained that the money needed to keep the aid flowing came from anonymous private doners in the U.S. and abroad. Meanwhile, Adolfo Calero, political leader of the largest contra force, Nov. 25 in Miami denied that the group had received any of the Iranian money. He said the rebels "have no access" to any Swiss bank accounts of the type described by Meese.

The Washington Post

Washington, DC, November 26, 1986

PERHAPS AN accident will save us, Louis XVI was supposed to have said as the French monarchy crashed around him. A kindred thought might have occurred to the Reagan administration as it disclosed the tale of the Israelis diverting part of Iran's arms payments to the Nicaraguan contras. Here at last was an opportunity to show command, to come clean, to feed the lions and still to preserve the defense of the administration's embattled policies respecting terrorism and Iran—although the disputed content of these policies appears to have been set aside for the duration. President Reagan did all of this yesterday, with the sturdy help of Attorney General Edwin Meese.

It begs belief that a mere lieutenant colonel on the National Security Council staff, even an ultimate gung-ho Marine such as the now-fired Oliver North, could have been, as Mr. Meese said, the sole person in the know. It invites further incredulity and dismay that his superior, the now-reassigned national security adviser, John Poindexter, could have known "generally" of the North operation and failed to look further into it or to inform his chief. Presumably the inquiry being pressed by the Justice Department—far from the only inquiry now under way—will shed more light on this bizarre affair.

In the meantime, it is good that President Reagan has finally, belatedly, seen fit to name a commission to look into the "role and procedures" of the NSC staff. It would serve the president poorly to appoint people of less than "wise man" stature. The commission will be under pressure to expand its study into and beyond the whole string of NSC operations with which elements of the Reagan administration have sought to plug the widening gap between presidential ambition and public acceptability over the past year. For it is evident that once again the secrecy option has encouraged the pursuit of policies that were not always accepted and were sometimes explicitly opposed by Congress, that were not always supported by or even disclosed to the full ranks of the administration and that trifled with the law.

The administration's sudden stumble upon the diversion scandal compelled the president to consider personnel changes he earlier had resisted. Col. North is gone; he became something of a notorious legend without ever becoming a known public man. Adm. Poindexter leaves with the reputation of having been too ready to offer the president salutes and shortcuts.

President Reagan was a man under pressure yesterday. The pressure is going to stay on. As his handoff of the podium to his attorney general showed, he is a president who puts immense reliance on subordinates. He needs strong Cabinet officers, especially a strong secretary of state; he is lucky to have one already. Incidentally, Mr. Meese, though he didn't seem happy with Secretary Shultz's acknowledged difference with administration policy on arms transfers to Iran, did "verify"—his word—the secretary's account of the fragmentary nature of his knowledge of events. The president also needs a strong national security adviser, one who understands the proper role of that ambiguous and difficult office, avoids the traps of secret power and helps Mr. Reagan recover from the damage he has sustained in the past few weeks.

Herald ❦ News

Fall River, MA, November 29, 1986

The latest twist in the disastrous arms deal with Iran is the disclosure that millions of dollars that came from Iran were diverted to the use of the Nicaraguan rebels.

It seems apparent that the President, let alone the Secretary of State and the Secretary of Defense, knew nothing of this appropriation of Iranian funds to the Contras.

Once Attorney General Meese had told the President about it, Mr. Reagan acted swiftly. Admiral John Poindexter, the National Security Advisor, and his aide, the mysterious Colonel Oliver North, have resigned, and a commission has been appointed to investigate the activities of the National Security Council.

In advance of that investigation, Congress and the American people can only surmise that the White House has been conducting its own foreign policy without reference to the State Department or this country's allies.

To a degree the President is within his prerogatives in doing so.

But for him to ignore the advice of the cabinet officers most intimately concerned in favor of the National Security Council was risky business at best, even though he was motivated by the desire to effect the release of American hostages.

As a result, when the Iranian deal misfired, he has found himself in a steadily worsening situation, which presumably reached a climax with the disclosure that funds from Iran were turned over to the Nicaraguan Contras.

No one is impugning the President's motives, but apparently activities that were compromising to the nation's official policies were carried on by virtue of his authority, even though without his knowledge.

It is no wonder the State Department felt unable to formulate or conduct a coherent foreign policy.

There is no way in which Donald Regan, the White House chief of staff, can make this set of circumstances look anything but damaging.

Admiral Poindexter and his aide may have believed that what they were doing corresponded with the President's real desire to liberate the hostages and, on the other hand, help the Contras.

But between them they have created a sitution which has embarrassed the President in the eyes of this country and the world.

They have also seriously called into question the value of the National Security Council, whose activities will now be reviewed by a special commission.

The nation is relieved that the President has jettisoned both Poindexter and North. The business of clearing up the damage they have done can now proceed.

It is to be hoped, however, that the President will not indulge in any more adventures of this kind without the full knowledge and explicit approval of his Secretary of State.

THE CHRISTIAN SCIENCE MONITOR

Boston, MA, November 28, 1986

FOR President Reagan, the quickest way through the deepening Iran affair is to support the process that already exists for confronting serious breaches of official conduct and policy.

That process includes:

● The appointment of a special prosecutor. Attorney General Edwin Meese's quick assessment of what went amiss – which revealed a diversion of Iranian payments for arms to the Nicaragua contras – might do as a first step for administrative purposes. But a half dozen important US laws may have been broken, for which Reagan officials may be accountable.

The attorney general gave a bravura performance Tuesday in responding to questions about discoveries to date. But he clearly thinks that for the White House team, loyalty to the President should come first. That may be true, politically speaking. But the attorney general first represents the law, not an officeholder or administration. This widening affair could pull in others in the President's Cabinet; the White House staff; the vice-president, who is in charge of National Security Council matters; and the President himself, in terms of knowledge or authorization of events. Appointment of a special prosecutor would ensure the requisite impartiality of the inquiry.

● Full cooperation with congressional inquiries. To avoid a protracted confrontation with Capitol Hill, the administration should decide at the outset to cooperate fully with the hearings and reviews that will preoccupy the 100th Congress when it convenes in a few weeks. There may be some rough moments. Still, in prior congressional reviews of administration performance, lawmakers ultimately rose to the occasion in fairness and responsibility.

● Thorough review of foreign policy decisionmaking and immediate clear allocation of authority. The announced blue-ribbon panel review of NSC activities can be useful. But the management crisis is immediate. If White House accounts are to be believed, neither the President nor his top people knew in detail what was going on. Any conclusion – that they knew or did not know, or some degree of both – is painful to contemplate.

Until someone is clearly in charge, other governments cannot with confidence deal with this administration. For the moment at least, George Shultz must step to the fore. It is argued by some that Mr. Shultz owed it to the President to have forced a showdown on the Iran arms-for-hostages issue long ago. Would his resignation have only permitted the NSC to run further amok? This dilemma is but one further piece of evidence of how this affair may have tainted the careers of dedicated public servants.

Sensible policy cannot be made while a scandal like this still runs at full tilt.

Crisis reveals character. Mr. Reagan's tolerance of internal feuding, his casualness with detail, his reliance on public promotion rather than consensus-building – the negative potential of all these, which a professional staff is supposed to offset, has been illustrated.

Through candor and cooperation, he can put the crisis behind him. Meanwhile, he must assemble a White House and foreign-policy operation worthy of bipartisan support, the confidence of allies, and the interests of the great nation he leads.

Los Angeles Times

Los Angeles, CA, November 30, 1986

Atty. Gen. Edwin Meese III began asking Reagan Administration officials last weekend what they knew about the secret arms-for-hostages deal with Iran. One of those he talked to was Lt. Col. Oliver L. North of the National Security Council staff. On Monday, Meese was able to tell President Reagan that profits from the Iranian arms sales had been channeled into a Swiss bank account used by Nicaraguan *contras* fighting the Sandinista regime. On Tuesday, Reagan fired North, allegedly a central figure in the profit-diverting scheme. Not until Wednesday, though, did Meese order the FBI and its investigative specialists into the case. In the meantime North had gone to his White House office and destroyed certain files. What was in those files? For all anyone knows, they may have been this Administration's equivalent of the Watergate tapes.

If the investigation of the Iran arms deal had been conducted from the beginning by dispassionate professionals, as it should have been, North would have been barred from his office the moment he came under suspicion. Instead, after being alerted by last weekend's questioning, he had 36 hours to dispose of whatever papers he wanted to. Do copies of these documents exist elsewhere in the bureaucracy? Perhaps. It may also be that because the Iran operation seems to have bypassed normal channels, North alone held the paperwork.

There is no telling yet how far guilty knowledge of the Iran arms scandal may extend. What is evident is that the impartiality and thoroughness of an investigation presided over by political appointees, loyal to the President who chose them, inevitably generates suspicion, and with the bungling that allowed North continuing access to his files that suspicion is off and galloping. The ethics-in-government law allows an attorney general to request appointment of an independent counsel if a political conflict of interest arises. A President determined to expose the whole truth as soon as possible would order that done now.

The Dallas Morning News
Dallas, TX, November 27, 1986

The most important thing that President Reagan can do now, in the aftermath of disclosures that funds from clandestine arms sales to Iran were used to support Nicaraguan rebels, is to be as open and cooperative with investigators as possible. No matter how difficult the forthcoming probes may be for him and his aides, the president needs to avoid the kind of stonewalling that brought down another administration.

As the president surely realizes, the way in which the White House reacts to the Iranian arms crisis may have as much bearing on the nation's ability to conduct foreign policy and on history as the incredible series of events that led up to the debacle.

The president has made an excellent start in reassuring the public by selecting former Sen. John Tower to head a study of what should be the future role and conduct of the National Security Council. Serving with Tower will be two other well-respected foreign policy experts: Edmund Muskie, secretary of state in the Carter administration; and Brent Scowcroft, national security adviser in the Ford administration.

In addition, the Reagan administration has promised to pursue a separate investigation under Attorney General Edwin Meese to determine whether any federal crimes were committed in the operation. But the president would be well-advised to go a step farther and support the appointment of a special prosecutor to examine any possible violations of law — someone who could not be accused of having an ax to grind or a job to protect.

Such a prosecutor must get all the facts surrounding the arms sale and bring to justice anyone within the administration who may have broken the law.

By most accounts, this may be the most serious crisis that the Reagan presidency has faced. But how successfully the nation untangles itself from the problem will depend not only on the candor and decisiveness of the president, but also on the statesmanship of members of Congress. As the forthcoming investigations proceed, the need to resist partisan politics will grow. If the dialogue degenerates into potshots by administration foes, nothing useful will be accomplished.

The nation must find out what, if anything, administration officials outside of the National Security Council staff knew about the *contra* funds. But equally important, Democrats and Republicans alike must help the president restore his credibility in foreign affairs as quickly as possible, for no one will have anything to gain if the United States becomes unable to protect its strategic interests around the world.

AKRON BEACON JOURNAL
Akron, OH, November 30, 1986

THE SHOCK waves from the secret Iran deal will surely be felt in Central America. Contra rebels seeking to overthrow the Nicaraguan government allegedly received the profits from the sale of arms to Iran. It was a tangled transaction involving Swiss bank accounts and, possibly, violations of the law.

The nation is being asked to believe that Lt. Col. Oliver North of the National Security Council acted on his own, without the knowledge of the rest of the administration. Maybe. In any case, the money trail bypassed Congress, which is supposed to have oversight in such matters.

There is reason to be skeptical of the entire Reagan policy toward Central America, which centers on funding the Contra guerrillas. But there should be no argument that the Sandinista regime in Nicaragua needs to be contained. And the fallout from the Iran debacle threatens the Central American effort in a couple of ways.

For one thing, the prestige and credibility of the United States has been damaged in that region as it has elsewhere. It will be much harder to work out regional cooperation on a common problem — Nicaragua — amid the mistrust.

Second, Congress only approved Contra aid in close votes and will be reluctant to renew any aid now. That can be a positive move if Congress finally switches emphasis from arms aid to economic aid, to help develop the Central American region and make it immune to communist overtures. But the congressional mood is more likely to be a cutoff of aid because there is little trust in the Reagan administration's ability to spend it wisely.

Other, private aid sources may also dry up now. Those providing aid might not want to risk getting caught up in the coming investigations into the entire NSC agenda. The Iran episode may help explain the mysterious Contra funding that has surfaced in recent months. But Col. North has surely hurt the cause he sought to aid.

The Oregonian

Portland, OR, November 26, 1986

Some time ago, President Reagan charged that there was a secret terrorist connection linking such distant countries as Iran and Nicaragua. The reaction at the time was skeptical, but the link has now been found: It was operating out of the basement of the White House.

National Security Adviser John Poindexter and his free-lance agent Lt. Col. Oliver North should have been removed last week, just because of the disastrous effect of their secret course of selling arms to Iran. Tuesday's revelations that the money from the sale went into a secret Swiss bank account for the Contras only shows how far out of control the foreign relations of the United States have gone.

Last week, the situation appeared appalling. This week, it got worse.

The president says, and there seems no reason to disbelieve him, that he did not know where the money had gone. It is hard to say whether this is better or worse than if he had. His ignorance may provide an alibi to some violations of law, but it suggests that his laxity of control is worse than his bitterest enemies had ever charged.

"Follow the money," was the moral of the last major presidential scandal, and in this case it did not need much following. It took the Justice Department at most three days to uncover the creative Contra financing, and the key figure was not exactly well-hidden: North worked directly for Poindexter, who worked directly for Reagan.

The president may claim to be shocked by North's activities, but hardly surprised. This administration repeatedly has declared itself to be above the law in foreign policy activities, especially regarding Nicaragua.

When Congress refused to provide aid for the Contras, the Reagan administration winkingly encouraged private American citizens to go to war. When the CIA decided to mine Nicaragua's harbors — an internationally recognized act of war — the agency ignored even its legal responsibility to notify Congress. When Nicaragua sued in the World Court, the United States declared itself outside the court's jurisdiction.

To Oliver North, the leap from this attitude to a course of embezzling against communism could not have seemed great. To the administration, and the Senate, and the American people, the lesson is underlined again: A foreign policy conducted under the table will go lower than ever expected.

THE COMMERCIAL APPEAL

Memphis, TN, November 26, 1986

PRESIDENT Reagan's arms-for-Iran crisis has taken a drastic turn for the worse with the disclosure that money from the sale was secretly — and probably illegally — used to support the anti-Sandinista guerrillas in Nicaragua.

In an uncomfortable announcement, Reagan admitted he did not know his National Security Council was running money to the contras, adding to the impression that he has lost touch with foreign-policy details.

The deepening scandal caused Reagan to accept the resignation of his national security adviser, Vice Adm. John Poindexter, and to dismiss Poindexter's key aide, Lt. Col. Oliver North, who handled the transfer of funds.

According to Atty. Gen. Edwin Meese, who investigated the matter for Reagan, Israel sold American weapons to Iran and deposited the proceeds in a contra account in a Swiss bank. Meese said no one higher than Poindexter and North knew about the maneuver, which, if correct, would be a bizarre way to conduct policy.

What makes the action perhaps criminal is that it took place after Congress passed and Reagan signed a law barring all but a bit of humanitarian aid to the anti-Marxist Nicaraguans. To slip them between $10 million and $30 million, which undoubtedly they used for arms, would violate both the spirit and letter of the law.

The bombshell comes at a dreadful time for the President. He is still reeling from criticism of the arms-for-hostages deal, which he is almost alone in defending. Now he faces a Watergate-style scandal involving White House wrongdoing.

Congressional Democrats have pledged a series of investigations, which they will try to keep running until the 1988 elections. The prospect is for serious damage to Reagan and his party.

Like all presidents in trouble, Reagan will appoint a commission — this time a board to review the work of the National Security Council. No review is needed; the NSC should act as it was meant to — giving the President all the options, not running covert operations like a mini-CIA without congressional oversight.

Instead of a review board, Reagan should appoint an experienced, respected figure to head the NSC — Brent Scowcroft, for example. Then the public would know that the council's advisory role was in good hands while the White House coped with the political crisis it brought on itself.

The Birmingham News

Birmingham, AL, November 27, 1986

The stunning revelation that profits from clandestine U.S. arms sales to Iran had been diverted to the anti-government Contras in Nicaragua left President Reagan with little choice but to fire the man responsible and to accept the resignation of that aide's supervisor, who knew something of the deal.

So Lt. Col. Oliver North, a can-do Marine officer on the National Security Council staff who had helped plan such successful operations as the Grenada liberation and the hijacking of the *Achille Lauro* hijackers, is out the door. With him goes Vice Adm. John Poindexter, who asked to be relieved of his assignment as assistant to the president for national security affairs.

And outside the White House, the critics are yelling for more bloodletting. They want Mr. Reagan's scalp, or at least Donald Regan's.

But what exactly has happened here? It appears that an overzealous operative in the administration has taken some of Mr. Reagan's laudable policy goals — opening new communication with Iran and providing support for the freedom fighters in Nicaragua — and mixed them together in an ingenious way that is certainly against the expressed will of Congress and most probably against the law.

Worst of all, North apparently did not tell his boss, Poindexter, exactly what he was doing. And Poindexter did not tell the president anything.

Many questions remain about the operation that Attorney General Edwin Meese described Tuesday. He says arms worth about $12 million were provided to Israel, which sold them to "representatives of Iran." Money to cover the full cost of the arms was given to the United States, while some $10 million to $30 million in profits were deposited in Swiss bank accounts for the Nicaraguan rebels.

Why did the Iranians pay so much more than the arms were worth? How much did the Israelis know about where the money was going? How much of the money is now in Contra hands, and how has it been spent?

But the most important question is why was a lieutenant colonel on the National Security Council staff making foreign policy? And why didn't the president know more about what was going on?

Mr. Reagan has always been more interested in the broad direction of foreign policy than in the details of its implementation. In most cases, this approach has worked well for him. While some leaders have been unable to see the forest for the trees, Mr. Reagan has been able to look over the whole landscape and map a strong and direct course to his foreign policy goals.

He trusted his aides to follow that course, and to steer around the political and legal pitfalls along the way. That trust was betrayed. The implementation of Mr. Reagan's policy was, in his own words, "seriously flawed."

Now Mr. Reagan has said he will name a special commission to examine the role of the National Security Council staff and the Justice Department will continue to investigate the money angle.

We hope these two probes will answer all the remaining questions about the Iran arms deal so that Mr. Reagan can put this foreign policy fiasco behind him and move on to more important matters of state.

Benjamin Linder, U.S. Volunteer, Slain by Contras in Nicaragua

An American volunteer working in Nicaragua was slain April 28, 1987. Benjamin Linder, 27, of Portland, Ore. was killed when contras attacked a work crew at La Camoleona in Jinotego province, some 30 miles from the Honduran border. Linder, a mechanical engineer, was working as a volunteer on a rural hydroelectric project. In a recent interview, Linder has said an acquaintance who was captured by the contras and later escaped had been told that the work crew, which was surveying the site of a hydroelectric project, had been targeted for death. Linder reportedly was the first United States civilian working for the Sandinistas to be killed by the contras. The Nicaraguan government said it held the U.S. government "directly responsible" for his death. Two Nicaraguans also died in the raid.

According to Nicaraguan government figures, 10 foreigners had been killed in the contra war. In October 1986, access to war zone for foreign volunteers had been restricted, but the restrictions only applied to those working on projects sponsored by foreign governments. Linder had been among a number of Americans on whose behalf the New York-based Center for Constitutional Rights in Spetember 1986 had filed a lawsuit seeking an end to U.S. funding of the contras. The suit was later dismissed.

Some 100 Americans and other foreigners protested Linder's death outside the U.S. embassy in Managua April 29, blaming U.S. support for the contras for the killing. Six members of the U.S. Congress urged Secretary of State George Shultz to call for an investigation and for a judgment on whether Linder's killers should be extradited. Linder was buried with honors in Nicaragua April 30. His family flew to Nicaragua for the burial, and was met on arrival by Foreign Minister Miguel D'Escoto Brockman and President Daniel Ortega's wife, Rosario Murillo. President Ortega attended the funeral.

The Record

Hackensack, NJ, May 1, 1987

Benjamin Linder, a 27-year-old mechanical engineer from Portland, Ore., died at the hands of the U.S.-backed contras in northern Nicaragua this week. Like so many thousands who have died in this undeclared war, Mr. Linder did nothing to deserve such a fate. He broke no laws in traveling to Nicaragua, did not violate the terms of his passport, did not aid or abet a hostile foreign power, and did not take up arms against his native land. He was in Nicaragua on a $4,500 grant issued by a small foundation in California that is also perfectly legal — even though, via people like Mr. Linder, it does assist a country that the Reagan administration regularly denounces as a Soviet outpost.

The contras who attacked the hydroelectric project on which Mr. Linder was working — killing him and two Nicaraguan co-workers — are armed, trained, and financed by the United States government. Indeed, the assault may have been in furtherance of the CIA's strategy (the subject of a recent report in The Miami Herald) of attacking and destroying Nicaragua's primitive electric-power system. The contras also may have attacked Mr. Linder because he is a foreigner, one of hundreds of young Americans and Western Europeans who have traveled to Nicaragua to offer their technical assistance and moral support — people whom the contras have taken to kidnapping and killing as part of their campaign to isolate the Sandinistas both politically and economically.

In the attack that killed Mr. Linder, the contras were pursuing strategies that the U.S. government has, at the very least, broadly endorsed. The young man's father was understandably bitter when he flew into Managua yesterday for his son's funeral. Benjamin, he said, was killed by "someone who paid someone who paid someone who paid someone and so on down the line to the president of the United States." Benjamin Linder did not, as White House spokesman Marlin Fitzwater suggested, die as a result of "internal strife in another country." He died as a consequence of military aggression by his own government.

WORCESTER TELEGRAM

Worcester, MA, MAy 15, 1987

All compassionate persons grieve for parents who have lost a son to violent death. So we feel sympathy for Dr. and Mrs. David Linder of Portland, Ore., whose 27-year-old son was killed in Nicaragua during combat between Sandinista troops and anti-government rebels.

But Americans must reject the Linders' claim, voiced by the father before a congressional subcommittee, that the young man's death was the "result of United States policy" and that somehow we should feel a collective guilt. That charge, and the manner in which it was delivered in subsequent television interviews, amounts to an attempt to politicize this tragic incident. That is unfortunate.

Benjamin Ernest Linder went to work in Nicaragua to help the Marxist, Soviet-supported regime because he believed in its cause and evidently rejected his own government's policy. He went there against repeated official U.S. warnings that Americans should stay out of combat zones. He knew the risks; so did his parents. At least seven other volunteers, all Europeans, have died in Nicaragua since 1983 as the result of warfare.

Assisting the Contra rebels is official U.S. policy. Helping the Ortega regime is not. Many countries would take a dim view of their citizens working for a hostile government at a time of a crucial struggle.

The American system recognizes political dissent and the principle of individual choice. Our government considers no retribution against the 200 or so U.S. volunteers on Ortega's payroll. But asking the American public to take responsibility for their safety is unreasonable.

Young Linder chose to contribute his talent to a cause in which he believed. He took a chance and paid with his life. We feel sorry for him and his family. But we certainly will not plead guilty.

FORT WORTH STAR-TELEGRAM
Fort Worth, TX, May 4, 1987

It was inevitable that one of the hundreds of American volunteers in Nicaragua sooner or later would get killed in the conflict between the Sandinista government and U.S.-backed contra guerrillas.

Benjamin E. Linder was the first. He probably won't be the last.

The nation should mourn for Linder, as it would for any American who loses his or her life while seeking to do good in a foreign land. Linder was an idealist, a believer in those principles of liberty and justice that are the bedrock of the society that nurtured him.

His convictions, rooted in the best American traditions, led him to go to Nicaragua to use his training as an engineer to help people in that impoverished and battered land build the foundations for a better life.

Those same convictions caused him to oppose the current administration's policy toward Nicaragua. Because he was an outspoken critic of U.S. aid to the contras, some now say that he was singled out for assassination by the contras. There is, however, no convincing evidence to that effect.

Linder simply appeared to have been at the wrong place at the wrong time. He was working on a project guarded by a unit of Sandanista militia that was attacked by a contra patrol.

Unfortunately, such tragedies are likely to occur again and again as long as the civil war in Nicaragua continues and Americans continue to go there and venture out into areas where combat is likely to occur. Americans who volunteer to work on projects in Nicaragua out of either a genuine desire to help or a way of showing disagreement with the policies of the Reagan administration must recognize the risk they take in doing so.

One can disagree with the Reagan administration's policy of aiding the contras without going to Nicaragua to work. But, if one does choose to go and run the risk of being killed, this nation cannot be expected to take responsibility for the tragedy.

The American people should mourn for Benjamin Linder. But the American government is not to blame for his death. The American public should not, therefore, fall prey to Sandinista propaganda that would portray Linder as a victim of America's Central America policy.

Omaha World-Herald
Omaha, NE, May 1, 1987

One of the ironies of the Nicaraguan situation is the involvement of Americans on both sides. While some anti-Communist groups raise money and send arms to the contras, other organizations with a political or religious orientation help the Sandinistas with money and volunteers. At one time more money had been raised in the United States for the Sandinistas than Congress was sending to the contras.

Pro-Sandinista Americans tend to be idealists who see the Sandinista regime as a benevolent reformist government dedicated to health, education and welfare improvements for the poor and underprivileged. The pro-contra groups have a view of the Sandinistas that more closely resembles that of the U.S. government, which, with good reason, considers the Sandinistas and their Soviet allies as a threat to nearby democracies.

The contras are not merely disgruntled remnants of Somoza's national guard, as their critics in the United States often assert. Nor are they mostly outsiders and mercenaries. With or without congressional support, they have consistently kept more soldiers in the field than the Sandinistas had when they fought and won the 1979 revolution against the corrupt Somoza regime.

Both sides now have their American heroes. Benjamin Linder, killed this week by contra forces while serving as a pro-Sandinista volunteer, is being widely praised in pro-Sandinista circles. He is not the first American to be caught in the Nicaraguan war. On the other side, Sam Hall and Eugene Hasenfus were taken prisoner, and the companions of Hasenfus were killed, while flying arms to the contras.

Linder's death is tragic. Indications are that one of his motivations was to make life better for the poor in Nicaragua. But what happened to him, as well as what happened to Hall and Hasenfus, is a reminder that Americans who go to Nicaragua against the advice of the U.S. government and align themselves with one side or the other in the Nicaraguan civil war do so at their own risk.

Winnipeg Free Press
Winnipeg, Man., May 3, 1987

The circumstances of the death of U.S. engineer Benjamin Linder in northern Nicaragua draw attention to the fundamentally worthless strategy being followed by the U.S.-backed Nicaraguan rebel movement that is trying to get rid of the Sandinista regime.

The rebels are not conducting a domestic guerrilla war that would bind them closer to the population while building the support that would justify their eventual seizure of political control in Nicaragua. They are indulging in a rather cowardly sporadic terrorist campaign against civilian targets that is planned in Langley, Virginia and that will have the effect of progressively alienating them from most Nicaraguans.

In the conspiratorial and paranoid atmosphere that prevails inside the Langley headquarters of the Central Intelligence Agency, the strategy imposed on the Nicaraguan rebels may seem to make sense. Outside, it makes no sense at all. It is a recipe for failure.

It has more advantages for the CIA than for the rebels. It gives the agency an excuse to use its limitless funds and apparently extra-legal status to practise covert action on real people. The CIA can write assessments of the effectiveness of training rebels to carry out such pointless attacks as the one that caught Linder.

Linder died in Jinotega province in a gorge from which he hoped to draw hydro-electric power to bring electricity to rural villages. Both the Sandinistas and the rebels lied about how he died. The Sandinistas first said he was deliberately shot in his village office by a six-man rebel assassination squad. Then they said he was kidnapped from his office and shot nearby by such a squad. The rebels said he died accidentally in the crossfire of an engagement between them and Sandinista troops.

U.S. journalists went to the spot and got the truth. Linder, armed with a Soviet AK-47 assault rifle, was with four similarly-armed, uniformed militia men, surveying the gorge for its hydro-electric potential when they were attacked with grenades and rifles by rebels higher up the gorge. Linder died immediately.

Both sides indulged in propaganda distortions for obvious reasons. The Sandinistas, eager to create inside the United States the maximum horror, made it appear that the rebels had deliberately set out to kill a U.S.

citizen. The rebels, eager to attract for this episode the minimum attention within the United States, made Linder's death appear to be a tragic byproduct of a legitimate military engagement.

The significance of what happened in that gorge has nothing to do with Linder's death, which is no more tragic than the deaths of thousands of Nicaraguans. The real point is that what happened was completely ordinary, a routine operation by the rebels not against a defended Sandinista barracks but against farmers in militia uniform trying to defend a foreigner who was helping them to get electric light in their huts.

Is this the kind of action that will bind rural Nicaraguans closer to the rebel movement? Will this encourage farmers to offer shelter, food and information to passing rebel patrols? Will this detach the sympathies of ordinary people from the Sandinista regime in Managua? The answers are self-evident.

Yet this is an ordinary example of the daily conduct of the rebels. They riddle civilian buses with automatic fire. They burn crops. They kill farm animals. They destroy farm equipment. They cut the throats of community leaders. They attack farm villages. They blow up electricity transformers.

The great brains in the CIA tell their rebel pupils that these acts are blows against the infrastructure by which the Sandinistas consolidate their grip on power. Common sense suggests that the only ones really suffering from these blows are poor, illiterate, rural peasants of exactly the type that an intelligent guerrilla campaign would be designed to protect and attract.

The rebel campaign is so ill-conceived, so badly executed and so certain of failure to achieve its goals that it might have been planned by a highly-placed KGB mole within the CIA. Instead, it is the expression of President Ronald Reagan's obsession with a tiny country posing no current threat to U.S. national security.

The Linder death would have some meaning if Mr. Reagan could separate it from its political, propaganda and even moral aspects. If he would simply see it as evidence that his Nicaragua policy cannot possibly work, he might come to his senses, call the whole thing off and let Nicaraguans settle their own fate.

The Idaho STATESMAN

Boise, ID, May 2, 1987

To the footnotes of that dirty business in Nicaragua, add the name of Benjamin Ernest Linder. He deserves to be remembered.

Mr. Linder, a 27-year-old from Portland, was killed Tuesday by contra rebels, supposedly the moral equivalents of our Founding Fathers. He is the first American volunteer killed while working in Nicaragua. His crime was being in the wrong place at the wrong time.

Mr. Linder, an engineer, was slain along with two Nicaraguan militiamen. He was working on a small hydroelectric plant in La Camaleona, a village 45 miles from the Honduran border. He apparently was caught in a firefight.

Contra and Sandinista leaders were quick to blame each other. The U.S. government paused briefly to express its regrets, but urged civilians to volunteer in "democratic countries" where their efforts will be appreciated.

Contra leaders implicitly blamed Mr. Linder for his own death by being in a war zone. They didn't mention that they initiated this war and determine daily where it is fought.

Regardless, Mr. Linder certainly knew the risks. He is one of 1,500 Americans working in Nicaragua. They do so either because they oppose the American government's policy of foisting war on the country or simply because they want to help.

There's evidence Mr. Linder was moved by the former motive. He was party to at least two lawsuits brought by groups trying to stop U.S. aid to the contras. Activist leaders charged that Mr. Linder was targeted for death because of that involvement. Prophetically, he said in one suit that he might "suffer irreparable physical harm as the result of the unlawful activities of the United States government."

Yes, Mr. Linder knew the risks. He decided to take them because he believed in what he was doing. Politics aside, Mr. Linder was committed to making life a bit better for peasants in a small Central American village.

His death is an embarrassment for the contras, a propaganda opportunity for the Sandinistas and an annoyance to the U.S. government. He will be missed by the people of La Camaleona. And by those everywhere who value helping others.

The Des Moines Register

Des Moines, IA, May 7, 1987

The death of an American civilian in Nicaragua is no more nor less tragic than the deaths of thousands of Nicaraguan, Honduran and Salvadoran civilians over the course of the five-year U.S. war in Central America.

But the slaying of Benjamin E. Linder by U.S.-backed contra rebels is different, because it epitomizes the self-destructive nature of the U.S. military adventurism in Central America.

The 27-year-old Linder was working as a mechanical engineer to provide hydroelectric power to impoverished Nicaraguan villages. In contrast, the Reagan administration is financing and advising the contras in a strategy of "low-intensity conflict," in which villages, hospitals and schools are razed and civilians terrorized.

Since 1982, more than 20,000 Nicaraguans have been killed, 10,000 wounded and 300,000 left homeless. This strategy has brought almost no support for the contras inside Nicaragua. But it has hindered efforts by the Nicaraguan government to promote economic development, which seems to be just fine with the Reagan administration.

Perhaps Linder and the 3,000 other American civilians in Nicaragua should know better than to live in a nation against which the United States is waging a war — albeit an unofficial one because the Reagan administration lacks the political courage to ask for a declaration of war.

Instead, the White House pursues a covert war, financing the contras with private and illegally diverted funds, and sending U.S. National Guard, Army and Army Reserve troops to Honduras to conduct "maneuvers" on the Nicaraguan border.

President Reagan even went so far as to declare himself an "official contra."

The dishonesty of this policy, by which officials profess their hope for peace while waging war, has created a political — potentially criminal — crisis for the administration.

It also has led to the death of an American civilian working in a country officially at peace with the United States.

"Who killed Ben?" asked David Linder, father of the slain American, "Someone who paid someone who paid someone who paid someone who paid someone and so on down the line to the president of the United States."

His voice broke and he wept.

ONE FOR THE GIPPER

MILWAUKEE SENTINEL

Milwaukee, WI, May 6, 1987

For even the most fervent supporters of US aid to the contra rebels in Nicaragua, there must be a sense of loss and frustration over the death of an American citizen.

That this death apparently came at the hands of contra forces that reportedly singled out Benjamin E. Linder for elimination is especially maddening.

Of course, it is proper to state, as some have, that Linder was "in harm's way" and that he was at risk in a land where a rebellion is in progress.

Yet there is a sense that Linder's efforts as a non-combatant to assist the rural population as a civilian hydroelectric engineer were sincere and of no threat to rebel or Sandinista.

Mix into the controversy reports that Linder was tortured before his death and the incident is particularly sad and brutal — if, of course, the charges of a Sandinista doctor can be believed. They cannot be, however, easily dismissed.

The attack near Jinotega, of course, comes at a time when administration credibility on aid to the contras is at its lowest point. Recent revelations in the Iran-contra affair and the start of congressional hearings account for that.

The incident can only further undermine administration efforts to appropriate money for the rebels.

Yet Linder's death and the discord in the rebel hierarchy justify this doubting attitude.

Throughout the time the United States has been aiding the contras, there have been charges of murder and other atrocities allegedly committed by the rebel group. Conversely, the Sandinistas themselves are no angels. They, too, have been charged with human rights violations.

But the death of Linder symbolizes all the brutality that comes with a war. And for that reason, charges of torture or assassination cannot be ignored by Congress — or the administration.

LEXINGTON HERALD-LEADER

Lexington, KY, May 1, 1987

The civil war in Nicaragua has dragged two young Americans into the news this week.

On Tuesday, Benjamin Linder was killed in an ambush in northern Nicaragua. The 27-year-old engineer from Washington was working as a volunteer, helping design power plants for the Sandinista government. He died in a grenade attack by anti-government guerrillas who enjoy the backing of the U.S. government.

On Wednesday, Carl R. Channell pleaded guilty to defrauding the US government while helping raise money for those same guerrillas. Channell had raised money for a tax-exempt foundation under the pretense of offering humanitarian aid to the Nicaraguan guerrillas. In reality, the money went to buy weapons.

It is hard to imagine two more contrasting individuals than these two young men.

Linder was a bearded and scruffily dressed figure with an odd sense of humor. Friends said he rode a unicycle under his gown at college graduation; when he went to Nicaragua in 1983, he worked as a circus clown until he could obtain an engineer's permit. He worked in the Nicaraguan countryside with the knowledge that he was always in danger.

Channell is nattily dressed and immaculately groomed, as befits one accustomed to moving in circles of wealth and power. His connections to the Reagan White House gained him entree with rich conservatives, who gladly contributed millions to his effort to help finance the Nicaraguan guerrillas. Perhaps he, too, has an odd sense of humor. One of his fund-raising projects claimed to be supplying toys to the guerrillas' children. In fact, it was buying guns and explosives for the guerrillas' war in the Nicaraguan countryside.

There is no reason to doubt either man's sincerity. In their own minds, both were working for larger causes. Linder seems to have been genuinely dedicated to helping the desperately poor people of rural Nicaragua, Channell committed to stopping the spread of leftist political ideologies.

Most Americans are probably reluctant to embrace the political views of either Linder or Channell. There are few blacks and whites in the gray world of Central American politics. Still, consider the rewards of these two young men.

Benjamin Linder put his beliefs on the line and paid with his life at the hands of guerrillas financed by his own government.

Carl Channell has plead guilty to defrauding that government, and is cooperating with prosecutors in hopes of escaping severe punishment.

Now ask yourself which man's life exemplifies the best traits of the American character. Or, to put it another way, which would you want on your side in a civil war?

The Knickerbocker News

Albany, NY, May 6, 1987

Benjamin Linder was one of thousands of Americans working in Nicaragua in support of the Sandinista government. Last week, he became the first American to die at the hands of Nicaraguan Contra rebels, who are supported by the Reagan administration.

Is his blood therefore on the hands of the Contra supporters? Is it proof the Contras are murderers of innocent civilians, far from President Reagan's image of them as freedom fighters?

Some critics of the Reagan policy are convinced the answer is yes to both questions, and are using this tragic episode to bolster their cause. They are the ones who are wrong.

Some facts need to be established up front: First, no matter where one stands on this issue, Mr. Linder's death is a cause for mourning. He was as committed to his political beliefs as he was skilled in the field of electronics. Even if one believes he was wrong to labor in support of the Marxist Sandinistas, as we do, that is no reason to trivialize his death.

Second, neither the Sandinistas nor the Contras have been totally forthcoming about the circumstances surrounding Mr. Linder's death.

Initial reports from the Contras indicated Mr. Linder was caught in a crossfire between government and rebel troops. That is not true. Reliable eye-witnesses say Mr. Linder had just reported for work and was seated and writing in a notebook when he was struck from behind by a rebel grenade. Neither he nor the government militiamen had time to fire back at their attackers.

Initial Sandinista reports said Mr. Linder was slain after he had been captured by the rebels. Obviously, that is not true either.

Nor is there any truth in the assertion by other Americans who support the Sandinista cause that Mr. Linder's death was "the murder of an unarmed humanitarian worker." In truth, Mr. Linder was armed — and apparently because he had heard reports that the rebels were gunning for him. Witnesses said Mr. Linder had just put down his AK-47 rifle when he was struck by the grenade.

That both sides would so distort the truth shows how desperate they are to sway world opinion to their side. That is one good reason for Americans on both sides of this issue to examine all claims with careful scrutiny.

It's also a reason to put this conflict in its proper perspective — not as a struggle between an upright revolutionary government in Managua and a band of ragtag killers intent on establishing yet another repressive military regime. Rather, it is whether Nicaragua should become another Communist base in our hemisphere.

We think the answer has to be no.

Mr. Linder obviously disagreed and, as an intelligent and thoughtful American, freely decided to put himself in harm's way for the sake of his convictions.

That he died is regrettable. That the Contras would try to excuse themselves is also regrettable. But that is no excuse for the Sandinistas' role in all of this. That Managua should now attempt to use an American's death for propaganda for their cause is an ugly attempt to distract the world from their true aim — to hold power forever, with Moscow's support.

Part III: El Salvador

A new cast of social groups and political actors emerged in the Central American spotlight by the 1960s. With the Cuban Revolution and the advent of Soviet influence in Latin America, United States policy in the region that the American elites had helped to foster could not be cured by democratic slogans. As a result, the few who had amassed privileges and political power were attacked. The United States, having been traditionally complacent about Central America, was unprepared to deal with the wave of social change that swept through the region. Many Latin Americans contend that the United States used the supposed communist threat as the latest in a cycle of convenient pretexts to maintain its dominant position in the region.

Historically, the middle class had been a small minority in Central America, but as it grew larger and became more diverse, it challenged the oligarchic structure, forcing the ruling elites to seek allies in the military, which in turn made appeals to the United States on the grounds of anticommunism. When the disaffected elements of the middle class followed the Cuban example and linked up with grass-roots organizations of peasants and workers, an explosive union was forged. Added to this was a progressive Catholic Church, moved by the doctrine of "liberation theology," which created a movement that was not merely politically motivated but spiritually inspired. All these factors merged in El Salvador, where guerilla forces met with relative success in the late 1970s and early 1980s.

The conditions necessary to produce social upheaval had existed in El Salvador for decades: poverty among the masses, extreme wealth held by a tiny oligarchy and a brutal and repressive political system. The rapid economic growth that came to El Salvador in the 1960s and 1970s proved to be the spark that ignited the fuse of revolution. The middle class, though tiny, was strengthened and expanded by the new economic activity. However, it had no political representation. The oligarchy attempted to preserve its political power by enlisting the military to protect its interests. The U.S. lost a valuable opportunity for reform in 1972 when it failed to respond to an election voided by the military when ballots cast for Jose Napolean Duarte threatened the oligarchy's hold on political power. "Popular organizations" of peasants, workers, students, church sectors and some elements of the middle class began to adopt nontraditional avenues of protest after the failure of the election to achieve change. But strikes and peaceful factory and foreign embassy sit-ins staged by the opposition were violently suppressed. In 1979, a series of reformist military coups unleashed a civil war that has left an estimated 50,000 people dead. Linked politically to democratic-minded politicians who had abandoned hope for peaceful reform, guerillas were able to occupy a quarter of the country by the mid-1980s. U.S.-backed government forces, however, have slowly forced a stalemate in the war and opened the possibility of a military victory over the guerillas as the 1990s approach.

Death Squads Kill Civilians; Aid to Country Debated

The pent-up forces in El Salvador's highly polarized society began mobilizing in the late 1970s and early 1980s. Some on the left used the political opening to try to push for more drastic changes while others prepared for a true socialist revolution. The traditional right and more conservative officers in the military sought to reverse the reformist movement within the military by initiating a massive repression employing the infamous *escuandrones de muerte* (death squads)—paramilitary gangs linked to the military and orchestrated by the oligarchy—that turned El Salvador into a slaughterhouse. Every day new piles of brutally murdered and mutilated bodies were found on street corners, garbage dumps and at the bottom of ravines. Many leaders of El Salvador's "popular organizations" were among the dead as a result of this program of political assassination that radicalized some leaders who had often been considered moderate in the Salvadoran context.

As the violence mounted many of the government's early supporters went into opposition as they sensed the junta being compromised by the repression and the resurgence of the right-wing officers. Salvadoran President Jose Napolean Duarte and the United States, however, did not. As hundreds of innocent civilians were killed by death squads each month and as the guerillas fought successfully in the provinces, the U.S. rushed assistance to the Salvadoran military attempting to strengthen a government verging on collapse. The Carter Administration delivered $10.7 million in "non-lethal" and lethal military aid plus a substantial economic-assistance package in 1980 and early 1981. That attempt and the subsequent aid packages granted by the Reagan Administration from 1981 to 1985 salvaged the government's power while periodic "general offensives" by the guerillas, modeled after those of the victorious Sandinistas in Nicaragua, failed to spark the mass uprising that the left in El Salvador had expected.

A coalition of right-wing parties led by former Major Roberto D'Aubuisson produced a victory in the March 1982 Constituent Assembly elections. D'Aubuisson, who had been dismissed from the army because of his extreme politics, represented a far-right response to El Salvador's civil war and was rumored to be linked directly to the death squads and to the murder of Archbishop Oscar Romero, a liberal church leader. Only strong pressure from the U.S. prevented D'Aubuisson from being named as a provisional president, being viewed as an unacceptable partner for the U.S. by much of the U.S. Congress. Not much more than a figurehead for the military, Duarte had his reformist credentials severely tested as the death squads continued to wreak havoc in the next two years.

U.S. State Department officials said December 31, 1983 that the Salvadoran government appeared to be complying with U.S. pressure to curb the activities of right-wing death squads. Salvadoran government officials and top officials in the armed forces had pledged Dec. 15 to crack down on the death squads. The Salvadoran government had reportedly asked for U.S. technical and investigative aid in bringing the squads under control, and the U.S. agreed. The Roman Catholic auxiliary bishop of San Salvador said Dec. 25 that 6,096 people had died in the nation's civil war to date in 1983. The bishop, Gregorio Rosa Chaves, said 4,736 of the deaths were attributable to the armed forces and right-wing death squads.

Supported by U.S. and reported Central Intelligence Agency funding, Duarte was elected president of El Salvador for the second time in 1984 and, this time, allowed to take office. During that 1984 campaign, the *New York Times* March 3 cited a former Salvadoran military official who charged that D'Aubuisson had organized and continued to direct right-wing death squads. The military official, who was not named for reasons of security, was described as a supporter of the Salvadoran government who had served "at the highest level of the security police." He was said to have known D'Aubuisson for many years and described him as an "anarchic psychopath" whose ascension to the presidency would lead to "uncontrolled violence" in El Salvador. He added that Salvadoran government officials kept police and soldiers from locations where political murders were to take place and aided assassins in obtaining refuge in Guatemala.

The Miami Herald

Miami, FL, January 19, 1984

TO BE successful, major-league pitchers must have a wide assortment of pitches. When a batter is expecting a fastball, a good pitcher is likely to deliver a curve, a slider, or a knuckleball. The purpose is to keep the hitters off balance. Three years into the Reagan Administration, that philosophy appears to be the guiding principle of the President's policy for dealing with Congress on El Salvador.

In San Salvador, Vice President George Bush warned Salvadoran President Alvaro Magana on Dec. 10 that there was no dichotomy of views in the United States about allowing government-condoned violence to continue. If death-squad murders persist, El Salvador would lose the support of the American people, Congress, and the Administration. First pitch: A fast ball, right across the plate.

Then came the other pitches. Now everybody is off balance, confused. President Reagan used a pocket veto of dubious legality to stave off legislation reimposing certification by Congress of human-rights programs in El Salvador as a condition to granting new military and economic aid. The Administration rejected similar advice by the Presidential Commission on Central America.

Instead, Deputy Secretary of State Kenneth Dam suggested the *possibility* of selective cutoffs in military aid to El Salvador unless human-rights violations cease. Then, on Monday, the Administration voluntarily submitted a report to Congress asserting that human rights conditions in El Salvador have improved. That came right after the President came up with his best change-up pitch: In his weekly radio speech to the American public, the President proposed sending another $400-million in military aid to El Salvador over the next 20 months.

Administration officials say that the message that Vice President Bush delivered to President Magana was successful; that indeed the level of violence in El Salvador has decreased dramatically. If so, there is no reason why the Administration cannot accept mandatory certification.

If it refuses, Congress has the obligation to set the signals straight when it reconvenes next week. The first priority should be to re-impose mandatory certification. That is the only language the violators of human rights in El Salvador would understand. No more curve balls to confuse the issue.

The Salt Lake Tribune

Salt Lake City, UT, February 7, 1984

U.S. Secretary of State George Shutz, speaking about developments in El Salvador, emphasized a particularly significant point concerning this nation's counter-insurgency policies. If not careful, the United States could be accused of condoning precisely what is deplorable when practiced by its antagonists.

Beginning a nine-day Caribbean and Latin American tour, the secretary commented on the so-called right-wing "death squads" operating in politically bloodied El Salvador. Contending this form of eliminating dissent was declining, Secretary Shultz candidly observed: "The tactics of terror, whether totalitarian terror or whether death squad terror, have no place in a democracy."

Then, making the reigning point, he said of the U.S. government: ". . . we oppose terror in all its forms." Just so.

Evidently, administration insistence that the Salvadoran regime discredit its followers' tendency to practice ex officio murder on the local opposition is making headway. Previously, during his stop-over in El Salvador, Vice President George Bush had also spoken harshly against "death squad" justice. Eventually, it was reported, those previously identified as connected with the roving, ad hoc executioners started leaving the country.

- Since El Salvador's military rulers rely heavily on U.S. financing for their power, they are obliged to accommodate some directives from Washington, D.C. On the matter of terror, the administration is definitely serious.

In trouble spots around the world, most prominently Lebanon, U.S. officials, civilians and servicemen, are the targets of terrorist attacks. Uniformly, such means of menace are hotly, properly denounced from this nation's capital. Terror, then, could hardly be a method endorsed or excused in the arsenal of besieged U.S. neighbors and allies.

If the administration is, as an example, to pressure for a Mideast peace by accusing Syria of aiding terrorist attacks against U.S. Marines in Lebanon, it can't be in the position of having the same allegation thrown back at it in El Salvador. Mr. Shultz' repudiation of terrorism was more than a handy remark. Let it be strenuously heeded as intended.

THE ATLANTA CONSTITUTION

Atlanta, GA, January 9, 1984

Events are closing in on El Salvador's government and army.

The White House's Jan. 10 deadline for demonstrable Salvadoran progress in combating right-wing death squad murders is fast approaching. And the administration is preparing to go back to the congressional well again, this time for a $100-million bucketful of military aid for El Salvador.

Meantime, the Salvadoran army is reeling from a successful rebel frontal assault on a supposedly impregnable garrison to the north of San Salvador, and the army's highly touted San Vicente pacification program is stymied because of the civilian government's inability to deliver promised services and the army's failure to prevent renewed guerrilla infiltration.

It's a time of testing for Salvadoran officialdom — with a skeptical U.S. Congress and an impatient American administration acting as flinty-eyed monitors. Increasing pressure is being exerted on the Salvadoran government to purge itself and the army of suspected leaders of the terror campaign.

The payoff, to date, is measurable but by no means definitive. The numbers of political murders have diminished. Several reputed hit-squad chiefs have been reassigned from their military posts, two to jobs outside the country. A suspect in the killings of two American labor advisers has been detained.

That's not nearly enough evidence that the Salvadoran government is an investment worth pouring additional money into. There's still a bit more time to make a case, but even these few salutory moves are meeting with clenched-teeth resistance from the bitter-enders.

The most feared of the terror groups, the Anti-Communist Army, has groused publicly that "we are not going to allow the *gringos* to make decisions on changes of military posts." And Roberto D'Aubuisson, the right-wing politician thought by many to be the death-squads' champion, thundered the other day: "I want to tell all those who have been unjustly named (as murder suspects) by those left-wing publications, *The New York Times* and *The Washington Post,* and repeated by the ambassador (Thomas Pickering), that we, the nationalists, are ever ready to back them."

One might make the case that the United States must maintain its commitment to the Salvadoran people not just to keep the guerrillas off their necks, but the "nationalists" as well.

AKRON BEACON JOURNAL

Akron, OH, January 19, 1984

THE Reagan administration has decided to buck the recommendation of the commission on Central America that military aid to El Salvador be directly tied to curbing human-rights abuses.

Instead, the administration will follow the lead of the commission's chairman, Henry Kissinger, who advised that if the link was made too rigidly, it might bring about a leftist victory.

Plainly, the administration has decided to fight communism first, and then go about protecting human rights.

The White House will provide periodic reports to Congress on the situation in El Salvador. The first report arrived Tuesday, and it drew some obvious conclusions.

For example, it said the civil war is at a stalemate, and that human-rights abuses remain a central problem, although it noted that progress had been made recently to reduce the killings of civilians.

But these voluntary reports lack the impact of the certification process. President Reagan ended with a pocket veto last fall.

It can't be disputed that the certification process was flawed. Every six months the State Department strained to show that the Salvadoran government was beginning to contain the military death squads. The killings usually slowed as certification approached, and then increased once it passed.

Still, certification was an important reminder of the fact that without taming the death squads, economic and social reform in El Salvador is a fantasy. The process focused attention on the administration's policy at regular intervals.

Now, the administration merely volunteers information. And there is already deep skepticism about its first report.

The State Department claims that the number of civilian killings dropped during the last year, from 177 each month in the first half of 1983 to 104 in the second half. The Catholic Church in El Salvador disagrees, arguing that three times as many civilians were killed each month, and the numbers increased during the year.

Whatever the numbers, it is certain that the death squads are a political tool in El Salvador. And the absence of a formal tie between their activities and American military aid gives them a blank check to roam the countryside.

Death squad leaders know that the Reagan administration is primarily interested in fighting communism, and that knowledge is the largest obstacle to change in El Salvador.

Rockford Register Star

Rockford, IL, January 19, 1984

We find nothing to cheer in the Reagan administration's claim that human rights are improved in El Salvador because fewer civilians are being murdered per month by the government for political reasons.

Nor are we overly concerned by the dispute between the administration and human rights monitoring groups over how many such murders there are per month in El Salvador.

As far as we are concerned, human rights do not exist in a nation if even one citizen is murdered by his government for political reasons. When such murders are measured in the thousands, as they are in El Salvador, any claim of "improved" human rights is ridiculous.

The Chattanooga Times

Chattanooga, TN, February 3, 1984

The Reagan administration began to press for action against the right-wing death squads in El Salvador only after the patience of this country with support for a government which murders its own people — or allows them to be murdered with impunity — had stretched to the breaking point. So it comes as no surprise that the administration puts the best possible face on reports that the right-wing violence has subsided a bit, at least temporarily. But was it necessary for Secretary of State George Shultz to go so far as to describe himself as "proud to stand together" with the Salvadoran government when he visited San Salvador this week?

Perhaps Mr. Shultz expressed his genuine feelings, and those of the president, but we do not believe the American people are by any means "proud" of our Salvadoran allies. And we do believe the American people are generally far more skeptical of the supposed progress made by that government against its anticommunist terrorists than is this administration or its officials. But if the administration is to secure the dramatic increases it seeks in military aid to El Salvador — $365 million this year and next, compared to the $65 million Congress approved for this year — it must at least pretend to be convinced of progress there, and must try to convince the Congress as well. And so, the charade will continue.

Meanwhile there is the question of whether the Salvadoran army can be transformed into an effective fighting force simply by the massive infusion of American dollars. The army is rife with corruption and ineptitude. It is pursuing a program of forced conscription which will net few enthusiastic fighters and more than a few guerrilla sympathizers and informers. Some of the army's more dramatic humiliations of late have involved units trained by this country. In short, there appears little evidence to inspire confidence in its performance, either from a military or a human rights perspective.

Pity the people of this beleaguered land. They are victimized on all sides. On the one hand are the guerrillas who do not shy from murder — as was evidenced recently by the shooting death of an American citizen at a guerrilla roadblock — and who pursue a program of intimidation and economic sabotage in their bid for power. On the other hand is their government. We wonder if these oppressed people would agree with Mr. Shultz that that government has earned praise for its commitment to a program that offers "peace, democracy and justice."

The Seattle Times

Seattle, WA, January 18, 1984

LAST November, President Reagan pocket-vetoed legislation that would have continued to link further U.S. aid to El Salvador to progress in human rights — meaning, for the most part, steps to put an end to killings by right-wing death squads.

The administration agreed instead to report every six months or so to Congress on the situation in El Salvador. One such report went to Capitol Hill this week. It says the "abuse of human rights remains a central problem" in the embattled little country, but claims progress is being made in both human rights and land reform.

The administration is seeking massive amounts of aid for El Salvador in line with the recommendations of the Central American policy task force headed by Henry Kissinger. But it remains cold to the task-force suggestion that the best way to keep pressure on the Salvadorans is for the direct linkage between aid and reform that the president vetoed.

Thus a special responsibility devolves upon Congress, in particular upon those committees directly concerned with foreign-aid appropriations. It is up to them to draw their own conclusions about whether lavish aid is likely to be cost-effective.

Vice President Bush and other administration figures have advised Salvadoran authorities that a failure to root out right-wing violence actually plays into the hands of left-wing insurgents.

But the administration thus far has refused to go a step further and face up to what that means, namely that U.S. aid to the power-holders in San Salvador is wasted unless the government cleans up its act.

The Kissinger commission has done its work. The administration has made clear its position. Now it is up to Congress to keep asking hard questions and then to make some tough judgments of its own.

EL SALVADOR DEATH SQUAD

Houston Chronicle
Houston, TX, June 18, 1984

Before and since his election as president of El Salvador, Jose Napoleon Duarte has pledged to combat the death squads that have claimed tens of thousands of lives during that nation's civil war. The disbanding of a police intelligence unit thought to be linked to the murders seems to be an encouraging development.

One of Duarte's first acts in office was to appoint a special commission to investigate alleged involvement of government officials in the death squads. Given the abysmal state of the Salvadoran judicial system and the government's minimal investigation ability, more steps need to be taken.

By disbanding the 100-agent S-2 unit of the Treasury Police, Duarte appears to have at least served notice that his government does not privately condone the right-wing death squads. Disbanding a suspect unit of the security forces falls far short of actual arrest, trial and conviction of death squad members, but transformation of El Salvador into a showplace for justice will not come overnight.

Aside from his professed belief in human rights and justice, Duarte has every reason to show his concern about the death squads. The American people and Congress have made it clear that they are reluctant to support a government that turns a blind eye to atrocity.

Detroit Free Press
Detroit, MI, February 20, 1984

THE STATE Department has decided to stop using the word "killing" in human rights reports. Perhaps that will make it easier for the United States to live with the Salvadoran death squads that make a mockery of human rights, just as Washington's bureaucratic language took some of the sting out of cutbacks in aid to this country's poor.

Henceforth, the department will call killing the "unlawful or arbitrary deprivation of life." But if the aim is truly more precision, as the State Department claims, such language simply won't do. A precise description of killing in certain countries must include the loud knock on the door, the kidnapping by security police, the long ride in the dark, the dumping of the victim from the rolling car. That would paint a compelling picture of reality for the hundreds of thousands of people living under totalitarian regimes.

One suspects, though, that it isn't clarity the State Department wants. From the first, this administration has displayed a particular facility for talking in the abstract, for reducing people and their problems to charts and graphs and Laffer curves, for employing the neat bloodless phrases that camouflage suffering and horror. Now it has decided to befog the brains of Americans concerned about our policy in Central America with some soothing bureaucratese.

Meanwhile, life, death and U.S. aid still proceed in El Salvador, and we will no doubt continue hearing that the country has made good progress at human rights. Yes, someone may respond, but are they still rounding up and killing people and ordering the assassination of archbishops? No, the State Department will say, though some "unlawful or arbitary deprivation of life" occasionally occurs. What a way to rid language — and U.S. foreign policy — of any real meaning or power.

ST. LOUIS POST-DISPATCH
St. Louis, MO, June 24, 1984

President Jose Napoleon Duarte of El Salvador promises that his government will investigate right-wing death squads and prosecute military officers found to be involved. He has undertaken a historically difficult task.

A few days ago a Salvadoran court sentenced five national guardsmen to the maximum penalty of 30 years in prison for the 1980 murder of four American Catholic churchwomen. The evidence indicated that the men were thoroughly guilty, the only question being to what extent their superiors were involved or tried to cover up the murders. In any event, it took three and a half years to bring the men to justice.

The salient point about this case is that it was the first trial in Salvadoran history for human rights violations committed by security forces. They and allied death squads have committed thousands of political and even nonsensical murders. No

Salvadoran has been found guilty of killing other Salvadorans in such cases. The case of the American churchwomen was exceptional because the victims were Americans, because the State Department insisted on a solution, and because Salvadoran authorities feared that the U.S. Congress would deny more arms aid unless something finally was done about the murders of the American women.

In attempting to exercise the same kind of justice for Salvadoran victims, President Duarte has disbanded a police unit accused of links to the death squads, and has created his own special unit to conduct investigations. But he is, in effect, challenging the military that has gone its own way for decades in El Salvador. If he is to succeed in behalf of his own people, Washington will have to demonstrate the same kind of support that it gave to the case of the American women.

The Washington Times
Washington, DC, March 20, 1984

Sen. Daniel Patrick Moynihan uses the phrase "semantic infiltration" to describe the way the liberal establishment, by picking up leftist terminology, creates a climate of opinion ripe for exploitation by communist propagandists. Remember "the corrupt Lon Nol regime" in Cambodia, since replaced by — oops — the government of Pol Pot? And the "corrupt and repressive" shah of Iran, succeeded by the Ayatollah Khomeini, who has failed so far to live up to Andy Young's prediction that he would come to be regarded as a "saint"?

A more recent example is the ritualistic use of "right-wing death squads" in reference to killings in El Salvador. That violence-ravaged nation has been struggling since 1979 against Marxist guerrillas who have killed tens of thousands of their fellow countrymen. Although much of this bloodletting has occurred in firefights with El Salvador's military, civilians have not been spared, and this Marxist terror has spawned counter-terror by groups dubbed "right-wing death squads."

You might suppose that, in the interest of even-handedness, Marxist killers would be dubbed "left-wing death squads," but this is not the case. In the past few days, three conservative members of El Salvador's Constituent Assembly have been gunned down in cold blood — two of them in the same 24-hour period. In one case the victim's 4-year-old daughter was severely wounded and clings to life by a thread. The perpetrators were described as "unidentified gunmen."

Lest it be supposed that these mere "anecdotes" fail to show a systematic tilt, we ran a computer check of stories on El Salvador in *The Washington Post* and *The New York Times* over the past several years. The *Post* used the phrase "right-wing death squad" 80 times, "left-wing death squad" not at all. The *Times* used the phrase "right-wing death squad" 126 times, "left-wing death squad" only once — in a column by William Safire complaining about endless media harping on "right-wing death squads" to the neglect of "left-wing death squads."

A similar check of the leading wire services, 15 major newspapers, more than 30 magazines, and more than 40 newsletters turned up a grand total of 1,655 references to "right-wing death squads," only nine to "left-wing death squads," four of them quotations from White House statements deploring *both* right- and left-wing death squads.

The prosecution rests.

El Salvador Land-Reform Progress Certified

El Salvador's Constituent Assembly December 13, 1983 voted, 34-25, to reduce by half the amount of land available for redistribution to poor farmers. The United States State Department said Dec. 14, "We are encouraged that an equitable compromise was worked out through the democratic process." The Constituent Assembly Dec. 27 voted to extend the third phase of the land-reform program, known as the "land to the tiller" phase. The assembly extended for six months a provision allowing peasants to buy up to 17.5 acres of land that they had previously rented. Of the roughly 117,000-120,000 peasants estimated to be eligible for this phase of the program, only about 57,000 had applied to buy land, largely because of threats from landowners and because of fighting in some areas.

The U.S. State Department January 25, 1984 certified to Congress that El Salvador's land-reform program had progressed enough to justify sending that country $6.8 million in military aid. Congress had granted El Salvador $64.8 million in aid for fiscal 1984, but 10% had been made contingent on land-reform advances. The Salvadoran land-reform program had long been criticized as corrupt, poorly run and a hinderance to farm production. U.S. Secretary of State George Shultz said in his report to Congress that production had declined since reform started, but added that reformed areas were keeping pace with areas not included in the program. Before land reform, 1% of the Salvadoran people owned 40% of the land. In his report, Shultz said that 25% of the rural poor had benefited from the program. The report also noted problems in compensating those whose land had been taken away. The government paid former owners in bonds as well as cash, but the owners contended that the bonds were just about worthless, the report said.

The Orlando Sentinel

Orlando, FL, February 19, 1984

So far, land reform in El Salvador is a flop. At least that's what U.S. auditors have just said, and maybe it is. But land reform, even with all its problems, is a critical element in the much broader fight to save El Salvador from a communist takeover. It can't be separated from efforts to win military battles or to protect human rights. To succeed, officials in Washington and San Salvador need to be candid, and citizens need to be patient.

According to the audit, the farm cooperatives set up under Phase 1 of the government's program aren't faring well. Many of them have huge debts, no capital, much unproductive land and bad management. Clearly, even in peacetime, breaking up huge holdings of farmland is no day at the beach. To make the change work in wartime is much tougher.

But there's no going back to the old status quo, with a few wealthy landowners running the show. The inequity of that concentration of power planted the seeds of revolution and made the rebels' recruiting more appealing. Admittedly, land reform puts the government in a cross fire between two groups that have no interest in seeing it succeed — the left-wing revolutionaries and the right-wing reactionaries — but that's the right place to be.

Henry Kissinger's commission on Central America is the latest group to make the point that failure on any of the many fronts in El Salvador jeopardizes success in all other areas. Thus redistribution of the land must proceed while much of the country is a battleground. Military aid must be increased while the Salvadoran army makes further steps at reforming itself. Economic assistance must be increased at the same time as random terror by rightists is reduced.

Certainly Americans, who are paying the tab for a good part of those efforts, cannot abide a self-defeating status quo: aid siphoned into private markets, bridges built only to be deserted under fire, right-wing death squads attacked in rhetoric but tolerated in reality.

The Kissinger report gave a realistic picture of the pluses and minuses in El Salvador and neighboring nations. It recommended a multibillion-dollar mix ranging from military and economic aid to initiatives in trade and education. Enacted comprehensively, the effort may be worth the price. Done piecemeal, done sluggishly by those in power there, done with the false hope of fast success, the U.S. role in El Salvador won't be worth a dime.

The Des Moines Register

Des Moines, IA, July 9, 1984

El Salvador's bumpy land-reform program took another bump when the conservative majority in the Legislative Assembly refused the other day to extend the "Land to the Tiller" law.

In the four years since land reform was first decreed, about 62,000 small farmers out of the 150,000 eligible have filed under that part of the law to acquire ownership of the land they were renting. Now the others will not get the chance.

President Jose Napoleon Duarte and his Christian Democratic Party have always favored land reform, and the United States has made land reform a condition for aid.

Nevertheless, the landowners who had run the country for generations were reluctant to give up their land in exchange for government bonds. They repealed or suspended portions of the land-reform law; they raised from 240 acres to 600 the portion a landowner could retain.

In some areas, after land was redistributed, local armed bands drove thousands of the new owners off. Farm co-operatives formed on big estates under Phase I of the land-reform law have suffered from under-capitalization and lack of know-how.

Duarte's party has a plurality but not a majority in the assembly; his government does not have full control of El Salvador. Rightist and leftist guerrillas roam the back country, and the army has not always been obedient.

Still, the fears of Jorge Camacho that the entire land reform will now be reversed may be exaggerated. Camacho heads the largest peasant union and is Duarte's deputy minister of agriculture. Duarte is still trying, but it isn't easy.

OKLAHOMA CITY TIMES

Oklahoma City, OK, February 16, 1984

PERSISTENT harping from the Left on human rights violations in El Salvador overshadows other developments in that small, beleaguered country that might be more significant.

A critical report by U.S. government auditors brings one of those developments — land reform — back out of the shadows, at least momentarily. It takes issue with the official Reagan administration line and warns that the future of the land reform program is bleak.

Despite some successes, the report states, most farm cooperatives created under the first phase of the program "are not financially viable." Many had massive capital debt, no working capital, large non-productive tracts of land, substantially larger labor forces than needed to operate the units and weak management.

The internal audit, prepared by the inspector general's office of the Agency for International Development, is not telling us anything new. The criticisms are similar to points already made by people with a close working knowledge of the situation in El Salvador.

The wonder is that the Reagan administration has allowed itself to be maneuvered into making Salvadoran land reform, instituted during the Carter administration, a cornerstone of its own policy there. The Reagan people see the program as the centerpiece of the Salvadoran government's effort to bring about more social and economic equality in the country.

But the intense desire of the present administration to shore up El Salvador's economic, political and military strength as a bulwark against further Marxist expansion in Central America may be blinding it to some realities there.

A new constitution completed in December by the Constituent Assembly sharply reduces the amount of land from medium-sized farms available for distribution among peasants. This approach has been severely criticized, but may be more feasible than the visionary efforts of the reformers.

The basic problem in El Salvador is that the land mass is too small to offer much of the country's dense population hope for ownership and a good deal of it is not suitable for crops grown economically in small plots. Dividing up the available land just squanders the scarce management ability and prevents production economies of scale.

The Oregonian

Portland, OR, January 6, 1984

The United States should demand successful land reform and land distribution among the peasants as a condition for continuing aid to El Salvador. Without spreading land ownership, any effort to democratize that nation is doomed.

Pressured by the United States, El Salvador initiated a three-pronged land reform program in March 1980. The rosiest thing that can be said about the results is that they are mixed.

Phase one is to convert large haciendas into peasant-owned cooperatives. Progress has been at a snail's pace.

Phase two, aimed at medium-sized farms, was effectively killed last month when the Constituent Assembly decided to write a provision into the new constitution that makes only 72,000 acres available for redistribution to farmers, instead of the originally targeted 173,000 acres.

Phase three was to be the "land to the tiller" program, which gives small tenant farmers the right to own the land they have been farming.

The United States based most of its hopes for progress on this phase. However, the large landholders in El Salvador also run the government and the military and have been reluctant to see their lands redistributed. Thus, this land-reform effort was discouraged through a combination of illegal evictions, violence and intimidation.

A survey last summer found that one of every eight peasant tenant farmers had been evicted. In some areas, the percentage soared dramatically. At San Francisco Chinameca, a rural town 25 miles from San Salvador, Juan Martinez Rojas reported that of 40 peasants who applied for ownership of the land they had worked, he was the only one still working his land.

Twenty-seven of the others were killed by right-wing death squads, according to a national peasants' organization. The rest either fled or renounced their land claims.

The United States can find many targets for improvement in El Salvador: stopping murders by right-wing death squads; control of abuses by the military; promoting free elections; prosecution of the murderers of U.S. citizens; rebuilding the nation's economy; resolution of the bloody and destructive conflict between Marxist guerrillas and the government.

Success with any of these endeavors, though, requires success first with land reform in order to build a base of support. The United States should insist on a truly energetic land redistribution strategy. In El Salvador, a nation with a population density greater than India's, a desire for democracy can be generated only by giving the 5 million workers and peasants a stake in the country's economic system. Land comes first, democracy follows.

ALBUQUERQUE JOURNAL

Albuquerque, NM, February 19, 1984

It is becoming increasingly clear that the last two U.S. administrations may have erred in pushing a no-ownership "land reform" on El Salvador. Latest indication is an Agency for International Development audit which says the land-reform outlook in El Salvador is "bleak."

Already some AID personnel have objected to the characterization by the AID inspector general's audit. But the anatomy of the land reform illustrates well why the IG is probably right. The fatal flaw: lack of a transferrable property right.

American Roy L. Prosterman, land-reform architect for Vietnam, had a hand in designing land reform for El Salvador. The Prosterman plan was first pushed in 1980 by the Carter administration and continues today under President Reagan.

In a *Wall Street Journal* piece last October, Prosterman noted that "attacks from both extremes" could slow the growth of agricultural productivity for Salvadoran peasants who were "given" plots of land formerly owned by wealthy Salvadorans. AID's inspector general said this indeed has happened.

But neither Prosterman nor the IG went beyond the obvious. The program also is hurt by the U.S. proviso that once land is confiscated from previous landowners, the title will be held by the government, not the peasant. Marxists among the Salvadoran guerrillas could not have brought a purer brand of socialism to Central America.

And Congress, as part of its certification process, wants assurances that the land reform is proceeding *as structured.* That is, peasants are said to be "given" a plot of land. But they do not have the right to realize the true value of what they "own" by selling it. Thus, writes Tom Bethell in a recent essay, the peasants "cannot be said to own it at all."

Private property rights would give peasants a personal property to defend. Since peasants are not titled property owners, they have little incentive to protect it, particularly since the land is actually owned by a government they know could just as easily kill them as protect them. The land reform — the structure of which we probably would never recommend for ourselves — has failure built into it.

Prosterman persuasively argues the connection between landlessness and political instability. In past land-reform cases, success has come to most nations that have built privately titled farms into their economies. But Prosterman does not mention the importance of private property rights in those nations that have successfully redistributed land.

Most Americans, perceiving Salvadoran social and political problems as stemming from a semi-feudal agricultural economy, favored land reform because it appeared to be the way to end oligarchical tyranny. But a central tenet of that "land-to-the-tiller" reform was never instituted. The land had not gone "to the tiller" at all.

Americans pushing for reforms may have had the right intentions. But they might better have urged on El Salvador tried-and-true values that have made the U.S. system one of the more productive and admired in the world. As it is now, the land-reform effort is bogged down and the prognosis is poor by AID estimates. The old landowners continue their repulsive practices. The new landowners have no transferrable private property right; it is "owned" by a government they distrust.

Good U.S. intentions have not helped in an area whose people want no more for themselves than their northern neighbors already have: freedom and the right to own a plot of land.

Duarte Declared Presidential Winner; CIA Election Role Reported

El Salvador's Central Election Council May 11, 1984 declared that Christian Democrat Jose Napolean Duarte had won the May 6 presidential election with 54% of the vote. Roberto D'Aubuisson of the ultraright National Republican Alliance (Arena) won 46% of the vote. Arena said it would refuse to accept the decision, but the Election Council May 15 rejected its petition for a recount. The May 6 runoff election went smoothly, free of bureaucratic difficulties that had plagued the first round of voting, although each party accused the other of trying to influence the result of the vote. Some clashes between the army and leftist guerillas were reported in the town of San Miguel, but there was no large-scale attempt by the left to interfere with the voting. Duarte, claiming victory May 7, said his government would call on all sectors of the population to help solve the nation's problems. Asked if he would accept the aid of United States troops in bringing about an end to the war he replied: "No, we won't have any troops here, not North American troops, Cuban troops or Nicaraguan troops." D'Aubuisson, refusing to concede defeat, referred to his rival as a "puppet...who they say has been bought by the U.S. Central Intelligence Agency (CIA) so they can maintain their interests."

Duarte's rival was not the only one to accuse the CIA of influencing the El Salvador elections. A *Washington Post* article datelined May 3 said the U.S. had worked to influence the vote in Duarte's favor, despite its claim of neutrality. The *Post* said the CIA had covertly supplied funds to a Venezuelan agency that had worked for Duarte free of charge. A May 10 *Wall Street Journal* article also cited U.S. intelligence officials who said the CIA had been involved in a two-year effort to promote elections in El Salvador and to assist moderate parties. The *Journal* said the Reagan Administration had secretly given $2 million to the effort, which primarily aided Duarte.

AKRON BEACON JOURNAL
Akron, OH, May 9, 1984

THE ELECTION of Jose Napoleon Duarte as president of El Salvador means Congress is more likely to approve additional U. S. aid to that nation. It does not, however, guarantee that better use will be made of that aid.

Mr. Duarte

The problem is not Mr. Duarte. He appears to be a true democrat, committed to improving human rights, promoting land distribution and controlling the rightwing death squads. The United States should certainly encourage those efforts and direct aid where it will help accomplish those worthy goals.

The problem is that Mr. Duarte still faces opposition within El Salvador from an ingrained power structure — primarily the military — that wants to see reform move slowly if at all. If the Reagan administration continues giving military and economic aid no matter how abusive the government is to its citizens, that opposition will see no reason to change. It will, in fact, become bolder.

That is the situation now, following the election. The House is debating military aid to El Salvador as part of a foreign-aid package. President Reagan, in a speech scheduled for tonight, is expected to push hard for military aid so the Salvadoran government can continue its fight against leftist guerrillas. And the President has implied Congress will be to blame if that fight is lost.

The truth is somewhere between Mr. Reagan's all-out support of the Salvadoran military and those who want us to drop all military help until El Salvador becomes a model democracy. A leftist victory in El Salvador — which, at the moment, seems unlikely — would do nothing for Salvadoran freedom. And, as the world's leading exporter of democracy, that should be our first concern.

But the aid package Mr. Reagan wants should be rejected. He wants no strings attached — only he would decide if the government has made progress in human rights. The Salvadoran military has not shown itself worthy of Mr. Reagan's unlimited support. The military aid too often has financed death squads. And killing civilians is not the way to build a popular government or to increase U. S. influence in Central America.

The way to do that is to grant the aid but make it clear that Mr. Duarte must be given a chance to build a stable, democratic government, as he was elected to do. U. S. aid should be directed toward strengthening the moderate forces that are coming into power. Guaranteeing U. S. aid no matter what the Salvadoran government does — which has been U. S. policy — will only give support to Mr. Duarte's hardline opponents.

Mr. Reagan is right in believing that the United States cannot concede El Salvador to the leftists. But he should offer the citizens a better alternative than they have had. By electing Mr. Duarte, the citizens are showing the way they want their country to go. The United States would do well to listen.

The Kansas City Times
Kansas City, MO, May 5, 1984

Let's not be naive about the U.S. presidential and congressional stakes in Sunday's run-off election in El Salvador. For the president and members of Congress, depending on whether they support or oppose Mr. Reagan's Central American policies, there's a lot at stake in the race between Jose Napoleon Duarte, the moderate Christian Democratic party candidate, and Robert d'Aubuisson, the rightist Arena party candidate.

It's not as though Washington doesn't care. Many in the White House and on Capitol Hill care intensely about what happens at the polls. Some may even have the interests of El Salvador at heart.

Caring is one thing, but the step taken by North Carolina Sen. Jesse Helms goes well over the line of discretion into the territory of meddling in foreign policy, an impulse many members of Congress cannot resist. Mr. Helms, a fringe-right Republican, is following a precedent recently refurbished by the likes of Sen. Daniel Patrick Moynihan of New York, who is pushing a bill to move the U.S. Embassy in Jerusalem from Tel Aviv to Jerusalem. Both men and their supporters are interfering in affairs they should avoid.

Mr. Helms has had the audacity and crude timing to write Mr. Reagan, demanding that the U.S. ambassador to El Salvador, Thomas R. Pickering, be replaced. Obviously hoping to influence the election outcome himself or bolster his image in his own re-election campaign, Mr. Helms charges Mr. Pickering with meddling in the El Salvadoran election.

Mr. Pickering may be meddling somehow (remember the experience with American ambassadors in Vietnam?), but Mr. Helms can only make matters worse at this point. It would be a blow to U.S. Central American policy if Mr. Duarte, whom the administration wants to win, were beaten by Mr. d'Aubuisson, the reputed leader of right-wing butcher squads.

Mr. Helms' interference now is most inappropriate. He seems to favor Mr. d'Aubuisson to win, which would wreck the moral underpinnings of Washington's policy. He and all the other men and women on Capitol Hill should keep their mouths shut and pray Mr. Duarte wins and then can assemble a government that can begin to sow the seeds of democracy against the greatest odds imaginable.

At this point, only a shallow opportunist would attempt to interfere so openly in El Salvador's fragile and threatened effort at democracy.

The Providence Journal

Providence, RI, May 15, 1984

His tiny tropical land is wracked by civil war. A sick economy has pushed unemployment to 40 percent. Political murders leave much of the population in terror. Extremists of the left and the right join in detesting him. With all this, what can Jose Napoleon Duarte hope to accomplish as the newly elected president of El Salvador?

With decisiveness, shrewd timing — and a good deal of luck — he could do plenty. But he is taking on a huge task at a dangerous time when a single slip can mean disaster. Some key factors:

● He takes office June 1 as the victor in a respectably free and non-violent election. This gives Mr. Duarte a claim on legitimacy that is unusual for El Salvador, where the democratic experience is meager.

● He is promising to end the officially condoned violence that has taken thousands of lives. The army, he reports, already has set up a unit to eliminate human-rights abuses by soldiers. More to the point, Mr. Duarte has pledged to eliminate the so-called "death squads" run by security forces. It's a tough job, but his credibility depends on his trying.

● He also has pledged to seek talks with the leftist insurgents. If he could strike a deal with the non-violent democratic left, and thus lead their parties toward a future coalition in parliament, Mr. Duarte could dramatically broaden his base of support (at the same time undercutting the guerrillas' appeal).

With a new U.S. military aid package forthcoming, Mr. Duarte has a chance to show that the money can be responsibly used. If it can buy antibiotics, say, to help reduce the appalling death rate (30 percent) among wounded Salvadoran soldiers, then he can show welcome results. By contrast, if the aid money gets frittered away, Mr. Duarte may find Washington unwilling to string along with him.

Opportunities, however, may matter less than the perils that confront Mr. Duarte from the right and the left. The far right is bitter at the defeat of its candidate, Roberto d'Aubuisson. Many businessmen and landowners view Mr. Duarte's reform ideas as dangerously radical. The leftist guerrillas, hoping to wear down the government's forces, see the moderate Duarte as a tool of Washington; they are expected to mount a major offensive next fall. Both extremes see Mr. Duarte as a threat to their chances of someday seizing control.

The United States has staked a great deal — conceivably too much — on the hope that this political veteran of 58 can breathe life into an infant democracy. For Washington, however, few other plausible options exist. Under Mr. Duarte, El Salvador has a modest chance of reducing chaos and pointing the way toward democratic processes that will endure. So long as he shows himself committed to this effort, he deserves the good will of the United States.

THE CHRISTIAN SCIENCE MONITOR

Boston, MA, May 8, 1984

THE apparent election of José Napoleón Duarte as El Salvador's new President is a victory for peace and moderation. Although the official results are not yet counted, it appears that the majority of Salvadoreans have voted for what many of them have long said they wanted: an end to the fighting.

Duarte has made this his top priority — halting his nation's war against communist-backed guerrillas through some sort of negotiation.

Duarte also seeks to rebuild El Salvador's tattered economy. He has indicated his willingness to remove Army officers who oppose his moderate leadership. And apparently he is willing to go to Washington to plead his case for United States aid in person. Such a visit would be useful to both sides.

The Duarte victory makes it much more likely that the Reagan administration can win support of a skeptical Congress for continued economic and military assistance to El Salvador. However, reaction to the role of the Central Intelligence Agency and the US military will also be crucial. The US House of Representatives had postponed action on aid proposals until it saw who won Sunday's Salvadorean election.

No one should underestimate the challenges ahead for Duarte. Most immediate, and perhaps most difficult, is gaining control of the Army and reforming it. Powerful elements within the Army are equally determined to control Duarte and limit his ability to reform either the nation or the military, despite the weekend order of the highest-ranking general that the Army should remain neutral during the voting. For decades the Army, and wealthy Salvadoreans, have controlled the nation.

Another extremely important issue: To what extent are negotiations possible with the guerrillas, who already are causing serious dislocations for the nation through military action? If talks do occur and prove successful, they then run the risk of permitting the guerrillas to share power and possibly to dominate or destabilize the government. To the majority of Salvadorean voters these risks seem preferable to the victory-through-more-war stance of Duarte's rightist rival, Roberto d'Aubuisson, which would have further polarized El Salvador.

Although the United States publicly took a neutral stance toward the election, privately it favored a Duarte victory. D'Aubuisson forces claimed that behind the scenes the United States and its ambassador to El Salvador, Thomas Pickering, were working to produce a Duarte victory. In the past, US embassies have been important in bringing about outcomes in Latin American nations that Washington favored. What is crucial here is whether Washington's intention is the best for the Salvadorean people, a point not lost on Congress.

For the election's promise to be realized, Salvadoreans must rally around Duarte. Ultimately this, and not US influence or aid, is needed to build a democratic consensus within El Salvador.

The Hartford Courant

Hartford, CT, May 8, 1984

Consider the situation during the presidential election Sunday in El Salvador:

Nearly 40,000 people have died since the late 1970s, mostly at the hands of the right-wing death squads whose members are known to have ties with El Salvador's regular military forces.

A state-of-siege law has been in force for several years. This law bans the freedom of assembly and the freedom of movement by individuals.

Public employee unions are illegal, and strikes are outlawed.

Telephone, water and railroad services are among the public utilities that are militarized by the state-of-siege law.

State security forces or the military is empowered to detain anyone, hold him or her for six months without charge or access to defense counsel. Military judges can extend the detention for six additional months.

All but one of the independent newspapers have been shut down. The exception, El Mundo, engages in self-censorship and its editors and staff have frequently been threatened with death.

No left-of-center party participated in the election, not even dissident factions of the Christian Democratic party.

Voting is mandatory in El Salvador. If a person's identity card does not show proof of voting, the military can detain the person.

In short, the circumstances are scarcely conducive to the free exercise of will. Elections did take place on Sunday, and the worst fears — the triumph of Roberto d'Aubuisson — have not materialized, at latest count. The apparent winner is Jose Napoleon Duarte, the Christian Democrat who probably would have the toughest and most dangerous job in the Western Hemisphere.

How does one run a civilian government when a quasi-government run by the military looms in the background? Can a president preside with honor when the ranks of government are dominated by the right-wing henchmen of Mr. d'Aubuisson?

Mr. Duarte would need considerable help from the United States, but how can he accept that help and avoid being reduced to a puppet?

Perhaps he can succeed, if he moves quickly to rescind the state of siege, if he persuades left-of-center forces to lay down their arms and help him form a government of reconciliation and if he persuades Washington that without participation by the left, there will be no end to the civil war.

These are big ifs.

Nevertheless, they are the requisites for making Sunday's election meaningful.

THE SAGINAW NEWS

Saginaw, MI, May 11, 1984

El Salvador has voted under — and against — the gun.

The apparent victory of centrist Jose Napoleon Duarte in El Salvador does not assure democracy for that Central American country, the focus of tensions in the region. But it's a far sight better than the alternative.

With almost 90 percent of 1.8 million elibigle citizens taking part in Sunday's presidential run-off, Duarte claimed about 55 percent of the vote against rival Roberto d'Aubuisson.

Americans puzzled about their country's role in that unhappy land should note both the numbers and the names. They underlie the urgency of President Reagan's plea Wednesday for a package of economic-military aid to Central America.

The strong turnout came in the face of repeated threats by the guerrillas, who had dubbed the election a "farce" — a label that represents the Marxist view of free elections anywhere, any time. True, Salvadorans are required by law to vote. So are Australians. The fact remains that citizens had to weigh the risks of a legal penalty against those of getting murdered. And they chose to vote.

The other significant point is that if Duarte's lead holds up, then they voted for the man who stands for reconciliation, reform, an end to wanton killing by both the left and the right — the latter symbolized, as it happens, by d'Aubuisson. In a land struggling to emerge from 50 years of bitterness and hatred, torn by civil strife, that choice was not as obvious as it might seem to innocent observers.

And there does seem to be a great deal of innocence about the Salvadoran situation. The backgrounds of the guerrillas, and their avowed affiliations, do not support any portrayal as liberators of the people. Their rebellion has far less legitimacy, actually, than that of Nicaragua's Sandinistas if Duarte, a democrat, not a dictator, takes leadership.

This election guarantees little — especially if d'Aubuisson presses his contention that no matter what the numbers say, he really won.

Yet it affirms that most Salvadorans are willing to give democracy a chance, perhaps in hope that those rebels who are not ideologues, who think their cause is popular justice, will take a chance as well.

Such an expectation may be naive. But the end of the civil war is the only hope for El Salvador — and for American policy. Better it be achieved by persuasion and example than by force of arms.

Either way, though, a Duarte government will get nowhere without aid, military as well as economic. Congressional Democrats who rebutted Reagan's speech are correct that domestic reform is central to a solution. But that fine position will be worth nothing if the elected government quickly loses the war.

While Washington debates, the people of El Salvador risk their lives on behalf of a free future. What risk is Congress willing to take in their behalf?

The Philadelphia Inquirer

Philadelphia, PA, May 9, 1984

If Jose Napoleon Duarte could only achieve his goals in El Salvador, that shattered country's prospects — and the outlook for U.S. policy there — would be much brighter. But the "if" is a big one. And the Salvadoran leader will need the right sort of U.S. backing if his chances are to improve.

Mr. Duarte, the candidate openly preferred by Washington, is claiming a narrow victory (with the totals still not final) in the Salvadoran presidential contest against right-wing extremists and the opposition of leftist guerrillas. That would make him the first popularly elected civilian leader in El Salvador in half a century, in astonishingly orderly elections labeled "fair and honest" by official U.S. observers.

Mr. Duarte is a moderate Christian Democrat who paid his dues for his faith in democracy. Elected president in 1972, he was tortured and exiled by the military. Made leader by a reformist military junta in 1980, he was undermined by uncontrollable right-wing death squads.

His courageous campaign platform — which some say is far more than he can deliver — boldly called for social reforms, a forceful crackdown on death squads and human-rights violations, and a dialogue with the left. These views will be hailed by President Reagan as he undertakes a new bid to coax stalled military and economic aid for Salvador from a dubious Congress, which has been awaiting the election results.

But Mr. Duarte will have tough going against the hostility of both the Salvadoran right and left. While the army, with an eye on U.S. congressional moneybags, has indicated it may remove two senior officers linked with right-wing excesses, it has served warning against any attempts at major reform. Conservative businessmen and landowners are hostile to Mr. Duarte's calls for the genuine land reform and social justice needed to rally support from workers and peasants. Attempts to woo the left into "dialogue" will no doubt spark accelerated violence from diehard guerrillas and risk a military coup on the right.

Mr. Duarte indeed deserves American support in his attempt to find a middle ground between military dictatorship and Marxism. But, as he recognized when he sharply rejected the idea of U.S. troops fighting in Salvador, hope for reconciliation ultimately lies not in military "victory" but in political "dialogue."

Some military aid for Salvador may be needed while serious efforts are made to get negotiations under way. (This does not speak to the very different question of aiding CIA-backed rebels fighting to overthrow the Nicaraguan government.) But in the long run U.S. arms will help Mr. Duarte less than will strong U.S. political support for keeping the Salvadoran army in check. Above all, if Washington really wants to strengthen Mr. Duarte's hand, it will focus on negotiated, not military solutions for Salvador and Central America.

The Virginian-Pilot

Norfolk, VA, May 6, 1984

If Christian Democrat Jose Napoleon Duarte wins in today's runoff for El Salvador's presidency, President Reagan will present the victory, with good reason, as a triumph of his administration's policy. But that a Duarte win will stop the Salvadoran bloodletting quickly is far from certain.

No one doubts that Mr. Duarte, who is popular both in El Salvador and at the White House, opposes the right-wing death squads who have killed tens of thousands of Salvadorans. But can he curb the killers in the armed forces and paramilitary forces who murder, rape and torture on behalf of the band of oligarchs that controls most of the riches of El Salvador? Nothing in Salvadoran history suggests he can. And as long as the killing goes on, many Americans will be unhappy about supporting any Salvadoran government against Soviet-bloc-supported revolutionaries.

The oligarchs have wealth and position and they long ago sealed a bargain with Salvadoran security forces conferring status and economic rewards upon the latter in exchange for keeping the restless peasantry in line. The slaughter seems destined to continue until the oligarchs no longer have anything to protect in El Salvador. And perhaps the only way to get the oligarchs out of the picture peacefully is for the United States to subsidize Salvadoran government purchase of large land holdings for distribution to the peasants.

Even that wouldn't necessarily halt the bloodshed right away. The leftist guerrillas, preferring revolution to reform, would probably choose to fight on. The death squads would go on killing to protect their own privileges and fight communism in their own counterproductive way. The death squads' reason for being is to maintain El Salvador's grossly unfair social and economic system. Reform that system, and the death squads would lose their patrons and, as they see it, rationale.

Moreover, the Salvadoran military — like armed forces generally throughout Latin America — would resist submitting to civilian authority. It regards itself as the primary agent of national stability and progress, reserving the right to step in to reverse political courses that it judges threatens itself and the national welfare.

A Duarte presidency would not diminish the military's life-and-death power in El Salvador unless the military consented — the armed forces control the guns. And an election victory by Mr. Duarte's right-wing opponent, ex-Major Roberto d'Aubuisson, would surely not change things; d'Aubuisson ties to the death squads are widely assumed.

Nonetheless, the freeish election (not "free," because failure to vote carries a stiff fine) and Mr. Duarte's broad following attest to profound yearning for constitutional democracy, peace and personal security among Salvadorans at large. If the Duarte cause carries this day, Mr. Reagan will have a weighty card to play in his efforts to gain congressional assent to further U.S. aid to crush the Salvadoran insurgency and bring justice and genuine tranquility to a suffering land.

ST. LOUIS POST-DISPATCH

St. Louis, MO, May 5, 1984

The White House is having trouble getting used to the idea of Sen. Jesse Helms opposing American intervention in Central America, but that is what the North Carolina Republican is doing. Or, at least, he is opposing one form of intervention.

Sen. Helms wrote a letter to President Reagan accusing Ambassador Thomas Pickering of attempting to manipulate tomorrow's election in El Salvador in favor of a moderate candidate, Jose Napoleon Duarte, against the ultra-conservative Roberto d'Aubuisson, who has been linked repeatedly with death squads. Sen. Helms turned that around by saying that Ambassador Pickering, in trying to rig the election, "is the leader of the death squads against democracy."

Now we can imagine what side Sen. Helms is on in the Salvadoran election. His letter to Mr. Reagan was first disclosed in San Salvador by a leader of the d'Aubuisson party. We also know what side the Reagan administration is on. A d'Aubuisson victory would be a disaster for it. Mr. d'Aubuisson is opposed to every reform in El Salvador and regards even Mr. Duarte as a communist. A suspicious Congress is holding up Mr. Reagan's request for more arms aid to El Salvador pending results of the election.

The White House has expressed Mr. Reagan's full confidence in Ambassador Pickering, and Sen. Percy, chairman of the Senate Foreign Relations Committee, says the envoy has been carrying out the policies of the president and Congress. "Unwarranted interference," Sen. Helms charges. After years of American interference in El Salvador, that is hardly the issue. Sen. Helms objects to the kind of interference.

The San Diego Union

San Diego, CA, May 9, 1984

The vote count from the final, runoff round of El Salvador's presidential election is not yet official but there seems little doubt that Christian Democrat Jose Napoleon Duarte has defeated conservative Roberto d'Aubuisson. That is prompting sighs of relief in the White House, where there was justifiable fear that a d'Aubuisson victory could result in Congress cutting off all aid for Salvadoran government forces fighting a communist-led insurgency.

The Reagan administration has reason to be elated, up to a point. The good news is obvious enough. For the third time in 27 months, Salvadorans have turned out in impressive numbers to vote in manifestly fair elections that the Marxist guerrillas had denounced and tried in vain to wreck. That says something important about whether a majority of El Salvador's 4.5 million people wants peaceful change or violent revolution.

These elections have given El Salvador a popularly elected legislature and president, and marked the country's passage in stages from military dictatorship to genuine democracy in five short years. This was no mean achievement. It is the most notable success to date in the Reagan strategy of democratizing Central America to help immunize the region against communism and against Soviet/Cuban penetration.

A Duarte victory also paints President Reagan's critics on Capitol Hill into a very tight corner. Heretofore, many had opposed at least military aid for El Salvador on grounds that the government there was not really democratic, or that it was not sufficiently committed to land reform and other ostensibly desirable changes, or that it was not really trying to stop the freelance violence of rightist death squads. Each of these arguments, questionable in any case, should now be thoroughly discredited.

Mr. Duarte's democratic credentials stretching back for two decades are beyond dispute. So is his advocacy of breaking up El Salvador's large estates and redistributing agricultural land to tenant farmers and agricultural workers. As for the death squads, Mr. Duarte denounced them fervently during the presidential campaign. He said Sunday evening that eliminating the death squads would be his first priority in office.

Given all this, even Congress's liberals will have trouble justifying votes to deny aid to the Salvadoran army. Put another way, it will be clearer than ever that such votes risk leaving a budding, if still imperfect, democracy helpless to defend itself against leftwing totalitarians bent on imposing a Castro-style dictatorship.

These are some of the points President Reagan will no doubt make when he delivers a televised address on Central America to the nation this evening. What he will likely omit is the darker side of a Duarte victory in El Salvador.

In much of the U.S. press, the Salvadoran presidential election was cast as a simple (and simpleminded) morality play. Mr. Duarte was almost invariably accorded such positive labels as "moderate" or "centrist." Roberto d'Aubuisson was almost as invariably made to seem the political equivalent of Darth Vader with such labels as "right-wing extremist," or "far right," or "ultra rightist."

And, of course, Mr. d'Aubuisson's name rarely appeared in the American press without drumfire repetition of the charge that he had been "linked to the death squads." Never mind that these allegations, made by Mr. d'Aubuisson's political enemies, have never been proven and that the candidate himself has denied them vehemently.

More to the point was what each candidate advocated. Mr. Duarte favors a partly socialized economy and striking a political deal with the guerrillas if possible. Mr. d'Aubuisson wants to defeat the guerrillas and rebuild El Salvador's threadbare economy with doses of free-market capitalism. Events may prove the d'Aubuisson approach to have been the better bet. Instead, Salvadorans and the Reagan administration are evidently stuck with the Duarte program; thanks in no small measure to the impression in El Salvador that a d'Aubuisson victory would mean a cutoff of American aid.

This is not to suggest, of course, that Jose Napoleon Duarte and his center-left Christian Democrats are not worth supporting against the Marxist-Leninist alternative offered by the guerrillas. Quite the contrary, as President Reagan is bound to argue this evening. Mr. Duarte's apparent election should make it harder for Congress to listen with a deaf ear.

United States Denies Visas to Activists

Emelina Panameno de Garcia November 20, 1984 accepted a Robert F. Kennedy Memorial Foundation award in Washington, D.C. on behalf of a group of Salvadoran women human rights activists who had been denied visas to the United States Nov. 12. The recipients of the award were members of the Committee of Mothers and Relatives of Prisoners, Disappeared Persons and Politcally Assassinated of El Salvador, a group that was critical of U.S. policy in that country. Visa applicants for four members were turned down on the grounds that the women had been involved in subversive activities. The four women denied that charge.

Officials of the Kennedy Foundation Nov. 18 said the State Department had suggested that if the foundation altered the award and canceled a lecture tour organized for the women, then the visas might be granted. The award of $30,000 was presented by Ethel Kennedy, wife of the late Robert Kennedy, and his brother, Sen. Edward Kennedy, Jr. (D, Mass.). In making the presentation, Sen. Kennedy praised the group for trying "with tireless resolve to save other families from the inexpressible ordeal which they have suffered—of sons and daughters taken from them forever by the terror in the night." Garcia had fled to Mexico from El Salvador after being raped and beaten in 1981.

In a related development, Roberto D'Aubuisson, leader of the ultra right National Republican Alliance, who had frequently been linked to right-wing death squads, had been granted a visa to enter the U.S., the State Department announced December 3, 1984. Responding to questions on why D'Aubuisson was granted a visa whereas the four rights activists had not, State Department officials said some degree of cooperation with D'Aubuisson was necessary to keep him and his supporters from undermining peace talks between the government of El Salvador and the leftist rebels.

THE TENNESSEAN
Nashville, TN, November 21, 1984

THE Reagan administration has, once more, made it clear that freedom of expression in this nation hinges on what philosophies are being expressed.

The State Department recently denied entry visas to four women who represent the Mothers' Committee in El Salvador. Ironically, they wanted to enter the country to receive the prestigious Robert F. Kennedy Human Rights Award.

The visas were denied under the 1952 Immigration and Nationalization Act which prevents aliens that would be "prejudicial to the public interest" from entering the country. It is the same law that was invoked to deny visas for Mrs. Hortensia Allende, the widow of former Chilean president Salvador Allende, and Ms. Bernadette Devlin McAliskey, the Irish political activist.

The State Department's motive was quite clear. According to the Kennedy Foundation, State Department officials agreed to grant the visas on the condition that the prearranged speaking tour be canceled. When the Foundation refused to cancel the tour, the visas were denied.

It would be understandable for the State Department to deny visas to those suspected of terrorist activity. But the representatives of the Mothers' Committee are not terrorists, and merely wanted to accept their award and speak to the American public about human rights in El Salvador.

The women threaten no one. But obviously, their message was threatening enough for the Reagan Administration to stifle. The State Department's action not only prevented four women from entering the country, it also denied Americans the right to hear different opinions about one of the most troubled nations in this hemisphere. It was, simply put, a case of censorship.

The Hartford Courant
Hartford, CT, December 5, 1984

When the first annual Robert F. Kennedy Human Rights Award was presented in Washington last month, four of the recipients were absent. Only Alicia de Garcia, a Salvadoran nurse, was able to attend. Four other leaders of CO-Madres — an organization of Latin American women who are asking for an end to political violence — were prevented from entering the country.

The State Department said the four "participated in terrorist activities," although the awards committee could find no evidence that was true.

It's more likely that the women were barred because through their protests, they expose the suffering caused by systematic violence to which the U.S. government is a party and which it cannot contain.

The full name of the group is the Committee of Mothers and Relatives of Political Prisoners Disappeared and Murdered of El Salvador. It was formed in 1977 by Archbishop Oscar Arnulfo Romero, who later was murdered. Twice a month, members of CO-Madres publicly demonstrate their opposition to violence against innocents and ask for amnesty for political prisoners and investigations into the fate of people who have disappeared during the civil war.

The Reagan administration has preferred to use a quiet, back-door approach to bettering the human rights records of U.S. allies. In that light, it might have better served the purposes of the administration had the women been allowed entry. Now there has been a publicity backlash.

The incident emphasizes again that the official U.S. view of Central America is peculiarly skewed toward ideological conflict, with people identified by their presumed location on the political spectrum.

Had the other members of CO-Madres been heard, they probably would have echoed Ms. Garcia's recollections of torture, rape and killing. Such stories are legion, and they're not necessarily framed in terms of left or right, government or guerrilla, but as simple expressions of fear, despair and a longing for peace.

These victims communicate at a very human, understandable level and they deserve to be heard.

The Philadelphia Inquirer
Philadelphia, PA, November 27, 1984

Four mothers from El Salvador were denied entry into the United States last week. They were to receive the first Robert F. Kennedy Human Rights Award at Georgetown University. They are members of CO-Madres, a group of 500 mostly poor and unschooled women whose brothers, sons and husbands have disappeared or been shot or dismembered in El Salvador's bloody civil strife.

The State Department said the women were wolves in sheep's clothing — that they had advocated violence, taken part in terrorism, that their group had said some stridently anti-American and anti-Duarte things. They were a run-of-the-mill pressure group, the State Department said, who hid behind human rights rhetoric.

Perhaps, a department emissary hinted to the RFK awards staff, something could be done if the award were broadened to include mothers from other Latin American nations. Perhaps, if a speaking tour were curtailed; perhaps, then the visas might not be such a problem.

On the record, of course, and officially, the State Department said it would never stoop to negotiate a visa or to suggest restrictions on the freedom to speak out or to dissent. And, in the end, one mother who was attending a conference in Argentina and who spent the day being vouched for by an English-speaking Catholic priest obtained a visa from the American Embassy in Argentina.

She was flanked by four empty chairs on the Georgetown University stage. She was, she said, no different from her fellow CO-Madres — a victim, not a subversive: She had been raped repeatedly, like many of the others; she had buried the bodyless head of a brother, like many of the others; she had catalogued horrors and protested and demanded investigations. But her compatriots were denied entry — denied the forum to tell their story.

The public might be "prejudiced," the State Department said; U.S. security might be endangered. Such is the language of the 1952 McCarran Act — Section 212 (a) (28) (f) — that stopped the mothers. Such is the shield of the immigration law's "ideological exclusion" provisions.

That U.S. security might be shaken by four mothers is an arguable proposition. But there is no doubt the American people might be "prejudiced" against certain Reagan administration policies in Central America were they to take the mothers' stories to heart.

In fact, a large number — perhaps the majority — of Americans already are disenchanted with the trend of U.S. involvement on the isthmus. And there are even more who are appalled at El Salvador's death squads and Washington's continuing inability — despite the leverage of millions of dollars of military aid — to pressure Salvadoran courts to punish their leaders.

Has support worn so thin that the Reagan administration fears a visit by four mothers will rip it to shreds? Does it fear that four mothers will hoodwink the American people if Big Government does not step in to protect them?

Or, and this is the most alarming, is the administration tinkering with Soviet-style information control, picking and choosing who will address the masses, granting the freedom to speak to those who toe the line, muzzling dissenting voices?

The McCarran Act's "ideological exclusion" provisions stand ready for abuse by the powers that be. They should be thoroughly rewritten. But this administration has not only abused them, it has fine-tuned them.

A case in point is the turnabout on El Salvador's most infamous right-wing leader, Roberto d'Aubuisson. He was turned down for a U.S. visa last year, discrediting his presidential candidacy before the Salvadoran elections. But he was approved for one last summer to be feted by Sen. Jesse Helms (R., N.C.) after the Duarte government was safely in office.

Save for civil liberties groups, there is little outcry.

The government will be emboldened by the silence. If it can cut the shape of speech at the margins, why not go for its heart?

That is the clear and present danger to the health of America's democracy: Not that four mothers would speak, but that Big Brother has gagged them.

ST. LOUIS POST-DISPATCH
St. Louis, MO, November 20, 1984

For reasons undoubtedly connected with its Central American policy, the Reagan administration has seized on the 1952 Immigration and Nationality Act to expand on an excuse for a kind of censorship. The State Department has denied entry visas to four Salvadoran women human rights activists of the Committee of Mothers and Relatives of Prisoners, Disappeared Persons and Politically Assassinated Persons of El Salvador.

The four women were to have received an $30,000 award from the Robert F. Kennedy Foundation, and foundation spokesmen say the State Department, in negotiating with them, offered to grant the visas if the women would cancel a speaking tour in this country. The offer was rejected

and so were the visas. The State Department says its decision was based on the women's advocacy of acts of violence and participation in terrorist activities.

In fact, the women were to be recognized for their courageous opposition to acts of violence and terrorist activities, in which more than 30,000 Salvadorans have been killed, mostly by right-wing death squads. A Kennedy Foundation awards committeewoman says the State Department has smeared them without evidence that would stand up in court. Beyond that, the department has prevented four women from telling Americans the story of the denial of human rights in El Salvador. The administration must not want the story told.

The Boston Globe
Boston, MA, November 28, 1984

Which is the longer-running farce: the pretense that law has returned to El Salvador, or US policy that mixes plaintive calls for justice in El Salvador with a habit of blaming victims and treating killers with deference?

Both sides of that argument got fresh ammunition last week. A Salvadoran army officer implicated in one of El Salvador's most outrageous political assassinations went free on a technicality. And four members of the "Mothers' Committee," a group of relatives of victims of disappearances and other political persecutions, were denied entry into the United States where they were to receive a human rights award from the Robert F. Kennedy Memorial Foundation.

The officer, Lt. Isidro Lopez Sibrian, was named by two triggermen as the one who gave them weapons and ordered them to gun down two AFL-CIO labor specialists and the head of the Salvadoran land-redistribution program in a hotel coffee shop in San Salvador in 1981. No one doubts that he did it, least of all US Embassy officials with inside information.

On the way to his "definitive stay of proceedings" by El Salvador's Supreme Court, Lopez Sibrian was allowed to dye his distinctive red hair and shave his mustache before appearing in a 1982 police lineup. He was acquitted because of Catch-22s built into the Salvadoran constitution under the influence of the ultra-right ARENA party.

The Salvadoran court's decision was not unexpected, but it deserves special notice. This case was one of five that caused international outrage and that President Napoleon Duarte singled out last summer for vigorous prosecution.

In each case substantial evidence points to clearly identified, well-connected Salvadoran military or security officers. In no case has an officer been convicted. In the only case that has produced a conviction – the killing of four American churchwomen – five national guardsmen served as scapegoats, a quid pro quo for a $19-million payoff in US military aid.

The shielding of higher-ups responsible for the most ostentatious examples of El Salvador's right-wing violence underlines the fact that, despite Duarte's democratic instincts, the fascists still run free.

As for the four representatives of the Mothers' Committee, the State Department denied them visas, charging they had engaged in "actual terrorist activities." They reportedly have lost 18 relatives to right-wing violence. Although the committee opposes US policy, and although these four may sympathize with the left, only one of the four has apparently ever been arrested – if "arrest" is a fair term to describe a detention, rape and beating during which she lost a breast.

This year the State Department has granted three entry visas to the ARENA leader, Roberto d'Aubuisson, widely believed to have been a prime mover in the initiation of death-squad terror in 1979-80 and in the 1980 murder of Archbishop Oscar Arnulfo Romero. He has never been charged with a terrorist crime.

This double standard sends out a message that makes the killers laugh ... and reminds leftists who may consider working within the system that they should expect no protection under law. That is no way to tame an insurgency.

Gunmen Slay 13 in San Salvador; Targets Were U.S. Marines

Gunmen shot and killed 13 people, including four United States Marines and two U.S. businessmen, in San Salvador June 19, 1985. The slayings occurred in the Zona Rosa district. A pick-up truck stopped at the curb outside a string of restaurants, and six to ten men carrying automatic rifles jumped out and fired at people sitting at sidewalk tables. Witnesses said the gunmen singled out the Marines and only began shooting at other people when a civilian pulled out a handgun and fired at them. The Marines were U.S. embassy guards, off-duty, unarmed and in civilian clothes. They were said to have visited the Zona Rosa cafes frequently, despite a security policy prohibiting embassy staff from patronizing outdoor cafes. The two U.S. businessmen who were killed worked for Wang Laboratories Inc. of Lowell, Mass. A group identifying itself as the Urban Guerillas-Mardoqueno Cruz June 21 took responsibility for the attack, and confirmed that the Marines were the intended targets. The group was reported to be affiliated with the Central American Revolutionary Workers' Party (PRTC), the smallest of the five groups within the Farabundo Marti National Liberation Front (FMLN), the umbrella organization of leftist groups battling the government. Salvadoran government and U.S. embassy officials said they believed the attack was further evidence that leftist rebels were returning to a policy of urban terrorism because they were losing the war in the field. White House spokesman Larry Speakes said there would be no military retaliation by the U.S. but added that the U.S. was prepared to provide El Salvador "with the assistance they need to do the job themselves." Speakes read a statement by President Ronald Reagan in which the President pledged to use his emergency powers, if necessary, to provide "additional military assets" to help the Salvadoran government in its war against the rebels.

THE LINCOLN STAR

Lincoln, NE, June 21, 1985

While the nation's attention fastened again on the Mideast, American lives were lost in El Salvador in a bloody terrorist attack upon a cafe in downtown San Salvador. The assassination of four Marines and nine others was a brutal reminder of our world commitments, as well as the pervasive use of terrorism.

Two other victims in the Wednesday attack were identified as Americans employed by Wang Laboratories. Five U.S. military men have now died in El Salvador since President Reagan increased our economic and military commitment in his first term of office.

The violence in El Salvador is unsettling, unexpected because we have recently come to expect that the moderate government under U.S.-backed President Jose Napoleon Duarte could bring the warring factions to peace.

Duarte emerged in clear control from the last election; war-weary, the majority of Salvadorans seem to want peace.

Guerrilla operations for the past four years have targeted rural areas. Intermittently, the two sides have engaged in talks. The violence, although continuing, has seemed insular. But this attack could signal a resurgence of urban violence and a new phase of fighting between Duarte's troops and the leftist rebels.

THE DEATHS come at a time when as a country we are vulnerable to thoughtless reactions and hungry for retaliation. We must not be tempted to act rashly and unbalance a tenuous situation in Central America.

President Reagan may be fretting mightily to press American might because of the frustrating stalemate in Beirut. Washington columnist Mary McGrory points out that during the last crisis in Beirut, when 240 Marines died, Reagan ordered the invasion of Grenada. Its success diverted us from the staggering loss in Beirut and the failure of U.S. policy in the Mideast. McGrory looks warily for a U.S. invasion of Nicaragua. Any military thrust from the United States in Central America would be a very grave mistake.

DUARTE HAS received heavy backing from the United States. Indeed it could be argued that he would not be president without our assistance. He bears a heavy debt to us and must feel the pressure of the American deaths.

For us the loss of American life, including three church women slain in 1980, must be kept in perspective. The five-year-old civil war has claimed some 34,000 Salvadoran lives. The reference book, "Latin American 1984" calls El Salvador one of the most dangerous spots on earth. The suffering of El Salvador continues; our loss there must be added to it but it does not change anything.

Solutions remain elusive. Lasting peace will never come without significant land reforms. Far-right extremists, backed by wealthy landowners and businessmen, will resist it tooth and nail.

Duarte has brought the right-wing into submission for now and he must be encouraged in efforts to bring the leftists into meaningful reconciliation talks. Until then, the bloodshed will continue.

Unfortunately, it is a price we'll pay for our involvement. It is a toll exacted daily from the Salvadorans.

THE CHRISTIAN SCIENCE MONITOR

Boston, MA, June 26, 1985

THE fatal shootings last week of 13 people, including six Americans, in an outdoor café in San Salvador signal two important messages.

One is that the struggle in El Salvador, while going well for the government of President José Napoleón Duarte, is far from won. This is no time for complacency.

The second is that the tactics of the guerrilla opposition are evidently shifting, which will require a similar flexibility by the government. After doing badly in general warfare in the countryside of late, the guerrillas are apparently going to resort to two kinds of terrorist tactics: urban terrorism, such as the café shootings, which are thought to be the work of leftist guerrillas; and attempts to sabotage the economy, such as recent bombings of electric transmission towers. Similar economic sabotage was effective in the past. The guerrillas are also attempting to take advantage of rising economic unrest among urban Salvadoreans.

In the United States, recent discussions of Central America have been dominated by the question of whether the US government should aid the Nicaraguan "contras." On this issue the Reagan administration recently scored a victory, and an undetermined amount of funds will be provided.

But three other nations of the region also require world attention: Honduras, Costa Rica, and El Salvador.

Both Honduras and Costa Rica are concerned about recent border skirmishes between contras based in their respective nations and Nicaraguan armed forces. Both neighboring nations fear that the longer the contra war against the Sandinistas continues, the greater the prospect they will be drawn into a war that they, especially Costa Rica, are not prepared to fight.

Costa Rica, long considered the region's most successful democracy, is trying to decide whether to make a major effort to build strong armed forces, at the risk of unbalancing its economy.

Honduras's greatest need now may be to strengthen its democracy; the nation is enmeshed in a lengthy and thus far divisive process of trying to select the successor government to President Roberto Suazo Córdova.

But it is El Salvador that faces the most immediate challenge. In 1983 the leftist guerrillas launched a major offensive which left the government troops on the defensive. They spent too much time in their barracks. When they did move into the countryside in search of guerrillas, they moved too slowly and cautiously.

Under prodding from American military experts, the government troops learned quickly. They became more aggressive and moved much more swiftly. Today it is the guerrilla forces that are reeling, unable to sustain significant pressure on government forces.

Now it is thought the guerrillas are retrenching, and — as in the early days of the struggle — reverting to urban and economic terrorism. The government forces will have to adapt again.

So will President Duarte. The guerrillas hope to feed off the unrest of several segments of the urban population. Medical workers are striking for higher wages. Water service employees are also on strike. University students are marching in an effort to get government financial help.

As President Duarte has gained increasing control of the government and brought about a substantial decrease in human rights violations, popular support and political freedom have increased. It is in this atmosphere, which stems from government successes, that the students and unions have begun to raise their voices.

All is far from perfect in El Salvador. But President Duarte has made major progress in social and military areas. With continued support from the United States there is no reason he cannot once again adjust to defeat this form of guerrilla attack, too.

The ✿ State

Columbia, SC, June 25, 1985

THE BRUTAL massacre of four American Marines, two American businessmen and seven others at a San Salvador cafe was designed to weaken American resolve at "a time for testing" of the United States, as one official called it.

The killings, for which an obscure leftist guerrilla group claimed responsibility, may well have been triggered by the plane hijacking in the Middle East. Violence tends to beget violence. But such murders are not unprecedented in El Salvador's urban areas. And guerrilla wars have no fronts.

Still, murder on the streets had declined significantly in the cities of the tiny, embattled Central American nation. Thus, this escalation is particularly tragic, not only for the United States, but also for Salvadorean President Jose Napoleon Duarte, who is trying to win a war with leftist insurgents, to negotiate with those same people and to fend off political sniping from his ultra-rightist foes, who claim he's too liberal.

The future of Mr. Duarte depends greatly on the support of the United States. The guerrillas know this, and undoubtedly they hoped their cafe slaughter would prompt cries in the United States "to bring our men home."

Instead, President Reagan immediately offered help from U.S. intelligence agencies and extra military aid to track down and punish the killers. The Administration ruled out use of U.S. military forces to retaliate — a significant display of moderation.

The President is correct in responding strongly and quickly. It is easier to react in El Salvador where the enemy is known, than in the Middle East, where the safety of the hostages is a major concern.

Of course, there are additional reasons — reasons of geography — for responding strongly to leftist, anti-American terrorism in Central America.

While it is almost impossible to draw the line at communist encroachment and terrorism in faraway places like Afghanistan and Vietnam, that line must be drawn at our doorsteps. The Soviet influence is already significant in Marxist strongholds like Nicaragua and among the El Salvador rebels, which Nicaragua and Eastern Bloc countries are backing.

The guerrillas might feel they took no chance when they singled out the Marines for death. Indeed, they might feel they taught America a lesson.

But if Mr. Reagan has his way, the insurgents will come to regret their cowardly act. This time, Congress should be highly supportive of the President.

Birmingham Post-Herald

Birmingham, AL, June 24, 1985

Four more U.S. Marines — one of them an Alabamian, Sgt. Bobby Joe Dickson of Tuscaloosa — have paid the ultimate price in defending democracy around the world. The four, guards at the American embassy at El Salvador, were killed by a group of terrorists, presumably Marxist rebels, as they sat in a sidewalk cafe in San Salvador.

This atrocity, in which two American businessmen and seven local citizens were also slain, appears to reflect a change of tactics by the guerrilla forces in El Salvador.

The attack indicates that the communist-aided guerrillas are getting desperate. They apparently hope that hit-and-run murder in the large population centers, particularly in the capital city, will unsettle the elected government of Jose Napoleon Duarte, as their large-scale military operations in the rural areas have not.

By targeting Americans, whenever possible, they also are seeking revenge against the United States for providing military and financial assistance to the Salvadoran government. And they may even think that killing Americans will turn U.S. opinion against maintaining a presence in El Salvador.

Even though he has been sorely tested by recurring acts of terrorism against Americans in various parts of the world, President Reagan's response to the slayings in El Salvador was appropriately controlled.

He made it clear that the United States will not be intimidated by Marxist thugs with guns, and he correctly ruled out any direct retaliation by U.S. military forces. The president said he will leave it to the Duarte government to find and punish the killers, offering whatever U.S. assistance that may be needed. He also said he would step up delivery of military equipment to the government.

Nothing can compensate for the loss of life, but the American families of the victims of this barbarous act in San Salvador should find some comfort in the knowledge that their loved ones were serving their country and the cause of freedom.

Roanoke Times & World-News

Roanoke, VA, June 25, 1985

THE BODIES of four U.S. Marine embassy guards, killed Wednesday night while relaxing off-duty in a San Salvador cafe, were brought home over the weekend. In a moving ceremony Saturday, with network TV coverage, President Reagan saluted their sacrifice, and pinned a Purple Heart to each of the four flag-draped caskets.

It is entirely appropriate, of course, so to honor those who die in the service of freedom and their country. But their deaths should not be exploited for political purposes, by the president or by anyone else. Such exploitation could occur if the slayings lead to ill-considered U.S. actions in Central America that encourage the public to forget about the deadlock in Lebanon over the continued holding of 40 American hostages by radical Shiite Moslems.

The Marines were neither the first Americans to die by terrorist hand in El Salvador nor the only people to die in the cafe on Wednesday night. Two other Americans — civilian employees of a U.S. computer firm — also were slain, as were two Guatemalans, a Chilean and four Salvadorans. In 1979, four American nuns were murdered in El Salvador; in 1981, two U.S. land-reform advisers were killed. Their memories, too, should not be forgotten.

Brutality is brutality; in that sense, the events in the Middle East — beginning with the hijacking of a TWA jetliner and murder of a U.S. Navy diver on board — are of a cloth with the machine-gunning in San Salvador. In other ways, however, they are not the same. In Lebanon, there is no effective national government; yet a known leader — Nabih Berri of the Shiite Amal movement — has taken at least temporary responsibility for the safety of the hostages. In El Salvador, the government under President Jose Napoleon Duarte is credible and democratically elected; yet the identity of the gunmen and their motives for the attack remain unknown.

Twenty months ago, in October 1983, there also were near-simultaneous "crises" in Lebanon and in the Caribbean basin. A suicidal Shiite fanatic drove a truck-bomb into Marine barracks in Beirut, killing more than 240 U.S. servicemen. Within hours, American troops were invading the tiny island of Grenada and overthrowing a short-lived, bloodthirsty communist regime.

The invasion of Grenada can be justified on its own merits, and the Reagan administration said the timing was coincidental. But though the bombing in Beirut and the invasion of Grenada were not connected logically, there was a chronological link: The effect, intended or not, was to divert public attention from a disastrous U.S. military operation to a successful one.

The wrong lessons should not be drawn from the events of 1983. The gunning-down last week of the Marines, and of the other nine people, was an outrage. But — barring the unveiling of dramatic evidence of, say, direct involvement by Cuba or Nicaragua — the outrage introduced no new factor into the Salvadoran equation: For years, Duarte and Salvadoran democratic centrists have been plagued by violence-prone, home-grown extremists of both the left and right.

Certainly, aid should be given the Duarte government, if requested, to track the killers. But the Marine deaths should not be used as a pretext for ill-considered moves in Central America, nor should they be used as a diversion to draw attention from the conundrum in Lebanon.

THE PLAIN DEALER

Cleveland, OH, June 24, 1985

While the attention of many in the United States was riveted upon the hostage situation under way in the Middle East, terrorists again were striking in another region known for its bloodshed and savagery. Six Americans—four U.S. Marines and two civilians—were among 13 persons killed by gunmen in San Salvador, El Salvador.

Who is responsible? The Reagan administration and Salvadoran officials immediately blamed leftist guerrillas for the assault. Indeed, a little-known leftist guerrilla organization has stepped forward to claim responsibility for the act. The Mardoqueo Cruz Urban Guerrilla Commandos said the attack was part of a campaign against "the yankee aggressor in El Salvador."

The escalation of violence in San Salvador was predictable. The war has been going badly in the countryside for the guerrillas. The superiorly equipped Salvadoran military has been able to keep the rebels off balance and incapable of mounting any significant offensive. In recent months the guerrillas had vowed to escalate the effects of the war in the capital.

Also predictable was the targeting, once again, of Americans. In past years, U.S. civilians have been targeted by right-wing death squads. Now American military personnel are being targeted by leftist terrorists. The rebels' clandestine Radio Venceremos has boasted: "The first Marines are starting to fall."

How must the United States respond? Revenge is tempting but can be blinding. While the urge may be to supply the Salvadoran military with more equipment to hunt down and kill more guerrillas, the better way is to work to strengthen the influence and control of the Duarte government.

Military assistance is not the most crucial need. If the Salvadoran government is to make further gains among the population and further erode the guerrillas' shrinking base of support, it must shore up the beleaguered Salvadoran economy, install fairness into an inept and inefficient judicial system, implement the remaining phases of land reform and work more aggressively to eliminate human rights abuses.

The most effective and long-lasting blow the United States can make against the leftist terrorists is to help the Salvadoran government achieve a system worthy of popular Salvadoran support.

DIARIO LAS AMERICAS

Miami, FL, June 22, 1985

La terrible tragedia que acaba de tener lugar en un restaurante al aire libre en la ciudad de San Salvador, cuando la República está regida por un gobierno que es el producto de elecciones auténticamente democráticas, demuestra, sin lugar a dudas, que el problema de El Salvador no es de carácter político, como lo dice una legión de liberaloides regados por el mundo cuando hablan sobre los problemas de Centroamérica. El asesinato colectivo perpetrado el miércoles donde murieron estadounidenses, centroamericanos y un chileno, responde a una específica realidad de subversión comunista, a la que no hay que llamar simplemente "izquierdista", como se empeñan muchos en definir vagamente así.

Las soluciones políticas sobre el caso salvadoreño se han ofrecido en elecciones de Asamblea Nacional Constituyente, presidenciales y municipales. Sin embargo, los comunistas dirigidos por Moscú a través de La Habana y Managua, no entienden, lógicamente, de esas soluciones. Se dice lógicamente, a la luz de lo que es el marxismo-leninismo y sus métodos. A la luz de la lógica civilizada sería distinto. A pesar de que todo esto es así, en cualquier conferencia internacional, incluyendo las de prensa, integradas por organizaciones democráticas, se encuentra el planteamiento y la defensa de la tesis de que el caso salvadoreño debe tener una solución política. Y la solución política implica compartir el Poder Público con los que representan la antidemocracia y el concepto antisocial.

Muchos liberales y liberaloides estadounidenses dicen que se han dedicado a estudiar el caso de El Salvador y hacen afirmaciones con respecto a muertes de personas atribuidas a los anticomunistas. Parece que sus investigaciones son profundas y que llegan a conocer mucho sobre el tema. Es de esperarse que esos conocimientos y esas experiencias se apliquen también a penetrar en la raíz de este crimen colectivo cometido el miércoles para que averiguen quiénes son —con nombres propios— al menos hasta donde ello sea posible, los responsables de esta matanza.

Y también es importante que se tenga como claro testimonio de la realidad, que la solución del gravísimo problema salvadoreño relacionado con la seguridad del Estado y de la sociedad en general no es de carácter político.

The terrible tragedy that has taken place in a sidewalk restaurant in San Salvador, when the republic is under a government that is the outcome of truly democratic elections, proves, without any doubt whatsoever, that El Salvador's problem is not political in nature, as is claimed by a legion of liberaloids throughout the world when they speak about the problems of Central America. The massacre of last Wednesday where Americans, Central Americans and a Chilean were killed, is a specific event of communist subversion, which should not be called simply "leftist", as many are set in vaguely defining things.

Political solutions for the Salvadoran case have been offered through elections for the National Constitutional Assembly, and presidential and municipal as well. However, the communists directed by Moscow through Havana and Managua, logically do not understand these solutions. And we say logically in the light of what Marxism-Leninism and its methods are. In the light of civilized logic it would be different. However, although this is the case, in any international conference, including press conferences with the participation of democratic organizations, we find the presentation and advocacy of the thesis that the case of El Salvador should have a political solution. And political solution implies sharing Public Power with those who represent antidemocracy and antisocial ideas.

Many American liberals and liberaloids say that they have studied the case of El Salvador in depth and they make firm statements regarding deaths attributed to the anti-comunists. Apparently their investigations have gone to great lengths and they get to the point of knowing practically everything there is to know. It would be desirable that they apply that knowledge and that experience to probe into the origins of this massacre of Wednesday so that they may find out —with names and surnames— at least up to where this be possible, who are responsible for these murders.

And it is important that everyone know as a clear testimony of what is a reality, that the solution to the very serious problem of security of the State and of society in general in El Salvador is not political.

The Kansas City Times

Kansas City, MO, June 22, 1985

American casualties should be expected in places where civil warfare and turmoil prevail. The point of terrorist activity in the Middle East, in Europe or in Latin America is to discredit democratic governments and push the United States into isolationism. The four Marines and two businessmen from Wang Laboratories who were murdered Thursday in El Salvador are the latest example.

According to witness accounts submitted to U.S. officials in San Salvador, the Americans were singled out first among the 13 victims at the outdoor cafe in that city's restaurant district. The Marines, guards at the U.S. Embassy, were off duty and in civilian attire. Five Salvadorans, a Chilean and a Guatemalan, all civilians, were also gunned down. They were virtual sitting ducks for the homicidal whims of their as yet unidentified killers.

By Friday, no group had claimed responsibility. All that is known is that the murderers wore camouflage uniforms and brandished machine guns. Some officials in the Salvadoran government and ours have been quick to identify the guilty as members of the Farabundo Marti National Liberation Front, an anti-Duarte rebel group. It is reckless to lay blame without having the facts.

In response to Thursday's malicious killings, President Reagan has ordered the swift delivery of congressionally approved military hardware to Salvadoran troops. The president also suggested using his emergency powers to give that government "additional military assets." But that does not mean sending in more U.S. troops, said National Security Adviser Robert C. McFarlane. We'll hold the administration to that assurance and to its decision to work with the Salvadoran government to curtail these acts of terrorism and find and punish the guilty.

The Honolulu Advertiser

Honolulu, HI, June 21, 1985

U.S. tensions with Nicaragua have dominated news from Central America in recent months. But that changed this week with the murder of 13 people at outdoor cafes in San Salvador, the Salvadoran capital.

Six Americans were among the dead, including four off-duty Marines assigned to guard duty at the U.S. Embassy. The Marines are the first U.S. military casualties in El Salvador since the May 1983 death of Lt. Commander Albert Schaufelberger, who was shot by left-wing assassins.

The U.S. Embassy and Salvadoran government charge leftist terrorists with the attack. It is believed that the guerrillas are turning to urban terrorism because their rural campaign against the government has gone poorly in recent months.

What did the terrorists hope to gain by their murderous act? Certainly not a change in Reagan administration policy toward the country.

Just a few hours after the killing, the U.S. Embassy issued a statement saying, "It was democracy that was attacked last night. The United States was among the victims. But the United States of America will not be intimidated by thugs with rifles."

Like all terrorism, the Salvadoran attackers' bloody deed was meant as a statement. The killings publicize the guerrillas' cause. Never mind that murder is used to gain the attention of others.

That is the hideous rationale of terrorism, which has been so prominent in Beirut this week before it raised its ugly head again in San Salvador.

Duarte's Daughter Kidnapped; Freed in Rebel Exchange

The eldest daughter of President Jose Napolean Duarte, Ines Guadelupe Duarte Duran, was kidnapped with a classmate by gunmen in San Salvador September 10, 1985. One of her bodyguards was killed in a gun battle with the kidnappers, and a second was seriously injured. No group immediately claimed responsibility. Salvadoran officers blamed leftist rebels but said the possibility that the extreme right was responsible could not be ruled out. In their search for Duarte Duran, police troops Sept. 11 raided what they said were 12 "safe houses" used by leftist rebels in San Salvador. Several people were arrested and arms and explosives were seized, but the whereabouts of the missing women remained unknown. Duarte Duran owned Radio Liberty and had managed her father's campaign in 1984.

Duarte Duran and her companion were freed by leftist rebels October 24 in an exchange in which the government released a number of captured rebels. Additionally, in return for the release of the two women, 23 mayors and a few other officials captured by the rebels, the government freed 22 rebel prisoners. It also permitted 101 wounded rebels to come out of hiding and be sent abroad for medical treatment. The exchange had been negotiated over a period of weeks by a three-member commission. All five groups in the rebel Farabundo Marti Liberation Front (FMLN) took part in the negotiations. The FMLN had not taken responsibility for the kidnapping until Oct. 21. A source said to be closely linked with the rebels was reported to have said that the military wing of the Communist Party, the Armed Forces of Liberation, was responsible for the abduction and that the FMLN command, which was not consulted, only took over responsibility for the exchange negotiations afterward.

The Detroit News
Detroit, MI, September 12, 1985

As we go to press, it is not clear whether Ines Guadelupe Duarte Duran, the eldest of El Salvador President Napoleon Duarte's six children, and a 35-year-old mother of three, has been murdered by the terrorists who kidnaped her Tuesday. Unfortunately, there is very little in recent Salvadoran history to suggest that she will survive the ordeal. Although the press once made much of the "right-wing hit squads" that fought back against Communist terror, political murder in El Salvador is now a leftist near-monopoly.

El Salvador is a close U.S. ally. We have committed vast political, economic, and military resources to helping the country fend off a well-armed Communist insurgency. And perhaps the best thing we can do to express our continuing support of Mr. Duarte in this trying hour is to ship him more guns.

Certainly, that's a more feasible option now than a year ago, when American politicians debated a question straight out of the moralistic 1970s: Should we help a country that, in fending off an insurgency aided and abetted from abroad, has used methods that the American Civil Liberties Union considers inappropriate in an American police department? Negative answers to this question brought to power, in Southeast Asia and beyond, some of the worst and cruelest regimes in history, which proceeded to claim millions of lives. From South Vietnam, Cambodia, and Laos, to Iran, Angola, and Nicaragua, the cost of keeping American hands clean has been unconscionably high for people whose only mistake was to invest trust and hope in America.

With that in mind, the administration prevailed over critics who said El Salvador's movement toward democracy was phony. And Mr. Duarte has not been a disappointment. The Salvadoran president, who was elected two years ago and whose party won control of the legislative assembly last year, has put together a broad consensus for democratic reform.

Mr. Duarte disproved critics on the right who predicted that he'd socialize El Salvador's economy and appease the guerrillas. By encouraging the army, with U.S. help and a renewed sense of national purpose, to seek out the guerrillas and destroy them, Mr. Duarte has rendered unnecessary the private violence that Salvadorans believed was the only means they had to defend themselves against the violent left. Though left-of-center on economic and social issues, he understands that above all what his country needs is growth, which cannot be attained without a confident private sector. What seemed a lost cause a year ago, now seems to be moving consistently toward an important victory.

That helps explain why the Communists, who have refused to participate in free elections, have fallen back on demands for "negotiations" and a fresh round of urban terror. They want to neutralize their ground losses in the countryside by getting the government to declare a cease fire and hold talks. At the same time, they want to create a climate of fear and insecurity that, they hope, will discredit the democrats and polarize the country, causing the United States once again to consider turning away in high moral indignation. Their campaign claimed the lives of several American marines this summer and now has struck El Salvador's first family.

In this difficult hour, President Duarte and his country deserve our attention and support. In several very important respects, El Salvador represents the kind of heroic, muscular, and self-confident democracy that Elliott Abrams, the U.S. Assistant Secretary of State for Inter-American Affairs, discusses in an exclusive interview with The Detroit News on today's op-ed page. It makes no apologies to extremists of the left or demagogs of the right. It offers political freedom and economic growth to its people and insists on maintaining its national independence.

That approach, we hope, represents the wave of the future. But as this week's kidnaping shows, violent forces will try to stymie reform. Indeed, recent history shows that fledgling democracies can fail if Americans refuse to help other nations build and protect the kind of government we already enjoy.

The Miami Herald
Miami, FL, September 14, 1985

EVEN IN a war-ravaged country where more than 55,000 people have died in the last five years, the broad-daylight abduction of Salvadoran President Jose Napoleon Duarte's oldest daughter had a numbing effect. In the simplest and starkest terms, the terrorists who kidnapped Ines Duarte Duran — whoever they might be — went beyond the pale this time.

Regardless of their political views, democratic world leaders — President Duarte's Latin American colleagues in the forefront — quickly issued strong statements condemning the attack. For these men, it makes no difference if the abduction — in which one of Ms. Duarte Duran's bodyguards was killed and another critically wounded — was carried out by a right-wing death squad or, as Salvadoran government investigators believe, by leftist terrorists. It imperils the moderate in the middle and his ability to govern a country torn by the extremes.

Ironically, the abduction also is a clear indication of Mr. Duarte's success in steering El Salvador to a more-moderate course. This success is anathema to those who need to radicalize society in order to impose selfish views predicated on hatred and violence.

On the day that Ms. Duarte-Duran was abducted, a guerrilla leader who identified himself as "Comandante Ulises" pledged to "annihilate" all American military advisers in El Salvador. He termed "a legitimate act of war" the killing of four U.S. Marines, two American civilians, and seven other people in an attack at a sidewalk cafe in San Salvador.

And on the day following the abduction, by contrast, the man whom Mr. Duarte defeated for the presidency issued a statement condemning the kidnapping and pleading for the safe and prompt release of his opponent's daughter. For Roberto D'Aubuisson, believed closely linked to right-wing death squads, the statement was unusual. He is not in the habit of condemning attacks on his political enemies, be those enemies from the left or from the center.

Regardless of the kidnappers' political affiliation, the attack strikes at Mr. Duarte both as a father and as president and U.S. ally. Washington should do all in its power to help Salvadoran security forces unmask and capture the abductors. And may world leaders continue condemning an attack on one of the pillars of the rebuilding of democratic institutions in the Western Hemisphere. If Mr. Duarte and his family are fair targets for terrorists, all other democratic leaders in Latin America will be too.

The Boston Globe

Boston, MA, September 13, 1985

Anyone who can empathize with a brave, vulnerable man, all the more vulnerable because he has a family, will be outraged by the kidnapping of the daughter of President Napoleon Duarte of El Salvador.

Once, such a deed would have been presumed to be the work of El Salvador's vicious right wing, which slaughtered thousands to terrorize political progressives. The ultra-right hates Duarte because he has edged toward political dialogue to end the war.

Today, however, suspicion falls heavily on elements linked to the left-wing Farabundo Marti National Liberation Front. Military pressure has forced the FMLN on the defensive, and some splinter groups are now turning to urban terror.

Duarte's 35-year-old daughter, Ines, a mother of three, was grabbed Tuesday when gunmen shot her bodyguards at a San Salvador university campus where she was taking classes. Duarte has canceled a trip to Boston and one to New York, where he was to address the United Nations.

Last year Duarte's surprise announcement in a UN speech led to peace talks at a dramatic meeting with the insurgents in La Palma.

This year, some persons had expected that Duarte would announce a new initiative at the UN to pump life into "dialogo."

Three high rebel officials have been captured in recent months. One possible motive for a kidnapping by the left would be to use Duarte's daughter as a pawn in a prisoner exchange. If the Salvadoran left wants bargaining chips for negotiations, let it snatch a colonel or capture soldiers in the field. Seizing a president's daughter is craven.

The Salvadoran left has earned respect and a serious hearing. Many of its leaders were moderates driven out of government and into the hills when there was no room for dissent within the system. Peace will not return to Salvador until their safety is again assured. That is Duarte's task.

If the kidnapping was the work of a leftist splinter group, the main insurgent forces must disavow the crime and hunt down the perpetrators. The Salvadoran left is as accountable for terrorists that lurk in its ranks as the army and Treasury Police are for their death squads. The rebels cannot condone the kidnapping of an innocent person without being tarnished by it.

THE LINCOLN STAR

Lincoln, NE, September 12, 1985

From El Salvador's political right and left have come kidnappings and killings that leave us stunned. The kidnapping of the daughter of President Jose Napoleon Duarte is an added shock to our system.

Of course, no one's injury or death by violence is any more or less tragic than another but there is an added dimension in the case of Ines Duarte. Her captors seek more than simply escalating the level of violence in a continuing war of attrition.

The added dimension in her kidnapping is the pressure it puts upon those people of El Salvador who have the ability and the willingness to effectively serve their country.

If a leadership role is an automatic invitation to personal disaster, such a role will be disdained. If one can lead only at the personal peril of ones family, the tendency is to avoid such a position.

Precisely such thinking is behind the

kidnapping. How steadfast can President Duarte remain if it seriously endangers his immediate family?

If it is possible through violence to coerce Duarte, revolutionary forces would be well on their way to ultimate victory. How could the government stand if there were none able and willing to lead it?

Thus, there is in the kidnapping of Duarte's daughter more to concern us than the threat of another act of deadly violence. While we abhor such a situation, we are left with a further concern for the future of a country and a region that threatens to do away with that element of its society in which the highest potential for achievement is to be found.

It is not an aristocracy for which we mourn but rather, a nationalism with its roots in men and women of purpose, learning, ability, integrity and dedication.

THE KANSAS CITY STAR

Kansas City, MO, September 12, 1985

Leftist guerrillas in El Salvador made a promise after they had claimed responsibility for the killing of 13 persons, including six Americans, at two adjoining outdoor cafes in San Salvador in June. Over the opposition radio station, Radio Venceremos, they broadcast a warning: "The present action is only the beginning . . ." They declared urban assaults would increase. They have kept their word.

On Tuesday leftists allegedly kidnapped Ines Guadalupe Duarte Duran, the daughter of President Jose Napoleon Duarte. Mrs. Duarte Duran, owner of Radio Liberty, a commercial station, was taken from the private university she was attending in San Salvador. One of her security guards was killed in what witnesses said was about a 3-

minute exchange of gunfire. Another guard was injured.

The Farabundo Marti Liberation National Front, the coalition of five guerrilla groups, said it killed the 13 in June. No one has yet claimed reponsibility for Tuesday's assault, but government troops believe it was the FMLN.

Mrs. Duarte Duran, mother of three, is as defenseless in this war as were other civilians who have been kidnapped, killed or made to "disappear" by both sides. Her apparent abduction is inexcusable and unacceptable. It served no useful purpose and, if anything, will only escalate the 6-year-old civil war because it has personally touched the elected head of the government. Peace talks may be a thing of the past.

The Wichita Eagle-Beacon

Wichita, KS, September 12, 1985

THE ongoing tragedy of the civil war in El Salvador now has touched the presidential family itself, with the kidnapping of Jose Napoleon Duarte's daughter. A classmate of Ines Guadalupe Duarte Duran also was kidnapped, and at least one bodyguard slain — acts of brutality that could backfire on the perpetrators. Nothing could have aroused the sympathy of the populace more for a family that already has known much grief, and that now is at the mercy of desperate and unprincipled people.

President Duarte properly has indicated he will remain "very firm" in any negotiations for his daughter's release. He should not let that keep him from negotiating, though. Any reasonable person would agree he should do whatever is within his power to ensure his loved one's safety, as long as it doesn't jeopardize the nation.

"That you, so respected an advocate of justice and democracy, should be attacked in this manner, along with your family, is a deep tragedy of our times," President Reagan wrote Mr. Duarte. It's ironic, indeed, that the person who most exemplifies El Salvador's quest for social justice should be subjected to an act of such social injustice. The kidnappings and related killing in San Salvador are only the latest expression of urban violence in a country that has seen the war in the countryside move increasingly into the capital city.

Mr. Duarte often causes his own bodyguards some nervous moments, with his propensity to walk the streets and plunge into crowds where his personal safety is hard to guarantee. He says he sooner would take the risk, though, than to be isolated from the people, inside the walls of the presidential house. His eldest daughter apparently shared that feeling, and now the Duarte family is paying the price for it. The family should know that people throughout the hemisphere are praying for a happy resolution of this act of cowardice and cruelty.

The Dallas Morning News

Dallas, TX, September 13, 1985

The kidnappers of the daughter of Salvadoran President Duarte are not yet known. The most plausible speculation is that it is the work of the Marxist guerrillas bent on destroying El Salvador's fragile democracy, though the Salvadoran right, too, has been less than pleased with Duarte.

The basis for an orderly society is that there be consensus on the means for resolving policy disputes. Whoever may be responsible for the kidnapping, there no longer should be any doubts about the guerrillas' real views on how policy should be made in El Salvador through bullets, not ballots. They want nothing to do with democracy.

Thus, after Duarte's election in 1984, an election in which they disdained to participate, the guerrillas have turned increasingly to economic sabotage and urban terrorism. They know that the more Salvadoran society works, the worse off they will become.

The latest news comes from an interview by the rebel radio station of "Commandante Ulises," one of those suspected of being responsible for the June 19 murder of 13 people, four of them U.S. Marines, at two outdoor cafes. The commandante said he intends to "annihilate" all American military advisers in El Salvador. Of course, this is not the first time nor will it be the last that Marxists with neither military superiority nor popular support have turned in desperation to wholesale murder.

The Arizona Republic

Phoenix, AZ, September 12, 1985

IF anyone is interested in learning something about the true character of the leftist guerrillas fighting the democratically elected government of El Salvador, they should ignore the rebels' rhetoric about justice, democracy, reform and liberation.

Watch, instead, what happens in the kidnapping of President Jose Napoleon Duarte's eldest daughter.

Of course, this shouldn't be necessary. The true character of the leftists should have been revealed to all the night of June 19 when the rebels indiscriminately shot and killed 13 people, including four U.S. Marines, on a busy street in the capital city of San Salvador.

It seems Marxists habitually kill the very people they are supposedly trying to liberate. Presumably that is a kind of liberation most people, given the choice, would prefer to do without.

The abduction of 35-year-old Ines Guadelupe Duarte de Navas — a divorced mother of three and head of the Christian Democratic Party's *Radio Libertad* — is another heavy burden President Duarte must now shoulder.

Duarte already has paid a heavy price for his patriotism, having survived in the past assassination attempts, a death sentence pronounced by the right-wing death squads, a military coup and imprisonment.

Duarte is a genuine hero, a courageous nationalist dedicated to the independence and freedom of El Salvador.

Although no group has yet claimed responsibility for the abduction or issued ransom demands, there can be little doubt that it is the work of leftist guerrillas.

There was a time when it would have been conceivable for the right-wing death squads to have carried out an operation of this kind in an attempt to discredit the lefists, but such activity has virtually ceased since Duarte took office June 30, 1984.

It is difficult to be optimistic about the eventual outcome of the kidnapping, given the vicious nature of the leftists.

It is an unfortunate fact of life that people of moderation must inevitably suffer at the hands of extremists both right and left, and Duarte has suffered his share from both ends of the political spectrum in El Salvador.

Once again, this patriot, his daughter and grandchildren must endure the unendurable.

The Record

Hackensack, NJ, September 3, 1985

One of the few areas where the Reagan administration can claim a foreign-policy success is El Salvador. Seemingly against all odds, the ostensibly democratic regime of José Napoleón Duarte has held onto power there longer than most observers had thought possible. The military has pledged him its support, right-wing death squads have let up on their rampage of terror, and leftist guerrillas seem to have lost momentum. A couple of years ago, when the extreme rightist Major Roberto d'Aubuisson was making his bid for power, El Salvador's choices seemed to be either fascism or revolution. Now a middle way appears viable for the first time.

But appearances can be deceptive. Mr. Duarte is less a leader than a tightrope walker of unexpected skill. He doesn't so much command as balance competing forces. Under his regime, violence has indeed subsided in the cities. At the same time, however, it has increased in remote areas of the countryside, where military activity is concentrated.

The rural violence has drawn less international notice simply because it takes place in remote, inaccessible areas, far from the international press corps in the capital of San Salvador. But the level of violence is fierce. Americas Watch, the respected (and politically neutral) human-rights group based in New York, has accused the Salvadoran military of employing wholesale terror to turn much of the rural population into refugees in order to deprive the guerrillas of a base of support. Americas Watch describes this as "draining the sea to catch the fish," and says it is accomplished through indiscriminate strafing, mortaring, and aerial bombardments and military sweeps employing thousands of troops. Perhaps a third of the countryside has been turned into a free-fire zone, the group contends, while perhaps a fourth of El Salvador's 4.8 million people have fled their homes.

The U.S. Embassy uses the term "surgical precision" to describe these air strikes. Americas Watch maintains that they are no less messy than in Vietnam. Since the guerrillas have no jungle command centers, the Salvadoran Air Force has had to content itself with raining down its fury on scattered rural hamlets where rebels are said to find refuge. Its preferred method of dealing with isolated jungle patrols of a half-dozen guerrillas is to hit them with 500- to 750-pound bombs dropped by U.S.-supplied jet fighters. Predictably, those who suffer most from this blunderbuss technique are innocent civilians, who are gunned down and blown up with shocking frequency.

Americas Watch bases many of its accusations on information compiled by Tutela Legal, the human-rights office of the Roman Catholic archdiocese in San Salvador. Tutela Legal has taken depositions from scores of refugees fleeing the free-fire zones, and their accounts are numbingly repetitious.

"When the planes and soldiers arrive, people disperse and run to the mountains, and they die wherever a bomb gets them or the soldiers find them," a 40-year-old man from the northern province of Cabanas recounted last fall. "This is the normal thing. They don't leave in peace anybody. They destroy houses, fields, animals and clothes, they leave one without anything. . . ." A widow from San Vicente, about 20 miles east of San Salvador, told of an "invasion" by the Salvadoran military last September: "The soldiers killed some people; five men, one woman, and two girls who were crossing a river; they killed the woman when she was running to the river. They caught her and hit her and her girls with machetes. . . ." Others tell of women raped, men stabbed, children killed, homes burned, all part of the normal course of events in the impoverished countryside.

President Duarte has issued military guidelines to discourage such abuses. Americas Watch says they are ignored. He has had better luck in restraining the military and security forces in the cities, but even there the repression, perhaps in response to renewed activity by leftist labor and student organizations, has begun to increase. Tutela Legal counted 80 political killings by right-wing death squads in the first six months of 1985, double the number in the preceding six months. The victims are tortured and killed, then deposited in garbage dumps on the outskirts of town, or are gunned down in broad daylight in offices or on city streets. Meanwhile, not one officer has been put on trial for *any* act of brutality since the orgy of killing began in 1979.

Democracy has not prevailed in El Salvador. The killing has merely shifted beyond the range of vision.

Los Angeles, CA, September 13, 1985

Guerrilla wars are by definition nasty. Unable or unwilling to fight in the open, insurgents employ hit-and-run attacks, often against innocent civilians. Lately, though, El Salvador's leftist rebels have begun specializing in the kind of deadly attempts at headline-grabbing that we are accustomed to seeing in the Middle East and Western Europe — and doubtless for the same reason: The war has not been going well for them, and the world's attention has shifted elsewhere.

The most recent example of their desperation was the kidnapping this week of President Jose Napoleon Duarte's daughter, Ines Duarte Duran. An employee of the government, her real value as a target lay in her relationship to the president. Her abductors, who also kidnapped her secretary and murdered one of her bodyguards, doubtless hope to provoke Duarte into a wave of general repression.

We trust that will not be his response — not now, with the search for the victims under way, and not later, when the temptation will be greater. It would be a shame to risk the progress Duarte has made by playing into the guerrillas' hands.

These days, the rebels are not eager to engage the better-trained and better-armed government troops. Instead, they strike against roads, power lines, bridges and local officials. They are also said to be forcing people into their service — hardly an indication that they think time is on their side. In fact, time may be running out. Duarte, who was elected in remarkably free elections, has created, with American help, a Salvadoran political center virtually out of thin air.

El Salvador is still far from being a showcase of democracy, but Duarte seems to be bringing many of the excesses of the former ruling oligarchy under control. Even the notorious right-wing death squads have been relatively quiet of late. Thus, the choice is no longer between two evils but, to a greater extent than ever, between a duly elected government with a claim to popular support and armed gangs with no claim at all.

The Birmingham News

Birmingham, AL, September 12, 1985

No one, regardless of sex, age or calling, is exempt from attacks by terrorists in El Salvador. The kidnapping of President Jose Napoleon Duarte's daughter, a university student, is another in a series of deadly crimes in the country's capital city.

While the terrorist kidnappers have not yet revealed their identities, it can be fairly safe to speculate that they are members of, or associated with, communist guerrillas in the countryside. That she will be held for ransom is almost a foregone conclusion, although one can speculate on the nature of the ransom: Money, release of communist prisoners or some other cherished goal of the guerrillas.

As deplorable as the kidnapping is, it also signals a general setback in the fortunes of the communist insurgents. Urban terrorism is perhaps the lowest level of communist insurgency. Retreat to urban terrorism from military engagement is an open admission of the failure of guerrilla forces in the countryside.

The purpose of urban attacks is to demonstrate the power of the insurgents at much smaller risk and at lower cost than in open combat between guerrilla strike forces and Salvadoran troops.

Urban terrorism is meant to show the powerlessness of the government to preserve order and protect the public and to force the government to take harsh measures against the terrorists. But more often than not, the innocent public gets caught up in those measures and loses some, if not many, of its freedoms.

The terrorists, of course, hope to trade on that discontent by creating sympathy for their cause among the public and even to recruit followers as a result of the discontent.

Of course, one hopes Duarte will do all in his power to locate his daughter and to set her free. One hopes also that the culprits are brought to justice and tried for their crimes. It is particularly important that Duarte succeed in this instance, the love he bears for his daughter being not the least consideration.

Prolonged harsh measures to seek out the terrorists can very well be used by the radical right to justify punitive acts against its enemies. People have not forgotten the so-called death squads. No doubt, the terrorists will make use of that history to discredit the Duarte government if the opportunity arises.

Again, it would be well to recognize that the change of communist tactics signals a setback, not an advance toward the insurgents' goals of toppling the Duarte administration and its constitutional government. It means that the insurgents are meeting heavy resistance from the people in the countryside and defeat at the hands of government troops.

THE PLAIN DEALER

Cleveland, OH, September 8, 1985

L less than three months ago, gunmen opened fire on customers at two sidewalk cafes in San Salvador, killing 13 people. Among the dead were six Americans, four of whom were U.S. Marines. Salvadoran officials now claim to have arrested three men who took part in the killings.

The officials have made quite a show of their prized catches. The three have appeared at a government news conference and on government television, confessing to the crime and providing highly detailed accounts of the attack. American officials, too, are convinced the three participated in the attack. Indeed, the FBI and CIA are believed to have assisted in the investigation.

What a contrast to previous efforts to find and bring to justice those involved in civilian killings. During the six-year civil war, more than 40,000 Salvadoran civilians have been killed. Yet, no one has been arrested and prosecuted for those crimes. Only in the murders of four American churchwomen in 1980 have there been prosecutions, and then nearly four years afterward, and only after intense pressure from the United States.

To an extent, the greater resources and efforts expended to find the killers of the U.S. Marines is understandable. In this country, police normally will spend more time investigating the killing of a colleague. And U.S. officials abroad routinely place a higher value on American lives than the lives of the native population, even when the killings of civilians is as commonplace as in El Salvador.

Part of the problem in El Salvador has been a historical connection between the atrocities and right-wing death squads connected to the military. While death-squad activity has been greatly curbed, the military and its officers still are mostly regarded as untouchable. Even when there is little doubt about the involvement of officers in a killing, loopholes in the law allow them to remain free. That happened in the case of the 1981 shooting deaths of two American labor advisers and a Salvadoran land-reform specialist.

Much of what is wrong in El Salvador revolves around the fact that neither that Salvadoran government nor Washington has placed sufficient emphasis on civilian lives. President Reagan pledged to "move any mountain and ford any river" to see that justice was obtained for the killings of the six Americans. Until San Salvador and Washington place the same importance on the lives of Salvadoran people, popular support for the government of El Salvador will remain tentative.

The Oregonian

Portland, OR, September 3, 1985

Vigorous prosecution of the many inactive and dusty death-squad murder cases in El Salvador's files could dramatically enhance the stature of President Jose Napoleon Duarte and his administration among that nation's middle class and peasants.

The new attorney general in San Salvador, Santiago Mendoza Aguilar, has reopened investigations of several notorious cases, indicating Duarte feels confident his government has enough support in the military forces to risk taking on the leaders of El Salvador's far right, who many believe directed death-squad operations.

Most notable of the cases reopened by Mendoza Aguilar is the 1980 murder of Archbishop Oscar Arnulfo Romero. His death is believed to have been ordered because of his outspoken opposition to government repression and right-wing death squads.

Other cases on Mendoza Aguilar's list include the murder of Michael Kline, 21, of San Diego, after soldiers stopped the bus he was on; the killing of journalist John Sullivan of New Jersey after he was taken from his hotel room in San Salvador in 1980; La Florida massacre in 1982, in which witnesses reported soldiers dragged seven peasants from their huts and hacked them to death; and La Hojas massacre in 1983, in which at least 18 members of a rural cooperative are reported to have been captured by soldiers and shot to death.

This activity coincides, possibly not accidentally, with Duarte's announcement of the arrest of three suspects in the June 19 San Salvador cafe massacre in which four U.S. Marines were killed. The investigation of those killings was the first case handled by a special 25-member unit trained by the FBI last year in Puerto Rico. This unit, which works under authority of the president, could be a big reason for the confidence of Mendoza Aguilar in reopening the old cases.

This demonstration that the government is willing to resurrect politically sensitive cases is bound to gain support for continued U.S. aid to Duarte among those who had been doubtful of his ability to stand up against the far right.

Rebels Raid Army Base, Slay Scores in El Salvador

Leftist freedom fighters March 31, 1987 staged their most successful operation in recent years, attacking a major military base and killing more than 60 soldiers. An American military adviser was also slain, the first U.S. adviser to die in combat in the guerilla war. The rebel Farabundo Marti National Liberation Front claimed responsibility for the attack, which destroyed much of the base, the 4th Infantry Brigade headquarters at El Paraiso, 36 miles north of San Salvador. The rebels attacked at a time when only 250 of the 1,000 troops usually stationed at the base were present. In the three-hour raid, they directed mortar and rocket fire at the center of the base, while rebel teams infiltrated the outer perimeter, raking soldiers with automatic weapons fire and hurling explosives. The guerillas targeted key offices and an intelligence center in the assault. The devastating success of the raid, described in some accounts as near-perfect, led military analysts to conclude that rebel infiltrators had entered the base to gain valuable intelligence and to assist in the assault from inside.

The slain American was identified as Staff Sgt. Gregory Fronius, 27, from Greensburg, Pennsylvania. He was a member of the U.S. Army Special Forces and was one of two U.S. advisers assigned to the base. The other adviser was not at the base at the time of the raid. According to some accounts, the rebels appeared to have deliberately sought out Fronius.

The military press office in San Salvador April 1 said 69 soldiers had been killed in the attack. About 60 were reportedly wounded. However, some officials put those totals closer to 80 and 100, respectively. At least 11 rebels died. All the dead soldiers were enlisted men. Officers reportedly retreated to an underground bunker during the assault. The army's performance in the battle, and the failure of a nearby army garrison to send reinforcements, prompted criticism from some military analysts and officers. The El Paraiso base was one of the most strongly defended in the country and it had been designed by U.S. Special Forces to be impregnable. It had been attacked and largely destroyed in 1983, when more than 100 soldiers were killed.

The San Diego Union

San Diego, CA, April 7, 1987

Some critics of President Reagan's Central American policy have been quick to take advantage of last week's guerrilla attack on a major Salvadoran army base that killed 78 soldiers, including a U.S. military adviser. These naysayers would have us believe that this recent setback demonstrates the inherent futility of trying to defeat the seven-year-old communist insurgency.

Such carping to the contrary notwithstanding, simple logic demands that the United States stay the course in El Salvador. In fact, the communists' chances of prevailing there have been diminished considerably during the last few years thanks to continued American assistance and a strengthened Salvadoran military.

Another reason for more stability in El Salvador is that the communist-led Sandinistas in Nicaragua have been too preoccupied with the contra freedom-fighters to send much help to the Salvadoran Marxist guerrillas.

The United States has been a strong backer of El Salvador since President Reagan assumed office in 1981, providing more than $500 million a year in military and economic aid. After Jose Napoleon Duarte became the nation's first democratically elected president three years ago, Congress became a supporter of the government as well.

Meantime, a change in El Salvador's military high command and its strategy has thrown the communist guerrillas off stride. Unable to mount a sustained offensive, they have resorted to sporadic assaults designed to generate maximum publicity. Thus the rationale for last Tuesday's hit-and-run raid on the government garrison in Chalatenango province.

President Reagan was on target when he said that the death of the first U.S. soldier in combat against Salvadoran guerrillas underscores America's responsibility to keep communism out of the Western Hemisphere. Clearly that responsibility also extends to neighboring Nicaragua, which the Soviet Union is turning into a mainland base for military and political subversion of all Central America.

The Dallas Morning News

Dallas, TX, April 2, 1987

The Marxist insurgents in El Salvador sought a dramatic way to revive world attention in their flagging struggle for power. So they attacked an army garrison, killing at least 65 soldiers, including U.S. military adviser Gregory A. Fronius, and wounding 100 others.

Whatever the message the guerrillas wished to convey, the one that rings clearest is that the United States must increase its resolve to support their defeat. For the lines of conflict are much more neatly drawn now than they have been at any time in

the history of this eight-year civil war. Prior to the election of Jose Napoleon Duarte as head of El Salvador 2½ years ago, congressional debate on support to El Salvador was dominated by an array of cynical pronouncements.

Some congressional critics insisted that a Marxist victory in that nation was inevitable and it was therefore futile for the United States to continue supporting the regime. Others suggested that the Salvadoran people lacked the political maturity to handle democracy and this nation should thus favor

the leftist guerrillas in their fight with the right-wing death squads.

El Salvador has faced tough problems in the interim. An economic crisis precipitated by the costs of combating the insurgency has been greatly exacerbated by last year's earthquake that killed 1,500 people and left tens of thousands homeless in the capital city of San Salvador. But the people of El Salvador also have shown a commitment to democracy — turning out to vote even in instances where their lives were being threatened by extremists — that defied and no doubt surprised the cynics in Congress.

The strife in El Salvador is no longer an issue of choosing sides between right-wing extremists and leftist guerrillas. It is in essence a war to defeat the enemies of its fledgling democracy. The Salvadoran people have shown great courage in the midst of violent opposition to hold on to their new democratic system. It is time for the United States to show like resolve by providing even more support if need be to help them do just that.

The Burlington Free Press

Burlington, VT, April 13, 1987

When a U.S. soldier was killed during a rebel raid on an army base in El Salvador two weeks ago, memories of Vietnam inevitably echoed through the reaction of many Americans.

That is sad, but convenient for the Reagan administration and its policy in El Salvador.

Like aging generals, Americans are trying to fight the last war all over again. Congressmen dwell on the importance of learning precisely how many advisers we have in El Salvador and whether it is more than last year. Are they really just advising? Are they going into battle? Should they be allowed to carry guns? •

These questions are all right, but they aren't the important ones.

Even Ronald Reagan hasn't forgotten the lessons of Vietnam, and the chances he would want — or that Congress would agree — to send combat troops to El Salvador are almost nil.

The United States isn't shoring up the Salvadoran government with the 55 military advisers now in the country, nor with the promise of troops.

American bodies aren't the issue. American dollars are.

So far, the administration has pumped $2 billion into El Salvador, $1 billion — $1 *billion* — of it into the country's military.

The money has brought the army plenty of weapons, but it has not bought victory — and is not l¹· ·ly to, as the rebels' successful attack on the El Paraiso army base demonstrated. Military victories will not bring land reform, will not wipe out the memories of the death squads, will not win the loyalty of terrified peasants.

The Duarte government has taken steps to curb the military's reign of torture and death, but has not fundamentally altered the equation in El Salvador: True power lies with a military that has brutalized the country.

It is difficult to imagine how the divisions in El Salvador can be knit into peace. Duarte has not begun to make the fundamental social reforms that might capture the hearts of his people. Even a victory by the Farabundo Marti National Liberation Front would likely create, as in Nicaragua, a new group of Contra-style rebels.

Vietnam does have a lesson to teach the United States in El Salvador: Each country's civil war is its own, arising from causes that grow from the soil of history. Each is a unique tragedy in which the curtain cannot be rung down by foreign military billions.

The Philadelphia Inquirer

Philadelphia, PA, April 6, 1987

More than a Salvadoran military barracks went up in flames last week in a devastating rebel assault whose casualties included the first U.S. adviser to die in combat in El Salvador's bloody, seven-year-old civil war. Another casualty was the perception — widely and wrongly held — that something of a *pax Duarte* had descended on that tortured land.

Peace has not come. And, though El Salvador's death squads are quiescent and last year's earthquake was distracting, that country remains in critical condition. It is victimized by its own class warfare and, to some extent, by a U.S. policy that has concentrated on defeating, rather than defusing, a leftist insurgency.

By some calculations, the war's destruction — close to $2 billion since 1980 — has matched dollar for dollar the total amount of U.S. economic assistance during the same period. Yet employment hovers around 50 percent and agrarian reform and democracy-building programs remain stalemated, perpetuating conditions that led to the insurgency in the first place.

Instead of expanding, the "democratic center" represented by President Jose Napoleon Duarte has shrunk, beset by a resurgent right wing and disenchanted numbers of peasants, workers and students. Salvadorans have lost confidence that there is a strategy for peace.

Instead, many see a U.S.-dominated strategy that emphasizes a long-term, low-intensity military effort while underwriting an economy that fails to deliver for the masses of impoverished Salvadorans. That strategy has relaxed the pressure on Mr. Duarte to build bridges to his dwindling natural constituency, those clinging to El Salvador's lowest rungs, while emboldening the right to resist reform.

It may have denied victory to the rebels, but it has not given them any incentive to stop fighting. Until U.S. policy addresses the political deadlock — and aims at broadening opportunity for the dispossessed while curbing the veto power of the oligarchs — the war will continue.

Last week the will and opportunity for social change seemed as sadly lacking as when the fighting began — seven years, $700 million (in U.S. military aid) and 62,000 lives ago.

Roanoke Times & World-News

Roanoke, VA, April 13, 1987

THE DEATH of a U.S. military adviser in El Salvador is a jarring and bitter reminder for Americans: Nicaragua is not the only country in that region with a civil war in whose outcome the United States has a sizable stake.

There are notable differences. In Nicaragua, the United States is backing an insurgent movement, the Contras, trying to overthrow an established (and popularly ratified) but left-leaning government. In El Salvador, Washington is backing the established government against a leftist insurgency. Fears persist that the United States will one day commit our own troops to the war in Nicaragua; there's been much less concern about that possibility in El Salvador, despite the presence of a handful of U.S. military advisers there.

In both countries, however, there have been recent setbacks for Washington. This is especially unfortunate in the case of El Salvador, where the United States has, for the most part, pursued an enlightened policy: resisting armed communism without embracing rightist militarism.

Our government has tried there to promote democratic ideals and practices while discouraging brutalities and vigilantism. We were rewarded with the election in 1984 of a centrist president, Jose Napoleon Duarte, who has kept the allegiance of the armed forces because they knew that to undermine him would jeopardize U.S. aid in the war against the insurgents. Duarte announced sweeping reforms and made bold overtures to the rebels for a negotiated end to the war.

Halfway through his five-year term, Duarte's efforts seem to have stalled on all fronts. The people have grown disenchanted. Reforms have produced few visible results. The economy is in terrible shape, with half the working force underemployed or on the streets. Negotiations with the rebels got nowhere; the war, which has killed 62,000 people, goes on. The audacious attack that took the life of American Staff Sgt. Gregory A. Fronius this week demonstrated the insurgents' capabilities: The raid, on a major army base considered very secure, also killed more than 40 Salvadoran soldiers.

Several months ago, the rebels visited pain and humiliation on Duarte himself by kidnapping his daughter and demanding ransom, which he paid. This was not the first time that Duarte, basically a good man, had been made to look ineffectual; and it bolstered his image as a figurehead leader controlled by events and by other people.

Even natural forces have worked against Duarte. Last October the capital, San Salvador, was rocked by an earthquake that killed 1,500 people and left tens of thousands homeless. Many still are living in tents and lean-tos, and piles of rubble from the quake still have not been cleared. The victims' plight feeds cynicism about the government's good intentions.

Meantime, the right wing — driven almost into hiding a few years ago — has been regrouping. The death squads still operate, although less openly than before. "People are sometimes tortured while in police custody," reports Newsweek magazine, "and no member of the army officer corps has ever been brought to justice for past abuses." The wealthy resist land reform and any talk of new taxes to pay for the war.

All that keeps El Salvador's fragile democracy afloat is U.S. aid: $545 million last year, as much as $770 million this year. Duarte governs with the help of a six-vote majority in the National Assembly; that margin could vanish in the legislative elections a year from now, with the far right making up ground it lost in 1984. Duarte's troubles in El Salvador may only have begun. So too for the United States.

THE INDIANAPOLIS NEWS
Indianapolis, IN, April 7, 1987

The news from El Salvador this week brings a reminder that the costs of involvement in a troubled world are dearly paid.

Before dawn on Tuesday, rebels attacked a military base at El Paraiso — about 40 miles north of San Salvador. The guerillas killed 43 Salvadoran soldiers and one U.S. military adviser. Staff Sgt. Gregory A. Frontius was the first U.S. soldier killed in El Salvador.

Frontius, 27, was a native of Greensburg, Pa., and was part of the 3rd Battalion, 7th Special Forces, U.S. Southern Command, which is based in Panama. His assignment was to help train and prepare the Salvadoran military to respond better to the threats the country's seven-year civil war presents.

That assignment brought Frontius to El Paraiso and — with the help of the Salvadoran rebels — it killed him. Doubtless, his death in the line of duty will create another round of questions about the United States' role in Central America.

This is as it should be. The United States has great power — economic power, military power, moral power — but the exercise of that power always has a price tag. Often, the price is measured in human lives.

That is all too clear in Central America. Nicaragua, which funnels arms and guerillas from the Soviet Union and Cuba to the Salvadoran rebels and their compatriots elsewhere in the region, can claim credit for an impressive number of corpses in recent years. The Sandinistas' war on human life and dignity, both inside and outside Nicaragua, practically demands a response from those who cherish both.

But, how and at what cost?

Those are the eternal questions about foreign involvement the American people always must ask — and answer — for themselves. The public cannot expect the president and the Congress to take sole responsibility for determining the United States' role in Central America, because the president and the Congress will not bear the burden of that involvement.

Unfortunately — tragically — that burden will be borne by the Gary Frontiuses of this country, and their mothers, fathers, sisters, brothers, wives and friends. It is a dear and costly burden.

And it is a burden no one should be asked to carry without careful consideration. Thus far, American policy in Central America has been muddled. Sometimes, the Reagan administration says it is simply attempting to contain Nicaraguan gun-running and terrorism. At other times, it has said the United States' goal is to topple the Sandinista government.

Through it all, the American public largely has been mute, depriving the Reagan administration of either a mandate to oppose the Sandinistas forcefully or a clear signal to get out quickly.

It's time for Americans to consider what they hope to accomplish in Central America and how they hope to accomplish it. Only when the country has answered those questions will it be fair to ask for the sort of sacrifices made by Gary Frontius and his family.

The Kansas City Times
Kansas City, MO, April 15, 1987

If the United States is to remain in a military advisory capacity in El Salvador, it should also insist that American advisers not be compromised by the Salvadoran military's inadequate security measures or the rebels' well-planned guerrilla initiatives. It should also consider how effective the advisers are in El Salvador. Judging by the rebels' success at El Paraiso, one may wonder if Americans are as useful as the administration may have hoped or believed.

The assault on the Salvadoran army's garrison at El Paraiso, where 69 Salvadorans and an American were killed recently, should not have occurred. At the very least, the rebels should not have been so successful, militarily speaking. Either Salvadoran troops and their American aides had underestimated the rebels' strength and capabilities, overestimated their own or simply were asleep on the job. The Paraiso assault demonstrates a severe breakdown in military preparedness on the part of Salvadoran troops and the American' support team.

It was at El Paraiso that Staff Sgt. Gregory Fronius, a Pennsylvanian, became the first American to die in combat in the five years of battle in El Salvador. As Fronius has made history of sorts, it seems appropriate at this time to re-evaluate the U.S. presence in El Salvador. That does not mean the withdrawal of U.S. support there, as the communist threat is real, but it may mean a possible restructuring of that presence and alterations in military strategy so that a more accurate appraisal may be made.

The rebel attack on the garrison has also put the Duarte administration on alert. El Salvador's civilian president has long tested the patience of the military which thinks he has been too soft on the rebels, even in the face of the kidnapping of his daughter. Duarte's inability to bring to trial and have sentenced soldiers accused of killing or violating the human rights of civilians, including Americans, is a constant reminder of his reluctance to ruffle the feathers of the military. Since El Paraiso, tensions between the executive branch and the armed forces have undoubtedly heightened.

The Miami Herald
Miami, FL, April 4, 1987

IT WAS probably inevitable. Send 55 U.S. military advisers to a nation where 60,000 people have been killed in a bloody civil war, and it's just a matter of time before one of the Americans gets killed.

This does not make the death of Green Beret Staff Sgt. Gregory Fronius during Tuesday's predawn guerrilla attack any less painful, to his family or to the nation. Nor do the thousands killed in the seven-year insurrection make the death of 64 Salvadoran soldiers during the attack on El Paraiso's army base any less regrettable.

The attack was the largest and most daring by Marxist-led Farabundo Marti National Liberation Front forces in more than two years. It was a jolting reminder that leftist Salvadoran guerrillas — believed by many to have lost military effectiveness recently — still represent a serious danger to the consolidation of democracy in El Salvador.

To be effective, guerrillas need public recognition. Their hit-and-run tactics are designed to frustrate their military opponents and thus to provoke a violent and blind retaliation. Killing an American military adviser was a bonus for the guerrillas, who seek to weaken America's resolve to help El Salvador.

Thus it's urgent that both Washington and Salvadoran President Jose Napoleon Duarte respond decisively and appropriately. El Salvador's army must act quickly to regain the military initiative lest the recent guerrilla upsurge escalate into a full-scale offensive. But they must avoid the understandable temptation to retaliate indiscriminately. That would only strengthen the guerrillas.

Washington's reaction must be measured as well. Sergeant Fronius's death should provoke neither a knee-jerk call for more U.S. forces nor for reducing U.S. aid to El Salvador.

Efforts to professionalize the Salvadoran military forces must continue without any further commitment of U.S. forces. That professionalization requires continued U.S. advice and economic aid. Most of all, it requires that both the Administration and Congress reaffirm this country's support for Mr. Duarte's efforts to rid El Salvador of guerrillas and strengthen its democracy.

The Washington Post

Washington, DC, April 5, 1987

THE FIRST American combat victim in seven years of civil war in El Salvador has died in a guerrilla raid in which some 60 government soldiers also were killed. It was a conspicuous success for the guerrillas, militarily and, perhaps more, politically. Americans have tended to let the struggle in Nicaragua obscure the longer, harsher, deeper conflict in nearby El Salvador, and an incident such as the one at El Paraiso brings El Salvador back into focus.

The death of Staff Sgt. Gregory Fronius, a military adviser, seems to have been the chance result of an unusual large-scale attack launched by the guerrilla command to show it can still stay in the field against the American-equipped and -trained armed forces of El Salvador. What is notable, however, is not that one American was killed, but that in seven years of providing aid and advice the United States has managed to stay in a support role and to do a fair job of helping Salvadorans better defend themselves. The prediction that the dispatch of a small number of advisers to this small Central American place would lead inexorably to a Vietnam-like involvement has not come true.

The guerrillas, however, hang on, reduced but resourceful and determined to block the government's strategy of wearing them down and writing them out of El Salvador's future. Until now, anyway, their assaults on military targets have been the lesser part of their activity. The greater part is their attacks on economic targets—coffee plantations, buses, electric pylons. These attacks have inflicted heartless damage on an already-staggering economy (whose latest burden is an American immigration reform that may close El Salvador's emigration safety valve). The attacks have also angered many Salvadoran citizens, thereby further narrowing the opposition's political appeal, souring what prospects there are for a political settlement and prolonging the war.

President José Napoleón Duarte hangs on too. His standing in Washington as the man who brought some political reforms to El Salvador ensures the flow of American aid that supports the anticommunist struggle. But his very success has had the effect of widening the political space in which ever-sharper challenges to him are mounted across the legal political spectrum—including challenges from the part of the spectrum that is most suspicious of trying to negotiate a political settlement. This is how his situation can get better and worse at the same time. The fact is that democracy is essential to the salvation of El Salvador, but so is an end to the war that no one knows how to stop.

Los Angeles Times

Los Angeles, CA, April 2, 1987

The deaths of two U.S. citizens in El Salvador's civil war is a sad reminder that the conflict is still unresolved more than seven years after it began. Worse, the conditions under which one of the U.S. advisers died suggest that the war could go on much longer than many analysts had thought.

One of the dead is an unidentified employee of the Central Intelligence Agency, killed when a helicopter crashed on a reconnaissance flight. The other was Army Staff Sgt. Gregory Fronius, 27, one of 78 persons who died in a surprisingly ferocious attack by leftist guerrillas on a major military base in the northern province of Chalatenango. The region is one of three that Salvadoran government forces have been trying to wrest from guerrilla control for several years.

Before Tuesday's attack, military officials in the Salvadoran government and at the U.S. Embassy in San Salvador had been suggesting that the guerrillas were facing an imminent demise because of the increasingly aggressive pursuit by an army that is larger, better trained and better equipped than it has ever been—thanks to U.S. support.

Yet since the start of this year, as if to respond to those confident claims, the rebels have begun inflicting serious damage on government forces with troubling regularity. Although the attack that killed Fronius is certain to get the most attention in the United States, it was only the most recent setback for the Salvadoran army.

Since Jan. 1 the guerrillas have launched four attacks in which they massed enough troops to strike at major military installations. They have also continued a strategy of methodically sabotaging the nation's electrical and transportation systems, and have expanded into areas where they had rarely operated before—such as El Salvador's western provinces.

So while they are not nearly as powerful as they were two years ago, the Salvadoran rebels are far from defeated. That sobering reality suggests that El Salvador's President Jose Napoleon Duarte should once again try to renew the long-stalled peace talks between his government and the guerrillas' political representatives. Unless he does, the war will claim many more lives—not just of North Americans but of many, many more Salvadorans.

Chicago Tribune

Chicago, IL, April 3, 1987

The death of S. Sgt. Gregory Fronius, an American Special Forces Green Beret killed along with 43 Salvadoran soldiers in a leftist guerrilla mortar attack on an El Salvador army base, was, as President Reagan says, "a tragedy."

But it should not affect basic U.S. policy in El Salvador or in Central America generally.

Almost before the casualties were counted, we began hearing and reading what have now become the ritual allusions to Vietnam. "Many members of Congress have expressed anxiety that in sending military advisers to Central America the United States is entering a quagmire similar to Vietnam," one news report said.

That is nonsense.

The United States has a strong and valid interest in seeking to help the democratically elected government of President Jose Napoleon Duarte survive and succeed against the long-running communist insurgency in El Salvador. The Reagan administration has self-imposed a limit of 55 U.S. military advisers assigned to help train the government armed forces and insists it has no intention of sending combat troops into the region.

There is no realistic comparison to be made with Vietnam and no sign of any administration intent to alter its involvement or up the ante.

Sgt. Fronius was the first American to die in a combat situation in El Salvador. He was not the first American casualty of the communist insurgency there. Another U.S. adviser was gunned down in downtown San Salvador in 1983 and four off-duty marines were killed at a cafe. Those were tragedies, too.

But they do not constitute a basis for policy change. What they do, as Mr. Reagan noted of Sgt. Fronius' death, is "bring home to everyone what we face" in the way of the communist threat in Central America.

The Des Moines Register

Des Moines, IA April 7, 1987

A rebel attack on a Salvadoran army base, which killed 43 government soldiers and one American adviser, put the international spotlight on U.S. military involvement in El Salvador. In the shadows, the beleagured presidency of Jose Napoleon Duarte is also under attack from rightists and leftists alike.

Preoccupation with Nicaragua and the election of the somewhat moderate Duarte has led to an assumption that El Salvador is no longer on the crisis list. Far from it.

Despite more than $2 billion in U.S. economic and military aid, Duarte has not ended the seven-year civil war that has killed 62,000 people and displaced 800,000.

U.S. assistance has enabled Duarte to quadruple the size of the army in just six years to more than 52,000 troops, but neither U.S. aid nor Duarte has addressed the underlying causes of civil war.

Among these are a 40-percent unemployment rate, rampant inflation, 1,000 political prisoners, malnutrition among 75 percent of the children and the highest infant-death rate in Central America.

The successful attack on the U.S.-built army base last month suggests that massive amounts of U.S. military aid have not prevented the Marxist Farabundo Marti National Liberation Front (FMLN) from building an effective fighting force.

But Duarte also faces opposition from the right. Large landholders and powerful businesses have effectively blocked land- and social-reform efforts promised by Duarte when he came to power, and there are reports that much of the U.S. economic aid has lined the pockets of the upper-middle classes.

Even so, the National Assembly cannot function because right-wing deputies are boycotting it in an effort to undermine Duarte's legitimacy. Last January, the right and left both participated in a one-day strike to demonstrate widespread opposition to Duarte.

Duarte's term runs out in 1989, but the United States had best not wait that long to review its policy in El Salvador.

Increased U.S. military assistance may prop up Duarte for a little longer. But a military-dominated U.S. policy does not relieve poverty in El Salvador and it certainly won't stop the killing.

Part IV: South America

For centuries the Inca empire in South America stood as one of the most advanced civilizations in history. But its rapid disintegration after the European "discovery" of the "New World" and subsequent colonization at the hands of the Spaniards ranks as one of history's more tragic episodes. The violent subjugation of the indigenous Indian civilizations accompanied the European's settlement efforts, particularly those of Spain. After penetration and exploration by Europe began in earnest in the 16th century, as Portugal claimed what is now Brazil under the Treaty of Tordesillas while Spain claims over the rest of the continent with the exception of the Guianas were recognized. Roman Catholicism and an Iberian culture were soon transplanted on the continent, as were some of the crops that would later become primary export staples. Since the 17th Century, the exploitation of the continent's resources and the development of its industries have been the result of foreign investment and initiative, especially that of Spain, Great Britain, and the United States.

But despite the many advances that have transpired in the region in the 20th century, South America is still rife with poverty, desperation and turmoil—individual, spiritual and political. This is in striking contrast to North America which, with its early-won political and economic independence, has become the leader of the developed world. This historical division in the New World is paradoxical since Latin America enjoyed the advantage of natural resources, agricultural growth and a labor force to work the mines and haciendas. However South America has remained dependent and underdeveloped while North America has steadily forged ahead.

The International Monetary Fund (IMF) plays a crucial role in the economies of South America, as in much of the Third World, by imposing strict disciplinary measures on debtor nations seeking new loans. But for South American countries already in straightened circumstances, austerity measures have triggered violent resistence, especially in Peru, Colombia and Ecuador. These upheavals have in turn lead to repressive measures, indicating that IMF-dictated austerity and repressive Latin American regimes are, at least casually related. For example, the 1976 military coup in Argentina, that led to the infamous years of totalitarianism, was directly influenced by an impending IMF credit opportunity.

Many factors have played in the instability of South America in the last ten years. The growth of the illegal drug industry throughout the region, the rise of revolutionary factions in Colombia and Peru and the 1982 Falklands War between Argentina and Great Britain have all contributed to the tension and misunderstandings between the United States and the nations of South America.

Argentina Rejects IMF Loan Term; Latin Nations Hold Debt Conference

In a letter of intent submitted to the International Monetary Fund (IMF) June 11, 1984, Argentina broke with tradition by bypassing the fund's negotiators to communicate directly with its managerial director. Rejecting harsher measures than had been proposed by the IMF in return for a loan, Argentina announced that it would raise wages in 1984 by between 6% and 8% after inflation and reduce the budget deficit to 9.16% of gross national product by the end of the year. The IMF had been demanding a smaller increase in wages and a budget deficit of no more than 8.5% of GNP. On Argentina's foreign debt, the letter said the government would pay the debt "within the framework of economic order, growth and social peace." Argentina said its plan was "strictly realistic" and would permit the nation to meet its obligations while at the same time avoiding social instability. In April, riots in the Dominican Republic over massive price increases, ordered by the government as part of an accord with the IMF, left scores of people dead.

Meanwhile, a United States guarantee to advance a $300 million loan as part of a rescue package formulated in March was due to expire June 15. The U.S. refused to extend the guarantee beyond June 15., indicating that a new loan might be arranged if and when Argentina and the IMF reached agreement. Argentina faced a June 30 deadline for paying some $500 million in past due interest to international banks. If the payments were not made, U.S. banks would be forced to classify many of their loans to Argentina as nonperforming. The U.S. banks with the largest outstanding loans to Argentina were Manufacturers Hanover Corp., Citicorp, Chase Manhattan Corp., and J.P. Morgan & Co., Inc.

Argentina's unprecedented move in submitting a unilateral austerity plan to the IMF was preceded May 19 by a joint statement issued by the presidents of Argentina, Brazil, Colombia and Mexico. The Latin leaders warned that their nations would not "indefinitely" accept the risks posed by high international interest rates and trade protectionism. The statement raised concern among international bankers that the Latin nations were considering the possibility of a debtors' cartel to negotiate with international banks. But when finance and foreign ministers from 11 Latin American nations attended a conference in Cartagena, Colombia June 21-22, the delegates said they would not renege on their debts and ruled out the possibility of forming a debtor's cartel. They proposed, however, that a new international structure to refinance the region's foreign debt be formulated, including an agreement to hold down interest rates on the debts. The delegates also proposed a change in the IMF conditions for refinancing aid, with priority given to reducing unemployment and encouraging economic growth instead of austerity measures. The new debt arrangements, it was proposed, would be formulated by a group of representatives from industrial and developing nations.

AKRON BEACON JOURNAL
Akron, OH, June 27, 1984

THE U.S. PRIME rate jumped another half point to 13 percent this week. That is the fourth such jump in four months, fueling concern that another recession could lurk behind the current economic boom.

The rise also worries debtor countries in Latin America, who met in Colombia last week to share notes on the debt crisis. Eleven Latin nations have borrowed roughly $360 billion from Western banks, mostly in the United States, and each time the U.S. prime rate increases a half point their debt grows by nearly $1 billion.

That, of course, adds to their already enormous economic problems, and it affects the United States. Weak economies in Latin America are less able to purchase American goods, costing Americans jobs and threatening the current recovery.

Indeed, the Latin debtors emphasized the connection between interest rates, debt and economic recovery. While hardly shirking responsibility for the current situation, the debtors stressed that any solution to the crisis involved more than austerity — tight budgets and lower wages.

Others could help. The United States, for instance, could be more aware of the fact that its policies have great impact on the region. Beyond the damage of high interest rates, U.S. protectionism keeps debtors from earning money for repayment from export sales. In addition, the banks that made the huge loans could take steps to sacrifice short-term profits to ensure long-term world banking stability.

Without cooperation and shared responsibility, the debtors realistically warned that many of the loans will never be repaid. That, they argued, would not be the result of a debtor plan to default on the loans, as many fear, but instead from their continued inability to repay because of depressed economic conditions.

Clearly, current belt-tightening is not enough, and the periodic rescue packages put together by the banks and the International Monetary Fund merely lend more money to debtors at higher interest rates.

Economic growth is needed to raise revenue. But to achieve that, bankers must be willing to lower their interest charges and grant longer periods for repayment. Slowly, debtors and lenders seem to be moving toward that kind of approach.

At the recent London economic summit, the industrialized democracies pledged more generous aid to the debtors, and in Colombia, the Latin debtors promised to repay.

Even Argentina, perhaps the most stubborn of the debtors, has offered a realistic proposal for repayment. Argentine president Raul Alfonsin, whose young democracy may be threatened by further belt-tightening, understands that many interests collide in the debt crisis. But he also recognizes that without cooperation and growth, few debts will be repaid at great political and economic risk.

Houston Chronicle

Houston, TX, June 26, 1984

These past weeks and months, reams have been written about the Third World debt crisis — and about the possibility of a so-called debtors' cartel.

Short of a cratering of the entire international monetary system, this latter is supposed to be about the worst nightmare keeping Western bankers awake nights. It's the old story: If a borrower owes enough, he owns the bank.

No doubt, then, the bankers are resting a little easier following last week's meeting of 10 Latin American debtor nations. No "debtor's club" came out of those sessions; and, despite the creation of a structure which could conceivably form the basis for a cartel in the future, no such move seems imminent. For the simple reason that it wouldn't work.

Mexico, for one, probably would not participate. That country's undersecretary of finance told his colleagues: "There can be no alternative to case-by-case resolution of the (debt) problem." Of course, that alone offers no guarantee such a strategy wouldn't ever be tried. If things got desperate enough, there's no telling what kind of deals would be cut. But things apparently aren't yet that desperate.

Cartels are fragile things anyway — witness the past few months with OPEC and oil prices. They are usually created to control the price and distribution of wealth — a scarce natural resource — not to share the misery. It is one thing for say, Saudi Arabia, to keep its oil in the ground in order to keep prices up; quite another for relatively solvent Venezuela to agree to lock arms with debt-ridden Brazil. Pity the politician who has to explain that one to the home folks. And that doesn't begin to take into account the complexities of the system — the very different deals between individual countries and individual banks.

That said, however, the subject remains a touchy one all the way around. As Henry Kissinger pointed out on last Sunday's Outlook page, there is little or no chance any of the Latin countries' debt principle will be repaid in the next decade, and even the interest payments will be politically difficult for some of the more impoverished. Already, in Argentina's case, the International Monetary Fund has been asked to renegotiate repayment terms and interest rates, and there will be more of that ahead. Much as anything, the bankers' tone will tell a large part of the story.

So maybe the Western bankers can sleep a little more soundly. But the smart ones will keep one eye open.

The Burlington Free Press

Burlington, VT, June 21, 1984

To default or not to default will be the question before the Latin American finance ministers when they meet today in Cartagena, Colombia, in an effort to work out ways and means of paying off their debts while retaining economic stability in their countries.

The seven participants in the meeting — Brazil, Mexico, Argentina, Venezuela, Colombia, Peru and Ecuador — owe $286 billion of the region's $340 billion in foreign debt.

Argentina is said to be leaning in the direction of default. Because of a raging 500 percent inflation rate in the country, today's peso will be worth half a peso in August. Ordered by International Monetary Fund to adopt austerity measures, Argentine leaders balked at the program because it called for wage cuts and an end to efforts to induce economic growth by inflationary means. Instead they offered their own program: increases in oil and utility prices, revival of the bankrupt social security system with employers' contributions and sale of some state-owned assets. It appears, however, that the international agency will not accept the Argentine solution. Unless agreement is reached, the nation could be cut off from further help from the fund. Banks might be equally reluctant to loan more money to Argentina.

Latin finance ministers will learn during the meeting that they will have to pay $22.5 billion in interest to their bankers, principally in the United States, this year and will receive only an additional $15 billion in loans. And they must continue negotiations to reschedule $160 million in bank debts. Default may be a tempting possibility, particularly with the Federal Reserve's bailout of the Continental Illinois bank in mind, but it could lead to harsh measures by bankers to recoup their loans. Banks could impound Latin American exports as a means of covering a portion of the debt.

Mexico, Brazil and Argentina, the countries most deeply in debt, apparently have but one choice; they must adopt the austerity measures set out by the International Fund in the hope that successful compliance will restore bankers' confidence in their economies.

At the same time, the United States must make efforts to hold interest rates down so that Latin American debtors will not be subject for further financial penalties on their loans.

Hemispheric stability depends on greater cooperation among Latin Americans and their affluent northern neighbor.

The Dallas Morning News

Dallas, TX, June 25, 1984

To the extent that international banking — for that matter, banking in general — is comprehensible at all to the uninitiated, topsy-turviness seems the rule. The case of 11 Latin American debtor nations is a classic illustration of the old joke about how it's your problem if you owe the bank $100, but if you owe it a million, it's the bank's problem.

Recently the nations met to set policy on the means of handling payments on their public debt to foreign banks, which has now reached, as Carl Sagan says of distances in space, "billions and billions." Argentina is the worst case, and may verge on default.

Not surprisingly, the nations decided that the thing to do was arrange more lenient terms of repayment. The U.S. Treasury's response was diplomatic — "We thought the whole thing was positive." But others not bound by diplomacy see something less positive, i.e., continued movement toward a "debt

cartel," which means the debtor nations' banding together and thumbing their noses at the banks.

The banks, of course, should be scolded for bad loans, but that doesn't solve the problem of how to get their money back from governments whose economies are basket cases. One way is for the taxpayers to cover the loss — hardly a just way, but some see it as inevitable. Another is for the debtor nations to adopt, in addition to the more lenient repayment schedules, pro-growth economic policies.

The fiscal austerity being urged by the International Monetary Fund, while needed, will not bring about the capital formation necessary for growth, nor will collectivist policies. But there is already evidence that those Third World nations where the market is allowed to do its stuff are progressing. This, along with austerity, is what the IMF should be preaching.

The Idaho STATESMAN

Boise, ID, June 19, 1984

The Economics 101 instructor explains the U.S. national debt — which now exceeds $1 trillion — in reassuring terms: It's not terribly important to retire it, because we owe the money mostly to ourselves, and we are able to service the debt.

The Third World situation cannot be described in such rosy terms because developing nations also owe their debts to us, but we have little control over those governments' revenues. With the Third World debt now exceeding $800 billion, a restructuring of the debt has become urgent.

At stake is a great deal more than the solvency of major American banks, which loaned at a breakneck pace until 1980. The Federal Deposit Insurance Corp. is at risk, having used 10 percent of its reserves to protect Continental Illinois depositors after concern about bad loans prompted an $8 billion run on the bank. Default by debtor nations could bankrupt the FDIC, throwing financial markets and banks large and small into turmoil, and landing a death blow on the economic recovery.

Outside the world of high finance, American employment adversely is affected by the debtor countries' contracting markets. Most importantly, the stability of Latin American governments is threatened by the economic gymnastics they must perform to make further payments.

Until recently, Third World countries generally had been able to secure loans that enabled them to make interest payments. Western loans are conditioned on IMF austerity programs that often lead to radical commodity price hikes, which have produced varying degrees of strife in the borrowing countries.

Latin American governments are beginning to feel that their populations have borne all the austerity that is politically or economically feasible. The Dominican Republic, after 50 people died in rioting inspired by IMF-mandated food-price hikes, in April became the first country to refuse an IMF measure. Inflation-riddled Argentina is resisting more belt-tightening. Ecuador and Bolivia have suspended payment on portions of their debt. The governments realize that asking people to pay more and more for the basics of life can inspire leftist insurgencies or military dictatorships.

The IMF, which is U.S.-led, and major banks must seek a long-term remedy.

The lenders could offer some relief by temporarily reducing interest rates while the debtor countries wait for the economic recovery to catch up to them and the IMF works on new, realistic agreements. Interest rates on Third World loans are tied to the U.S. prime rate, which has added billions to Latin American debt as it has been pushed up by the U.S. budget deficit. If they don't lower interest rates temporarily, the banks will have to loan more, as has been the past crisis response, which increases their exposure to default and adds to the risk that they will end up like Continental of Chicago.

If renegotiation is not forthcoming, the debtors will be pushed even closer to their only alternative, which is default en masse. If more realistic repayment terms are not approved and debtors do not take the radical step of default, the United States faces the prospect of non-Communist dominoes to the south crumbling from within.

Detroit Free Press

Detroit, MI,
June 16, 1984

ARGENTINA'S democratic forces won the presidential elections last fall, but Argentines are still far from achieving a consensus on how to turn their country's shattered economy around and on how to eliminate the deep-seated political attitudes responsible for 55 years of dreadful military rule.

The patriotic euphoria of the election has subsided under the pressure of economic chaos and record-high inflation. The moderate government of President Raul Alfonsin is under attack from all sides, especially from the Peronist trade unions. The Argentine president is squeezed between the need to impose dramatic — and unescapably painful — economic reforms and the diminishing support for carrying them out.

Argentina has an overmanned public sector, a huge budget deficit and a staggering foreign debt it cannot handle, the legacy of a succession of military juntas that indulged in wasteful public spending. Wages and salaries for the money-losing state enterprises consume one-third of the state budget. The inflation rate reached 600 percent this year.

The remedies are clear, and have already been recommended by the International Monetary Fund: Slash military spending, kill the plans for grandiose nuclear or hydropower plants and similar projects, cancel the subsidies to the money-losing state enterprises and step back from the election-time promise to raise real wages in the public sector. But those actions are precisely what organized labor opposes. The Peronist unions have already started undermining the government with strikes and strong-arm methods.

Nor is Mr. Alfonsin safe from Argentina's military, who, although forced from power after the lost Falklands war, have already recovered from the shock. The generals defend the military budget and exhibit growing opposition to the trials of their colleagues responsible for the atrocities of the late '70s, when some 6,000 Argentinians were tortured and killed for alleged subversive activities.

It is hard to reverse the tradition of populist demagoguery and economic mismanagement that has dragged once-prosperous Argentina down to its current Third World status. Mr. Alfonsin is meeting the challenge with a moderate, common-sense political course. He has not let the trials of the military turn into a large-scale witch hunt. He has persuaded American banks to provide much-needed short-term loans. He is building a coalition against the rightwing Peronist forces, a coalition that includes the leaders of 14 other parties and even Mrs. Isabel Peron.

Everything now depends on some flexibility on the side of the IMF and the patience of the Argentinians themselves. If they will support the necessary austerity measures and spurn the Peronist rhetoric, and if the IMF gives Argentina some breathing space, President Alfonsin — and the democracy he has come to symbolize not only in his country but throughout the hemisphere — may emerge the victor again.

The Washington Post

Times Herald

Washington, DC, June 26, 1984

THE REAGAN administration keeps saying that interest rates will fall—but instead they keep going up. The banks' prime rate, to which some of the Latin American debts are tied, rose half a point yesterday. Rates have generally gone up two percentage points since mid-March, raising the Latin countries' interest payments something like $5 billion a year. The danger here is that the Latin countries' interest payments will continue to rise faster than the export earnings that are their only means of paying them.

The effects of these rate increases chiefly fall abroad. Here in the United States each increase sets off a ripple of grumbling among borrowers, but it's hardly audible in the general celebration of a strong economic recovery. Most of Latin America, in contrast, is in a severe recession.

To say that the higher interest rates over the past several months will cost Latin debtors $5 billion more a year substantially understates the full cost. Another effect was also visible yesterday, as higher interest pushed up the exchange rate of the U.S. dollar. For foreigners whose debts are denominated in dollars, it means that each dollar of repayment will cost more in terms of their own money and the output of their economies.

Eleven of the indebted Latin countries met a few days ago in Cartagena, Colombia, to try to decide what to do next. There was some concern here that there might be an attempt to organize a debtors' alliance. That did not happen, for the very good reason that the 11 countries differ enormously in their economic strength and their intentions. But the 11 agreed that they need better consultation with their creditors and wider discussion of reforms in the financial system. The suggestion was deliberately pitched in a low key, but it deserves an active and affirmative response here in Washington.

There are two competing views on the solution to the Latin debts. One view holds that the normal process of a strong economic recovery will soon generate sufficient earnings to bring the debts down to safe proportions. The other argues that, forced rapidly upward by the recovery and the large American budget deficit, interest rates will rise faster than the debtors' ability to pay. If that is the case, the debts will become unmanageable without much more forceful intervention by the governments of the rich countries.

Until last winter the evidence seemed generally to favor the first possibility—that growth would resolve the crisis. Since then the rise in interest and exchange rates has made it seem less certain. This latest rise in the prime rate, three days after the Cartagena meeting ended, strengthens the case for thinking that further intervention may become necessary.

Los Angeles Times

Los Angeles, CA, June 27, 1984

International bankers were relieved this past weekend when 11 Latin American nations ended a major meeting on the Latin debt crisis without forming a debtors' cartel. But by raising the prime lending rate to 13%, as they began doing Monday, the banks are pushing the Latin debtors closer to the brink.

The meeting at Cartagena, Colombia, was unprecedented because it marked the first time that the deeply indebted Latin nations came together to talk about their mutual problems on a political level, including their foreign ministers as well as their finance ministers and other economic specialists in the discussions.

There had also been tough action by some of the Latin debtor nations before the Cartagena meeting. Bolivia and Ecuador suspended payments on their debts, and Argentine President Raul Alfonsin cut off negotiations with a team from the International Monetary Fund rather than accept tough austerity measures that his government would have to impose in order to qualify for IMF aid in paying off a $45-million foreign debt.

Those actions led some bankers to fear that the Cartagena meeting would result in some drastic moves by the participants—Argentina, Bolivia, Brazil, Chile, Colombia, the Dominican Republic, Ecuador, Mexico, Peru, Uruguay and Venezuela. Collectively, those nations owe $350 billion to foreign banks and lending institutions like the IMF. A collective decision to repudiate their debts, or even to delay payment for a time, could wreak havoc with the international financial system.

Luckily for the bankers, the actions taken at Cartagena were admirably moderate. The 11 nations did close ranks on the debt issue by establishing a permanent consultative group that will hold regular meetings in the future. But they issued no ultimatums. Instead, they compiled a list of 17 proposals to relieve the debt crisis. That list includes some constructive ideas that have already been advanced by farsighted economists and diplomats, even conservatives like Federal Reserve Board Chairman Paul A. Volcker and former Secretary of State Henry A. Kissinger.

Among the Cartagena proposals: a ceiling on interest rates, the elimination of commissions and penalties in refinancing agreements, more time to repay their debts, a limit on how much of their export earnings debtor nations can use in order to pay off foreign debts, less emphasis on austerity as a short-term cure for debt problems, and more emphasis on economic growth as a long-range solution.

Finally, and most important, they repeated a request that Mexico's President Miguel de la Madrid recently made to President Reagan: Cut the massive U.S. budget deficit because it, more than any other single factor, is forcing interest rates up. The reason for Latin America's concern about the U.S. deficit and rising interest rates is clear: For every one-point rise in the prime rate, the collective Latin debt increases an estimated $2.5 billion.

Some banks have begun to respond to Latin America's moderation on the debt issue. Several banks that are owed money by Brazil and Mexico, the largest debtors in the region, rewarded them for imposing harsh austerity on their citizens by extending new loans at lower interest rates. That politically astute decision probably kept Brazil and Mexico from taking more forceful roles in the Cartagena discussions.

More recently, banking leaders like Richard Flamson, chairman of Security Pacific Corp., have started talking favorably about limiting interest rates for debtor nations. That would be a difficult step because it would force his bank and others to suffer loan losses. But that is precisely the kind of decisive and courageous action that will have to be taken by the banks before the debt crisis is over.

The Philadelphia Inquirer

Philadelphia, PA, June 23, 1984

Politics — both South and North American — have become as big a factor in the Latin debt crisis as balance sheets. And the problem won't be solved until the banks and the U.S. administration admit it.

The current focus of the crisis once again is Argentina, a country newly returned to democratic rule via free elections, and struggling to reverse the 500 percent inflation inherited from corrupt military rulers.

The Argentines are being asked by the International Monetary Fund (IMF) to impose draconian economic measures at home, such as slashing wages. This, in order to give foreign banks the confidence to lend them more money with which to pay overdue interest on their $43 billion debt. But newly elected President Raul Alfonsin believes the IMF formula would be political suicide, setting off nationwide labor strikes and social unrest; he has suggested milder economic medicine that the IMF and the United States have rejected as inadequate.

The longer Argentina holds back payment, the more the earnings of several major U.S. banks will drop, sending tremors through a system already unnerved by the recent near failure of the Continental Illinois National Bank.

THE  SUN

Baltimore, MD, June 29, 1984

"Dead men," a Peruvian legislator said recently, "don't pay debts." That remark sums up the concern of Latin American nations trying to find their way out from under a crushing burden of foreign debt — and fearing that if they are pressed too hard to meet their obligations, they will destroy their own economic and political systems instead. If that happens the international banking system, or large parts of it, could wind up in ruins.

Last week's conference of 11 Latin American debtor nations in Cartagena, Colombia, announced a fairly moderate series of decisions, indicating that the debt-crisis bomb is not quite at the point of detonating. Yet the meeting also showed clearly that the world must find new ways of thinking about the issue.

The nations at the Cartagena meeting disavowed any plans to form a "debtors' cartel" or to repudiate their obligations. The conferees instead adopted a non-confrontational agreement to act as a coalition to seek debt-crisis solutions. Ideas discussed included an International Monetary Fund mechanism for compensatory financing when interest rates rise (as they did this week), placing a "cap" on increasing rates and more generous formulas for stretching out repayments.

On a more philosophical level, the conferees discussed whether the IMF and international financial and development institutions should put less emphasis on austerity and more on policies to reduce unemployment and produce growth. This may go against past economic orthodoxies, but it recognizes the reality that the belt-tightening traditionally demanded of debtor nations may now be politically impossible. That is the claim of Argentina, where President Raul Alfonsin rejected austerity proposals by IMF negotiators for his young democratic government. In an unprecedented move, Mr. Alfonsin made his own counter-proposal directly to the IMF's managing director, thus moving the issue to a level where the political leaders of the major creditor nations will be involved — not just the fund's technicians.

The short-term result of Argentina's stand will probably be another compromise, similar to that which averted a default earlier this year. Mr. Alfonsin's action may be most useful in pointing out the fact that foreign debts are no longer a technical financial matter between each debtor nation and its creditors, but a political problem affecting the political stability and development hopes of Third World nations. That is the reality which lenders, borrowers and regulators must all face as they seek a way out of the present crisis.

Is Mr. Alfonsin playing politics with debt? Perhaps, but not more than are the banks and the American administration. How so? No one factor is more responsible for the current crisis than the huge U.S. deficit that has driven up U.S. interest rates. Most of the Latin nations' debt is linked to the U.S. prime rate, so each one percentage-point rise boosts their annual interest payments, the Argentines' by about $400 million.

The administration denies the link between the deficit and interest rates. This denial is given little credence in a new report by central banks of all the major non-Communist industrial nations, which says the deficit threatens economic recovery throughout the world. But the Reagan administration, with its political agenda geared to an election year, is unwilling to administer tough economic measures of its own to bring the deficit down. This led the Argentine labor minister, Juan Manuel Castella, to charge heatedly that "the populations of the Third World have been subsidizing the finances of the Western countries of the Northern Hemisphere."

The banks also played politics with debt, refusing until recently to accept their share of the blame — and the losses — for reckless overlending in the 1970s. They finally turned to new tactics this month to try to calm Latin resentment and prevent the debtors from forming a united front at a meeting this week in Colombia. The strategy is to reward those countries, such as Mexico and Brazil, that have swallowed the IMF prescription, by giving them lower interest rates and easier repayment terms — despite the loss in bank profits — while standing firm against recalcitrant governments such as Argentina.

No doubt Argentines will have to swallow bitter economic medicine to get their economy back on track. But the medicine won't help if it kills the patient, in this case Argentine democracy. Finding a formula that bankers and Latin debtors can live with won't be easy. But it will be much harder until the administration faces up to the political havoc played by the deficit with debt.

Nation Paralyzed by Death of Popular President-Elect

President Tancredo de Almeida Neves, 75, died April 21, 1985 after an illness that had prevented his inauguration as Brazil's first civilian president in 21 years. On his death, Vice President Jose Sarney automatically became president. Sarney had been sworn in as acting president March 15.

Neves, an opponent of five successive military governments, had come to personify the Brazilian people's desire for a return to democracy and for economic improvement. His illness had traumatized the nation. Since he was hospitalized on the eve of his scheduled inauguration, religious groups of all persuasions—from Roman Catholics and Protestants to spiritualists—had gathered outside the hospital to pray and conduct rites to bring Neves health. Neves' death resulted from intestinal problems and complications arising from seven operations to control infections, internal bleeding and a hernia. As his condition had deteriorated, Sarney April 12 canceled a trip to the north to inspect damage caused by flooding there and ordered all ministers to remain in the capital. Neves was buried April 24 in the town of his birth, San Joao de Rei.

In an address to the nation April 21, President Sarney pledged to carry out Neves' political program. Under the existing constitution, Sarney could remain in office until 1991. Neves, however, who had been chosen president by an electoral college, had pledged that he would introduce direct elections in 1988. Many politicians believed that Sarney, who lacked wide popular support, would in any case not be able to hold on to power for long and that presidential elections would have to be held as early as 1986. Until 1984, Sarney had been the chairman of the Social Democratic Party (PDS), the government party that had held office until March 1985. He had turned against the PDS over its choice of a presidential candidate, joining a group of dissidents to form the Liberal Front Party. The party had given its support to Neves in return for Sarney's appointment as vice presidential candidate. Sarney was a member of the Brazilian Academy of Letters and published a novel and several collections of poems and short stories.

BUFFALO EVENING NEWS
Buffalo, NY, April 26, 1985

THE EUPHORIA that swept Brazil with the return of democracy last January has been replaced by grief and uncertainty with the death of the man who had personified the nation's hopes, President-elect Tancredo Neves.

Mr. Neves, 75, was the most popular leader in the nation's history, but he was stricken just before taking office, setting off an anxious 38-day deathbed vigil. His death leaves the newly installed government in disarray just as it is beginning to handle the delicate problems of transition from the 21 years of military rule. Brazil, with 130 million people, is by far the largest Latin American country, and its return to civilian rule had seemed to confirm the recent trend toward democracy in all Latin America.

The vice president, Jose Sarney, has now become president, but he does not have either Mr. Neves' charisma or his broad political support. As a former supporter of the military leadership, he was accepted only grudgingly as a compromise vice presidential candidate. However, all parties, possibly fearful of a return to military rule, have pledged their support of the new president.

Mr. Sarney has acted in a conciliatory manner in an attempt to bring the country together. He is working with the Cabinet chosen by Mr. Neves and has promised to carry out his program to write a new constitution and possibly hold new presidential elections before the end of his six-year term.

Beyond these formidable political problems is the continuing economic crisis. Brazil had a 230 percent rate of inflation last year and its foreign debt is a staggering $102 billion. Strong leadership is needed to put the economy in order.

Brazil's political stability is highly important to the other nations of Latin America. The uncertainty caused by the death of Mr. Neves has caused international bankers to wonder about Brazil's ability to repay its vast foreign debt, and such doubts could become self-fulfilling by undermining the new government. Brazil needs time to regain both political and economic stability, and the International Monetary Fund, in its continuing surveillance of the Brazilian economy, should exercise understanding and restraint.

A Brazilian archbishop recently referred to Mr. Neves as a kind of Moses leading the people to a promised land. President Sarney cannot possibly measure up to the exaggerated hopes and dreams the people envisioned in a Neves presidency. But in time he may be able to lead Brazil through this difficult transition period.

The Washington Post
Washington, DC, April 23, 1985

BRAZILIANS HAVE suffered an unkind blow in the death of their recently elected but uninaugurated president, Tancredo Neves. Mr. Neves, who endured a month-long medical ordeal, had appointed only some of the top members of the government he intended to run before he fell ill. In the month since, the man elected vice president with him, Jose Sarney, has taken some further steps to get the democratic system and the new government in place. But Mr. Sarney, necessarily, moved slowly, waiting for public pressure to build for him to take actions and proceeding with immense caution.

There were a couple of reasons for this. The obvious one was that the vice president (who became, while Mr. Neves was ill, the acting president) did not wish to appear overeager or in any way ambitious to assume Mr. Neves' place. Another reason was that Mr. Sarney, who came over from the military government's party to run with Mr. Neves against a man that military government favored, does not begin to enjoy the popularity or support that Tancredo Neves did. Mr. Sarney will now have a huge political chore to accompany his formidable task of governing.

Although there seems to be no prospect of an effort to revoke or overturn the new democratic dispensation, there will be much controversy as to how soon direct elections for a successor government should be held. There will probably be an effort to have them held very soon. And there are also politicians in Brazil of Tancredo Neves' party who are stronger and more popular than Mr. Sarney, politicians who will be very much trying to arrange things for the new president.

None of this will make Mr. Sarney's ability to preside any easier, and the new president has much to do. Brazil, as other countries in the region, is obliged to fight a ferocious inflation with steps that are alienating workers and threatening a part of the population that is already inordinately poor. Its export earnings, spectacularly high last year, may be sharply reduced this year. Brazil has sent one failed letter of intent after another to the International Monetary Fund, and is now in another round of negotiations with it. The emergency measures that have enabled the country to carry its debts so far will not be adequate indefinitely—particularly if and when the North American economy, with its gigantic demand for Latin exports, begins to slow down.

Governing Brazil is going to require immense skill and steadiness. It is going to require a high degree of trust between the people at the top and the people at the bottom. It is not an opportune moment for a long hiatus or a debilitating quarrel over who's in charge and who possesses the title to legitimate authority. The country's financial position requires decisions that cannot be postponed. The sudden death of the man who won the election, in the moment of his triumph, puts enormous tests ahead of Brazil and its new democracy. But Brazil and its political leadership have shown, over the past year, that they are capable of great things.

THE PLAIN DEALER

Cleveland, OH, April 20, 1985

A month ago, with the swearing in of Brazil's new civilian government, that nation's generals returned to the barracks after 21 years of military rule. But Brazil's return to democracy has been strained by the serious illness of President-elect Tancredo Neves. The newly elected Neves has yet to be sworn into office. There is doubt that he ever will be.

Shortly before he was to take the pledge of office the veteran politician was forced to undergo an emergency abdominal operation. During the last four weeks, he has undergone six more operations. The prospects for his recovery are not optimistic.

Neves is a shrewd, well-liked politician, and a craftsman at constructing coalitions. His skills are needed at a time when Brazil faces a $100 billion foreign debt and inflation soaring above 200%.

Neves would stand a good chance of mustering popular and political support needed for such unpleasant medicine as new austerity measures.

The spotlight now falls on Jose Sarney, the vice president. Sarney is not even a member of Neves' Brazilian Democratic Movement. He was chairman of the military backed Democratic Social Party, and left his post just prior to the Jan. 15 election to become Neves' running mate. His presence on the ticket was designed to add strength and support for the delicate coalition Neves had built.

It is uncertain whether Sarney could command the coalition's support. He may not be able to provide the kind of leadership Brazil so desperately needs. For the reborn democracy, the task ahead will be immense.

Birmingham Post-Herald

Birmingham, AL, April 24, 1985

Brazil's struggle to govern itself democratically after 21 years of military rule has received a severe setback with the death of President-elect Tancredo Neves, the most popular and trusted politician in that vast nation of 132 million persons.

Neves, who had held virtually every elective office in 50 years of public life, had the backing and hopes of 80 percent of Brazilians for his policy of implanting civilian government and fighting inflation and recession.

Unfortunately, it took Neves, 75, too long to wiggle the generals out of power and maneuver himself through the Electoral College. He was hospitalized a few hours before he was to be inaugurated March 15 and died after seven emergency operations.

His running mate, Jose Sarney, 54, has succeeded to the presidency amid doubts that he has the experience and political skills to lead the country through dangerous times.

Among other problems, Brazil has a foreign debt of $100 billion, the highest in the developing world. It suffers from runaway inflation, which hit 230 percent last year, and could face severe social strains if the government moves to restrain spiraling prices by cutting demand.

Neves in fact had planned an austerity program to slow government spending and bring down inflation. It is thought that only he had the prestige to succeed with such a painful policy.

Although he has pledged to carry out Neves' policies, Sarney carries a reputation as a free-spending governor and congressman. In addition, he supported the coup that brought the military to power in 1964 and cooperated with the soldiers until quite recently.

So age and illness have cheated Brazilians of the president they wanted, and now they are to be led by a flexible (opportunistic?) politician, whose devotion to sound money and civilian rule is open to question.

Herald News

Fall River, MA, April 23, 1985

The death of Brazil's president-elect, Tancredo Neves before he could be sworn into office is an extraordinary stroke of ill luck for the country which had elected him with such high hopes.

Neves by his political victory at the polls had embodied the desire of the Brazilian people for a return to civilian rule after years of dominance by a military junta.

It is tragic that because of the intervention of fate, he was unable to prove his capacity to rise to the demands of his high office and reesstablish a truly free political atmosphere in Brazil.

But it does not follow from this tragedy that the country will be unable to make a successful transition back to civilian and parliamentary rule.

Clearly, much of the reeponsibility for leading Brazil in the direction of democracy will rest with Jose Sarney, who was elected vice president when Neves was elected president, and has already been sworn into office.

All of Brazil's political factions have agreed that Sarney has been constitutionally elected. There is no significant dissent from the agreement that he has been duly installed.

But misgivings are being expressed in Brazil and in other countries about his commitment to the democratic principles Neves stood for and which were the basis for his election.

Those misgivings are based on Sarney's close connections with the military junta that ruled Brazil prior to the election.

It remains to be seen whether the uneasiness about Sarney's commitment to democratic rule are well-founded.

He himself has publicly stated that he will abide by the principles and policies of Neves, and there is surely no reason to doubt his sincerity in that respect, at least as yet.

Yet it must be admitted that the situation he finds himself in is one that contains a great many pitfalls.

First of all, Brazil's economic situation is far from ideal, and the combination of the huge national debt and the high rate of inflation will surely test his ingenuity as well as his political integrity.

Then, too, his association with the former military rulers of the country will make it tempting to fall back on their advice in the current period of major economic strain.

He will be hard-pressed to maintain an even course that will rely on civilian advisors and parliamentary support rather than on the former ruling clique.

In this respect the help he can receive from Brazil's allies, including above all this country, will be absolutely indispensable.

Since it became obvious that Neves was unlikely to recover, he and the Brazilian government have presumably already made overtures for economic assistance to Washington.

It is important, not only for Brazil's own sake, but for the future of democracy in Latin America, that Sarney get as much help as is possible from here.

The people of this area share many cultural ties with the people of Brazil.

Many of our own residents have relatives there.

They will hope that Brazil in its current troubled effort to find its way back to democracy, will have the sympathetic assistance of the United States.

And they will certainly wish Jose Sarney success.

The Houston Post

Houston, TX, April 23, 1985

The return to civilian government in Brazil came a day late for that country's president-elect Tancredo Neves, felled by an abdominal disorder only hours before he was to be sworn in March 15. The 75-year-old statesman, who enjoyed broad popular support, died Sunday of complications of that illness.

It would be tempting to say that at least part of the hope for a democratic Brazil died with Neves, but that might be unduly pessimistic. During Neves' protracted illness, the vice president, Jose Sarney, adopted an increasingly assertive role in dealing with the country's multitude of pressing problems. Among them are a massive foreign debt, 200 percent annual inflation and the great gap between the country's rich and poor.

Neves, who called his country "the friendliest nation the United States has in the hemisphere," listed those three factors as his most pressing tasks. He vowed to make repayment of his country's $100 billion foreign debt a top priority. He termed himself "an old, unrepentant liberal" who believed Brazil could function as a capitalist society and at the same time provide for all its citizens.

Sarney inherits not only those tasks, but support from across the political spectrum that Neves enjoyed as well. Much of the support was, and is, rooted in dissatisfaction with the 21 preceding years of military rule and the loss of confidence in government. And there has been a rallying around Sarney, just as people rally around any leader in time of crisis.

Sarney is a former chairman of the military-backed Democratic Social Party and was on the ticket with Neves, head of the Brazilian Democratic Movement, to attract broader support. Despite those credentials, close Neves allies are among those rallying around him. Political and military leaders promise support.

Perhaps the tragedy of Neves' death will not become the feared political tragedy of a Brazil recaptured by military rule. If the new Brazilian democracy can overcome the death of its most popular leader and support the institution of the presidency rather than the person of the president, it will have taken a giant step toward permanency.

THE DENVER POST

Denver, CO, April 24, 1985

AMERICANS share in the hopes of Brazilians that the fledgling democracy in our great southern neighbor will survive the passing of the man who did so much to foster it, President-elect Tancredo Neves. But Brazil's uncertain future also should make Americans reflect on just how lucky we are to enjoy the political system whose stability we so often take for granted.

When President Kennedy died, Americans mourned — and then speculated on what policy shifts his successor, Lyndon Johnson, might initiate. But no one seriously doubted our democratic institutions would survive the transition. Should Ronald Reagan die tomorrow, our national grief would be eased by the knowledge that George Bush, and our system, would carry on — with the support of all loyal Americans.

Brazil, just returning to democracy after 21 years of military rule, has no such assurance that former Vice President Jose Sarney will enjoy similar support. The United States can best honor the glorious legacy of our constitutional architects by strongly supporting Sarney's struggle to similarly institutionalize democracy in Brazil.

THE BLADE

Toledo, OH, April 27, 1985

SUPPORTERS of democracy in Brazil cheered a few weeks ago as a civilian was poised to take the presidency after 21 years of military rule. Now, despite the death of Tancredo Neves, the vision of a civilian government remains intact.

On the eve of his inauguration Mr. Neves became ill; a few days later the popular president-elect had died, leaving interim president Jose Sarney to take the oath of office.

Mr. Sarney will inherit both a shaky political environment and an economic crisis. The latter in particular will require immediate but painful counterattack.

Inflation, the primary culprit, is at an annual rate of 230 per cent, while unemployment remains at high levels as well. It will be necessary for Mr. Sarney to impose the kinds of controversial austerity measures that will impress the International Monetary Fund, which can provide additional aid and stretched-out interest repayments.

It is little wonder that the military is less interested than it once was in governing, even though the nation has made substantial progress in recent years in becoming an agricultural and industrial power in the region.

Brazil's development in those areas will help impress U.S. and IMF officials who may hold the key to the country's future progress, but the harsh steps that Mr. Sarney must take are not going to go down well with the Brazilian people. They could cause the pro-military Democratic Social party, from which Mr. Sarney defected last year, to wonder if the military should be back in control.

Foreign governments can do much to help Brazil travel the rocky route to democracy. The Reagan administration, which appears eager to counter the influence of Cuba and Nicaragua in Latin America, should be equally concerned about bolstering democracy in countries where it has been given a new lease on life.

The Kansas City Times

Kansas City, MO, April 23, 1985

Tancredo, as Brazilians affectionately called president-elect Tancredo Neves, was the future. The centrist politician and former governor of Minas Gerais, spoke of great things like reducing inflation, improving social conditions and, most important, *diretas ja*, direct elections.

Mr. Neves, 75, was hospitalized on the eve of his inauguration and never got a chance to keep his campaign promises. They were kept by his vice president, Jose Sarney, who was sworn in as acting president on March 15. Now he has automatically become the president of Brazil.

Mr. Sarney's adeptness at making Brazilians and international bankers content during Mr. Neves' absence is perhaps what has kept South America's largest country from falling apart at the news of Mr. Neves' death on Sunday. Mr. Neves had undergone seven operations since mid-March. He had intestinal problems and died of heart and lung complications.

Mr. Sarney should find the transition from vice president to president an easy one because he has been doing Mr. Neves' work all along. Brazilians can also find a friend in Mr. Sarney who has adhered to the Neves prescription for democracy despite former ties to the military-backed Social Democrats.

Mr. Sarney, who joined Mr. Neves' Brazilian Democratic Movement Party, assured Brazilians he would continue with plans for democracy, which includes a call for a special assembly to rewrite the constitution to allow the people to vote in direct elections. Mourning Brazilians, especially those who now feel their nation is in political purgatory, need such assurances.

The government has set aside eight days of mourning for Mr. Neves. Although it is a delicate time and his memory deserves such a lengthy honor, Mr. Sarney would be wise to get things in gear by the ninth day. Brazilians need a speedy exit from this limbo.

President Sarney's old ties to the military and recent alignment with the civilian party may make him a great stabilizer. Whether he likes it or not, he is the new hope for Brazil.

THE  SUN

Baltimore, MD, April 23, 1985

Brazil has suffered a tragic blow in the death of its president-elect Tancredo Neves, the man who was to lead South America's largest nation back to civilian government after 21 years of military rule.

That transition would not have been an easy one even had the 75-year-old Mr. Neves lived to assume the presidency to which he was indirectly elected in January. Though Brazil avoided the extremes of violence and polarization that occurred under military regimes in neighboring Argentina and elsewhere in the region, it still faces grave social and economic problems. Half of its 130 million people live in dire poverty, while perhaps 40 per cent of the labor force is unemployed or underemployed. The inflation rate exceeds 200 per cent a year, while the foreign debt of over $100 billion is the world's largest.

To cope with the conflicting pressures for economic discipline, social progress, and consolidation of democracy would have taken all the conciliatory talent for which Mr. Neves became known in nearly a half-century of political life. Now, those pressures fall on his successor, Jose Sarney, who has neither the stature nor popular affection commanded by Mr. Neves. Because he was never associated with the ruling generals' Democratic Social Party, Mr. Neves embodied the national desire for a return to democracy. Mr. Sarney, by contrast, belonged to the official party until he defected during pre-election maneuvering last year. That move left a legacy of distrust both in the Democratic Social camp and in Mr. Neves's Brazilian Democratic Movement. The former sees Mr. Sarney as a traitor and the latter regards him with misgivings because of his past links with the military government. Thus, instead of a leader with enough popularity to take necessary but unpopular decisions without destroying the consensus for orderly political change, Brazil's future rests on a president without broad support and without the mystique that seemed to be Mr. Neves's strongest political weapon.

One probable consequence of Mr. Neves's death and Mr. Sarney's succession to the presidency will almost certainly be increased pressure for direct elections, replacing the indirect system under which Mr. Neves was chosen. Mr. Neves had promised to restore direct elections, possibly as early as 1988. Speeding up that timetable could involve both opportunities and risks. It could provide a leader with a stronger mandate than Mr. Sarney now enjoys, but it could also lead to demagogic politics raising unrealistic hopes and possibly reopening the political rifts – between liberals and conservatives and between military and civilians – that Mr. Neves's personality and talents seemed to bridge. Whatever happens, Brazil's political maturity will be subject to tests far more severe than anyone would have imagined before Mr. Neves's illness and tragic death.

The Honolulu Advertiser

Honolulu, HI, April 14, 1985

Even if Brazil's President-elect Tancredo Neves, 75, defies two-to-one odds and survives his seventh round of abdominal and chest surgery, it seems clear his country will have to do without his leadership for some time, if not forever.

This is a great loss for Brazil, the world's sixth most populous country, which this year is in transition from military to civilian government after 21 years of authoritarian rule.

MEANWHILE, Vice President Jose Sarney has been a figurehead leader though lately politicians of all parties as well as business and military leaders have called for Sarney to take charge more forcefully.

One problem is that Sarney, 54, is nowhere near as popular with the people as Neves, an urbane and pragmatic conciliator who had come to symbolize the restoration of democracy in Brazil.

Further, the Cabinet of 26 civilian and military ministers was selected by Neves before he was stricken on the basis of personal ties and political compromises. It now appears Neves had no written program for his government, reserving for himself the flexibility to settle disputes between ministers.

Some of these have surfaced since the inauguration. The basic conflict is between the desire for generous social spending to deal with Brazil's many problems and the need for fiscal austerity dictated by a $100-billion foreign debt and inflation which could hit 300 percent this year.

Neves would likely have resolved such differences through strong leadership, but Sarney's presidency is expected to be much weaker, requiring more political tradeoffs.

INABILITY TO solve economic problems has been the main cause for Latin American military dictators to return their countries to civilian rule. (Brazil is the seventh such case since 1981.) But political chaos and contention among would-be leaders is the classic situation in which the military believes it must take control "to restore order."

The months ahead are thus likely to be quite perilous for Brazil's newly reborn democracy.

The Dispatch

Columbus, OH, April 24, 1985

The death Sunday of Brazilian President-elect Tancredo Neves follows a tumultuous period in the nation's efforts to become a full democracy, but Neves' death does not mean that the dream of full self-determination for the people of Brazil must die, too.

Neves was 75 years old when he died of severe heart and lung complications. His death followed seven operations during the last 39 days, operations that started only hours before he was to be inaugurated as the country's first civilian president in 21 years. His 50-year public career had been dedicated to the service of his people. Death has cheated him of the honor and opportunity the presidency offered him.

Neves promised to do something about the country's terrible financial condition, a condition that includes a $100 billion foreign debt — the Third World's largest — 234 percent inflation and combined unemployment and underemployment of 40 percent.

More important, perhaps, was Neves' vow to advance democracy in his nation of 122 million people. He was elected through an electoral college. Direct presidential elections are scheduled for 1990, but millions of Brazilians have demonstrated during the last year for a change in that schedule: They want the right to choose their own leaders now. Neves promised to work for that change.

The responsibility of the presidency and the hope of a nation now rests with Jose Sarney, the man who was elected vice president with Neves and has been in charge of the government during Neves' illness. He assumed the presidency upon Neves' death. Sarney has told his mourning countrymen that he will make good on Neves' promises. "Our program is Tancredo Neves' program," Sarney said, promising to govern with "morality, austerity, honor and responsibility."

The next months will be difficult for Brazil. Its high hopes have been abused. But its people have the will to be free. That will is stronger than any one man, no matter how revered he may be. It is a testament to that will — and to Neves' long public career — that the transition of power was smooth and non-violent. Social order and prosperity were what Neves sought; he was successful.

Garcia Sworn in as President; Alarms Bankers With Debt Plan

Amid tight security, Alain Garcia Perez was sworn is as president of Peru July 28, 1985, succeeding President Fernando Balaunde Terry. It was the first time in 40 years that an elected president had handed over power to an elected successor in Peru. Garcia, 36, of the left-of-center American Popular Revolutionary Alliance (APRA), inherited a nation with a debt-ridden, chaotic economy and beset by strikes and political violence. The nation's foreign debt was between $13.5 billion and $14 billion. Peru had made only token payments on its debt since early 1984, and interest arrears amounted to $450 million. In his inaugural address, Garcia announced that his government would limit foreign debt payments to 10% of the nation's export earnings—a sum that amounted to about $301 million—for the next 12 months, while his government renegotiated the debt. He said Peru would directly deal with its creditors and not with the International Monetary Fund, which he described as "an accomplice" in Peru's economic difficulties. Garcia warned Peruvians that a tough economic program would have to be implemented but said the nation would not accept "imposed economic policies."

United States Treasury Secretary James Baker, responding to Garcia's debt payment plan, July 29 said so-called "political solutions" to debt problems were "counterproductive" and would reduce the willingness of banks to give loans. U.S. Federal Reserve Board Chairman Paul Volcker issued a similar warning July 30 and international bankers expressed consternation that other Latin American debtors might follow Peru's example.

The Detroit News
Detroit, MI, August 2, 1985

Alan Garcia Perez, the new president of Peru, announced in his inauguration speech on Sunday that Peru would repay its $14 billion in international debts its own way. Debt service would be limited to 10 percent of export earnings, which the creditors could divide up any way they see fit. Without endorsing the specific formula he proposed, 16 Latin American countries promptly backed the general idea in a "Declaration of Lima." These countries owe the rest of the world $360 billion, so this ain't beanbag.

Export earnings are the key to repaying loans. But 10 percent of annual export earnings in Peru's case represents $300 million, far less than the country owes. If Peru won't raise the percentage it will pay, the only way it can service its debts on schedule is to improve its export earnings. Can Peru do it?

Probably not, if Peru follows the recommendations of the International Monetary Fund (IMF) or tries to implement the kind of programs Mr. Garcia says he favors. Peru is, to understate the case, in poor shape economically. When some left-wing soldiers took over in 1968, they nationalized International Petroleum (an Esso subsidiary) and ITT (copper). They broke the back of the old oligarchy, which had smothered private enterprise, but they replaced it with a heavy-handed state sector which now is estimated to be responsible for 70 percent of GNP. The country has also suffered from changes in the ocean currents that have played havoc with its fisheries industry as well as its agriculture. And a vicious guerrilla insurgency diverts resources while maintaining a climate of fear.

Mr. Garcia, declaring himself a socialist in his inaugural speech, says he wants more statism, not less. He speaks of conciliation with the subversives, which will simply embolden them. Under these conditions, the economy will contract, not expand. And it is especially unfortunate, because there has emerged in Peru over the past few decades a new middle class which will do well if it is left alone.

A very substantial part of Peru's economy is now underground, simply because the state, through crippling taxation and suffocating regulations, will not allow it to thrive openly. Virtually all new construction takes place in neighborhoods that do not exist on official maps, for example. Enterprising Peruvians are doing things aplenty, but they are increasingly forced to do it by barter.

The IMF, for its part, will ask Mr. Garcia to raise taxes further and enforce austerity programs on Peruvians. Understandably, he says he does not want to deal with the IMF any more (only with individual banks), but he is already playing the austerity game by imposing foreign currency exchange controls and requiring that savings be in sols, the national currency.

Offered socialism from within, austerity plans from without, the Peruvians don't have too much to look forward to. The banks and the U.S. government should take a tough stance. Peru should be expected to pay its debts. If they cave in to Garcia's unilateral rescheduling, other debtor governments will demand the same or even more favorable treatment. The international credit structure could suffer a severe shock.

At the same time, the creditors, particularly the IMF, should be listening carefully to the debtors. What they are being told is that austerity programs don't work, politically or economically. In this, the debtors are correct. IMF and bank conditions for rescheduling of debts need to stress growth — and that means lower taxes, less government, and stable currencies. These are the conditions that the creditors should be laying down on the troubled debtors. Otherwise there will be more Perus.

The Dispatch
Columbus, OH, August 4, 1985

Alan Garcia, the new president of Peru, faces some criticial decisions in the early days of his presidency. There are indications that he may be inclined to make the wrong decisions.

The 36-year-old Garcia was recently sworn in as the country's youngest president, succeeding Fernando Belaunde Terry. His inauguration marked the first time in 40 years that a democratically elected president handed over power to another democratically elected president.

One of the first announcements Garcia made was that he was limiting his nation's foreign debt payments to a fraction of the scheduled repayment amounts. He said he intends to hold debt payments to about 10 percent of the value of the country's exports. As the debt is currently structured, Garcia said, Peru would have to repay $3.7 billion in 1985. But exports, the source of foreign exchange income, will generate only around $3 billion. A cap of 10-plus of export earnings, or around $300 million, would leave Peru far short even of meeting overdue interest payments. He said there are pressingh needs of the country's poor that must be addressed before the foreign debt commitments can be honored.

Garcia's concern for the poor is commendable and it is certainly proper for him to want to help solve the problems facing the needy. However, he must realize that he, as president, has inherited commitments made by prior governments — commitments that can be abrogated only at Peru's peril. Loans were made to the nation by foreign governments and banks in good faith. They were accepted by Peruvian leaders because they were viewed as necessary for the country's development. Changes in Peru's domestic political situation, or the failure of past development projects to meet expectations, do not lessen the nation's responsibility to honor its word. And deciding not to satisfy present loan commitments can only serve to limit the availablity of future loans that may be necessary to fund new projects.

Garcia, understandably, wants to improve the lot of his people. He should move carefully, however, realizing that a decision that may appear beneficial now could have devastating consequences.

DESERET NEWS
Salt Lake City, UT, August 1-2, 1985

When Peru's new president, youthful Alan Garcia, took the oath of office this week, he said his country would limit its payments on $14 billion worth of foreign debt — and never mind what the foreign banks that loaned the money might say.

This action is understandable because Peru is in the midst of an economic crisis described as the worst in its history. The country has an inflation rate of more than 100 percent a year, and two of every three workers are without a steady job.

Peru is already $475 million in arrears on interest payments, and another $3.7 billion in payments falls due this year. It's obvious the country cannot pay what is due, at least under present circumstances.

Garcia wants to limit foreign debt payments to an amount equalling 10 percent of his nation's exports. Last year, those exports totaled $3.1 billion, and a tenth of that isn't going to go far in paying the debt.

Garcia at least is trying to repay some of the debt and wants to negotiate a new payment schedule. Other Latin nations, however, think even that is too much and are talking about simply canceling the $360 billion that Latins owe to foreign banks, most of them U.S. banks.

At a conference in Cuba this week, delegates from 17 Latin nations said their countries should stop making payments on the foreign debt. That practice, if adopted, would have devastating impact on American banks and could cause an unprecedented banking crisis. No nation is so well off that it can afford to forget about $360 billion in loans.

Such a repudiation of debt seems unlikely, though, if only because those Latin nations still need a lot of help. Refusing to pay what they owe would quickly mean the end of future aid. How many banks are going to "lend" money to people — or countries — that won't pay it back?

That's not entirely a rhetorical question. Many Latin debtors are so slow to repay that it's clear some U.S. banks have incurred far more risk than was prudent.

If the economy does not improve in many Latin countries, they may be faced with the same sitation that confronts Bolivia. The Bolivian government has not made payments on its foreign debt since last year. Payments amount to 175 percent of Bolivia's entire export earnings, the source of dollars to make payments. "It is not that we do not want to pay," government officials say. "We just cannot pay."

By all means, the banks should start negotiating new terms of repayment. Otherwise, some Latin countries will soon feel there is no way out except to simply cancel the debt — and take their chances in the future. That would make losers out of all the Americas, north and south.

The Philadelphia Inquirer
Philadelphia, PA, August 5, 1985

Two loud messages have been heard recently from Latin American leaders — Cuba's Fidel Castro and newly elected President Alan Garcia Perez of Peru — about how debt-ridden nations south of the border should deal with the burdensome problem of repayment. U.S. banks and the Reagan administration would do well to listen to Mr. Garcia's message if they don't want to get ultimately stuck with Mr. Castro's.

Cuba's leader has been preaching the gospel of default to his neighbors. He says that the debts are a form of oppression and that payment should be suspended. Mr. Garcia's message is much more startling. In his inaugural address he announced that Peru henceforth would continue to pay off its $14 million debt but would limit payment next year to 10 percent of its export earnings. Moreover, Peru will make its repayment arrangements directly with its creditors without the intervention of the International Monetary Fund.

What Mr. Garcia has yanked out into the open is a concept that financial analysts have whispered about but no one has yet tried. He seeks to break the vicious circle by which debt-burdened Third World countries pay out so much of their scarce hard-earned currency to banks that little is left for the development needed to break out of the cycle of debt. Often they have to borrow more money to keep up, thus sinking further into debt.

The IMF's formula has been to demand that Third World nations impose harsh austerity measures at home in order to cut domestic consumption and generate more capital for expansion. That formula makes economic sense on paper but in reality causes such widespread hardship that it threatens the survival of many newly democratic Latin governments.

For banks to cap annual debt payments and stretch out the time for repayment may cut into profits. However, the alternative — at a time when little new capital is available for borrowers and when protection tendencies in America threaten their export earnings further — is political instability, and possibly default. Far better to get the money back slowly than not at all. If Mr. Garcia's formula doesn't appeal to the banks or to Washington, perhaps it will prod them to finally come up with some creative and realistic formula of their own.

THE CHRISTIAN SCIENCE MONITOR
Boston, MA, July 30, 1985

NEWLY inaugurated President Alan García Pérez is quickly putting his own stamp of authority on Peru's political and economic agenda. In the process, President García may be setting a unique precedent for other financially troubled Latin American nations eager to find innovative ways to restructure their massive foreign debt obligations.

What Mr. García is doing — and what will be closely watched by other nations as well as the international financial community — is to attempt to link the level of payments on the nation's foreign debt to a fixed percentage of its overall export earnings. President García says that Peru will not pay out more than 10 percent of its export earnings during the next 12 months to satisfy its debt obligations, which now total more than $14 billion. In the meantime, he says, the nation will seek to refinance its debt, although dealing directly with the nation's overseas bank creditors rather than dealing first with the International Monetary Fund, as is common in most debt refinancing agreements.

If successful in this effort, Mr. García would in effect be providing a new model for debt refinancing agreements in Latin American and other third-world nations.

That he is acting with such vigor at this juncture is understandable. Peru is beset by a number of serious problems: 100 percent annual inflation, high unemployment, a flaccid economy, the aforementioned foreign debt on which there is little immediate prospect of repayment, heavy migration of rural Indians from the interior mountains to the urban coast, and an increasingly grave security threat from two violent guerrilla movements. Peru is considered the most fragile of the continent's endangered democracies, besieged by armed factions.

One guerrilla group is Sendero Luminoso, or Shining Path; Maoist-oriented, it has operated primarily in the countryside. Last year an urban terror group, the Tupac Anaru, arose. It claimed responsibility for several bomb explosions last week in Lima. The explosions came despite unprecedented security operations by some 50,000 troops and police in the days leading up to the Sunday inauguration.

Peru was one of the leaders of the current Latin American move away from authoritarianism toward democracy: In 1980 a democratically elected government replaced the nation's 12-year military rule.

But the country's problems did not yield to the regime headed by outgoing President Belaúnde Terry, and the national joy at the return of democracy dissipated. One of President García's major immediate tasks is to convince his citizenry that democracy can deal with Peru's problems — and then prove it by deed.

If the García regime were unable to make major progress, both the left and right would be strengthened, and democracy's immediate future in the country would be endangered.

García's task is challenging but not impossible. Circumstances demand that Peru take firm steps to control inflation; at the same time, the United States and Peru's other international creditors must be understanding of the problems of unemployment and a sluggish economy, and not try to force the Peruvian government to take steps that are too fiscally restrictive.

President García must unshackle his nation's businesses by stripping away the many layers of counterproductive regulations. Not only would such action permit existing companies to operate more robustly, but it would encourage would-be entrepreneurs to register and operate in the official, tax-paying economy. In turn this could enable Peru to begin to take advantage of what is potentially one of its major economic assets — a thriving underground economy — by encouraging these small businesses to move to the official sphere.

Significantly improving the nation's economy would rob both guerrilla movements of some of the popular support on which they depend for survival. At the same time, the government must take strong action to defend itself militarily from the guerrillas.

Peru's straits call for a leader who radiates confidence in himself and his nation. García apparently does that. We wish him well.

Winnipeg Free Press

Winnipeg, Man., July 31, 1985

Peru's new president displayed remarkable self-confidence in his inaugural address, lashing the United States government, international bankers and his own country's security forces as if he had an unshakeable grip on political power.

In fact, 36-year-old lawyer Alan Garcia is the first civilian in 40 years to succeed another elected civilian. His leftwing Aprista party is not an obvious candidate for automatic support from a military establishment that has considerable experience in dictatorship.

Nevertheless, surrounded by massive military protection to protect him from assassination by the Maoist Sendero Luminoso movement, he felt it appropriate to condemn "illegal executions and torture" by security forces fighting the movement's terror campaign. He said he will set up a peace commission to talk with the Maoists, is ready to give their leaders amnesty and wants faster trials of those accused of terrorist outrages so that those who are innocent can go free.

Each of these ideas has merit. Utterance of them together on the day he was being inaugurated in a downtown Lima transformed into an armed camp gives cause to wonder about his judgment.

Similarly, there are grounds for questioning the wisdom of his brash public talk about standing up to those to whom his country owes $13.6 billion and to whom $425 million in interest payments are outstanding. He will not bend, he says, to pressure from the International Monetary Fund to impose austerity measures to restore the economy to health. Presumably, then, he will not ask for the loans that are the only reason why such austerity measures are ever requested.

He also says that he will limit debt repayments to foreign banks. During the next year, they will get only ten per cent of the value of Peru's export earnings. Higher payments will be made only when the economy grows. Presumably, he also has decided that he will need no further private foreign loans.

His bluster about the "imperialism" of industrialized countries and of international capitalism, as well as his call for an end to Peru's close alignment with U.S. policies, may be part of his strategy for convincing the Maoist guerrillas to abandon terror in favor of electoral politics. The trouble is, he may fail to persuade the Maoists, but anger the armed forces enough to tempt them out of their barracks.

la presse

Montreal, Que., August 15, 1985

La dette extérieure de $360 milliards de l'Amérique latine n'est pas une mince affaire; elle n'est pas non plus la fin du monde. Elle met, certes, des pays comme le Mexique et l'Argentine dans l'embarras économique. Les pays endettés, comme leurs créanciers, doivent trouver le moyen de diminuer cet embarras. Il ne s'agit toutefois pas d'une tâche surhumaine à condition de ne pas se laisser divertir par des solutions extrêmes.

En premier lieu, il faut insister sur le fait que ces dettes ne doivent pas être nécessairement remboursées. Tout ce qu'il faut c'est que l'économie des pays endettés puisse supporter le service de la dette, paiements d'intérêt et de capital. Une des façons d'y parvenir est de diminuer le montant de la dette; une autre est de permettre à une croissance forte de l'économie de diminuer l'importance relative de la dette. Cette dernière solution est de loin celle qui est préférable car elle combine l'amélioration du niveau de vie avec la diminution du fardeau de la dette.

La répudiation pure et simple de la dette, telle que prônée par le président cubain Fidel Castro, n'est pas une solution car elle isolerait commercialement les pays endettés et affaiblirait les finances des pays industrialisés, les marchés dont ils dépendent. M. Castro ne semble pas être très sérieux quand il évoque cette possibilité car Cuba n'a aucune intention de répudier sa dette de $3 milliards à l'égard de banques occidentales et encore moins les $10 milliards dus à l'Union soviétique.

C'est le nouveau président du Pérou, M. Alan Garcia, qui a présenté une solution vraiment révolutionnaire: le Pérou, suggère-t-il, ne consacrerait que 10 pour cent de ses revenus des exportations au service de la dette. La suggestion est intéressante mais inacceptable pour les créanciers. En effet, le Pérou a une dette de quelque $14 milliards et des exportations d'environ $3 milliards. Un propriétaire qui a une dette hypothécaire de $14,000 et qui propose à sa banque de payer $25 par mois serait considéré un farfelu par son banquier; or la proposition de M. Garcia est du même acabit.

M. Garcia a, cependant, parfaitement raison de lier le service de la dette aux revenus des exportations car il n'y a que ces revenus qui peuvent être utilisés à cette fin sans qu'il y ait une augmentation automatique de la dette. Il est bon que les banquiers occidentaux et les pays industrialisés se le fassent rappeler: le seul moyen de mettre fin à la crise de la dette est d'ouvrir nos marchés aux exportations des pays de l'Amérique latine et de favoriser les échanges entre les pays endettés eux-mêmes.

Jusqu'à présent, l'attitude des pays occidentaux et du Fonds monétaire international a été d'encourager les pays endettés à avoir un excédent de la balance des paiements grâce à des mesures d'austérité qui diminuent la demande interne: on se serre la ceinture et on paie ses dettes.

Pour beaucoup de pays, l'austérité était nécessaire mais elle ne constitue pas une solution à long terme. À bon droit, M. Garcia nous rappelle que la crise de la dette ne se résorbera de façon satisfaisante que si nous sommes prêts à développer notre commerce avec les pays endettés et à importer leurs produits, surtout leurs produits manufacturés.

The Courier-Journal

Louisville, KY, August 1, 1985

ALAN GARCIA, Peru's new president, is making U.S. bankers nervous. His announced plan to limit Peru's debt payments this year to only 10 percent of its export earnings could prove contagious in debt-ridden Latin America. But the proposal also deserves close and sympathetic attention in Washington.

Peru itself doesn't represent much of a problem, since only $2.2 billion of its $14 billion over-all foreign debt is owed to U. S. banks. But if Mr. Garcia gets away with his bold plan — which includes rejecting any role whatsoever for the International Monetary Fund (IMF) — bigger Latin American debtors, such as Brazil, Mexico and Argentina, are sure to get ideas.

The IMF is deeply resented by these countries — and by many debtors in Africa, too — because of the austerity measures it demands as the price for helping borrower nations reschedule their bank loans. But most commercial banks won't reschedule loans without IMF participation.

In practice, a failure

As a result, Latin American economies are being put through the wringer. Country after country has been forced, under IMF agreements, to curtail imports and domestic spending, while devoting an increasing share of their resources to expanding exports.

The idea, of course, is that debtor nations need export income with which to repay their loans — or, as is more often the case, to keep fairly current on interest payments.

In theory, this seems a sensible approach. In practice, it has been a painful failure. A strong dollar and falling prices for most commodities produced in Latin America have combined to erode export earnings at the same time that the prices of many imported goods were rising. For instance, Peru's entire income from exports in 1985 is projected at $3.1 billion — which is less than the $3.7 billion it will owe this year in interest and principal payments on its foreign debt.

To cover such shortfalls, many debtor nations are forced to reschedule

their loans, which means getting fresh bank credits. And that, in turn, means they must go even deeper into debt.

This madness has the blessings, open or implicit, of the Reagan administration, the Federal Reserve Board, the IMF and the banks. President Garcia is saying, "Enough is enough."

Unlike Cuba's Fidel Castro, he is not urging Latin American debtors to band together and renounce their combined debt of $350 billion. (Despite Mr. Castro's tough talk, Cuba has been very reliable in repaying its own loans.) But Mr. Garcia, newly elected, believes he owes the Peruvian people more than a stiff dose of IMF-imposed austerity.

And as democracy spreads in Latin America, replacing inept and frequently brutal military regimes, other elected heads of state are saying the same thing. They want to be able to invest in schools, hospitals, roads and other badly needed public projects and services. And they want temporary debt relief so their economies can grow.

That's where Washington comes in — or should come in. The U. S. government should be eager to nurture democracy in Latin America. But present policies could undermine the democratic trend if elections seem to bring no relief from the crushing burden of debt — and from the painful sacrifices that go with it.

So President Reagan should take the lead in calling together lenders and borrowers to arrange new, extended repayment terms. And while he's at it, he also could do more to promote direct investment in Latin America by U. S. firms. As *The Wall Street Journal* reported last month, the days when U. S.-based multinational companies were resented as exploiters seem to be over. More and more Latin American governments are begging for direct investment, as a way to create jobs and generate income without incurring still more bank debt.

This new mood, though born of desperation, meshes nicely with Mr. Reagan's upbeat faith in private enterprise as the engine of economic growth. He should grab the opportunity to replace Fidel Castro as a hero to millions throughout Latin America.

The San Diego Union

San Diego, CA, August 2, 1985

Peru's newly elected president, Alan Garcia Pérez, took office this week vowing to renegotiate his country's $14 billion foreign debt and slash debt payments in the meantime. This defiance of such stock villains as gringo bankers and international lending agencies should play well with Peruvians and, perhaps, with such other Latin debtors as Argentines, Brazilians, and Mexicans.

But Mr. Garcia also has an opportunity, if he will but seize it, to do something more than jeopardize his country's future credit worthiness. He can demonstrate that reforming Latin America's typically inefficient, statist economies could begin shrinking the region's $360 billion foreign debt while simultaneously raising living standards for poor and middle class alike.

Few Latin economies are more desperately in need of fundamental reform than Peru's. Start with the tax structure. Incredibly, any Peruvian earning more than $40 per year is subject to the top income-tax rate of 65 percent. Corporations are subject to a top rate of 70 percent. These immense disincentives to work, save, and invest choke off growth and actively discourage the creation of wealth. They help explain why Peru's economy not only failed to grow but actually contracted by 1.3 percent from 1980 to 1983.

The next target for reform should be the Peruvian government's vast, constricting bureaucracy and its stranglehold on entrepreneurship. A recent study by a private Peruvian think tank, the Institute for Liberty and Democracy, concluded that it took an average of 289 days of work — and as many as 24 bribes — to obtain all the bureaucratic authorizations for establishing a small clothing factory. Getting the permits necessary to start up a bus company took more than 1,000 days. Eight years was required for starting a food market. And, on average, would-be entrepreneurs would have to wait 15 years for permission to begin building houses in the suburbs of the capital city of Lima.

Is it any wonder that housing, for example, is in critically short supply in Lima, especially for the poor? And, given confiscatory taxation and the dead hand of the bureaucracy, is it any wonder that an estimated 60 percent of Peru's economy consists of underground, illegal enterprises that employ two out of every three working Peruvians?

In an average year, the Peruvian government issues 30,000 new regulations restricting economic activity. The government owns 174 major enterprises that are operated — invariably at a tax-subsidized loss — either as monopolies or as subsidized competition against private companies. Three-quarters of Peru's banking industry is owned or controlled by the government. Clearly, it is not free-market capitalism that has failed in Peru and in other Latin countries but the sort of state intervention, excessive taxation, and overregulation so commonly found in Latin America.

Sixty percent of Argentina's economy is state owned and the remaining 40 percent is heavily regulated, mostly in ways that discourage growth. The list of Argentine industries controlled by government monopolies includes oil, natural gas, minerals, telephones, airlines, railways, subways, shipping lines, shipyards, petrochemicals, steel, explosives, insurance, banking, broadcasting, warehouses, port activities, plus nuclear, hydraulic, and electrical energy.

In Peru and other Latin countries, state intervention and de facto mercantilism are legacies of the Spanish conquest and culture. In Argentina, they are the more recent products of the Peron dictatorship following World War II. It is a measure of their destructiveness that Argentina has declined from the seventh wealthiest country in the world in 1945 to a ranking of no better than 60th today.

What Latin America's sickest economies need is not less capitalism and fewer free markets but much more of both. Absent these liberating reforms, it is doubtful that such debtors as Peru and Argentina can ever pay what they owe. And more doubtful still that life can improve much for the millions of Latins effectively kept poor by the economic misrule of their own governments.

The London Free Press

London, Ont., August 12, 1985

In his first week in office, Peru's new president took daring action on the nation's $14-billion debt crisis that may encourage imitation by other Latin American debtors.

But Alan Garcia Perez's radical plan to bypass the International Monetary Fund (IMF) and deal directly with creditors, and to allot no more than 10 per cent of annual export earnings for debt payments to, industrialized countries, doesn't go far enough for Cuban President Fidel Castro, who has insisted again that only cancellation of Latin America's $360 billion debt would solve the region's crisis.

Garcia's proposal comes at a critical time. Debt-ridden Third World nations struggling to cope simultaneously with awesome domestic problems and IMF austerity pressures have surely been tempted to follow Castro's advice. Fortunately, no nation has done so.

Now, Peru has suddenly become the focus of an experiment which could set a precedent in changing debt rules realistically while avoiding the foolhardy course of default.

Understandably, there's concern that if debtor countries start bypassing the IMF, banks and the rest of the Western financial system would lose an anchor vital to monetary stability.

Although some observers argue that IMF austerity measures put debtor countries in better shape to repay, it's questionable whether growth-limiting measures that often result in lower real wages and price increases improve economic stability. In the Dominican Republic and Jamaica, for example, the high economic, social and political costs of austerity have been blamed for internal turmoil.

It's significant and reassuring that Garcia has not suggested reneging on Peru's debt. Indeed, his whole thrust has been toward a solution that would keep domestic economic and social unrest to a minimum.

In contrast, there is little doubt that Castro's suggestion is aimed at destabilizing Western financial institutions, to whom his nation owes $3.2 billion. Although he has promised to repay Cuba's loans, Castro is obviously looking for backing in an excuse to not pay.

Under Garcia's plan, payments on the debt this year will be about $300 million. That doesn't seem like much considering Peru is already $475 million in arrears on its $14 billion debt. Still, it's double the rate managed by Garcia's ineffectual predecessor, Fernando Belaunde Terry. Western nations could help by buying more from Peru and other Third World debtors instead of protecting uncompetitive domestic industries.

Garcia was democratically elected and is immensely popular. Should his program succeed, he may well achieve the regional leadership role he covets. Like Castro, however, he will have to demonstrate he can sort things out at home before offering advice abroad.

That will be no easy task. Nonetheless, Garcia has already offered peace talks with leftist guerrillas, promised to clean up corruption and narcotics trafficking and called for an end to the arms race in the region. But with per capita income down to 1965 levels, two out of three workers without full-time jobs, the annual inflation rate approaching 200 per cent and the debt, the economy is the first priority.

In response to Peru's economic crisis, Garcia has also introduced an emergency program to freeze prices, devalue the currency, slash loan rates, tighten exchange controls and boost minimum wages by 50 per cent.

It will take time to measure the effectiveness of Garcia's initiatives over the next five years. For the moment, however, the eyes of all debtor nations are on Peru,

Alfonsin Party Wins Mid-term Elections Amid State of Seige

In Argentina's mid-term congressional elections November 3, 1985, President Raul Alfonsin's Radical Civic Union maintained its commanding position. The poll marked the first time in 20 years that mid-term elections had been held and the first time an election had been held under a state of seige. Alfonsin declared a state of seige October 25, after a civilian judge disputed his order to arrest 12 rightists suspected of involvement in a month-long spate of bombings. All the suspects, including six civilians and six military officers, were known rightists with links to former military governments. Their arrests were ordered Oct. 22, but a judge Oct. 24 had declared the arrest decree unconstitutional and ordered the release of a principal suspect, arguing that the president could make arrests without proof of guilt only under a state of seige. The bombings continued as the executive and legislative branches sought to resolve the issue of the legality of the arrests. Alfonsin responded by declaring a nominal state of seige under which constitutional liberties would not be withdrawn as long as they did not interfere with the government's crackdown on violence. Argentina had lived under a state of seige under military regimes from 1976 to 1983, when Alfonsin took power.

More than 84% of Argentina's 18.7 million eligible voters went to the polls Nov. 3 to elect 127 members to the 254-seat House of Representatives, 97 provincial senators and over 6,000 other officials. With 99% of the votes counted Nov. 4, Alfonsin's party had won about 42%, compared to 52% in the general election, but it had added one seat to its previous majority of 129 in the House. The poll was widely viewed as a referendum on Alfonsin's economic program, which had been successful in bringing down inflation but at the cost of higher unemployment and falling real wages. It was conducted peacefully, except for some scuffles in Buenos Aires between rival party members. President Alfonsin Dec. 9 lifted a 45-day state of seige imposed in October after a wave of bombings by suspected right-wing terrorists.

Five former military junta members December 9, 1985 were found guilty of crimes committed during a campaign against leftists in the 1970s, and four other junta members were acquitted. Two of those found guilty were sentenced to life imprisonment, and the other three received terms ranging from four and one half years to 17 years in prison. Reaction to the sentences was mixed, but human rights organizations expressed anger and extreme disappointment at what they regarded as lenient sentences for most of the defendants. Hundreds of people marched through Buenos Aires on the evening of Dec. 9 to protest the verdicts. An organization of relatives of the victims said its members would press to bring to trial all those implicated in the crimes, a reference to the lower-level military men accused of involvement in the abuses. An estimated 1,700 cases were pending against as many as 400 officers. Echoing the opinion of many observers, Simon Lazara, a lawyer and vice president of Argentina's Permanent Assembly for Human Rights, said the trial was "an historical event almost without precedent in Latin America and the world." He continued, "A constitutional government has tried and obtained a conviction against a dictatorship that used the horror and terror of the state to exile and disappear thousands of Argentines."

Richmond Times-Dispatch
*Richmond, VA,
November 5, 1985*

Argentines are familiar with states of siege: They have been a fact of life in Argentina for almost half of the past 50 years, under both civilian and military governments. President Raúl Alfonsín, two years into his term as Argentina's first elected leader after eight years of military rule, insists that the 60-day state of siege he has declared is different. It has been invoked to protect, not to prevent, democracy; to restore order, not to rescind civil liberties.

People the world over have heard that one before, and have come to regret believing it. If Mr. Alfonsín begs indulgence, he will also have to endure some skepticism.

The case for indulgence rests on a presidential premise and a presidential promise. Mr. Alfonsín's premise is that a recent wave of terror, widely believed to be the work of 12 right-wing civilian and military men, requires this extraordinary measure. When the lower courts ruled that the president lacked the evidence and the power to arrest the 12, he had no choice but to declare a state of siege empowering him to suspend civil liberties and bypass the judiciary temporarily. Otherwise, the court now reaching verdicts in the trial of nine military officers for human rights abuses might be intimidated. Voters might have been frightened away from Sunday's mid-term congressional elections, the first in 20 years.

Mr. Alfonsín's promise — borne out, so far, by his performance — is that the state of siege will end in 60 days and that meanwhile, for all but those 12, "constitutional guarantees and rights will remain in effect."

Exit democracy, even to that dozen degree, and enter the skeptics — and, ordinarily, civil libertarians.

The extraordinary measure Mr. Alfonsín has selectively invoked on behalf of democracy were last invoked by military governors who went on to wage a "dirty war" against leftist terrorists, some real, most imagined. Mr. Alfonsín cites extraordinary circumstances, also cited by the nine former military leaders on trial for their alleged role in that war. Argentines have their president's word that past excesses against one end of the political spectrum won't eventually be repeated against the other. And most Argentines, from Sunday's early election returns, believe him.

Had it been, however, President Duarte who had taken such steps against El Salvador's leftist terrorists, the world's watchdogs of civil liberties would be howling the hard questions with which every nation beset by terrorism is struggling. Is due process not a staple of democracy, the right of even the most minute and distasteful minority? Are the loftiest goals — protecting democracy, ensuring justice, curbing terrorists — justification to suspend rights? Are the best motives necessarily a bar to the worst results? If democracies resort to undemocratic methods, can they survive as democracies?

Mr. Alfonsín's answers to those questions are those a committed democrat thinks best for Argentine democracy. Few Argentines disagree; those who do point to a past in which extraordinary measures taken ostensibly to preserve democracy ended up serving only the power of the incumbent. Only time can prove who is right.

BUFFALO EVENING NEWS
Buffalo, NY, November 1, 1985

NINE THOUSAND men, women and children "disappeared" during the eight years of Argentine military rule that ended in 1983. When turning over power to the civilian government, military leaders said the armed forces should be absolved of charges of murder, torture and kidnapping, saying the troops were following orders. Now nine former military leaders, including three former presidents, are on trial for allegedly giving those orders.

The trial is a time of reckoning for the military leaders and for the Argentine people, most of whom are finding out for the first time the details of what the generals dismiss as a necessary "dirty war" against communist guerrilla forces. The trial prosecutor disputed that characterization, saying: "The juntas behaved like common criminals or terrorists and deserve to be punished accordingly."

Argentina is a tense nation as the trial nears an end and an organized terrorist campaign of bombing and bomb threats is being conducted, apparently with the goal of destabilizing the democratic government and intimidating the trial court.

As a counter-measure, the government of centrist President Raul Alfonsin has declared a state of siege, hoping to show it is in control and seeking, with the emergency decree, to keep 12 suspected terrorists in jail. Such a state of emergency, while commonplace in Latin American dictatorships of the past, is a drastic measure for a democracy.

Alfonsin's bold move has not been a complete success. It has been challenged in the courts, and so far it has not succeeded in stamping out the terrorist bombing. Nevertheless, he has remained popular since his resounding election victory in 1983, and his drive to seek those responsible for the atrocities under military rule has stirred widespread support.

Hopefully, the current state of siege will be brief, and Argentina will be able to resume its democratic course, strengthened by its confrontation of the evil of an unsavory era.

The News Journal
Wilmington, DE, November 7, 1985

FREE ELECTIONS are an essential step toward lawful, democratic government, but no more. Aside from violence in Colombia, there is backing and filling on this process in Latin America.

For elections to be meaningful, different factions and candidates must be able to get on the ballots. Voting has to be secret. Victors and losers must abide by the outcome. Victors must try to carry out campaign promises.

Last weekend's parliamentary elections in Argentina, with supporters of President Raul Alfonsin getting more than 40 percent of the national vote, bode well for democracy in that South American nation. Alfonsin's election two years ago put an end to Argentina's repressive military regime.

While the president's Radical Party was unable to get a clear majority, it has enough strength in the legislature to carry forward the programs begun by Mr. Alfonsin. These center on efforts to rebuild the Argentine economy through austerity measures that are painful for the present but are expected to benefit the country in the long run.

There is still fear of resurgence of the military. But for the time being, the first midterm congressional elections in 20 years offer hope that Argentina may have taken more than a first step toward democracy.

In Guatemala, where elections were also held last weekend, the situation is more tenuous. The military government has promised to return this strife-ridden Central American nation to civilian control. Last Sunday's presidential election showed the sincerity of that promise.

The Christian Democratic candidate, Vinicio Cerezo, received 40 percent of the votes. According to Guatemalan law, there has to be a runoff election. The winner of the runoff is to be installed as president in mid-January.

Mr. Cerezo and his opponent, Jorge Carpio, have pledged to improve human rights. Neither expects to bring to justice those in the military responsible for wanton killings in the last few years. "We are not going to be able to investigate the past," said Mr. Cerezo in a realistic appraisal.

Civilian rule and respect for human rights are more than an internal necessity for Guatemalans. They also are the determining factor for U.S. aid, which was halted several years ago because of human rights violations.

In Panama, democracy took a step backward this fall when President Nicolas Barletta resigned after only 11 months in office. He was replaced by Panama's vice president, Eric Arturo Delvalle. For the vice president to step into the presidency was in accord with the constitution.

But what makes events in Panama worrisome is that Mr. Barletta resigned due to pressure from the military and also because of inability to implement measures to pull Panama out of its economic difficulties.

Panama was ruled by a military strongman all too long. Is there a serious danger that that could happen again soon?

THE INDIANAPOLIS STAR
Indianapolis, IN,
November 2, 1985

Dictators are accustomed to boasting that they are too tough to be dislodged by democracies because democracies are "too soft."

When push comes to shove, democracies can be much tougher than their enemies. In crises they may have to resort to extraordinary measures to prove it.

In Argentina, the election of President Raul Alfonsin ended a bloody dictatorship's state of siege and restored democracy two years ago.

Now Alfonsin has imposed a state of siege. His intention is to halt bombings and bomb threats blamed on right-wing terrorists.

Purportedly the bombings are meant to scare Alfonsin into granting amnesty to nine ex-members of the junta, including three former presidents of Argentina, who are on trial in Buenos Aires.

The nine are charged with involvement in the ghastly state of siege that began in 1976 after the military junta ousted Eva Peron amid accusations of corruption.

During the next six years the junta's forces fought populists and guerrillas and killed some 9,000 people. Many thousands of people simply disappeared during those years. The Inter-American Human Rights Commission in 1980 issued a report charging the junta, which had Soviet cooperation, with widespread arbitrary detention, torture and illegal killings. The government rejected the report.

Amid worsening economic conditions, including inflation of more than 300 percent, the junta sent a military force to invade the British-held Falkland Islands 250 miles off the Atlantic coast in 1982. British defeat of the invasion forces led to the collapse of the junta.

Alfonsin's Radical Civic Union gained an absolute majority in the electoral college and Congress in 1983. Democracy was restored.

The new wave of terrorism seems to prove that Alfonsin's foes intend, by one means or another, to remain a powerful force in Argentinian politics.

Congressional elections are set for tomorrow, Nov. 3. Alfonsin's party hopes to enlarge its thin majority in the Chamber of Deputies.

Argentinian democracy is new growth. Its survival demands toughness in its leaders. There was a plot to kill President Alfonsin late last year when he visited Cordoba. Then a bomb exploded in a Buenos Aires stadium where he was to speak. The latest bombing wave is a challenge that demands powerful counter-measures.

It would be hard to deny that Alfonsin is using his state of siege not to destroy democracy, as his predecessors did, but to defend it. It is proof of a toughness that is essential if the young democracy is to endure.

Edmonton Journal

Edmonton, Alta., December 12, 1985

For a country rich in resources and people, Argentina has endured some horrendous experiences usually seen in less developed nations.

In the last decade, the South American country has been rocked by vicious military rulers, an out-of-control economy and a disastrous war with Great Britain over the Falkland Islands.

When President Raul Alfonsin was elected two years ago, he immediately crushed the military's power by placing top officers on trial for the torture and murder of thousands of people who disappeared in the anti-subversive campaigns of the late 1970s.

The move resulted in the conviction this week of five key military officers who helped run the country after the military takeover in 1976. Ex-president Jorge Videla and former navy commander Emilio Massera were each sentenced to life imprisonment. The three other military strongmen received lesser sentences.

The convictions don't ensure a more prosperous future for Argentina. Alfonsin's greatest challenge lies in repairing a broken-down economy suffering from a tremendous debt load. But the sentences may help restore a sense of justice and order to a society long terrorized by military commanders and dictators.

The crimes committed by Videla and his colleagues were horrifying. Faced with a wave of left-wing terrorist attacks, the military reacted by arresting everyone suspected of subversive tendencies. The insurrection was crushed but at a tremendous cost. About 9,000 people, many of them innocent, disappeared or were murdered.

Surprisingly, the general who led Argentina into the Falklands War was acquitted. General Leopoldo Galtieri, responsible for the deaths of 712 Argentinians in the war, was apparently guilty of nothing more than stupidity. Maybe the fact that he surrendered power to an elected civilian government after the war helped save his skin.

The Argentinian courts have sent the military a clear message it isn't likely to forget. The civilians have had the final word; the tortured have turned on the torturers.

Now, it's up to the Alfonsin government to show Argentinians they have a future with democracy.

The Houston Post

Houston, TX, December 11, 1985

While Guatemala celebrated the election of its first civilian president in 15 years this week, a civilian court in Argentina sentenced five of the country's former military rulers to prison.

The Argentine generals and admirals were convicted for their roles in the country's "dirty war" against leftist insurgents in the 1970s, during which more than 9,000 people disappeared. Gen. Jorge Videla, who headed the ruling junta during that period, and another junta member were sentenced to life imprisonment. Three other junta members received stiff prison terms.

The trial of the Argentine brass sends a message seldom heard in Latin America: The military is not above the law. That could have repercussions throughout the region, particularly in countries like Guatemala, which faces a transition from military to civilian rule next month.

President-elect Vinicio Cerezo must try to revive Guatemala's moribund economy and improve its deplorable human rights record. He can take courage from Argentina's popular President Raul Alfonsin, who has coped with similar problems since he took office in 1983 after a decade of military rule. Government by law has just won a pair over government by gun in Latin America.

LAS VEGAS REVIEW-JOURNAL

Las Vegas, NV, December 12, 1985

The new constitution called for summary executions for "enemies of the people," a dissolution of the capitalist state and the establishment of a Vietnamese-style peoples republic.

It was 1976, and this was the constitution adopted by Argentina's Montoneros, the communist guerrilla force whose leadership was an amalgam of Maoist intellectuals from the universities, radical students, some leftist blue-collar factory workers and others seeking to overthrow the government.

In Argentina that year inflation screamed upward to almost 20 percent — a week. Leftist guerrillas stormed rural police stations, seized control of the universities, and assassinated scores of military and civilian leaders. Bombs spewed flak almost daily in the streets of Buenos Aires and machine gun fire raked the night.

Finally, the military grabbed power, arresting the ineffectual President Isabel Peron. The generals suspended the Argentine constitution — modeled on that of the United States. The junta disbanded Congress and restricted the courts' jurisdiction to minor criminal and civil matters. All political activity was outlawed. The generals and admirals now ruled.

Then the army moved, in force, to put down the insurgency.

The Dirty War was on.

Secret military police and non-uniformed death squads began impromptu executions of their own.

The Argentine military strike against the guerrillas and guerrilla sympathizers was quick, savage and effective. Thousands of Argentines whom the army suspected of being Montoneros or of aiding them spent their last seconds on earth staring down into an improvised grave or looking into the swift muddy waters of the Parana River, waiting for a lead slug.

Others writhed in secret dungeons while their torturers gave them blasts of electricity, beat them, raped them, murdered them.

The insurrection was crushed. But the cost was high. Thousands — not just revolutionaries but also many simply suspected of being sympathizers — vanished into clandestine military prisons, never to be heard from again. It was the most brutal chapter in Argentine history.

In the wake of the Dirty War, the military proved itself to be incompetent at handling the economy, and inflation raged. The last straw for the military government was the Falklands War against Britain in 1982. The junta gravely botched it, and Argentina was humiliated. The military government fell.

This week, Argentina marks its second year of democracy. A popularly elected moderate — Raul Alfonsin — is in power. The economy is stabilizing, and the nation seems well on its way toward recovery from its brutal, chaotic recent past.

In a move unprecedented in Latin America, the former military rulers were put on trial. From all appearances, the trials were fair, above board and public.

This week came word that five former junta members — including Jorge Videla, who ruled during the Dirty War — were found guilty of kidnapping, torturing and murdering their adversaries. Videla was sentenced to life. (Argentina has no death penalty.)

Perhaps the guilty verdicts will not satisfy the craving for revenge among those many Argentines whose relatives were murdered at the hands of state torturers. Many Argentines may view the sentences, ranging from 54 months to life, as too light. But the trials demonstrate that the rule of law has been reestablished.

Developments in Argentina are good news for the hemisphere. Perhaps few Americans realize the great potential and inherent wealth of Argentina. The country is immense — seventh largest nation in the world. Its climate is mostly temperate. It has a wealth of resources, and is one of those rare countries which is self-sufficient in food. It possesses another much valued resource — oil. Its cities are clean and modern, its transportation system up to date, its social programs progressive. The Argentine populace is as literate as that of the United States and the middle class dominant, as in the U.S.

This is no banana republic. Potentially — with its vast area, wealth of resources and population of only 30 million — Argentina is one of the wealthiest countries in the world.

Now that Argentina has returned to democracy and taken steps toward exorcising the demons of the past, perhaps the nation can develop that potential.

The Honolulu Advertiser

Honolulu, HI, December 24, 1985

Something unprecedented in Latin America is happening in Argentina. After a long, public trial, five former military junta leaders — including two past presidents — were stripped of their rank and sentenced to prison for human rights violations including murder, illegal detentions and torture.

One former president got life; another 17 years. During the junta years more than 9,000 people disappeared in a secret "dirty war" aimed at opponents of the regime. Most have never been accounted for.

THE END OF the trial coincided with the second anniversary in office of Raul Alfonsin, the country's democratically elected president. His party made a strong showing in midterm elections last month, indicating support for his actions.

On taking office Alfonsin reversed an immunity law the junta had hastily pushed through, and when military tribunals last year found no case against the former rulers, he moved their trials to civilian courts.

Alfonsin has been equally audacious on other fronts. Left with an economy severely damaged by the junta's mismanagement and facing a foreign debt crisis, he adopted a program more austere than that proposed by the International Monetary Fund to end the country's 2,000 percent inflation.

MORE DIFFICULTIES may be ahead. The trial of Leopoldo Galtieri, another former military president, and two others for mismanaging the doomed Falklands War is under way and trials of 300 junior officers accused of crimes in the "dirty war" are scheduled. There is a danger the military's restraint might snap.

But holding off the military and the anti-democratic Peronists should be easier because Alfonsin's government has shown Argentinians the potential when true justice and the rule of law are paramount.

Argentina is setting an example to other nations in Latin America and elsewhere — including the Philippines — that even after a period of dictatorship, democracy is an achievable goal. And that example should be supported in any way possible, including on the economic front, by the United States.

The Philadelphia Inquirer

Philadelphia, PA, December 12, 1985

Argentine President Raul Alfonsin has much to celebrate after completing two years in office. All those who cheered Argentina's return to democracy, and the example it provided for other Latin countries that have since restored civilian rule, can share in that celebration.

The most immediate cause for kudos is the conviction on Monday by a civilian court of five ex-military rulers for crimes of murder and torture committed during Argentina's undeclared war on left-wing guerrillas during the 1970s. About 9,000 people were seized and disappeared, presumed dead.

Argentine human rights activists and the families of those abducted protest that the sentences are too mild. Only two ex-junta members received life terms and three others were acquitted. But this cannot obscure the fact that the rule of law triumphed as, for the first time in recent Latin American history, a civilian court sentenced military leaders for serious crimes.

Moreover, the court has transferred massive documentation to the country's top military court for cases against lower-ranking commanders accused of involvement in the repression. Further trials appear likely despite opposition from the armed forces and conservative civilian groups. In fact, President Alfonsin felt confident enough to lift early a temporary state of siege imposed after a wave of bombings attributed to right-wing paramilitary cells opposed to the trial.

But the biggest boost to Argentina's democratic renewal has come from President Alfonsin's success in checking his country's hyper-inflation, which was soaring toward 3,000 percent at midyear and threatening to destroy chances for political stability. His team has managed to slash inflation to 1.9 percent in October and get interest current on its enormous foreign debt, without causing a severe recession or unemployment.

Economists agree the toughest economic tests lie ahead and progress to date could still unravel. But President Alfonsin already has earned the respect of his people and of the administration. He deserves American support in his struggle to re-establish a firm basis for Argentine democracy.

The Boston Globe

Boston, MA, December 14, 1985

The people of Argentina can take only partial satisfaction from the conviction of former officers and junta leaders who conducted a reign of terror in that country from 1976 to 1983.

Gen. Jorge Videla and Adm. Emilio Massera, chiefs in the first of three blood-drenched juntas, were convicted on dozens of counts of murder, kidnapping and torture, and sentenced to life in prison. They were also absolved of hundreds of other alleged crimes, however, while four more officers belonging to military juntas were acquitted.

Only a few years ago thousands of innocent men, women and children were suffering from the sadism of right-wing officers who nearly turned Argentina into a South American version of Hitler's Germany in the 1930s. Mothers and fathers still grieving for sons and daughters who were kidnapped, tortured and killed by fascist death squads can never have their children returned to them; they are entitled to feel that the mixed verdict of a civilian court was hardly commensurate with the crimes committed against their kin.

Justice was done, but it is an incomplete justice. Only a few crimes and a small number of the criminals have been punished. The ruling of the judges allows for further prosecution, though, and the trial itself can become a precedent − not only for Argentina, but for other countries in this hemisphere that have suffered under fascism.

President Raoul Alfonsin has demonstrated the personal and political courage required of a leader who must come to terms with a dictatorial past in order to construct a democratic future. Though removed from power, the same forces that carried out the juntas' terror still exist in Argentina, as demonstrated by a recent series of bombings.

Because the US government and American officials have had a shameful history of collaboration with the Argentine officers responsible for state terror, a similar display of political courage should be required in Washington.

The American authorities who contracted with Argentine fascists to train guerrilla bands to overthrow the Sandinista regime in Nicaragua ought to apologize. American officials who defended the Argentine torturers as mere "authoritarians" and worthy friends of a democratic people ought to admit they brought shame on American ideals.

IMF Groups Hold Semiannual Meetings

The main policy committees of the International Monetary Fund (IMF) and the World Bank held their semiannual meetings in Washington, D.C. in late March and early April, 1986. A number of other meetings of international groups connected to the IMF and the World Bank were also held there during that time. Among the actions taken during the meetings were the backing of the current floating system of exchange rates by the major industrial nations, the approval of a new $3.1 billion IMF-World Bank lending pool for the world's poorest nations, and a call for a nearly twofold rise in lending by the World Bank within the next five years.

Finance Ministers representing the Group of 10 industrialized nations met April 9 and 10, 1986 and once again backed the current system of floating exchange rates. The ministers also decided not to establish a new group for studying monetary reform, but to leave the question to the IMF executive board.

Outstanding external debt of Third World nations totaled some $950 billion at the end of 1985 and was likely to top $1 trillion in 1986, according to data released by the World Bank March 26. A key finding in the survey was that during 1985, debtor nations had repaid about $22 billion more to banks and other lenders than they had received in new loans—meaning that the new flow of capital was from developing nations to industrialized ones. The World Bank also estimated that some $93 billion in debt principal repayments had been rescheduled during 1985.

The Miami Herald
Miami, FL, February 7, 1986

THE U.S. Commerce Department has confirmed what many a South Florida businessmen already knew from his own balance sheet. The drop in trade with Latin America that began in 1982 continued through last year, and there's no end in sight.

Exports through the Port of Miami, Port Everglades, and West Palm Beach totaled $6.1 billion in 1985, or 21 percent below the $7.7-billion worth of exports registered in 1981. The 1985 exports' value was unchanged from the year before, frustrating predictions that South Florida's exports would rise 10 percent last year.

"The new figures reflect the continued difficulties that Latin American countries are having in finding dollars to maintain their imports," notes Ivan Cosimi, head of the Department's Miami-district office. The increase in exports that was predicted but not realized last year was expected to come largely from replacement of machinery and spare parts, whose purchase foreign users had deferred because of foreign-exchange difficulties.

One reasonably bright note in this region's trade dirge is that imports through the three ports totaled only $4.6 billion, unchanged from 1984. Since exports also didn't change from 1984 to 1985, the ports together showed a foreign-trade surplus of $1.5 billion each year.

Given the United States's staggering foreign-trade deficit — it totaled $148.5 billion during 1985 — it's at least some solace that South Florida showed a surplus. Would that both the value of the surplus and of South Florida's exports increase markedly in 1986.

The Washington Post
Washington, DC, January 21, 1986

THE WHITE HOUSE is wasting time over the choice of the next World Bank president as though it didn't make any difference, but the World Bank is crucial to the plan that the secretary of the Treasury, James Baker, has proposed for dealing with the Latin debts. If the delay over the appointment continues, Mr. Baker will eventually begin having difficulty persuading the rest of the world that the White House is prepared to give his plan active and vigorous support.

It has now been more than three months since the World Bank's current president A. W. Clausen, said that he would not seek reappointment when his present term ends in June. He made the announcement, incidentally, at the same meeting in Seoul, Korea, and on the same day as Mr. Baker's address outlining the Latin debt plan. Since then, inevitably, Mr. Clausen has become something of a lame duck at the bank, and the bank itself has been losing momentum.

But the Baker plan's emphasis on the World Bank is loaded with significance for the Latin borrowers. Of the two great international lending institutions that face each other across 19th Street, governments and commercial banks concerned with the Latin debts have so far been mainly working through the other one—the International Monetary Fund. Because the IMF's job is to deal with the foreign exchange emergencies, its remedies tend to be addresssed to the short run, and because balance-of-payments trouble usually involved overspending they tend to begin with restraint and austerity. Mr. Baker's references to the World Bank were a signal to Latin America that the United States is prepared to take a longer perspective in dealing with the debts and, instead of austerity, it wants to rely more heavily on economic growth to balance accounts. To Latin America, that is a highly welcome change.

But the Baker plan has never been spelled out in any great detail. For example, the World Bank has the funds to maintain its role for only perhaps a couple of years. What happens then? The Reagan administration has never been enthusiastic about expanding the international banks' resources, and Congress has never voted them money without a long and onerous struggle.

In formal terms the next president of the World Bank will be chosen jointly by all the governments that belong to it. But tradition holds that the nominee will be an American, and as a practical matter, he will be named by the Reagan administration. Who should it be? Clearly, it needs to be a person of sufficient international standing to have the confidence of both the Latin Americans and the commercial bankers. It needs to be a person of sufficient breadth to speak to the large issues of fairness and social justice raised by the repayment of the debts. It has to be a person capable, here in Washington, of coaxing further support from a Congress laboring under the shadow of Gramm-Rudman.

It would be reassuring to think that the White House was energetically searching for the right candidate. But there are no visible signs of it.

THE WALL STREET JOURNAL.
New York, NY, March 5, 1986

The "Baker plan" for supply-side rehabilitation of debtor nations is obviously a good idea. But as soon as it was announced in Seoul last fall, everyone wondered whether it's realistic to expect the IMF and World Bank to press debtor nations to make politically sensitive economic reforms. Brazil, the biggest debtor nation of all, has just answered the question: When the right options are put on the table, democratic politics works for economic reform, not against it.

In Brazil, as in Argentina earlier, a military regime had made such a mess of things that it voluntarily surrendered to democratic, civilian rule. In Argentina, the election of Raul Alfonsin to the presidency quickly led to economic reform—primarily an attack on inflation. Now the same thing is happening in Brazil.

Brazil has been a marvelous laboratory for disproving a theory, once seductively popular among some economists, that a country can accommodate to inflation and thereby enjoy its stimulative benefits at no cost. Brazil, during its long era of authoritarian rule, happily printed cruzeiros to finance government subsidies and the losses of state industries. Wages and about everything else in sight were indexed upward to offset inflation. In fact, Brazil had been financing its seeming prosperity with enormous external borrowing, as the debt crisis made clear.

Jose Sarney, Brazil's president, ascended to that office from the vice presidency last April after Tancredo Neves was elected but died before inauguration. Mr. Sarney tried initially to boost his prestige, and deal with debt-service needs, by simultaneously shutting down imports and printing

still more money. Factories hummed but inflation got worse. Brazilians voted heavily against his party in some important municipal elections. The lesson: Voters don't like inflation, even indexed inflation.

So Mr. Sarney and his finance minister, Dilson Funaro, have frozen prices and wages, created a new currency unit called the cruzado that presumably will be printed more sparingly, and abandoned indexing. As with any such policy, the real test will be whether the government can remove the controls before they do economic damage, while at the same time making deindexation stick. The next test will be whether it can start opening up the market to competition again, cutting state subsidies. We'd like to see more attention to tax rates and incentives for the private sector.

So far, though, initial results are promising: The Brazilian stock market rose, and the official and parallel exchange rates for the cruzado are converging. Over the weekend Brazil worked out a $31 billion debt restructuring plan with 14 banks that represent its external creditors.

Significantly, Mr. Sarney has taken the fundamental reform of ending indexing not to please Jacques de Larosiere of the IMF or the Baker-Volcker team but to try to strengthen his slipping grip on the Brazilian presidency. The Washington-based money triumverate will in no way frown on his efforts, but President Sarney and his economic policy makers have taken pains to tell Brazilians that what they are doing is their own idea.

The Baker plan may not be working quite the way it was initially envisioned, but if debtor governments can do the job themselves, so much the better.

THE CHRISTIAN SCIENCE MONITOR
Boston, MA, March 27, 1986

COMING off a week in which unilateral action once again seems to characterize the affairs of nations, the World Bank's interest in providing a hefty infusion of new loans to Latin America comes as a reminder that global problems are best resolved by international cooperation.

The billion-dollar-plus bank action — expected to be approved during the next month — is particularly timely, given the mixed signals in the global economic picture. It is also an achievement for US Treasury Secretary James Baker III, who has urged the bank to increase its lending to third-world nations.

Capital infusions are absolutely essential to third-world nations. The economic recovery is still on track. But a slowdown of consumer spending in industrial nations, as is now taking place in the United States, has an adverse impact on export-oriented developing nations. Moreover, the downturn in the value of the dollar against other currencies makes imports more expensive for Western consumers. Granted, it would take time for the

World Bank to actually disburse new loan funds for Latin America, assuming they are quickly approved. But the awarding of the loans would be a signal to private lending agencies — commercial banks that have already extended credit to the region — that they should consider new loan packages as needed.

Latin America, unfortunately, is one of the trouble spots in the world economic setting. The economies of the region vary widely, but in far too many nations there is high unemployment, and underemployment; continuing high inflation, despite improvements; overdependence on revenues from low-priced export commodities, including oil; and national practices based in large measure on corruption. Moreover, of the total third-world debt, over one-third, some $380 billion, is owed by Latin American nations.

The overriding economic priority for Latin America — as, indeed, for the world economy — remains growth. New loans earmarked to Latin American job creation and trade are essential to reach that objective.

Minneapolis Star and Tribune
Minneapolis, MN, April 11, 1986

A lot of people are talking constructively about Latin America this week. Consider a report by several dozen leaders from throughout the hemisphere who offer creative proposals on subjects ranging from peace to debt to narcotics. Gathered under a nongovernmental umbrella called the Inter-American Dialogue, that group is not the only source of the week's pronouncements on Latin America, but the high quality of its work commands special attention.

For example, the report realistically warns of Nicaragua's "menacing" military buildup and aid to revolutions elsewhere. But the Dialogue's bankers, industrialists, scholars and former officials also recognize the wrongheadedness of current U.S. policy. Accordingly, they wisely advocate an end to U.S. aid for the contras warring on the Nicaraguan government. With that issue pending in Congress, the advice is timely.

Latin economic development is less dramatic but equally timely and, in the long run, more important. Appropriately, the crisis of debt and growth heads the Dialogue's agenda. Its solutions are ambitious and in some cases unrealistic: The recommended stretchout of *all* Latin debt seems unnecessarily sweeping, and the proposal for writing off portions of some countries' debts would further impair the credit of those borrowers. But the call for Latin economic expansion coupled with economic reform deserves strong support.

The Dialogue envisions new lending of $20 billion annually to all of Latin America from all sources. Nearly three times the amount proposed last year by Treasury Secretary James Baker, that goal also is ambitious. But careful studies by the nonprofit Institute for International Economics suggest that such a figure is attainable.

The Dialogue report gets surprising reinforcement from another direction: the conservative Heritage Foundation. Such criticisms of Latin economies as "bloated public sectors" and "inefficient state enterprises" come from the Dialogue, though they parallel many Heritage comments. The Dialogue and Heritage differ on important principles, including the role of the World Bank. But with Latin America suffering extraordinary economic duress, it's encouraging to see even a few similar recommendations from such disparate groups.

THE BLADE

Toledo, OH, August 16, 1986

A LATIN-AMERICAN economic common market has long been an elusive dream in the lands of South America and the Caribbean. But an agreement signed last month by leaders of Brazil and Argentina, the two giants of that region, promises to lead nearer that goal.

They are not talking about peanuts. Eleven protocols signed by Brazilian President Jose Sarney and Argentine President Raul Alfonsin should double annual trade between the two nations to $3 billion by the end of this decade.

Both nations have a combined gross national product of $300 billion a year. Success of the program is not a foregone conclusion, by any means, but the hope is that, as the bilateral relationship matures, neighboring countries such as Uruguay, Paraguay, and Bolivia will be drawn into the alliance and contribute to it.

It is particularly interesting to note that the accords were facilitated by the fact that both Brazil and Argentina restored democratic governments at about the same time after long periods of military dominance. Both economies languished under the dictatorial rule of Juan Peron and his military successors in Argentina and their repressive counterparts in Brazil.

The painful history of the European Common Market, going back to its beginnings in 1957, illustrates as well as anything how long and difficult a road lies ahead for the Latin American nations. And they are much poorer to start with than were the western European partners.

But any journey must begin with a first step, and the Brazilian-Argentine agreement represents just that for a region of the world in dire need of economic progress.

The Houston Post

Houston, TX, March 12, 1986

Sweeping economic reforms in Brazil aimed at reducing inflation were followed two days later by an announcement of agreement with commercial banks restructuring nearly a third of the country's $104 billion foreign debt. Argentine inflation is down, too, and both countries are benefiting from lower oil prices.

Even oil-exporting Mexico apparently is hurting less than expected: Officials revised downward the amount they say they will need to borrow to meet this year's needs. So the prospects of those developing countries with massive foreign debts being able to pay what they owe are perhaps better now than they have been in recent years.

Brazil has the largest debt, but boasted an economic growth rate of 8.3 percent last year. It has had trade surpluses totaling $32 billion over the last three years.

Argentina, with a foreign debt of $50 billion, introduced its own economic reforms last June. There has been some erosion of enthusiasm, and strikes are becoming more frequent. Economic activity has decreased — the gross domestic product was down 4 percent last year — and public confidence is down. Still, inflation has been slowed from 25 to 30 percent to 2 or 3 percent per month.

Mexico owes $96 billion. It earns 70 percent of its foreign exchange from oil exports, and thus suffers greatly from low and falling prices. Yet, its reduction in the amount of new money it says it needs to borrow is encouraging, and perhaps the lengthy anti-corruption campaign may be bearing some fruit.

No one can rule out default of one or more of the debtor countries. Yet there are positive elements. Apparent willingness of commercial banks to restructure some of those debts further eases pressure. All in all, things may not be as bad as they were.

The Philadelphia Inquirer

Philadelphia, PA, August 15, 1986

Simon Bolivar, the patriot soldier who joined the struggle for Spanish-American independence 175 years ago, ultimately became cynical about his dream of a unified Latin America. Nationalist jealousies have blocked the attempts of many subsequent leaders to achieve that same dream. But the 12-point common market pact recently signed by Brazil and Argentina holds promise that an interdependent Latin America could develop into an economic powerhouse.

The two nations linked in the agreement, known as the Act of Buenos Aires, only recently have emerged from disastrous military dictatorships. Yet their commitment to democracy seems deeply rooted. Indeed, in inviting the continent's other nations to join their union, they excluded the tyrannical regimes in Chile and Paraguay.

For fragile democracies to thrive in a fiercely competitive world, pragmatic approaches like a supportive common market are essential. Brazil and Argentina already have been cooperating. Their austerity measures, exemplified in currency and spending reforms, came about after extensive interchange of ideas. Now they hope to become mutually self-sufficient in foodstuffs, connect their auto and aeronautics industries and counter growing world protectionism by liberalizing trade policies.

Although they contain vast resources, skilled workers and large middle classes, Brazil and Argentina also have a host of political, social and structural economic problems.

Moreover, these rich partners were tense rivals as recently as 1982, and they must overcome formidable obstacles such as Brazil's industrial-cost advantage. Suppressing local interests for the common good always is tough, as the European Economic Community has learned. Necessity, on the other hand, is the mother of cooperation.

Brazil and Argentina seek to avoid the old cycle of undelivered promises of reform followed by anti-democratic rule. If they can succeed in attracting Peru, Bolivia, Colombia and Venezuela to join their common market, there is hope that a commitment in the economic sphere will extend to scientific and political endeavors as well. Then, perhaps, Bolivar's ancient dream will become reality.

AFTER THE DELUGE

The Dispatch

Columbus, OH, September 4, 1986

Argentina and Brazil have taken the first step toward creating a South American "Common Market" to promote trade between the nations. The move is welcomed.

Leaders of the nations recently signed a pact by which they agreed to:

● Lift trade barriers and tariffs on $2 billion worth of capital goods to be exchanged over the next four years.

● Give preference to each other's products in bidding on government contracts.

● Create special funds for the promotion of bi-national companies.

● Jointly pursue advances in technology and industry.

● Rely on each other's food products to make up for seasonal shortages.

Brazil and Argentina are longtime economic and political adversaries and the strengthening of economic ties can only increase the incentives for both nations to maintain friendly relations.

Furthermore, each nation is faced with economic problems that can be addressed through enhanced trade. Argentina has a $10 billion foreign debt and Brazil's is $103 billion. While Brazil is better situated to deal with this burden (its gross national product is growing at an annual rate of 6 percent), Argentina is faced with an economy that is shrinking at a 4 percent annual rate.

In addition, the two countries have opened talks with Uruguay about that nation joining in the regional market, but has rejected queries from Chile and Paraguay, saying that a condition of membership is a democratically empowered government. Both Paraguay and Chile are ruled by military dictators. "Integration is a will of the people and not just of those who command," Argentine President Raul Alfonsin said. "It only makes sense when they (the people) are consulted and asked to participate."

The economic accord will enhance relations among South American nations and will also encourage a broadening of social and political liberty across the continent. The agreement between Argentina and Brazil should go a long way toward enhancing the quality of life in South America.

Los Angeles Times

Los Angeles, CA, August 26, 1986

From the outside, the common view of Latin America's debt is that it is a $370-billion albatross around the necks of governments and banks. From the inside, that debt is a maternity ward in Mexico City where the hospital cannot afford to repair an incubator and a public school teacher in Brazil quitting because inflation cuts her paycheck below the survival level.

Troubling as the outside view may be, the inside view, as described in a recent series by Times writer John Broder, is worse. It shows the onset of an economic depression and a failure of hope that could leave at least one generation of Latin Americans ill fed, uneducated, unemployed and in poor health. That is a recipe for dynamite in a region with a long history of political instability.

The debt means that nations as big as Brazil and as small as Costa Rica, as democratic as Venezuela and as dictatorial as Chile, must cut government spending in order to pay off loans from international banks and lending agencies. It means not enough capital for growth, and that in turn means not just hard times but hard times for a long time.

From the outside, "capital flight" brings to mind the wealthy and the corrupt smuggling money into Swiss bank accounts. From the inside, it also means maids and taxi drivers hoarding precious dollars to deposit in little banks from San Diego to Miami—a sign of a basic lack of confidence that pervades Latin America.

Latin America needs economic reforms that will ease governments out of the market, increase competition and lead to more free trade. But if the reforms also mean not just a few bad years but hard times for as long as anyone can see, then any short-run gains will mean long-run social losses.

Henry A. Kissinger, former U. S. secretary of state, and others argue persuasively that it is more important to lend a hand to Latin America while it works its way out of debt than it is to stick to a rigid schedule of interest payments. International bankers argue, also persuasively, that they cannot be too lenient without eroding their own finances.

One choice is more of the same, but indefinite austerity gambles on causing political instability from the Rio Grande to the Rio de la Plata. Many demagogues already want Latin America to repudiate its debt.

Kissinger points to another way. He has called on the United States and other industrial nations to revive the Marshall Plan that helped Western Europe rebuild after World War II and apply it in Latin America. Kissinger thinks the psychological effect—a reason to hope for better times—would be just as important as its economic effect.

A Marshall Plan for Latin America would also give banks and creditor nations reason to hope. Even if they cut interest rates and gave Latin America more time to repay short-term loans, their investments would be repaid as Latin America's economy grew.

Kissinger is on the right track. Easing Latin America's economic agony is not something that banks can take on by themselves. Western governments must join bankers in implementing decisions that are both political and financial. It would cost the West, but Latin Americans, from presidents to peasants, already live with those costs. And the cost to the West would be lower than the cost of chaos.

Chilean Crisis Mounts; 7 Slain in Strike

Chileans staged a two-day general strike July 2-3, 1986 to demand a return to democracy. At least six people were shot to death during the strike, and a Chilean-born resident of the United States who was set on fire died later of his burns. Human rights groups blamed the military police for the deaths. The strike had been called in June as the culmination of a month-long series of planned boycotts and other acts of civil disobedience against the government of President Augusto Pinochet Ugarte. The protests and strike were organized by the National Civil Assembly, a recently formed coalition of union confederations, professional associations, students, community organizations and other groups, led by Juan Luis Gonzalez.

The strike began violently July 2, with most of the incidents occurring in Santiago's poor neighborhoods, where the Communist Party was active. Barricades were built and rocks were thrown at passing vehicles. Police acted quickly to quell any signs of protest. Of the three people who died in Santiago that day, two of them were reportedly shot by police in the capital's poor neighborhoods. The third person who died was a 13-year-old girl shot while going to buy bread. There was also a number of bomb blasts around Santiago July 1-2. These were the latest in a series of bombings, many of which were claimed by the leftist Manuel Rodriguez Patriotic Front. In the three largest cities, Santiago, Valparaiso and Concepcion, 95% of cargo trucks stayed off the roads during the two days of the strike, according to a union spokesman, and public transport was scarce. Absenteeism July 2 was about 60% in some industrial areas in Santiago, according to Rodolfo Seguel, leader of the National Workers Command. However, many shops factories and offices were open as normal.

The American killed in the violence was Rodrigo Rojas de Negri, 19, a Washington, D.C.-based photographer who July 2 was set on fire by uniformed police. Negri died July 6. The youth and a friend, Carmen Quintana Arancibia, 19, had been cornered by uniformed men with blackened faces, according to witnesses. The men beat the two youths with rifle butts, doused them with flammable fluid, set them on fire and then wrapped them in blankets and drove them away in a truck. The two were later found wandering in the northern district of Quilicura. Charges emerged later that the authorities had refused to allow Rojas and Quintana to be transferred from the poorly equipped clinic where they were first taken to a hospital with better facilities. The authorities reportedly said the two could not be moved because they were under arrest. At Rojas's funeral July 9 in Santiago, riot police used tear gas cannons to disperse mourners in a 2,000-strong funeral procession. Four people were injured.

The Washington Post

Washington, DC, July 9, 1986

THE CHANCE DEATH of a 19-year-old with Washington connections has given Americans a rare glimpse of the condition of state terrorism prevailing in Chile. Rodrigo Rojas graduated from Woodrow Wilson High School and recently returned to visit his native country, which his mother had fled as a political refugee. He was in a group of students entering one of the slums that army units regularly invade and terrorize. Soldiers grabbed him and a companion, beat them, doused them with an inflammable fluid, set them afire and dumped them by a road. When they were finally brought to a hospital, they were denied suitable treatment. Mr. Rojas died last Sunday.

Gen. Augusto Pinochet in 1973 overthrew an elected government that had seen the country slide into civil war. He set up shop as a dictator and, in 1980, wrote a constitution that could yet keep him in power for the extraordinary span of 25 years. At first many Chileans at least tolerated his rule as a relief from chaos. Their toleration has since thinned, but their efforts to find a path back to Chile's traditional stable democratic ways have foundered. Democrats from across the spectrum agreed on a broad blueprint called the National Accord a year ago, but have yet to follow through. President Pinochet has played on the opposition's divisions and on a general apprehension about violence on the left—violence that he partly provokes by closing off normal political outlets. Nor has he shrunk from using the security forces for political viciousness.

Successive American administrations have sought a way to help restore democracy. Jimmy Carter carried the human rights cause, but it is fairly said that his policy of sanctions and toughness did not budge Gen. Pinochet and may have left him the stronger for having shown he could weather American disfavor. President Reagan, after an unsuccessful experiment with friendly persuasion, chose Chile as a place to demonstrate that he cared about advancing human rights and democracy not only in left-leaning and communist countries but also in right-wing, ostensibly anti-communist countries. Especially since Gen. Pinochet rejected the National Accord, the administration has hardened its line. The general, however, has also hardened his.

One possible result in Washington is to strengthen congressional sentiment for, and to diminish the force of administration opposition to, new economic sanctions. Chile and South Africa could become kind of a matched pair of targets. In both cases, the test should be whether sanctions will likely take the United States beyond expressing outrage into actually moving the political process in the direction of democracy.

THE KANSAS CITY STAR
Kansas City, MO, July 8, 1986

There's a cruel touch of irony in knowing that while Vanessa de Negri, a Chilean activist forced into exile in 1976, protested in the United States against torture in her homeland, her 19-year-old son would become a victim of it during a visit to Santiago.

By most unofficial accounts, the Chilean military is to blame for the tortures of Mrs. De Negri's son, Rodrigo Andres Rojas de Negri, and Carmen Quintana Arancibia, 18, a university student. According to reports to Amnesty International and Americas Watch, the young people were seized by men in uniform, doused with a flammable liquid and set afire. Mr. De Negri, a photographer who lived with his mother in the District of Columbia, received burns over 66 percent of his body, according to the human rights groups. He died Sunday. Miss Quintana was also severely burned.

The U.S. was right to insist on an investigation of these tortures, not only because Mr. De Negri is a permanent resident of the United States, but because no nation, particularly one friendly to the U.S., must be allowed to exist under a form of government where human cruelty has become so much a way of life that any protest against it seems abnormal.

According to the human rights groups, Miss Quintana and Mr. De Negri had accompanied 60 students from the University of Santiago on a tour of a shantytown where anti-government protests were common. Mrs. De Negri had demonstrated in Norfolk, Va., against the participation of a Chilean tall ship allegedly used for torture, the Esmeralda, in the Fourth of July and Statue of Liberty rededication ceremonies. The human rights groups have not determined whether there is a connection between Mrs. De Negri's activities in the U.S. and the abuse of her son.

Soon it will become difficult to separate Mr. Pinochet from what he fears most: the Communists and their methods. Chileans will begin to ask one another: "Which side are you on? That of the people-burners or that which would do away with their madness?"

President Reagan must know that the Marxist-Leninist Sandinistas were propelled to popularity and the presidency by the abuses of another right-wing ally, President Anastacio Somoza. Chile is becoming ripe for a Sandinista equivalent, more dangerous than the Allende government Mr. Pinochet replaced.

Detroit Free Press
Detroit, MI, July 14, 1986

DEATH IS death, but there was something especially repulsive about the recent murder in Chile of Rodrigo Rojas de Negri, who was beaten, doused with gasoline and then set on fire during anti-government protests. Our repulsion was increased when Chilean police turned tear gas and water hoses on 2,000 mourners at Mr. Rojas' funeral Wednesday.

The tragedy has prompted the harshest criticism yet from the Reagan administration of Chilean President Augusto Pinochet. Elliott Abrams, assistant secretary of state for inter-American affairs, sharply condemned both the murder and the police response at the funeral, saying the incidents make the need for democratic elections in Chile more urgent.

Although the administration began distancing itself from the Chilean dictator earlier this year, it is unfortunate that such horrors must occur before U.S. officials respond with sufficient outrage to the Pinochet government's human rights abuses. Mr. Abrams' angry condemnation, however, appears to represent an important step. President Reagan may finally have realized that he cannot credibly campaign for aid to the contra rebels against Sandinista repression in Nicaragua while giving Mr. Pinochet kid-glove treatment. Although tardy, the administration's response to the continuing oppression in Chile is welcome.

The Virginian-Pilot
Norfolk, VA, July 13, 1986

Veronica de Negri, formerly of Valparaiso, Chile, came to Norfolk two weeks ago to speak out against the inappropriate inclusion of the Chilean four-masted barketine *Esmeralda* in the Liberty Sail of the Americas event celebrating the restoration of the Statue of Liberty. Since the military coup that brought it to power in 1973, the dictatorship of President Augusto Pinochet has routinely tortured and terrorized Chileans. Official savagery is still the norm.

Veronica de Negri brought that message to Hampton Roads. At a press conference at the Holiday Inn/Waterside in downtown Norfolk, she spoke of the repeated torture and rape she suffered at the hands of Chilean security personnel who seized and imprisoned her for six months in the mid-1970s. The news photograph of her standing on the Elizabeth River waterfront, the palms of her uplifted hands sending a "no-blood-on-my-hands" message to the *Esmeralda* and its crew and the Chilean government, was published internationally.

Last week, Veronica de Negri flew from the Washington area, where she lives and works, to Santiago, Chile, to sit beside the hospital bed of her 19-year-old son, Rodrigo Rojas. Young Rodrigo and an 18-year-old woman companion were at a bus stop in a Santiago shantytown when they were attacked by a gang — eyewitnesses described the attackers as soldiers with grease-darkened faces — who beat the two with sticks, poured flammable liquid on them, set them afire, then wrapped the burned victims in blankets and carried them off, dumping them miles away. Rodrigo subsequently died of his injuries.

In such ways does the Pinochet regime deal with its critics — in this case, with students who go into the Santiago shantytowns to comfort families terrorized by roving military patrols.

But the poor and those who would help the poor are not the sole targets of the regime: The mayor of Valparaiso, for example, was among the scores of men and women who were tortured aboard the *Esmeralda* in the days after the 1973 military coup in Chile. Veronica de Negri was a public-works employee involved in labor-union and feminist activities when she "vanished" — whisked away to the torture cells of the Chilean regime.

Aided by the International Rescue Committee, Veronica de Negri and her son left Chile in 1975 — she had been released from jail after signing a "confession." Chilean novelist Ariel Dorfman, who teaches at Duke University, said at a Washington press conference last week that Rodrigo had returned to his homeland in May in quest of his roots. The youth was not a U.S. citizen when he died, but the U.S. State Department expressed the hope "that a complete and thorough investigation into this tragic incident will be conducted" and "appropriate action . . . taken to see that justice is done."

The Chilean government denies Army complicity in the attack on the youth and his companion. It voiced regret and "condemned in the strongest of terms this irrational act" — and promised a probe by an independent prosecutor.

But skepticism is in order: Amnesty International, Americas Watch and the Human Rights Commission of the Organization of American States have documented a long list of Pinochet-regime crimes against human beings. The Chilean judge assigned to look into the Rojas case tends to see no evil when government personnel are charged with wrongdoing. Meanwhile, the pro-government press reports that Rodrigo and his companion were burned while handling a Molotov cocktail.

When efforts were made to remove Rodrigo Rojas from the hospital to which he had been taken to another hospital where he could have received better treatment, the police said that could not be done because the victim was under arrest. Told of this, the Chilean information minister in Washington replied: "That is impossible. . . . If he is burned, how can you say he is under arrest?"

Nonetheless, a U.S. State Department officer attests that authorities blocked removal. So blatantly does the Pinochet dictatorship practice cruelty against Chileans that Washington — which encouraged the toppling of the government of Marxist President Salvador Allende 13 years ago — has distanced itself from General Pinochet and called for speedy restoration of constitutional democracy.

But General Pinochet stays put. Were Washington to employ its large influence in international banking circles to curtail economic assistance Chile, as it did to bring down Mr. Allende, it might expedite the Pinochet regime's demise. Meanwhile, both Washington and ordinary people everywhere must make clear to Santiago by word and dead that governments sustained by murder, torture and terror are beyond the pale.

The Hartford Courant
Hartford, CT, July 7, 1986

Even as the Chilean tall ship Esmeralda entered New York Harbor to join in America's celebration of liberty, the military dictatorship of Gen. Augusto Pinochet was clamping down on new protests by Chileans seeking an end to his brutal rule.

The unrest began as a general strike by tens of thousands of workers asking for a return to civilian government, but riot police equipped with tear gas and water cannon escalated tension in the streets of Santiago, and three people, including a teenage girl, were shot to death.

"The authorities cannot allow small, irresponsible groups to create an artificial climate of insecurity," said Santiago's military governor, Gen. Osvaldo Hernandez. It's a familiar story.

As is usual in countries whose governments derive authority only from brutality, the regime's accounts of the strike and accompanying police violence were the only ones to be reported in the Chilean media.

But Gen. Pinochet's press censorship is only one aspect of his repellent rule. Since seizing power in a bloody coup almost 13 years ago, the strongman has systematically crushed all opposition. He is a despot who considers democracy to be as bad as communism.

Gen. Pinochet not only refuses to negotiate, he has perfected the tools of torture as well as repression. The Esmeralda, once a floating detention center, has become a notorious symbol for human-rights groups because of the brutal tactics used on those imprisoned on it.

Gen. Pinochet has on occasion put on a more democratic face — particularly when he has most ardently sought aid from the United States. Some U.S. help has indeed been given his regime — Washington seems to think that the Chilean junta poses less of a threat to Latin America than the Nicaraguan Sandinistas, for example.

U.S. officials are aware of the repression — the Reagan administration last year pledged stepped-up efforts to "engage more seriously in the process" of moving the dictatorship toward democracy. What has happened since? How serious is Washington's purpose?

Mindful of what happened to brutal rulers in the Philippines and Haiti earlier this year, the United States should seize on the new and courageous Chilean protest to pressure Gen. Pinochet for immediate reform, starting with free congressional and municipal elections.

Otherwise, the repellent spirit of the Esmeralda can only spread in a land that has known no liberty for more than a decade.

San Francisco Chronicle
San Francisco, CA, July 15, 1986

SENATOR JESSE HELMS, the conservative Republican from North Carolina, does not run this country's foreign policy, much as he would like to. That, happily, is up to the president and the State Department. But the senator seemed determined to undercut this country course of action with his recent intemperate and thoughtless public statements from Chile.

Helms strongly criticized U.S. Ambassador Harry G. Barnes Jr. for having attended the funeral of a young Chilean from Washington, D.C., who was fatally burned during anti-government protests on the outskirts of Santiago. Helms accused the career Foreign Service officer of having "planted the American flag in the midst of a Communist activity," adding that if President Reagan had been there he would have sent Barnes home.

This was a case in which witnesses reported seeing soldiers pour something flammable on the young man and his companion and set them afire. The French ambassador attended the funeral, as did senior officials from the Spanish, Belgian and Italian embassies. Besides, Barnes' presence was authorized by the State Department and has been backed by the White House.

THERE IS ANGUISH and anger in the air of a Chile whose repressive leader, Augusto Pinochet, now says he expects to stay on until 1997. America needs all the expertise it can muster for the delicate diplomacy ahead. It would help immeasurably if Senator Helms could keep his mouth shut.

Edmonton Journal
Edmonton, Alta., July 4, 1986

The civil disobedience campaign by the Chilean labor and opposition coalition, Civic Assembly, has drawn the expected response from General Augusto Pinochet Ugarte's regime: arrests, crackdowns on opponents, censorship and other odious features of the police state.

Hopeless though the situation may seem, civil disobedience is ultimately a more effective protest than the violent bombs-and-bullets campaign favored by a minority of extremists.

Peaceful resistance to an unjust government gives the protesters moral power that armed rebels cannot claim. It lays a groundwork for democracy in the sense that it is not led by people whose authority is established by gunpoint.

Chile remains a totalitarian anomaly in a continent that is rediscovering democracy, but it may not take much to re-establish democratic government. The government of Dr. Salvador Allende Gossens, overthrown by Pinochet with U.S. help in September 1973, was the first elected Marxist government in the Western Hemisphere. Had it been allowed to stay in power, it may have followed the tradition of Marxist governments in India, which respect the rule of the ballot box and are voted in and out of office like any other party.

But the Chilean middle class was nervous of Allende's intentions to get more power for the presidency in the face of an unstable national assembly that could not produce an unassailable majority. At the same time, Allende's efforts to give Chile direct control of its own economy were opposed by international business interests.

Yet the cost of toppling Allende's government was a brutal civil war and one of the most repressive military dictatorships South America has seen.

With Pinochet firmly in control of the armed forces, any violent challenge to his government invites bloody retribution. That's why Civic Assembly's peaceful campaign is realistic.

But no mass protest can work in isolation. Chile's democrats need the world's help. Canada must consider diplomatic and political pressures to restore democracy to a once-proud land.

The Courier-Journal & TIMES
Lincoln, NE, July 15, 1986

SENATOR JESSE HELMS of North Carolina evidently sees himself as the last obstacle to a Communist takeover of the State Department.

During President Reagan's first term, Senator Helms fought doggedly to block the nominations of several ambassadors whom he suspected of being too liberal — even though those nominations were made by the most conservative President since Calvin Coolidge. Now the Senator has gone a very big and potentially dangerous step further by criticizing the U. S. ambassador to Chile — thereby giving aid and comfort to the ruthless regime of General Augusto Pinochet.

Ambassador Harry Barnes's offense was to attend the funeral of a 19-year-old resident of Washington, D. C., who was burned to death during recent anti-government protests in Santiago. Witnesses say the youth, a Chilean exile, was seized by uniformed men, doused with a liquid and set afire.

Quite properly, the U. S. government expressed serious concern about the incident and demanded a full investigation by Chilean authorities. Meanwhile, Elliott Abrams, assistant secretary of state for Inter-American Affairs, says the State Department was fully aware that Ambassador Barnes planned to attend the funeral, which was broken up by police using tear gas.

None of this deterred Senator Helms from going on the state-run television network in Chile Saturday to accuse Ambassador Barnes of "planting the American flag in the midst of Communist activity" by attending the funeral.

What Ambassador Barnes was actually trying to do, of course, was show U.S. concern over what has all the signs of being a political murder. Beyond that, the Ambassador has been carrying out Reagan administration policy in Chile, which calls for increasing U. S. pressure on General Pinochet in hopes of making an orderly transition to democracy.

If Senator Helms objects to that policy, he should direct his complaints to his fellow Republican in the White House. And if President Reagan objects to meddlesome lawmakers undermining U. S. diplomacy in Chile, he should direct *his* complaints to Senator Helms.

The News and Observer
Raleigh, NC, July 15, 1986

Senator Helms is giving aid and comfort to one of the most brutal dictatorships in the Western Hemisphere. In a disgraceful performance, Helms flew off to Chile, cast aspersions on the U.S. ambassador and put himself at odds with the policy of his own nation's government.

Since 1973, when the elected government of Salvador Allende, a Socialist, was overthrown, Chile has lived under a repressive military regime led by Gen. Augusto Pinochet. Opponents of the Pinochet government have been executed, jailed and tortured.

As if blind to its record, Helms has now blessed the Chilean dictatorship in an interview with a government-owned newspaper. "The U.S. ought to understand that Chile is one of two countries in the entire Latin American area that resists communism," he said. "Its transition to democracy is on an orderly course."

On the same day Helms spoke, Pinochet illustrated again his own disdain for free elections. The general said he planned to rule until 1997. The Chilean constitution, approved in a disputed plebiscite in 1980, provides for an election in 1989 in which voters have the choice merely of approving or disapproving a single candidate named by the military commanders. "This is going to continue beyond 1989," said Pinochet. "We are not going to hand over the government for the pure pleasure of it."

In an interview on the state-run television network, Helms accused U.S. Ambassador Harry G. Barnes Jr. of having "planted the American flag in the midst of a communist activity." What Barnes did was to show up at the funeral of Rodrigo Rojas, a Chilean native and resident of Washington, D.C. On a visit to his native land, the young man was burned to death. Eyewitnesses said that men in uniform had doused Rojas and a companion with a flammable substance.

The State Department swiftly put distance between the Reagan administration and the maverick senator. Spokesman Bernard Kalb said the U.S. government supported an impartial inquiry into Rojas' death, and he termed "completely false" the implication by Helms that Ambassador Barnes had encouraged the street violence that broke up the funeral procession

Moreover, Elliott Abrams, the Reagan appointee who is assistant secretary of state for inter-American affairs, also made clear that Helms spoke incorrectly when he said that, if President Reagan were in Chile, he'd send Barnes home. Abrams said that "the policy he (Barnes) is pursuing is the president's policy."

By standing so publicly on the side of an authoritarian regime, Helms disrupts his own government's efforts to foster democracy and human rights in Chile. Once again Helms' actions call into question his judgment on foreign policy and his own understanding of democracy and freedom.

Wisconsin State Journal
Madison, WI, July 15, 1986

To his political friends, Jesse Helms is an able advocate of right-wing conservatism; an idealogue who knows the right moves. To his enemies, he is a loose cannon, an obstructionist more than a maverick, who gets away with a lot.

But he is highly skilled at obstructionism, or "sending them a message." Helms has ably represented the state interests. And the North Carolinian who is not in even partial agreement with the senator on the issues might still conclude, as Vermont Royster has, that the Congress needs a few Helmses.

When Helms engages in foreign policy, holding up nominations or treaties, he is exercising his senatorial rights and playing his role of the great dissenter. This has infuriated the State Department but has produced some pluses. Helms forced needed debate on the Anglo-Irish extradition treaty, for example.

When Helms discovered there was corruption in Mexico, it was perhaps greater news to him than many. What the purpose of some of the senator's Mexico-baiting was, is unclear. But Helms pointed out that the list of his committee witnesses was balanced, and that many problems in Mexico and in Mexico-U.S. relations were flushed out. Helms is not Joseph R. McCarthy reincarnate. But he's getting closer. In recent days he has gone from maverick to wrecker.

The subject is Chile. Jesse Helms likes the dictator there: Augusto Pinochet. Helms says the general, who is one of the globe's great tyrants and worst abusers of human rights, helps stave off communism. His theory is that said authoritarianism can more easily be followed by democracy than could communism. His-

torical evidence, recent experience and sense refute the theory. All democratic emotions should belittle it. But this is Helmsian foreign policy, the policy of many on the right and sometimes of our government.

Now Jesse, in addition to articulating this theory and traveling to Chile to bear it witness, has intruded himself into a diplomatic affair.

A young Chilean man, Rodrigo Rojas de Negri, whose home was in Washington, D.C., was taken by police during an anti-Pinochet strike, doused with gasoline and burned to death. The government says the young man was an agitator and got what he deserved. The U.S. government was outraged. As an expression of this, U.S. Ambassador Harry G. Barnes attended the boy's Santiago funeral, a move approved in Washington.

A call was made for an impartial investigation, of which there is, of course, fat chance. The surprise was that Helms took *our* government, State Department and ambassador to task — while in Chile. The funeral was just "a communist activity," said the senator.

Assistant Secretary of State Elliot Abrams called the Helms attack "indefensible." Abrams pointed out that if Helms thought the gestures wrong he ought to have talked privately, and on our shores, with the president.

What was Jesse Helms trying to accomplish? What cause does he think justifies this breach of diplomatic propriety and common humanity? Helms-haters have created an image of a mean and irresponsible man. His disgraceful meddling in Chile makes it seem as if Jesse Helms wishes to live up to that image.

Minneapolis Star and Tribune
Minneapolis, MN, July 14, 1986

So sparkling were the fireworks of this country's Liberty Weekend that a grim flash elsewhere in the Americas was easy to miss. Early in July a torch flared briefly in Chile — a human torch named Rodrigo Rojas, burned to death by men in uniform. His murder is an ugly reminder that the Reagan administration too long looked away from the repression that makes Chile an exception in dominantly democratic South America.

U.S. officials in recent months have come to realize that quiet diplomacy has only encouraged Chile's Gen. Augusto Pinochet to hammer harder at his opponents. In doing so he has fomented increasing support for the most radical and violent opposition. An article in Foreign Policy magazine describes the problem Pinochet presents: "The longer he clings to power, the greater the threat of upheaval and the appeal of the far left become."

The soundness of that analysis was borne out this month when a 48-hour strike left six people dead and dozens wounded. Acts of violence by the military and police were reported, as were bombings of buses and power stations by guerrilla groups. Rojas became a victim at the start of the strike. A 19-year-old who had lived for a decade in the United States, the young exile was on his first visit as an adult to his homeland. Witnesses described the apprehension of Rojas and a companion, the beatings given them and, finally, their immolation. The Chilean army denied any responsibility. A judicial investigation has begun. We would not bet heavily on conclusive results.

But no one need prejudge the Rojas case to conclude that the Chilean government has a reprehensible record. Last year the Organization of American States reported a pattern of "deliberate and systematic" torture in Chile. Even the Reagan administration, which for years had said little about such matters in Chile, helped draft a U.N. resolution strongly critical of Pinochet.

Nor is there any doubt that Chileans want a return to representative government. Polls show a public yearning to return to civilian rule. And last August the leaders of 11 political parties representing 80 percent of the electorate reached a remarkable accord: remarkable in that it reconciled historic differences among the parties in order to unite them in a call for democratic government. But Pinochet shows no intention of resigning before elections scheduled for 1989, and evidently plans to ensure that he remains president thereafter.

The United States cannot impose democracy on Chile. But it can sustain and increase the volume of its protest; sponsorship of the U.N. resolution was a good precedent. And, except for direct humanitarian aid to the poor, it can sponsor cuts in loans from international organizations like the World Bank. The United States probably can do no more to help Chile. It should do no less.

U.S. Troops Aid Attack on Cocaine Targets in Bolivia

United States Administration officials July 15, 1986 said U.S. Army personnel and equipment had been sent to Bolivia to help in the war on drug traffickers. Six Black Hawk helicopters and some of the roughly 160 pilots, officers and support personnel to be involved in the operation had arrived in Santa Cruz July 14 from their U.S. Southern Command bases in Panama, the officials said. They would assist the Bolivian military in raids in the Beni region in north-central Bolivia, where a large part of the world's cocaine is produced. The helicopters, equipped with M-60 machine guns, would transport Bolivian troops to drug installations, according to the officials. A U.S. Drug Enforcement Administration officer would be aboard each helicopter. U.S. Army personnel would not be involved in the raids but would be permitted to return fire if shot at. The 60-day operation would be directed at 35 targets.

The U.S. had wanted to keep the operation secret until Bolivian troops could be trained, but news of the arrival in Santa Cruz of a U.S. C-5A transport plane carrying the U.S. troops and helicopters quickly appeared in the local press. The lead allowed drug traffickers time to flee, with their equipment and drugs. The raids, due to start July 16, had to be delayed because of "logistical problems," according to the Bolivian embassy in Washington, D.C.

Bolivian President Victor Paz Estenssoro reportedly had been prompted to request U.S. aid in part because of the growing political influence of drug traffickers, who had financed candidates for local and national office. In addition, drug abuse among Bolivian young people was increasing, and legitimate business operations were being threatened by the growth of illigitimate businesses to launder drug money.

The Bolivian operation was the first under an April 8 national directive approved by U.S. President Ronald Reagan. The directive described the international drug trade as a threat to U.S. security and permitted U.S. military personnel to aid American agencies in planning raids on narcotics traffickers, and equipping police forces and transporting them to the sites of the raids. Critics questioned the administration's assertion that the involvement of the military in law enforcement was not covered by the War Powers Act of 1973. Under the War Powers Resolution, the president has to consult Congress whenever U.S. troops are to be introduced into hostilities or "situations where imminent involvement in hostilities is clearly indicated by the circumstances."

The Washington Times

Washington, DC, July 21, 1986

Crack Bolivian anti-drug forces, aided by U.S. troops and helicopters, swooped down on a couple of ranches over the weekend amid much hoopla and press releasing. As it turns out, the raiders hit the wrong addresses, leaving the arrest count in this operation in the single digits, and the lowest of the single digits at that. There won't be many ballads written about this military escapade.

Bolivia, however, seems determined to cook up some ill will toward Washington, perhaps to cover its bungling. Jacobo Liebermann, closest adviser to President Victor Paz Estenssoro, says Bolivia wanted help "of a different nature, entirely run by Bolivians. But instead we got the invasion of Normandy."

This is a bold statement, suggesting that the U.S. is eager to send troops into Latin America with or without invitation. The truth is that billionaire drug pushers won't be beaten on the cheap and, as admitted by its own government, Bolivia is broke. "The operation was very closely coordinated over a period of months with President Paz and the government of Bolivia," says Elliott Abrams, assistant secretary of state for Inter-American Affairs. "The plans were joint plans, and had they disliked any part of the plan, we would have changed it."

The U.S. is obviously eager to take the war to the source. Together with Colombia, Peru, and Brazil, Bolivia is a wellspring of a cocaine empire that makes $100 billion in the United States alone. The cost in human life and productivity is immeasurable, therefore demanding Washington's best efforts.

This has primarily been a symbolic operation. Press releases eradicated the element of surprise, and now the Bolivian government has decided to engage in some Yankee-bashing, sounding the American invasion theme so dear to Daniel Ortega and bringing into question its commitment to fighting the cocaine lords. The earlier U.S. decision to withhold $7.2 million in economic aid until Bolivia reduced its huge coca crop was justified, and without a change in attitude in La Paz, Bolivia's "invaders" should hold onto their cash.

THE LINCOLN STAR

Lincoln, NE, July 18, 1986

The Bolivian government, with the aid of the U.S. Army, will again tackle its cocaine producers. The effort would be the economic equivalent of wiping out Nebraska's corn and wheat growers, so entrenched is the cultivation of coca leaves, used to produce cocaine, in Bolivia's economy.

But this is in keeping with Bolivian President Victor Paz Estenssoro's pledge when voted into office last year to crack down on cocaine trafficking and to eliminate government corruption. So the effort proceeds.

If nothing else, a 1983 law making U.S. aid contingent on efforts to curb drug exporting has held Paz Estenssoro's fingers to the fire. Cutting off the aid we send to Bolivia, of course, would not stop the drug traffic, but it would probably be the end of the current government.

Paz Estenssoro also pledged economic relief. Without foreign aid, the drug money rules. In recent news accounts, Paz Estenssoro expressed the well-founded fear that the growing power of what he called the drug Mafia could become a political force, even governing the country. One has only to look at the brazen actions of the drug ring in Colombia to know the truth in his fears. Bolivia's history of political instability would not hinder such a development, either.

WHILE ECONOMIC reform remains elusive, the "informal" economy of cocaine remains dominant.

Bolivia is largely dependent on the export of tin, which has suffered in the soft world market. Bolivians have seen their meager purchasing power more than cut in half since 1982. The country has suffered devastating bouts with inflation, despite a continual devaluing of the Bolivian peso. After the last devaluation in January, their peso stood at 2.17 million to one U.S. dollar. Bolivia's foreign debt stands at $4 billion.

The country is poor — the poorest in South America — and cocaine is a lucrative demand export.

Clearly, stopping the supply of cocaine abroad is as complex as reducing the demand at home.

PRESIDENT REAGAN has called drug trafficking a threat to national security. In an unusual move, he has authorized the use of U.S. military to enter a country — at Bolivia's request — for the sole purpose of providing assistance in raiding cocaine labs.

Now, other Latin American countries have voiced interest in a continental effort against the drug trade. The signals sound good.

But to emerge victorious is to wage war on many fronts: to face the economic reality of a poor country addicted to the drug trade for its survival; to face a layer of our own society willing to risk death for an hour's thrill.

To battle drugs is to battle poverty, disillusion, boredom, wealth and power. To ignore any aspect or concentrate on one aspect to the exclusion of others would assure defeat.

If we do not now address the poverty that makes a country dependent on coca, then it also means that next year at this time, our military will again be raiding the jungles of Bolivia.

THE SAGINAW NEWS

Saginaw, MI, July 20, 1986

Every president at least since Nixon has declared war on drugs. Rambo Ronald Reagan is the first to actually go to combat.

For once, few in Congress can complain about a presidential decision to send U.S. troops and helicopters into a Latin American country. The cocaine epidemic is, as Reagan said, a matter of national security. Hundreds of Americans are dying. Millions more are wasting their minds, lives and families.

It makes you wonder what happened to good old LSD and even heroin; at least most people recognized the perils inherent in those substances. The lure of cocaine, however, cuts across all age, class and income groups, evidently because it was touted as "safe." Well, Los Angeles County alone counted 118 cocaine-related deaths in 1985. More than 1,000 users required hospitalization.

"The drug epidemic is as dangerous, if not more so, than any of the terrorists we face," said Sen. Alfonse D'Amato, R-N.Y. Congressional testimony last week compared the spread of "crack," a highly potent, smokable form of cocaine, to a tidal wave.

While Congress was conducting hearings, Reagan got cracking to try to roll back the wave. At the request of the Bolivian government, he sent soldiers and choppers into that South American country, the source of half the cocaine reaching the U.S. The targets of the combined U.S. and Bolivian forces were the refineries which process raw coca leaves into a narcotic powder.

But this war is as much economic and social as military.

Some 50,000 Bolivian peasants subsist from 100,000 acres of coca leaves. The refining plants can be rebuilt as long as the growers keep producing raw material.

Meanwhile, Peru is an even larger source. Top officials in Mexico and Thailand, as well as Cuba and Nicaragua, are reportedly involved in the drug trade. In poverty-stricken Bolivia itself, cocaine is a $2 billion industry, operating with the collusion, bribed or voluntary, of high-level government officials.

The armed assaults can be useful as a holding action, to reduce the availability and raise the price of cocaine.

But the drug warriors should not confuse sources for causes. As long as there is demand, there will be supply. The roots of the problem are right here in the United States. And not not even the president can declare war on the human weakness of millions of Americans.

The anti-drug crusade will not succeed unless it works on at least two fronts.

Abroad, not just the cocaine refineries, but the fields, have to be eradicated; if Bolivia is truly serious about ridding itself of its own dependency, it must agree to go all the way, including finding substitute crops.

At home, young people, especially, have to be told bluntly that even if the first snort or puff doesn't kill them, it's the first step to a living death. Socially, drug use must be made the thing not to do.

Persuasion cannot be achieved at gunpoint. The process is necessarily slow. But America will not regain its mental health without rehabilitating its collective mind on drugs.

The Dallas Morning News

Dallas, TX, July 17, 1986

The decision by the United States to provide military support for drug raids in Bolivia serves notice that this nation intends to take strong steps to stem the flow of narcotics from South America.

The planned use of U.S. Army troops and helicopters in raids on Bolivia's primary cocaine-processing plants is an unusual move that already is causing debate in legal circles. Military personnel are not normally used for police-related activities.

But the unchecked stream of drugs from Bolivia and Colombia to the United States has indeed grown to become a national security issue. When the Bolivian government requested assistance in trying to battle the powerful drug traffickers who control that nation's economy, the Reagan administration had a public responsibility to accept.

It is important that U.S. troops assigned to this detail be kept out of any law enforcement activities during the raids. Bolivian authorities should take full responsibility for any fighting or apprehensions that occur. The role of U.S. military personnel should be limited to a backup capacity.

News reports of the planned raids may have been deemed necessary by federal officials, who knew the decision to assist the Bolivian government would be controversial. But the advanced warning has provided too much time for drug traffickers to be prepared.

As the spread of cocaine use continues throughout this country, federal authorities may be forced to take measures that never would have been considered a few years ago. Sending troops to Bolivia to assist in stamping out cocaine-processing plants was a difficult decision — but it was the right one.

ST. LOUIS POST-DISPATCH

St. Louis, MO, July 17, 1986

President Reagan's decision to send some U.S. troops to help Bolivian forces make cocaine raids is hardly on the scale of previous administration searches for a military solution. These would include sending Marines to Lebanon, conducting an attack on Libya, invading Grenada, using military advisers in El Salvador and flying Honduran forces to defense positions against Nicaraguans.

Against these ventures, most of which have cost American lives, how great are the risks involved for the 160 U.S. Army pilots and supporting personnel who are to lift Bolivian troops in raids against drug traffickers? Officials in Washington think the risks are slight; the U.S. soldiers, they say, will be allowed to fire only when fired upon. Unfortunately, they may be fired upon. Cocaine is big business in Bolivia, so big that a previous Bolivian military government was accused of involvement in it.

The administration insists that Bolivia asked for U.S. troops. But did the administration ask Bolivia to ask for them? Last month the State Department decided to withhold half of Bolivia's economic aid for the year because the Bolivians had not undertaken any significant coca eradication. The invitation to U.S. troops followed.

Moreover, President Reagan asserts that a military role in fighting the drug traffic is justified by a threat to national security. No one will deny that the drug trade is a major national concern, but it hardly fits the usual definition of a threat to the nation's security. The nation has, unfortunately, been living with drug trafficking for many years. While Bolivia or Peru may ship drugs here illegally, it is Americans who buy and use them illegally. Defense against drugs requires a home front.

The Reagan administration, even more than some of its predecessors, has expanded the concept of national security to justify the exercise of broad presidential authority. In the case of drugs, this has resulted in eroding traditions and laws separating the military from law enforcement, which is to say, smudging the distinction between military and civil law. The military itself has resisted being used as police.

There is also a question of the War Powers Resolution, which more and more looks like a dead letter. That 1973 act requires the president to consult with Congress whenever he introduces the armed forces into hostilities "or into situations where imminent involvement in hostilities is clearly indicated...." The administration says it briefed congressional committees but denies that the Bolivian operation falls under the War Powers Resolution.

Congress has not been bold in upholding the war powers law and it seems unlikely now to challenge the use of U.S. soldiers in Bolivia. But it could at least question whether their use serves any rational purpose. The last time the Bolivian army tried to raid drug centers, the drug traffickers were forewarned and fled. American officials say they wouldn't be surprised if the same thing happened again. Such an expedition hardly justifies another unusual expansion of executive power, much less any risk to American lives.

Seattle Post-Intelligencer

Seattle, WA, July 18, 1986

In answering Bolivia's cry for help in stopping cocaine production by sending U.S. military personnel and helicopters, the Reagan administration has taken a bold and necessary step to stem the flow of drugs into this country and to protect the Bolivian government from possible takeover by its powerful narcotics empire.

Bolivia, whose poverty level is second only to Haiti, produces about one-half of all the cocaine that reaches U.S. and European markets. Bolivian President Victor Paz Estenssoro says cocaine brings $600 million a year illegally into his country, compared to $500 million for all legal exports, and he fears for the future of his fragile democracy.

"If we do not address this problem decisively," Paz Estenssoro said recently, "the day could come when the economic power they (the drug producers) wield could result in their governing the country, including via democratic means."

Thus the dispatch of a U.S. Army troop and helicopter task force to Bolivia serves to meet a dual threat from the cocaine trade — a threat to the stability of the Bolivian government, as well as to the fabric of American society. It is hard to quarrel with President Reagan's declaration that the U.S. mission, code-named "Operation Blast Furnace," serves the interest of national security.

Previous U.S. efforts to prod Bolivia into halting its illegal exports of cocaine itself include 1982 legislation which prescribed reducing foreign aid money to those countries which fail to eradicate their coca crops. Late last month the State Department decided to withhold $7.2 million in such aid from Bolivia, because of lack of significant progress against the drug trade. Obviously, if the Bolivian government was capable of effective measures it would take them. But it is not and U.S. assistance has become essential.

The Bolivian problem is special and unique. We see no cause to fear that the U.S. mission will lead to an improper law-enforcement role for the U.S. military in the fight against narcotics, nor apparently does a majority of Congress where there is strong bipartisan support for the Bolivian operation.

TULSA WORLD

Tulsa, OK, July 18, 1986

U.S. ARMY troops and aircraft are being moved to Bolivia to help that country's drug agents in a campaign against dozens of jungle-based cocaine labs.

Since Bolivia produces about half the cocaine sold in the United States, this extraordinary step is welcome news, even if it does not make an immediate measurable dent in the dope trade.

It is good news because by accepting U.S. military help in the war against drug dealers, the Bolivian government has shown that it takes the drug problem seriously. For the Bolivians, this is no easy decision. Cocaine accounts for more national income than all other exports combined. In moving against the coke trade, President Victor Paz Estensoro is attacking not only criminal activity, but his country's biggest industry.

"If we do not address this problem decisively," said Paz Estensoro, "the day could come when the economic power the drug traffickers wield could result in their governing the country."

U.S. personnel will not take part directly in the raids and arrests, but will provide transportation and support. U.S. helicopters and transport planes can make a big difference in the jungle drug war. And the time has come to use every possible resource.

If the dope trade cannot be crippled, the result will be government by criminals not only in Bolivia, but in other impoverished Latin countries as well.

The Star-Ledger

Newark, NJ, July 20, 1986

The decision to use U. S. troops in foreign operations must not be taken lightly. But the assignment of American Army personnel and aircraft to assist the Bolivian armed forces ought not be looked upon as an instance of U. S. expansionism. Instead, it is evidence that we are putting our money—and our military might—where our mouth is.

For some years, we have been demanding that governments in nations where there is extensive drug trafficking put a stop to it. The response has been that the drug traffickers are so powerful that there is not enough firepower on hand to halt them.

So, when Bolivian military officials began raiding the major cocaine traffic that is conducted in the north-central section of their country, the Reagan Administration gave them some needed help, in the form of military personnel and helicopters. If we are serious about attacking the drug trade, it will be more and more necessary to go to the source, not wait until the drugs arrive on our streets.

Washington, DC, July 21, 1986

The action last week was a scene reminiscent of the Vietnam War: U.S. Army helicopters clattered over the jungle; heavily armed men ran to raid an enemy stronghold.

This time the jungle was not in Southeast Asia but in South America. The target was not the Viet Cong, but international drug smugglers. Our helicopters were not carrying GIs, but Bolivian commandos. It was the first time our military has been used to fight drugs in a foreign country.

Critics of this new tactic in the drug war are already mounting their own search-and-destroy missions.

They say it's wrong to send our troops to another nation, that it's a waste to declare war on drugs. They're hallucinating. It's a far greater waste to stand by and do nothing.

Think of the lives that killer cocaine has trashed. Think of Len Bias and the grief his family feels, as told in this newspaper today. That's the real tragedy, the real waste.

Bolivia is the second-poorest country in the Western Hemisphere. It has been trying, without success, to slow its flourishing cocaine trade. It exports $600 million worth of cocaine a year, more than its $500 million legal exports bring. It wanted to attack cocaine processing labs in remote jungles but had no way to transport troops. So Bolivia's president asked the USA for help.

Declaring that the flow of illegal drugs is a threat to the USA's security, President Reagan sent six Black Hawk helicopters and 160 soldiers. Almost all are support troops, needed to keep the ships flying.

The president did the right thing. This mission is not dramatically different from the support our military already gives civilian police here and in the Caribbean. Military planes have flown thousands of drug surveillance missions.

The careful guidelines are wise, too. Both the USA and Bolivia have emphasized that our men will do everything possible to avoid combat; they will only fire if fired upon.

But there must be limits on military drug missions. It would be foolish, as some suggest, to turn soldiers into full-time drug cops. That would erode the separation between civilian and military power and hurt national defense.

That's why our mission to Bolivia must be strictly limited — in time as well as scope. Our soldiers must avoid combat and leave as soon as the raids are over.

These raids were no surprise to the smugglers, so they haven't turned up much cocaine. But at least one large cocaine lab has been dismantled, and others are targeted.

Attacking the supply of illegal drugs is important, but it's just part of the answer. We must attack demand, too, with enforcement, education, and peer pressure. By now, it's obvious that using cocaine is no "victimless" crime.

To remember the Vietnam War, a group of veterans built a wall with 58,000 names on it. Maybe it's time we listed the names of all the victims illegal drugs have killed. How many names would there be? Would there be thousands? Hundreds of thousands?

If we could ask all of those victims what we should say about drugs, their answer would be just one word — No.

"I LOVE THE SMELL OF NAPALMED COCA PLANTS IN THE MORNING!"

The Providence Journal

Providence, RI, July 17, 1986

It is becoming increasingly clear that illicit drug use is not only producing personal tragedies, like the recent death of basketball star Len Bias, but also threatening to create a nationwide social disaster.

Last April, President Reagan underlined the gravity of the situation when he signed a directive declaring drug trafficking a national security threat that could warrant military responses. This week the administration escalated its battle against drugs by announcing that U.S. military personnel will be assisting an anti-drug operation in Bolivia. A C5-A transport plane, carrying six Black Hawk helicopters and a company of about 100 military pilots and support personnel, was sent to Bolivia on Monday. The American force, which will be under the supervision of agents of the U.S. Drug Enforcement Agency, will be used primarily to help ferry Bolivian personnel. The Americans are expected to be in Bolivia for about two months.

The administration's action seems to have been well designed to meet any serious objections. Next to Peru, Bolivia is the world's largest producer of coco leaf. The site of the planned operation, the Beni region in north-central Bolivia, contains that country's most extensive illegal oper-

ations involving the cultivation of the coco leaf and its processing into cocaine. Most Bolivian cocaine ultimately finds its way to the streets of the United States.

Nor is this a matter of the United States intruding where it is not wanted. On the contrary, the use of American military transport capabilities was explicitly requested by Bolivian president Victor Paz Estenssoro, who recognizes that the criminal conditions surrounding the drug trade — gang violence, corruption of public officials, tax evasion, etc. — pose a grave threat to the stability of that nation's democratic system. In fact, it seems only fair that we respond to Bolivia's request for such assistance since, by the terms of a 1982 Congressional enactment, the State Department was recently forced to put a halt to American economic aid to Bolivia in response to that nation's inability to make sufficient progress in stemming the drug trade.

While each operation's details differ, the general principle of using U.S. military personnel and equipment to assist in anti-drug operations in foreign countries is unusual but by no means unprecedented. In 1984, the American armed forces provided

communications support during a major drug raid in Colombia, and since last year a U.S. Air Force helicopter patrol has been stationed in the Bahamas to help that nation's anti-drug operations.

Of course, it is possible that Americans may be killed or injured in Bolivia. That has occurred to American troops stationed in the relatively calm nations of Western Europe; there is certainly no way to be sure it can't happen in the Bolivian situation. However, extensive precautions have been taken in the agreement between the American and Bolivian governments. American troops will be armed, but only for self defense. They are not to fire unless fired upon. The actual apprehension and arrest of drug traffickers will be carried out by the Bolivian officials.

The Reagan administration briefed key congressional committees before dispatching the American contingent to Bolivia. Congress should continue to keep a watchful eye on this operation. However, it should do so only in the interests of suggesting ways of improving President Reagan's latest maneuver in a worldwide war that the United States cannot afford to lose.

Reputed Top Colombian Drug Trafficker Extradited to U.S.

Colombian police and military personnel February 4, 1987 captured a reputed leader of the world's largest drug trafficking ring and immediately extradited him to the United States. The trafficker, billionaire Carlos Enrique Lehder Rivas, 37, considered one of the world's most violent and successful drug traffickers and had long been sought by the U.S. Lehder and 14 bodyguards were captured in a predawn raid at a mansion in the Rionegro area near Medelin after a brief exchange of gunfire. Lehder was flown later that day to Tampa, Florida, arriving amid heavy security early Feb. 5. He appeared the same day in U.S. District Court in Tampa on drug-trafficking charges. Lehder was wanted in Jacksonville, Fla. in connection with a 1981 indictment charging him with importing 3,000 kilograms of cocaine. An August 1986 indictment returned in U.S. District Court in Miami charged him with a further 13 counts of drug smuggling and racketeering. Lehder became the 10th Colombian national and the 14th person overall to be extradited to the U.S. under a 1979 extradition treaty signed with Colombia. An order for his extradition to the U.S. had been signed in 1984.

Lehder was said to have begun his trafficking career selling marijuana in New York. In time he became a leader of the so-called Medilin Cartel, which was said to be responsible for 80% of the cocaine entering the U.S. In the late 1970s, Lehder bought a Bahamian isalnd, which was reportedly used as a base for his drug-trafficking activities before moving his operations to Colombia in 1981. In 1982, Lehder, who was a former senator, reportedly formed the Latino Nacionel political party, which sought to end the U.S. extradition treaty. The Colombian was said to be a political theorist who admired Adolf Hitler and the political philosophy of Friedrich Nietzche. In a 1985 television interview, he had called cocaine Latin America's "atom bomb," capable of destroying the U.S. He called on army officers and leftist revolutionaries to join the "cocaine bonanza," which he described as an "arm of the struggle against America" and the "Achilles heel of American imperialism."

U.S. Drug Enforcement Administration (DEA) chief John C. Lawn Feb. 5 said security at DEA offices worldwide had been intensified after Lehder's arrest. In 1985, Lehder had offered a payment of $350,000 to anyone who killed or captured the DEA chief and had also issued death threats against other law enforcement officials. He reportedly had threatened that if arrested, he would kill a judge a week until he was freed.

LEXINGTON HERALD-LEADER
Lexington, KY
February 8, 1987

The United States has managed, with the help of Colombian president Virgilio Barco Vargas, to extradite the man federal officials think is one of the world's biggest drug traffickers, a king of cocaine. What's important now is that Colombia be encouraged to stand firm with the United States in rounding up the rest of Colombia's cocaine royalty.

Carlos Lehder Rivas, a political disciple of Adolf Hitler, makes a fine trophy for the U.S. Justice Department and Drug Enforcement Administration: Serving up an alleged top dog in the world cocaine trade will stress to those who would follow in Lehder's footsteps that the United States and Colombia are serious about their drug-busting. But even more important is that Lehder can provide information about his friends in the drug business. Without a comprehensive, well-informed effort to rout the Colombian drug trade, it would be all too simple for another cocaine distributor to fill the gap left by Lehder.

Rounding up such men is not a tidy or safe business. Already death threats have apparently been made against law enforcement officials in connection with Lehder's capture. There are rumors that Lehder threatened to kill a federal judge a week if arrested. The DEA is tightening security at its field offices in response to the Lehder arrest.

With luck and the continued cooperation of Colombia, the arrest of Lehder will serve as a prelude to the arrest of Colombia's other top three drug dealers. Leon Kellner, the U.S. attorney in Miami, noted that the Lehder arrest means, "One down, three to go."

With continued help from Columbian officials, the other kingpins of the international cocaine trade may yet be brought to justice.

The Kansas City Times
Kansas City, MO, February 10, 1987

Colombia and the United States do not trade insults the way this country does with Mexico. There are no U.S. troops burning coca plantations in Colombia, as in Bolivia, where their presence has raised a domestic furor. America's misguided narcotrafficking policies in Bolivia and Mexico waste more time and money than results can justify. They mostly serve to scatter traffickers from parts of the country where enforcement assumes a high profile to parts where this presence is next to nil.

The arrest and extradition of Colombian Carlos Lehder Rivas, a reputed cocaine kingpin, is a good example of how a bilateral anti-drug policy should work. Colombian and American officials negotiate a way to net the big fish and rid their countries of a common plague. Negotiation would be ineffective were it not for conscience-minded officials who cannot be baited by traffickers' lavish offerings. That seems to be a key to Colombia's success.

Lehder is a very big fish. This former parking lot attendant with a fifth-grade education is believed to be one of the wealthiest drug barons in Colombia. He is a gangster with many low-life high-placed friends in the U.S.

Allowing Lehder to face the American judicial system was perhaps the bravest thing that a president could have done. Colombia President Virgilio Barco is now the most wanted man in Colombia because he has abided by legislation passed three years ago by Colombia's Conservative Party and which legalized deportation of drug fugitives to the U.S.

There are many who want Barco dead, just as they wished death for former President Betancur, who also netted big fish for the American courts. Betancur lives. The same cannot be said of his friends, relatives and those who assisted his anti-drug campaign. Elected officials, judges and journalists are among those hit by paid assassins or drug-financed leftist rebels. Since Lehder's extradition, more than a dozen Colombian notables, including Bogota Councilman Jorge Guzman, have been killed.

The Reagan administration must give Colombia more than a supply of funeral wreaths and kudos for its troubles. When Colombians "Just say 'No,'" they often sign their death warrants.

Los Angeles Times
Los Angeles, CA, February 2, 1987

Colombia is losing its war against illegal drug traffickers, and losing it badly. A poor but proud nation of 28 million people is literally under siege by a relative handful of powerful and violent criminals.

In a world plagued by illicit drugs, and the corruption and other social problems that they cause, no other nation has suffered the way Colombia has in recent years. Judges there are being murdered at the rate of one a month, according to a recent dispatch from Bogota by Times correspondent William Montalbano, and even a Supreme Court justice was killed by assassins. Three newspaper editors who crusaded against drug traffickers have been murdered, as have several top police officials —including one sitting attorney general. Even a former attorney general who was given an ambassadorial post behind the Iron Curtain to help protect him from restribution was tracked down in Hungary and killed by a hired gunman. And those are only the most extreme examples of the arrogant lawlessness of the Colombian drug gangs.

So rich and powerful have Colombia's drug lords become (they control an estimated 80% of the cocaine sold in the United States) that they have even begun spending their ill-gotten gains to try to win support from Colombia's poor. They have built social centers, funded food programs and tried to run for public office, portraying themselves as modern-day Robin Hoods. Some have gone so far as to suggest that they might repatriate the money that they have hidden in foreign banks to help bolster the Colombian economy—if the government of President Virgilio Barco lets up on the legal pressure that it has put on them.

To their credit, Barco and many other honest Colombian officials have resisted all efforts by the drug lords to intimidate them or to seduce them with the fantastic wealth that their filthy trade produces. Last month, in a particularly courageous act, Barco signed into law a new extradition treaty with the United States under which any arrested drug kingpins can be sent to this country for trial. It is the legal system in the United States, still largely beyond their corrupt and violent reach, that the Colombian drug lords fear most.

But the Colombians will not win their war on drugs by themselves. They need more help than they are getting from their allies, especially the United States. How sad and ironic that, as Colombia's president was exposing himself to physical danger by signing an extradition treaty with the United States, President Reagan was submitting to Congress a budget that would reduce the Administration's spending on drug-education and drug-eradication programs.

It should come as no surprise that, as in Mexico and Peru, prominent Colombian politicians are starting to ask why their nation should bear the pain of the drug war when the rich nation that consumes most of those illegal drugs is not doing enough to control the problem within its own borders. Until the United States is willing to do more to fight the war on drugs in this country, such as spending more to educate potential consumers about the dangers of drug use and to help police crack down on drug traffickers here, smaller and poorer nations like Colombia will fight a bloody but losing battle against the brutal drug kingpins of this world.

The Virginian-Pilot
Norfolk, VA
February 10, 1987

The capture in Colombia and extradition to the United States of a man alleged to be among the world's biggest, richest and most vicious cocaine tycoons represents a major victory on a strategically important front in the war on drugs. Carlos Lehder Rivas, 37, former Colombian senator, admirer of Adolf Hitler and reputed billionaire kingpin of 80 percent of the U.S. cocaine trade, now sits in a Florida jail, awaiting federal prosecution on multiple counts of drug smuggling and racketeering. If convicted, he could be sentenced to life in prison.

Mr. Lehder's *modus operandi* makes him an especially choice war prize. When not combining their peculiar form of business and pleasure on Mr. Lehder's privately owned island in the Bahamas or at his estate in the Colombian resort city of Medellin, Mr. Lehder and his cohorts in the "Medellin cartel" — the OPEC of the drug trade — are busy intimidating and murdering Colombian government officials and private citizens who stand in their way.

Among those gunned down in the nation's streets since last July were a Colombian supreme court justice; a district-court judge who has ruled against Medellin traffickers; a police colonel who was head of the country's anti-narcotics unit, and two newspaper editors who opposed the cartel in print. The cartel's hired killers have roamed as far as Budapest, where a former Colombian justice minister was the target of an assassination attempt last month. Mr. Lehder also has placed bounties on the heads of top U.S. Drug Enforcement Administration officials.

Though Mr. Lehder is safely in custody, his countrymen remain at risk. Before his capture, Mr. Lehder warned that his minions would kill a judge a week until he is freed. The six-month-old government of drug-fighting President Virgilio Barco Vargas concedes that it is no match for the cocaine cartel's armed caravans.

Vice President George Bush, chairman of a federal anti-drug project, has sent a message to Colombian President Barco praising his courage. But words are not enough. Colombia deserves no less than Bolivia has received in its war on cocaine traffickers: U.S. military equipment, technicians and pilots last year assisted Bolivian officials in a major drug-eradication assault on cocaine fields and laboratories.

Such assistance has not yet saved Bolivia from narco-terrorists. Colombia cannot expect a quick blitz to victory, either. But of the Reagan administration's many fronts in its war on drugs, none has produced results so spectacular as the capture of Mr. Lehder.

Such advances may never vanquish foreign drug traffickers. But if Colombia seeks U.S. reinforcements, the Reagan administration should be prepared to shift resources from its overemphasized domestic drug-testing front to fight the war on drugs — and terrorism — at its source in places such as Colombia.

THE SACRAMENTO BEE
Sacramento, CA, February 7, 1987

Carlos Lehder, allegedly the biggest drug dealer in the world, is in U.S. custody at a secret location in Florida after being arrested in Colombia and quickly extradited. If he is convicted, it would be the first time a kingpin of one of the boldest and most violent outlaw organizations of modern times — one that's believed to control the flow of 80 percent of the cocaine and marijuana that reach American streets — has been brought to justice.

Yet Lehder's arrest, important as it is, also is cause for apprehension. Other big Colombian drug dealers remain at large and, in the violent and intimidating atmosphere that pervades Colombia, virtually a law unto themselves. They have made and kept threats to kill anyone who tried to shut down their operations: Two Colombian justice ministers, a supreme court justice, 20 judges, hundreds of policemen, a newspaper editor and two informants for the U.S. Drug Enforcement Administration are among the victims of the cocaine cartel's savagery. One Colombian official was even tracked down and murdered in Communist Hungary.

Paradoxically, the same thugs who now threaten to avenge Lehder's arrest may be the ones who turned him in because of the high profile he had assumed as a crackpot politician and admirer of Hitler who also supports some left-wing causes and describes illicit cocaine trafficking as an arm of "the struggle against America." Whether his fellow gangsters betrayed him or not, their threat to exact reprisals cannot be ignored, either in Colombia or in this country.

Colombian President Virgilio Barco has shown great courage in extraditing Lehder after his arrest last week in a shootout with police. U.S. officials must follow that example in prosecuting him and in standing firm against all attempts to thwart the course of justice by threats of reprisal. The joint Colombian-U.S. campaign against Colombian drug merchants has had little to show for the $70 million spent over five years. The arrest of Lehder thus is an important psychological breakthrough. Now it's vital to stand firm by refusing to let gangsters cow civilized society into backing down against this lawless threat.

The Washington Post

Washington, DC, February 9, 1987

IN THE WAR against drugs, Colombia has just set a very brave example. It arrested and extradited to the United States a man named Carlos Lehder Rivas, who is accused of being one of the great cocaine traffickers in his country. Drug dealers there have used their immense riches and their command of armed men to practice an arrogance unheard of in more fortunate places. Of the police, officials, judges, editors and others who have resisted their vast criminality, those they cannot buy they have sought to murder or intimidate, reaching out even to attack a conscientious justice minister who had been sent off for his safety as ambassador to Hungary.

Americans know the menace of drugs at home, but in such a country as Colombia, where the institutions of law enforcement and administration are weaker, the very integrity of the nation comes to be at stake. There is actually a proposal that the leading drug dealers, in exchange for a presumably friendly prosecution in Colombia, pay off the country's $13 billion foreign debt.

The extradition process in Colombia is infinitely delicate. It provides Colombians with a way to bring to justice and to send out of the country suspects who may be more dangerous when they are in official hands—because of the violence their thugs take to reclaim or avenge them—than when they are at large. Yet retaliation against those who take part in extradition is always a threat—see what happened to the ambassador in Hungary. There also seems to be a feeling, halfway between shame and nationalism, that makes Colombians hesitate to hand off these desperadoes to others, especially to the United States. The newly arrested Mr. Lehder had been known to characterize cocaine as a weapon against "American imperialism." He is only the first of the accused kingpins to be extradited. Florida has him now.

Cooperation in law enforcement with Colombia and other source countries is increasingly central to American drug policy. Colombians who look at the comparative costs to the two countries, however, can be forgiven for asking whether the United States yet does its full share. American diplomacy stresses the idea that drugs are a shared hemispheric concern; this is the basis for common action. This is so, but it is also so that many Latins see the United States, with its huge demand for drugs, as the principal cause of their terrible drug costs, including increasing rates of addiction among their young. The readiness of such a country as Colombia to take the risks of cracking down on the biggest traffickers deserves appreciation in this country—and matching seriousness.

The Miami Herald

Miami, FL, February 6, 1987

ONE DOWN, three to go." U.S. Attorney Leon Kellner applied these words to report the capture of drug lord Carlos Lehder Rivas, one of four leaders of the "Medellin Cartel." The Colombia-based organization is reputed to supply 80 percent of the cocaine consumed in the United States. Mr. Lehder was captured this week at a ranch near Medellin and immediately extradited to the United States, where he faces multiple drug-trafficking charges.

Only a few weeks ago the U.S.-Colombia extradition treaty was virtually nonexistent. A legal technicality — the document did not bear the actual signature of a Colombian president — had reduced the treaty to wet paper. Showing his commitment to the bitter anti-drug war, President Virgilio del Barco rescued the accord with his immediate signature.

Equal swiftness characterized the capture and extradition of Mr. Lehder. Colombian National Police moved fast on an informant's tip and made the arrest after a 15-minute gun battle. Once Mr. Lehder was under the custody of the Colombian government, President del Barco lost no time in handing him over to the U.S. Justice Department.

President del Barco and the Colombian police deserve praise for an excellent job done under strenuous and dangerous circumstances. The cooperation of American authorities is also to be commended. The U.S. Justice Department has been persistent in activating the extradition treaty. Also, Drug Enforcement Administration agents have stood behind Colombian agents in their difficult drug war.

Now it is up to U.S. authorities to carry this victory all the way. While Mr. Lehder is processed for trial, extreme security measures must be taken to avoid an escape attempt. This man counts his fortune in billions gleaned from street-corner drug sales, quite enough to buy his way out of most situations. Further, the U.S. Embassy in Bogotá should take special security measures, lest the cocaine king's vassals seek hostages or threaten other violence in pursuit of their boss's release.

It has taken a long time to bring Mr. Lehder in. Now the United States must keep him.

Miami, FL, February 13, 1987

THE CAPTURE of Carlos Lehder Rivas, one of four co-leaders of the Medellin cocaine cartel, brought justifiable exultation both here and in Colombia. One down, three to go? Yes — and no. For the cartel's reach is so broad, its ruthlessness so bestial, its illicit wealth so staggering that even this law-enforcement coup is unlikely to deter it much or for long.

That may sound pessimistic, but it isn't. It's simple realism.

Cocaine is a scourge. It's as deadly as the plague for Colombians who dare oppose it, as endemic as the sniffles among all strata of American society.

American demand drives the Colombian supply. American users lie, cheat, steal, and sacrifice family, career, and health to obtain cocaine. The Medellin Cartel viciously kills anyone — police officer, judge, cabinet minister, journalist — who attempts to loosen its pernicious grip on Colombian life.

So yes, it is exhilarating to have one of the Medellin Cartel's principals at last in the embrace of the American justice system. Yet whatever the result of Mr. Lehder's trial on multiple cocaine-trafficking charges, it will lessen neither the demand at South Florida's squalid "crack" houses nor the cartel's resolve to fill the demand.

Mr. Lehder's arrest is significant in another respect that could be — pray that it is — both telling and enduring. It came scant days before The Herald began to publish an exhaustive investigative report on the cartel on Sunday.

That was indeed a serendipitous confluence of events. It prompted the two national newspapers, El Tiempo and El Espectador, and the five regional newspapers in Colombia to request permission to reprint simultaneously the entire series — text, photos, charts, everything. Request promptly granted.

That request took great courage, because the cartel reputedly has assassinated 15 Colombian journalists since 1984 — most recently Guillermo Cano, editor of El Espectador, last Dec. 17. These newspapers' presentation en masse of The Herald's wealth of information, supplemented with their own reporting on the cartel, will blanket Colombia with facts on the menace emanating from Medellin.

Thus Mr. Lehder's arrest already has galvanized the Colombian press. Perhaps that effect will suffuse itself throughout Colombia and create nationwide revulsion against the cartel. Revulsion — against suppliers in Colombia, against cocaine use in America — is the only true antidote to this scourge.

The Seattle Times

Seattle, WA, February 6, 1987

THE capture of cocaine king Carlos Lehder Rivas in a shootout at one of his luxurious Colombian hideouts and his immediate extradition to the United States provide a deeply satisfying example of the kind of cooperation this country has long sought with Latin American authorities in the war on illegal narcotics.

That sort of cooperation has often been hard to come by. Latin governments at times have taken the attitude that the drug problem is strictly a U.S. concern. Some Latin authorities have been bought off or scared off by the powerful drug racketeers, who can offer fortunes in bribes and do not hesitate to use assassination and torture as tools of intimidation.

Nowhere has the power of the narcotics barons been more brazenly on display than in Colombia, whose most lucrative export is not to be found among international-trade statistics, because it happens to be cocaine.

Former President Belisario Betancur showed great courage in signing Lehder's extradition order in May 1984. Lehder, described by U.S. officials as "the most violent of the Medellin Cartel," has thumbed his nose at U.S. and Colombian justice. The Medellin Cartel, a group of billionaire drug lords, is believed responsible for processing, shipping and distributing more than 80 percent of the cocaine consumed in the United States.

During the past year it appeared that Colombia had backed away from Betancur's resolve. But the killing of a fearless anti-racketeering editor, Guillermo Cano, last Nov. 17 prompted Colombia's current president, Virgilio Barco Vargas, to open a new offensive against the cocaine kings. The result was the capture of Lehder and 15 bodyguards.

Lehder is indeed a big prize. But final victory in the war on the international illegal drug trade will never be achieved as long as North American users continue to show contempt for the law and their own physical well-being.

The Saginaw News

Saginaw, MI, February 11, 1987

The arrest and extradition of alleged Colombian drug kingpin Carlos Lehder Rivas is extraordinary, as columnist Georgie Anne Geyer explains in her commentary today. Her fear — and ours — is that, for quite different reasons, this reputed controller of 75 percent of the cocaine traffic may escape justice in the United States as he has in Colombia.

Consider that drug dealers have tried to make a deal with the Colombian government: In exchange for lenient legal treatment, they would pay off the entire $13 billion foreign debt.

The drug trade is that lucrative. It is that dangerous. The dealers, and not only in Colombia, threaten to take over the country. Whom they cannot bribe, they kill.

Colombia's lightning transfer of Lehder to answer a U.S. indictment was a desperate, courageous bid for both self-preservation and self-respect. Its legitimate institutions are in jeopardy. No modern nation truly wishes to live off the suffering of others.

But now the American system of justice is under scrutiny, not because it is being bought off, but because of its traditional regard for the niceties of proper procedure. Already one attorney has questioned the manner in which Lehder was extradited.

That respect for the rights of the accused is a matter of pride in a civilized society. But Lehder, by all accounts, thinks and acts by other rules: He recognizes none that apply to him. How does society handle such a man?

Very carefully. Marshals ringed the Florida courtroom. Sharpshooters were posted atop nearby buildings. And the judge denied bail pending the scheduled March 23 trial.

If he did not, there almost certainly would be no trial. To men with incomes of $300 million a year and up, what does bail mean?

The further danger is that life also means little. In Colombia, the drug cartel has murdered dozens of policemen, judges, even ministers — and, yes, the journalists who expose their activities. What is its influence in the U.S.? This case may tell who holds the true balance of power.

It needs to be said once more that Americans are not entirely innocent in this matter. This country's appetite for illicit drugs engorges the dealers and undermines neighboring nations.

But the Lehder case goes to the source of the problem, and to the heart of justice. The U.S. alleges that he is one of the greatest drug dealers in the world. "Prove it," says his lawyer. It will be a trial that will allow, in many ways, no room for error.

San Francisco Chronicle

San Fransisco, CA, February 9, 1987

WITH THE ARREST and extradition of billionaire Carlos Lehder, believed to be one of the world's biggest cocaine dealers, the government of Colombia seems at last to have seized the initiative against a widespread narcotics traffic that tears at the country's vitals.

Recently, those who spoke out and acted against the drug business — journalists, judges and prosecutors — were threatened and often murdered. Traffickers made good their appalling boast: "We can kill whom we want." Fear did its work and the drug dealers went about their trade with arrogant openness.

By seizing Lehder, Colombian authorities have taken one of the reputed leaders of the so-called Medellin cartel, which U.S. Justice Department officials say is responsible for 75 per cent of all cocaine smuggled into America.

In mid-January, every newspaper in Colombia published on its front page a declaration of principles. Coming after assassination of the respected editor of El Espectador, this stated that the country was in danger of falling under "complete control" of traffickers. The government, political parties and Colombian society were urged to unify behind effective action against the criminals.

COLOMBIAN OFFICIALS and the American community in that country naturally fear reprisals now that this big fish is behind bars in Florida. But it took courage to grab him, and it will take continued courage and perseverance to turn the tide in this desperately-important battle.

Argentine Rebellion Ends, But New Unrest Emerges

A rebellion triggered by an army officer who refused to appear before a civilian court to answer charges of human rights abuses ended peacefully April 19, 1987. However, a new revolt April 21 by a group of disgruntled army engineers spread alarm throughout Argentina. The second rebellion, in the northern province of Salta, was suppressed hours after it began. The earlier revolt, by middle-ranking officers occupying an army school at the Campo de Mayo base, ended April 19 after President Raul Alfonsin went to the base and persuaded the remaining 130 officers to surrender. A group of officers had taken over the school April 17 in support of Ernesto Guillermo Barreiro, an army major who was cashiered for refusing to appear before a civilian court on charges of human rights abuses in the 1970s. Barreiro had taken refuge at an army base in Cordoba but later fled.

President Alfonsin had ordered the 2nd Army Corps., stationed in Rosario, 200 miles to the northwest of the capital, to retake the Campo de Mayo base. However, by the time of the rebellion, most of the force of up to 2,000 men still had not reached the capital. Some observers attributed the delayed response to the unwillingness of middle-ranking officers to move against the rebels. Adolfo Gass claimed April 28 that Campo de Mayo had not yet been attacked because of resistance in the middle ranks of the army. According to some accounts, Alfonsin was obliged to intervene personally because of the resistance. Before leaving for Campo de Mayo, Alfonsin had addressed a cheering crowd of tens of thousands of people in the Plaza de Mayo, and spoke of the people's desire to live in democracy. After gaining the rebels' surrender, Alfonsin returned to tell the crowd that the rebellion was over and that those involved would be detained and "put to justice."

The rebels, most of them captains, apparently had said they were not seeking a coup and that they continued to recognize the authority of the president. Although Alfonsin denied having made any deals, the leader of the the Campo de Mayo rebels, Aldo Rico, spoke of an "agreement" made with the government that he said could mark the start of a process of national reconciliation. Throughout the rebellion, mobilization of popular support had been part of the government's strategy in confronting the insurgents. At the the height of the crisis, labor, business and political leaders and members of professional and other organizations April 19 had signed a Democratic Pact committing themselves to defending democracy. The pact also recognized distinct "levels of responsibility" in the military with regard to the abuses of the 1970s.

The Washington Post

Washington, DC, April 21, 1987

AS POLITICAL theater, the end of Argentina's brief military rebellion was superb. President Raul Alfonsin told the crowd in Buenos Aires to wait for him, as he took off in a helicopter to confront the rebels. Several hours later he returned to announce that they had surrendered.

But it was deadly serious theater. The size and fervor of the public demonstrations supporting Mr. Alfonsin suggest that if his nerve had failed, and if the rebels had actually attempted to take over the government, the country might well have slid toward civil war. As it has turned out, the display of allegiance both by civilian crowds and by the great majority of the military officers is likely to leave Argentina's new democracy stronger than before.

The reasons for the rebellion aren't hard to understand. The present elected government under Mr. Alfonsin is leading the country through an extraordinary process of cleansing and renewal—a prof und repudiation of the bloodstained military regime that collapsed in 1983. It's no surprise that some of the military officers bitterly resent the democratic government and have good reason to fear the courts.

Under the juntas some 9,000 people were illegally arrested and, usually after being tortured, were murdered by the state's security forces as the juntas went after their enemies, real and imagined. The government is prosecuting the people it considers responsible for those crimes. Two of the country's former military rulers are now serving life sentences, and the courts are working their way through the lists of charges against several hundred military and police officers of lower rank. The uprising began when one of them, Maj. Ernesto Barreiro, accused of having been a torturer at an interrogation center near Cordoba, fled from a court's summons and took refuge with a military unit that refused to hand him over. A day later the major went into hiding elsewhere and the resistance at Cordoba collapsed. Sympathizers meanwhile had seized a military school not far from Buenos Aires, the scene of their dramatic surrender to Mr. Alfonsin on Sunday.

Not all of the questions about these events have yet been answered. The army's chief of staff has resigned, and the reason isn't clear. Perhaps he was forced out because he couldn't control his officers. Or perhaps, less reassuringly, it might have been a concession to the rebels, who detested him. A good deal depends on the answers. But a dangerous crisis has passed, one that the Alfonsin government met with fortitude, skill and success.

THE DAILY HERALD

Biloxi, MS, April 22, 1987

Democratic rule is still precarious in Argentina, as in most of Latin America. But it has emerged stronger than before from a mutiny by discontented army officers, which President Raul Alfonsin succeeded in ending peacefully on Easter Sunday.

The crisis began when a civilian court summoned Maj. Ernesto Guillermo Barreiro, one of about 280 officers charged with violating human rights during the military rule that ended with Alfonsin's election in 1983. When Barreiro refused to appear, he was immediately dismissed from the army. Then some of his fellow officers gave him sanctuary at a base in western Argentina and defied orders to return to barracks.

The mutineers, who also took over an infantry school near Buenos Aires, objected to the use of civilian courts to try military personnel for kidnappings and murders committed during Argentina's campaign against terrorists and other opponents of the regime in the 1970s. They sought an amnesty for such crimes, claiming that it is unfair to punish middle-echelon officers for obeying orders from high command.

Two encouraging signs: First, the leaders of this mini-rebellion insisted they were not attempting a coup. Sincere or not, the fact they felt obliged to make such a declaration suggests the democratic spirit is stronger in Argentina than one might have guessed from the nation's turbulent history over the last half-century.

Second, Argentina's top military leaders — whatever their private feelings — publicly sided with the civilian government. So did party leaders from across the political spectrum and the peaceful crowds that gathered across the country, including several hundred thousand in the capital's Plaza de Mayo.

In a dramatic climax, Alfonsin took a helicopter to the infantry school to persuade the last of the mutineers to lay down their arms. Flying back to the Plaza de Mayo, he told the cheering crowd, "The house is in order, and there is no bloodshed! Go home and kiss your children and celebrate Easter in peace."

So this victory for democratic institutions is also a personal triumph for Argentina's democratic president. He deserves it.

The Record

Hackensack, NJ, April 22, 1987

In the barracks, the officers are restless. But in the main square, Argentina's first freely elected president in more than a decade is defiant. Before a cheering crowd of hundreds of thousands, he declares that the nation will no longer allow itself to be intimidated by rebellious military men. No longer will the government pay obeisance to the army. The people cheer again, and the president vows to deal with the rebels firmly. A short time later, the mutineers surrender. Democracy is victorious.

Or is it? In the United States, the dramatic confrontation between Argentine President Raul Alfonsin and a small group of rebellious army officers has been hailed as a triumph for popular democracy. On closer inspection, it appears to be something less. The mutineers gave in, but the army major whose threatened arrest for human-rights violations triggered the rebellion escaped moments earlier; sympathizers are believed to have him in hiding. Mr. Alfonsin has fired officers who took part in the uprising, but he also dismissed Army Chief of Staff Gen. Hector Rios Erenu and other top officers whom the rebels found objectionable. General Erenu's successor, meanwhile, is Gen. José D. Caridi, who human-rights organizations say may have assisted in the 1983 torture death of an army conscript. In the wake of the uprising, the government has also moved to limit the prosecution of junior officers for murder, torture, kidnappings, and the like committed during the so-called "dirty war" against Argentina's left in 1976-83.

The crisis has thus ended on an uncertain note. Democracy and civilian government have apparently pulled through for now, but Mr. Alfonsin's concessions could cost him dearly in the months ahead. As an Argentine economist told The Wall Street Journal: "If this leads to a series of barracks revolts, we are right back where we started — the most developed banana republic in Latin America."

Few countries have started out so high and fallen so low as Argentina. Sixty years ago it had a standard of living comparable to Australia or Canada; today its per-capita income is just slightly ahead of Mexico. In 1929 it accounted for 10 percent of global wheat production; today it accounts for about 2 percent. Proportional to its population, Argentina exports 25 percent less today than it did on the eve of the Great Depression.

The Depression, in which tariffs and other import barriers mushroomed throughout the globe, hit Argentina's export-oriented economy particularly hard. So did World War II. Nonetheless, Argentina's problems have been chiefly of its own making. Juan Peron, who set the tone for a whole generation of Third World misleaders, took power in 1946 and in a few short years managed to squander the national treasury on a host of ill-conceived public works. A fervent admirer of Mussolini, he also suppressed civil liberties and fostered a grotesque political cult around his wife, the famous "Evita." By the time he went into exile in 1955, Peron denuded Argentina not only financially, but culturally and politically as well.

Three decades later, Argentina is still living in Peron's shadow. It has vast natural resources and a well-educated population. Raul Alfonsin is struggling to free his country from his predecessors' legacy of authoritarianism and military rule. But as recent events show, victory is not yet within his grasp.

Los Angeles Times

Los Angeles, CA, April 21, 1987

Argentina's President Raul Alfonsin took a giant step over the weekend toward easing his countrymen's fear of military coups when he faced down a rebellion by junior officers who objected to his human-rights policies.

Argentina has suffered through six such coups since 1930, the most recent and bloodiest in 1976. It looked as though yet another civilian government might fall when officers at two military bases last week said that they would fight rather than allow civilian authorities to judge military men suspected of human-rights violations. The rebellion began when a major, accused of having exceeded his authority during the so-called "dirty war" against subversion in the late 1970s, refused to face trial. Fleeing to the provincial city of Cordoba, a center of anti-government activity in the past, he was joined by sympathetic colleagues. A day later, officers at another base near Buenos Aires joined the brewing rebellion.

Alfonsin called on the rebels to surrender, and ordered loyal troops into positions from which they subdued the plotters. More important, Alfonsin rallied behind him the support of virtually every important sector of Argentine society and politics —even opposition parties that often attack him. On the fourth day of the crisis, hundreds of thousands of Argentines marched in the streets of Buenos Aires and other cities, cheering not just Alfonsin but civilian government and democracy as well.

Those street demonstrations, more than anything else, made it clear to the rebellious officers that this time the civilians would not be easily pushed aside. Alfonsin delivered the coup de grace on Easter Sunday when, at no small personal risk, he entered a rebel stronghold and persuaded the officers to give up.

It was a splendid display of patience and courage by a man who is the antithesis of the political strongmen who have often dominated politics in Argentina and elsewhere in Latin America. Alfonsin is no decorated hero, but a portly grandfather with an bland and unimposing presence. He also is a tenacious democrat, however, who insists that Argentina must exorcise the ghosts of an often-bloody past that includes not just the "dirty war" but also the dictatorships of Juan Peron and others in uniform if it is to live up to democratic ideals. Alfonsin showed on Sunday how inspiring even a bloodless stand for the rule of law can be. He set a magnificent precedent that may well be a turning point for democracy and civilian government in a country that has known too little of either for more than half a century.

The Burlington Free Press

*Burlington, VT
April 23, 1987*

Democracy in Argentina isn't out of the woods yet. The military wolf pack that has hounded down half a dozen governments still bays in the underbrush.

Nevertheless, weekend events in Buenos Aires provide grounds for hope that, this time, a freely elected government will survive.

President Raul Alfonsin provided riveting leadership in overbearing a rebellion of middle-level army officers. Opposition leaders and trade unions that have been critical of his government rallied in support.

Most importantly, Argentinians by the hundreds of thousands flocked to the streets on Easter day, apparently ready to face down the military by sheer weight of numbers.

That inspirational sight shouldn't obscure the tests that still face the Alfonsin government.

In ending the rebellion, Alfonsin did not fully address its cause: the refusal of the military to accept the authority of civilian courts to try officers for atrocious human-rights abuses during the so-called "dirty war" of the late 1970s.

The middle-level officers argue they shouldn't be held responsible for carrying out orders. They want amnesty.

But at least part of the current public enthusiasm for democracy is the result of revulsion at past military excesses, including torture, kidnapping and the "disappearance" of at least 9,000 Argentinians. Argentinians want to clean house.

To keep the military under control, the Alfonsin government will likely have to acknowledge different levels of responsibility for human-rights abuses — thus allowing some officers to avoid trial — and then sell that arrangement to the public.

Beyond the challenge of exerting civilian control over a powerful military, Argentina faces economic problems that will put dangerous stress on a democratic government in a country without a strong tradition of democracy.

There is little enough that outsiders can do, but what the United States can provide in terms of economic and moral support of the Alfonsin government should be offered unstintingly.

THE INDIANAPOLIS STAR

Indianapolis, IN, April 23, 1987

Argentine President Raul Alfonsin has retired the army chief of staff and eight other generals. The purge of top army ranks followed by one day his act of cool determination and courage in personally entering a military base held by rebel officers and obtaining their surrender.

Afterwards he told 100,000 citizens gathered outside the presidential mansion, "These rebellious men have changed their attitude. As is fitting they will be detained and submitted to justice."

Argentina has lived in a climate of tension since April 15 when long simmering animosity flared between the armed forces and the government over trials for officers accused of human rights crimes during the 1976-83 military dicatorship.

First a renegade major, who refused to honor a court order to testify about abuses at a detention center, was cashiered and ordered arrested. He took refuge at a barracks in Cordoba and persuaded other officers to join him. Although the situation seemed resolved when he fled the base on April 17, other officers took up the cause and seized the base under leadership of Lt. Col. Aldo Rivo, a Falkland Islands war veteran.

Declaring that democracy means not only liberty but also "submitting absolutely and without exception to the juridical system," Alfonsin said he would refuse to negotiate with the rebels but details of what quid pro quo, if any, the surrender entailed are not known.

Tens of thousands of citizens, including many of Alfonsin's political opponents, took to the streets during the crisis to support his insistence that law applies to all — the armed forces not excepted.

It was Alfonsin's finest hour in his three and one-third years as the elected chief executive of a nation with a long history of military intervention in government.

The Argentine victory of civilian rule over military bullying followed a similar victory in Peru two weeks previously. Peruvian President Alan Garcia dismissed the head of the air force after the officer continued to lead military opposition against a parliament-approved plan to restructure the military system.

The plan places the joint chiefs of staff under a single defense minister similar to the U.S. secretary of defense.

Garcia lined up armed forces loyal to the democracy and made the firing stick. Further, last week he offered Alfonsin military aid in the event it was needed to bolster Argentina's democracy against the rebel officers.

To its credit the Reagan administration made clear that it backed Alfonsin totally in the crisis.

In many Latin American nations, the armed forces have often been "the political party with guns," rather the defender of an elected government.

Alfonsin and Garcia were chosen in free, honest elections. Members of the military who don't like the administrations have the same right as other citizens — to vote against them at the next elections. Ballots, not bullets!

MILWAUKEE SENTINEL

Milwaukee, WI, April 23, 1987

Argentine President Raul Alfonsin brought a peaceful end to two military mutinies which broke out in his country last week and a third ended without incident Tuesday. But did the president compromise on his resolve to deal harshly with human-rights abuses that occurred under the military regime which he succeeded?

"The men in the uprising have backed down . . . they will be detained and put to justice," he told a cheering crowd of 200,000 on his return to Buenos Aires Monday following a personal appeal to rebellious troops at an army infantry school.

But part of the bargain was the apparent forced resignation of his army chief, Gen. Hector Rios Erenu, whose ouster had been demanded by the mutineers because he had insisted that officers accused of human-rights abuses be tried in civilian courts. It was also Erenu who couldn't get loyalist troops to march on the mutineers.

And Erenu's replacement, Gen. Jose D. Caridi, has been included in a list of military officers identified by human-rights groups as suspects in the so-called "dirty war" on leftists under military regimes that ruled Argentina from 1976 to 1983.

There is some hint here that it is Alfonsin who is backing down. And, possibly, pleas of middle-level officers that they were only following orders during the repression may have some credence. But this requires some sorting out of those who were truly left without a choice.

It is estimated that between 9,000 and 30,000 Argentines simply vanished during the military rule and the 40-month-old democracy will lose its credibility unless all those responsible are called to account. Currently, 250 military men face charges on human-rights abuses.

In the words of Adolfo Perez Esquivel, who won the 1980 Nobel Peace Prize for his work in human rights, yielding to rebel demands would court "future suicide." Alfonsin should squelch such dire predictions by reasserting civilian control over the government and proceeding swiftly with the human rights trials.

BUFFALO EVENING NEWS

Buffalo, NY, April 21, 1987

NEWS OF the military revolt in Argentina last week sounded like a return to the dismal cycle of dictatorship and military rule that has plagued the country for generations.

But this time, skillful leadership by President Raul Alfonsin and massive support for the nation's new democratic institutions ensured that the cycle would not be repeated.

Argentina has many problems, but its democracy has shown itself to be hardy and well established in the 3½ years since Alfonsin was elected in the wake of the military disaster in the Falkland Islands war.

One of the president's first acts was to bring to justice the military leaders responsible for the reign of terror that took at least 9,000 lives of political opponents in the previous eight years of dictatorship.

Remarkably, the trials sent a former president and other top leaders to prison, and the investigation into human rights abuses is continuing.

Last week's revolt broke out over the refusal of an officer to answer a summons to testify in court. Fewer than 300 troops were involved in the mutiny, but the atmosphere was tense for a time as one group of rebels held off 2,000 troops outside a military base.

But the rebellion did not spread throughout the armed forces as similar efforts have in the past. Meanwhile, Alfonsin received the support of the political opposition, labor, business and other groups in the crisis. Before flying to talk with the rebels, he was hailed by a massive crowd of 400,000 in Buenos Aires.

The outpouring of popular support was reminiscent of the groundswell that swept President Corazon Aquino into power in the Philippines last year.

Alfonsin has tried to take a reasonable course on the trials of human rights violators, bringing the guilty to justice but showing flexibility regarding low-ranking personnel. The rebellious officers were seeking a general amnesty. They are now in jail.

There was an air of celebration in the country with the suppression of the military threat. Argentina has suffered through generations of bad government by military leaders and the charismatic Juan Peron who dominated political life for four decades, including a period after his death in 1974. Economic ruin, repression and political instability are the legacy of those years.

Today, however, from the wisdom gained in those grim years and in response to the democratic trend on the entire continent, Argentina appears to have found itself. Military leaders have seized power six times in the past 57 years, but perhaps for the last time.

An opposition political leader declared after the rebellion was defeated: "There will never be another coup in Argentina." If so, this potentially wealthy country could move toward a position of economic and diplomatic leadership among Latin nations.

"THE CIVILIANS ARE GETTING OUT OF HAND"

ARGENTINE MILITARY REVOLT

PHILIPPINE COUP ATTEMPT

©1987 HERBLOCK

Houston Chronicle

Houston, TX, April 21, 1987

The strength and resiliency of democracy in Argentina and the Philippines got another test over the weekend, and in both instances the results were encouraging.

In both countries, military groups attempted to use force to upset the orderly process of democracy. In both, the government quickly responded and the mutineers gained no civilian support.

The mutiny in Argentina had the potential for causing the government serious trouble, and not many years ago likely would have. In nearly 60 years the military has overturned civilian government six times, the last military dictatorship lasting nearly a decade. The mutiny grew out of that military rule, with the officers involved trying to force an end to the trials of military men in civilian courts for atrocities committed while the military was in power.

But the mutiny, involving two military bases, ended without a shot fired. President Raul Alfonsin personally negotiated with the officers, and a cheering crowd of several hundred thousand, waving banners supporting democracy, greeted Alfonsin when he returned with the good news that the mutiny had ended.

The weekend mutiny in the Philippines was an attempt by 13 soldiers to free more than 100 soldiers jailed at army headquarters after a January coup attempt. The incident lasted only eight hours. The military acted quickly and decisively, and the mutineers received no support beyond that of some of the prisoners they were trying to free. This bodes well for Mrs. Corazon Aquino, who has been diligently working to rebuild democracy and restore a sensible civilian-military balance in the Philippines.

The failed mutiny in the Philippines also provides a message to the communist insurgents, that they must contend with a democracy that is growing stronger. The military at last is seriously pursuing these insurgents, who derided Mrs. Aquino's attempts at negotiation.

The democracy of Argentina and the Philippines will be tested further. Both have serious problems to overcome. But the weekend victories indicate the campaign is moving in the right direction.

ALBUQUERQUE JOURNAL

Albuquerque, NM, April 23, 1987

Two springs ago, Argentine President Raúl Alfonsín came to Albuquerque to accept an honorary degree from the University of New Mexico.

In a stirring speech to an audience that included some 100 Argentine immigrants, Alfonsín implored New Mexicans to be advocates for his troubled country. "We need to be free, once and for all," he said.

Alfonsin has been fighting for that freedom ever since. Over the past week, his 3 ½-year-old democratic government weathered its most serious test. Three army revolts ended peacefully, thanks to Alfonsín's charismatic leadership and the widespread support of his countrymen.

Alfonsín's 1983 election brought an end to military rule. But not since 1930 has a civilian president completed his term.

The recent uprisings were sparked by the Argentine president's pledge to bring military leaders to trial for human rights abuses committed during the "dirty war" against suspected leftists in the mid-1970s. Thousands of Argentines were kidnapped, tortured and murdered then. Many simply disappeared, never to be seen again.

Several former *junta* leaders already have been tried and convicted. The week of uprisings came about when mid- and low-level officers rebelled at having to face trial for their roles in the dirty war killings. They were, they contend, just following orders.

Alfonsín now must keep the mighty military in check while living up to his precedent-setting promise to bring those responsible for the killings to justice. It takes a courageous and committed leader to tread that narrow path.

We in New Mexico had a glimpse of Alfonsín's fortitude two years ago. Then, his speech brought the Albuquerque audience to tears and to its feet.

In Argentina last week, Alfonsín — and the democratic ideals he represents — brought hundreds of thousands of citizens out to rally in his support and plead with military leaders to abandon their mutiny.

We New Mexicans musn't forget Alfonsín's call to be advocates for Argentina. Latin America's brightest hopes ride on this government that is neither totalitarian nor authoritarian, but democratic and free.

The Seattle Times

Seattle, WA, April 21, 1987

THE administration in Washington points with justifiable satisfaction to the flowering of democracy in South America and the Philippines during the Reagan years. The depth of the roots is open to question, however.

The ease with which democratic governments in Buenos Aires and Manila snuffed out military rebellions over the past few days bolsters confidence.

Argentine President Raul Alfonsin flew to an army base over the weekend and talked dozens of officers into peacefully ending a three-day mutiny. There remains some speculation over whether Alfonsin made any concessions to the rebels, who were protesting the trials of officers charged with violating human rights during military rule that ended in 1983.

Philippine President Corazon Aquino had little trouble putting down the latest pocket revolt by disgruntled soldiers loyal to former President Ferdinand Marcos. But Aquino's offers of peace and reconciliation still are met by what she calls "bloody and insolent rejections by the left and the right."

One thing military insurrectionists in both Argentina and the Philippines clearly lack is popular support.

Brazil Suspends Interest Payments

In what was widely perceived as a threat to the international financial system, the government of Brazil February 20, 1987 announced that it was unilaterally suspending payment of interest on debt to foreign commercial banks. The suspension aimed at protecting the nation's shrinking supply of hard currency reserves, which had fallen to $3.96 billion in January compared with $11 billion a year earlier. In a further move Feb. 24 that indicated to some observers a carefully planned program to change the terms for discussion of Latin America's $380 billion debt, Brazil ordered its commercial banks not to repay foreign banks that sought to recall short-term credits and deposits at Brazilian institutions. President Jose Sarney announced the payment suspension in a televised address to the nation. He said his government was not adopting an "attitude of confrontation" but explained that "for reasons of sovereignty and national security, our reserves have to be preserved." Sarney expressed the hope that upcoming negotiations with creditor banks would produce a "definitive and lasting solution" to the nation's debt problem.

Some $67 billion in medium- and long-term credit was affected by the suspension. Short-term commercial debt and all debts to governments and international institutions were not affected. With a foreign debt of some $108 billion, Brazil was the largest debtor nation in the developing world. About $81 billion of the total debt was owed to private commercial banks, including $24 billion owed to American banks. Brazil's biggest United States creditor was Citicorp, which headed Brazil's bank advisory committee. If the suspension lasted longer than 90 days, U.S. banks would be required to set aside currency reserves to cover overdue payments, thereby hurting their quarterly profits. In each quarter, U.S. banks would usually receive about $500 million in interest payments from Brazil. Brazil normally made a total of some $1 billion a month in interest to more than 600 banks. In the wake of the suspension of interest payments, stocks of major U.S. banks tumbled.

The Honolulu Advertiser
Honolulu, HI
February 26, 1987

Brazil's decision to suspend indefinitely interest payments on its $108 billion foreign debt is an ominous reflection of the world financial system's continuing intractable problems.

Like many other debtor nations, Brazil has long since stopped paying back principal on its debts. But its new moratorium on payment of interest — Brazil's second in four years — again highlights the depth of many nations' financial woes.

What's frightening, yet by no means improbable, is that Brazil's crisis will trigger other bankrupt nations to suspend interest payments. If that happens, it would spur a crisis of confidence and trust in the U.S. and world financial communities.

Already, Argentina, which has $52 billion in foreign debt, is balking at paying interest unless banks lend it more money. Some suggest the Philippines might also suspend its payments.

It was only a matter of time before the world debt crisis again emerged in public. Now that it's back, and with a vengeance, there's a need for new agreement on steps to solve the problem.

From all indications, Treasury Secretary James Baker's 1985 plan for dealing with international debt problems is flawed. That initiative called for banks to offer $20 billion in new loans to debtor nations in return for their adoption of market-oriented economic policies.

Unfortunately, adoption of free-market policies is no guarantee of economic growth. And by offering new loans, many banks have exposed themselves further to dangers of default.

Part of Brazil's problem is political. By placing the burden on foreign bankers and governments, from whom it wants to extract concessions, President Jose Sarney avoids — for the time being — further belt-tightening by his nation's 130 million people.

Such a Band Aid solution merely avoids the inevitable. With inflation hovering around 20 percent a month and its trade in poor shape, Brazil is in need of comprehensive economic restructuring if it's to recover its economic zest.

THE  SUN

Baltimore, MD, February 25, 1987

In suspending payments on interest as well as principal on its $108 billion foreign debt, Brazil was quick to note it was asking neither cancellation of its obligations nor concessionary interest rates. Words like "default" and "moratorium" never appeared in government pronouncements, which stressed instead that Brasilia's negotiators would be forthcoming in seeking a new agreement with international banks.

So what's going on here? Nothing to celebrate, to be sure, but not quite the ultimate crisis doomsayers have predicted since the dismal Mexican August of 1982. Since the Third World debt problem emerged in all its staggering proportions, nations have discovered an interesting phenomenon. It's called interdependence. No one government — either debtor or creditor — can act with complete unilateral abandon for the simple reason that the consequences would be self-defeating.

While President Jose Sarney was disrespectful to the banking fraternity, and especially to the International Monetary Fund, his gestures were more for domestic than foreign consumption. As Brazil's first popularly elected leader in this generation, he needed a political lift to offset an economic downspin that threatens him and his fragile democracy. So Mr. Sarney pushed the buttons of Brazilian nationalism, stating that his country's well-being was not compatible with the current "massive outward transfer of resources."

His were tough measures. If they were to be enforced with impunity, the world would be witness to a sizable North-South power shift. But, in fact, Mr. Sarney was only moving a few key pieces in a gigantic chess game. He is in desperate need of new short-term credits from the very banks he is bearding. He therefore shares their desire to maintain the solvency necessary in big money centers to keep loans flowing.

Even though there is a certain confidence that the international financial system will muddle through, there are no grounds for complacency. The banks will wind up lending more money on more favorable terms that will increase Brazil's debt — a debt no one really believes will ever be repaid in full at stated interest rates.

For a while, this arrangement will preserve the fiction that there will be a good-faith effort to repay principal and interest. But truth eventually will overtake fiction unless both sides come up with more creative solutions. Instead of debt buildup that puts Third World countries on a treadmill, the emphasis somehow has to shift to measures that will spur trade and economic growth. What Brazil's challenge tells us is that while the world's financial ship has been kept afloat through diligent pumping, it is still deeper in the water than it was when Mexican alarm bells sounded in 1982.

Herald News
Fall River, MA, February 25, 1987

Brazil, facing an economic crisis, has suspended the payment of interest on its mountainous foreign debts.

The action was neither unexpected nor unprecedented. Mexico took a similar step a year ago for similar reasons.

All the same, it had an immediate, though temporary, effect on stock market speculation because so much of Brazil's indebtedness is for loans from banks in this country.

There is no reason to think the suspension of interest payments on the Brazilian national debt will go on indefinitely.

Yet President Sarney is hardly building confidence among his country's creditors by, in effect, refusing to consider the austerity measures Brazil's situation calls for.

Admittedly he is in a difficult situation, with his public support dwindling and the nation's economy incapable of generating the profits needed to pay off its debts.

What he seems to be looking for is a rewriting of the terms of the repayments on the national debt.

In itself, that is not out of the question. It has been done before with other countries, and in all probability will be done again.

The stumbling block is that the rewriting of repayment terms is usually contingent on the acceptance of austerity measures by the government seeking the revision.

Mexico is a case in point.

But the Brazilian government, at least at the moment, seems unwilling to guarantee economic measures which it knows will be unpopular with its own people.

This is not wholly unreasonable, or at least it is not sheer obstinacy. The government's stability is by no means assured, and could be weakened even further by restraints on wages and prices intended to bring the economy back into balance.

But restraints will certainly be part of the price for restructuring the national debt.

What Sarney seems to want is a restructuring of the debt without restructuring the economy, and his country's creditors will hardly agree to that.

For that reason the crisis precipitated by Sarney's decision to suspend interest payments on the national debt may be more prolonged than initially supposed.

It may indeed be the beginning of a showdown between major Third World countries and the international banking institutions, many of them American, which have financed their economic growth.

That showdown has been averted several times in the past, and it is to be hoped it will be again. But at the moment the signs are not favorable.

The Washington Post
Washington, DC, February 25, 1987

BRAZIL'S MORATORIUM on its interest payments brings the international game of chicken over the Latin debts to a new and dangerous phase. In this test of wills and nerves, each side has a great deal to lose if it overplays its position. If Brazil treats its obligations recklessly, it will be cut off from all further foreign credit—with dire economic consequences for President Jose Sarney's government from which no amount of nationalistic chest-thumping can rescue it.

As for the banks that are Brazil's creditors, their situation is better than when the crisis began. They have had time to accumulate reserves against these debts. But that seems to have made some of them arrogant and inflexible. In particular, Citicorp of New York, head of the lenders' committee, has carried its intransigence, and its insistence on the last nickel, to a point that has begun to draw sharp objections from the Reagan administration.

Brazil is not an isolated case. The banks agreed in principle to the Mexican refinancing nearly five months ago, but have yet to come up with the actual money they promised. The same banks—with Citicorp apparently in the lead once again—have been carrying on a long, corrosive quarrel with the Philippines over its debts. If the banks cannot bring these cases to reasonable conclusions, they will invite a solution imposed by the government. They won't like it, but there's too much at risk to leave the outcome, or lack of it, to bankers grappling for another eighth of a point in interest.

The banks might usefully reflect that they have a lot at stake in Washington these days. If, to take the worst case, Congress should decide a couple of years from now that the banks were collectively responsible for a collapse of a struggling new democratic government in Brazil, those banks will have difficulty persuading anyone in Congress that they are fit to hold the broad new powers for which they are now lobbying.

But Brazil has responsibilities as well. It won't help to get sentimental over Brazil's distress, which is largely self-inflicted. Brazil has used more than $100 billion of the world's savings to build dams, factories, railroads and all the rest. Those investments were, in general, good ones and can repay the lenders. President Sarney says defiantly that Brazil is entitled to grow. That's true, but it's not the issue. Brazil grew last year at a phenomenal rate, perhaps 12 percent. Its spectacularly successful export drive has faded because Mr. Sarney has been trying to buy popularity with grossly inflationary wage increases. The goods that were being sold abroad two years ago are now being consumed at home. Brazil's present inability to make its debt payments is the result of its internal economic troubles, not the cause of them.

The outlines of the necessary compromise are pretty clear. The banks are going to have to put up some new money, with no foot-dragging, and on better terms than in the past. Brazil, for its part, is going to have to keep up its payments. It is not entitled to default. But it is entitled to generous treatment from the banks, which have been profiting mightily from these loans.

THE TAMPA TRIBUNE
Tampa, FL, February 28, 1987

If a secretary in Interbay decided to "suspend" her car payments, or an elderly widow in Sulphur Springs her mortgage payments, within a few months the banks would have repossessed the car and evicted the widow.

International finance, however, is not consumer finance. Brazil will probably get away with suspension of payments on $78 billion of its $108 billion debt, the largest in Latin America.

Brazil's action is neither the first nor simply the "other" shoe to drop in the international debt crisis. Peru's President Alan Garcia last year announced his nation would pay only 10 percent of its export earnings against its foreign debt of $14 billion. The Dominican Republic says if things get tougher it will follow Brazil's lead on its own $4 billion debt. Mexico, which owes $100 billion, Argentina ($52 billion), Venezuela ($32 billion), and Ecuador ($8 billion) are busy conferring on suspension of payments.

The $350 billion Latin American debt is spread around. Brazil's private creditors number about 750 U.S., Canadian, Western European and Japanese banks. And suspension now is not as much a threat to banking stability as it would have been several years ago. Banks have adjusted their policies to provide much more resiliency than they had then.

U.S. Treasury Secretary James Baker says the Reagan administration regards Brazil's default as "only temporary" and no cause for panic. Federal Reserve Chairman Paul Volcker shares that assessment. He and Baker have urged the bankers to work out something with their debtors.

That, of course, is just what the Brazilians, and others, have in mind: to extract more favorable repayment terms, over which Peru and its creditors are now dickering. The banks know that if they don't, they have no recourse to repossession or eviction.

Nor is the problem solely financial. Brazil's President Jose Sarney said his action was necessary to avoid "political instability, recession, unemployment, and social chaos." The presidents of the other Latin American debtor nations can say the same. Since all except Garcia are moderate centrists, their downfalls would pose grave security problems for the United States. The prospect of 135 million Brazilians under communist rule is clearly unacceptable. Short of political overthrow, the prospect of long-term default of the $123 billion owed U.S. banks would blow Jim Baker's and Paul Volcker's cool.

So chances are that the industrial world's banks, nudged by their governments, will help their debtors put those dropped shoes back on. No doubt they now know they never should have provided such expensive shoes in the first place.

'NO, YOU MAY NOT CANCEL THE INTEREST PAYMENTS ON YOUR DEBT. WHO DO YOU THINK YOU ARE? BRAZIL?'

San Francisco Chronicle

San Francisco, CA, February 24, 1987

THE ANNOUNCEMENT that Brazil was suspending payment on its privately-held foreign debt for an indefinite period sent shock waves around the world. The Brazilian government's assurance that it had every intention of repaying its lenders in full is not of much reassurance as trading in banks stocks indicated on Wall Street yesterday. Stocks of the big international banks all took a battering, much-troubled Bank of America among them.

Brazil's predicament is typical of that of many emerging nations. Falling exports have sharply limited its foreign earnings. The fairly-new democratic government inherited huge loan balances, placed at $109 billion, from the generals who preceded it. The government has been on a dangerous tightrope trying to satisfy the expectations of its lenders against the expectations of a poor electorate.

The government's assertion that there will be eventual full repayment is little comfort to American banks which are required to report bad loans if interest repayments are in arrears more than 90 days.

IT IS OBVIOUSLY a time for some serious horse trading. A Brazilian default must be avoided at all costs. It would, in effect, cut off Brazil from the rest of the world and cause chaos in world financial circles. It would, additionally and quite seriously, tempt other debtor nations to follow dangerous precedent.

The Courier-Journal & TIMES

Louisville, KY, February 26, 1987

MAJOR U.S. banks and their shareholders have reacted with surprising calmness, so far, to the Brazilian government's announcement last week that it will suspend payments on $67 billion of its $108 billion foreign debt. Banks that have lent most heavily to Brazil and other Latin American countries saw their stock prices drop sharply, but the reaction has been well short of panic.

Does that mean everything's okay? Not quite. While most of the affected banks have been stashing away reserves against the possibility of such a default, Brazil's action could be emulated by other nations in the region. Latin America's total debt is around $350 billion, much of it owed to U.S. banks.

Even before Brazil acted, Peru had restricted its debt payments to 10 per cent of export earnings. Argentina and Ecuador have warned they will need more time and fresh infusions of credit to meet their commitments. Meanwhile, Fidel Castro, as one might expect, has been cheering Brazil's stand — even though Cuba itself has a good repayment record.

Throughout Latin America, political leaders are under intense pressure to defy Washington, renege on their debts and spurn the budget austerity that Yanquis preach but do not practice.

This sort of thing has happened before. In the 1920s, Latin American countries borrowed heavily in the United States, but usually by selling bonds to individual investors instead of taking out bank loans. In the following decade, unable to raise fresh capital or export their way out of debt during the Great Depression, many of these debtor nations defaulted.

Even the U.S. record has its blemishes. Individual states sometimes failed to pay off bonds sold abroad. For instance, British holders of $7 million worth of bonds issued by Mississippi before the Civil War are still trying to collect.

Like it or not, today's debtor nations have too much political and economic leverage to be cut off by lenders. Washington doesn't want the widespread social unrest that would result if Latin American governments either (1) imposed the austerity programs necessary to meet their obligations, or (2) were denied new loans.

So some sort of deal will be worked out with Brazil. But before the U.S. government offers relief to Latin debtors, either directly or through the International Monetary Fund, the banks should be required to accept some of the losses. After all, they took the risks, and some have already gotten part of their money back — in the form of deposits by Latin politicians and businessmen who pocketed loans intended for "development" of backward economies.

The Christian Science Monitor
Boston, MA, February 26, 1987

BRAZIL's decision to halt repayment of part of its $108 billion foreign debt underscores the seriousness of the Latin debt challenge as well as the need to develop creative new investment tools for the region in general.

Brazil is only the latest in an unfortunately long line of Latin nations unable to meet existing loans or seeking refinancing, including Peru, Ecuador, and Argentina. There is rising concern that Mexico may soon face new difficulties in meeting refinanced loan obligations. All told, the region owes $380 billion in external debt.

The issue is not just responsibility. Latin debtor nations have indicated an eagerness to honor long-term obligations. The deeper issue is protecting the new democratic governments in place throughout most of Latin America. In many cases, debt obligations go back years – to the days when nondemocratic governments were in power in such nations as Brazil and Argentina.

The economic situation for Latin America is not entirely unpromising.

What is working: Recent oil price declines make energy and industry costs somewhat cheaper. US-European currency adjustments make Latin exports to the United States less expensive than many European products. Many US companies are shifting production to the region.

Still, the US needs a comprehensive Latin America policy that recognizes debt repayment as but one component in a framework aimed at strengthening democratic government. US Treasury Secretary James Baker's plan to provide some $30 billion in new commercial and international credits to debtor nations, while those nations undertake structural reforms, is a step in the right direction.

Commercial banks and Latin nations, including Brazil, will presumably work out refinancing packages. But that doesn't get at the larger challenge: Latin American democratic governments need faster, more productive growth. That means new industrial, technological, and – yes – financing assistance from the US and other Western nations.

The Virginian-Pilot
Norfolk, VA, February 26, 1987

When Brazilian President Jose Sarney announced last week that his country would suspend interest payments to foreign commercial banks, U.S. bankers and government officials worried. They should.

Although the move's timing contains elements of gamesmanship (since international talks on renegotiating terms of the various loans are due shortly), Brazil's problem is real. The Latin-American nation's trade surplus shrank to $129 million in January from last year's average $1 billion per month. The equation is simple: No trade surplus, no hard-currency reserves; no reserves, no way to pay for imports or pay interest on outstanding loans. (Forget about repayment of principal: Brazil has been unable to repay a dime of principal since 1983.)

Nor can the move be blamed on a lack of Brazilian *will* to pay. Mr. Sarney's previous good-faith efforts to meet interest payments while reviving the Brazilian economy are well-known. The plain fact is that Brazil just can't make interest payments equaling 5 percent of the country's gross national product when inflation is running at a rate of 700 percent and the interest rate is so high that every seven years Brazil pays, in interest, an amount equal to the entire amount of the principal.

And although a moratorium on Brazilian interest payments is bad in itself, the precedent it sets is considerably worse. Brazil's $108 billion in foreign debt is accompanied by Argentina's $52 billion and Mexico's $103 billion. That's $263 billion owed by just three countries. An estimated additional $120 billion is owed by other Latin-American countries. What if (as is likely) Brazil's move serves as precedent for Mexico, Argentina and other Latin nations?

The fact is that most or all of the money loaned to Latin American nations is lost, and the only question remaining is when the lenders will be forced to admit it.

But this the banks are reluctant to do. Ever since the dimensions of the crisis became clear in August 1982 — when Mexico became the first Latin American nation to run into repayment trouble — the banks have been buying time, hoping that something would soon turn up. They've also been augmenting capital and loan-loss reserves to improve their ability to deal with the day of reckoning. But they are still dangerously overextended: while Third World debt is down from its 1982 level of 290 percent of the creditor banks' capital, it still measures 190 percent. In other words, banks loans to Third World nations still amount to nearly twice the banks' capital.

Nobody can quite figure out how those loans can be written off without (a) bankrupting several very large banks, thus probably bankrupting the Federal Deposit Insurance Corp. or (b) requiring a federal bail-out of the banks through an infusion of additional funds into the FDIC from general revenues, which would have to come either from a tax hike or, more probably, from additional inflation (i.e. printing of unbacked dollars), and thus would be nearly as popular as doubling congressional salaries.

Therefore the administration and the bankers prefer to pretend that the debts can still somehow be repaid. To continue that fiction, they have repeatedly renegotiated postponements and restructuring of the debt. Governments have pressured banks to grant additional loans to debtor nations, so that the principal of the new loan can be used to "repay" part of the previous loan or, more usually (insanely). can be used to make payments of *interest* due on previous loans. Does anyone think this can go on forever?

The Miami Herald
Miami, FL, February 24, 1987

A YEAR ago it was baptized Brazil's new economic miracle. Today it has become Brazil's economic nightmare.

Brazilian President Jose Sarney caught international banking officials off guard with Friday's decision to suspend interest payment to foreign banks. This was not supposed to happen; not to Brazil. Last year Brazil's oil imports declined by $8 billion and its trade surplus exceeded the $9 billion to $11 billion that the country needs to meet its annual interest payments. Inflation appeared to be under control.

Brazil's undoing was a government-sanctioned domestic-spending spree. Trade surpluses, more than $1 billion a month in mid-1986, became a scant $129 million in January. Foreign-exchange reserves dropped from $11 billion to less than $4 billion. Inflation is again galloping at an annual rate of more than 700 percent.

President Sarney said that the decision to stop interest payments does not imply that Brazil will be making radical demands of creditor banks in New York at meetings scheduled to begin in March. So much for understatement.

American banks hold $24 billion of Brazil's $108 billion in foreign debt. Brazil's interest payments to those U.S. banks total $2 billion a year. If Brazil misses its interest-payment deadline by more than 90 days, those banks may have to write the loans off. That could be calamitous both for Brazil and the U.S. banking system.

Both Brazil and its creditors therefore have urgent reason to try to resolve this particular crisis. Yet the larger problem of developing countries — Mexico is another — having to reduce their people's standard of living drastically to meet interest payments on foreign loans remains unresolved. The hope that these countries' economies will grow their way back to health is illusory so long as their export earnings, rather than being reinvested in productive enterprises, are siphoned off in interest payments.

No, the only solution — difficult but in time unavoidable — is for Congress to devise a way for U.S. banks systematically to begin writing down their foreign loans. If the United States does not take the lead in helping to lift these nations' insuperable foreign-debt load, it one day will crush the debtors — and underneath them, the U.S. lenders as well.

Index